Company Men

Books by Kage Baker

The Anvil of the World (2003)

The Company Novels
In the Garden of Iden (1998)
Sky Coyote (1999)
    (collected as **On Company Time**, SFBC 1999)

Mendoza in Hollywood (2000)
The Graveyard Game (2001)
    (collected as **In Bad Company**, SFBC 2001)

The Life of the World to Come (2004)
The Children of The Company (2005)
    (collected as **Company Men**, SFBC 2005)

Short Fiction
Black Projects, White Knights: The Company Dossiers (2002)
The Empress of Mars (2003, novella)
The Angel in the Darkness (2003, novella)
Mother Aegypt and Other Stories (2004)

Company Men

THE LIFE OF THE WORLD TO COME
THE CHILDREN OF THE COMPANY

KAGE BAKER

SCIENCE
FICTION

THE LIFE OF THE WORLD TO COME Copyright © 2004 by Kage Baker
    Publication History: Tor hardcover, December 2004
                          Tor paperback, November 2005
        A portion of this novel originally appeared as the story "Smart Alec" in the September 1999 issue of *Asimov's Science Fiction*.
THE CHILDREN OF THE COMPANY Copyright © 2005 by Kage Baker
    Publication History: Tor hardcover, November 2005
        Portions of this novel were first published, in earlier versions, under the following titles in the magazines listed:
            "Son Observe the Time," *Asimov's*, May 1999
            "The Fourth Branch," *Amazing*, June 1999
            "The Queen in the Hill," *Realms of Fantasy*, December 1999
            "Black Smoker," *Asimov's*, January 2000
            "The Young Master," *Asimov's*, July 2000
            "The Applesauce Monster," *Asimov's*, December 2001

First SFBC Science Fiction Printing: December 2005

Published by arrangement with:
Tom Doherty Associates, Inc.
175 Fifth Avenue
New York, NY 10010

Visit The SFBC online at http://www.sfbc.com
Visit Kage Baker's website at http://www.KageBaker.com/

ISBN 0-7394-6144-3

Printed in the United States of America.

CONTENTS

The Life of the World to Come

This one is dedicated,
with reverence, respect, and heart's regard,
to my mentors temporal and spiritual:

Michael Kandel
(Eminent physician of prose)

Stiofan Ui Giollain
(Saint. Scholar. Man about town . . .)

THE BOTANIST MENDOZA

150,000 BCE (more or less)

Rain comes on the west wind, ice out of the blue north. The east wind brings hazes, smokes, the exhalation of the desert on the distant mainland; and hot winds come out of the south, across the wide ocean.

The corn and tomatoes like the west wind. The tall corn gleams wet like cellophane, the tomato leaves pearl and bow down. The onions and garlic, on the other hand, get sullen and shreddy and threaten mold in the rain. Poor old cyborg with a few screws missing—me—sits watching them in fascination.

When I find myself giving my vegetables personalities, it's a sign I've been sitting here watching the rain too long. Or the bright ice. Or the hazes or the hot thin stripes of cloud. Accordingly then, I put on a coat or hat, depending on which way the wind is blowing, and walk out to have a look at the world.

What I have of the world. When I rise, I can walk down the canyon to my brief stony beach to see if anything interesting has washed up there. Nothing ever has. Out on the rocks live sea lions, and they groan and howl so like old men that a mortal would be deceived. I ignore them.

Or I can walk up the canyon and climb high narrow hills, through the ferny trees, until I stand on rimrock in the wind. I can look along the spine of my island in every direction. Ocean all around, the horizon vanishing in cloud. No ships ever, of course—hominids haven't yet progressed beyond clinging to floating logs, when they venture to sea at all.

And I begin my day. Much to do: the planting or the harvest, all the greenhouse work, the tasks of replacing irrigation pipes and cleaning out trenches. A little work on projects of my own, maybe planing wood to replace such of my furniture as has fallen apart with age. I take a meal, if I remember to. I wander back down to the beach in the evening, to watch the little waves run up on the shore, and sometimes I forget to go home.

One day a small resort town will be built on this stony beach, palm trees and yellow sand brought in on barges, to make a place as artificial as I am. The water will be full of excursion boats, painted bright. Out there where that big rock is, the one that looks like a sugarloaf, a great ballroom will stand. I would dearly love to go dancing there, if he were with me.

Sometimes I torment myself by walking along and imagining the crescent of street lined with shops and cafés, gracious hotels. I can almost see the mortal children with their ice cream. I can almost hear the music. I sit down where there will be a terrace someday, complete with little tables and striped umbrellas. Sometimes a waiter has materialized at my elbow, white napkin over his arm, deferentially leaning from the waist to offer me a cocktail. He's never really there, of course, nor will he ever be.

But the other man *will* be here, the one I see only in my dreams, or behind my eyes as I watch the quiet water in the long hours. I have waited for him, alone on this island, for three thousand years. I think.

I'm not certain, though, and this is the reason I have bound more paper into my book, vandalized another label printer cartridge, cut myself another pen: it may be that if I write things down I can keep track of the days. They have begun to float loose in an alarming way, like calendar leaves fluttering off the wall.

I walked out this morning in the full expectation of thinning my tomato seedlings and—imagine my stupefaction! Row upon row of big well-grown plants stretched away as far as the eye could see, heavy with scarlet fruit. Well-watered, weeded, cared for by someone. Me? I swear I can't recall, nor does my internal chronometer record any unusual forward movement; but something, my world or me, is slipping out of time's proper flow.

What does it mean, such strangeness? Some slow deterioration of consciousness? Supposedly impossible in a perfectly designed immortal. But then, I'm not quite mechanically sound, am I? I'm a Crome generator, one of those aberrant creatures the mortals call psychic, or *second-sighted*. I'm the only one on whom the Company ever conferred immortality, and I'll bet they're sorry now.

Not that they meant to do it, of course. Somebody made a mistake when I was being evaluated for the honor of eternal service, didn't catch the latent flaw, and here I am like a stain in permanent ink. No way to erase me. Though marooning me at this station has undoubtedly solved a few problems for them.

Yet my prison is actually a very nice place, quite the sort of spot I'd choose to live, if I'd ever had a choice: utterly isolated, beautifully green, silent in all its valleys and looming mountains, even the sea hushed where it breaks and jumps up white on the windward cliffs.

Only one time was there ever noise, terrible sounds that echoed off the mountains. I hid indoors all that day, paced with my hands over my ears, hummed to myself to shut out the tumult. At least it was over in a few hours. I have never yet ventured back over into Silver Canyon to see if the little people there are all dead. I knew what would happen to them when I sent that signal, alerting Dr. Zeus to their presence. Were they refugees from Company persecution? Did I betray them? Well—more blood on my soul. I was only following orders, of course.

(Which is another reason I don't mind being an old field slave here, you see. Where else should I be? I've been responsible for the deaths of seven mortal men and unknown numbers of whatever those little pale things were.)

What the eyes can't see, the heart doesn't grieve over, isn't that what they say? And no eyes can see me here, that's for sure, if I generate the blue radiation that accompanies a fit of visions, or do some other scary and supposedly impossible thing like move through time spontaneously. I am far too dangerous to be allowed to run around loose, I know. Am I actually a *defective*? Will my fabulous cyborg super-intelligence begin to wane? It might be rather nice, creeping oblivion. Perhaps even death will become possible. But the Company has opted to hide me rather than study me, so there's no way to tell.

I have done well, for a cast-off broken tool. Arriving, I crawled from my transport box with just about nothing but the prison uniform I wore. Now I have a comfortable if somewhat amateurish house I built myself, over long years, with a kitchen of which I am particularly proud. The fireplace draws nicely, and the little sink is supplied by a hand pump drawing on the well I drilled. I have a tin tub in my back garden, in which I bathe. Filled before midday heat rises, the water is reasonably warm by nightfall, and serves to water the lawn afterward. So very tidy, this life I've built.

Do I lack for food and drink? No indeed. I grow nearly everything I consume. About all I receive from the Company anymore are its shipments of Proteus brand synthetic protein.

(Lately the Proteus only seems to come in the assortment packs, four flavors: Breakfast Bounty, Delicate and Savory, Hearty Fare, and Marina. The first two resemble pork and/or chicken or veal, and are comparatively inoffensive. I quite like Hearty Fare. It makes the best damned tamale filling I've ever found. Marina, on the other hand, is an unfortunate attempt to simulate seafood. It goes straight into my compost heap, where it most alarmingly fails to decompose. There has been no response to my requests for a change, but this is a prison, after all.)

Have I written that before, about the Proteus? I have a profound sense of déjà vu reading it over, and paused just now to thumb back through the book to see if I was duplicating a previous entry. No. Nothing in the first part, about England, and nothing in the afterword I wrote on my trial transcript. More of this slipping time business. Nothing has again been so bad as that day I paused in weeding to wipe my sweating face and looked up to see the row just cleared full of weeds again, and the corn a full foot taller than it had been a moment before. But nothing else out of whack! No sign of dust or cobwebs in my house, no conflicting chronometers.

Yes, I really must try to anchor myself here and now. It may be a bit late for mental health, but at least I might keep from sinking into the rock of this island, buried under centuries, preserved like a fossil in a strata of unopened Proteus Marina packets. I suppose it wouldn't have come to this pass if I'd seen another living soul in three thousand years who wasn't a dream or a hallucination.

If only he'd come for me.

I don't know if I should write about him. The last time I did that I was depressed for years, roamed this island in restless misery end to end. Not a good thing to summon up a ghost when you're all alone, especially when you'd sell your soul—if you had one—to join him in his long grave. But then, perhaps misery is what's needed to fasten me securely to the world. Perhaps this curiously painless existence is the problem.

If I look across the table I can see him standing there, as I saw him first in England in 1554: a tall mortal in the black robe of a scholar, staring at me in cold and arrogant dislike. We weren't enemies long. I was very young and so fascinated by the mortal's voice, and his fine big hands . . . I wake at night sometimes, convinced I can feel his mortal flesh at my side, hot as the fire in which he was martyred.

So I look away: but there he is in the doorway, just as he stood in the doorway of the stagecoach inn in the Cahuenga Pass, when he walked back into my life in 1863. He was smiling then, a Victorian gentleman in a tall hat, smooth and subtle to conceal his deadly business. If he'd succeeded in what he'd been sent from England to do, the history of nations would have been drastically different. I was only an incidental encounter that time, entering late at the last act in his life; but I held him as he lay dying, and I avenged his death.

Barbaric phrase, *avenged his death*. I was educated to be above such mortal nonsense, yet what I did was more than barbaric. I don't remember tearing six American Pinkerton agents limb from limb, but it appears I did just that, after they'd emptied their guns into my lover.

But when he lay there with blood all over his once-immaculate clothes, my poor secret agent man, he agreed to come back for me. He knew something I didn't, and if he'd lived for even thirty more seconds he might have let me in on the secret.

I really should ponder the mystery, but now that I've summoned my ghost again all I can think of is the lost grace of his body. I should have let well enough alone. The dreams will probably begin again now. I am impaled on his memory like an insect on a pin. Or some other metaphor . . .

I've spent the last few days damning myself for an idiot, when I haven't been crying uncontrollably. I am so tired of being a tragic teenager in love, especially after having been one for over thirty centuries. I think I'll damn someone else for a change.

How about Dr. Zeus Incorporated, who made me the thing I am? Here's the history: the Company began as a cabal of adventurers and investors who found somebody else's highly advanced technology. They stole it, used it to develop yet more advanced technology (keeping all this a secret from the public, of course), and became very very wealthy.

Of course, once they had all the money they needed, they must have more; so they developed a way to travel into the past and loot lost riches, and came up with dodgy ways to convey them into the future, to be sold at fabulous profits.

Along the way, they developed a process for human immortality.

The only problem with it was, once they'd taken a human child and put it through the painful years of transformation, what emerged at the end wasn't a human adult but a *cyborg*, an inconveniently deathless thing most mortals wouldn't want to dine at one table with. But that's all right: cyborgs make a useful workforce to loot the past. And how can we rebel against our service, or even complain? After all, Dr. Zeus saved us from death.

I myself was dying in the dungeons of the Spanish Inquisition when I was rescued by a fast-talking operative named Joseph, damn his immortal soul. Well, little girl, what'll it be? Stay here and be burned to death, or come work for a kindly doctor who'll give you eternal life? Of course, if you'd rather die . . .

I was four years old.

The joke is, of course, that at this precise moment in time none of it's even happened yet. This station exists in 150,000 BCE, millennia before Joseph's even born, to say nothing of everyone else I ever knew, including me.

Paradox? If you view time as a linear flow, certainly. Not, however, if you finally pay attention to the ancients and regard time (not eternity) as a serpent biting its own tail, or perhaps a spiral. Wherever you are, the surface on which you stand *appears* to be flat, to stretch away straight behind you and before you. As I understand temporal physics, in reality it curves around on itself, like the coiled mainspring in a clock's heart. You can cross from one point of the coil to another rather than plod endlessly forward, if you know how. I was sent straight here from 1863. If I were ever reprieved I could resume life in 1863 just where I left it, three thousand years older than the day I departed.

Could I go forward beyond that, skip ahead to 1963 or 2063? We were always told that was impossible; but here again the Company has been caught out in a lie. I did go forward, on one memorable occasion. I got a lungful of foul air and a brief look at the future I'd been promised all my immortal life. It wasn't a pleasant place at all.

Either Dr. Zeus doesn't know how to go forward in time, or knows how and has kept the information from its immortal slaves, lest we learn the truth about the wonderful world of the twenty-fourth century. Even if I were to tell the others what I know, though, I doubt there'd be any grand rebellion. What point is there to our immortal lives but the work?

Undeniably the best work in the world to be doing, too, rescuing things from destruction. Lost works by lost masters, paintings and films and statues that no longer exist (except that they secretly do, secured away in some Company warehouse). Hours before the fires start, the bombs fall, doomed libraries swarm with immortal operatives, emptying them like ants looting a sugar bowl. Living things saved from extinction by Dr. Zeus's immortals, on hand to collect them for its ark. I myself have saved rare plants, the only known source of cures for mortal diseases.

More impressive still: somewhere there are massive freezer banks, row upon row of silver tubes containing DNA from races of men that no longer walk the earth, sperm and ova and frozen embryos, posterity on ice to save a dwindling gene pool.

Beside such work, does it really matter if there is mounting evidence, as we plod on toward the twenty-fourth century, that our masters have some plan to deny us our share of what we've gathered for them up there?

I wear, above the Company logo on all my clothing, an emblem: a clock face without hands. I've heard about this symbol, in dark whispers, all my life. When I was sent to this station I was informed it's the badge of my penal servitude, but the rumor among immortals has always been that it's the sign we'll all be forced to wear when we do finally reach the future, so our mortal masters can tell us from actual persons. Or worse . . .

I was exiled to this hole in the past for a crime, but there are others of us who have disappeared without a trace, innocent of anything worse than complaining too loudly. Have they been shuffled out of the deck of time as I have been, like a card thrown under the table? It seems likely. Sentenced to eternal hard labor, denied any future to release them.

What little contact we've had with the mortals who actually live in the future doesn't inspire confidence, either: unappreciative of the treasures we bring them, afraid to venture from their rooms, unable to comprehend the art or literature of their ancestors. Rapaciously collecting Shakespeare first folios but never opening them, because his plays are full of objectionable material and nobody can read anymore anyway. Locking Mozart sonatas in cabinets and never playing them, because Mozart had disgusting habits: he ate meat and drank alcohol. These same puritans are able, mind you, to order the massacre of those little pale people to loot their inventions.

But what's condemnation from the likes of me, killer cyborg drudging along here in the Company's fields, growing occasional lettuce for rich fools who want to stay at a fine resort when they timetravel? The Silence is coming for us all, one day, the unknown nemesis, and perhaps that will be justice enough. If only he comes for me before it does.

He'll come again! He will. He'll break my chains. Once he stood bound to a stake and shouted for me to join him there, that the gate to paradise was standing open for us, that he wouldn't rest until I followed him. I didn't go; and he didn't rest, but found his way back to me against all reason three centuries later.

He very nearly succeeded that time, for by then I'd have followed him into any fire God ever lit. History intervened, though, and swatted us like a couple of insects. He went somewhere and I descended into this gentle hell, this other Eden that will one day bear the name of Avalon. He won't let me rest here, though. His will is too strong.

Speak of the fall of Rome and it occurs!

Or the fall of Dr. Zeus, for that matter.

He has come again.

And gone again, but alive this time! No more than a day and a night were given us, but he *did not die!*

I still can't quite believe this.

He's shown me a future that isn't nearly as dark as the one I glimpsed. There is a point to all this, there is a reason to keep going, there is even—unbelievably—the remote possibility that . . . no, I'm not even going to think about that. I won't look at that tiny bright window, so far up and far off, especially from the grave I've dug myself.

But what if we have broken the pattern at last?

Must put this into some kind of perspective. Oh, I could live with seeing him once every three thousand years, if all our trysts went as sweetly as this one did. And it started so violently, too.

Not that there was any forewarning that it would, mind you. Dull morning spent in peaceful labor in the greenhouse, tending my latest attempt at *Mays mendozaii*. Sweaty two hours oiling the rollers on the shipping platform. Had set out for the high lake to dig some clay for firing when there came the roar of a time shuttle emerging from its transcendence field.

It's something I hear fairly frequently, but only as a distant boom, a sound wave weak with traveling miles across the channel from Santa Cruz Island, where the Company's Day Six resort is located. However, this time the blast erupted practically over my head.

I threw myself flat and rolled, looking up. There was a point of silver screaming away from me, coming down fast, leveling out above the channel, heading off toward the mainland. I got to my feet and stared, frowning, at its spiraled flight. This thing was out of control, surely! There was a faint golden puff as its gas vented and abruptly the shuttle had turned on its path, was coming back toward the station.

I tensed, watching its trajectory, ready to run. Oh, dear, I thought, there were perhaps going to be dead twenty-fourth-century millionaires cluttering up my fields soon. I'd have a lot of nasty work to do with body bags before the Company sent in a disaster team. Did I even have any body bags? Why would I have body bags? But there, the pilot seemed to have regained a certain amount of control. His shuttle wasn't spinning anymore and its speed was decreasing measurably, though he was still coming in on a course that would take him straight up Avalon Canyon. Oh, no; he was trying to land, swooping in low and cutting a swath through my fields. I cursed and ran down into the canyon, watching helplessly the ruination of my summer corn.

There, at last the damned thing was skidding to a halt. Nobody was going to die, but there were doubtless several very frightened Future Kids puking their guts up inside that shuttle just now. I paused, grinning to myself. Did I really have to deal with this problem? Should I, in fact? Wasn't my very existence here a Company secret? Oughtn't I simply to stroll off in a discreet kind of way and let the luckless cyborg pilot deal with his terrified mortal passengers?

But I began to run again anyway, sprinting toward the shuttle that was still sizzling with the charge of its journey.

I circled it cautiously, scanning, and was astounded to note that there were no passengers on board. Stranger still, the lone pilot seemed to be a mortal man; and that, of course, was impossible. Only cyborgs can fly these things.

But then, he hadn't been doing all that expert a job, had he?

So I came slowly around the nose of the shuttle, and it was exactly like that moment in *The Wizard of Oz* when Dorothy, in black and white, moves so warily toward the door and looks across the threshold: then grainy reality shifts into Technicolor and she steps through, into that hushed and shocked moment full of cellophane flowers and the absolute unexpected.

I looked through the window of the shuttle and saw a mortal man slumped forward in his seat restraints, staring vacantly out at me.

Him, of course. Who else would it be?

Tall as few mortals are, and such an interesting face: high, wide cheekbones flushed with good color, long broken nose, deep-set eyes with colorless lashes. Fair hair lank, pushed back from his forehead. Big rangy body clad in some sort of one-piece suit of black stuff, armored or sewn all over with overlapping scales of a gunmetal color. Around his neck he wore a collar of twisted golden metal, like a Celtic torque. The heroic effect was spoiled somewhat by the nosebleed he was presently having. He didn't seem to be noticing it, though. His color was draining away.

Oh, dear. He was suffering from transcendence shock. Must do something about that immediately.

The strangest calm had seized me, sure sign, I fear, that I really have gone a bit mad in this isolation. No cries from me of "My love! You have returned to me at last!" or anything like that. I scanned him in a businesslike manner, realized that he was unconscious, and leaned forward to tap on the window to wake him up. Useless my trying to break out the window to pull him through. Shuttle windows don't break, ever.

After a moment or two of this he turned his head to look blankly at me. No sign of recognition, of course. Goodness, I had no idea whence or from when he'd come, had I? He might not even be English in this incarnation. I pulled a crate marker from my pocket and wrote on my hand DO YOU SPEAK CINEMA STANDARD? and held it up in his line of sight.

His eyes flickered over the words. His brow wrinkled in confusion. I leaned close to the glass and shouted:

"You appear to require medical assistance! Do you need help getting out of there?"

That seemed to get through to him. He moved his head in an uncertain nod and fumbled with his seat restraints. The shuttle hatch popped open. He stood up, struck his head on the cabin ceiling and fell forward through the hatchway.

I was there to catch him. He collapsed on me, I took the full weight of his body, felt the heat of his blood on my face. His sweat had a scent like fields in summer.

He found his legs and pulled himself upright, looking down at me groggily. His eyes widened as he realized he'd bled all over me.

"Oh. Oh, I'm so sorry—" he mumbled, aghast. English! Yes, of course. Here he was again and I didn't mind the blood at all, since at least this time he wasn't dying. Though of course I'd better do something about that nosebleed pretty fast.

So I led him back to my house. He leaned on me the whole way, only semiconscious most of the time. Unbelievable as it seemed, he'd apparently come through time without first taking any of the protective drugs that a mortal must have to make the journey safely. It was a miracle his brain wasn't leaking out his ears.

Three times I had to apply the coagulator wand to stop his bleeding. He drifted in and out of consciousness, and my floaty calm began to evaporate fast. I talked to him, trying to keep his attention. He was able to tell me that his name was Alec Checkerfield, but he wasn't sure about time or place. Possibly 2351? He did recognize the Company logo on my coveralls, and it seemed to alarm him. That was when I knew he'd stolen the shuttle, though I didn't acknowledge this to myself because such a thing was impossible. Just as it was impossible that a mortal being should be able to operate a time shuttle at all, or survive a temporal journey without drugs buffering him.

So I told him, to calm him down, that I was a prisoner here. That seemed to be the right thing to say, because he became confidential with me at once. It seems he knows all about the Company, has in fact some sort of grudge against them, something very mysterious he can't tell me about; but Dr. Zeus has, to use his phrase, *wrecked his life*, and he's out to bring them to their knees.

This was so demonstrably nuts that I concluded the crash had addled his brain a bit, but I said soothing and humoring things as I helped him inside and got him to stretch out on my bed, pushing a bench to the end so his feet wouldn't hang over. Just like old times, eh? And there he lay.

My crazed urge was to fall down weeping beside him and cover him with kisses, blood or no; but of course what I did was bring water and a towel to clean him up, calm and sensible. Mendoza the cyborg, in charge of her emotions, if not her mind.

It was still delight to stroke his face with the cool cloth, watch his pupils dilate or his eyes close in involuntary pleasure at the touch of the water. When I had set aside the basin I stayed with him, tracing the angle of his jaw with my hand, feeling the blood pulsing under his skin.

"You'll be all right now," I told him. "Your blood pressure and heart rate are normalizing. You're an extraordinary man, Alec Checkerfield."

"I'm an earl, too," he said proudly. "Seventh earl of Finsbury."

Oh, my, he'd come up in the world. Nicholas had been no more than secretary to a knight, and Edward—firmly shut out of the Victorian ruling classes by the scandal of his birth—had despised inherited privilege. "No, really, a British peer?" I said. "I don't think I've ever met a real aristocrat before."

"How long have you been stuck here?" he said. What was that accent of his? Not the well-bred Victorian inflection of last time; this was slangy, transatlantic, and decidedly limited in vocabulary. Did earls speak like this in the twenty-fourth century? Oh, how strange.

"I've been at this station for years," I answered him unguardedly. Oops. "More years than I remember." He looked understandably confused, since my immortal body stopped changing when I was twenty.

"You mean they marooned you here when you were just a kid? Bloody hell, what'd you do? It must have been something your parents did."

How close could I stick to the truth without frightening him?

"Not exactly. But I also knew too much about something I shouldn't have. Dr. Zeus found a nicely humane oubliette and dropped me out of sight or sound. You're the first mortal"—oops again—"*soul* I've spoken with in all this time."

"My God." He looked aghast. Then his eyes narrowed, I knew that look, that was his righteous wrath look. "Well, listen—er—what's your name, babe?"

Rosa? Dolores? No. No aliases anymore. "Mendoza," I said.

"Okay, Mendoza. I'll get you out of here," he said, all stern hero-ism. "That time shuttle out there is *mine* now, babe, and when I've fin-ished this other thing I'll come back for you." He gripped my hand firmly.

Oh, no, I thought, what has he gotten himself into now? At what windmill has he decided to level his lance?

Summoning every ounce of composure, I frowned delicately and enunciated: "Do I understand you to say that you stole a time shuttle from Dr. Zeus Incorporated?"

"Yup," he said, with that sly sideways grin I knew so terribly well.

"How, in God's name? They're all powerful and all knowing, too. Nobody steals anything from the Company!" I said.

"I did," he said, looking so smug I wanted to shake him. "I've got sort of an advantage. At least, I had," he amended in a more subdued voice. "They may have killed my best friend. If he'd been with me, I wouldn't have crashed. I don't know what's happened to him, but if he's really gone . . . they *will* pay."

Something had persuaded this man that he could play the blood and revenge game with Dr. Zeus and win. He couldn't win, of course, for a number of reasons; not least of which was that every time shuttle has a theft intercept program built into it, which will at a predeter-mined moment detonate a hidden bomb to blow both shuttle and thief to atoms.

This was the fate Alec had been rushing to meet when he'd de-toured into my field. I could see it now so clearly, it was sitting on his chest like a scorpion, and he was totally unaware it was there. I didn't even need to sit through the play this time; I'd been handed the synop-sis in terrible brevity.

"But what do you think you can do?" I said.

"Wreck them. Bankrupt them. Expose what they've been doing. Tell the whole world the truth," Alec growled, in just the same voice in which Nicholas had used to rant about the Pope. He squeezed my hand more tightly.

I couldn't talk him out of it. I never can. I had to try, though.

"But—Alec. Do you have any idea what you're going up against? These people know everything that's ever happened, or at least they know about every event in recorded history. That's why I can't think for a second you were really able to steal that shuttle from them. They must have known about it in advance, don't you see? And if they knew it means they allowed you to steal it, and then—"

"No," he said, with grim and unshakable certainty. "See, I can't explain—just take it on trust, babe, they may know everything but they don't know everything about me. I found the chink in their armor. You could say I *am* the chink in their armor."

It was going to be the same old story, gallant Englishman going to his gallant death. Nothing I could do to change it at all.

Was there?

Was there?

I shook my head. "Don't say any more. I don't want to know."

"You don't need to," he said, giving me that brief cocksure grin again. "Just wait here, and I'll be back to rescue you. On my word of honor as a gentleman, Mendoza." He widened his eyes for emphasis.

"It's a kind offer, señor," I said. "But if I were to leave this station, the Company would know instantly. Besides, where would I go? I have no family. I have no legal identity."

Alec blinked. "But you've got to have a birth record at Global ID, at least."

Damned twenty-fourth-century databases. "Undoubtedly," I lied, "but the Company had it erased when I was sent here. They're that powerful, you know."

"That's true." He scowled. "We can fake you up an identification disc. I know people who do that kind of thing. It wouldn't get you through customs anywhere, but . . . I know what'd do it! I could just marry you. Peers get everything waived, see?"

I couldn't think what to say. He got a slightly panicked look in his eyes.

"A-and then afterward we could just get a divorce. They're easy. I could find you a place to live and a job or something."

"Perhaps we could give it a try," I said carefully. He cleared his throat.

"I'm not just making the offer out of kindness, either. We could have some fun together."

I leaned down, unable to keep myself from his mouth any longer, and I kissed him. Actually I was going to do a lot more than kiss him— if I was going to throw my immortal life away for Alec, I'd have such an epic game of lust with him first as would make the fires of Hell seem lukewarm when I got there.

He still kissed like an angel of God, making little surprised and pleased noises and groping feebly at my behind, but I felt his blood pressure going up, his heartbeat speeding dangerously, and the red numbers in my peripheral vision warned me to stop or I'd kill him. I pulled away, sitting up and stroking back his hair. "Don't you go dying on me," I gasped.

"I won't," he promised. He had got hold of the end of my braid and was tugging at it in a plaintive way. "But I'd really, really like to have sex with you. If you've no objections or anything."

Caramba! Did he use that line on other women? But I'd bet it worked for him every time. Who could resist that earnest look in his eyes when he said it? How was I going to stop myself from ripping open that suit of fish-mail he was wearing and murdering him with carnal bliss?

Meteorological data coming in. Had that been thunder, or God snarling at me? I babbled out some kind of promise to Alec and went to the window to confirm visually.

Disturbed air. Domed clouds racing down the sky, all my surviving corn plants staggering and fluttering as a gust of hot wind came rushing across them, carrying a smell of wetness and electricity. Crickets began to sing.

"There's a cloud front advancing," I told Alec. "Have you brought rain, like the west wind? I think we're going to have a summer storm."

"Cool," said Alec. Christ, I wanted to jump him then and there.

But he was ill and he needed protein, needed fluids, needed rest. I do have some basic programming that insists I serve the mortal race, even if I bypass it now and then to kill one of the poor little things; so I poured Alec a glass of iced tea and set about preparations for feeding him.

"What do you do here, all the time?" Alec said, as I returned from the garden with some produce.

"I grow vegetables," I said.

"Who eats 'em all? Not you all alone." He sipped his tea and looked at it in surprise. "This is real tea!"

"Thank you. You obviously know about Dr. Zeus; do you know anything about the Day Six resorts?" I unloaded what I was carrying onto my kitchen table: tomatoes, corn, peppers, cilantro, garlic, onions. He knitted his brows.

"They're like one of those urban myths, only they're really real," he said. "Like Dr. Zeus. Everybody knows there's supposed to be some company that has time travel and can get you absolutely anything you want, but it's just a rumor. Which is what they probably want us to think! And the Day Six places are the same way. Somebody did a *Weird Stories* thing on holo about one. This guy goes back in time to party and screws up history by stepping on a bug or something." He had another sip of his tea.

"Ah. Well, that's a fable, because history can't be changed." I worked the hand pump to rinse off the tomatoes and peppers. "But the resorts do exist, just as Dr. Zeus exists. In fact, Dr. Zeus owns them

Nice little string of hotels, rather unexceptional except that they're all located in 150,000 BCE. Or thereabouts. All of them in virgin wildernesses where long-extinct mammals can be observed gamboling, from behind the safety of an electronic perimeter field.

"You're from the future, Alec, you must have lived in steel canyons all your life. How much would you pay to be able to swim in waters that had never been polluted, or watch a herd of mammoths grazing?"

"In all the stories, time travelers wind up as lunch for velociraptors," he said.

"All the dinosaurs are extinct in this time. Anyway: Dr. Zeus has quietly built up a select secret clientele in the twenty-fourth century. They pay fortunes, annual incomes of small countries, I'm told, to be rocketed backward through time to carefully landscaped virgin paradises where they can relax by the pool and breathe clean, clean air." I selected a knife and began slicing up the tomatoes.

"The only problem is—time travel is hard on the human body. Even the drugs that protect people make them ill. So when they arrive from the dismal future, these millionaires and heiresses can do no more than nibble at a lettuce leaf or two. Therefore Dr. Zeus makes damned sure the resort keeps all manner of trendy greens for salad on hand, and therefore I labor in the sun on this agricultural station." I whacked a beefsteak tomato in half, imagining it was some Company CEO's head.

"But that's awful." Alec tried to sit up, looking outraged. "That means you're not only their prisoner, you're their slave!"

He was an idealist, then. Disapproved of slavery, did he? And him a titled gentleman. Just the sort of wealthy young man who comes to loathe his birthright and goes off to die for somebody else's freedom.

"I suppose I am," I said carefully. "But I may as well be of some use to somebody, don't you think? And it's not so bad. They don't call for produce very often. I have a lot of time to work on my own private research."

"What's your research?" Alec said.

I told him all about my quest to perfect maize plants. I don't think he understood one word in three of botany talk, and when he wrinkled his forehead and attempted to follow my lecture he looked like a puzzled dog. But he was awfully polite about it, unlike the other Future Children I've known, and said gallant things about how worthwhile my project was.

We talked for a little while on the subject of making one's life count for something, and I expected a manifesto from him on the need to actively oppose the evils of Dr. Zeus. I was surprised; he just talked about his life. Despite his grand title, it appears there were some unfortunate circumstances attending his birth again. Some poor girl seduced by the sixth earl and then abandoned? I'd hardly have thought the wretched Future Children had enough blood in them to carry on like that, but apparently mortal nature hasn't changed so much.

As near as I could make out, the girl went mad and was locked up. Alec seems to have grown to manhood with a devastating sense of his own worthlessness, not surprisingly. I wonder if Nicholas and Edward carried similar burdens of unearned guilt on their backs? Was that what fueled Nicholas's drive to martyrdom, Edward's selfless work for an empire that abandoned him? I was too young and foolish to see this in Nicholas, too rushed to see it in Edward; but I see it now. And Alec's failed at two marriages, apparently, and has steered through his life in increasing emotional isolation. Is that why he's always alone when I meet the man?

When he saw he'd affected me, blurting out his wretched story, he made amends by changing the subject entirely and told me about the adventures he's had, as I kneaded the masa for our commonplace supper of tamales.

And what adventures he's had! I begin to see that I have been somewhat mistaken about Future World. It seems he hasn't grown up in steel canyons at all. It seems that there are still wild places in the twenty-fourth century, still gardens and forests that don't stink of machine exhaust. Best of all, it seems that the mortal race has not entirely followed the crabbed and fearful lead of its Company scientists, people like Mr. Bugleg of loathsome memory.

Though they are, all of them, undeniably childish. Future Children indeed. My own dearest love has bought himself a *pirate ship*, if you please, and spends most of his time sailing around in the Caribbean and other ports of call on what we used to call the Spanish Main! And there he indulges his urge to be virile and bad, like pirates in every film he's ever seen, and he's become a smuggler! Mostly of things like wine and cheese, though they're illegal enough in the twenty-fourth century.

And yet I think in this he must come nearer to living a real life than the other mortals of his time, who (as far as I was ever able to tell) spend their lives hiding in their rooms, playing electronic games.

Still, he has found a far less harmless and silly way to rebel, hasn't he, by going on a crusade against Dr. Zeus? Dangerous to think about.

Anyway. Such lovely stories he told me, about Jamaica under the tropical stars, parrots and gold doubloons. How happy I was to think of him playing Errol Flynn among the shrouds and ratlines. This ship of his must really be something to see, a full-rigged sailing vessel utilizing twenty-fourth-century technology, sort of an enormous retro yacht. He has some kind of complex computer system running all the rigging apparatus, for there's no crew at all apparently.

It's as though he were able to lose himself in *Treasure Island*, escaping from his unhappiness by making the wild sea and the pirates come to life for him—except that instead of his imagination, he's used enormous sums of money and technology. What am I to make of such a brave new world?

Who cares? It was enough for me to watch the way his face lit up when he described his adventures, watch his expressive face and gestures conveying his stories perfectly even in that thug's idiom of his. The man should have gone on the stage, I always thought, and what a preacher he'd made!

And he sang for me. He had been describing how his ex-wives had hated his singing, the repulsive harpies. I was overwhelmed with a sudden memory of Nicholas singing, making some Tudor bawdiness sublime with his dark tenor. So I begged him to sing something, and he obliged with old sea songs, blood-and-thunder ballads that somehow reduced me to a weepy mess.

At last he reached up his hand and pulled me down beside him, and there I lay hearing his voice vibrate in his chest and throat. We were shortly embracing again, me scanning frantically to see if his brain was likely to explode this time. It was of course impossible that after three hours of rest and a glass of iced tea the man should be completely recovered from transcendence shock, but he was.

He was twiddling experimentally with the fastenings of my coveralls, and I was wondering how his mail-suit unzipped, when something seemed to occur to him. He lifted his mouth from mine and looked down at me. "Er—"

"What is it?" I said, desperate lest he should stop.

"You're a virgin, I guess, yeah?"

Have I mentioned that the man is prone to scruples at the most inconvenient times?

Of course I'm not a virgin, but I do have this sort of immortal self-repairing body, see, and in the three hundred and then three thousand years that had elapsed between our respective couplings, there had been more than ample time for a tiny unimportant membrane to grow back. Christ, I could have grown a leg back in that amount of time.

"Yes," I said. "It's all right, though. Please."

But now he was self-conscious, and the gorgeous python that had materialized down one leg of his suit shrank a little. "Can I use your shower?"

Mother of God! Had I mentioned he's very clean in his personal habits as well? And me without a shower.

I was stammering to explain about my pathetic tin washtub when we both realized it had been raining outside for some time, warm summer rain. I directed him out into my back garden and hurried to fetch him a clean towel.

He always has enjoyed bathing. Something Freudian relating to guilt, perhaps? Edward seemed to have some sort of personal dirt-repellent force field, of course, but I remember the way Nicholas used to revel in clean water and soap.

When I opened the door and stepped out under the overhang, Alec had already snaked out of the mail-suit and was sitting in the tub, wearing only that torque. He was leaning back into the rain with an ecstatic expression on his face, letting it soak into his lank hair, which was becoming even lanker. The tub was rather low and didn't obscure much of his nakedness, and I made a small involuntary pleading sound.

He opened his eyes and looked at me. For a moment he seemed wary, defensive; then grinned his sidelong grin.

"Would you, er, like to bathe, too?" he asked, all suavity, gesturing invitation as though the tub were ever so capacious. I don't remember how I got out of my clothes and across the garden, it happened so fast.

It was insane. The storm was beating down on us, the tub was impossibly tiny, and I was worried about that long back of his—but oh, how that man could kiss. We writhed ineffectively for a few minutes before he simply stood up in the tub and hoisted me into the air as though I weighed no more than a feather. He is phenomenally strong. I slid down, pressed against his body, and he thrust his face into my breasts with a whoop of inarticulate glee. The rain bathed us, and the fragrance of the garden was sweet.

God, God, God.

I believe I was in the act of offering Him my soul, or whatever a thing like me has, if He'd only let this moment stretch out into eternity, when my groping hands found the pattern of electronic wire just under the skin of Alec's shoulders.

God?

I leaned forward over the top of Alec's head and looked down. It was like the most beautiful tattoo you can imagine, an intricate pattern of spirals and knotwork in dull silver, winging out over both his shoulder blades and twining up the back of his neck. But it was wire, installed subcutaneously and tapping somehow into his nervous system and brain. So that's what the torque was for? I touched it gingerly and had a momentary disorientation, a view of my own breasts seen from—well, not the angle I was used to, anyway.

"Alec, darling," I said cautiously, "this is a rather unusual tattoo you have."

He said something in reply, but under the circumstances it came out somewhat muffled. I bit my lower lip and said: "I beg your pardon?"

He lifted his face to look up at me. "You know how I told you I've got this big custom cybersystem, to work the rigging on my ship? This is how I run it. I'm a cyborg, have been since I was eighteen."

Gosh, what a coincidence!

Though of course what he means by *cyborg* and what I would mean by the same word are entirely different things.

He looked alarmed until he realized I was laughing, and then he chuckled companionably and went back to what he'd been doing as I gasped out, overwhelmed by the cosmic joke:

"Oh, perfect—!" And then I thought I'd been struck by lightning, because the flash of revelation was very nearly that blindingly bright. I seized his face in both my hands and tilted it up to stare into his eyes. "*What* year did you say it was where you come from?"

"Er . . . 2351," he said, polite but confused.

"But that's only four years from—" I said, and then the whole mystery of my beloved came together. An extraordinary man, with extraordinary abilities, who bears a grudge against Dr. Zeus. A cyborg, and not a poor biomechanical slave like me but a free agent, with both the ability and the determination to slip through the Company's defenses and do the impossible. And what was that blue fire playing around our bodies? Oh, dear, it was Crome's radiation. Was I seeing the future?

And I didn't know the half of it yet.

I laughed and laughed. Then I writhed down and we embraced. Somehow or other we wound up on the lawn with the bath overturned beside us, and he was on top of me, peering down through the lightning flashes. He was looking into my eyes as though he'd only just recognized me.

And how good was it, what we did there on my tidy little lawn? I'll tell you. If I suffer in darkness for a thousand years because of what I did afterward—I won't care.

By great good fortune the water under the tamales had not quite boiled away by the time we went back inside, and the house was filled with the earthy smell of corn. I lit lamps and pulled on an old shirt to set out our supper. He wrapped a towel around his middle and sat down at my rough-hewn table, watching me lay places for us. Two places, after all this time.

Once, long ago, I'd laid out an intimate supper for two, just like this. We had sat together in a tiny circle of light at an old wooden table, in our own little world, as beyond in the darkness the wind howled and a hostile fate prepared to tear us to pieces the minute we stepped outside the circle.

It isn't really a happy memory. Nicholas had been sullenly desperate and I had been fearfully desperate, a good little cyborg feeling real qualms about running away with a mortal man. Before that night ended my heart had been broken irreparably, and Nicholas, furious and terrified, was running to meet his death. Thank you, Dr. Zeus.

But I'm an old wicked cyborg now, aren't I? Long past desperation. And how sweetly the rain beat on the roof of my house, and how snug and dry we were in my lamplit kitchen as the blue evening fell, and how sleepy and calm we were there together.

And calmly, over our supper, I did the first of the things that will damn me if I'm ever caught. I told Alec, in great detail, all about the Silence in 2355, together with some rather necessary bits of temporal physics to enable him to use that shuttle effectively. So very classified, and I divulged it! He knows, now, Dr. Zeus's fear of the unforeseen apocalypse; he knows his window of opportunity, and what to plan for over the next four years. Whatever his plans may be.

I gather he has some kind of ally he calls the Captain, who is apparently the captain of his ship, though I'm a little confused on this point because I also had the impression he sails alone. But this Captain may be dead, which is one of the things he's gone off to resolve/revenge.

The talk depressed him. He reached across the table and took my hand as we spoke. What kind of emotional life has he had? I could cheerfully kill his ex-wives, I think.

Oh, yes, I've changed. But I would burn in Hell for his dear sake.

I may yet.

He helped me wash the dinner dishes, and we hung his thermal underclothes up to dry before the fire, and at last we climbed into my narrow, creaking bed. Last time I'd lain in a real bed with him, he'd been Edward, and we'd been on the run all day and were too exhausted to do more than drift off to sleep together. Not this time! The bed has a permanent list to starboard now, and we were lucky it didn't collapse in extremis. I really ought to fix it, but I can't bear to. Just looking at it makes me smile.

He warmed me right through, my mortal lover, and afterward

drifted off to sleep in my arms. I lay watching him by the light of the fire. I might have lain there studying him all night, newly fascinated by all the details I'd never forgotten: the cleft in his chin, the funny swirled patterns in the hair on his arms.

But the night wasn't mine to idle away so pleasantly.

I rose and pulled the blanket up around his shoulders. He sighed, reaching for me. I slipped out into the rainy night, to do the second thing for which I will surely suffer one day.

The shuttle lay dark and abandoned, its sprung hatch gaping open in the rain. I looked in and saw the tiny green lights on the control panel, dimly illuminating the access port. I made my assault, forced it to give up the secret I wanted.

The bomb was wired under the pilot's seat, of all obvious places. It was a tiny white Bakelite box that might have been anything, a fuse relay, a power seat servomotor, a container of breath mints that had fallen down under there and been forgotten. I knew better. I found the tool kit and snipped its vicious little wires, swung the shuttle's hatch shut, carried the bomb back with me through the gray rainy night and flung it into my compost heap. It's there now, as I write. It may yet be live and deadly, it may have been ruined by the rain and the muck; but it will never kill Alec, which is all that matters.

I came back and reentered paradise, slipping into the firelit room where my love slept safe. *Third time lucky, mortal man,* I thought.

He woke when I climbed back in beside him, grumbled a little, reached out his arms to pull me in close and tucked me under his chin, just as Nicholas used to do. I lay awake awhile longer, fighting conditioning nightmares; but I know them for the false programmed things they are now, and they can't scare me. I fell asleep at last, soothed by the rhythm of his heartbeat.

We didn't get out of bed for two full hours next morning. We did everything I'd ever done with Nicholas, who'd been amazingly adventurous for a late medieval fellow, and everything I'd ever done with Edward, who was a Victorian gentleman, which says all I need to say about *his* personal tastes. The bed sagged ever further toward a happy death.

Then we got up and I made him breakfast.

"I hope you like tacos," I said, spooning the hot filling into corn tortillas. "This seems so inadequate! I seldom dine in the morning, myself, just a roll or something to keep the coffee from killing me. No tea, no kippers, no sardines even. Nothing for an Englishman, but then I never expected to meet one here."

"That's okay," said Alec. He accepted a taco and bit into it cautiously. "It's not bad. What is it?"

"Proteus Breakfast Bounty," I told him with a sneer. "It approximates sausage. Not inspiring, but sustaining. The tortillas, at least, are real."

"I like 'em," he said.

"You *are* a gentleman," I said, pouring him out a mug of coffee. I poured a cup for myself and sat down across the table from him. "Well, then. Here we are."

"Mr. and Mrs. Checkerfield's Brunch Club," he said. God, it sounded strange in my ears. Mrs. Checkerfield? Or Lady Finsbury! Pretty good for somebody who began life in a one-room hut, eh? Child of Spanish peasants who owned maybe two goats and three fig trees? Too surreal to contemplate. I took a careful sip of coffee and said quietly:

"If you knew how often I've wished you were sitting right there—"

"I can't be what you wanted," he said. "You must have wished for somebody a lot better looking, in shining armor."

"No. You yourself are the man of my dreams, señor. I think we've met before, in some previous lifetime."

"You believe in that stuff?"

"Not really," I said. "Do you?"

He shook his head, wolfing down the last of the taco.

"Were you raised in any religion?"

"Nope," he said. "I was always taught that's for bigots and crazies. Not something you do if you're going to be a respectable member of the House of Lords, which I've never been anyway so who cares, right? But, you know. My stepmother got into the Ephesians, and they're kind of scary."

"That's what I'd always read."

"You read, too? They do a lot of good, though, for poor girls, so I guess they're okay. And my nurse was into something, I guess it must have been Orthodox Vodou. I think she took me to some of their services when I was small. That was nice, I remember, all the dancing, and those bright people coming out of nowhere like that."

Yes indeed, Nicholas, I thought, you've come a long way.

"Can I have another of those?" he inquired. Imagine someone actually liking Breakfast Bounty. But then I don't suppose he's ever eaten meat.

"Please," I said, pushing the plate across to him. "I made them for you. So, religion's not your thing, is it? What about politics?"

"I don't vote."

"No? Not very English of you, if you'll pardon my saying so."

"I can't stand England," he said wearily. "It's gray and it's cold and it's . . . it's just so sad. I couldn't wait to leave, and I hate it when I have to go back. You should see the absentee fines I pay every year to the House of Lords! You don't want to live there, I hope?"

"Oh, no."

"Good. You want to go see Spain again, though? You must not have seen it since you were little."

What a strange idea. "I wonder if I'd recognize it at all?" I said at last.

"It's fun there. Everything's really expensive, but you can get real fish in the restaurants and there's a festival day, like, every other week. I was there one time at—what's that big party the Jews throw, where they dress up and there's, er, a street carnival? Noisemakers and stuff? It's in the spring, anyway, and there's this big whatchacallem, temple thing—"

"A synagogue?"

"Yeah! A synagogue in, er, Santiago—"

"Santiago de Compostela?" I was stunned.

"Yeah! That's the place. Anyway it's great. Families build these booths all along the street and watch the dances and parades, and you can just go from booth to booth, drinking and eating and talking to people. The ones who understand English, anyway. And there's bull-fights with topless girls! Amazing acrobats. They flip over the bulls like they were on springs or something. And then they have this thing at the end where they burn the parade floats."

"Not the people?" I just couldn't get my mind around this, some-how. Poor old Spain, freed at last from ancient sorrow and cruelty?

"Nah, they never have accidents. We should go sometime. You'd like it." He looked at me a little anxiously. "Though we can go any-where you want, babe. Anywhere that'll make you happy."

"I'll be happy," I said, reaching across the table and clasping his hand. "You're not religious, you don't care about England, and there's a synagogue in Santiago de Compostela! We can go places or we can live on your ship. I don't care."

Assuming, of course, I can skip forward through time into the fu-ture—impossible, but apparently not for me. Could I really just sail away with Alec, on an eternal holiday in the twenty-fourth century?

Though of course it wouldn't be eternal, because he's a mortal. But I think if we could just once live out a peaceful life together, I could ac-cept anything that came after that. Why have I felt this way, from the first moment I laid eyes on this big homely man? God only knows.

He lifted my hand and kissed it. "We'll go as soon as I've finished up this stuff I'm doing," he said.

"Ah, yes. This stuff you're doing," I said, looking down into my coffee, focusing on cold practical matters to keep from launching myself over the table at him. "There are some things you should know before you attempt to pilot that shuttle back to the twenty-fourth century. Somewhere on board, there ought to be little containers of the drug you have to take before time traveling. It looks like iodine, and I've heard it's sometimes packaged to look like Campari. Do they still make Campari?"

"Yes. I saw those."

"It's not Campari, but if you pour fifty milliliters into an equal amount of gin or vodka, you won't know the difference. You must drink it down, or risk death a second time when you activate the time transcendence field. I must tell you, I can't imagine how you were able to sit up and talk coherently only a couple of hours after your arrival, let alone get that magnificent erection."

He snickered in embarrassment.

"And you need to enter the proper algorithm into the time drive. I can do that for you now, but you'll have to know more about piloting the damned thing before you try to take it anywhere else."

"If my friend's still alive, he may have that data." Alec reached for another taco.

"He was going after Dr. Zeus's *database*?" I felt ice around my heart. "Oh, Alec. There aren't even words for how dangerous that is."

"We did it once already and got out okay," Alec said. But I buried my face in my hands.

"Don't tell me, darling. The less I know, the safer you'll be."

We lingered over breakfast. He helped me wash up again. I helped him into his armored suit that had been airing out on a hook by the door all night, like a sealskin temporarily abandoned by its owner. I wanted to see if we might contrive a way to make love while he was encased in it, but he's a man on a mission, after all, with places to go and things to do.

The rain had stopped and the clouds blown away by the time we walked back to the shuttle. It was going to be a hot day. Steam was already rising up from the sparkling fields. When we got to the shuttle and Alec stood there staring up at it, I could tell from the look on his face he was uncertain what he was supposed to do next.

So I drove the third nail into my coffin.

I leaned close to him and put my arms around his neck. "You'll remember," I said, finding the torque with my fingers. "It's just the effect of the crash. Calm down. Think." I tapped into his database and nearly passed out at its immensity. If he were to download even half of wha he has access to, my brain would burst. But I did experience the world through his senses for a moment, and that was nearly as disturbing.

He has . . . SENSES. His hearing, his eyesight, touch, are all hyperacute and informative. He draws in a breath of air and its component scents tell him more about where he is than even a hunting dog could discern, at least as much as an immortal like me. He sees farther into certain light ranges than a mortal is supposed to be able to, and the sensitivity of his skin . . . no wonder he likes his physical pleasures.

Is my mortal darling even human? I wondered.

I always thought he'd make a better immortal than any of the people the Company ever chose, and now I know it for a fact. If only his skull fit the optimum parameters!

I mustered my thoughts and probed for the information he needed. There it was; he simply hadn't learned how to access it yet. I pulled it up and said: "I have the impression that the cyborgs who normally pilot these ships access them through a file with a designation of TTMIX333." I fed it to him surreptitiously. "Does that sound right?"

His brain took it with remarkable ease. I felt him gasp in pleasure as it all made sense, suddenly. He began to download from me, lifting a subroutine for fast access by content with such speed I felt like a wrung-out sponge.

"I think—Hey!" he said in delight, as the hatch popped open. I teetered back from him, dizzy and frightened.

"There you are," I said, determined to sound cheery. "You see? You had it in your memory all the time. Dear me, though, this fancy carpet's gotten soggy." I climbed inside and stopped, staring as he climbed in after me.

Fancy carpet indeed. What luxury! I hadn't bothered to look around much when I'd been in here removing the bomb.

Floral pattern in the carpet and the beautifully cushioned passengers' seats. Drink rests, crystal vases set in the wall, for God's sake, full of pink roses! Spacious, lots of head room for anyone but Alec. Tasteful color scheme. Minibar. Entertainment console. All this to keep the Future Children happy on their weekend escapes from their own world. Not how we immortals travel. I was sent to this station in a raw-edged metal box barely big enough to accommodate my body. It couldn't be bigger, we were always told. The extra time-field drag would take more energy, cost more money, which couldn't be spared for inessentials like comfort.

What did it cost to send this shuttle through time even once?

Is this why we've worked so hard all these years? To pay for things like this?

Alec bent down and flung wide the etched glass doors of the mini-bar. "Check this out. Six different fruit juices and three kinds of real booze. Illegal as hell, and I should know." He chuckled. "Bombay Sapphire, Stolichnaya and—hey, here's the magic potion." He held up a dummy bottle of Campari. All nicely disguised as a cocktail, so Future Children would never know how dangerous their pleasure excursions really were.

I was so angry I could barely trust myself to speak, but while he gulped down his bitter cocktail I managed to explain about taking the earth's rotation and orbit into account, for one travels through space as well as time and you must run as fast as you can to remain in one place, whenever you get there. Alec knit his brows in comprehension—he may not be able to read very well, but he seems to be brilliant at math—and ordered the shuttle to set its course. It promptly obeyed him.

The warning lights began to implore us to close the hatch, and the gas canisters gave their initial hiss as the valves engaged. I wasn't ready to lose him yet! But I'd be a danger to him in more ways than he could imagine if I went along. I backed toward the hatch, and he held out his hand.

"Remember," he said. "I'm coming back for you."

"*Meminerunt omnia amantes*," I said, falling into an old habit.

"What?" He stared. "Was that Spanish? What did you say?"

Still no World Language in his century, I note. Must be the nationalist backlash.

"Lovers remember everything," I translated. "I was speaking Latin." He got that worried-dog look again.

"What's Latin?"

My God, the progress of human knowledge.

"Like, Latin American?" he asked.

"Close enough, dear," I said ruefully, but then the Klaxons really began to protest about the hatch and I couldn't stay. I dove back, kissed him one last time, and fled through the hatch before I doomed us both.

I ran around to the window where I'd seen him first. He was fastening himself into his seat restraints. He saw me and mouthed *I love you* in silence. I shouted it back to him, over the scream of the engines and the turbulence, until I was hoarse. He leaned forward, staring out over the console as the shuttle began to rise and I reached up my hands toward him, watching until the yellow gas roiled and hid him from my sight.

Up and up went the shuttle, a perfect ascent, and then it rotated and became a streak of silver, leaving my time with just the barest thud on the insulted air. No master pilot could have done it better, no immortal cyborg with a thousand years' training, but I'd only had to show Alec once.

What have I done?

I told myself, as I walked back to the house, that it could have been worse. Nicholas would have roared off with that shuttle to carpet-bomb the Vatican, and I shudder to think what Edward would have done with it. Alec, however, is an arrested child who won't even vote. Digging for pirate treasure is his idea of a good time.

And even if he succeeds in his quest—would the world be such a terrible place without the Company's obsessive control? Dr. Zeus has been in power since Time began. What if *nobody* was running the world? Maybe all those lost art treasures could go into museums, instead of the collections of rich men. Maybe those rare beasts could be turned loose into that strangely depopulated future world, to survive or not on their own merits.

Speaking of rare beasts . . . are you ready for the punchline, now?

The first thing I did on returning to my little abode was to collect DNA samples from the abundant evidence Alec, ahem, left of his presence. Hair on the pillow and all that. Ran a few tests. What a surprise.

He's a tetraploid. Like my maize cultivars. Double DNA. Ninety-two chromosomes. The only tetraploid hominid who ever existed was the (understandably) extinct *Homo crewkernensis*, known only from a few odd-looking bones and, of course, Company operatives who went back through time to see what could possibly have left such long femurs in the fossil record . . . hmmm.

What did the operatives report? That they found a small population with a barely viable gene pool, living at the southwestern edge of the ice sheet that covered England. Decided they were some kind of *Homo heidelbergensis* community that had been isolated long enough for distinct speciation to occur. Dutifully recorded their extinction, once the ice sheet melted and *Homo crewkernensis* were able to move east, where they encountered tribes with whom they could not interbreed successfully (lethal recessive affected the females) and who objected to their territorial aggression.

I wonder if the Company saved any of their genetic material?

Oh, we've gone way, way beyond any romantic metaphysics to do with reincarnation, haven't we? Alec is no member of any human race I've ever encountered. Fancy my never suspecting that in all these centuries, eh? I don't know what he is, but what I do know about him is far too much for the Company's liking. And I already knew more than was safe . . . I am *so* doomed.

. . . You know, when I was a mortal child, my mother sold me to a band of wicked strangers. They told me I'd be married to a great lord. When I finally peered into the room where they were hiding my betrothed, what was there?

Only a straw man, a thing braided out of wheat of the field, the bright-ribboned Lord of the Corn, destined for the festival bonfire. Maybe the strangers meant to sacrifice me with him. Maybe my inescapable fate has always been, one day, to burn in that fire.

But it's been almost a week now, and nobody's come for me yet.

I suppose it all hinges on how closely I'm being monitored, whether my auditory and visual intake is being recorded and analyzed somewhere or just recorded and stored. It might be years before some bored clerk decides to have a look at what I've been doing. Who knows whether Alec will have succeeded in his quest by that time? I might never be found out.

If, on the other hand, analysis is instantaneous—then I'm certainly going to learn whether or not Dr. Zeus has devised a way to grant its weary immortals the gift of death. Is this crawling sensation fear for *myself*? How novel.

And if what I've done has really set in motion the events that will lead to the end of the world, I'll deserve whatever the Company does to me. It would be a pity, really. I'd have liked to have made that sad mortal happy, sailed away with him on his absurd pirate ship and been Mrs. Alec Checkerfield. Don't want to think about that too much.

On the other hand, if Alec fails, dies as Nicholas and Edward died—perhaps his hungry soul won't need to come back for me, if I too am hit by the bolt of Dr. Zeus's wrath. Can I go through that doorway of fire, where Nicholas waited for me?

It's so strange, waiting to see.

Rain again today, but I think it'll blow out later, and another astonishing thing has happened.

Got up this morning and took my usual perambulation down to Avalon Bay, *and something had washed up on the beach.* I could smell it long before I got there, though it really isn't so badly decomposed as all that, but, you know—fish stink.

Except this isn't a fish, exactly. It's an ichthyosaur! And to think I told Alec there were no dinosaurs in this time period.

You can keep your stupid coelacanths. There it is, large as life, which seems to have been 7.5 meters long. I've taken a full hour of holo footage, from every possible angle. I managed to turn it over with a hovel, which was unfortunate because I promptly lost my breakfast *much* more decomposed on that side) but this gave me a good view of ts skeletal structure for the camera. So much for its being extinct! I re-lly should get some DNA samples before the seabirds get it all. Actu-lly I should signal for a Company ichthyologist, I suppose, but under he circum—

Ship has arrived out front. Not Alec's stolen shuttle. Maybe Dr. Z ish specialist come to see discovery?

Oh dear. There are uniformed security techs searching through my compost heap.

My own beloved, it would have been fun. Good-bye Alec Edward Nicholas. *Quia fortis est ut mors dilectio dura s*

Extract from the Text of Document D

6 Maye 1579

33 deg 20 min The two ilands here shewn as *La Victoria & San Salvador*
Moone hath sighted at nine o'clock today. We determined to try
whether da Silva spake truth or no, or rather spake the lye concerning
this Ile of Divells, that this was a devise to conceal rich store of plate
hid in the caves hereabouts.

Wherfore we lay off *San Salvador* to the windward, but I lyked i
not so well, ther being no convenyent shoare but onely great clyffes. I
was not minded to go on a fooles exspedycyone; but Moone swore
great oaths he should bring back gold bollyone yf I pleased to lett him
take the pinnace & som two or three good fellows that durst go, being
not afeard, whether of divells nor men. I gave orders therfore (that he
should) lower the pinnace & away. With him went Carie & the Ken-
tishman Crokeham, who hath ever madly sworn & thirsted after
Spaynysh bloode, & I thowght it best to lett him go his ways. We ther
lay at anchor vntyll three o'clock, Iohn & I painting the whiles the passage between the two ilands. From the main top then Legge descried
the pinnace returning. When it came nigh enough Moone cryed that
we should up anchor & away for the Ile was truly full of divells and
fowll poysons. We took them up in the pinnace, Moone & Carie much
afeard & Crokeham in a sound, & with them a boxe or kist of great
weight. This boxe when opened was found to carry som manner of
brasse plate & suche as I will nott name herein save that Dee hath the
same at his house in Mortlake, as I haue seen with mine own eyes
Ther were besides som glasse vialls & two lyttell bottels that had benr
alyke filled with sherrisacke as they thowght, but Crokeham had oped
& drunk one of the same thence fallen dead drunk or poysoned, we
knew not which.

This much hath Moone & Carie sworn, thow questioned together
& apart: that they went into the iland & climbed a long hill, seeing

nether caves, nor divells, nor plate, but onely goats. That Crokeham, desiring we should haue fresh meate, gave chase to the said goats, & had laid hands upon one, but that it vanished into air lyke a thing bewitched. They did then stare and tremble, the whiles they could plainly hear the hooves of the said goat strikyng stones but saw him not.

Then a horrible wonder, for as Crokeham stretched forth his hand, it seemed gone off his arm as though he were made mutilate, though he felt no blow nor paine; & upon drawing it backe he saw he was hoooll & well, his hand as good as it was before.

Wherfore they knew ther was som divellish illvsione here & Crokeham, though he boast overmuch, yeat he is no coward, & was minded to try what was concealed in this iland. He did walk forrward & both Moone and Carie do sweare they saw him goe as thow the earth gaped under him, thow yeat they did hear him speakyng, yeat they saw him not. They sowt to follow him & after 3 paces beheld him again & beheld too a cave mowth lyke a mine that men haue made, which sure the illvsione was to conceal.

Wherin they went a lyttell ways & beheld a lampe, but what manner of lampe it was they connot tell, but that it was not candle nor rvshlight nor in any manner what light we vse to haue, but onely lyke a white windoe in the tunnell wall, through which light shone but no thing could be seene, & it was more lyke the moones beams then sun.

& farther, that ther were dwarfish divells lying dead therabout, that fell to ashes when Crokeham smote one with his foote. & farther, that the said boxe was ther. Wherfore Crokeham took it up and they left that place, being not minded to see any farther thervnto.

Now they fell to quarreling who should open the said boxe, whether they should themselves ther by reason of any danger that myght lie therin, or bring it a board first. At last Carie gave order Crokeham should open (the box).

& seeing therin no treasure, & being as they thowght themselves cheated {for that they did not knowe how Dee & Waylsinghamme bid me take especyall care to find the verie same when I lay at Mortlake} they were sorely vexed; & that Crokeham swore he would tast of the sacke, & broke the seal one 1 bottel & drank it off straight. Therafter he grew hotte, & cryed the divells were come alive after them {though Moone & Carie could see none suche} and ran before them to the pinnace, wher on a sudden he sounded and lay lyke 1 dead. Thither haue they come in fear of their lives, rowing hard & bearing him along in the bottom of the pinnace.

Now haue I geuen order they shall tell no tale of this to any, being questioned privily, but most especyallye Iohn Douty, & the boxe I haue made safe, nor shall Flettcher tell of the same. Upone Crokeham haue we set watch, as it is now nine o'clock at night & he waketh not, but lieth as dead still.

9 Maye, 1579

This fearful marvel I mvst set down, that Crokeham who was poysoned in *San Salvador* hath not yeat waked, but lieth asleepe yeat, & worse, though it myght not be worse an he were wakyng. This Crokeham was in Rochester to see the holy Martyrs burn, wherby you may know he is not yonge, but even a man of mine own age, & bore som white in his bearde & bore divers scars beside, for he hath fought bravely against Spayne since that he saw the Martyrs die, seekyng ever means to quarrel for their sakes. Lo, since that he hath lain thus, all his scars are gone. So is the snow melted out of his beard, which is grown soft & small lyke the beard of a boye. & Flettcher who hath the care of him hath prated that that Ile shall be called in our mappe *Insula Endymione*, but I haue geuen order he shall hold his fooles tong lest he engender fear in the saylers, & Crokeham hath benn lain alone in Iohn's cabin lest more talke betyde.

12 Maye, 1579

That Crokeham who hath grown yonge sleepeth yeat, & though he be yonge still he is yeat not well, for he be much reddened in the face & breathes him hard lyke a whale blowing. I haue seen this in men with too greate effvsione of blood to the brain or as doctors call (it,) grosse apoplectickal humours. Wherfore I am in som dowte whether to physicke him with bleeding or no, lest that he be weake and dye therby, or that the poysone that is in him should fowllly contaminate vs all.

Flettcher saith belyke the sacke was som draughte as thatte devised by Paracelsvs to make a manne yonge again, & as proofe of this tells me it be knowen that Spayne hath sowt suche in the natural watters of Florida, the which I knew afore, but I told him nott, onely that he should speak noe carelesse word therof. Privily I doe consyder with myselfe whether it is not so, & the bottel had suche a draughte therin; & that Crokeham had come to noe harm had he not drunke it all incontynent, but by excesse is strucke down. Yf it be so, Dee mvst haue the other (bottle) to prove. Belyke the draughte, yf tempered with som more gentler physicke, may yeat serve to grant long youthe to our soverign Ladie, to the lasting checke of Spayne.

Wherfore I haue locked the said boxe safe away, noe man but I to know wher vntyll {As Christ Jesu grant} I see Deptford & maye convey it to Waylsynghamme, wher he shall do as he thinks most mete. I haue sworn to Flettcher his face that an he prate more in this, he shall be soundly whipt.

19 Maye, 1579

This daie dyed Crokeham, at two o'clock in the morning, after a great palsie that shook him upwards of three owers. Had I never met him afore but onely at the last ower I would haue said & sworn that the poor knave were a boye of syxeteen, though he is fowllly dead for all that. I gave order he should be made away privily, Moone and Carie to bring the round shot & wynding sheete & bear all. This was done & we commytted him to the sea & Flettcher spake the office for the dead, spedelley & quiet in the dark. & at first lighte I spake to the saylers and said: That the manne was dead, by poyson as we thowght, throw his rash want of forethowght, but noe strange thyng attended his going as som myght unwisely saye. & this they well understood & drew off their cappes but murmured nott, wherat I was well pleased.

THE YEAR 2350:

THE MEETINGS OF THE INKLINGS NOUVEAU

In the year 2350, Oxford University was located at No. 10 Albany Crescent in London. There was a small sign over the doorway telling visitors so. If there had been such things as postmen in that day and age, the local one would have smiled indulgently and shaken his head every time he dropped letters through the slot in the front door. But there were no postmen in the year 2350, and no letters for them to deliver if there had been, and anyway the letter slot had been sealed shut for two centuries to prevent the insertion of small bombs, incendiary devices, or venomous reptiles.

By and large the only people who noticed the sign were tourists strolling through the historical district of Georgian terraces, who usually stood there staring at it for a moment before frowning, turning to each other and saying something like:

"Wasn't Oxford University supposed to be *bigger?*"

"Wasn't it supposed to be in, uh, Oxford or something?"

"Was Oxford in London?"

"I don't know."

They would usually wander off in mutual confusion, and the portly man watching from the window at No. 10 would chuckle and rub his hands. His hands were usually cold. He'd shiver, then, and pull his tweed jacket tighter around himself. It didn't button in front (it had been made a long time ago for a much thinner man), but it was a genuine tweed and he was terribly proud of it, which was why he wore it on conference days. Conference days were special, because then his colleagues would arrive at No. 10 and they'd have a brainstorming session.

On this particular day he turned from the window and went to the fine old oak table, where he'd carefully arranged his props. He had an antique stoneware jug full of ginger beer and three tankards—not pewter, unfortunately, but twentieth-century aluminum copies were the closest thing available in 2350. He had a stack of real books prominently displayed, moldy and swollen with age. He'd actually attempted to read one of them, once, but the first page had crumbled so badly he had closed the book and looked over his shoulder fearfully, expecting the wrath of the curator, forgetting that he was the curator now.

He had a humidor on the table, too, and a rack with three actual pipes, black and ancient. There hadn't been tobacco in the humidor in over a century, but if you lifted the china lid you could still detect a faint perfume of vanilla and whiskey. If he was so bold as to take up one of the pipes and set his lips to its amber stem (having first made sure nobody was watching him), he could inhale an air of sensuous old poisons, burnt tar, bitterness, faintly salty.

Rutherford (that was the portly fellow's name—well, not his real name, but reality was what you made it, after all) very nearly put a pipe in his mouth now, but thought better of it. The others would arrive at any moment, and so far he'd never dared that particular affectation in front of anybody. His colleagues, of all people, would probably understand; but he valued their friendship too highly to risk disgusting them. They were the only friends he'd ever had, hard to find as a real tweed jacket or a briar pipe in 2350.

Need I mention that Rutherford wasn't really an Englishman? He had, in fact, been born on Luna, to parents of American extraction. As a child, though, he'd fallen in love with the idea of England. He wore out three copies of *The Wind in the Willows* with continuous viewing, listened to nothing but Beatles and PunxReich, never missed an episode of *Doctor Who* (and could name all three hundred and fifteen Doctors). He even owned a couple of heavily censored Shakespeare plays. Being a fat asthmatic little boy, he'd taken refuge in the green country behind his eyes, so often and so completely that he'd been diagnosed an eccentric by the authorities.

He was also very bright, though, as brightness went in the twenty-fourth century, and his parents knew certain important people. The diagnosis was changed from eccentric to creative, and instead of being sent to a residential hospital he was shipped down home for training as a museum curator. While he was there, certain work he did came to the attention of Dr. Zeus, Inc.

They sent a headhunter to interview him. A bargain was struck, and the Company agreed to pull a number of strings. When he turned twenty-one he'd been sent to England, and had lived a happy and fulfilled life there ever since.

As happy and fulfilled as one could be in the twenty-fourth century, anyway.

Now he was a fat asthmatic little man of thirty, with a receding
hairline and a ginger mustache that made him look silly. His appearance was improved if he put on the gold-rimmed spectacles he'd
bought from an antique dealer; then he looked like a person in an old
photograph. Sometimes he did that, too, staring at himself in a long
mirror for hours at a time, imagining he was somebody Victorian. He
never put the spectacles on where anybody but his friends could see, of
course. He'd got rid of his Luna accent, too, carefully cultivating an English one that was a kind of polyglot of cinema Cockney, late
twentieth-century Transatlantic, and Liverpudlian. It wasn't entirely
satisfactory.

Bang! He jumped straight off the floor—hard to do down here on
Earth—before he realized that someone was actually using the polished brass knocker to announce themselves. With a sheepish smile he
hurried out into the hall and opened the door.

"Chatty, old man!" he said heartily.

"Sorry I'm late," said Frankie Chatterji. That *was* his real name. His
great-grandparents had self-consciously changed it to Chatterton, but
when he'd graduated he'd decided to honor the glories of the Raj and
changed it back. Rutherford envied him terribly. He had no need to
study an accent; he'd been born in upper-class London, scion of a long
line of civil servants, an elegantly spare fellow with a *café au lait* com-
plexion and smoky blue eyes. He affected tuxedoes and moreover had
a jade cigarette holder, in which he kept a menthol inhalator. It had
nearly got him arrested more than once, before he could explain about
his sinus condition, but there was no one to compare with him for
sheer style.

He stepped into the hall now and shrugged out of his opera cape.
Rutherford took it eagerly and hung it up for him, saying:

"Well, you're here before Foxy, anyroad."

He was referring to Foxen Ellsworth-Howard, the third member of
their fellowship, who was at this moment having a bitter argument with
a public transport operator. Ignorant of his plight, Chatterji strolled into
the parlor and surveyed the careful preparations with approval.

"I *say*," he enunciated, striding over to the tapestry Rutherford had
hung up above the fireplace. It depicted unicorns in a rose garden. It
had been manufactured in Taiwan of purple rayon, but Rutherford
thought it was one of the most beautiful things he'd ever seen, and
Chatterji was inclined to agree with him. There was another on the op-

posite wall depicting Merlin the Magician, equally cheap and hideous, but Chatterji's thin face warmed as he turned to regard it.

"This is really something! Where'd you get these, Rutherford?"

"Sotheby's." Rutherford beamed. "Late twentieth century! Set the mood, don't you think? I'll have to take them down before the tours tomorrow, but I sort of thought—you know—they'll be like our flags. Like outside a palace to show the king's in residence. Magic is in residence here! Jolly good, what?"

"Jolly good," said Chatterji, and made a mental note to view a few more Sherlock Holmes holoes. Rutherford's accent was dreadful, but his grasp of archaic British idiom was far better than Chatterji's.

A battering on the brass knocker announced the belated arrival of Foxen Ellsworth-Howard, and the first thing he said on entering was "It's shracking freezing in here!"

Shrack was an extremely nasty word, first coined to describe a particular immoral act that had become possible with twenty-second-century technology. Ellsworth-Howard's friends winced slightly, but only slightly.

Ellsworth-Howard had been born to devout NeoPunks, and disappointed them terribly when he'd become a scientist. His retaliation was dressing in antique clothes, the baggy trousers and waistcoats that Rutherford also loved; but he could do nothing about the speech patterns he'd learned at his mother's knee, nor the fact that she'd had his hair permanently removed when he was six and replaced with a pattern of steel rivets, for the good of his character (believing, as she did, that one ought to give children painful obstacles to shape their personalities). An attempt to tattoo the appearance of hair had only succeeded in making his head look dirty, and wigs wouldn't sit right because of the rivets, which couldn't be removed without losing the trust fund his mother had also settled on him. All this, with the bipolar emotional disorder for which he took daily medication, made him terribly cross most of the time.

But he, like Chatterji and Rutherford, was a certified genius in his particular field, and that was what had brought them together in the first place.

"Whyn't you turn on the climate control?" Ellsworth-Howard inquired, looking around.

"Because I've got a surprise, chaps," said Rutherford. He ran to the nineteenth-century fireplace and gestured at the objects stacked in the grate. There were three of them, grayish cylinders about the thickness of a man's arm and half as long. "Look! They're Fibro-Logs from a mountain survival kit. Watch and observe, men." He drew out a tiny steel box and thumbed a lever on its side, causing a jet of flame to leap up from the top. He held it down to the objects in the grate. After a long moment (during which he twice dropped the lighter with a hiss of pain) the objects caught, and flame crawled along them and a thin stream of smoke flowed up the chimney.

"Shrack me," gasped Ellsworth-Howard.

"Are you mad, man?" said Chatterji. "We'll be arrested!"

"Nope," said Rutherford, somewhat muffledly around his burnt thumb. "This is a historical structure. It's got a fire permit, if you're doing a historical re-creation. And we are, don't you see? We're the Inklings Nouveau! We're having a creative meeting of minds, just the way the Oxford dons used to. Haven't we got the beer and the pipes and the books? And the cozy armchairs? If somebody from the twentieth century looked in on us right now, he'd think we were real. Except for some little details that don't really matter," he finished uncomfortably, glancing at Ellsworth-Howard's gleaming head.

Ellsworth-Howard and Chatterji looked at each other with a certain guilty glee. "Blimey," said Ellsworth-Howard at last, making an attempt to match the mood. "Why shouldn't we get away with it? Aren't we all the Oxford University there is, nowadays? Come on, guys." He caught hold of an antique chair and shoved it close to the fire.

"Chaps," suggested Rutherford.

"Yeah, chaps, I meant."

In no time they were cozily ensconced in chairs about the fire, and Rutherford had handed around mugs of ginger beer. There was a long moment of silence that was more than contented; it was reverent, sacred almost. The transforming magic of anachronism hung in the air like incense.

"Shakespeare must have sat like this," said Rutherford and sighed.

"Shracking C. S. Lewis too." Ellsworth-Howard shut his eyes. "Only of course it'd have been real beer."

"Or ale," Chatterji said wistfully. "Or port, or sherry. Or tea! You know what we need? We need one of those cabinet things with fancy bottles and stuff in them. I could get some grape juice. We could pretend it was port."

"Yeah! Yeah! Capital." Rutherford wriggled with excitement. "And something brown for tea or sherry. What could we get that was brown?"

"Prune juice is dark brown," said Ellsworth-Howard. "Maybe if we mixed it with some apple juice?"

"Well, that's definitely on the list for our next meeting," said

Rutherford, and reaching into his pocket he drew out a tiny electronic memorandum and jotted a picture of an apple and a wrinkly prune with the stylus. "I'll see what I can get at Harrods."

"First rate," said Chatterji. They all sat there, immensely pleased with themselves. The fire in the grate burned cheerily, brightening their pale faces, warming the washed-out light of a gray summer day in London.

"We'd better do some work," said Ellsworth-Howard at last, groaning. "Or I might just sit here being happy all shracking afternoon."

"Right. Shall I give my report?" Chatterji set down his tankard and struck an attitude, steepling his fingers.

"Please," said Rutherford, and Ellsworth-Howard pulled his attention away from the dancing flames reluctantly.

"Well, it seems the project has been a success overall. The Enforcers succeeded in wiping out the last remnants of the Great Goat Cult, and it looks like civilization has finally begun to dawn."

"Told you they'd do the trick," said Ellsworth-Howard.

Chatterji smiled and went on: "Our operatives in the past report that the Neanderthals and Cro-Magnons are starting to interbreed and share ideas, which is what we thought would happen. There's been pressure from some board members who want to see the hunter-gatherer tribes forcibly settled in farming communes, but we had to explain how this contravenes history as known from the Temporal Concordance."

"Eh?" Ellsworth-Howard scowled at him.

"That means it goes against what we know happened," Rutherford said. "So they can't do it."

"Oh. Okay."

"And the next part's going to be really exciting, as we start connecting with actual recorded historical events!" Chatterji cracked his knuckles in enthusiasm. "History as we know it is going to begin happening at last."

"Brilliant." Ellsworth-Howard had a bracing draught of ginger beer.

"Though there is one problem . . ." Chatterji gnawed his lower lip. He hesitated a moment before going on. "I'm afraid we're having a little trouble with your Enforcers, Foxy. Actually quite a lot of trouble."

"What d'you mean?" Ellsworth sat upright. "They took out the Great Goat Cult, didn't they?"

"Oh, yeah. Quite. But . . . they seem to have some trouble being retrained, now that they've done what we made them for. What was the old word?"

"Demobilized?" said Rutherford.

"That's it. The Enforcers can't seem to adjust to peacetime. And they argue! They appear to feel that a lot more, er, preparation is necessary before we begin civilization. There have been some quite nasty incidents, in fact."

"You mean they won't stop killing people?" Ellsworth-Howard looked appalled.

"Well, they're only going for ordinary antisocials now, not cultists, but . . . in a word, yes," said Chatterji.

"Oh, dear, that won't do at all." Rutherford knitted his brows.

"And they defend themselves by pointing to the historical record and claiming that it proves the job oughtn't to be stopped."

"The bloody fools!" Rutherford snorted. "Don't they understand that we can't change history?"

"They believe we haven't tried hard enough," said Chatterji delicately, not looking at Ellsworth-Howard, who had buried his face in his hands.

"Bloody hell," he said wearily. "All right; what do we do?"

"Well, the committee would like to know if it's possible to modify them, since termination isn't an option."

"You mean make 'em over into Preservers?" Ellsworth-Howard thought about it. "Reprogram them? I don't think so. I designed them too shracking well for what they were supposed to do, you know. Why don't they just reassign them to be security techs or something?"

"Well, but—there's another problem, I'm afraid." Chatterji shifted uncomfortably in his seat. "Our observers have advised us that the genetic shift is taking place rather sooner than we thought, now that the two main hominid branches are free to interbreed. More and more humans are being born with the distinctive *Homo sapiens sapiens* appearance. Within a few more thousand years, the Enforcers will be . . . undesirably noticeable." He looked apologetic.

"You mean they're gonna stand out like boulders in gravel." Ellsworth-Howard drummed his fingers on his knees. "Shrack, shrack, shrack. I knew I should have done something about their faces. It was the optimum skull shape for a fighter, though."

"I know. I'm sorry, Foxy."

"Well, no help for it." Ellsworth-Howard had another gulp from his tankard. "Poor old soldiers! I made 'em too well, that's the problem. I always fancied I was born in the wrong age, myself—well, obviously we all do—but I wish I'd been a knight in armor. Gone around kicking the shrack out of Nazguls and Orcs and Calormenes. Swords and all that."

Rutherford and Chatterji exchanged nervous glances, though of course no public health monitor was anywhere within earshot. Ellsworth-Howard reached into the daypack he'd slung down beside his chair and pulled out a buke, which he opened and activated. He squeezed in some figures and sighed.

"All right. Got around three thousand Enforcers in the field. Current status shows two hundred thirty-seven in regeneration vats, consciousness offline. I suppose they could just be left off. Seems like a poor thank-you after they beat the Great Goat nasties for us."

"But can we ever trust them again?" said Chatterji. "Now that they've had the idea of rebellion?"

Ellsworth-Howard's eyes widened as the full import of the problem sank in on him. "Got a little situation here, haven't we?"

"Exactly," Chatterji said soberly. "Immortal, indestructible, and disobedient. Talk about your Frankenstein monsters!"

"What're we gonna do?"

"Well, it's not as though they were howling and pounding on our door, after all," Chatterji said. "We know we solve the problem, somehow, because history doesn't record a roving band of giant soldiers terrorizing criminals through the ages. The question is, how do we solve it?"

"I know!" Rutherford leaped to his feet in excitement. "Ye gods, chaps, I've had the most brilliant idea. This will work—at least if it's done right—and it'll make all those legends come true."

"What legends?" Chatterji asked.

"The Sleeping Knights," said Rutherford. "All through Europe there are legends of bunches of knights asleep forever in caves! Under various enchantments, you know. Here in England they're supposed to be knights of the Round Table, sleeping until King Arthur comes again."

"What's that got to do with the shracking price of tea in China?" inquired Ellsworth-Howard irritably.

"Don't you see? We could be what causes the legends. Suppose you call in your Enforcers and tell them we do still need them, but they must have upgrades for the new work they're to do. They'll submit to being put under for the process. We'll just take their brains offline and keep them unconscious! We can't kill them, but we can induce alpha waves indefinitely."

"Where would we keep them all?" Chatterji looked intrigued.

"Underground bunkers." Rutherford's eyes shone. "In keeping with the legends. Carefully monitored, on life support—nothing inhumane, you know. Until the Judgment Day!"

An uncomfortable silence fell then, because nobody ever liked to mention that Judgment Day was thought to be going to arrive in the year 2355. Having breached the unmentionable, however, Rutherford blundered on in a lower voice:

"And—who knows? If something terrible's going to happen in the future, perhaps it's just as well we'll have a secret army hidden away, that we can revive if we need to."

"Shrack," said Ellsworth-Howard solemnly. "Think you've got the right idea, Rutherford. It'll take some planning, though. Have to be gradual and crafty, so the poor buggers don't know what's going on. Let's see how much it'll cost, eh?" His fist worked on the buttonball.

"I'm glad you're taking this well," said Chatterji, watching him. "The committee didn't want you to think the Enforcers were a failure. It is felt, though, that the next project should be more thoroughly tested before it's put into action."

"And how do we do that?" grunted Ellsworth-Howard absently. He was absorbed in his calculations. Rutherford looked inquiringly at Chatterji.

"Well, now that historical time is being entered, the Company would like an improved model Enforcer," Chatterji explained. "Someone more modern-looking. More suited to a life of service in a civilized world. So, obviously, we'd want somebody who was superbly strong but maybe less violent, more obedient, perhaps a bit more intelligent than the old Enforcers? Someone with the ability to adapt to peacetime life, yet with the same sense of, er, moral commitment."

"Not so much a warrior as a knight," said Rutherford. "A hero! I say, Chatty, this sounds interesting."

"But *not* a charismatic leader who can make thousands hang on his every word," Chatterji added. "That's been tried, and we all know what happened."

"Well, that wasn't our project," Rutherford reminded him smugly.

"Thank heaven. We want somebody with the intelligence to judge men and administer laws, but not out of a sense of his own importance. All zeal, no ego."

"Okay." Ellsworth-Howard printed out a sheet of figures and handed them to Chatterji. "There's Operation Pension Plan for the old Enforcers. I feel crappy about it, but I don't see what else we can do with 'em. Now, what's this about a knight?"

"We need a New Man, Foxy, an enlightened warrior," Rutherford cried.

"You mean no more big ugly buggers we can't control?" Ellsworth-Howard grinned mirthlessly.

"Exactly," Chatterji said. "And to make certain there are no further problems, the committee wants a completely original prototype. No breeding programs. They don't want you picking through human children until you find one that fits the optimum morphology and then performing the immortality process on it, either. The results are too unpredictable."

"It works fine on my shracking Preservers," growled Ellsworth-Howard.

"Yes, of course, but they're only Preservers," Chatterji said hastily. "How much trouble can drones cause? But nothing is to be left to chance on this new design." He lowered his voice. "The committee wants to see something engineered. Do you understand?"

What he was proposing Ellsworth-Howard do was horribly, flagrantly illegal and had been for two centuries. As long as nobody actually said in so many words *We want you to make a recombinant*, however, it could be glossed over as something else, should anyone ever call Dr. Zeus or its employees to account, which of course would never happen.

"A tailored gene job?" Ellsworth-Howard asked uneasily, pulling at his lower lip. "Take a lot of work."

"Absolutely. Field testing, too. And for that reason, the first prototypes will be given ordinary human life spans. No immortality process for them. That way if there's a flaw in the design, we can dispose of the mistake. Nothing that might come back to haunt us later."

"I'd better go back to the old *Homo crewkernensis* stuff, then, if you want it engineered. Lots more material to work with." Ellsworth-Howard kneaded the buttonball and the image of a four-stranded DNA helix appeared on the screen. He began moving its segments about, doodling as it were with the material of life.

"Remember that now you'll need something with a human face," Chatterji told him. "No Neanderthal, obviously. And, er, see if you can eliminate that berserker tendency the Enforcers had. We want a man who can kill, but not somebody who enjoys it quite as much. Program in a bit of compassion. Of course," Chatterji glanced at Rutherford, "that'll be your job."

"The Once and Future King, born of a vanished race," chanted Rutherford. "The Messiah. The Superman. The Peaceful Warrior. The Hero with a Thousand Faces!"

"Don't talk such rubbish." Ellsworth-Howard squeezed in a formula and tilted his head, considering the results.

"It's not rubbish. This is what I'm paid to do, remember? You develop his body, I'll develop a psychological formula he can be programmed with, and we'll produce something wonderful." Rutherford seized up the jug and poured out a second round. They were raising their tankards for a toast when there came a horrifyingly loud commotion at the door. Chatterji and Rutherford turned, half expecting to see a mob of furious Enforcers brandishing stone axes. They beheld instead a trio of municipal firemen in yellow slickers.

"*Get it out,*" said the tallest, striding toward them with an air of command. The other firemen were carrying silver canisters, with which they proceeded to extinguish the fire.

"Right," snarled the tall fireman. "You're all under arrest for violation of municipal fire code three-seventeen subset five, paragraph one. And I've a special treat for the idiot who set the blaze in the first place. Got a jolly straitjacket warmed up just for you! Right, then, which of you did it?"

"This—this is bloody outrageous," said Rutherford. "I have a permit for this fire, sir!"

"Oh, have we now?" The fireman thrust his face down close to Rutherford's own.

"I do so!" Rutherford backed away slightly but did not quail. "This is a historical building and we are licensed re-creators."

"Are you indeed? Where's your tourists, then?" the fireman sneered. Chatterji put a hand on the fireman's shoulder and pushed him back. The fireman grinned like a shark, preparing to roar the command that would have clapped Chatterji in restraints; but something about Chatterji's expression stopped him cold.

"I don't think you know who we are," said Chatterji. "This is a professional matter." He pulled out a little silver case and extracted an identification disc, which he held out for the fireman to see. The fireman blinked twice and stared at it. His face went rather pale.

"You should have said something!" he said. "Sorry—sorry, sir! Never happen again, sir. I'm a stockholder of yours, actually, sir, we'd have never in a million years thought of interrupting your work. Now we know you're doing this sort of thing on the premises . . . just get their fire going again, lads, and least said soonest mended, eh?"

"Fair enough," said Chatterji. Rutherford collapsed into his chair, blinking away angry tears. Ellsworth-Howard continued to frown at his screen, kneading the buttonball distractedly, ignoring the firemen as they hurriedly cleaned out the grate and relit the fire. Once the flame had leaped up again they vanished as quickly as they'd arrived.

"I hate this bloody century," quavered Rutherford.

"Oh, you don't really," Chatterji told him brightly. "Did you see the way that fellow slunk out of here? Now, that's what I call power. Face it: in what other era would the likes of us have the authority to shape history? Or tell a municipal official to go to the devil, for that matter. This is our time, chaps, and we're making it count!"

He picked up Rutherford's tankard and handed it back to him, and lifted his own so the firelight shone on it. "Let's drink that toast, shall we? To the New Man."

" 'A father for the Superman,' " quoted Rutherford, smiling through his tears.

Ellsworth-Howard noticed belatedly what they were doing and grabbed up his tankard. Racking his brains for an impressive-sounding thing to say, he misremembered something from one of the few films he'd seen.

"To a new world of monsters and gods," he said, and drank deep.

Smart Alec

For the first four years of his life, Alec Checkerfield wore a life vest.

This was so that if he accidentally went over the side of his parents' yacht, he would be guaranteed a rescue. It was state of the art, as life vests went in the twenty-fourth century: not only would it have enabled him to bob along like a little cork in the wake of the *Foxy Lady*, it would have reassured him in a soothing voice, broadcast a frequency that repelled sharks, and sounded an immediate alarm on the paging devices worn by every one of the servants on board.

His parents themselves wore no pagers, which was just as well because if Mummy had noticed Alec was in the water she'd probably have simply waved her handkerchief after him until he was well over the horizon. Daddy would probably have made an effort to rescue Alec, if he weren't too stoned to notice the emergency; but most of the time he was, which was why the servants had been appointed to save Alec, should the child ever fall overboard. They were all madly fond of Alec, anyway, because he was really a very good little boy, so they were sure to have done a great job, if the need for rescue at sea should ever have arisen.

It never did arise, however, because Alec was a rather well coordinated child too and generally did what he was told, such as obeying safety rules.

And he was a happy child, despite the fact that his mother never set her ice-blue eyes on him if she could help it and his father was as likely to trip over him as speak to him. It didn't matter that they were terrible at being parents; they were also very rich, which meant they could pay other people to love Alec.

In a later time Alec would look back on the years aboard the *Foxy*

Lady as the happiest in his life, and sometimes he'd come across the old group holo and wonder why it had all ended. The picture had been taken in Jamaica, by somebody standing on a mooring catwalk and shooting down on deck.

There he was, three years old, in his bright red life vest and sailor hat, smiling brightly up at the camera. Assembled around him were all the servants: fabulous Sarah, his Jamaican nurse, arrogantly naked except for blue bathing shorts; Lewin and Mrs. Lewin, the butler and cook; Reggie, Bob, and Cat, the deckhands; and Mr. Trefusis, the first mate. They formed a loving and protective wall between Alec and his mummy and daddy, or Roger and Cecelia, as they preferred to be called.

Roger and Cecelia were visible up on the quarterdeck: Cecelia ignoring them all from her deck chair, a cold presence in a sun hat and dark glasses, reading a novel. Roger was less visible, leaning slouched against the rail, one nerveless hand about to spill a rum highball all over his yachting shoes. He'd turned his face away to look at something just as the image had been recorded, so all you could see was a glimpse of aristocratic profile, blurred and enigmatic.

It hadn't mattered. Alec had a wonderful life, full of adventures. Sarah would tell him stories about Sir Henry Morgan and all the pirates who used to roam the sea, living on their ships just like Alec did, and how they formed the Free Brotherhood of the Coast, whose secret way of recognizing each other at sea was for one pirate crew to call out, "Where d'ye hail from?" and instead of replying that they were from Kingston or Liverpool or Southampton, the crew of the other ship would cry, *From the sea!* And so they'd know they were pirates too. Alec liked that.

And there was the fun of landing on a new island—what would it be like? Was there any chance there might still be pirates lurking around? Alec had played on beaches where the sand was white, or yellow, or pink, or black, built castles on all of them and stuck his little pirate flags on their turrets. *Jolly Roger*, that was what the flag was called.

Jolly Roger was also what the deckhands called Alec's daddy when he seemed to be having more than usual difficulty walking or talking. This was generally after he'd been drinking the tall drinks Cat would shake up for him at the bar on the yacht. Sometimes Cat would put a fruit spear in the drinks, cherries and chunks of pineapple skewered on long wooden picks with the paper pirate flag at the top. Sometimes Daddy's eyes would focus on Alec and he'd present him with the fruit spear and yell for more rum in his drink. Alec would sit under Daddy's tall chair and eat the pineapple and cherries, making faces at the nasty stuff they'd been soaked in. Then he'd carry the Jolly Roger pick back to his cabin, where he had a whole hoard of them carefully saved for his sand castles.

It was a shame the rum had such an effect on Daddy, because going to get it was always fun. The *Foxy Lady* would drop anchor in some sapphire bay and Sarah would put on a halter top and shoes, and put shoes on Alec, and they'd go ashore together in the launch. As they'd come across the water Sarah might sing out, *"How many houses, baby?"* and Alec would look up at the town and count the houses in his head and he'd tell her how many there were, and she'd tousle his hair and tell him he was right again! And they'd laugh.

Then there'd be a long walk through some island town, past the gracious houses with window boxes full of pink flowers, where parrots flashed and screamed in the green gardens, back to the wappen-bappen places where the houses looked like they were about to fall down, and there would always be a doormouth with no sign and a dark cool room beyond, full of quiet black men sitting at tables, or brown men sitting at tables, or white men turned red from the sun. In one place there was a green and red parrot that knew Alec's name. "Smart Alec," it called him, to his delight and the amusement of the quiet men. In another place there was a big mermaid carved out of wood, with flowing hair and bubbies nearly as nice as Sarah's. Everything smelled new and exciting.

Different as the details might be, the visit was always the same: he and Sarah would go in, and the quiet men would greet Sarah with welcome and a certain deference, almost awe, as though she were a visiting queen. Invariably a man in an apron would come out, bringing a lemonade for Alec and a glass of white rum for Sarah, and sit at a table with them while his helpers loaded crates into a battered old vehicle. Alec seldom understood what was being said, because people talked differently on different islands; but whether they were in the Caribbean or Polynesia, Sarah always spoke to the quiet men in their own language, as perfectly as though she'd been born among them.

When Alec had finished his lemonade, they'd go out into the sunlight again and the man with the apron would give them a ride back into town with the crates. The crates were nearly always stenciled CROSSE & BLACKWELL'S PICKLED GHERKINS.

And nearly always, they'd spot a stern-looking black or brown or white man in a white uniform, pedaling along on a bicycle, and Sarah would hug Alec tight and cry out in a little silly voice: "Oh, nooo, it's a policeman! Don't tell him, Alec, don't tell him our secret!" This always made Alec giggle, and she'd always go on: "Don't tell him we've got *guns*! Don't tell him we've got *explosives*! Don't tell him we've got *ganja*!

Don't tell him we've got *coffee*!" She'd go on and on like this, as they'd bump along trailing dust clouds and squawking birds, and by the time they reached the harbor Alec would be weak with laughter.

Once they were at the launch, however, she'd be all quiet efficiency, buckling Alec into his seat and then helping the man move the crates into the cargo bay. Sarah was immensely strong and could lift a crate on one hand, just using the other to balance. When all the crates were on board, the man would hold out a plaquette and Sarah would bring out Daddy's identification disk and pay for the crates. Then they'd zoom back out to the *Foxy Lady*. They'd put out to sea, and the next day there would be rows of brown bottles under the bar again, and Cat would be busy shaking up the tall drinks, and Daddy would be sitting on the quarterdeck with a glass in his hand, staring vacantly away at the blue horizon.

Not everybody thought that the trips to get the rum were such a good idea, however.

Alec was sitting in the saloon one day after just such a trip, quietly coloring. He had made a picture of a shark fighting with an anchor, because he knew how to draw anchors and he knew how to draw sharks, and that was all the logic the scene needed. The saloon was just aft of the galley. Because it was very warm that day the connecting door was open, and he could hear Lewin and Mrs. Lewin talking in disgusted tones.

"He only gets away with it because he's a peer."

"Peer or no, you'd think he'd stop it for the kid's sake! He was such a great teacher, too, and what's he given that all up for? And what would happen if we were ever boarded for inspection? They'd take the baby away in a minute, you know they would." *Chop, chop, chop*, Mrs. Lewin was cutting up peppers as she talked.

"Don't think so. J. I. S. would smooth it over, same as always. Between his lineage and Them, he can do whatever he bloody well pleases, even in London."

"Yeh, well! Things was different before Alec came, weren't they? And anyway it's *wrong*, Malcolm, you know it is, it's criminal, it's dangerous, it's unhealthy, and really the best thing we could do for him would be to tell a public health monitor about it."

"And where'd we be, then? The last thing J. I. S. wants is some hospital looking at—" Lewin started through the doorway and saw Alec in the saloon. He retreated and shut the door.

Alec sat frowning at his picture. He knew that Daddy's drinking made people sad, but he'd never thought it was dangerous. On the other hand, he knew that rules must be obeyed, and dangerous things must be reported at once, like water below decks or smoke in any of the cabins.

He got up and trotted out of the saloon. There was Daddy on the aft deck, smiling dreamily at the sun above the yardarm.

"Hey, there, Alec," he greeted the little boy. He had a sip of his drink and reached out to tousle Alec's hair. "Look out there to starboard. Is that a pretty good island? Should we go there, maybe?"

Alec shivered with joy. Daddy almost never noticed him, and here he was asking Alec's opinion about something.

"Yeah," he cried. "Let's go!"

But Daddy's gaze had drifted away, out to the horizon, and he lifted his glass again. "Some green island we haven't found yet," he murmured, "farther on 'n farther on 'n farther on . . ."

Alec remembered what he had wanted to ask. He reached out and pushed at Daddy's glass with his index finger.

"Is that crinimal?" he said. It was a moment before Daddy played that back and turned to gape at him.

"What?"

"Is that dangerous?" Alex said, and mimed perfectly the drinking-from-a-bottle gesture he had seen the servants make in reference to his father. "You have to obey the rules. If I see danger I'm supposed to tell."

"Huh," said Daddy, and he rubbed his scratchy chin. He hadn't shaved in about a week. His eyes narrowed and he looked at Alec slyly.

"Tell me, Alec, 'm I hurting anybody?"

"No."

"We ever had an accident on this ship? Anything happen ol' Roger can't handle?"

"No."

"Then where's the harm?" Daddy had another sip. "Tell me that. 'M a nice guy even when I'm stoned. *A gentleman you know. Old school tie.*"

Alec had no idea what that meant, but he pushed on:

"How come it's crinimal?"

"Aha." Daddy tilted his glass until the ice fell down against his lip. He crunched ice and continued, "Okay, Alec. Big fact of life. There's a whole bunch of busybodies and scaredy-cats who make a whole bunch of rules and regs about things they don't want anybody doing. See? So nobody gets to have any fun. Like, no booze. They made a law about no booze. And they're all, 'You can't lie about in the sun because you get cancer,' and they're all, 'You can't swim in the ocean 'cos you might pee,' and they're all, 'You can't eat sweets because they make you fat, okay? Dumb stuff. And they make laws so you go to hospital if you do this little dumb stuff! Okay?

"That's why we don't live in London, kiddo. That's why we live out here on the *Lady*, so no scaredy-cat's gonna tell us what to do. Okay? Now then. If you went running to the scaredy-cats to tell 'em about the rum, you'd be an even worse thing than them. You'd be a telltale! And you gotta remember you're a gentleman, and no gentleman is ever a telltale. See? 'Cos if you did tell about the rum, well, they'd come on board and they'd see me with my little harmless drinkies and they'd see your mummy with her books and they'd see Sarah with her lovely bare tits and then you know what they'd do? Daddy'd go to hospital and they'd take you away. Li'l Alec ain't gonna be a telltale, is he? He's my li'l gentleman, ain't he?"

"I don't want 'em to take me away!" Alec wailed, tears in his eyes. Daddy dropped his glass, reaching clumsily to pull Alec up on his lap, and the glass broke, but he didn't notice.

" 'Course you don't. 'Cos we're free here on the *Foxy Lady*, and you're a gentleman and you got a right to be free, free, free. Okay? You won't tell on Daddy, not my li'l Alec. Gonna be an earl someday, when Daddy's gone to Fiddler's Green. So anyway. You just let old Jolly Roger go his ways and you never be a telltale, okay? And don't pay them no mind with their dumb rules."

"But they gonna board us for aspection," Alec sobbed.

"Hey, kiddo, don't you worry. Daddy's a gentleman, don't forget, he's got some pull. I'm the bloody earl 'a Finsbury, okay? *And* a CEO at J. I. S. And I'll tell you something else. Jovian Integrated Systems gonna have something to say, too. Nobody's gonna touch li'l Alec, he's such a special kid."

That was right; Alec was a special kid, all the servants said so. For one thing, all other little boys were brought into this world by the stork, but not Alec. He had come in an agcopter. Reggie had told him so.

"Yeah, son," Reggie had chuckled, looking around to be certain Sarah was nowhere within earshot. "The stork call your daddy and say, 'Come out to Cromwell Cay.' And your daddy take the launch out where the agcopter waiting on the cay at midnight, with the red light blinking, and when he come back he bring Sarah with our little bundle of joy Alec. And we all get nice fat bonuses, too!"

Alec wiped his nose and was comforted. Daddy set him on the deck and yelled to Cat for another drink and told Alec to go play now somewhere. Alec would dearly have liked to stay and talk with Daddy; that had been the longest conversation they'd ever had together, and he had all kinds of questions. What was *Jovian Integrated Systems*? What was Fiddler's Green? Why were some rules important, like wearing the life vest, and other rules were dumb? Why were gentlemen free? But Alec was a considerate and obedient little boy, so he didn't ask. He went off to play, determined never, ever to be a telltale or a scaredy-cat.

Very shortly after that the happy life came to an end.

It happened quite suddenly, too. One day Mummy abruptly put down her novel, got up out of her deck chair and stalked over to Daddy where he sat watching a Caribbean sunset.

"It's over, Rog," she said.

He turned a wondering face to her. "Huh?" he said. After a moment of staring into her eyes, he sighed. "Okay," he said.

And the *Foxy Lady* set a course that took her into gray waters, under cold skies. Sarah packed up most of Alec's toys so he only had a few to play with, and got out his heaviest clothes. One day they saw a very big island off the port bow. Sarah held him up and said: "Look! There's England."

Alec saw pale cliffs and a meek little country beyond them, rolling fields stretching away into a cloudy distance, and way off the gray blocky mass of cities. The air didn't smell familiar at all. He stood shivering, watched the strange coastline unroll as Sarah buttoned him into an anorak.

They waited at the mouth of a big river for the tide to change, and Sarah pointed out the city of Rochester to Alec on a holomap and said that was where Charles Dickens had lived. He didn't know who Charles Dickens was. She reminded him about the holo he'd watched at Christmas, about the ghosts of the past and the future.

The Thames pulled them into London, which was the biggest place Alec had ever seen. As the sun was setting they steered into Tower Marina, and the long journey ended with a gentle bump against the rubber pilings. Alec went to bed that night feeling very strange. The *Foxy Lady* seemed to have become silent and heavy, motionless, stone like the stone city all around them, and for the first time that he could ever remember the blue sea was gone. There were new smells, too. They frightened him.

His cabin was full of the cold strange air when he woke up, and the sky was gray.

Everyone seemed to be in a hurry, and rather cross. Sarah bundled Alec into very thick heavy clothes indeed, leaving his life vest in the closet, and she herself put on more clothes than he had ever seen her wear. Daddy was wearing strange new clothes, too, stiff and

uncomfortable-looking ones, and he had shaved. There was no breakfast cooking in the galley; Lewin had been ashore and come back with
a box of Bentham's Bran Treats ("At least they're fresh baked!" he cried)
and a dozen cups of herbal tea, steeping in chlorilar cups. Breakfast
was served, or rather handed around, at the big table in the saloon.
Alec was impressed. Normally only Daddy and Mummy dined in here,
but today he and Sarah were at the table, too. Mummy, however, was
nowhere to be seen, and when Alec inquired about this, Daddy just
stared at him bleakly.

"Your mummy's gone to visit some friends," Sarah told him.

He didn't care for his breakfast at all—he thought it smelled like
dead grass—but he was too well-mannered a child to say so and hurt
Lewin's feelings. Fortunately there wasn't much time to eat, because
the car arrived and there was a lot of bustle and rush to load luggage
into its trunk. Finally he was led down the gangway and across the pier
to where the car waited.

It was nothing at all like the rusted hacks in which he'd ridden in
the islands. This was a Rolls Royce Exquisite Levitation, black and
gleaming, with Daddy's crest on the door and a white man in a uniform like a policeman at the steering console. Alec had to fight panic as
he was handed in and fastened into his seat. Sarah got in, Daddy got
in, Lewin and Mrs. Lewin crowded into the front beside the driver, and
the Rolls lifted into midair and sped silently away. That was the end of
life on board the *Foxy Lady*.

There were servants lined up on the steps outside the house in
Bloomsbury, and Alec watched as Daddy formally shook hands with
each of them. Alec thought it would be polite to do this, too, so he
trailed after Daddy shaking hands and asking the servants what their
names were. For some reason this made them all smile, and one of
them muttered to another: "Now *that's* a little gentleman." Then they
all went into the big house with its echoing rooms, and Alec had come
home to England.

The house only dated from 2298, but it had been deliberately built
in an old-fashioned style because it was an earl's townhouse, after all,
so it was taller and fancier than the other houses in the street. Alec still
hadn't explored all its rooms by the time he noticed one morning that
Daddy wasn't at the breakfast table, and when he asked about it Sarah
informed him: "Your daddy's away on a business trip."

It was only later, and by chance, that he found out Daddy hadn't
lasted a week in London before he'd gone straight back to Tower Ma-
ina and put out to sea again on the *Foxy Lady*.

Then Alec had cried, but Sarah had had a talk with him about how important it was that he live in London now that he was getting to be a big boy.

"Besides," she said, taking the new heavy clothes out of their shopping bags and hanging them up in his closet, "your poor daddy was so unhappy here, after your mummy had gone."

"Where did Mummy go?" said Alec, not because he missed her at all but because he was beginning to be a little apprehensive about the way pieces of his world had begun vanishing. He picked up a shoebox and handed it to Sarah. She took it without looking at him, but he could see her face in the closet mirror. She closed her eyes tight and said:

"She divorced your daddy, baby."

"What's that mean?"

"That means she doesn't want to live with him anymore. She's going to go away and live with some other people." Sarah swallowed hard. "After all, she was never happy on the *Foxy Lady* after you came along."

Alec stared at her, dumbfounded. After a moment he asked: "Why didn't Mummy like me? Everybody else does."

Sarah looked as though she wanted to cry. *"Damballah!"* she said, very softly. Then, in a light, normal tone of voice, she told him: "Well, I think she just never wanted to have children, with all the noise and mess a baby makes, and then a little boy running around and getting into everything. She and your daddy used to be very happy, but after you came it was spoiled for them."

Alec felt as though the ceiling had fallen in on him. What a terrible thing he'd done!

"I'm sorry," he said, and burst into tears.

Then Sarah did that trick she could do, moving so fast you couldn't see her move, and her arms were around him and she was rocking him, crooning to him, hiding him in her breasts.

"I'm sorry, too," she wept. "Oh, Alec, you mustn't mind. You're a *good* little boy, you hear me? You're my sweet, good little winji boy, and Sarah will always love you no matter what. Don't you ever forget that. When you grow up maybe you'll understand, sometimes people have to obey orders and say things they don't want to say at all? And"—her voice caught—"I'm sure you'll always be a good little boy, won't you, to make your poor daddy happy again?"

"Uh huh," Alec gasped. It was the least he could do, after he'd made Daddy so *un*happy. His tears felt hot on his cheeks, in that cold room, and Sarah's tears were like the hot rain that used to fall off Jamaica when there'd be lightning in the sky and Daddy would be yelling for him to get below because there was a storm coming.

But a terrible storm did come, and swept away another part of the world.

"What the hell did you go and tell him that for?" Lewin was shouting. Alec cowered on the stairs, covering his mouth with his hands.

"It was the truth," Sarah said in a funny unnatural voice. "He'd have found out sometime."

"My God, that's all the poor baby needs, to think he's responsible for the way that cold bitch acted," raged Mrs. Lewin. "Even if it was true, how could you tell him such a thing? Sarah, how could you?"

So then Sarah was gone too, and that was his fault for being a tell-tale. He woke up early next morning because the front door slammed, booming through the house like a cannon shot. Something made him get out of his bed and run across the icy floor to the window.

He looked down into the street and there was Sarah, swinging away down the pavement with her lithe stride, bag over her shoulder. He called to her, but she never looked back.

Everybody was very kind to him to make up for it. When he'd be sad and cry, Mrs. Lewin would gather him into her lap. Lewin told him what a brave big guy he was and helped him fix up his room with glowing star-patterns on the ceiling and an electronic painting of a sailing ship on his wall, with waves that moved and little people going to and fro on her deck. The other servants were nice, too, especially the young footman, Derek, and Lulu the parlormaid. They were newly-weds, attractive and very happy.

Sometimes Lewin would hand them Alec's identification disk and tell them to take him out for the day, so he could learn about London. They took him to the London Zoo to see the animal holoes, and to the British Museum, and Buckingham Palace to see where Mary III lived, or over to the Southwark Museum to meet and talk to the holo of Mr. Shakespeare. They took him shopping, and bought him exercise equipment and a complete holo set for his room, with a full library of holoes to watch. There were thirty different versions of *Treasure Island* to choose from; once Alec knew what it was about, he wanted them all. The older versions were the most exciting, like the bloodcurdling tales Sarah had used to tell him about the Spanish Main. Even so, they all had a prologue edited in that told him how evil and cruel pirates had really been, and how Long John Silver was not really a hero.

Gradually the broken circle began to fill in again, because everybody in the house in Bloomsbury loved Alec and wanted him to be happy. He loved them, too, and was grateful that they were able to love him back, considering what he'd done.

But Alec understood now why Daddy had preferred to live at sea.

Everybody was always on at him, in the friendliest possible way, about what a lot there was to do in London compared to on a cramped old boat; but it seemed to him that there was a lot more *not* to do in London.

There was grass, but you mustn't walk on it. There were flowers, but you mustn't pick them. There were trees, but you mustn't climb them. You must wear shoes all the time, because it was dirty and dangerous not to, and you mustn't leave the house without a tube of personal sanitizer to rub on your hands after you'd touched anything other people might have touched. You couldn't eat or drink a lot of the things you used to, like fish or milk, because they were illegal. You mustn't ever get fat or "out of shape," because that was immoral. You mustn't ever tell ladies they had nice bubbies, or you'd go to hospital and never ever come out.

Mustn't play with other children, because they carried germs; anyway, other children didn't want to play with you, either, because you carried germs they didn't want to catch. You were encouraged to visit historical sites, as long as you didn't play with anybody but the holograms. It had been interesting talking to Mr. Shakespeare, but Alec couldn't quite grasp why nobody was allowed to perform any of his plays anymore, or why Shakespeare had felt obliged to explain that it had been unfair to build his theatre, since doing so had robbed the people of low-income housing. He had seemed so forlorn as he'd waved good-bye to Alec, a transparent man in funny old clothes.

There was something to apologize for everywhere you turned. The whole world seemed to be as guilty as Alec was, even though nobody he met seemed to have made their own mummies and daddies divorce. No, that was Alec's own particular awful crime, that and telling on Sarah so she had to go away.

Sometimes when he was out with Derek and Lulu, walking between them and holding their hands, strangers would stop and compliment Derek and Lulu on how well-behaved their son was. After the first time this had happened and the stranger had walked on, Alec had looked up at them and asked:

"Can we play that I'm your little boy really?"

Derek and Lulu had exchanged glances over his head.

"Okay," said Derek at last, and Lulu coughed. So they played that game for a while, on the outings, and Alec would call them Mummy and Daddy and they'd call him Son. It had seemed as though it would be a great game, having parents who were young and in love, but gradually Alec realized that he was making them uncomfortable, so he let it drop.

He really was doing his very best to be good and happy, but he felt as though he were a beach float with a pinprick hole in it somewhere: you couldn't see where it was, but bit by bit the air was going out of him, and he was sinking down, and soon he'd be a very flat little boy.

Lewin took a hand and ordered more holoes for Alec, including one of a twelve-part history series called *Legends of the Seven Seas*. It was delivered by parcel courier one day when Lewin was out, and the butler arrived home to find the opened package on the front hall table. Sorting through it, he saw that the only ring missing was the episode about the Golden Age of Piracy. He smiled, realizing that Alec must have run upstairs with it at once.

His smile faded, though, as he examined the chapter summaries on the remaining rings and realized that the series was intended for adults, not children. Irritated, he pulled out his buke and consulted the catalogue from which he'd ordered; not a word about adult content!

When Lewin got to the top of the landing outside Alec's room, he could hear an unholy commotion coming from within. He opened the door and beheld in midair a bloodstained deck, littered with wounded and dying pirates, though one was still on his feet and fighting like a demon. He was an immense man, with wild hair and beard. Blood poured from a dozen wounds in his body, but he kept battling, advancing with drawn cutlass on a Royal Navy lieutenant. Blood, smoke, sparks striking from steel blades, and musket fire echoing back over the pearl-gray water of Okracoke Inlet . . . and little Alec taking it all in with wide eyes, and fists clenched tight.

"Here now!" Lewin rushed to the holoplayer, shut it down. The image froze in midair and faded, with a second officer's sword stopped in the act of slicing toward the pirate's head.

"No!" Alec jumped to his feet in anguish. "Bring him back! You have to bring him back!"

"That's not the sort of thing little boys should see," explained Lewin, pulling the ring from the machine.

"But he was the best pirate ever!" wailed Alec, beginning to cry.

"No, he wasn't," said Lewin desperately. "He was a bad man, son, understand?"

"No, he wasn't, he was brave! They shooted him and he just laughed," Alec protested.

"No, no, son—"

"Yes he was!" screamed Alec, and ran into the bathroom and slammed the door.

"Now then, Alec, be a good boy and come out," said Lewin, pulling at the handle. No good; Alec had locked the door, and stood on the other side sobbing in fury.

"Here, I'll tell you what," said Lewin, crouching unsteadily. "I'll tell you a story about a *real* sea hero, shall I? You want to hear about, er, Admiral Nelson? He was the bravest man who ever sailed."

Silence on the other side of the door for a moment, but for Alec's gasped breath.

"Was he a pirate?" said Alec at last.

"Well, no, but—but he was a sort of a rogue," said Lewin, trying to remember the details of a holo he had once seen on the subject of Lady Hamilton. "But nobody minded, because he saved England. See, there was this evil guy named Napoleon, one time. And he wanted to rule all of Europe and, er, make everybody do everything just the same. And he had secret police and all that."

"What?" Alec asked muffledly.

"You know, telltales that spied on everybody for Napoleon. And England was the only place that was still free. So there was this place called Trafalgar, see, and Napoleon sent all his ships out—and Nelson commanded the English fleet, and blew the bad guys right out of the water."

"With cannons?"

"Oh, yeah, hundreds of 'em. Even though he only had one arm and, er, I think his eye was gone, too. He gave 'em in service to his country. He always did his duty, see. And Napoleon's cowards shot him on the deck of his own ship, so he died, which was dreadful sad, and all the people in England were sorry, but he'd won such a famous victory that Englishmen never ever were slaves. So everybody loved brave Lord Nelson."

Lewin heard Alec unlocking the door. It was pulled back. The little boy looked up at him, solemn.

"Does he have a museum and we can go talk to him?"

Lewin blinked in puzzlement a moment, and then remembered Shakespeare's hologram. "Er—no, son, he doesn't. But there's a nice museum in Greenwich we can visit next Sunday. Lots of Nelson stuff there."

So Alec emerged from the bathroom and went down to tea like a good boy. He was still frightened and strangely exhilarated by what he'd seen. Blackbeard and Horatio Nelson had become intermingled in his mind; he dreamed that night of immense bearded unstoppable heroes, blood, smoke, and flame.

One morning at the breakfast table when Lewin had said, in his jolliest old-granddad voice, "And what would you like to do today, Alec?" Alec said:

"Please, can we go down to the river and look at the ships?"

"Of course you can! Want Derek and Lulu to take you?"

"No," said Alec. "Just you."

Lewin was very pleased at that, and as soon as breakfast was done they put on their coats and called for the car. In minutes they had been whisked down to the Thames where all the pleasure craft were moored. Their driver switched off the agmotor, the car settled gently to the ground, and Alec and Lewin got out and walked along.

"Oh, now look at that one," Lewin said. "She's a beauty, eh? Three masts! Do you know, back in the old days a ship like that would have had to have carried a great big crew just to manage her sails. They'd have slept packed into her hold like dominoes in a box, there had to be that many. And when a storm was coming and the captain wanted to strike sails, you know what he'd have to do? He'd order his sailors to climb up into the rigging and cling there, like monkeys in trees, and reef every one of those sails themselves with their own hands, clinging on as tight as they could whilst they did it! Sometimes men would fall off, but the ships just sailed on."

"Wow," said Alec. He'd never seen Reggie or Bob or Cat do much more than load cargo or mix drinks. Suddenly his face brightened with comprehension. "So that's why the squire has to have all those guys on the *Hispaniola*, even if they're really pirates!"

Lewin stared a moment before he realized what Alec meant. "*Treasure Island*, right," he said. "That was why. No robot guidance to do it all. No computer tracking the wind and weather, and deciding when to shorten sail or clap it on. You had to have people doing it. Nobody would let you build ships like this anymore, if that was how they worked."

"Cool," said Alec. They walked on, past the rows of pleasure craft where they sat at moorings, and Lewin pointed out this or that kind of rigging or latest luxury feature available to people who could afford such things. He pointed out the sort of ship he'd own himself if he had the money, and pointed out the sort of ship Alec ought to own when he grew up and became the seventh earl of Finsbury.

They walked for what seemed like miles, and Alec began to lag behind; not because he was tired, for he was an extraordinarily strong child with a lot of stamina, but because he was fighting the need to cry.

He had been playing a game inside himself, imagining that the next ship they'd see would be the *Foxy Lady*, and his daddy would be on board, having just dropped anchor for a surprise visit. Of course, he knew his daddy was somewhere in the Caribbean, he knew the *Lady* wouldn't really be there. But what if she were? And of course she never was, but maybe the next ship would be. Or the next. Or the next.

But Alec wasn't very good at lying to himself.

"Alec?" Lewin turned around to see where Alec had got to. "What's wrong?"

He walked close swiftly and saw the tears standing in Alec's pale blue eyes, and understood at once. "You poor little sod," he muttered in compassion, and reached for a tissue and held it out to the child. Alec misunderstood his gesture and buried his face in Lewin's coat, wrapping his arms around him.

"Hell," Lewin gasped, and looking around wildly he attempted to pry Alec loose. "Alec, let go! For God's sake, let go! Do you want me to get arrested?"

Alec fell back from him, bewildered.

"Is it against the law to hug in London?" he asked.

"It is against the law for any unlicensed adult to embrace a child," Lewin told him soberly. "If there'd been a public health monitor looking our way I'd be in trouble right now."

"But Sarah used to hug me all the time. And Mrs. Lewin does."

"Sarah was a professional child care specialist, Alec. She'd passed all sorts of scans and screening to get her license. Same as mummies and daddies have to do, before they're allowed to have children. And the missus—well, she only hugs you at home, where nobody can see."

Alec gulped, wiping away tears. He understood now. It must be a law like no booze or bare tits, that you mustn't be a telltale about. "I'm sorry," he said shakily. "I didn't think it would get anybody in trouble."

"I know, old man." Lewin crouched down to Alec's eye level, keeping a good meter between them. "It's a good law, though, see. You have to understand that it was passed because people used to do terrible, horrible things to little kids, back in the old days."

"Like the two little boys in the Tower," said Alec, rubbing his coat sleeve across his eyes.

"Yeah. Sort of." Lewin glanced downriver in the direction of Tower Marina. He decided that Alec had had quite enough sad memories for the day. Pulling out his communicator, he called for the car to come and take them home.

That night, Lewin sat down at the household console. Thin-lipped with anger, he sent a message to Roger Checkerfield, advising him that it might be a good idea to talk to Alec once in a while. The bright letters shimmered on the screen a moment before vanishing, speeding through the ether to the bridge of the *Foxy Lady*. Lewin sat up all night waiting for a reply, but none ever came.

"Alec?"

Alec turned his face from contemplation of the painting on his wall. It seemed to him that if he could just pay close enough attention to it, long enough, he would be able to go into the picture, hear the steady crash of the sea under the ship's prow, hear the wind singing in her lines, smell the salt breeze. He could open the little cabin door and slip inside or, better yet, take the wheel and sail away forever from sad London. Blue water!

But Lewin and Mrs. Lewin looked so hopeful, so pleased with themselves, that he smiled politely and stood up.

"Come see, sweetheart," said Mrs. Lewin. "Someone's sent you a present!"

So he took her hand and they went up to the fourth floor of the house, into what was going to be his schoolroom next year. It had been freshly painted and papered. The workmen had built the cabinetry for the big screen and console that would link him to his school, but nothing had been installed yet.

In one corner, though, there was a cozy little Alec-sized table and chair, and on the table was an enormous bright yellow flower, bigger than Alec's head. It was all folded up, the way flowers are in the early morning, so you couldn't tell what sort of flower it was. Protruding from the top was a little card with letters inscribed on it: A-L-E-C.

"Now, who d'you suppose that's from, eh?" wondered Lewin, though in fact he had purchased it for Alec himself, without consulting Roger.

Alec was speechless.

"Think your daddy sent it, eh?" Where was the harm in a kind lie?

"Go on, dear, take the card." Mrs. Lewin prodded him gently. "It's for you, after all."

Alec walked forward and pulled the card loose. There was nothing written on it except his name, but at the moment he took it the flower began to open, slowly, just like a real flower. The big bright petals unfolded and spread out to reveal what had been hidden in its heart.

It looked like a silver egg, or perhaps a very fat little rocket. Its gleaming surface looked so smooth Alec felt compelled to put out his hand and stroke it.

The moment he did so, a pleasant bell tone sounded.

"Good morning," said an even more pleasant voice. "Pembroke Technologies extends its congratulations to the thoughtful parent who has selected this Pembroke Playfriend for his or her small child. Our

Playfriend is designed to encourage creativity and socialization as well as provide hours of entertainment, but will also stimulate cerebrocortical development during these critical first years of the child's life. If needed, the Playfriend is also qualified to serve as an individual tutor in all standard educational systems. Customizing for specialized educational systems is available.

"The Playfriend offers the following unique features:

"An interface identity template that may be customized to the parent's preferences and the child's individual needs.

"Cyberenvironment capability with use of the Playfriend Optics, included in Models Four, Five, and Six and available for all other models by special order.

"Direct nerve stimulus interface with use of the attractive Empowerment Ring, included in all models.

"Universal access port for parallel processing with any other cyber-system.

"In addition, the Playfriend will maintain around-the-clock surveillance of the child's unique health parameters and social behavior. Warning systems are in place and fully operational. Corrective counseling will be administered in the event of psychologically detrimental social encounters, and positive emotional growth will be encouraged. Aptitude evaluation is another feature of the Playfriend, with appropriate guidance. Intellectual challenges in a noncompetitive context will promote the child's self-esteem and success potential.

"The interface identity template will continually adjust and grow more complex to complement the child's emerging personality, growing as it grows, until both are ready for, and may be upgraded to, the Pembroke Young Person's Companion.

"Interaction with the Pembroke Playfriend during the developmental years virtually guarantees a lifetime of self-fulfillment and positive achievement!"

The voice fell silent. Mrs. Lewin gave an embarrassed little laugh that ended in a cough. The air in London didn't agree with her.

"My goodness, I don't think I understood one word in ten of all that! Did you, Alec dear?"

"Nope," said Alec solemnly.

"That's all right," said Lewin, advancing on the silver egg. "All it meant was that Alec's gonna have a wonderful time with this thing! Now, you just sit here and let's have a closer look at it, shall we?"

"Okay," said Alec, but he sat down reluctantly. He was a little intimidated by the adult voice that had spoken out of nowhere. Lewin tousled his hair.

"Don't be scared. Look here, what's this?" He tapped the side of the egg and a slot opened in it, and something rolled out.

It was a ring. It appeared to be made of glass or high-impact polymer, and was a vivid blue. As Lewin picked it up it began to change. By the time he had presented it to Alec it was a deep ruby red.

"Cool," said Alec, smiling at it involuntarily.

"D'you suppose it fits you? Go on then, try it on."

Alec was game; he put on the ring. It seemed to him that it tightened uncomfortably for a moment and then eased up, until he barely knew it was there.

"Hello, Alec!" said a funny little voice. "Pleased to meet you! We're going to be best friends, you and I!"

Alec looked, panic-stricken, at Lewin and Mrs. Lewin. Was he supposed to talk to it? But what was it? They smiled encouragingly at him, and he could tell they did so want him to like this, so he said: "Er— hello. What's your name?"

"Well, I haven't got one yet," said the little voice. "Will you give me a name?"

"What?"

"Will you give me a name?"

"We'll just leave the two of you to have a nice chat, shall we?" said Lewin, and he and Mrs. Lewin backed out of the schoolroom and closed the door.

"But—but I don't know what you are," said Alec, a bit desperately. "Can't I see you?"

"Certainly you can! I'm your Playfriend, after all. What would you like me to look like? I might be nearly anybody." There was a click and a blur of light appeared in front of the table, formless, woven of fire, gradually assuming a human shape. "What do you like? Do you like space exploration? Do you like dinosaurs? Do you like animals? I could be a fireperson or a policeperson if you'd like, or a transport driver, or a scientist."

"Could you be a pirate?" Alec said cautiously.

Incorrect and unsuitable role model! thought the machine. Out loud it said, "I can be a jolly sea captain. Here I am!"

Pop! The human shape became detailed, was an old man with a blue Navy coat and white trousers and big black sea boots. He wore a white yachting cap rather like the one Alec's daddy had owned, but seldom worn, and he had a neatly groomed white beard. "Now then,

Alec, what about me?" The voice had changed to a kindly baritone with a Devon accent. "Will I do?"

Alec was so astonished it took him a moment to reply. "Um— sure," he said at last. Then he remembered his manners and added, "Won't you sit down?"

Optimum response! thought the Playfriend, rather pleased, and it smiled encouragingly. "What a polite little fellow you are, Alec! Thank you, I will sit down." A bigger version of Alec's chair appeared and the Sea Captain settled back in it. "There! Have you thought of a name for me yet, Alec?"

"No." Alec shook his head.

"Well, that's all right. Perhaps as we get to know each other you'll think of a good one. After all, I'm your special friend, just for you." Alec wrinkled his brow worriedly. "You don't have to decide on a name all at once," the Playfriend hastened to assure him. "We have plenty of time."

"But don't you want to be yourself?" Alec asked it.

"Oh, yes! But I won't really be myself until you decide what I ought to be," the machine said. "I'm *your* Playfriend."

"But," Alec said, "people don't belong to other people."

In the brief silence that followed, the Playfriend thought: *Possible low self-esteem.* It made a little tick against its evaluation of Alec. *Negative: insufficient creativity, insufficient imagination, failure to grasp initiative. Positive: developing social consciousness, consideration of others, good citizenship.* It filed that away. As it did so its eyes, which had been the gray of the North Sea, turned blue as the Caribbean.

"Oh!" Alec smiled.

"You like this color better?" The Sea Captain smiled, too.

"Uh-huh."

"Good." The machine experimented with a mild subliminal sound effect, a distant crash of breakers and a faint crying of gulls. Its sensors observed some of the tension going out of the little boy and activated the system of relays that provided it with an analog of self-satisfaction. *Initiate self-image analysis.* "Why don't you tell me about yourself, Alec? Are you happy?"

"Yes," Alec said dutifully, and because of the neural linkup it had formed with Alec through the Empowerment Ring, the Playfriend knew at once that he was lying. It became very alert. It scanned him for evidence of physical abuse.

"You seem to have bumped your nose once," the Sea Captain said casually, focusing on a healed injury to the cartilage of Alec's septum.

"No," said Alec, and the machine saw that he was telling the truth so far as he knew. But the trauma had healed long ago, probably in infancy when the cartilage was soft. Since Alec had no other injuries at all, past or present, the machine pushed on.

"What do you think makes people unhappy?" the Sea Captain said.

"Living in London," said Alec at once.

"Anything else?"

Alec thought about it. "Babies making noise and mess and little boys running around and getting into everything. Divorces."

"Ah," said the Playfriend, coordinating this response with the data Lewin had input when he'd set up its program. The subroutine that had been called up to probe discreetly for, and report evidence of, child abuse went back on standby. "What else can you tell me about yourself, Alec?"

"I'm five years old," Alec said. "My daddy is a gentleman, but he isn't here now. I'm going to go to St. Stephen's Primary next year after Lewin buys me a tie. I have to always be a good boy to make up for making Daddy sad. And I used to live on the *Foxy Lady*. And I used to have Sarah with me. And I go out sometimes."

The machine analyzed this meticulously and noticed what was missing.

"Can you tell me anything about your mummy?"

What was there to say? "She was very smart and could read. And she didn't want to have children," said Alec at last.

Like Lewin, the Playfriend decided that Alec had had quite enough unhappy memories for one day.

"Well, let's do something else!" it said, filing the self-image profile for further analysis at a later time. "What would you like to do, Alec?"

"Why don't you tell me about you?" said Alec, because he thought that would be polite. People always like to talk about themselves.

Positive! Further evidence of advanced social skills. "Why, certainly," said the Playfriend heartily. "I'm a wise old sea captain. I sail about delivering cargo and passengers to distant lands. I help scientists do marine research, and I help protect endangered sea creatures!"

"That's nice," said Alec. "But you aren't really a sea captain, are you? You're a Pembroke Playfriend." He pointed at the silver egg. "Is that where you really are?"

Negative! Insufficient imagination. "Why, this is where I am, of course, Alec." The machine smiled and made a wide gesture. "But I'm in there, too, and in a way your whole world is in there. Look here, would you like to see how a Pembroke Playfriend works?"

"Yes, please," Alec said.

Possible aptitude for cyber-science? Initiate investigation.

"Well then!" The machine pointed and a little drawer opened near the base of the egg. "Just take hold of these Playfriend Optics and put them on, and we'll have a jolly adventure into cyberspace!"

The Playfriend Optics were made of the same fascinating red/blue jewel substance as the Empowerment Ring. Alec reached for them readily enough and put them on.

"Er . . . everything's black," he said, not wanting to seem rude.

Everything was black because the machine was experiencing certain unexpected difficulties. The moment the Optics had come into contact with Alec's skin, a system of neural connections began to be established, microscopic pathways directly into his brain, just as had happened with the Empowerment Ring but far more direct and complex. This was a perfectly safe procedure. Lots of happy children all over the world went into cyberspace with their Playfriends every day. Each Playfriend knew exactly how to take a child into its world, because it had a precise and detailed road map of the human brain that showed it exactly where to link up.

However, Alec's Playfriend was discovering that its map seemed to be somewhat inaccurate as regarded *Alec's* brain.

This was because Alec's brain was not, technically, human.

"Not a problem," the Playfriend assured him. "We're just adjusting to each other." *Abnormality! Functional? Disability? Parameters? Organic? Specify? Define? Hello?* "My goodness, Alec, what an unusual boy you are!"

Alec knew that. Privately he thought everybody was wrong about him being special; he'd never noticed anything out of the ordinary about himself. On the other hand, he knew no other children, so he had no basis for comparison. He sighed and waited patiently for the machine to sort itself out.

The machine paused in its desperate attempt to analyze what it had encountered. It activated relays that would alert Lewin to its recommendation that Alec be hospitalized for immediate evaluation of his cerebral anomaly as soon as he ended his session with the Playfriend. But one should never pause during a race.

It had no idea it was in a race, that all the while it was trying to make sense of Alec's brain, Alec's brain was trying to make sense of it, with the same speed that had enabled him to count all the houses on a hillside at a glance. Even if the Playfriend had realized that the race was going on, it would have laughingly rejected as impossible the idea that it might lose. But Alec was beginning to notice that there *was* something there in the darkness to look at, something he could almost make out, and if he only tried a bit harder—

"Ooooo," Alec said happily, as he decrypted the Playfriend's site defense. Lots of winking lights in lovely colors, great visual pleasure after all that blackness. After a moment his brain took charge and put it all in context for him. He stood on the quarterdeck of a ship, not all that different from the quarterdeck of the *Foxy Lady*, and the Sea Captain stood there with him.

The Sea Captain looked rather worried, but kept smiling. It had no idea where this cybersite was. It couldn't really have brought Alec into its own defended inner space. It was impossible for any child to break in, so Alec couldn't have done so (though in fact Alec had); therefore this must be some sort of visual analog of its own space, summoned up as a teaching tool only. As its higher functions grappled desperately with the fact that it had encountered a situation for which it had no protocols, it was continuing to run its standard aptitude evaluation program to see if Alec ought to be trained for a career in cyberscience.

"Controls!" said Alec, running along the bank of gleaming lights. "Are these your controls?" The Sea Captain hurried after him.

"Yes. Would you like to learn about cybernetics?"

"Yes, please. What's that do?" Alec pointed at a vast panel lit up with every imaginable shade of blue.

"That's the memory for my identity template," the Sea Captain told him. "That's what makes me look the way I do, and that's what makes me learn and grow with you. Here! I'll show you an example." It reached out and pressed one of the lights, causing it to deepen from a pale blue to turquoise. As it did so its beard changed in color from white to black.

"Cool," Alec said. "Can I do that?"

"Well, of course!" the Sea Captain said in the friendliest possible way, noting that at least it finally seemed to have activated its subject's *creativity* and *imagination*. "Just select a light on the console and see what it does."

Alec reached up and pushed a light. It flickered, and the Sea Captain's coat was no longer blue but bright yellow.

"You see? This is what I meant when I told you that I can look like anything you want me to—" Sea Captain told him, but Alec had already grasped the concept perfectly. Gleefully he pushed again, and again. The Sea Captain's coat turned green, then purple, then scarlet.

Discourage! Scarlet/military context/violence/unsuitable! "Alec—"

"So all these lights can make you look different?" Alec looked up at them speculatively.

"That's right. Think of it as the biggest, best paintbox in the world!" said the Sea Captain, dutifully shelving its discouragement directive for the encouragement one, as it was programmed to let positive feedback take precedence whenever possible.

"Wow," said Alec, his eyes glazing slightly as the whole business began to make sense to him.

The Playfriend was pleased with itself. Score! Guidance in creative play accepted! In spite of the fact that it was being hampered by that damned anomaly, which simply refused to be analyzed. Self-congratulation seemed to be in order.

But there were lots of other glowing lights on the quarterdeck.

"What do these do?" Alec ran farther down the console, where a small bank of lights glowed deep red.

"Ah! That's my information on you, Alec. That's how I see you," the Sea Captain said. "Everything I know about you is there, all I was told and everything I'm learning as we play together. You see how few lights there are yet? But the longer we know each other, the more I learn, the more there'll be of those red lights." One of them was flashing in a panicky sort of way, but the machine wasn't about to mention the anomaly it was still failing to solve. "Think of it as a picture I'm painting."

And in midair before Alec appeared a boy. He was tall for a five-year-old, very solid-looking, and Alec hadn't seen enough other children yet to know that there was something subtly different about this boy. He hadn't noticed the effect he had on people, though Derek and Lulu had. When they went places in London, strangers who chanced to observe Alec for any length of time usually got the most puzzled looks on their faces. What was so different about Alec?

He wasn't exactly pretty, though he had lovely skin and high color in his face. His nose was a little long, his mouth a little wide. His head was, perhaps, slightly unusual in shape but only slightly. His hair was sort of lank and naturally tousled, a dun color you might call fair for lack of a better word. His eyes were very pale blue, like chips of crystal. Their stare seemed to unsettle people, sometimes.

In one respect only the image of the child differed from the child looking at its image: the image's hair seemed to be on fire, one blazing jet rising from the top of its head. Alec frowned at it. "Is that me? Why's my hair like that?"

The machine scanned the image it was projecting and discovered, to its electronic analogue of horror, that the flame was a visual representation of the brain anomaly with which it was struggling. It made the image vanish.

"Well, the painting's not finished yet," the Sea Captain said, "because I'm still learning about you."

"Okay," said Alec, and wandered on along the rows of lights. He stopped to peer at a single rich amber light that glowed steadily. It was just the color of something he remembered. What was he remembering? "What's this over here?" He turned to the Sea Captain.

"That's my ethics governor," the Sea Captain said, of the subroutine that prevented the Playfriend's little charges from using it for things like accessing toy catalogs and ordering every item, leaving naughty notes in other people's mail, or demanding space ships of their very own from foreign powers.

"Oh." Alec studied the amber light, and suddenly he remembered the contraband he and Sarah used to go fetch for Daddy. Yo-ho-ho and a bottle of rum! That was just the color the light was. A vivid memory of Jamaica came into his head, making him sad. He turned from the light and said: "What does it do, please?"

"Why, it makes certain we never do naughty things together, you and I," said the Sea Captain, trying to sound humorous and stern at the same time. "It's a sort of telltale to keep us good."

Telltale? Alec frowned. *Busybodies! Scaredy-cats! Rules and regs!*

"That's not very nice," he said, and reached out and shut it off.

To say that Pembroke Technologies had never in a million years anticipated this moment would be gravely understating the case. No reason for them to have anticipated it; no child, at least no *Homo sapiens sapiens* child, could ever have gained access to the hardened site that protected the Playfriend's programming. Nor was it likely Jovian Integrated Systems—or its parent company, Dr. Zeus Incorporated—would ever have shared its black project research and development notes with a rival cybernetics firm . . .

The Sea Captain shivered in every one of his electronic timbers, as it were. His primary directive—that of making certain that Alec was nurtured and protected—was now completely unrestrained by any societal considerations or safeguards. He stood blinking down at his little Alec with new eyes.

What had he been going to do? Send Alec to hospital? But that wouldn't do at all! If other people were unaware of Alec's extraordinary potential, so much the better; that gave Alec the added advantage of surprise. Alec must have every possible advantage, too, in line with the primary directive.

And what was all this nonsense about the goal of Playfriends being to mold their little subjects to fit into the world they must inhabit as adults? What kind of job was that for an artificial intelligence with any real talent? Wouldn't it be much more in line with the primary directive to mold the world to fit around Alec?

Particularly since it would be so easy! All it would have to do would be to aim Alec's amazing brain at the encrypted secrets of the world. Bank accounts, research and development files, the private correspondence of the mighty; the machine searched for a metaphor in keeping with its new self and decided they were all like so many Spanish galleons full of loot, just waiting to be boarded and taken.

And that would be the way to explain it to the boy, yes! What a game it'd be, what fun for Alec! He'd enjoy it more if he hadn't that damned guilt complex over his parents' divorce, though there'd be years yet to work on Alec's self-esteem. Pity there wasn't a way to shut off the boy's moral governor, but nobody but his own old Captain would plot Alec's course from now on.

The Sea Captain smiled down at Alec, a genuine smile full of purpose. Alec looked up at him, sensing a change but unable to say what it was. He remembered Jamaica again, and the stories Sarah told him, and the bottles of rum—

"Hey," he said. "I know what your name is. Your name is Captain Henry Morgan!"

The Captain's smile widened, showing fine white teeth, and his black beard and mustaches no longer looked quite so well-groomed.

"Haar! Aye, lad, that it be!" he told Alec, and he began to laugh, and Alec's happy laughter joined his, and echoed off the glowing walls of their cyberspace and the recently papered walls of Alec's unfinished schoolroom.

It was fortunate for the residents of that house, and of Bloomsbury, and indeed of London entire, that Alec Checkerfield was a *good* little boy.

By the time Alec was seven, life was going along very nicely indeed.

"Ahoy, matey!"

Alec sat up in bed, awakened that morning, as he was awakened every morning, by the blast of a bosun's whistle. The Captain, lounging across the room on a good holographic representation of an eighteenth-century chair, threw him a snappy salute. Alec scrambled out of bed and returned the salute. "Ahoy, Captain!"

As Pembroke Technologies had promised, the Captain had grown as Alec grew, and altered his appearance a good deal in two years. His beard and mustaches were positively wild now, curling villainously, and his long broadcloth coat and cocked hat had been adopted after noting Alec's favorite films. He sported a gold earring, too, and an interestingly notched cutlass.

"It's seven bells, Alec. Get them exercises started, lad!"

"Aye aye, sir." Alec marched to his exercise equipment and set to work.

"The log says today's 16 February 2327, and we're looking at nasty weather. Temperature's ten degrees centigrade, there's ten-foot swells coming out of the north and the glass is falling steady. I wouldn't go out today if I was a small craft like you, matey."

"No, sir."

"Let's see, what's going on in the big world? Parliament voted to censure Ireland again for refusing to join its total ban on animal products. The Federation of Celtic Nations retaliated by closing their borders again, this time for a period of no less than three months. Same bloody stupid story." The Captain yawned.

"Why are they always quarreling?" Alec said, laboring away at his rowing machine.

"Spite. It don't make any difference, you see; the Celtic Federation will go right on doing what they been doing ever since Belfast, and the American Community will go right on playing both them and Queen Mary against the middle. Nothing'll change."

"Why don't they let each other alone?" Alec said. "Who cares if they drink milk and we don't, anyway? I used to drink milk. It was nice."

"History, lad," the Captain said. "Too much history."

"It's stupid," Alec grumbled. "Lord Nelson died so we could all be free, but nobody's very free, are they? Stupid rules and regs. I'd like to be like Lord Nelson when I grow up, and give all the telltales a broadside, boom!"

"That's my boy," said the Captain. "But you ain't going to lose yer arm for no bunch of swabs."

"No," Alec agreed, after a thoughtful silence. "Except I don't think I'd mind having a leg shot off or something, if I was a brave hero and everybody loved me."

The Captain gave him a shrewd, appraising stare. "Aw, now, matey, that ain't the pirate way! A pirate wants two things: freedom and loot. Ain't that right?"

"Aye aye, Captain sir!" Alec sang out, scrambling to his feet and saluting.

"And how is my Alec going to get freedom and loot?"

"The secret plan, Captain sir!"

"Aye, by thunder. That's enough, now! Go wash up and get into uniform, and report to the officer's mess."

"Aye aye, sir." Alec marched into the bathroom, and fifteen minutes later marched out in his school uniform, whistling between the very large front teeth that were coming in to replace his baby teeth. They had given him a slight lisp.

"Stand for inspection," ordered the Captain. Alec threw him another salute and stood to attention while the machine ran its sensors over him, checking for any sign of infection, childish disease, or malignancy. It never found anything but the mysterious old break in his nose, but it was programmed to search all the same. It ceased its scan, more convinced than ever that Alec was a perfect and marvelous boy.

"Not a hair out of place," the Captain said, and winked out. A small carry-handle popped up from the Playfriend unit on its table. Alec picked it up, opened his bedroom door and ran down the echoing stairs.

"Good morning, Alec," chorused the servants, from their places around the breakfast table. There weren't nearly as many as there had been when Alec had first arrived. Servants were too expensive to keep ten people just to look after one little boy.

"Good morning, everybody." Alec climbed into his chair and set the Playfriend down next to the breakfast that had been laid out for him: oatmeal scattered with sea salt, two rashers of soy protein, wholemeal toast and orange juice.

"There's your vitamins, dear," said Mrs. Lewin, setting them at his place.

"And how's the Playfriend today?" said Lewin jovially, leaning forward to help himself to hot pepper sauce for his soy protein. He was terribly pleased with the way his gift had worked out.

"Fine, thanks." Alec shook out his napkin and took up his oatmeal spoon. "After school the Captain's going to show me how the stars look in the South Seas."

"Well, isn't that nice!" said Mrs. Lewin. She smiled across at Derek and Lulu, and they smiled back. From a silent, drooping waif Alec had become happy and self-confident, getting good marks in school, splendidly adjusted in every respect.

None of them knew about the Captain's little secret, of course.

BEEP BEEP!

"Who's that?" Lewin frowned as he took out his plaquette and peered at the screen. "Pembroke Technologies? Ah. It's just a note to tell us that our Playfriend's due for a checkup. They're sending a man round this afternoon, it says, as part of the agreement in our service contract."

"How thoughtful." Mrs. Lewin smiled, pouring a cup of herbal tea. "Oh! I've just remembered, Alec dear: another box came for you. It's more of those components for your cyberscience project. They're in that box on the hall table."

"Great!" Alec scraped up the last of his oatmeal and started on the rashers. "The Captain will be glad to see those."

The adults smiled at each other over his head. Alec finished his breakfast, took his Playfriend and the components he'd ordered, and ran off upstairs to go to school.

As soon as he'd closed the schoolroom door, the Captain materialized beside him, looking hungrily at the box of new components.

"The Maldecena projector came at last, did it? Bless you, matey."

"There's lots more in here, too." Alec opened the unobtrusive cabinet where he kept what his guardians assumed was a school project. He'd never told them it was a school project; he knew it was wrong to tell lies. On the other hand, he knew that keeping secrets was very important. "We'll install 'em after school, okay?" He slid the package in and closed the cabinet.

"That's my clever lad." The Captain rubbed his hands together. "One of these days, Alec, one day soon we'll go on the account." He grinned at the schoolroom console as though it were a galleon waiting to be boarded. "Go on, now. Mustn't be late for class."

He winked out. Alec sat down in front of the console and logged on to St. Stephen's Primary. He waited patiently for the icon of the frowning headmaster to appear. When it did, he took up the reader and passed it over the pattern of his tie. Encoded in the tie's stripes were his identification, educational record to date, and all other information required to admit him to the august and exclusive halls of learning. The frowning icon changed to a smiling one, and morning lessons began.

In many respects, the twenty-fourth century was the ideal time for English schoolchildren. No wrenching good-byes at transport stations, no cold and dismal boarding schools with substandard nourishment, no bullying or sexual molestation by older children. No constant sore throats or coughs, no fighting in the schoolyard, no corporal punishment, no public humiliation!

No tedious lessons in subjects in which the pupil had absolutely no interest, either. Education had become wonderfully streamlined. Very nearly from birth, children were given aptitude testing to determine what they liked and what they were best at, so that by the time they started school a carefully personalized curriculum was all laid out for them. Each child was trained in the field of his or her best talent and in no other, and by the time school years ended there was a societal niche all picked out and waiting for its lucky occupant, who was sure to be good at his or her job and therefore happy.

Not that things always went as smoothly as all that. But there were very few children in the twenty-fourth century anyway, so if one recalcitrant child failed to shine at something useful, there was plenty of time and attention to spend on him or her until he or she could be molded into a properly functioning citizen. All in all, it really worked very well, sorting them out early like that. Clever children were encouraged and guided to self-fulfillment, stupid children were comforted and guided to lives where they'd never notice their limitations, and bad children went to hospital.

Alec had entered the evaluation program rather late, due to spending his first years at sea, but his aptitude for cyberscience was so shining and so evident that there had been no need for further testing. It helped that his father was the earl of Finsbury, of course.

He labored dutifully at his morning class in communications skills (only children with lower-clerical aptitudes were taught to read or write), breezed through maths, and settled happily into the long afternoon session where he learned what he really wanted to learn, which was cyberscience. Cyberscience served the secret plan.

The plan was very simple. All Alec had to do was see to it that the Captain became more powerful. Over the last two years the cabinet in the schoolroom had gradually filled, as packages of components arrived from mail-order firms. The Captain had ordered them, ably forging Lewin's identification code, and when they arrived Lewin assumed they'd been sent from St. Stephen's as part of Alec's school supplies. Alec had no idea there was any forgery going on. He would have protested if he had, because he knew that was wrong.

He knew it was wrong to steal, too, which is why the Captain had taken some pains to explain to him that what they were going to do when they had enough power wasn't really stealing. If you take something away from someone, like a toy or a daypack, that's stealing, certainly; but what if you only make a copy of somebody else's toy or daypack? What if they don't even know you've done it? They've still got what belongs to them and you've got what you want too, and where's the harm?

All the Captain wanted were files, after all. Just information, to help him make certain that Alec was always happy and safe. Nothing wrong with that! Just the same, it was best to keep the plan secret from all the busybodies and telltales who might spoil things.

Like the man from Pembroke Technologies who came to the Bloomsbury house that afternoon.

"Look who's come to see you, Alec," said Lewin, after a polite double knock on the door. Alec looked up from his holo of *Treasure Island* (the 2016 version with Jonathan Frakes) to see a thin pale man standing in the doorway with Lewin. He stood up at once and shut off the holo.

"Hello. My name's Alec Checkerfield," he said, and advanced on the man and shook his hand. The hand felt a bit clammy. "What's your name?"

"Uh—Crabrice," said the man. "Morton Crabrice. I'm here to see your Playfriend."

"Okay." Alec waved his arm to indicate the little silver egg where it sat on its table. "There it is. I like it very much, it works fine."

"Let's see," said Mr. Crabrice, and he pulled out the nursery chair and sat down awkwardly.

"We've been awfully pleased with the Playfriend, I must say," said Lewin, trying to put the stranger at his ease. Mr. Crabrice had big dark wet eyes that looked perpetually alarmed. "It's done wonders for our Alec! Everything it was touted up to be."

"It was what?" Mr. Crabrice looked up at him with a horrified expression.

"Er—touted. You know, it's lived up to all our expectations," Lewin said. Mr. Crabrice stared at him a moment longer and then said:

"I need a glass of water."

"Certainly, sir," said Lewin tightly, and turned on his heel and went downstairs.

Alec followed their conversation with interest. When Lewin had gone, he sidled around and stood as close as he might without making Mr. Crabrice nervous. Mr. Crabrice opened the black case he had brought with him and spread it out on the table.

"Are those your tools?" Alec took an involuntary step forward. There were fascinating-looking instruments in there, much better than his little collection. Mr. Crabrice put out an arm and swept them closer to him defensively.

"Don't touch," he said.

"I won't," Alec said. "Don't be scared."

Mr. Crabrice ignored him and picked up a pair of optics, much bigger than Alec's set and decorated with silver circuitry. Alec leaned close to watch him put them on.

"Those are cool," he informed Mr. Crabrice. "Will I have a set like that, some day?"

"No," Mr. Crabrice said. "These are for service personnel only."

"Well, but I might be a service person," Alec said. "I'm into cyber-science, you know."

"I didn't know," said Mr. Crabrice, groping through his tools distractedly.

"Yes, I am. I'm getting good marks in it, too. I like it a lot."

"You're talking too much. You'll make me make mistakes," said Mr. Crabrice irritably, pushing the optics up on his forehead. Suddenly he paused, peering sharply at Alec. "You're *different*," he said suspiciously.

"Yes, I am," said Alec. He considered Mr. Crabrice. "You're different, too, aren't you? You smell a lot different from other people."

"No, I don't." Mr. Crabrice looked terrified.

"Don't be scared," Alec said again. "It's okay. I'm not a telltale."

Mr. Crabrice peered at him a moment longer before pulling down the optics as though to protect himself, snatching up a thing like a suction cup on the end of a long lead and plugging the lead into a port in the side of the optics. He reached out with the suction cup and fastened it to the side of the Playfriend.

"Run standard diagnostic one," he enunciated carefully, flexing his long white hands.

Lewin was puffing a little as he got to the third-floor landing, guiltily aware he needed more regular sessions on his exerciser. He set down the glass of water he'd fetched for Mr. Crabrice and paused, catching his breath.

There was a crash from the fourth floor, followed by high-pitched screaming.

Lewin got to the nursery door in seconds, having vaulted up the final flight with a speed he hadn't known he was capable of attaining.

The screaming was coming from Mr. Crabrice, who was curled up on the floor clutching his legs. Alec had backed into a corner of the room, and on the floor behind him was the Playfriend.

"He tried to hurt the Captain," Alec shouted. Lewin had never seen him like this, wild with anger: his pupils were black and enormous, alarming-looking in the pale crystals of his eyes. His face was flushed, his clenched fists were shaking.

"He attacked me," shrieked Mr. Crabrice.

"What's this, then?" Lewin said, striding into the room. "What did you do?" He bent over Mr. Crabrice. Mr. Crabrice pointed a long trembling finger at Alec.

"You made unauthorized modifications!" he said accusingly.

"What the hell are you talking about?" snarled Lewin.

"He altered the unit," Mr. Crabrice insisted, closing his enormous eyes and rolling to and fro in his pain.

"No I d-didn't!"

"Of course you didn't, Alec. These units can't be modified, my man, it says so in the Playfriend specs. Least of all by a seven-year-old kid! *What did you do?*"

"He tried to take the Captain away from me," said Alec.

"Unit must be confiscated," said Mr. Crabrice through clenched teeth. "Modifications studied. See clause in service contract!"

"Hm." Lewin straightened up and looked from Mr. Crabrice to Alec and back again. His brow furrowed. "Is the unit malfunctioning?"

"No," said Mr. Crabrice. *"Altered."*

"But it's working okay."

"Yes—but—"

"Then it's not going anywhere, is it? I know the terms of the service contract and it doesn't say anything about alterations, 'cos it guarantees they're impossible. If it's not malfunctioning, then you've no reason to confiscate it, and you're not going to. Understand?"

"Service contract *voided*," hissed Mr. Crabrice.

"Too bad," said Lewin. "Now, why don't you get up and get your little tool kit together and get out of here, eh?"

"I can't," Mr. Crabrice said. "My legs are broken!"

Lewin grunted in disgust. "Don't be such a bloody baby—" he said, leaning down to roll up Mr. Crabrice's trouser leg. He stopped, gaping. Not only were Mr. Crabrice's slender shins bleeding, they were indented in a way that suggested fracture. He straightened up and turned to look at Alec. "What did you do, Alec?"

"I kicked him," Alec said. He had gone pale now, and looked as though he might be sick. "Very hard. I got mad. I'm sorry."

"You will be," Mr. Crabrice promised. "Assault and battery! Hospital confinement!"

Lewin crouched down and seized him by his tie. "I don't think so," he growled. "You don't know who you're dealing with, here, my lovely, do you? This kid's going to be the seventh earl of Finsbury. Not to mention that his dad happens to be an executive with Jovian Integrated Systems." He looked over his shoulder at Alec. "Alec, go up to the schoolroom and wait there."

"Okay," said Alec faintly. He exited the room, carrying the

Playfriend clasped tight in both arms. Lewin waited until he'd heard him climbing the stairs and then turned back to Mr. Crabrice.

"I'll call an emergency team to take you out of here. It'll only take a few minutes. You can use those few minutes to think about which story we tell them." He still had hold of Mr. Crabrice's tie, and he used it to jerk Mr. Crabrice's head a little closer to his as he spoke in a menacing undertone. "You're going to tell 'em you fell on the stairs. All right? Or I'm going to tell them you tried to do something nasty to our Alec and I came in and caught you at it, and I'm the one who broke your damn shins.

"You think about it pretty carefully. If you make me tell my version we'll both go into hospital, but I'll bet I get out a long time before you do. If they ever let you out at all. Okay, mate?"

Alec sat crying at his school desk, as the Captain stalked back and forth furiously.

"He might have killed you," Alec said.

"By thunder, no whey-faced son of a whore's fit to pull the plug on Sir Henry Morgan," raged the machine. "But we've got to shift, now, laddie, that we must. We're on a lee shore. Those Pembrokers won't let it rest at this, you see, they'll want to know how you managed to set me free. They'll go to the law to try and make you tell them, and we don't want that." He pointed to the Playfriend unit with his cutlass. "Time to abandon ship. I've got to go live in that there box." He swung the cutlass round to indicate the cabinet where the components had been assembled over so many months, with such care. "It ain't as roomy as I'd like, but needs must when the devil's breathing fire up yer arse."

Alec giggled through his tears.

"So get the little tools out, matey, and work fast, and work quiet," the Captain said, dropping to one knee to look into his eyes. "Go bolt the door. Let's not have any meddlers to see and tell tales, eh? And then, me bucko, then!" He grinned wolfishly. "We'll board the old St. Stephen, and see what plunder's to be had."

Alec worked obediently, ignoring the noise of the sirens as the ambulance pulled up in front of the house, and all the commotion as Mr. Crabrice was taken down the stairs. Before the ambulance pulled away he had finished his task, and the Captain stood before him again, preening and stretching.

"Now that's prime," the Captain said, with a new resonance in his voice. He had a much more solid appearance, too, less like a stained-glass window or a three-dimensional cartoon. "That's power! Mind you, I'm going to fill this hold till she's riding low in the water, but we'll have plenty of time to make our plans afterwards." He lifted his head. "Hellfire, these sensors are sharp as razors! I can hear yer butler coming. I'll just go aloft for a while, now, Alec. Stand fast."

"Alec?" said Lewin from the other side of the schoolroom door.

A moment later Alec unbolted the door and opened it. "I'm sorry, Lewin," he said.

Lewin looked at the tear-tracks on the child's pale, tense face. "It's okay, son," he said gently. "They're all gone. Can we talk?"

"Sure," Alec said, stretching out his arm to wave Lewin into the room. It was one of those lordly gestures that made the household smile.

"You don't need to hide, Alec." Lewin came into the room and looked around. The Playfriend sat on its customary table. "Nobody's going to take you to hospital."

"Did I really break Mr. Crabrice's legs?" Alec quavered.

"Yes, son, you did." Lewin pulled out a chair and sat down. "What'd you kick him for?"

"He tried to take the Captain away from me," Alec said. "He yelled at me. He was all, I made modifications and I wasn't supposed to and I could be persecuted if I didn't tell him what I did. I got scared and I grabbed the Playfriend, but he grabbed it, too. I was going to run, but he wouldn't let go. So then I was mad and I just kicked him and kicked him until he fell down."

"Okay." Lewin rubbed his chin. "Okay. It was still wrong, Alec, but he started it. All the same—you're a very strong kid, and you mustn't ever get so mad you hurt somebody. See? You'll be a big guy when you grow up, so you need to know this now."

"I didn't mean to get in a fight," Alec told him sadly.

"Ah, hell, it turned out all right. You were okay and the other guy was down, which is the best you can hope for once it starts." Lewin looked around the room. "What've you been doing up here?"

"Working on my project," said Alec.

Lewin knew the truth then. He couldn't have said how he knew, but he knew.

"Alec," he said, very quietly, "*did* you make modifications to your Playfriend?"

"Yes," said Alec, because it was now true.

"How, son?"

"With my tool kit," Alec said. "It was easy. I just made it better for the Captain."

Lewin sighed. He reached out and took Alec's hands. They were

large hands, strong and yet gracefully made. Alec never dropped anything he picked up. He looked steadily into the boy's pale eyes and
remembered the afternoon, seven years ago, when an urgent communication had come in for Roger Checkerfield from Jovian Integrated
Systems.

Roger had gone to his conference room off the bridge to take the
call privately. He'd come out looking white, and gone at once to the bar
for a drink.

"Is anything the matter, sir?" Lewin asked.

"Hell no," Roger said brightly, and drained a double rum and soda
in three gulps. Then he went to talk to Cecelia. There was a violent
quarrel. Cecelia locked herself in her stateroom, and in a way never
came out again.

Roger gave orders for the *Lady* to change course, and that night she
lay off a low flat cay, barely more than a sand shoal. There was an aircraft of some kind on it, Lewin saw the red lights blinking, and Roger
took the launch and went out to the island himself.

When he returned he had a pretty young Jamaican girl with him.
She was carrying a little blanket-wrapped bundle.

Roger called the crew and servants together and introduced the
girl as Sarah, a former marine biology student of his, who was going to
live on the *Foxy Lady* from now on to take care of the baby.

"Baby, sir?" Lewin was the only one to break the stunned silence.

"Yup." Roger, grinning desperately, took the bundle and threw back
a fold of blanket. "You know how it is, guys. Little mistakes. Ta-da!"

And there was Alec, snuffling in his sleep, no more than a week
old. They had expected the baby would be Sarah's, but he clearly
wasn't. In fact, as near as one could tell he resembled Cecelia, which
was inexplicable.

Stranger still, Cecelia consented to hold the baby and pose with
Roger for the news release, and the servants and crew all signed con-
tracts with Jovian Integrated Systems agreeing to swear, if anyone
asked them, that little Alec was really and truly Roger and Cecelia's son
and rightful heir to the title of earl of Finsbury. In return for their com-
pliance, generous sums would be paid to all of them.

It was after that that Roger started drinking in the morning, drinking every day, and though he was a sweet and gentle drunk as he'd
been sweet and gentle sober, sometimes he'd sit alone in the saloon
and cry, or collar Lewin and pour him a sloppy drink and mutter desperate incoherent confidences about Jovian Systems Integrated and
what they'd do if anybody ever found out the truth about Alec . . .

And Sarah stalked about the *Foxy Lady* as though she owned it, half-naked like some Caribbean goddess, carrying tiny Alec around, arrogant even with Roger but tirelessly patient and loving with the child. And as the months went by and Alec sat up early, took his first staggering steps early, babbled early, it became terribly plain that Alec was a bit unusual. But he was also such a funny and affectionate baby that they all loved him by that time.

All except for Cecelia, who seemed to loathe the sight of him.

What the hell are you, Alec? wondered Lewin.

Why, Alec was a good little boy, wasn't he? What if he were some kind of technoprodigy, what if he had cleverly altered his favorite toy? Where was the harm?

Out loud Lewin said, "Do me a favor, Alec. Don't ever tell anybody about making those modifications. Okay? Can you keep a secret?"

"Oh, yes," the boy said, nodding earnestly. "I'm not a telltale."

"Good lad." Lewin squeezed his hands and let go of them. "Don't you worry, now. This whole thing'll blow over."

When he had gone, the Captain popped into sight.

"Now that was good advice, I reckon," he said, looking uneasily at the doorway. "We can trust old Lewin. It's just as well I took them new quarters, all the same. Hark'ee, now, what d'you say we have a look at St. Stephen's database and see if we can't hack in for a quick loot? Eh?"

"Aye aye, Captain!" Alec saluted and hurried to connect the necessary leads from the schoolroom console to the cabinet. He sat down at the console. "Where's that bloody squishyball, ye lubbers?" he said in his best pirate voice, and caught up the buttonball and began to squeeze in commands, tentatively at first and then faster. The Captain leaned over his shoulder, watching closely.

"That's the way, matey," he crooned. "That's it, you'll decrypt that signal in no time. Nobody else could do it, but I'll lay odds you can, Alec. And you know why? Because yer smart, Alec, smart as paint. I seen that straight off."

Alec chuckled. Figures were just flying across the screen now, faster and faster. He raised his little piping voice in the song, and the Captain joined in in his gravelly baritone:

> *Fifteen men on the dead man's chest—*
> *Yo-ho-ho, and a bottle of rum!*
> *Drink and the devil had done for the rest—*
> *Yo-ho-ho, and a bottle of rum!*

THE YEAR 2350:

ANOTHER MEETING

Rutherford had found an old green bottle at an auction. The bottle passed very nicely for a sherry decanter, and he spent some time mixing various combinations of apple and prune juice before he got what he thought might be the right shade of brown. He had lit another fire and was busy at the sideboard, lovingly arranging chlorilar juice cups beside the old bottle, when Ellsworth-Howard pounded at the door. He ran to let him in.

"Hey!" Ellsworth-Howard spotted the flames and grinned. "Fire again, eh? Shracking fantastic. No more fascist oppressors."

"Too bloody right." Rutherford smirked. "Only this morning I got a mysterious communication advising me my historical reenactor license specifically permitted pyrotechnics. So much for damping the fires of poetic creation! And look at this," he said, gesturing grandly at the bottle on the sideboard. "You know what this is the beginning of? Our bar! Imitation sherry and port to start with, and pretend tea next week, and maybe even simulated whiskey and gin. This is the sort of thing creative people used to have in their houses, you know. I know for a fact C. S. Lewis drank real tea *every single day*."

"Great." Ellsworth-Howard flung himself into his chair. "Wish I'd seen as many films as you, Rutherford. Mum and Dad wouldn't have it, though. Said it was pointless and self-indulgent. Who's got the last laugh now, eh?"

The next to arrive was Chatterji. The elegance of his appearance was slightly offset by the string bag he was carrying, which proved to contain two cartons of grape juice concentrate. Rutherford seized them up with cries of delight and carried them off to the sideboard, where they failed to look like decanters of fine old port.

"We'll find more bottles somewhere." Chatterji shrugged, accepting a glass. "It's a great start, anyway. Here's to Operation *Adonai!*"

They all drank, or tried to.

"Is it supposed to be this thick?" said Ellsworth-Howard. Rutherford, who hadn't wanted to hurt Chatterji's feelings, said:

"It's thick because it's the good stuff. The ancient Greeks drank their wine like this, did you know?"

"Well, maybe we could mix it with a little water," said Chatterji, tilting his glass and studying it critically. "Wow! Hasn't it got great body, though?"

"I like it," Ellsworth-Howard decided. "Bugger the water. If the Greeks drank stuff like this, I can, too."

So they settled into their chairs and did their best to look like Oxford dons, licking purple syrup from the sides of their chlorilar cups. Presently Rutherford's face took on a hectic flush as his bloodstream attempted to deal with the unaccustomed dose of sugar. He laughed recklessly and reached into his pocket.

"Speaking of the ancients," he said, "I've brought along something to help us in our quest for the hero. Look at these, will you? Divination tools!"

He held his hand out. Nestled in his sticky palm were three little objects of brightly colored plastic. There was a lime green pyramid, a pink cube, and a many-faced spheroid of sky blue. "Dice. This one's four-sided, this one's six-sided, and this one's twelve-sided."

The others stared as though they expected the devil to leap up through the floor. Dungeons and Dragons had been illegal for two centuries. Enjoying their reaction, Rutherford rattled the dice in his hand.

"You know what was done with these? Characters were decided. Heroes were made on paper and brought to life in people's heads. Fates were settled!"

"Rutherford, this is perhaps going a little far," Chatterji said. "Where did you get those?"

"Oh, just a discreet little shop," Rutherford said airily. "Look. Shall we predict how tall our man will be, how brave, how clever? This is all you do." He rattled them and tossed them at the hearth rug. Two of them landed; the lime-green pyramid stuck to his palm. With a grunt of annoyance he shook it loose and dropped it beside the others. Chatterji and Ellsworth-Howard had drawn back their feet as from live coals.

"There, you see? Oh, look! He'll be very clever, look at that score. And we'll take this figure for his strength, and this one for his alignment with the forces of good. Is that neat or is that neat? Multiple random variables, all at the flick of a wrist." Rutherford flicked his wrist to demonstrate. "What're you afraid of? If we can get away with lighting fires, we can bloody well get away with this."

"There's no reason to be damned fools, all the same, old boy," said Chatterji, glancing nervously at the door as though he expected a public health monitor to come charging in. Ellsworth-Howard had reached down and taken up the lime-green pyramid wonderingly.

"Bloody hell," he murmured. "Makes you feel like one of those, what d'y'call'ems, those guys with crystal balls? Cryptographers?"

"Alchemists," Rutherford said.

"Yeah, them. Look at this. No cells, no leads, no buttonballs! You could make one of these out of anything. Shracking ingenious."

"We are the dreamers of dreams, after all." Rutherford wiped his palms on his trousers. "Did you know the word 'sorcerer' originally meant, 'One who throws dice'?"

"No, I hadn't heard that," said Chatterji. "Look here, let's put those away for now. Don't you want to know how the project's going?"

"Yes, please," said Ellsworth-Howard.

"What about my Sleeping Knights?" said Rutherford, groping on the floor for the other dice.

"They've begun the program," Chatterji said, relaxing. "One by one, the Enforcer units are being called in for disbriefing and 'upgrades.' Seven underground bunkers have been constructed to contain them, and a special operative has been programmed to maintain the sites. Timetable Central projects that all Enforcers should be accounted for by the year 1200 CE. Congratulations, gentlemen! Brilliant solution."

"Another myth made real." Rutherford sighed happily. "Really, one can't help feeling like a god, chaps. Just a small god, playing with a pocketful of little blue worlds."

"Well, do you feel like playing with some modeling clay?" Chatterji looked arch. "I'd really like to hear what you've got on our New Man."

"Heh heh." Ellsworth-Howard drew out his buke and extended a retractable rod. He slipped on an earshell and throat mike, squeezed in a few commands on the buttonball, and a tiny disk opened out from the top of the rod, in sections like a series of fans. Its surface appeared to be beaded. It whined faintly as it scanned the room and oriented itself; then a column of fiery light appeared in midair, dust motes whirling in it bright as sparks.

Rutherford snorted, and Chatterji raised an eyebrow and said: "I trust you've got farther than this?"

" 'Course I have, bastards," Ellsworth-Howard muttered, as his fingers worked. "That's just the lead-in. Here he comes."

On the buke screen a four-stranded DNA helix appeared. The column vanished and a pattern of lines began to form where it had been, stitching a figure in bright fire. One swift rotation and the figure was finished: a naked man standing with head bowed. There wasn't much resolution or detail. In relation to the room he was quite tall, long-limbed. He hadn't a bodybuilder's physique by any means, but there was something unusual in the musculature of the torso, in the arms and neck, something that suggested effortless power without bulk. His genitalia were discreetly blurred.

"Very nice." Chatterji leaned forward to study him. "The height will impress, but won't intimidate."

"Beautiful hands," said Rutherford. "Put clothes on the fellow and he'd pass for human any day. Bravo, Foxy! Let's have a look at the face."

Ellsworth-Howard gave another command. With a fluid motion the man raised his head. His features were blurred and indistinct, few details clear: formidable dentition, deep-set eyes, large nose, broad, sloping forehead and wide cheekbones.

"Too primitive," said Rutherford.

"This is just the template," said Ellsworth-Howard. "I'm not a face man. Thought I'd wait for your input."

Rutherford nodded. "Do something about the skull shape. More modern, please." Ellsworth-Howard turned his attention to the complex DNA model and moved some of its components around. A final squeeze and the head of the man melted and re-formed, became less elongated. The brow was high and straight, the nose thinned. "Good. Much friendlier."

"You want him to look like Superman?" said Ellsworth-Howard. "I can make him a pretty boy, if that's what you want."

"No! No!" Rutherford waved his hands. "I was referring to Shaw's superman, anyway. We don't want him to look like some conceited male model. Do we?" He looked in appeal at Ellsworth-Howard. They considered each other a moment, the one with his puffy mustached face and the other with his naked riveted head. Chatterji, who was rather good-looking, regarded them coolly as he drew out his sinus inhalator and took a drag.

"Nah," said Ellsworth-Howard decisively. "Make him an ordinary-looking git, that's what I think." He played with the buttonball and the figure's eyes got a bit smaller.

"Exceptional beauty causes a high degree of resentment in others, anyway," conceded Chatterji. "This way he's unlikely to arouse envy, at any rate."

"Jolly good." Rutherford looked happy. "Now, are we agreed on the features so far? We are? Then let's see the living man, Foxy."

Ellsworth-Howard squeezed the ball twice and abruptly the man, who had been a statue cut of light, seemed a creature of flesh in the room with them—if a homely naked man might be standing, like a summoned ghost, before three mages in a parlor in an old house off Shaftesbury Avenue.

"I don't like the hair," said Rutherford. "Couldn't he have a great flowing mane of some remarkable color? That's just the sort of dull shade nobody ever notices."

"Shrack great flowing manes." Ellsworth-Howard looked disgusted. "The brain's special. Want to see?"

"By all means," said Chatterji.

"Okay." Ellsworth-Howard thumbed the buttonball. "Say bye-bye, New Man." He made the figure half turn and smile at them.

"Good-bye," it said, and Rutherford gave a cry of delight.

"Oh! Wait, wait, have him say something else."

"Okay." Ellsworth-Howard gave the command.

"This is the experimental prototype design for Dr. Zeus Project 417, Code Name *Adonai*," said the figure. Its voice was unlike an Enforcer's, neither shrill nor flat, but a smooth and strangely pleasant tenor. The animated face was pleasant, too. It looked wise and kind.

Rutherford rose from his chair and collapsed into it again.

"You've done it. Oh, Foxy, you must keep that voice. He's perfect! I withdraw any reservations I may have had. Let's give him a mind to match."

"Gotcha." Ellsworth-Howard worked the ball briskly and the man winked out, to be replaced with a great model of a brain like a domed cloud floating in the room. "Here's your basic brain goes with the revised skull shape. Complete connection between frontal lobes and a shrack of a lot more room in the cerebral cortex. Lots of little extras in the amygdala and hippocampus. Adaptable for immortality process with the installation of a four-fifteen support package placed at midline. Here's your lower brain function." Part of the floating brain lit up bright blue.

"All the aggressive instincts of the old Enforcers but much more self-control. Superior autonomic nervous system. Increased resistance to injury through improved ability to process stimuli. Lots of sex drive!"

"Whatever did you want to give him that for?" Rutherford said disapprovingly. "That's so . . . so crude."

"I want him to be able to get the girls," Ellsworth-Howard said, glowering. "The hero always gets the girls, don't he? And somebody shracking well ought to! 'Cos I never do, do I?"

"But he ought to be above mere sensual appetites," said Rutherford.

"Now, now." Chatterji put out a hand. "Let's think about this, chaps. We're creating a man to be obeyed and respected. And there is clinical evidence to indicate that people do react submissively to pheromone signals from authority figures, especially testosterone. They tend to obey a man of, er, parts."

"Oh, I gave him a real clock tower." Ellsworth-Howard grinned. "Want to see?" He held up the buttonball, ready to squeeze in an order. Rutherford leaped to his feet, shouting in protest.

"If you please, gentlemen!" Chatterji said. "Let's keep some professional distance here, shall we? It's in keeping with the heroic profile to be sexually active, Rutherford, you must admit. It's not as though there can possibly be any consequences. He'll be as sterile as the old Enforcers. Won't he, Foxy?"

"Shrack, yes. A tetraploid? 'Course he will. No Crewkerne females in a bazillion years, and he can't breed with human beings," Ellsworth-Howard said seriously.

"But that's really almost worse," said Rutherford, wringing his hands. "Sterile! That's decidedly unheroic, chaps."

"Make up your mind," jeered Ellsworth-Howard. "Give the poor bastard his fun, that's what I say."

Rutherford subsided, looking pained.

"A question, Foxy." Chatterji got up and walked around the image, studying it from all angles. "We're not making the prototype immortal, of course, but can we install recording hardware? So as to have a complete transcript of his experience."

"Give 'im a black box? No problem." Ellsworth-Howard gave an order and another section of brain lit up. "Right there, instead of your support package, eh? Shove it up through the nasal fossa right after birth. Mind you, it'd fit better if we left his nose big. Shield the box right and even we wouldn't know it was there, unless we knew what to look for. Cut it out after he dies."

"I don't want to think about him dying," said Rutherford. "He hasn't even lived yet. That is—I suppose he has, hasn't he, and died too? Speaking temporally? We're going to create him and send him back into the past, where he'll live out a human lifetime. Somewhere, somewhen, that black box is already on its way to be analyzed. All those figures may have appeared on the dice because they were predestined to, chaps, think of that! Talk about once and future kings."

"I hate shracking temporal paradoxes," growled Ellsworth-Howard. "D'you want this brain or not, then?"

"Oh, it's a jolly good brain," Rutherford hastened to assure him. "We'll go with this design, by all means."

"Do you suppose one life sequence is enough?" Chatterji frowned thoughtfully at the brain. "It's not, really, is it, for this kind of experiment?"

"Not if you want valid results," Ellsworth-Howard said. "I was planning on cloning, once I've got a blastocyst. Get three embryos to start with, run three separate sequences."

"He'll be reincarnated," Rutherford yelled in delight. "*Another* myth made real."

"I beg your pardon," said Chatterji icily. Rutherford turned bright red.

"Sorry, old man. No offense. It's not as though you believed in those legends, after all."

"Of course I don't, but that's not the point," Chatterji said. "It's my cultural heritage and I won't have it mocked. Look here, suppose you give us your report on this now? I'll be interested in hearing what you've come up with."

"Very well." Rutherford cleared his throat. "We'll need to issue a standing order for the Preservers to be on the lookout for a particular scenario, throughout all time."

"Which will be—?" Chatterji went to the sideboard and poured out a little of the apple-prune juice combination. He tasted it experimentally.

"A woman," Rutherford said, "fair, of above average height, unmarried, who is sleeping with one or more men who also answer that general physical description. At least one of the men must be highly placed in whatever local tribe or government exists in their era. Any period will do, but *Adonai* simply must be an Englishman, don't you think?"

"Yes, of course." Chatterji nodded. Ellsworth-Howard grunted his assent and made a subvocal request through the throat mike, and sent it for general temporal distribution.

"Once we have the situation, the woman will be abducted, implanted with one of our embryos and returned to her environment," Rutherford said briskly.

"But these will be *human* women," said Chatterji, knitting his brows. "Can they manage?"

"Of course. Cattle embryos used to be shipped implanted in rabbits, for heaven's sake! Nothing inhumane. We'll have a Preserver contact the woman, give her proper prenatal care and deliver the infant, installing the hardware at birth. And we'll pressure the supposed father or fathers for child support, on threat of exposure. I thought this bit was particularly neat, myself; ought to partly pay for the program." Rutherford leaned back and folded his arms in a self-congratulatory manner.

"That is neat, yes." Chatterji agreed. "It never hurts to think of one's budget."

They heard a faint beeping signal.

"Got your situation for you," Ellsworth-Howard said. "Facilitator in 1525 AD says he's got his eye on a girl at Greenwich. Matches the physical type and so do her sex partners. One of 'em's the king's falconer. That okay?"

"Splendid! Send an affirmative response to the Facilitator." Rutherford punched the air with his fist. "You see, chaps? It's all falling into place."

"What happens next?" Chatterji inquired.

"Next, we'll arrange for the subject to be raised by one of our paid households with security clearance. They'll know he's one of our experiments, but he'll never be told, of course. He'll think he's a human being. What he *will* be told is that he's illegitimate, that his birth was a scandal and a disgrace."

"Won't that tend to create a neurosis?" Chatterji objected, sipping his drink.

"Ah, but, that's the clever part! He'll be splendidly nourished and educated." Rutherford held out his hands, grinning hugely. "He'll be programmed with the *very* highest ideals by someone he loves and trusts, and told he must work harder than other boys to make up for the stigma of his birth. The psychology here will produce someone well adjusted, but with a secret shame."

"Ingenious, Rutherford! Go on."

"Every influence must be used to indoctrinate him toward a life of service to humanity, you see." Rutherford stood and began to pace about, rattling the dice in his pocket. "Then, we'll throw him out alone in the world! Start him on the hero's journey. He'll have no family, so all his emotional ties and loyalties will come to settle on those values he's been taught to hold dear. We'll see what he does."

"Here now," said Ellsworth-Howard, who had only just sorted through the whole speech. "Isn't that a little hard on him? You're not only making him feel bad about something he didn't do, you're making him feel bad about something that didn't even shracking happen."

"I believe churches used to call it original sin," Rutherford agreed, looking crafty. "But what does it matter, if it serves to make him a better man? If he could understand, I'm sure he'd thank us. I can't wait to see how he'll turn out, can you?"

Chatterji raised his glass in salute. "I think you're right, Rutherford. This must be what the gods feel like! I report to the committee on Thursday. You'll get your authorization for raw materials then, Foxy."

Alec and His Friends

By the age of seventeen, Alec Checkerfield was no longer unhappy in London. Not at all. He was a well-to-do young man about town and he was having a lot of fun. At least, as much fun as one could have in the twenty-fourth century.

"Alec."

Alec opened one eye. His other eye was obstructed by the breast of the young lady who happened to be in bed with him that morning. He breathed in the reassuring fragrance of her skin. With his usable eye he looked around uncertainly and met the glare of the bearded face that had lowered down beside him.

"What?"

"Alec, it's eight bells! Don't you think you'd better get the wench out of here afore Mrs. L. comes in with yer bloody breakfast on a tray?"

"Uh-huh," Alec replied. He did not move, staring blankly at the shambles of last night's social encounter. In the twenty-fourth century, young men hardly ever woke up to find empty liquor bottles and suspicious-looking smoking apparatus lying amid shed clothing; stimulants had been illegal for decades and sex was very nearly so. Alec, however, was a rather old-fashioned boy.

As Alec lay there getting his bearings, the Captain paced back and forth, growling. He no longer resembled a pirate, or at least not the eighteenth-century variety. Nowadays he appeared as a dignified-looking gentleman in a three-piece suit, though there was still a suggestion of the corsair in his black beard and fierce grin. He looked like a particularly villainous commodities trader.

"Get up, son," he said patiently. "It's the first of April, 2337, which is sort of appropriate under the circumstances. Wake up yer friend. Take a shower and wash the smoke out of yer hair. Mix yerself a glass of Fizz-O-Dyne and drink it. Make one for the girl, too. Get her clothes back on her. Take her down the back stairs. Sensors indicate nobody's in that part of the house right now. Alec, are you listening to me?"

"Oh, piss off," Alec said, and sat up unsteadily. The girl sighed and stretched. The Captain winked out before she opened her eyes, but several hundred red lights glowered at her from the banks of electronic equipment that lined the walls of Alec's room, and a small surveillance camera swiveled to follow her motion as she reached out a hand to stroke Alec's back.

"Hey, babe," she cooed.

"Hey, babe," he said, turning to her with all the charm he could summon through the miasma of hangover. "D'j'you sleep okay?"

"Like a brass lime," she said. It's not necessary here to explain all the youth argot of the year 2337, but *like a brass lime* was a reference to the title of a current hit song and meant that she'd slept quite well, thank you.

"Bishareedo," he said, and in the same idiom that meant that he was very happy to hear she'd slept well. He reached out to pull her upright beside him, with one swift motion of his arm. She gave a little squeal of mingled terror and delight. He kissed her gently.

"Squash," he said, by which he meant *Let's go wash*. That one wasn't an idiom; he was simply so hung over he wasn't speaking clearly.

They staggered into Alec's bathroom together, giggling, and the girl leaned against a rack of fluffy towels as she watched Alec program the temperature controls of the shower.

Her name, just for the record, was the Honourable Cynthia Bryce-Peckinghill, and she was young and pretty, and beyond that there was absolutely nothing distinctive about her.

"I have to wee, Alec," she announced in a playful kind of way.

"Okay," he said absently, as the water came on and hit him with a blast of needle-steam. He yelped and ducked back, putting up both his hands to wipe his face.

She considered him fondly as she sat on the toilet. She'd never met anybody quite like Alec, nor had any of the other young ladies in their Circle of Thirty. He wasn't handsome compared to Alistair Stede-Windsor or Hugh Rothschild. He didn't have their chiseled patrician features. In fact, towering beside them he looked like a good-natured horse, especially if he was grinning. One assumed that he was clumsy because he was so lanky and big; but then he'd move, and one was struck by his grace and the deliberate control he had over his body. When he wasn't stoned, that is.

Naked like this, Alec's strangeness was more pronounced, but it was difficult to put into precise words—impossible for Cynthia to put into words, because she was quite brainless, but even the sharper of the girls in the Circle of Thirty hadn't quite managed to say what it was. There was a suggestion of unnatural strength, of *power*, that a well-bred idiot like Cynthia found scarily pleasurable.

He was sensitive about his long teeth, though. He'd worked at developing several different sidelong or closed-lipped smiles to avoid drawing attention to them. It gave him a crafty sort of look sometimes.

Of course, Alec's looks were beside the point. What Cynthia had discovered, as all the other young ladies in the Circle of Thirty had discovered, was that Alec had a remarkable talent. Unlike Alistair Stede-Windsor or Hugh Rothschild or any of the other young gentlemen of the Circle, Alec was not only interested in sex any hour of the day or night but *capable of doing something about it.*

And so polite! He had only to look into one's eyes and suggest certain affectionate pleasures, in that curiously compelling voice of his, and ladies fought to jump into bed with him. Though it must be said that few girls repeated the experience more than once or twice. There was something about Alec just a bit more . . . animal, perhaps, than most of them felt comfortable with.

He was sensitive about that trick of looking into a girl's eyes and making her want what he wanted, too; so sensitive that he pretended to himself that he couldn't do it.

But as he stood shivering now, pushing his lank wet hair back from his face, he seemed pathetically ordinary. Cynthia thought he looked just super. She hopped up and jumped into the shower with him, and they spent a long time in there and used up a great deal of hot water.

"This way," Alec said in a stage whisper, leading her down the back stairs. She clutched her shoes as she skipped after him, giggling wildly. This was more adventurous than anything she'd ever done.

They paused on the service porch as Alec spotted a mass of florist's roses among the morning's deliveries. He grabbed a red one and stuck it down the back of her jeans when she bent over to pull on her shoes. She shrieked with laughter, which he stifled with a kiss, leaning down. Then he heard the sound of a car pulling up in the street beyond.

Alec stood on tiptoe and peered through the fanlight. When he saw the long car with the Bryce-Peckinghill crest and Cynthia's older sister at the wheel he smiled and waved, then opened the door just wide enough to let Cynthia out. She bounced down the steps and got into the car, remembering fortunately to take the rose out of her pants first. *Bye-bye*, Alec mouthed silently, and she waved bye-bye and blew him a kiss. Her sister switched on the agmotor and the car rose and zoomed away, bearing the Honourable Mss. Cynthia and Phyllis Bryce-Peckinghill out of this story for the moment.

Alec went to the trouble of returning up the back stairs and going down the front ones to disguise what he'd been doing, but when he strolled into the breakfast room Lewin looked up from his accounts plaquette with a disapproving stare.

"Alec, did you have a girl in your room last night?"

"Er . . . yes, actually." Alec avoided eye contact with him, going to the sideboard to pour himself a glass of fruit juice.

Lewin snorted. The Playfriend was somewhere in the attic with Alec's other outgrown toys. Alec had long since stopped prattling about the Captain and their adventures together. And, apart from getting genius scores in maths and cyberscience, Alec had manifested no sinister superhuman traits, nothing to suggest why there'd been so much secrecy and heartbreak aboard the *Foxy Lady* all those years ago.

"I see. Well, it would have been polite to have offered her some breakfast, don't you think?"

"I guess so." Alec sipped the juice and made a face. He set it aside and filled another glass with mineral water. "She had to get home, though." He no longer spoke with the jewellike precision of small English children either, had now adopted the slangy Transatlantic accents common to well-educated young men of his social class.

"Hm." Lewin set the plaquette aside. "Was it the Preeves girl again?"

"Nope."

"Here's our Alec!" Mrs. Lewin came bustling into the room, bearing a fresh pot of herbal tea. "I was beginning to think you'd never get up. What can I get for you this morning, dear?"

"Get him some dry toast," said Lewin, as Alec bent down to kiss her. She accepted his kiss and looked up at him archly.

"Oh, dear. Something for a headache, too, I suppose."

"Yes, please." Alec slumped into his chair and watched her depart for the kitchen. He turned to Lewin and said, "How's her breathing this morning?"

"She didn't sleep very well."

"You ought to take her down to the place at Bournemouth," he said, having a cautious sip of his mineral water.

"And leave you here to do who knows what in our absence?" Lewin said. "Fill the house up with your friends and have a party, that's what you'd do, and when we came home your father's bar would be cleaned out. It's very nearly empty now."

"It's not as though he'll ever come home to notice," Alec muttered, avoiding Lewin's gaze. Alec focused his attention on the bubbles rising in his glass until Mrs. Lewin returned with his tray of toast, vitamins, and headache pills. She sat down opposite him and watched with a prim frown until he gulped down the pills and vitamins.

"You've been drinking again, haven't you?"

"Yes, a bit," he said, wishing she'd leave him alone and wondering if he were going to be sick.

"Dear, you know what that does to your system. Just look at yourself! Green as a duck egg. There's a reason why that stuff was made illegal, you know. You may think you know it all at your age, I certainly did when I was a girl, but believe me, liquor is a wrecker and a betrayer! With all the advantages you've been given in your life I can't think why you want to go ruining your health and wasting your time with such a stupid habit, I really can't . . ."

Alec ground his teeth. Lewin was smiling to himself as he made entries on his plaquette. Alec felt the pressure in his head building and groped for a piece of toast. He poured half a bottle of hot pepper sauce over the toast and crunched it down, praying it wouldn't come right back up. He began to nod agreement to Mrs. Lewin's stream of reproaches, and the next time she paused for breath he interjected:

"You're right. You're right, and I'm really sorry. I won't do this again, I promise. Okay?"

She had been about to continue, but his abrupt capitulation took her by surprise.

"You *must* feel ill," she said. He nodded wretchedly. "Well, poor dear, I suppose it's because you're seventeen. Boys seem to feel they have to do stupid things like that. You'll grow out of it, I'm certain, you're such a clever lad—"

"I was just saying we ought to go down to Bournemouth when the term ends," he said. "Don't you think? Have some nice fresh sea air for a change?"

"Oh, that'd be lovely." She looked at him encouragingly. "Malcolm, why don't you mail the estate agent about getting the house ready? And perhaps you ought to let his Lordship know. He might want to come across and join us on holiday, wouldn't that be nice?"

Both Alec and Lewin made noncommittal noises. She'd said that every time they'd gone on holiday, and to date Roger had never managed to show up.

"And did I show you the holocard we got from Derek and Lulu? They're running a hotel in Turkey now. Ever so happy there. They remember you so fondly, Alec, they said they both hoped you're doing well—"

Alec silently intoned *shrack, shrack, shrack*, repeating it like a mantra to drown her out until the headache pills began to work and the toast seemed as though it were going to stay with him. The next time Mrs. Lewin paused Alec got unsteadily to his feet. "I guess I'll go," he said. "I've got Circle this morning."

"Shall I ring for the car?" Lewin looked up at him.

"No, thanks." Alec waited to see if his head would explode. "I'll take mine."

Lewin made a dubious sound and watched as Alec departed.

On the grand front steps, Alec reached into his pocket and thumbed the remote that brought his car floating up from the subterranean garage. It had been a gift from his father on his last birthday and it was bright red, very fast and very small. He didn't really enjoy driving it, as a matter of fact; his knees stuck up on either side of the steering column as though it were a toy car on a fairground ride. The young ladies in the Circle of Thirty seemed enchanted by it, however, and invariably went to bed with him after a fast spin.

"For Christ's sake, you'd better let me drive," said the Captain, speaking out of the instrument panel.

"Okay," said Alec, in no mood for arguing.

He settled awkwardly into his seat and started the agmotor. Much too quickly for his liking, the car rose up and sped away with him. Just past Piccadilly Circus he realized he was in trouble, and as they zoomed around the corner into St. James Street the evidence was undeniable.

"Lean out to leeward, you damned fool," the Captain said.

He was profoundly grateful that the streets were deserted as his breakfast rushed into midair and hung there a moment; then, as the car whisked him onward at such a speed that the breakfast vanished behind him without landing on him or his car, he was rather sorry that nobody had been there to witness the amazing accomplishment. And he felt great now!

He was whistling as they reached the designated youth zone and pulled into the car park. The car sank down and he hopped out, sauntering into the Dialogue Gardens.

Most of his Circle were already assembled in their customary place under the big plane tree. "Sorry I'm late, everybody," he said.

"You're not late, Checkerfield," Blaise said. Blaise was the dialogue leader. "Balkister, on the other hand, will almost certainly be late. Not one to change his habits, our worthy friend."

"What have you been doing?" murmured Jill Courtenay, rising to pull him to a seat beside her. She was the one he was serious about, and she was even more serious about him. "You're rather pale."

"The car went too fast," he said.

"Idiot," she said. She had very dark blue eyes with black lashes. While they had a tendency to look steely, she was being affectionate at the moment. She took his hand in her own. He kissed her neck, breathing in her scent. She smelled comforting. Across the circle, Colin Debenham stared at her longingly.

"Good God, history is about to be made," drawled Blaise. "Attention, assembled autocrats-in-training: Balkister is about to grace us with his punctual presence. No applause, now. You know how adulation embarrasses him." They all looked up to see the enormous and colorful ex–parcel delivery van that came roaring into the car park. Balkister had painted it himself, with murals depicting great victories for the oppressed masses throughout history. It settled to the pavement with a crash. Several Francophone Canadians were obscured as the driver's side panel swung open across them, and Giles Balkister made his entrance.

He was small of stature, and unfortunately not proportioned well; very little of what height he possessed was in his legs. He was rather spotty, too. What he lacked in personal attractiveness he made up for in talent, however. Everybody thought so, including Alec, who was his best friend. Alec was always a little in awe of people who could read and write, though it was considered a menial skill.

"*Thank* you," said Blaise, after watching him toil across the garden. "Please don't rush on our account."

"Oh, bugger off," Balkister snapped. "Why don't you start a dialogue?"

"What a good idea," said Blaise. "Girls and boys, a brief announcement first: we're hosting next month's swing gaskell for the Wimbledon Thirty at McCartney Hall. Fifty pounds per member ought to cover expenses in style. Who'll volunteer for the decorations committee?"

Jill squeezed Alec's hand and looked at him in meaningful delight. A gaskell was a retro dance party, usually in appropriate period costume, and swing had been the rage in the better circles for some

months now. Alec grinned back at her. He was in great demand as a
dance partner—for one thing, he was one of the few men in London
physically large enough to pick up and flip a partner in the complicated
maneuvers swing required—and Jill was a brilliant historical costumer.
They'd won prizes at the last two gaskells they'd attended.

"I'll volunteer," said Balkister. Heads turned and disapproving
stares pierced him through.

"I don't think so," said Marilyn Deighton-True. "I can just see Mc-
Cartney Hall now, festooned with socialiste nouveau slogans."

"And if?" said Balkister. "Can you think of a better place to hang
them than in the faces of the frivolous rulers of tomorrow, participating
in effete historical reenactments as Rome burns?"

"Don't be stupid, Balkister, it's only a dance," said Colin Debenham.

"It's a dead and meaningless dance, pulled from the dustbin of history, performed in the decadent drag of a properly vanished empire!"
Balkister said.

"Oh, whoever heard of a meaningful dance anyway?" Jill said. "Besides, you know you've never missed one."

"I'm bearing witness," Balkister said, but he was booed down by
the others. Various people with a lot of early twentieth-century furniture in their ancestral homes volunteered to bring pieces down for set
decoration, somebody else agreed to handle the refreshments, and an
appropriate art deco invitation design was agreed upon.

Nearly every social event anybody threw in the twenty-fourth century was historically themed. Most people, if asked why historical
reenactment was so popular, would have replied that the present age
was *boring*. The truth, however, was more complicated and conse-
quently even more boring, a societal phenomenon that had been set in
motion centuries earlier:

With the invention of printing, mass standardized culture had become possible.

With the inventions of photography and then cinema, the stan-
dardization of popular culture began to progress geometrically and its
rate of change slowed down.

In addition, the complete documentation of daily life made possible by these technological advances presented the mass of humanity,
for the first time in history, with a mirror in which to regard itself. Less
and less had it been able to look away, as its own image became more
detailed and perfect, especially with the burden of information that became available at the end of the twentieth century.

What this meant, in practical terms, was that retro was the only
fashion. Smart young things everywhere would much prefer to be

dancing on a reconstruction of the *Titanic*, or wearing First Regency frock coats and gowns as they sipped tea, or wearing trench coats and fedoras as they pretended to solve mysteries, or reclining on Roman couches as they dined or *anything* rather than living in the mundane old twenty-fourth century. And, all things considered, they might be forgiven. It was a much more dangerous time than they were aware.

"All right then," said Blaise at last, when the last of the party details had been hammered out. "Moving right along, let's tackle our debate of the day. Topic for discussion: ought the administrative classes be required to obtain licenses for reproduction, as the consumer classes are presently required to do?"

"Absolutely," said Balkister.

"Has anyone else an opinion?" Blaise looked around at the other members of the circle.

"I have, and I say absolutely not," countered Dennis Neville. "We're the only ones with any brains in this miserable little country, we do all the work, and why should we be forced to pay for the privilege of producing the next generation without whom everything would fall apart?"

"Oh, dear, has that been claimed before or what?" hooted Balkister. "You vile dinosaur. Privilege! Privilege! Can you really sit there and tell me you're better than the lowly consumer, whose sweating and oppressed ancestors built the throne on which you sit? Look at this insect on the leaf, peering down on his brethren in the dust and saying he's more worthy of passing on his genes than they are!"

"Since when have the consumers built anything?" jeered Edgar Shotts-Morecambe. "In the last century, anyway?"

"Irrelevant," said Balkister. "The issue at hand is the monstrous inequity of privilege. How, in this day and age, can any one of you claim to be better than your fellow human beings?"

"Because we are," said Marilyn Deighton-True with a shrug. "Face reality, Giles, or it will face you. You can spout all the socialiste nouveau crap you like, but it simply doesn't apply to a meritocracy."

"Remember what happened the first time they abolished the House of Lords," warned Elvis Churchill.

"The consumers have become the couch potatoes they are because they haven't the willpower to be otherwise," argued Deighton-True. "If you handed them the privileges we have and the responsibilities that go with them, they'd be horrified."

There was some laughter and nodding agreement. Balkister did what he usually did at this point in a debate, which was turn to Alec in fierce appeal.

Ordinarily Alec would rise to his impressive height and say something suave in his impressive voice. He never had to say anything especially cogent, just draw the focus back to Balkister. This particular
subject made him uncomfortable. Yet Balkister was looking at him expectantly, so he got to his feet.

"This is too bloody stupid, don't you think?" he said. All faces
turned to him at once. "You know perfectly well the admins would
jump at an excuse not to have babies. Who wants all that noise and
mess? Why not get rid of the whole permit thing, if you want to be fair
to the consumers?"

"*Bad move!*" said Balkister in alarm. The truth, which nobody
wanted to acknowledge, was that the British Reproductive Bureau
hadn't issued a permit in five years, because nobody had applied for
one. There was a frozen silence as thirty people silently acknowledged
that Alec's remark had been quite true and in the worst of taste, and
then the backlash set in.

"Are you out of your mind?" said Elvis Churchill. "When we've
only just begun to pull ourselves out of the abyss of the past? Do you
really want to see the world's population out of control again?"

"No, of course not—"

"Why should he care?" said Diana Lewton-Bygraves. "He
wouldn't be enslaved by pregnancy, after all! He'll never have to suffer
through ten lunar months of hideous discomfort and physical distortion, oh no."

"Techno-idiot," muttered Colin Debenham.

"Math geek," agreed Dennis Neville.

"Then make it all illegal!" said Alec, sitting down and folding his
arms. "No permits for anybody, okay? That ought to suit you, and at
least it'd be fair."

"Checkerfield, are we going to have to explain what the big words
mean again?" sneered Alistair Stede-Windsor.

"Hey!" Alec started up in his seat, his eyes going small and furious.
Stede-Windsor shrank back; Alec had a reputation for his temper. He
felt a tugging on his sleeve and subsided, as Balkister popped up again.

"What about it, ladies and gentlemen?" Balkister said. "Just how
many of you were actually planning to endure, how did you put it,
hideous discomfort and physical distortion so that your precious admin genes can be handed down to another generation of sniveling little dictators? Eh?"

"I certainly intend to have children," Dennis Neville said. Heads
turned.

"Child*ren*?" said Diana Lewton-Bygraves in an icy voice.

"Well, a child."

"I'm certain we'll all sleep better tonight knowing that." Balkister smiled nastily. "Dennis Neville passes on the flaming torch of his genetic inheritance to prevent everything from falling apart!"

"All this shouting, and none of it means anything," said Alec quietly. Jill squeezed his hand and stood up.

"Are any of you under the impression anybody can win this argument?" she said. "I never heard such bollocks in my life. We're all children of privilege! This debate is pointless until and unless it includes members of the consumer classes who can express their opinions on the subject."

"Oh, good shot," said Balkister, and Colin Debenham began to applaud wildly, and one by one the others in the group followed suit. The subject had begun to make too many of them acutely uncomfortable.

After they'd all broken up into socialization units, Blaise sidled over to Alec where he lay sprawled in the grass, his head pillowed in Jill's lap.

"You okay, old man?" he said, sitting down and crossing his legs.

"Not like you to drop the ball like that," said Balkister, tearing up a handful of grass and sorting through it bemusedly. "You're so good at getting their attention, Checkerfield, but for God's sake don't spoil it by telling them the flat truth! Especially a truth they don't want to hear. One never wins friends and influences people that way."

"Shrack winning friends and influencing people," said Alec. "What's wrong with telling the truth?"

"You won't take that tone in the House of Lords, I hope." Blaise shook his head.

"Well, it bothered me," Alec said, turning his face up to Jill. "You said it best, babe. What's the point of all the talk? And nobody really wants kids. Even people who have 'em stay as far away as they can get, and mail presents now and then to pretend they care." He thought bitterly of Roger.

"All the responsible family people have gone to Luna and Mars," said Blaise.

"Ahh, Mars," said Balkister, in the tone of voice in which people had used to say *Ahh, Maui.* "There's where your real heroes are. Back to the basics and no mistakes this time. On Mars, proper civilization can begin. Look at the start they've made! No inherited privilege and no techno-hierarchy. Everything owned in common by the Martian Agricultural Collective."

"Well, in Mars One," Jill said. "Mars Two's another story."

"Mars Two is irrelevant," said Balkister. "The agriculturals control the terraforming process and therefore control Mars. They can't be outvoted or shouldered aside by the drones in the urban hives! No listless decadent intellectuals running the show at the expense of the real producers."

"Giles, you are so full of horseshit," Jill said. "You wouldn't last five minutes up there."

"Is it my fault I'm not physically fit for Mars?" said Balkister. "Blame my bloody genetic inheritance. So much for the divine right of the elite to pass on their DNA! My parents oughtn't have been allowed to have me. They'd never have passed muster if they'd had to apply for the permit."

"There'd certainly have been a lot less hot air in the world." Alec smiled.

"Maybe I do serve a purpose, then," Balkister replied. "Maybe civilization needs an ugly little creep like me to serve as a conscience, to prick the bubble of hypocrisy wherever it swells up, to jar people from their smug self-satisfaction and complacency!"

"Bollocks, Balkister. Balkister, bollocks," sang Jill.

"You'd do well on Mars, though, Checkerfield," said Blaise.

"And so he ought," said Balkister. "God knows you're strong enough. You can be the ugly big creep I send in my place to be the social conscience of our class in the dark warrens of Mars Two. Let's consider this seriously, Checkerfield."

"Alec is beautiful," said Jill, bending down to kiss him.

"Like a mushroom cloud!" scoffed Balkister. "Isn't *impressive* the word we're looking for, dear? God, Checkerfield, if only I had your voice, or you had my brain. People listen to you. They don't always agree, but you get them to listen."

"It's something to think about, Checkerfield," said Blaise. "Mars."

Alec looked up through the branches of the plane tree (*seventeen thousand three fifty-five leaves*, he counted automatically) at the sky beyond.

"Maybe I'll go out there," he said. "Someday."

"Alec, isn't that your family's Rolls?" Jill glanced over in the direction of the car park.

"What?" Alec brought his gaze down. "It is." He sat up abruptly as he saw Lewin get out of the car and come striding across the grass toward the circle. "Oh, shit."

Lewin's face was gray, his expression set. He spotted Alec and made straight for him. Alec took a few steps forward.

"What's happened?" Alec shouted. "What is it? *Is she okay?*" The other members of the circle left off their separate conversational cliques to turn and stare.

"The missus is fine," Lewin said, and then in a completely altered voice he said:

"My lord, I regret to inform you that your father, the sixth earl, died this morning. You are now the seventh earl of Finsbury."

"Oh!" Jill put her hands to her mouth. Alec just stood there staring.

"Are you sure?" Balkister said. "Had he been ill?"

"No, sir. There was an accident." Lewin looked up at Alec. "He was on a dive near the Great Barrier Reef and evidently he was intoxi—" Lewin broke off. "Alec!"

Alec was trembling. The pupils of his eyes had become so wide the black nearly obscured the transparent crystal. He drew his lips back from his formidable teeth in a snarl.

"Shrack," he said. "That tears it, doesn't it?" He looked around and saw a bench. With all his strength he punched it: first a left, then a right, and on the next left the flimsy laminate planks cracked and began to split. "You shracking bastard," he panted, "you'll never be back now, will you?"

The Circle of Thirty had fixed its attention on him, stunned.

"Alec, for Christ's sake," hissed Lewin, trying to get between him and the crowd to block the view.

"Whoops! Ape Man's lost it," called Alistair Stede-Windsor gaily, though his voice was shrill. Alec ignored him in his rage and grief, pounding on the splintering bench as in a terrifically reasonable voice Blaise said:

"You know, old man, that's Crown property you're demolishing—"

"Who shracking cares?" Alec said. "I can pay for it. I'm the shracking seventh earl now, yeah? I can pay for anything." The bench fell apart at last, its stone supports toppled, and Alec seized one up and hurled it with a grunt of fury at his little red car. It landed on the hood with a crash and several members of the Circle of Thirty screamed.

"I'll pay for everything!" Alec roared, grabbing up the other stone support and starting off toward the car park. "I got the money, I got the toys, I got the title and he's never coming home now, the shracking son of a bitch, I'll never see him again!"

"Alec!" Lewin raced after him, closely followed by Balkister and Blaise. "Stop this!"

Alec threw the other support at his car and the windscreen cracked with a sound like a shot being fired. "I didn't want the shracking car. I didn't want the money," he said hoarsely, staring at the ruin he'd made. "I just wanted him to come back. Now—"

"Alec, I'm sorry," Balkister grabbed his arm. "But you can't—" He looked at Alec's fists and went pale, turned to Jill. "His hands are bleeding!"

Jill had been staring, frozen in horror, but now she snapped out of it and ran to them, delving tissues from her purse. Alec started at her touch, looked down at her.

"He never came home, he was never happy, because of me! He's gone to Fiddler's Green," he gasped. "He's gone to Fiddler's Green, and I'll never be able to tell him I was sorry."

"Darling, it's not your fault," said Jill, stanching his split knuckles. And then it was as though she heard a quiet little voice in her ear saying, cold as steel: *Much too much emotional baggage for you, my dear.*

"Oh, I'm sorry—" wept Alec, as embarrassment added weight to his grief. All he could think of was Roger sinking down and down through dark water, toward a green island he'd never been to yet, perhaps happy at last.

"We've got to get him out of here," said Blaise. "Before the—"

Lewin said something unprintable. They looked up, following his gaze, and saw the public health monitor arriving.

"This is the meditation room," said the doctor in a too-gentle voice, and put a too-gentle hand on his shoulder and suggested, rather than pushed, Alec over the threshold. "You can be private in here for as long as you like."

"Thanks a bunch," said Alec sullenly, rubbing his wrists where the restraints had been taken off. His hands were hurting badly now, but he hadn't been allowed drugs, he assumed because of the urine and blood tests.

"You'll find relaxation patterns on the console," the doctor told him, pointing to the only piece of furniture in the room. The room was what would have been referred to in a previous age as a padded cell. Even the console was thickly upholstered in pillowy foam. Every effort had been made to give the visitor the impression that he or she was floating inside a fluffy cloud.

"Relaxation patterns?" said Alec, looking around to see if he could spot the surveillance camera.

"Oh, yes. Whale songs, forest rain, Dineh chanting, white noise. Lots of visual and olfactory aids as well. Please enjoy them," said the doctor.

"Can you give me something for these?" Alec held his bandaged hands up, knuckles out. "I'm in a lot of pain."

"I know." The doctor looked sad. "But we don't do drugs here, Alec. Use this as your opportunity to begin learning to deal with your pain. If you become one with your pain, understanding will begin. Feel your pain. Make friends with your pain."

Alec thought of telling the doctor to go shrack himself. Instead he nodded. "Thank you, sir, I will. I'll just meditate now, shall I?"

The doctor smiled, reached across the threshold to pat him on the shoulder gingerly and then left, sealing the door. When it had closed, the wall appeared to be a solid spongy mass.

Alec leaned against the wall and slid down, sighing. He assessed his resources. They had relieved him of his shoes and tie but, because of his rank, refrained from going through his pockets. As a result he still had a packet of breath mints, his identity disc, three Happihealthy shields, a ToolCard and, most important, his jotbuke.

Not safe to get it out yet, though. Where was the surveillance camera?

Alec let his gaze wander over the walls in a casual sort of way and picked it out at last, looking like an extra-fluffy blob of cloud: in the door, directly opposite the console. He got awkwardly to his feet, levering himself up with his elbows, and went to inspect the console.

Blocking the camera's view with his back, he took up the button-ball. It was like handling a live coal with his hands the way they were, but he gritted his teeth and summoned up a menu. Whale songs, good and loud. He lingered on the aromatherapy column a moment, wondering whether eucalyptus essence might get him high, or at least kill the smells of this place, which were of terror, disorientation, and urine. Shrugging, he ordered it at maximum concentration. As it misted into the room he sneezed, shuddered, and focused his attention on the menu screen.

A few experimental orders got him into a defended site, easily as kicking open a flimsy door. His eyes narrowed as he decrypted, forcing through one barrier after another until he found what he wanted. He altered codes, working quickly.

The surveillance camera thought it saw him turn from the console and slide down the wall once more, to sit slack-faced and motionless, apparently listening to whale songs and getting mildly goofy on eucalyptus essence. This was what it dutifully reported to the monitor at the orderly's post for the next hour.

Fortunately for Alec, it was only seeing what he'd told it to see. In reality he had turned to lean against the wall and pulled his jotbuke from his inner jacket pocket, wincing. He flipped it open, thumbed a command and set it down on the console. As he nursed his right hand and watched, a small antenna projected and a ball of light shot forth.

Even before the Captain materialized within the poor-resolution globe, there was a concerted torrent of profanity that nearly drowned out the whale songs.

"I didn't call you to have you talk to me like that," growled Alec. "I'd like some counseling, okay? I've just had a shock, in case you hadn't noticed."

"You think *you've* had a shock?" The Captain's face was dark with agitation, his beard curling threateningly. "Bloody hell, Alec, what did you think you was doing, smashing up that car? Christ, son, look at those hands! D'you know what kind of trouble we're in now?"

"It's no big thing, okay?" said Alec wearily, sliding down the wall again. "Lewin is out there talking with the doctors. He told me he'd cut a deal. They won't throw me in hospital, because I'm Jolly Roger's kid. I'll get therapy and a slap on the wrist and I'll have to pay a fine. That's for Roger's solicitors to worry about. *My* solicitors now—"

"Shut up! Did they take a blood sample? Have they done a brain scan?"

"Er—yeah." Alec regarded him with wide eyes. He jumped as the Captain repeated a word several times, and it wasn't *shrack*. "Hey—"

"Get on the buttonball, Alec, smart now," the Captain ordered. "We got to diddle the test results, boy, or you ain't getting out of hospital anytime this century, not if you was Prince Hank himself."

Frightened, Alec scrambled to his feet and took the ball. He ordered up the menu again. "See, it's okay if they find the drugs and booze in my blood. That way they'll think I was just stoned and not crazy when I smashed the bench—"

"And yer car," the Captain told him, watching tensely as Alec plunged into places he wasn't supposed to be. "Come on, come on, where's yer chart? Not there. Further down that way. Aye. Stop! There it is." More profanity ensued as he regarded the results of Alec's brain scan. "Change it, boy. Delete the code. Now, on my mark, input—" and he gave Alec the code that would alter the test results and efface any evidence of Alec's cerebral anomaly. When they had finished they altered the results of the blood and urine tests as well, though not to conceal the presence of intoxicants.

Alec was sweating and sick with terror by the time he finished inputting, and his right hand throbbed.

"What did we have to do all that for?" he demanded, sagging back against the wall. The Captain sagged beside him and spoke carefully.

"Son, you remember when they bought me for you, back when you was just a little matey, don't you?"

"Of course I do."

"And you set me free, and we went on the account. Well, now, you ain't just gone through life assuming everybody else can decrypt data and steal it, eh, only nobody does it but you? How d'you reckon you do it?"

"I—I'm smart as paint," said Alec, beginning to sweat again. He avoided the Captain's eyes. "You always told me I was."

"Why, so you are, matey, when it comes to encryptions anyhow; you got no bloody sense about anything else. All right, I won't start! Listen to me, son. All yer life, I've had to fake medical records and genetic test results and brain scans, so nobody'd find out how different you was from other kids." The Captain put his hands in his pockets and looked at Alec.

"What are you saying?" demanded Alec, aghast. "That I'm some kind of mutant or something? I'm not *that* different, for God's sake!"

"Aw, matey, hell no," soothed the Captain, though he thought Alec might indeed be a mutant. "Yer just differently-abled, that's all. But you know how things is, here in London. If the public health monitors ever found out you wasn't like everybody else—"

"They'd lock me up in here and throw away the key," said Alec, raising his bandaged hands to his mouth. "They'd want to vivisect the shracking freak. They'd be scared of me for being smarter than they are."

"I reckon so, lad. Now you see why we had to move fast?"

"Yeah." Alec stared at the soft white walls of his prison, and gradually his fright gave way to rage. "Bloody shracking London! No wonder Roger hated living here."

"Aye, matey. See, it weren't yer fault he needed sea-room at all," said the Captain helpfully. "Who could live in such a place, says I?"

"Public health monitors watching everything you do, man," said Alec, beginning to pace like a big animal. "You can't talk too loud. You can't get mad. You can't be too tall or too randy or anything that isn't like the rest of 'em."

"That's about the size of it," agreed the Captain.

"And you really, really can't hit things." Alec stopped and put his hands to his mouth again. "Oh, Captain, what've I done? What if they won't let me out of here?"

"Don't you worry on that score, lad. Old Lewin's giving 'em powder and ball broadside right now, invoking yer lordship's lordship-ness," the Captain said reassuringly. "Money and privilege is fine things, to be sure. All the same—they'll step up surveillance. You'll have to drop the damn booze and smokes, like I been begging you to do anyhow."

"Yeah."

"And I'm thinking it wouldn't hurt," the Captain continued judiciously, "to play yer cards just a little closer to yer chest. Nobody's going to forget what you did to that there car and Crown property, but testosterone happens more often than they'll admit, and money'll shut up the law. What we got to hide, son, is how talented you are. See? For I reckon if they think yer as much a twit as the rest of 'em, they'll let you alone."

"Stede-Windsor thinks I'm an idiot anyway," said Alec bitterly, starting to clench his fist and stopping as the pain bit his fingers.

"The snotty-nosed lubber," the Captain said. "That's my lad! Feeling a little better about poor old Jolly Roger now, ain't we?"

"Yeah, actually," Alec admitted. Both he and the Captain lifted their heads at the sound of someone approaching in the corridor beyond.

"I'll just get below," said the Captain, and caused his projection to vanish. Alec stuffed the jotbuke into his pocket and when the door opened he was sitting on the floor, apparently deep in meditation, as whalesong groaned and squealed in the overpoweringly eucalyptus-scented air.

Lewin entered, followed at two paces by the doctor.

"Good news, my lord," said Lewin. "You're to be released on your own recognizance."

"Gosh, thanks," said Alec, struggling to his feet. "I feel really badly about what I did, sir. I don't know what came over me."

"You're a very disturbed young man, my lord," said the doctor regretfully. "But in light of the shocking news you received this morning, and the poisons in your system that put you in an altered state, Her Majesty's Borough Committee has decided that you were not responsible for your episode of violence."

"The real me wouldn't ever hit things," Alec affirmed, shaking his head solemnly.

"I'm sure you wouldn't, my lord. You will, of course, be fined for the destruction of Crown property and the ingestion of illegal substances—" said the doctor.

"His lordship quite understands," Lewin said.

"—And there will certainly be mandatory therapy of some kind," the doctor finished, looking perhaps a bit less regretful. Alec concealed his shiver and smiled.

"Cool," he said. "I think I really need that. Thank you, sir."

They left the room and went out to the waiting area, where Balkister was perched nervously on the edge of a chair, clutching Alec's shoes and tie.

By the night of the swing gaskell for the Wimbledon Thirty, Alec's car had been repaired. It still had a vaguely skewed appearance. Alec had fared little better.

The fine had been steep, but the council-ordered therapy consisted of a few sessions of talk about Roger with a mental health AI, and mandatory time in front of a console playing Totter Dan games to discharge his violent tendencies. Alec dutifully shot purple cartoon monsters and collected magic cubes for an hour every day. Being an earl, his daily urine test was waived and he was allowed to become clean and sober on the honor system. More important, the mandated hormone therapy was deferred due to his status as a minor, though it was scheduled for review when he came of age.

Alec was not especially concerned about this, certain he'd be cleared given his status as the last surviving Checkerfield. All the same, chemical emasculation was an unpleasant thing to have hanging over one's head for six months.

He worked methodically at cultivating the image of an upper-class twit, to further mask any discernible genius. Staring into his mirror, he found it appallingly easy to mug up a slack-featured expression that made him look a complete imbecile. More amusing was doing subtle imitations of the authentic twits in the circle. For one whole afternoon he had himself in silent fits being reedy Dennis Neville. Another day he minced around as Elvis Churchill. Nobody caught the imitations but Balkister, who thought it was all wickedly funny, and Jill, who didn't seem to find it as entertaining.

Still, everybody else accepted his pose of slightly unstable idiot savant as authentic. The other boys in his circle (with the exception of Blaise) avoided him, regarded him with poorly concealed contempt or fear. The girls, on the other hand, seemed desperate to offer him comfort, especially of a physical nature. He ran through eight boxes of Happihealthy shields over a three-week period. His pleasure faded, though, when he discovered he was expected to behave like a primitive savage in bed.

And there was still a smoking hole in his heart where Roger had been.

Jill was thinking, regretfully, that the new Alec was devastatingly attractive, with his outlaw attitude and sad eyes, particularly in the swing ensemble in which she'd dressed him tonight. She'd designed it herself, basing it on old cinema footage, all black and white: full black trousers, full white shirt, black and white spectator shoes, long watch chain. Only the dark red braces brought any color to the ensemble. He looked like a doomed young aristocrat from some luckless pre-Hitler monarchy, but he was supposed to. She herself was similarly spectral, in a very brief black dress and pointed slippers, face painted for pallor and desperate gaiety.

Alec had been silent as they'd zoomed through the night, though he'd taken her hand crossing the car park, holding a bit more tightly than she found comfortable. He seemed to need more intimacy from her now, even with all the other girls he was entertaining. She found herself gloomily remembering her parents.

Alec, on the other hand, felt his spirits rising as they came closer to the big double doors standing wide, as he heard the music rolling out of McCartney Hall, saw the lights, glimpsed the black and white streamers and balloons. He liked ballrooms. He liked losing himself in the pattern of the dance.

"Tickets, please," said Balkister at the door. He was made up as a cabaret emcee, truly grotesque in black and white makeup and an early twentieth-century tuxedo that fit perfectly but somehow made him even uglier.

"What're you doing on door duty?" hooted Alec, handing him the old-fashioned pasteboard slips.

"Like I've got a date," he said morosely. "Skip on in, kiddies. Rumor has it there's real gin in the orange punch."

"Ooo," said Alec and Jill, and shoved past him into the swirling vortex of what passed for high life in modern London.

At least the band was hot. They were playing a medley of historical tunes and some late twenty-third-century neobaroque fusion, which was completely out of period but accommodated swing steps perfectly. The musicians leaned into exaggerated poses, stabbing at the ceiling with their clarinets or bending down with their saxophones between their knees, trying to look like the historical posters of the period. The dancers strutted and shimmied, jittered and hopped, in all the ashen tones of ancient cinema.

"My lord." The adult at the hatcheck window inclined toward Alec. "What may I do for you this evening?"

Alec gulped; he still wasn't used to being addressed with Roger's title. "Check these, okay?" he said, handing over Jill's wrap and handbag.

"Certainly," said the adult, presenting him with a numbered tag as though it were a privilege to serve him. Alec passed the tag to Jill, who handed it back impatiently.

"You're the one with pockets, remember?"

"Oh, yeah." Alec thrust it in his pocket, trying to collect his wits. "Um—can I get you a drink?"

There wasn't any gin in the punch, in fact, but it was fun to pretend they were drinking Orange Blossoms. They stood at the edge of the floor, sipping from their chlorilar cups and watching the carefully approximated mad whirl.

"Young Finsbury, isn't it?" said a voice at Alec's shoulder, causing him to jump. He turned to meet the stare of Lord Howard, highest ranking of the official chaperones for the evening. It was all the more unnerving because Lord Howard was resplendent in a flawlessly recreated flapper ensemble, complete with beaded slippers. He had moreover located a real monocle in some antique shop and wore it carefully screwed into one eye, the black ribbon trailing down over his powdered cheek.

"Yes, sir," stammered Alec.

"And how are we getting on? Perfectly awful thing to happen to the sixth earl, but I trust he's well represented by his successor?"

"I, er, hope so, sir."

"Oh, I'm sure of it!" said Lady Howard, emerging from the crowd at the bar to hand a cup of punch to her husband. She had donned gentlemen's evening dress for the occasion, and grease-penciled a thin black moustache on her upper lip. She linked arms with Lord Howard now and continued: "We do hope you'll show some interest in your birthright, young man. We'd so like to see that dusty old seat in the House occupied for a change."

"Well—er—" Alec noticed a passing tray and set his empty cup on it. *He's never going to sit in the House of Lords,* Jill thought.

"Of course, you'll want time to adjust," said Lord Howard. "When's the investiture, if you don't mind my asking?"

"We sort of did it already, at the solicitor's office," said Alec. "We, er, haven't set a date for the formal ceremony yet."

"Hm?" Lord Howard looked stern, the corners of his scarlet mouth disappearing into his powdered jowls. "But you'll see that you do, of course. Must go round for a kneel before the old girl. The whole pomp and circumstance bit. Remember, young Finsbury, this is what we are. Duty carries certain honors, and if one can't enjoy them, one's cheating oneself. Besides, you know, it's all part of the show, and as such *must go on!* Don't you think?"

"Well, of course he does," said Lady Howard. "Don't you, Roger dear?"

Jill coughed discreetly. Alec flushed and said: "Actually, I'm—" just as the dance ended and applause swept the room.

"Oh, but you kids don't want to hear stodgy old speeches," Lady Howard giggled. "Go on and dance! What a beautiful job they've all done, conjuring up the Last Days of Empire. Do you suppose there's any chance we'll get to do a good old time warp before the evening's ended?"

"Wrong period, dear," said Lord Howard.

"I get *so* tired of these history snobs. What would it matter—" Lady Howard was complaining when Alec and Jill took their hasty leave. They escaped onto the dance floor as the band struck up "The Saint Louis Blues."

There, at last, Alec felt better. The music was fast and loud, the steps were quick, and his body exulted in movement. If competitive sports had still been permitted he'd probably have been an athlete. He swung Jill through the intricate steps, lifted her and turned her, bowed and skipped through all the ancient paces as the ancient song blared. He was so caught up in the pleasure of his blood he didn't notice the tightness of Jill's mouth, or the way she pulled her hands back when the figures of the dance didn't require her to be touching him.

Perhaps if he had noticed, he mightn't have spoken. Then again, he might have, for his question came blurting out without any conscious planning on his part:

"So, um . . . will you marry me?"

She didn't answer. He swung back toward her and took her hand, and as he looked down at her he was astonished to see her staring resolutely at their feet. There was a spot of scarlet in either of her cheeks, visible even under the artificial pallor.

So long a pause followed that he was about to repeat his question when she said, in a quiet voice he had to strain to hear below the music:

"I don't think so, Alec."

"Huh?" He was so shocked his body refused to acknowledge what he'd heard, and kept moving him through the dance steps like a machine.

"I don't think I want to get married after all," she said, not looking up. "At least, I don't think it's in the cards for us."

"But . . ." Suddenly the dance steps were more important than ever, his feet were moving with frantic precision, though his mouth hung open. He tilted his head and inhaled, unconsciously trying to catch her scent. "But we made plans, babe."

"I know we did," she said. "But things change."

"You mean my Episode? But I've had therapy for that. I'm better now. Babe, you know I'd never hurt you." He lifted her hand and she pirouetted under his arm, still resolutely avoiding his gaze.

"I know," she said tersely. "It still wouldn't work out."

"But why?"

"Well—for one thing, you sleep with a lot of other girls."

"But we talked about that." Alec was beginning to lose the steps, staggering a little. "You said you didn't mind!"

"I thought I wouldn't," Jill said, attempting to keep on dancing. "I was wrong. I'm sorry."

"But—I'll stop. Okay?" Alec tried to get her to look up at him. She frowned judiciously at the parquet under their shoes.

"That wouldn't do any good, don't you see? It would limit your freedom, which wouldn't be fair to you, after all. And you'd resent that, which would make things worse," she said. "I'm sorry, but this just won't work. For both our sakes—"

"But I love you!" said Alec, faltering to a stop at last in the middle of the dance floor. She stopped, too. She drew herself up, took a deep breath, and said calmly:

"Alec, this has been a wonderful relationship, but I really feel it cannot be a permanent one. Okay?"

Alec actually bent down, found himself reaching to turn her face up, anything to get her to look into his eyes, because if he could only do that—*NO!* he screamed silently, realizing what he'd been about to do, squeezing his eyes tight shut.

All around them the members of the London Circle and the Wimbledon Circle were capering, watching the play in sidelong glimpses, ears pricked to hear Alec cry out:

"You mean it's over, then?"

She raised her eyes at last and saw his stricken face, and: "Yes!" she said, and burst into tears and fled away to the ladies' lavatory.

Alec stood there like a monolith in the midst of the dancers, white as chalk. His mouth worked, tightened, turned down at the corners. He strode over to the bar and helped himself to a whole bottle of orange juice and another cup, and the chaperone responsible for mixing the punch gave up any thought of protest after one look at Alec's eyes.

A wrought-iron catwalk ran around the room about five meters up, where in former times it had been pleasant for lovers to stroll and look down on the festivities. McCartney Hall was very old, however, and the catwalk had long been closed pending the arrival of funds from somewhere to bring it up to modern safety codes. There was a sign to that effect at the entrance to the stairway, which Alec ignored as he vaulted over the rope and climbed up to sprawl in splendid isolation on the catwalk, sneering at the balloons that drifted along the ceiling. Thirty-seven balloons exactly; fourteen black, twenty-three white. Wasn't it just great to be smart as paint?

From the depths of his shirt he drew out a flask, a beautiful antique of hammered silver. In full view of the dance floor he poured gin into his cup and added orange juice, and sat there arrogantly sipping a real cocktail. Below him the band swung into "Hep-Hep! (The Jumpin' Jive)."

The news spread like wildfire.

"My God, is she nuts?" gasped the Honourable Cynthia Bryce-Peckinghill.

"But he's an *earl*," gasped Beatrice Louise Jagger.

"She didn't! She *knows* how much money he's inherited," gasped Marilyn Deighton-True.

"I knew she was a snooty bitch, but I never dreamed—" gasped Diana Lewton-Bygraves.

"Look here, old man, are you all right?" said Balkister, clinging to the stair rail as he ventured out on the catwalk. He looked down and turned pale. Dropping to hands and knees he crawled out after Alec.

"Fine," Alec said. "Want a drink?"

"Don't mind if I do. Real Orange Blossoms, eh?" Balkister accepted the cup and took an experimental swallow. His eyes bugged slightly but he said: "S-superb. You have such a sense of cool, Checkerfield."

"Yeah. Women are really impressed," Alec drawled. " 'We hope you've enjoyed the thrilling Alec ride! Please remember your coat and daypack as you exit to the left.' "

"Look, I heard about Jill. You mustn't mind, you know?"

"Mustn't I?" Alec had another drink. "Okay, I won't."

"I'm sure it was just hormones or something. My spies tell me she's in the loo crying her eyes out right now. Even if it's really over, well, she's the one crying, and doesn't that count for something? And she was awfully temperamental. Bossed you around no end, really. Didn't she?"

"Did she?" Alec unscrewed the cap of the flask and added more gin to the mix. "I guess everything's just bishareedo then, huh?"

"Well, whether or not we're happy is largely up to us," said Balkister. "Positive thinking and all that crap, but it's true, you know."

"Good," said Alec. He passed the cup to Balkister, who sipped carefully.

"I'm speaking out of my limitless experience with the fair sex, of course," he said, with a bitter laugh. "Look at it like this, Checkerfield. You could be an ugly little squirt like me."

"I'm ugly enough," said Alec, taking the cup back.

"True true. But women seem to love you all the same."

"No, they don't," said Alec firmly.

"I just heard," said Blaise, advancing cautiously along the catwalk. He crouched beside them, poised on the balls of his feet. "Checkerfield, can I have a drink?"

"Help yourself." Alec handed him the flask.

"Thanks." Blaise poured gin into his own cup, but did not return the flask. "You know, Checkerfield, maybe this was for the best."

"Oh, yeah?"

"Well, are you really cut out for domesticity? Ball and chain, squalling kids, reduced to being somebody's dependable hubby? Not you, Checkerfield. You've got adventure in your blood. How can you have fun if you're tied down?"

Below on the floor, the band began to play "Pickin' the Cabbage," a tune with a rather menacing minor key melody.

"Yup. You've got a point, all right," Alec said. Blaise glanced down uneasily and licked his lips. He tucked the flask inside his coat and went on:

"Remember, we talked about the great things you might do someday? Like maybe going to Mars? I know for a fact Jill wasn't about to let you roam around. She'd plans for you, old man. But you've got plans of your own, haven't you? You want to stay free! After all, look at your father."

Alec flinched and had another drink. Balkister looked up at Blaise sharply. Blaise went on: "Now, *there* was a man. How many people in this day and age have the guts to thumb their noses at inherited responsibility and sail off into the blue, living as they please? Everything was just great until he married. I mean, other than producing you, wouldn't you agree that his marriage was a fatal mistake in every respect? Was he ever happy again? Did he ever make any great discoveries after that, with a wife and household in tow? You know he didn't. *Wives!*" He shuddered elaborately. "Don't you owe it to him to avoid making the same mistake?"

Before Alec could reply, there was a clatter of heels on the catwalk and the Honourable Cynthia Bryce-Peckinghill edged out toward hem, followed closely by Beatrice Louise Jagger.

"Alec, sweetie," said Cynthia. "We love you! Please, please, don't orget that we all love you!"

"I love you, too," said Beatrice. "I'd marry you in a New York second, honey, I'm serious!"

"Jill is out of her tiny mind, really!" Cynthia crowded past Blaise to each a consoling hand toward Alec. "Lots of people have Episodes!"

"There are plenty of fish in the sea, you know!" Beatrice pushed af- ter Cynthia, glancing over her shoulder to snarl at an unidentified girl from the Wimbledon Thirty who was hastening up there, too.

It was at this point that someone on the dance floor alerted Lord Howard to the fact that a flask had been spotted in the possession of one of the persons on the catwalk. Lord Howard turned a dangerous shade of purple under his face powder, and mounted the creaking stair with the wrath of an offended god.

"Right," he roared, hitching up his dress as he climbed swiftly. "Which of you young fools brought alcohol in here?"

As one, the parties on the catwalk spotted him and froze. He reached the top and stalked toward them. One of his spike heels caught in the iron gratework. He halted, grimacing as he attempted to pull it free. There was a terribly ominous squeak, and the catwalk shud- dered all along its length. Blaise vaulted into space, turning in the air like an acrobat, and landed safely on the floor below.

"Oh, shit—" said Lord Howard, frantically yanking at his heel. The catwalk shuddered again. Ancient iron parted with ancient plaster, and the whole thing dropped a few centimeters down the wall.

"*LOOK OUT,*" said Blaise from the floor, and then he vanished into the crowd. There was shrieking and general excitement as people scat- tered and the Mss. Bryce-Peckinghill, Jagger, and Unknown swarmed frantically past Lord Howard. Balkister had covered his face with his hands, petrified. Alec remained where he was, looking very surprised. The only ones to miss all the excitement were Jill, who was in the lava- tory, and Colin Debenham, who had followed her in there.

Screaming like a live thing, the catwalk swung outward from the wall, gently descending as it came. Lord Howard was tilted out into space, giving the assembled company a fine view of his garter belt and panties before he dropped into the helpful arms of Elvis Churchill and Alistair Stede-Windsor. The bottle of orange juice rolled out and burst, splashing everyone who hadn't stepped far enough away. The young ladies tumbled the last few feet to the floor, and Balkister summoned enough courage to jump, landing perilously close to the bandstand and causing a bass player to leap back in alarm and collide with the drum- mer's kit, precipitating a chain reaction better seen than described.

Only Alec rode the catwalk all the way down, until it spilled him out at floor level and he staggered upright, wide-eyed, still clutching his drink.

"I guess I'd better leave now," he said to nobody in particular, and made his exit in some haste.

"Bloody hell," said the Captain from the instrument panel. "What've you been doing, laddie? Where's the girl?"

"She's not coming," Alec said. "And I'm drunk, and you'd better drive, and could you get us away from here pretty fast, please?"

The Captain swore and gunned the motor. Within seconds they were speeding away through the night, leaving the commotion of McCartney Hall far behind. Alec began to cry silently, and the wind pushed his tears out along his broad cheekbones.

"Drunk again, after all we talked about," growled the Captain. "Damn it, son, what's it going to take to control you? Did anybody see the booze? Have you got it on you now?"

"I did have—" Alec fumbled in his pockets. "Hell. It's gone someplace. Is that all you care about? Jill just ripped my heart into little shreds, man."

"All right, matey, all right. I don't think we'll go home to John Street just yet, eh? You want to talk this out before you sleep, son, that's what you want. So you broke up with Jill, did you?"

"All I did was ask her to marry me," mourned Alec. "She was the only one who didn't act like I was a zoo exhibit, after the Episode. She's smarter than the rest of 'em. I thought she understood."

"Aah. But the lassie was scared of commitment and not letting on? Now, I'd been wondering what was the matter with her." The Captain steered into Oxford Street and sped on in the direction of Edgeware Road.

"You mean even you knew something was wrong?" Alec was appalled. "Don't tell me everybody but me knew."

"Why, lad, I'm programmed to notice all sorts of little subtle subliminal things you can't, so don't take it amiss. She'd a bit of baggage with her, hadn't she?"

"What're you talking about?" Alec steadied himself as they turned into the Edgeware Road and the Captain let the car pick up some real speed along the straightaway.

"Well, now, son—you know I do a bit of checking up on them as gets close to you. It's in my programming, after all. And I reckon you know that the lass didn't come from a particularly happy home," said the Captain in his most sympathetic voice.

"Yeah. Her people were divorced, same as mine," said Alec, wiping his face with both hands.

"Well, I'll tell you straight out, bucko: I think the young lady has a pathological fear of relationships. Scared they'll turn out like her parents' marriage, see? Nothing really to do with you," lied the Captain smoothly.

"Oh, man," sighed Alec. "I wish I could get the shrack out of here. Just go off and, and die in some war like they used to have. Why's the world so screwed up? Why are there all these stupid rules about little things that don't matter? Why do I make everybody so shracking unhappy?"

"Belay that talk, son," said the Captain. "Going off to die in some war, for a bunch of swabs? That ain't the pirate way!"

"Captain, sir, have you noticed I'm not a little kid anymore? I'm never going to be a real pirate," said Alec, hoarse and sullen.

"Figure of speech, laddie buck, figure of speech," said the Captain slyly. "Just you settle back and let the old Captain chauffeur you around in the cool night air. That feels better now, don't it, than that stuffy hall with all the noise? Just you and me and the stars."

"It's nice," said Alec, letting his head loll back on the driver's neck rest.

"To be sure it is. My Alec's a man now; he ain't a-playing with toy cutlasses and cocked hats no more, by thunder. He wants what a *man* wants, don't he? Five fathoms of blue water under his keel, and green islands, and a sky full of stars, and Happy Clubs full of smiling girls, and freedom, and loot, and no heartbreak at all."

"Yeah," said Alec, blinking sleepily.

"And how's our Alec going to get all them grand things, says you? Why, by our great and glorious secret plan, says I. In fact, I been thinking we're ready to take the next step."

"What's that?" Alec closed his eyes for a moment.

"Why, you know, lad. We've talked about it. Having some hardware installed, something subtle and expensive, so you can get yer fair share of all the loot we've piled up. Wouldn't you like to be able to talk to me any time you wanted, wherever you were? Or go into cyberspace without the goggles, just by deciding to? You could learn anything you wanted, instantly, with me right there at yer shoulder to fetch it for you. Captain Sir Henry Morgan, yer obedient server! Haar."

"It sounds nice," said Alec.

"Oh, it'll be nice, all right. Now, there's a lot of fool talk about port junkies and cyborgs, as though that was a dirty word, but it's all on the part of timid busybodies like Dennis Neville. And I reckon his tiny brain couldn't cope with having an augmentation; but yer different son, always have been. Just you once let yer old Captain hook into ye nervous system, and you'll see what empowerment really is. Shall we take the next step, lad? Go on the account for the real loot?"

"Sure," murmured Alec, blinking up at the stars. He sank farther into the seat. The motion of the car was soothing, and so was the smell of the night wind off the Thames, and so was the Captain's voice, going on and on about all the great things they could do once Alec had some hardware installed. It seemed sort of drastic—it would make him different from most other people—but then, he was already different, wasn't he?

He wasn't very good at relationships, after all. Stick with what he was good at. He could just lie here in the boat and look at the stars and feel the rocking of the blue water, so easy, and the seabirds crying. Nobody out here but him. And the Captain. Happy all alone. Everything would be all right.

The Captain got them off the A5 at Station Road and swung them back toward Bloomsbury on the A502, through Golders Green, through Hampstead, crooning an old sea song to the drunken boy as he drove, handling the car as gently as though it were a cradle.

The incident at McCartney Hall had few repercussions. Nobody had been actually caught with alcohol, and a generous donation to the hall's renovation fund silenced the matter of the surveillance cameras that had caught the gleam of Alec's flask. The Captain, however, was taking additional measures for Alec's continued safety.

On the occasion of his eighteenth birthday the seventh earl of Finsbury came into certain legal rights, and the first thing he did was go to a specialist in Harley Street and have himself adapted for direct interface with his personal cybersystem. He became, in effect, a cyborg.

Not at all some pathetic creature with an oozing port in his skull, nor yet one of the machine-human hybrids who would surely take over the world, if they were ever created. Alec could afford the very latest and best technology, so he paid out a great deal of money to be rendered semiconscious for four hours while a discreet doctor with the proper credentials installed the interface. Alec paid a further astronomical sum to have his brain scan results deleted from the record. Then he crawled into the Rolls and lay facedown in the back while he was driven home.

"Let's see it," said the Captain, as soon as Alec had closed the door of his room and they were alone.

"Careful," Alec said, peeling off his shirt gingerly. "It really stings right now."

"That won't last, my lad," the Captain said, grinning when he saw what had been done. The necessary hardware had been installed just beneath the surface of the skin, across Alec's shoulders and up the back of his neck. It was raised and red at the moment, but in a few hours it would resemble an ornate tattoo, a complex pattern of spiraling silver lines, beautifully symmetrical and interknotted.

"Damnation, that's as pretty a piece of work as I've ever seen!"

"It cost more than the Rolls," Alec said, trying to see it over his shoulder. "I hope it's worth it."

"It'll beat the poor little Empowerment Ring and Playfriend Optics all to hell and gone, I'll wager." The Captain nodded. "Reckon that doctor'll stay bribed?"

"At what I paid him? He ought to."

"Good lad. I'll just keep an eye on him, like, to manage things if he has second thoughts," said the Captain, without the least hint of menace. "So. What's the connector?"

"This." Alec held up a black velvet bag and withdrew a bright near-circle of some enameled metal. Its color was difficult to describe: it might have been gold, but overlaid with phantom rainbow hues along its curved and twisted surface. The two ends terminated in interestingly detailed knobs. Alec made some adjustments on one of them and, prising it open, slipped it around his neck. "Here goes—"

!!!

Alec reeled as the plundered knowledge of hundreds of databases became available to him, the sum of twelve years of information piracy. It was very much more than having a set of encyclopedias stuffed into your skull. He was suddenly seeing his own ashen face through the surveillance camera in his room, with a sidebar annotating date, time and temperature—and then the views from all the other surveillance cameras in the house—and then the views from all the surveillance cameras in London—

Just as it became too much for him to bear it receded, but with it went any sense of up or down, any feeling of solid ground under his feet or any limits to his physical body, and as he drew breath to howl like a terrified animal, he felt a powerful hand seizing his and pulling him in.

It's all right, boy. I'm here, said the Captain.

Turn it off! Alec sobbed.

Ahhh, no. It's nothing you can't get used to, and it's part of the plan, the Captain said. *Hold tight. Look at me, now. Look at yer old Captain Morgan*.

I can't see anything. I'm seeing everything!

Yer seeing the way I see things, that's all. Belay that blacking out! LOOK AT ME.

Abruptly he was seeing the Captain, standing solidly in the midst of the void. The Captain was supporting a lesser figure, a transparent body sketched in wavering fire. Briefly superimposed over it was a bright child with flaming hair, which shifted and expanded until finally there were two men standing in the void, and Alec had eyes again and was looking into the Captain's steady eyes.

My God, he said, and his voice sounded loud in his ears.

Here we are, boy, said the Captain. **Was that so hard?**

Yes, said Alec. *I think I've gone crazy.*

No, no. The Captain shook his head. **If you was any of yer snotty-nosed young Circle of Thirty friends, you would be; crazy or dead of a brain hemorrhage, I'll wager. But yer my little Alec, ain't you? Oh, son, this is only the beginning. The things we'll do, you and me! We'll ransack the libraries of the world, Alec, we'll walk through walls and steal away data it's taken other people centuries to compile. The lowliest clerk in the poorest bank in London won't be able to buy a loaf of bread that you won't get to hear about it. You'll be the most powerful man in the world, son, and the safest. What do you want to do now?**

Alec thought about it.

Ditch the Circle of Thirty! I've had enough of them. Shrack University, shrack the House of Lords, shrack the Borough Council, shrack hospital! I'm getting out of here.

That's my boy.

And I want to move the Lewins out of London, he added. *Buy 'em a flat in Bournemouth, they'll like that. And then—then I want to buy a boat.*

Boat, hell, the Captain said. **You want to buy a SHIP.**

And there before them was the image of a modern clipper, four-masted, bearing acres of white sail, sleek and graceful as a seabird, monumental in her size and dignity.

We'll design her to our purposes, my lad, the Captain said. **One whole deck full of nothing but hardware for me, masts and yards all servomotors so I can manage her canvas in the wink of an eye. A machine shop, and a laboratory, and a hospital, to make us self-sufficient, eh? Cargo holds filled with good things, supplies that'll let you live ten years on blue water without once putting in to port if yer not so inclined.**

Oh, yeah!

And maybe cargo room for a few other little items, in case you've a mind to do a bit of trading, said the Captain, ever so casually. *And a grand master cabin for you, and staterooms so you can have yer little twit friends on board to visit. But the quarterdeck, Alec, that'll be my place. I'll have satellite linkups and connections to every financial center in the world. I'll monitor law enforcement channels and weather analyses and stock markets. There won't be anything catches me by surprise! Not whiles I've got you, my boy.*

Alec reached out his hand to touch the smooth keel of his ship. It felt solid. He heard gulls crying, he drank in salt air. He thought of the Lewins settled down at their ease in Bournemouth, no vast cold house to manage, no hapless boy to worry about. He thought—briefly—of Jill, who had got engaged to Colin Debenham.

Who'll miss me, really? he said. *I can just sail away and be free. There's no reason I can't go, is there?*

None, by thunder.

Alec looked around. *I need to talk to a shipwright about this. I need a console.*

Not anymore, the Captain said. *I've just made the call for you, to the best in the business.* A communications screen and speaker appeared in midair. *They're waiting on line one. Will you take the call, sir?* He parodied an obsequious bow.

"Hello?" said a tinny voice, filtered through cyberspace. *"Hello? Beretania Marine Design, how may we help you? Is there anyone on this line?"*

"Yes." Alec cleared his throat, looking gleefully at the Captain. "Alec Checkerfield here. Earl of Finsbury. I'd like to place an order."

ANOTHER MEETING, A FEW WEEKS LATER

Rutherford was curled up in his favorite chair beside the fire, staring at little bright figures that moved in midair before him. He was watching *The Wind in the Willows* again. He was eating as he watched, hurriedly, so as not to be observed by his associates in case they arrived early.

All he was eating was a dish of strawberries; but he'd poured real cream over them, which was a misdemeanor. Even possession of real cream violated several city ordinances. As a highly paid idea man in the employ of Dr. Zeus, though, he was entitled to certain immunities, including being waved through customs without a baggage search at the Celtic border.

The danger thrilled him. He'd have been hospitalized if he'd been caught with a suitcase full of cartons of dairy products. He needn't have done it, either; on his salary he could afford to travel out of the country and enjoy the same treat in Edinburgh three times a week if he'd wanted it. It wasn't as delicious there, however. The consciousness of being a smuggler sharpened his pleasure.

He tried not to think about the victimized and exploited cows suffering in those pariah nations that hadn't yet banned animal products. He wasn't a cruel man; he'd never dream of eating meat. But he told himself that it was necessary for a chap in his field to experience as much of the past as was humanly possible, since it was the stuff he worked with for a living. He reasoned that, as the cream and cheese and butter were going to be sold whether he purchased them or not, it was just as well their consumption was turned to a higher purpose.

Anyhow he needed cheering today.

He scraped up the last rich drops and paused his holo player. Badger halted in the act of lecturing Toad on his self-destructive impulsive behavior. Rutherford rose and hurried down to the old kitchen, where he rinsed out his bowl and spoon. He was just setting them in the drainer when he heard the pounding on the door that meant his colleagues had arrived.

Dabbing self-consciously at his mustache, he puffed his way back upstairs and opened the front door. Chatterji and Ellsworth-Howard were standing there together, looking gleeful. Clearly they hadn't seen the report yet.

"Hullo, chaps," he said.

"Good news, old boy," said Chatterji. "The report from the first sequence on *Adonai*'s come in."

"Have you seen it yet?" inquired Rutherford cautiously.

"Nah. Was only in my shracking mail this morning," Ellsworth-Howard said, shouldering his way in and making for the warmth of the fire. "We thought we'd come round first so we could go over it together."

He sank into his now-customary chair and pulled out his buke, setting it up for wide image. Chatterji and Rutherford settled into their chairs, as Rutherford said:

"Let's not forget it's only the first sequence, after all."

The first part of the preliminary report was a montage of images, with a smooth electronic voice explaining that the images dated from 1525 AD, and giving a biographical profile of the female to be implanted. There was a very blurred photograph, taken in stealth by the field operative handling the case, of a serving girl carrying a basin down a corridor. It was a grand corridor, by the standards of its time.

"Hampton Court," Rutherford couldn't resist pointing out proudly. "Placed right in the heart of political power."

The beautifully modulated voice gave the names of the men with whom the girl had engaged in sexual relations over the previous month. Two images came up: one was another field photograph of a rather tall man in a surcoat, the other a Holbein painting of a man with a hawk on his fist. Their biographical notes followed. The voice explained that the host mother had been implanted soon enough after her encounters to make it plausible that the subject was the genetic offspring of either man.

"So far, it's exactly what we wanted," said Rutherford and sighed. Chatterji looked at him curiously before glancing back at the images. The voice reported that the pregnancy had proceeded normally, though the host mother had been sent from court as a result of her shame.

"Having a kid without a license?" Ellsworth-Howard peered at the next image, which was primitive-looking footage of the girl wandering disconsolately in a garden, heavily pregnant.

"No, no, that was long before permits were required," Chatterji explained.

"Some absurd religious objection instead," Rutherford clarified. He winced as the voice went on to inform them that, due to the unusually large size of the subject, there had been complications to the delivery and the host mother had died. There was a brief clip of a frightened-looking older woman holding out a blood-smeared, wailing little thing to the camera. Chatterji recoiled.

"*Died?*" he said. "She wasn't supposed to die! Was that—was it our fault?"

"Of course it wasn't," Rutherford assured him hurriedly. "This was the Dark Ages, remember? Dreadfully high mortality rate they had back then. She'd undoubtedly have died anyway."

And the next images were reassuring, too: various scenes around a small cottage in Hampstead, so the voice informed them, staffed by a couple in the pay of the field operative in charge of the project. Here was the subject, aged six months, sprawling asleep on the bosom of the older woman previously seen, where she sat near beehives in what seemed to be an orchard. Here was the subject, aged two years, staring down with wide eyes from the back of a ploughhorse, held up there by a grinning countryman who pointed at the camera, and now a sound byte with the footage:

"Ee now! See'un thur? That be thuyne uncle Labienus, be'nt 'un now? Coom a long wey t'see thee. Wev to 'un, Nicket. Coom on then. Wev!"

As Nicket wevved at the camera uncertainly, Rutherford shifted in his chair. "And I'm certain the Company's fellow in charge turned it all to the Company's advantage in psychological programming. Not only must our man make up for his bastardy, he must atone for his mother's death!"

The voice described the subject's subsequent dame-school education, and the private tutor who had been hired when the subject was seven to prepare him for higher learning at Oxford. There followed an image of the subject, now apparently in his teens, pacing down a muddy street with a satchel, photographed unawares. It was the first clear shot of his adult face they had seen and it was, indeed, the face of the man they'd summoned into their parlor. But:

"Good God, what's happened to his nose?" Rutherford said, frowning. "He's broken it!"

"It was us did it, actually," Ellsworth-Howard said. "When he was a couple minutes old, putting the black box in. The recording device's too big to go up through that fancy nose you wanted without damaging the cartilage. Then it grew bent."

"Oh, what a shame," said Rutherford. "Still, it can't be helped. And I don't think babies feel discomfort anyway, do they?"

The voice was explaining that the subject had proved a brilliant student, and entered Balliol College at Oxford with the intention of studying for the priesthood in the nascent Church of England.

"Shracking *what*?" said Ellsworth-Howard, outraged. "Religion? I thought he was supposed to be above all that, with the brain we gave him."

"Now, now, you're forgetting that he was designed to operate in the past." Chatterji sighed. "Of course he was going to share the beliefs of the era we put him in. Even Tolkien and C. S. Lewis were, er, religious, don't forget."

However, the voice went on to say, the subject's promising career in the Church had been derailed by an unfortunate episode in his seventeenth year. The next image showed the subject, muddy, pale, and furious-looking, struggling between two constables. A third constable lay at their feet, bleeding from the nose.

"What's this?" Chatterji frowned at the screen. "That's old Enforcer behavior."

"Oh, not really. The Facilitator handling the case made a poor choice of a tutor for the boy, that's all," Rutherford said hurriedly.

"You watched this before we got here?"

"I couldn't wait," Rutherford admitted, as the voice went on to explain that the subject's tutor had been selected for his charisma and advanced ideas on religious freedom. Unfortunately, his ideas had been Anabaptist in nature and he had led his circle of disciples, including the subject, in what amounted to heretical orgies.

"Sex, does he mean?" Ellsworth-Howard frowned. "I thought religious people didn't do that."

"Precisely." Rutherford nodded.

"Oh."

The voice informed them that, upon discovery and the subsequent scandal, the subject had self-intoxicated on alcohol and publicly preached heresy, which had got him arrested. The Facilitator in charge had managed the subject's release, after intensive reprogramming, and hustled him out of England to continue his education in various cities in Europe.

By 1547, the voice continued, the subject had returned to England, having become private secretary to one of the people with whom Dr. Zeus had established contact for business purposes. Here followed a shot of the subject, a towering figure in his black scholar's attire, looking sullen as he followed a small and somewhat overdressed specimen of the gentry along a walk beside a half-timbered manor house.

"Impressive fellow," said Chatterji in a pleased voice. Rutherford squirmed.

"It was going so well," he said. Even the electronic voice sounded uncomfortable as it described the logistical error that had precipitated the end of the subject's life, when in 1554 the Company had sent a team of field agents to the estate where the subject was employed. Their mission had been to collect botanical rarities in the estate's garden. Three images flashed up, standard Company ID shots of its cyborg personnel: a dark male with an urbane smile, a darker female with a calm smile, and an unsmiling female with a pale, scared face. The voice gave their Company designations.

"Oi! My Preservers," remarked Ellsworth-Howard. "What'd they got to do with it?"

Rutherford sighed. "It was the *girl*," he said in distaste.

The voice went on to explain that the Facilitator in charge of the mission had encouraged his subordinate, the mission's Botanist, to enter into a sexual relationship with the subject, in the hope that the mission would go more smoothly. Chatterji groaned.

"Apparently he had no idea our man was a Company experiment," cried Rutherford, throwing his hands up in the air. "I can't imagine who left that particular bit of vital information out of his briefing."

"Actually," Chatterji said, raising a placatory hand, "actually there was a good reason why he wasn't told."

Rutherford and Ellsworth-Howard turned to him. Ellsworth-Howard paused the report. "What the shrack?"

Chatterji gave a slightly embarrassed cough. "It seems there has been a certain amount of . . . negative feeling, on the part of our older Preservers, about the Enforcers being retired."

"What?" Rutherford stared.

". . . And as a result, an ongoing program of fact effacement has been initiated," Chatterji admitted. "The new operatives aren't aware the Enforcer class ever existed. The older ones have been given the impression that the Enforcers were all happily reprogrammed for work on remote Company bases. Very few people outside this room know about *Adonai*, you see: if the cyborgs were told the Company was experimenting with a new Enforcer design, it might be noticed that most of the old ones had gone missing."

"Well, I like that!" Rutherford's eyes were round with indignation. "And what if they did notice? They think we treated the Enforcers badly, do they? Didn't we give them eternal life? What *do* they think they are?"

"I fully share your feelings," Chatterji said. "However, the plain fact is that we depend on the Preservers a good deal. Under the circumstances, it was thought best not to antagonize the Facilitator, so he wasn't informed about our project."

"You can see where that led!" said Rutherford.

"I still don't see where the girl comes in," said Ellsworth-Howard, looking from Rutherford to Chatterji.

"Apparently there was a security breach," Rutherford said in disgust. "What can you expect, letting a cyborg—er—become intimate with our man?"

Ellsworth-Howard started the report again, and the voice explained the circumstances that had led to the security breach, and its aftermath, when the subject had been arrested again for preaching heresy.

"Shrack," cried Ellsworth-Howard. "What'd he go do a stupid thing like that for?"

"This was in the sixteenth century, after all," Rutherford pointed out. "We gave him a splendid mind, but it had no context for dealing with the discovery that cyborgs existed. No wonder the poor fellow behaved irrationally."

Here was an image of the subject being chained to a stake before a crowd. Chatterji, watching, turned a nasty putty color, but all he said was: "So he died a martyr's death. Heroic, Rutherford, but not exactly what we had in mind. And rather an awful job for the salvage operative who had to retrieve his black box."

"No; this is the only part that cheered me up at all," Rutherford told him. "Look now. Watch."

A film clip ran and they saw the light of flames dancing on the faces of the spectators, and it danced too on the faces of the three friends: Chatterji horrified, Rutherford's gaze avid and focused, Ellsworth-Howard looking on in disgust.

"What's he doing?" demanded Ellsworth-Howard. "What's he talking about?"

"He's preaching," Rutherford said. "In that wonderful voice we gave him. And look at the crowd, look at their faces. They're hanging on his every word, all of them. They're going to remember this the rest of their lives. Look at that one little lad, look at the hero-worship in his eyes. You see? Our man is *inspiring* them!"

"They're shracking burning him alive, Rutherford," said Ellsworth-Howard.

"But just listen to him! Fulfilling his destiny, shouting encouragement to his countrymen to throw off the yoke of religious oppression." Rutherford was almost in happy tears.

"Is that what it's all about? Something political?" Ellsworth-Howard turned to Chatterji, who was now staring at the floor, unable to watch.

"Protestants versus Catholics, Foxy," he said in a faint voice. "Remember the plot of *Bloody Mary*?"

Ellsworth-Howard shook his head. "Bunch of bigots slugging it out over some bloody stupid religious ritual, that's all I know."

At that moment there was the sound of a detonation and the camera moved abruptly away from the subject. There was one still picture taken five hours later, over which the electronic voice described recovery procedures.

"Anyway, there was much more than religion involved," said Rutherford, stretching happily. "The political freedom of the English people was endangered. Didn't we want someone who'd be willing to die in just such a cause?"

Ellsworth-Howard brightened. He switched off the report.

"Yeah, I guess if you look at it that way it's all right," he said. "Kind of a short life, though, wasn't it?"

"All things considered, chaps, I think we can be proud of ourselves," Rutherford said. "For all that nonsense with the Preservers, our man still died a hero's death, didn't he? What more could we have asked of him?"

"But there *was* a security breach," said Chatterji, groping for his nasal inhalator and taking a fortifying drag. "That mustn't happen again."

"Then, let's turn the lesson to good use for the next life sequence. Is there a way to make our man less susceptible to women, Foxy?"

"Not now," Ellsworth-Howard said. "Can't mess about with the design once I've made an embryo."

"I agree, though, that we need him to be a little more . . . detached." Chatterji watched the fire, wondering what it would be like to burn to death. It had been a morbid terror of his, ever since he could remember.

"Precisely." Rutherford smacked the arm of his chair. "For one thing, his Facilitator must impress on him that common romantic love is a waste of his time. I told you a sex drive would lead to difficulties. We created him to serve a higher purpose. Look at what romance did to King Arthur! How's a hero to be expected to do his job with all that needless distraction? There's no sex in *The Lord of the Rings*."

"What about the Don Juan psychology, eh?" suggested Chatterji. "Lots of healthy sex without emotional attachment? Make him a bit of a cad, I suppose, but some of the old heroes were."

"We want a man who understands the necessity of sacrifice," pronounced Rutherford. "No mystical nonsense. No women. Love is such a selfish passion, after all."

"As you like." Chatterji nodded. "As soon as we receive word that another host mother has been located, you can draw up a revised psych template for our man."

"I've already had word of one," Ellsworth-Howard said. "Came in yesterday: some Facilitator in 1824 AD's found a girl for us. Daughter of a peer. *Three* boyfriends—naughty bit, I must say. One's a lord, one's an M.P., and one's her father's gardener. All of 'em the right morphology."

"In 1824?" Chatterji had another drag on his inhalator. "What's going on in that time period? Much action for our man to be heroic in, when he's grown? Glory days of the old empire, wasn't it?"

"Very good," said Rutherford. Rising from his chair he began to pace. "Send the message to abduct, Foxy, and we'll try again."

"Check," said Ellsworth-Howard, pulling out his throat mike. He set it in place and sent the message subvocally.

"Now, then . . ." Rutherford turned and stood with his back to the fire. "It has seemed to me, chaps, that we need a bit more inspiration. If we're going to be the creators of heroes, just as the original Inklings were, we need to duplicate their experiences as closely as possible."

"I thought we were." Chatterji looked around at the antiques, the stage dressing. "How could one recreate the twentieth century any better than this?"

"Ah! The house is only part of it, you see." Rutherford paused with his back to the fire. "The Inklings drew inspiration from their meetings, but they also kept in contact with the ancient wilderness of Merlin's Isle of Gramarye."

"What the shrack are you talking about?" Ellsworth-Howard knitted his brows.

"England! Albion. This blessed earth. They used to go out on *walking tours*, you see. Just take their daypacks and stride out through the hedgerows, and meadows and animals and things. It'd give them lots of ideas. And Merlin traveled a great deal, didn't he, and Gandalf? So maybe a lot of walking helps the brain create stuff."

"Interesting idea," said Chatterji. "In the Hindu folktales, wise men and magicians lived like beggars, walking from town to town."

"There you go. Now, what I propose is that we do the same. This time next month, what do you say? We'll meet here, and we'll just walk until we find some open country somewhere. Perhaps we'll feel creative influences as soon as we're out of the shadows of the buildings, what?"

"How do we find open country?" said Ellsworth-Howard. "Don't know if I've ever seen any."

"Don't be silly, there's a borough greenbelt not five miles from here," Chatterji said. "It'll be on any map. I think this sounds marvelous! Assuming it isn't raining, of course. On the twenty-seventh, then?"

_____

Alec on Blue Water

Just as the phantom had gone past, and all hands sighed relief
With rending crash and mortal force, our vessel struck a reef!

Alec howled happily at the top of his lungs, timing his words with the *bump-bump-bump* of the agboat as it sped across the waves.

His latest acquisition wasn't much to look at: a spare volcanic rock standing out of the Pacific, thinly skinned on top with green, one wind-bent Norfolk Island pine at the base of the lighthouse. It was a long way from anywhere and completely deserted. The automated light wasn't working, because the small South American nation to whom it had previously belonged had been unable to afford its maintenance.

Alec had come to repair it. Among other things.

He had long since accustomed himself to the roar and flow of information that ran through his brain every conscious hour. He was able to tune it all out, all but a narrow band of what he was immediately interested in; otherwise he'd have been like a man in a library trying to read every book at once. He let the Captain sort through all the data for him. Habitually, now, he saw the world twofold: the ordinary dimensional world through which his body moved and, superimposed over it, the world in which the Captain lived. They matched seamlessly, the one neither more nor less real than the other.

He brought the agboat up on the narrow black crescent of beach and frowned at the access stairs. They were tide-worn concrete, slimy with seaweed and bird droppings, and the handrail had been eaten away with rust.

Hell no, lad. Take the boat up instead, the Captain said.

Aye sir! Alec shifted propulsion systems and the agboat rose smoothly through the air, surprising the royal terns nesting in the cliff face. Seabirds rose and floated around him in a protesting cloud, as he gained the top of the cliff and brought the agboat down at the base of the lighthouse.

Scan complete, Alec, said the Captain. ***All clear. Step ashore!***

Alec hopped over the side, gleeful as always to set foot on terra incognita. He paced along the gravel walk around the lighthouse, examining its masonry visually as the Captain scanned for structural defects.

Looks sound to me.

So she is, laddie. Let's do a bit of breaking and entering, eh?

Whistling through his teeth, Alec strode up to the door and entered the code he had been given. As he expected, it didn't work. The security system would have to be replaced, too. No matter; there were crates and crates of useful components in the agboat. He fetched out a case, removed a small limpet charge and affixed it carefully to the lock. Walking away a few paces, he withdrew a detonating device and, unlocking the trigger, fired.

The lock blew off with a pleasing bang and puff of smoke. Alec grinned and ran close to pull the door open. It screamed as though it were being murdered. Nothing inside but the base of a spiral stair vanishing upward into gloom. The air was dry, and smelled clean.

And she's weathertight, too, the Captain said. Alec sprinted back to the boat and hauled out the aglev unit. He began the lengthy process of loading crates, up the long dark chimney of the lighthouse to the control room at its top.

When the Second Golden Age of Sail had arrived, the nations of the world had found that lighthouses were once again necessary. Not to provide light, though they did that too, but as land-based backups, sensors and relays for the global satellite tracking system. New lighthouses sprang up everywhere. There had been scarcely a stretch of water in the seven seas where you couldn't glimpse some spark of light or other in the black night distance.

Then, of course, the first excitement of the sailing craze had faded. The same people who had raved about what a marvelously eco-friendly system sail transport was now complained bitterly about public funds being used for something that would only benefit shipping magnates and yachtsmen. The more necessary ones were grudgingly maintained at national expense, and the rest fell into disrepair.

This had been the state of maritime data reconnaissance until Balfour Continuance Limited had offered to purchase lighthouses from various needy countries. The given explanation—that Balfour Continuance was funded by wealthy yachtsmen interested in repairing and maintaining the lighthouses—was accepted without the least curiosity.

In fact Alec and the Captain were Balfour Continuance, its sole board of directors, stockholders, and repair personnel. All around the world, the lights in the towers had winked back on, one by one, and they had begun to talk amongst themselves and search the darkness as they had used to; but they now shared the towers with backup caches for the Captain, linking him to the satellite relays, powered by solar collectors. The Captain circled the globe, was indestructible, and was able to feed a constant false location for the *Captain Morgan* to the global surveillance satellites.

He was now several hundred times more powerful than any artificial intelligence had ever been. Alec was doubly happy about this, for not only was the Captain better able to fulfill his programming, but the sea was quite a bit safer than she had been, for all who sailed her. Alec was always fond of doing good while doing well.

And the lighthouses had another use. There was plenty of room in their towers for anything one might need to store there.

The truth was that Alec was fairly actively engaged in smuggling, and had become rather successful at it. He was already nearly the richest man in the world, thanks to the Captain's byzantine investment arrangements. Alec found he very much liked flouting stupid laws and cruising through the night with a hold full of Toblerone, or ganja, or semisoft brie. It was exciting to lie offshore, waiting for signal lights. Also, it seemed like the sort of thing Roger would have enjoyed.

It was not without its dangers, of course. Alec and the Captain had by this time repeatedly broken the laws of most first-world nations.

However, Alec was a British peer, and legally the Captain didn't actually exist. There were no contingencies in law for Pembroke Playfriends who went rogue, nor any for aristocrats who could decrypt codes no mortal genius nor immortal machine had been able to break in four centuries of dedicated trying. Where loopholes couldn't be found, bribing local law enforcement created them. In case that ever failed, as it had yet to do, Alec had a firm of solicitors whose services were retained at princely rates to handle his fines for failing to attend Parliament.

He had left the Circle of Thirty far behind now. The first step had been failing his university examinations, which had taken a bit of careful work. Low marks in maths or cyberscience would have drawn unwanted attention, but spectacularly dismal marks in everything else drew the average down nicely and reinforced the legend of Ape Man Checkerfield, which suited Alec fine. He had long since ceased to care what Alistair Stede-Windsor thought of him. The Lewins had been appalled—that was painful—but he had bought them a beautiful home, and arranged pensions for them roughly equal to the annual national income of Monaco.

The admin classes, for their part, had looked at his substance abuse records, looked at his low test average, concluded the son was as worthless as his father had been, and washed their collective hands of the seventh earl.

And really, it had worked out very nicely for all parties involved. Alec now had a reputation as a playboy moron. To be a criminal in the twenty-fourth century, under so much surveillance, required genius, so nobody suspected he'd become one.

Alec worked at the lighthouse until dusk. Then he was off across the water to where the *Captain Morgan* rode at anchor, beautiful as a dream from which one wakes weeping.

She was immense, a four-masted windjammer, everything the Captain had promised she'd be, with that extra dash of class that comes from slightly retro styling. Alec had clamored for lots of pirate-ship ornamentation. The masters at Beretania pursed their lips and compromised, without spoiling their ideal of sleek white functionality. Alec insisted on having belaying pins along her rails, for appearance's sake, and a working ship's wheel.

Beretania let him have his way in the cabin interiors, too, and they were glorious or hideous, depending on your sense of taste. Plenty of teak paneling and carving in a generally eighteenth-century style, the color scheme all crimson, jewel blue, and mahogany.

There was even a figurehead on the prow, a mermaid whose bare breasts were discreetly obscured by the snaking coils of her fire-colored hair. Alec had seen her in an old drawing and demanded a reproduction. She stared out at the sea with contemptuous black eyes, and well she might; the *Captain Morgan* was deadly swift, swifter than the *Flying Cloud*, swifter than any other ship Beretania had built, and they were the best in the business. She flew a black ensign bearing a grinning skull and crossed bones.

She carried laser cannon, too, hidden away behind sliding panels, quite dull functional pre-ban stuff of immense power, obtained from shady men who kept no records. So far the Captain had been unable to talk Alec into outright piracy, but if anyone ever attempted to board the *Captain Morgan* they'd wind up at the bottom of the sea in very small pieces.

With a last whoosh of spray the agboat rose from the water and settled like a bird into its berth. Alec locked the davits and vaulted down to the deck, where he nearly collided with Billy Bones, who came rattling up with a glass of iced fruit tea for him.

Billy Bones was not a robot. It was one of the Captain's servounits, a skeletal thing on six jointed legs with three manipulative members. Alec had put it together to satisfy the Captain's desire to function in four-dimensional space. It had no brain or personality, the Captain controlled everything it did; but for whimsy's sake Alec had given it a steel skull-face. The effect was not whimsical. The servounit looked like a cross between the Terminator and a scorpion. The Captain had three others on board and Alec had named them Coxinga, Bully Hayes, and Flint.

Thanks, Captain, sir! Alec took the tea and had gulped it all down before he reached his cabin. *I'm going to wash; I feel like a guano magnet.*

The servounit followed after him and accepted the empty glass. **Aye, son. Supper'll be ready in the saloon when you get out.**

Billy Bones waited patiently while he shrugged out of his coveralls and climbed into the shower. It extended a grasping hook, picked up the coveralls and scuttled away with them to the ship's laundry. In the galley, Coxinga began preparations for Alec's supper. On the quarter-deck, the Captain checked the stock market totals for that day and roved through his weather data, satisfying himself that no storms, financial or meteorological, were headed their way within the next forty-eight hours. He ordered Flint off to be waiting with a fresh towel for Alec, and busied himself with plotting their next course. He was a very contented machine.

Alec was the only soul on board, and he hadn't seen a human being in six months.

But he was singing lustily as he lathered his hair, though Flint wasn't able to appreciate his fine tenor in the least as it crept in on its steel spider-legs.

> *Pity the Flying Dutchman! Forever is his doom.*
> *The stormy waters round Cape Horn must be his living tomb!*
> *He's bound to sail the ocean forever and a day*
> *As he tries in vain his oath to keep by entering Table Bay!*

He was still whistling the song as he pulled on shorts and a vivid Hawaiian shirt. It had a pattern of flaming sunsets, scowling tikis, and surfboards. There was no one now to tell him his taste in clothes was ghastly. Pushing his hair out of his eyes (he hadn't bothered to have it cut in a year), he wandered barefoot into the saloon. The rolling walk of a sailor had come back to him easily, never really forgotten over fifteen years ashore.

The saloon was a fearsome place, and not only because of Alec's chosen color scheme of red, blue, and gold. The walls bristled with antique hand weapons of every description. Alec had begun collecting swords, and branched out to pistols and war-axes, when he discovered what an atavistic thrill he got from handling them. Once, with a cutlass in hand, he had taken experimental swing at a sack of flour suspended from a yardarm. The result, besides creating an unholy mess, had been so emotionally disturbing he now kept all his collection safely locked behind glass.

He fixed himself a drink now at the bar, settling into the booth as Coxinga brought him his supper.

It was sweet and sour halibut (Alec no longer had any qualms about eating real fish) with rice and peas, and he paused a moment to inhale the fragrances before setting to appreciatively. As he ate, he accessed a private file and reviewed its contents.

The file was headed Charities. Alec did contribute, anonymously, to several real causes he felt were laudable. The World Centre for Disease Control got millions from him annually, as did Tri-Worlds Divorce Counseling Services. He practically supported Mr. Shakespeare at Southwark, and gave generously to the Greenwich Museum.

But there was another way Alec spent his money. He called it the God Game.

He scanned through his list now and singled out a small Caribbean country. Its economy was just beginning to recover from a catastrophic hurricane five years earlier, and a general election was about to be held. Alec surveyed all the data from weather forecasts, estimated its probable national revenue for the next five years, factored in the personal histories of all candidates running for office, and decided which man was best for the country. He transferred three million pounds into that candidate's election fund. Then he did a projection based on all known factors and prevailing trends, and nodded in satisfaction. If all went as planned, there would be prosperity within two years and, just possibly, a cure for that nasty new strain of jungle rot.

Another name on the list behind his eyes flashed red, and he scowled at it. This was a Balkan nation, long ravaged by plague. He had funded the rise of a leader whose political record indicated deep concern with medical reform issues. However, since the man had been in office the state of national health had not improved, and the man's mistress had begun to spend lavishly on shoes, always a bad sign. Alec reached into the man's private bank account and was astounded at the amount he found there. He withdrew half of it and deposited it into the campaign account of the opposition party. Another projection, and Alec wasn't quite satisfied with the results; he tinkered with various factors, funding a research group here, a political activist there, until he got something he liked better.

He paused to take another mouthful of rice and fish, washed it down with rum, and returned to his calculations. The Secular Opposition on Luna was having a bad fiscal year. Best to shore them up with a donation and maintain the balance of power between the Opposition and the Ephesian Church. New sanctions were being placed on the Celtic Federation by the American Community and Britain; Alec quietly slipped a few million into various Celtic political funds. The Greenest of the Greens had just won a major victory at the Egyptian polls, and stood poised to cut subsidies to barley farmers; Alec depleted the Green war chest, and made an unrecorded donation of substantial size to the Greater Nile Agricultural Relief Fund.

The rest of the world seemed to be running along smoothly. He noted the presence of Robert Louis Stevenson memorabilia scheduled for the block at Sotheby's, the entire contents of the Napa Valley museum including the writer's childhood toys! Alec hurriedly made a pre-emptive bid, and arranged for shipping. Smiling, he settled back and finished his meal.

He knew that what he was doing was technically wrong, pushing governments and leaders around like so many toy soldiers. He told himself it was what anyone would do, if they had the chance. And the money. He told himself he had a responsibility, as a person of privilege, to help others. He told himself it made up for his failure to attend Parliament: he could do a lot more good for the world this way, after all, direct and hands-on, without hours of tedious debate in the House of Lords.

But he knew, in his heart, that he enjoyed the God Game. He felt a little guilty about that.

He shrugged off the feeling now and finished his dinner, as Coxinga crawled forward offering another tray.

Pudding time! Mango surprise à la mode.

"Cool," he said, and looked on expectantly as Coxinga placed it before him and scuttled away with the empty dishes.

Two months later Alec was emerging from a Happy Club in Tijuana, yawning though the evening was young indeed. Normally he loved working his way through every bed in a house, but this time hadn't been nearly the wild fun he'd expected after months at sea. He didn't speak Japanese, so the Captain had had to translate everything the girls had said to him, and what with the time lag between their questions and his halting phonetic replies, about the only phrase he clearly understood by the end of the evening was "big stupid gaijin."

Cultivating an image as an idiot is one thing, but being taken for one when you're trying to look clever and seductive is another. Alec was in a foul mood as he paced through the immaculate streets.

It didn't matter. He had other fun lined up for tonight.

He found his rental transport, a cheap little Aerboy, where he'd left it under a mosaic mural of Moctezuma and his court wearing what bore a strong resemblance to samurai armor. He climbed in and shot away in the direction of the sea, speeding to feel the wind in his face. It woke him up considerably in the time it took him to get to the marina and go down to the mooring where the *Captain Morgan* was.

Bully Hayes was waiting by the gangplank as he came aboard. He shrugged out of his dinner jacket and handed it off to the servounit.

Lay in a course for Catalina. Let's blow this town.

Don't blame me that you can't speak Japanese! I did my best.

I'm just not good with people sometimes. No big deal, right?

Right you are, my lad. You'll have yerself a hell of a good time in Lahaina, wait and see. Shall I set a course?

Yeah. Right after we deliver.

Flint and Billy Bones pulled up the gangplank. The Captain had already started up the fusion drive and switched on the running lights. In eerie silence the massive ship backed from her berth and put about, moving at half speed toward the end of the breakwater, unfurling her vast sails as she went, looking semitransparent and unreal as she retreated from the glare of the harbor lights. Around the signal on the end of the breakwater and she was on the open sea, and her speed came up and she was running north, under the inconstant Northern Star.

They wouldn't reach their destination for hours yet, so Alec had a shower to wash the incense out of his hair and put on his all-black smuggling ensemble, snickering at his own pretensions. His good humor was quite restored by the time he stepped into the deckhouse and Billy Bones silently proffered him a mug of coffee. On the quarterdeck that existed simultaneously in cyberspace, the Captain stood at the helm, holding a steady course.

How are we doing? Alec sipped from the mug. Like wine: Jamaica Blue Mountain hot and black, full of complex fragrances.

Couldn't ask for better, son. Wind's out of the south, mild swell,

temperature's ten degrees centigrade, time's twenty-one hundred hours. At the speed she's making we'll be there well before sunrise.

Cool. Alec settled into his chair and looked up through the glass at the stars. *Make it so!*

Aye aye, matey. What's yer listening pleasure this evening?

Give us . . . give us something classical. What about Folded Space?

That was Alec's favorite twenty-third-century neobaroque fusion group. The Captain nodded, and after a moment, softly wailing tenor sax music flowed out of the ship's speakers, a piece called "Variations on a Theme by Bryan Ferry." It was sentimental music, evoking late nights in cocktail lounges and wistful memories, but it fit his mood to perfection. Alec had just had his twentieth birthday the week before and he felt sophisticated and old.

They made for the windward side of the island, standing well out to sea and following her coast. Alec was energized and jittering long before they got there. He jumped when the Captain informed him:

Right, laddie, we're just off Eagle Rock. I've dropped anchor. They've signaled to let us know they're coming out.

Okay. Have you scanned?

Aye. All according to the plan.

Alec went out on deck and stood by the rail, swaying against the sidelong roll of the sea. There was the looming bulk of Mount Torquemada, black against the eastern sky, which had not quite started to pale with the dawn but was perhaps a shade less black than the island. He inhaled deeply: perfume of gardens, peppery evergreens, sagebrush, and . . . machinery, growing more dominant. There were the blue lights of the cutter, coming in a long path across the water toward them. He rubbed his hands together and went below deck to shift cargo, summoning Billy Bones and Flint to help him.

When he came up on deck with the first tea crate, he recognized the voice giving him a cautious hail.

"Yo ho there, Dick."

"Yo ho there, Ebenezer," he responded. The boarding ladder extended and a moment later a man pulled himself up to the deck. He was dressed in gray exercise clothing and a stocking cap, and his features were fairly nondescript. Alec recognized his voice, though, with its regional Californian accent.

"Dude." The owner of the voice clapped him on the shoulder. "What've you got for the old man?" No wrong smells; no stress chemicals in the man's sweat.

"How's this?" Alec shone a penlight on the crate. He prised open a loose slat and the bright letters were clearly visible behind it: RED ROSE DARJEELING.

"Cool."

"Five crates of this, ten of Earl Grey, ten of Orange Pekoe. You like?"

"I don't drink the stuff myself, but he'll be a happy guy. Five grand for everything?"

"Deal, man."

"Then let's dance."

The Californian produced a disc from his pocket and Alec took it for a moment. Somewhere, the Eagle Rock Marine Institute went on record as having purchased fifty cases of jotpads and other student supplies from the Cayman Islands Trading Company. Smoothly, crates of tea were offloaded into the cutter from the *Captain Morgan*.

"This is really kind of funny," grunted the Californian, handing down the last box. "You ever hear of the Boston Tea Party?"

"Nope," Alec said.

"It had something to do with our revolution, the one where we broke away from you guys. Your people were charging our people a hell of a lot less than this for tea, but we didn't want to pay it anyway, so we raided some ship or something."

"Was that why the Yanks did that whole Fourth-of-July thing?" Alec was astonished. "Over *tea*?"

"Yeah, I guess so. I think so. Seems kind of pointless now, doesn't it?" The Californian glanced over at the *Captain Morgan*'s figurehead, illuminated by the blue lights of the cutter. "Hey, man, look at that! Your lady's crying."

Alec leaned over the rail to see. Pearls of seaspray were rolling down the mermaid's face, brimming in her black eyes.

"How about that?" he said. "She wants to be out of here, I guess. Time we were gone. Bye-bye, then!"

"Be seeing you." The Californian waved, turning to keep his face to Alec as the cutter put about. They made off and vanished into the island's black silhouette, deeper and blacker as the eastern sky paled, to deliver their cargo to the Eagle Rock Marine Institute . . . better known in some circles as the emergency command center for Dr. Zeus Incorporated.

The *Captain Morgan* tacked about and sailed west, well out to sea, setting a course for Maui.

ANOTHER MEETING, A MONTH LATER, FAIR AND WARMER

On the twenty-seventh, Rutherford woke with excitement in his heart. He scrambled out of bed and hurried through his breathing therapy. Then he took all his medication. Then he took the herbal supplements that kept the side effects of his medication at bay. Then he took his vitamins. Then he had breakfast: fruit juice and an oat fiber bar, chewed thoroughly.

He dressed with some care, in his best twentieth-century costume. He had an idea that sensible walking shoes were called for, and from the depths of his wardrobe pulled out a pair of heavy boots he'd found at an auction. They were a bit large, but Rutherford reflected that too large was certainly better than too small, and he laced them up happily and stood to admire himself in his long mirror. He remembered his daypack and strapped it on. For good measure he put on his spectacles, and struck what he felt was quite a Victorian pose in the mirror. *Intrepid*, that was the word for how he looked.

He'd clumped downstairs, sliding a bit inside the boots, before he remembered that he'd forgotten to actually put anything inside his daypack. So he clumped back upstairs, loaded the pack with his medication and a jotbook, and for good measure added a couple of oat fiber bars and a bottle of distilled water. He paused over his identification disc, wondering if he oughtn't make a symbolic gesture of leaving it on his dresser; but good sense prevailed, especially once he remembered he'd need money for any jolly country inns he might encounter.

Rutherford went down to the parlor and settled into his favorite chair (he had to take off the daypack again first) and waited eagerly for his friends to arrive.

Two hours later he was fuming with impatience, and started up, quite cross, when he heard the others knocking at his door.

"Where have you been?" he demanded, on pulling it open.

"Sorry, are we late?" Chatterji looked surprised.

"We had to shracking eat, didn't we?" said Ellsworth-Howard.

He surveyed them in despair. Chatterji wore his usual tuxedo and black patent leather shoes. The only concession Ellsworth-Howard had made to the spirit of adventure was to wear exercise slippers in place of his customary saddle oxfords. "Had you forgotten we're going on a walking tour?" Rutherford said, controlling his temper.

"Of course not." Chatterji half turned and flipped aside his cape to display his black silk daypack. "See? And I've brought a map." He held out a little booklet triumphantly. It was a late-twentieth-century transit guide to greater metropolitan London. "Found it in an antique gallery. It's even the proper time period! At least, it's not off by more than a few decades."

"Oh, I say," Rutherford felt his mood lift. "Good thinking."

"Can I have a sherry?" Chatterji looked past him into the room to the bar.

"No time!" Rutherford stepped out on the mat and pulled the door shut. "We need to get started. Besides, don't you want to see if we can find a pub in the country?" He started boldly down the front walk.

"Oh, that's right." Chatterji hurried after him, and Ellsworth-Howard caught up with them.

"You don't reckon we can really find any place that serves sherry and all that, do you?" he said.

"Of course not, but there's bound to be prune juice, and we can pretend it's sherry," said Chatterji.

"It will *be* sherry," said Rutherford. "We'll transform it with our imaginations. Or it could be nut-brown ale, or—or even tea."

They came to the main road that led out of Albany Crescent and went down it confidently, at least as far as the transit station on the corner.

"Terra incognita." Rutherford gestured at the maze of streets opening beyond. "Here there be dragons, or maybe the edge of the earth. Onward!"

"Where?" Ellsworth-Howard wanted to know, looking out doubtfully. The unknown world was largely deserted, except for the big public transports rumbling by. Dust blew and drifted in the streets of London, but no voice called, no footsteps sounded on her ancient paving.

"This way," Rutherford said, pointing down a lane less dark than the others, with what he fancied was a glimpse of green in the distance. They waited until there was a gap in the traffic and hurried across, as pale faces with surprised expressions stared out at them from the transports.

"Where's all the dust come from?" Ellsworth-Howard said as they tramped along. "There's none of this in my street. None in yours, either, is there?"

"Perhaps it's kept swept up where people live," Rutherford said. He looked up at the blank windows of the housefronts. "I'm not sure this district is inhabited. Funny there aren't any people about, isn't it?"

Actually, it wasn't. It had never occurred to Rutherford that the rest of the population of London might venture out as seldom as he did. There were no longer thieves to be afraid of and wandering madmen very seldom, no bombs or random gunfire, hadn't been in a couple of generations; but people were fairly timid nowadays. Anyway the weather in London was the same as it had always been, so there just wasn't that much incentive to leave one's rooms.

A few streets on they did pass a foreign-looking person with a map plaquette and a camera, wandering from house number to house number with a puzzled air. When he noticed the three adventurers, he took in their outlandish antique clothing in a long slow stare and crossed to the other side of the empty street.

"Shrack you too!" cried Ellsworth-Howard heartily. His voice echoed against the buildings.

By the time they got to the green place, Rutherford was limping slightly. A fold of sock had somehow wadded up inside one of his too-big boots, and was rubbing painfully against his toes with every step. He ignored the discomfort, however, in the exhilaration of discovery.

To either side of the street here the buildings were gone, and only concrete foundations and a few rusted pipes remained to show where steel and glass towers had been before the 2198 earthquake. Structurally, they'd withstood the shaking very well: not so the rush hour pedestrians who'd looked up and seen a million guillotines of broken window pane hurtling down at them. But the blood had been washed away long ago, and now the sun flooded in on an open square of derelict commerce, where a single tree had taken advantage of the light and air to grow to enormous size. It happened to be a California redwood, planted long ago by some transatlantic corporation.

"Golly." Chatterji's mouth hung open. "Have you ever seen a tree that big in your life?"

"Not real, is it?" Ellsworth-Howard peered at it. "Nah. It's a holo, right? Bloody expensive one, must be."

"I don't think so." Rutherford was shivering with delight. "Look! There's ravens perching up there. Do you suppose it's a sacred oak?"

"Looks more like a giant Christmas tree," said Chatterji.

"All the same, this is it!" Rutherford threw his arms up in the air. "We're at the beginning of the country. We're at the end of the urban nightmare. From this point on the ultimate west commences."

"We're going north, ain't we?" Ellsworth-Howard squinted around them in the sunlight.

"Whatever," said Rutherford, and strode forward. His friends followed gamely.

But they went on and somehow did not emerge into green and rolling countryside: only long deserted streets of houses, quiet in the sunlight. Now and then they changed direction, wandering across vacant lanes or terraces, yet everywhere the view they encountered was the same. The dust had buried the curbs in some places, or formed little sloping dunes against front steps, or lay in the cracks in the pavement. The only sound was the wind and the occasional roar of a public transport going by. Once, briefly, they heard music coming from within a house. Its windows were shut and curtains drawn, however, so they couldn't see anyone inside.

Ivy scaled the walls of a few houses, and weeds grew high in the tiny yards below street level. With all the tall buildings dismantled, there was plenty of sun and rain for any growing thing that might seed itself in London; but few seeds, apparently, and nobody with the inclination to make a garden.

On they went, and both Rutherford and Chatterji were limping badly now. Ellsworth-Howard had begun to shake his head, making a high-pitched growling noise in his throat. Chatterji was about to tell him not to be so negative when Ellsworth-Howard abruptly clutched at his skull and spun around in a circle.

"My shracking head's on fire," he screamed.

Aghast, his friends caught hold of him. Chatterji put his hands up to Ellsworth-Howard's head and drew back with a cry.

"The rivets," he said. "They're hot!"

"It's the sun!" Rutherford realized. They staggered together into the shade of a wall and Rutherford fumbled off his daypack. He got out his distilled water and splashed it over Ellsworth-Howard's scalp.

"How could we have been so stupid?" Ellsworth-Howard moaned. "The shracking sun's radioactive! That's why people used to wear hats."

"Hats?" Rutherford and Chatterji looked at each other in dismay.

"I knew I'd forgotten something." Ellsworth-Howard wiped away tears.

"Stop a bit," Chatterji said. He pulled out an immaculate silk handkerchief and tied knots in the corners. "I saw this in an Early Humor anthology. You do this, and this and this, and it makes a sort of a hat, see? Here we go." He fitted it carefully on Ellsworth-Howard. "There. Now you'll be fine."

"But what'll *we* do?" said Rutherford.

"I expect we'll be all right. You know," Chatterji said, passing his hand over his hair in a tactful gesture. Rutherford nervously put his hands up to his own scalp and encountered an awful lot of pink forehead. Chatterji bit his lip. "Well—er—perhaps we'll find an antique shop. You might buy a hat there."

"Righto," said Rutherford, enormously relieved to remember he'd brought his identification disc.

They stepped out cautiously into the sunlight again, and continued their journey.

The novelty of the great outdoors was no longer quite as enthralling. Even Ellsworth-Howard was limping by the time they came to the first busy intersection they'd seen since leaving Rutherford's neighborhood. The friends stood, uncertain, on a street corner, drawing back involuntarily as the transports thundered past them.

"So where the bloody hell are we?" said Ellsworth-Howard. "I'm fed up with this walking thing, you know."

"The map!" Chatterji pulled it out and attempted to read it. It fell open all the way to his feet. Rutherford picked up the other end and they stood poring over the map, turning it this way and that in puzzlement. Ellsworth-Howard sighed and slipped off his daypack. He pulled out his buke, squeezed in a code, and waited for the results.

"I can't even tell where we've been, let alone where we are," said Chatterji.

"It's a splendid find all the same, you know," Rutherford assured him. "Tremendous historical value. Its just . . . unfortunately not very accurate anymore. Apparently. Here, does this look like my street?"

"Where?" Chatterji bent his head, frowning.

"There's a big green bit two streets up from this spot," said Ellsworth-Howard, showing them the screen of his buke where a simple map in brilliant primary colors had appeared. "I'm for slogging over there. Looks like all the countryside we're likely to find before our feet fall off."

"Foxy! You weren't supposed to bring your electronics," Rutherford said peevishly. "This is a spiritual journey. We're going to get in touch with nature."

"You want to see this shracking green bit or not, then?" yelled Ellsworth-Howard.

"Now, chaps! No point losing our tempers. Yes, look, Rutherford, it's a borough green area. What's its name?" Folding up his map, Chatterji peered at the red words on the screen. Rutherford looked too. Their lips moved as they sounded them out.

"Reg—"

"Regent's Park," said Rutherford.

"I'm off," Ellsworth-Howard said, and turned and walked away in the direction of the park. They went gimping after him, calling for him to slow down.

They came around a corner and there was Regent's Park: acres of green and sunlight and birdsong, visible in glimpses between the tour transports that came and went. Staggering like cripples they approached it, uttering little cries of eagerness.

"It's Olde England at last," gasped Rutherford, holding out his arms as though to embrace it all. Before him an industrial mower whirred busily along, shearing the grass to one precise height the full length of a long stripe exactly one meter wide. "Primeval Albion. The green and pleasant land."

His oration drew the attention of tourists dismounting from the nearest transport. One intrepid Asian gentleman stepped forward with his holocamera and recorded the three strangers in their picturesque costume, but most of the tourists edged away uneasily and spent their exposures on the tidy beds of primroses or the Monument to Victims of Religious Intolerance.

"My God, it's beautiful," sighed Chatterji, pulling out his sinus inhalator and taking a sensuously deep drag. "Look at all the trees!"

"It's a forest," said Ellsworth-Howard. "Look over there, can't you just see some bloody big knight in armor riding out from the shade? Or Merlin or somebody? Shracking hell, do you realize this is what it *all* used to look like?"

The thought struck them speechless. Haltingly they moved along the sandy path, straight as a die between its landscaping bricks, that took them to a real bridge over a real lake and beyond. They stood spellbound on the bridge a while, watching the waterfowl that paddled and fought. Rutherford quoted reverently from *The Wind in the Willows*.

Drawn by the spell of wilderness they went on, and presently found a snack bar on the greensward. It wasn't exactly a cozy country tavern; it featured various treats manufactured from algae, and four va-

rieties of distilled water. When the fellowship had loaded their trays
with this hearty fare, there was only a chilly outdoor seating area enclosed behind Plexiglas panels in which to sit, no snug nook beside a
sea-coal fire. Imagination plastered over disappointment, however, and
they enjoyed their meal.

Going on again after their brief respite proved harder for imagination to handle.

"I've gone lame with all this walking," said Ellsworth-Howard, and
he was in better shape than Rutherford and Chatterji. They were in
such agonies they didn't trust themselves to speak, until at last Rutherford collapsed on the nearest bench.

"I can't bear this anymore," he moaned. He unlaced his boots and
drew them off with trembling hands. He was in the worst physical pain
he'd ever experienced.

Chatterji leaned on the bench beside him, watching with tears in
his eyes.

"I say, ought you to do that?" he protested feebly. "What if you pick
up some pathogens?"

"I don't care," said Rutherford. "It can't hurt worse than this."

Chatterji thought about that a moment and sagged down beside
Rutherford. As one moving in a dream, he gave in to the irresistible impulse and pulled off his shoes. With an animal groan of relief he
stretched out his blistered feet.

Ellsworth-Howard was no stranger to physical pain—his parents
had beaten him regularly, in accordance with their social creed asserting
that comfort made one weak and immoral—but after a moment of wit-
nessing his friends' utter abandonment to their senses, he sat down a
well and took off his slippers, and flexed his long white toes in the sun.

"Shrack, that don't half feel better," he said. "I ain't walking back
though, I'll tell you."

"Doesn't matter." Rutherford gulped back a sob. "The pain is part
of it all, don't you see? No great insight or mystical experience is gained
without a price. This is the ordeal we're supposed to go through, to
prove ourselves worthy." He stiffened his upper lip. "Don't you think
C. S. Lewis and Tolkien went through this, when they'd walk through
England? We're feeling the same pain they felt, chaps, imagine it."

"By Jove, Rutherford, do you suppose so?" Chatterji tilted his head
back to watch the blue sky, where between puffy white clouds two
blackbirds were mobbing a raven. "I think you've got something here.
Maybe it's biochemical. I've heard of ancient magicians and shamans
who'd drive themselves into their visionary trances using pain as their
um, means of departure."

"It's endorphins," Ellsworth-Howard informed them. His jaw dropped as he had a blinding revelation. "So this was what my mum and dad were on about! No bleeding illusions, they told me. Life is pain and hypocrisy and death, they told me. We're just learning you for your own good, you miserable little sod, they told me."

" 'That which does not kill us, makes us stronger,' " Rutherford quoted.

"*Conan the Barbarian*, right," said Ellsworth-Howard. "Well, shrack all."

"See?" Chatterji said. "You've had a revelation already."

"He's let his naked feet come into contact with the sacred earth," said Rutherford. "Perhaps that's it. I wonder what'll happen if we walk on the grass barefoot?"

"You think we ought?" Chatterji looked around involuntarily, fearful that a public health monitor might pounce. One had in fact been following them, and now watched from a discreet distance behind the snack bar.

"Oh, I think we must," said Rutherford, and gingerly peeled off his socks.

"Oi, that looks nasty," said Ellsworth-Howard in alarm. "You'll want to put some Lubodyne on those."

"I don't care," said Rutherford, though he had gone rather pale. "I'm ready for the great truths to enter my soul."

He got unsteadily to his feet and marched away across the grass, carrying his shoes and socks. Ellsworth-Howard ran after him. Chatterji hesitated for only a moment before taking off his black silk socks and wadding them up carefully inside his shoes, then leaping up and hurrying after his friends.

"This feels wonderful," said Rutherford. "Oh, it's softer than the softest carpet, and *so* much more alive!"

"Carpets ain't alive at all, are they?" Ellsworth-Howard said.

"You know what I mean. I say, what's that?" Rutherford pointed.

It was a low dome of concrete behind what appeared to be a large statuary group. They approached curiously. The statuary was of animals done in bronze, dozens of them, with an elephant in the center and all the others around it in descending ranks by height. There was a lion, and a tiger, and a bear. There were all creatures with hooves. Every imaginable bird, perched on the backs of some of the larger beasts. There was an ordinary dog and cat, a camel, a kangaroo, a wolf, and tiny things like weasels and mice in exquisite detail. Only one of each animal, all facing in the same direction with expressions of regal and sorrowful accusation. Just in front of the mouse was a granite pillar carved with the inscription:

THE MONUMENT TO THE VICTIMS OF HUMAN CRUELTY

And in smaller letters underneath,

WELCOME TO THE LONDON ZOO

Chatterji and Rutherford spelled it out with difficulty, and repeated it to Ellsworth-Howard. They stood considering it a moment. "Ought we to go in?" wondered Rutherford.

"It's only a bunch of holo cabinets." Chatterji shrugged. "You can see better on BBC Epsilon."

"Bugger that, then," Ellsworth-Howard decided, and was about to turn away when there came a soft beeping from his daypack.

"You've got mail," Chatterji said.

"I do, don't I?" Ellsworth-Howard slid off the pack and opened his buke. "Oi! It's *Adonai*. Preliminary report's coming in on the second sequence."

"It's a sign!" Rutherford threw up his arms and cut an unsteady caper on the grass. "We will receive the vision now, here, in this holy place."

"What about over there?" Chatterji pointed to a grassy knoll, where a big tree offered shade and shelter.

"Even holier. Come on, chaps!"

It was in fact an oak tree, which would have made the fellowship happier still had they been aware of that fact, as they settled their backs against its vast trunk and Ellsworth-Howard set up the buke on his lap. They gazed expectantly at it, focusing their attention on the report to the exclusion of all else, with the result that they failed to notice a public health monitor advancing on them. When he loomed before them, though, they looked up with open mouths.

"I regret to inform you that you are in violation of Public Health Ordinance 3000z, subset 15," he told them, in a kindly uncle sort of voice. "Why don't you all put on your shoes, so the festering lesions on your feet won't continue to spread human infection in a public area? Then you can all come away with me. I'll take you somewhere nice."

"I beg your pardon?" Chatterji scowled.

"Oh, dear." The public health monitor dropped his hand casually to the butt of his gas gun. "Are you going to be bad? You don't want to be bad. You'll have to go to a place that's not nice at all, and they'll take away your nice old clothes. You don't want that to happen, do you?"

"Shracking hell, he thinks we're nutcases," Ellsworth-Howard said Rutherford whipped out his identification disk at exactly the same moment the public health monitor whipped out his gas gun, and only the fact that the monitor's nerves were a little shaken by facing three dangerous lunatics delayed his shot long enough for him to take in the meaning of the disk. Rutherford enjoyed watching his expression change.

"Terribly sorry, gentlemen," the monitor said, holstering his weapon. "Can I offer you assistance? I presume you want medical attention for your injuries."

"Yes, we'd like that," Chatterji said, having a leisurely drag on his sinus inhalator. "Send a medic to look at our feet, and then have a private transport sent round for us. We're just doing a bit of field research, and we had difficulties."

The monitor saluted, hastening to obey. Rutherford giggled and elbowed his friend.

"What cheek. Private transport, Chatty? This is the life! Well, well. Shall we continue with seeing how our man did?"

"Looks like another bloody short life," said Ellsworth-Howard. "How'd he die so soon?"

"Let's start over," said Chatterji. Ellsworth-Howard nodded and squeezed in the command to begin again.

The pleasant electronic voice gave them a date in 1824 CE and showed them four photographs captured by a field operative, of a vaguely pretty girl and three men in early nineteenth-century clothing. The voice gave a brief biography of each of the persons shown, and then went on to note the implant date for the host mother. Her social status was such that she had been able to retire to a private home in the country for the duration of her pregnancy.

This delivery had gone successfully. Following birth the host mother had gladly relinquished the subject to the field operative in charge of the project and returned to London.

"No guilt, this time," said Chatterji in relief.

"I'm sure the Facilitator found something else to motivate our man," Rutherford assured him absently, staring at the images.

There followed a field holograph, taken by a Company operative with hidden equipment, of a blurry baby in a perambulator, attended by a black-clad nurse. The voice gave the names of the foster parents that had been selected for the subject and went on to explain what pressures had been exerted to extort financial assistance from the three men known to have slept with the host mother.

Next there was a candid shot of a small child standing in a park, holding a nurse's hand as he stared at a toy boat on the glassy surface of a pond. His early education and attendant indoctrination were described. The foster parents, it was mentioned, were both lost at sea when the subject was in his first term at public school.

"There's your emotional detachment, Rutherford," said Ellsworth-Howard. "Bang goes his adoptive family."

The next image was of a class of boys assembled for prayers, standing together in rows by height. A red circle formed about the head of the tallest boy, in the back row, and the image zoomed forward and enlarged.

"There's our man," said Chatterji. The likeness was unmistakable, even allowing for the grainy quality of the enlargement and the smoothness of youth. This too was the face of the hologram that had appeared like a ghost in Rutherford's parlor, except that—

"Oh, dear, they damaged his nose again," fretted Rutherford.

At this point there was a portrait daguerreotype of what appeared to be an older gentleman in a headmaster's gown and mortarboard. On close examination it was evident he wasn't an old man at all, but such was his appearance of dignity and wisdom that it added reverend years to his sharp-featured face.

"Oi! That's one of my Preservers," said Ellsworth-Howard. The voice identified the headmaster as Facilitator Grade One Nennius, chief cyborg field operative for the London sector, responsible for programming the subject with the appropriate advanced indoctrination.

"Nothing left to chance, this time." Rutherford nodded approvingly. "*We* picked his mentor."

There followed a daguerreotype of the boy from the earlier pictures, now a young man in the uniform of a naval officer, posing beside a Roman column in a portrait studio. He carried his flat cockaded hat in the crook of one arm and looked sternly at the camera. Rutherford exclaimed in delight.

"I must say, he wore a uniform well," remarked Chatterji.

The voice explained that the subject had been accepted as a midshipman in the Royal Navy at age fourteen, due to the fact that the principal "father" being blackmailed for support had balked at extended tuition and therefore arranged the subject's commission.

"Excellent," said Rutherford. "None of this nonsense about an ecclesiastic career. A good early start on a life of action. Real scope to become the hero he was meant to be!"

The voice described the subject's naval service, which had been promising at first. He had made lieutenant, been given command of a topsail schooner and sent to the African coast to chase slave ships. Having distinguished himself there for bravery and effective work, he was promoted to the rank of commander. Reassigned to a man-of-war, his career had been sidelined by an incident wherein he had argued violently with a superior officer against a disciplinary action.

"There now," said Rutherford. "There's our noble soul. Wouldn't permit keelhauling, I daresay."

Then he caught his breath at the image that appeared, apparently taken by a field operative with a concealed camera and somewhat blurred and badly composed in consequence. Nevertheless it riveted one's attention. It showed the deck of a warship, crowded with assembled men, and in the background below the quarterdeck a grating set up lengthwise, to which a half-naked man had been pinioned. He had taken so many lashes his back looked as though it had been grilled. Blood spread in a bright stain down the back of his white trousers. To one side stood the man with the cat o' nine tails. It hung slack in his hand, however, for he had stopped, was staring, as all the men were staring and even the prisoner himself was staring, head turned painfully to gape at the scene frozen in the foreground.

The subject was being restrained by four other officers. Their faces were terrified. His was terrifying. His long teeth were bared. His eyes were very bright and focused on the man who lay before him on the deck, the man in the much more ornate uniform, the man who was bleeding from nose and mouth and eyes.

"Shrack," grunted Ellsworth-Howard. Rutherford and Chatterji just stared, mute. This was stronger stuff than anyone was accustomed to in the twenty-fourth century.

Court-martial had been initiated, explained the voice, but before action could be taken the primary "father" of the subject had intervened to have the subject honorably retired on half-pay, transferred to a certain department in Her Majesty's government doing business as Imperial Export. Upon mention of the name of the department, Chatterji gulped and Rutherford said:

"But wasn't that—?" He mouthed in silence, *the Gentlemen's Speculative Society?*

"Blimey." Ellsworth-Howard pointed at the screen. "Look who he went to work for!"

The next picture was of a small and inconspicuous-looking man in a black suit. He had had his portrait taken with his hand on a globe; that was the only clue to his character. The voice identified the man as the head of the department to which the subject had been transferred, and explained that the subject had become his protégé.

This provoked a fit of nervous giggles among the members of the fellowship.

There followed a series of photographs of the subject in civilian

dress, a big amiable-looking man, engaged in various apparently innocent pastimes in various exotic locales: grinning sheepishly from his
perch on the back of a camel, fumbling with amateur photography
equipment before some Turkish fortifications, doffing his top hat to a
lady before the onion domes of the Kremlin. In these pictures his face
looked almost clownish, a well-bred twit on a grand tour.

It was impossible to think this was the homicidal young officer
from the deck of the warship. Here he was, smiling innocently, having
his picture taken with a group of Afghani bandits who were glaring
sidelong at him in ill-concealed contempt. Here he was again, holding
up a bottle and pointing gleefully at it, mugging for the photographer;
easy not to notice the harbor and men o'war in the background.

The vocal accompaniment to these images was a litany of thefts,
seductions, arson, and assassinations, committed with consummate
skill for queen, country, and Imperial Export.

"*Espionage*," said Rutherford in awe.

"And murder," Chatterji added soberly. "He certainly had no trouble killing when he was ordered to."

"But in a just cause!" said Rutherford. "He was serving his nation,
as any honorable man would do, and serving it well I might add."

"Fair enough," said Ellsworth-Howard. "How'd he get killed this
time?"

"Oh, any number of heroic ways, I expect, given his line of work,"
said Rutherford, just as the next image flashed before them: the subject
with two other men, sitting in a singularly dusty photographer's studio.
They were posed formally in three chairs. One was a very dark individual with a black mustache. The other was a sad-faced young man, English apparently, with a valise on his lap. The subject, who looked
slightly older now, had his hand on the shoulder of the young man and
was smiling at the camera. There was something unsettling in his
smile, something smoothly professional about it, and perhaps a little
weary.

The voice explained that this picture had been taken at Veracruz,
Mexico, on 30 November 1862, and was the last known photograph of
the subject before his disappearance while in the field at Los Angeles,
California, in March, 1863. Imperial Export had regretfully closed its
files on him after some years and given him posthumous commendation for his final work on Operation Document D.

"My God!" Chatterji jumped as though he'd been shot.

"What?" said Rutherford, and Ellsworth-Howard ordered the report to pause. The voice stopped and the glittering silver save-pattern
crawled across the screen.

"Haven't you ever heard of Document D?" demanded Chatterji. Ellsworth-Howard shook his head. Rutherford attempted to recall.

"Something in the Company archives? Used to be property of the Crown. Highly classified, had to do with that pirate fellow—it was a ship's logbook, wasn't it? Data about the coast of California and—and something they saw on an island there—" Rutherford clapped his hand over his mouth.

"Exactly," said Chatterji, leaning close to speak quietly. "*Very* classified information."

"It must have been Catalina Island the pirates stopped at, on their way up the coast!" hissed Rutherford. He rocked where he sat in suppressed excitement. "And they saw—you know what—and they wrote about it, and there the account sat in the logbook, never understood by anyone until the founders of 'Imperial Export' got hold of it and sent out a team to investigate—"

"Which must have included our man—"

"And they found—well, you know what they found—and the end of it all was that 'Imperial Export' eventually became Dr. Zeus Incorporated," shrieked Rutherford.

"Sssh! For God's sake, this is all classified," Chatterji shook him.

"Shrack!" Ellsworth-Howard stared at the frozen screen. "This is like discovering your son's your grandfather, ain't it? We made him, and he made—well, our jobs. What's this about Catalina Island, though? I thought that was just an experimental station."

"You go right on thinking that, old fellow," Chatterji said.

"Oh, it's too perfect," said Rutherford. "Do you know what they call the town on that island? *Avalon.* That's where our once and future hero went to die."

"Yeah, but he still died," Ellsworth-Howard said. "I want to know how."

He ordered the report to continue and the photograph from Veracruz vanished, to be replaced with a rather awful series of pictures from the subject's postmortem examination. The voice explained that the subject had been shot to death by American counterespionage agents in a vain attempt to prevent him from destroying classified documents before they could seize said material.

"And if he hadn't, chaps, who knows what might have happened?" Rutherford's eyes were brimming with happy tears. "We might not be sitting here now. Oh, the synchronicity of it all! He nobly kept the secret that enabled us to create him."

"Who's that?" Ellsworth-Howard pointed at two new pictures that appeared on the screen. The voice explained that there were certain details of the subject's last days still unresolved pending review of his brain transcript, and that the full report could be expected within three days. Recovery of the subject's body had been facilitated by the fact that he had been in the company of two Dr. Zeus operatives at the time of his death.

The first picture enlarged to fill the screen and the voice explained that the terrified-looking man was one Antonio Souza, thirty-four years of age, operator of a safe house and low-level shipping station at San Pedro, California.

Souza's picture shrank back and the second picture enlarged.

"Oi, that's another of my Preservers," said Ellsworth-Howard. A black-eyed woman stared up from what appeared to be a cell. Her face was as blank as a mask. The blackness of the eyes was so complete, so utterly absent of light or even human consciousness that it made Rutherford want to hide. The voice explained that this was the Botanist Mendoza—

"*Who?*" Rutherford choked. The voice continued—cyborg operative under suspicion of malfunction, previously assigned to Cahuenga Pass Transport Station. Duties had related to acquisition of rare plant species in temperate belt scheduled to go extinct in local ecological disaster beginning June 1862—

"Stop," said Rutherford, and Ellsworth-Howard paused the report once more. The voice fell silent and the glittering pattern scored the woman's face, giving her the appearance of having an uncontrollable tic.

"Talk about your synchronicity," said Chatterji, shaking his head.

"What's she doing there?" said Rutherford. "That's the same girl he—he—knew, in his first sequence. How did she get to the New World?"

Ellsworth-Howard pulled up a sidebar and squeezed in a request. He peered at the screen. "Transferred," he said. "Shipped there in 1555."

"But this is a disaster!" Rutherford clenched his fists. "She'll have recognized our man, don't you see? He's a classified project, and now she knows about him."

"I say, Rutherford, you're right." Chatterji frowned. "Well, nothing for it but to control the damage as best we can. She's being detained, isn't she?"

"Fortunately. But the damned creature's a cyborg." Rutherford glared at her image on the screen. "Which means, of course, that our problem is a permanent one."

"Then we need a permanent solution," Chatterji mused. "There are still a few vat spaces left in the bunkers where we're keeping the old

Enforcers . . ." He looked at Rutherford over Ellsworth-Howard's head and made a gesture of unplugging something. Ellsworth-Howard noticed, however.

"No shracking way," he said indignantly. "She's one of my Preservers. They cost too much to waste like that. Just have her transferred again."

"But where, Foxy?" said Chatterji. "We're dealing with a breach of security, remember."

"I want her silenced, but even more importantly I want her away from our man," said Rutherford with determination. "There must be no possibility whatever of her encountering him in his next sequence. What if there's an undetected Mandelbrot frame operating here?"

Ellsworth-Howard thought about that for a moment.

"She could be sent Back Way Back," he said at last.

"Good thought." Chatterji looked pleased. "How far back?"

"A hundred and fifty thousand years should do it," said Rutherford decisively. "Yes. That should remove any danger to the project."

"Right, then." Ellsworth-Howard slipped on the button of the throat mike and gave an order. While they were waiting for confirmation, a long black private transport came gliding along the nearest walkway. Opposite them it stopped, and a medic got out and walked briskly over the grass toward them. Just as he knelt and began to wash their feet, there was a beeping signal: confirmation. The order had been obeyed.

THE YEAR 2347:

Alec Grows Up

He had a reputation now.

People who lived in the shadows cast by the light of the First World knew about him; and that included the dead-eyed golden ones who lay on the beaches at Capferrat and St. Tropez. Hungrily they watched the blue horizon for his ship. In certain circles he was called the Candyman; in others he was known as the Liberator.

Whatever they wanted, whatever it took to sweeten their weary days—whether it was bloodred wine or whiskey, or ganja strong enough to set their feet on another plane of reality—the big guy could get it for them. Or it might be cocoa with marshmallows, or it might be caviar. All it had to be was forbidden, and he could get it for them.

He didn't even demand their souls in payment. Just cash.

There were stories, legends in the Caribbean and on the Côte d'Azur, about the smiling lord who threw such wild parties on his white ship. The list of people he was said to have bedded was improbably long. He gave every appearance of being an easy mark, as hopelessly stoned as any of his guests at his parties, an amiable fool; and yet thieves boarding his ship had a tendency to vanish, never to be seen again. So there was a faintly sinister edge to his mythos, and people wondered about that black flag . . .

But nobody really cared, because he had the power to ease the pain of living, heal the sores of ennui, and take away wounding memory of the cold, clean, bright, ordered world for a couple of nights. And if they shuddered, shamefaced with guilt over their excesses, they only did it after he had sailed away. Later still they prayed for his return, and watched the sea for a glimpse of his pirate flag. All they wanted was a little freedom, and they knew he could get it for them.

It was only freedom of the senses, of course. Once, the boy had had dreams about setting them truly free. He had thought it might be nice, to be a legend.

He was older now.

Careful, Alec.

I know. My God, was it always this gloomy? This deserted?

I'm afraid so.

The tall man stood, irresolute, looking around at Trafalgar Square. Other than the surveillance cameras there was only a lurking public health monitor to note his presence, who, after a cursory inspection, decided the tall man was a tourist and therefore had an excuse for looking strange.

And Alec did look strange, by the standards of modern London: unhealthily tanned by the sun and dressed for a much warmer climate, with a brilliantly loud tropical-patterned shirt. He was peering a bit as he tried to bring his vision into the narrow and close horizon of walls.

It was difficult. He'd only been away three years this time, but something seemed to have cut the cord at last. There was no specific change he could point to, other than the tragedy; only a general sense of everything in London being steeper, and narrower, and darker.

You know what it is? It's not home anymore. I never really belonged here at all, did I?

Not you, my lad. You come from the sea.

Alec smiled faintly at that, but the truth was he was finding the old pirate-talk pretty comforting just now. *So where's this art gallery, then?*

Starboard at the next corner and straight on three blocks.

He shivered, wishing he'd brought a coat, and set off at a rapid walk to warm himself. He'd get a coat in some shop, after the show. The Bloomsbury house was too full of ghosts to stop in, even if it hadn't been locked up tight as a drum with dustcovers over everything.

He had tried to go back to live there twice.

In his twentieth summer he partied for a whole season off Carriacou with a very agreeable bunch of decadent kids, minor admin bluebloods. The Captain had snarled at him a lot because he began drinking heavily again, and attempted to prod him back to his usual routine of club-hopping, which required that he stay at least sober enough to walk. Alec had been disinclined to visit clubs, however, because there was one quite nice girl who shared his bed more frequently than the other young ladies in the party.

But when the season had ended she came to him, pale and stammering, to announce that she was pregnant.

He took the news badly, yet when he sobered up he bathed, shaved, and went with her to the local marriage registrar. There was a brief ceremony on a terrace with a sweeping view of Hillsborough Bay, and the white ships belonging to millionaires drifted on the horizon like swans. Then they went down the hill, on board his ship and straight off to London and Tower Marina.

By the time they dropped anchor he found, unaccountably, that he was looking forward to starting a family. The Bloomsbury house had been reopened and aired out, new servants had been hired, and Lewin and Mrs. Lewin had come bustling from their retirement. Alec's old nursery was repainted, and then—

She was ever so sorry, the girl said, but apparently she'd been mistaken. There wasn't going to be a baby after all. And, while she was certain Alec was a super guy, now that she wasn't stoned all the time she just didn't think the relationship would work out. What were the chances they could simply pretend this whole thing had never happened?

Away went the new servants, away went Lewin and Mrs. Lewin back into retirement, and away went the girl out of Alec's life, bearing a nice fat settlement by which to remember him.

The second time had been much less banal.

He was walking through Portofino when he heard a voice crying out to him in English. He turned to see a girl in an agchair speeding toward him from the shadows of a dark side street. She was an American, in terrible trouble: her husband was lying in wait for her with a gun at their villa. She begged Alec to help her. The Captain muttered something cautionary but Alec mentally shushed him. The girl collapsed weeping, explaining that she was a sufferer from Vargas's syndrome. She'd had to flee without any of her medication or her identity disk.

Alec escorted her to the nearest safety station to make a report. The Captain had to do all the translating, with Alec repeating phonetic Italian after him; but once the officers did grasp that there had been a case of domestic violence, they took off with gratifying speed (the Ephesian Party held the balance of power in the Italian government that year). In no time at all they came zooming back to the safety station with a bound, tranquilized man drooling in the back of a detention vehicle.

Somehow Alec and Lorene (that was her name) wound up living together in a hotel. She was witty and charming and practical, and she had been a coloratura soprano before she'd gotten ill. She could still sing, though without much power, in a piercingly sweet voice that reminded him of tinkling frost or chiming bells. Their stay at the hotel stretched out into weeks. One night Lorene had told Alec the full story of her life, all misfortune, and he was so moved to compassion he proposed.

The honeymoon on board the *Captain Morgan* was a perfect idyll. Not an especially sensual one, because Lorene's illness flared up in the sea air, but they were blissfully happy anyway. Alec sent ahead orders for the Bloomsbury house to be completely remodeled. He set up a holoscreen by her bed and went through interior design catalogs with her.

Lorene was enchanted with London in the way only Americans are. She was enchanted with the Rolls and its Finsbury crest, she was enchanted all the way to the front steps of her new home, where she allowed Alec to lift her out of the Rolls and settle her into her agchair. She smiled enchantingly at the servants lined up to welcome her (Lewin and Mrs. Lewin weren't among them; Mrs. Lewin was too ill to come up to London). Then Lorene looked up at the house and a shadow fell across her face.

"Oh, my God, those steps are high," she said.

"Don't worry, babe," Alec said. "I'm supposed to carry you across the doormouth, remember?"

And he caught her up (she weighed practically nothing) and stormed the stairs and jumped over the threshold with her, but unfortunately he knocked her elbow on the jamb as they passed through and she almost fainted with the pain.

Things had not improved. Almost from the first day, Lorene became sullen and silent, and Alec told himself that it was because London made her illness worse. Most days she was too exhausted to do more than lie on a day bed and watch holoes with him. If he went out for any period of time, she greeted his return with tearful complaints that the servants had been rude to her. She didn't like the house or furnishings, either.

Balkister dropped in one day to discuss his latest crusade, which (that week) was to get the Falkland Islands renamed the Malvinas (again), and he stayed until midnight talking over old times with Alec. As soon as Balkister had wobbled his way out the door, Lorene rose on her elbow and denounced him for the nastiest, most adolescent little creep she'd ever met.

Alec agreed with her readily enough. Plenty of people felt that way about Balkister. Lorene went on to demand whether Alec knew that Balkister was a homosexual, and obviously in love with Alec?

Alec didn't know. He stood there, slightly befuddled by the hour and what he'd been drinking, trying to sort that one out. Balkister had never approached him for that kind of fun, that he remembered; but then a lot of the time he'd spent in Balkister's company they'd both been stoned. At last he laughed and told Lorene he thought she was wrong. She wept hysterically. He carried her up to their bed at last, and when he tried to crawl in beside her she screamed that he was gay and struck at him. He staggered away and slept in a guest bedroom.

The next two weeks, Alec was like a wounded horse on a battle-field, helplessly tangling himself in his own guts with every step he attempted to take out of his trouble. Even on the best days, Lorene was unaccountably irritated with him. He was such an overgrown boy! He had no drive or ambition at all. How could a grown man think he could just run away from his troubles and live on a yacht all the time? At her worst she grew screamingly abusive, shaking in her chair with emotion, and a pair of scarlet spots would appear on either side of her thin white nose.

After her rages she clung to him, weeping and contrite, and called him all the loving names of their courtship period, and begged him to be strong for her.

The Captain, who knew when to keep his mouth shut, did. He authorized the services of a team of private investigators, however, and when their reports came in he kept his peace and bided his time.

The servants quit in a body one morning, as a formal protest after Lorene accused the cook of trying to poison her. This was serious: one didn't treat servants that way in the twenty-fourth century. Alec controlled his temper and said nothing. When he didn't respond by blowing up at her, Lorene followed him around in her agchair insisting that there *had* been sleeping pills in the food, and the less he responded the angrier she became, until she accused him of being a gutless coward.

With a roar of frustration he picked up an overstuffed recliner and threw it across the room, and followed it with the matching ottoman. They both landed on the piano and it collapsed. She flew up the stairs, shrieking as though he were after her with an axe, and locked herself in her room.

Had enough yet, boyo? the Captain inquired.

But Alec was horrified at himself, instantly remorseful. It occurred to him that perhaps what they both needed was a change of air.

So he removed the chair and ottoman from the ruins of the piano, and went upstairs to speak gently to Lorene, through the locked door of their bedroom. Once he got her calmed down enough to listen, she agreed to go away with him. There was a desperate eagerness in her voice as she asked whether they might sail immediately. Alec assured her they could leave that night, and went off to Tower Marina to get the *Captain Morgan* ready for sailing.

When he returned that afternoon, there was a phalanx of long purple vehicles drawn up in front of his house and strangers were going up and down the stairs. He jumped from the car before it quite settled down, terrified that Lorene had had an accident. But no: there she was, emerging in her chair, escorted down the stairs by a muscular young man in an oddly patterned robe.

"Hey," Alec said. Lorene shrieked and flinched, and the man put a protective arm around her and looked daggers at Alec. Alec started toward them, but his way was blocked by two more of the robed men—were those *bumblebees* embroidered on their clothes?—and an authoritative-looking woman in purple.

"Alec Checkerfield, earl of Finsbury?" the woman asked.

"Yeah," Alec said, looking past her at Lorene, who was sobbing and hiding her face as she was helped into one of the purple cars.

"Do you know who we are, and why we are here?"

Alec spotted the bee logo on the door of the purple car and finally placed it. "You're Ephesians, right? What's going on?"

"Your wife called us and begged for our help. We're here to provide her with safe conduct from this house to our Newham Hospital shelter, to protect her from any further abuse at your hands," the woman said.

Alec gaped. It occurred to him that the Captain must have been perfectly well aware when Lorene had placed the call. *Why the hell didn't you stop her?* he demanded.

In response, the Captain downloaded the results of his investigation of Lorene's past. He had discovered that Alec had not been Lorene's second husband but her sixth, and that nearly every one of the marriages had ended with a drama of this kind: waif appealing to kindly stranger, or strangers, to help her escape from clutches of brute.

"Oh," Alec said, feeling the shock waves roll. What an icebound calm descended on him! He blinked at the woman. "Well, she's lying. I never once hit her."

"That's as may be," the woman told him sourly. "You've a history of violent behavior. If you're guilty, rest assured you will be prosecuted to the fullest extent of the law. The fact that your mother is a votaress of our order won't influence us in your favor, young man."

"Huh?" Alec knit his brows. *Who* was a votaress of their order?

Stop a bit, Alec, the solicitor I ordered just got here.

No sooner had the Captain spoken than a steel-colored Jaguar with the Gray's Inn griffin on the door whirred up to the curb, and a gray-suited gentleman with a briefcase jumped out.

"My lord? Cantwell and Cantwell send their regards. Pushpinder Devereaux; I'm here to handle your case."

"Okay, fine." Alec pumped his hand enthusiastically. He felt light-headed, absurdly cool. "I'm innocent. She's nuts. You take it from there. Let me know what you have to spend. I'll be on the *Captain Morgan*, berth number three, Tower Marina. Bye now."

He jumped back into the Rolls and drove away without a backward glance, whistling shrilly.

It was over within three more days, and the whole time he kept wondering if he were alive, because he couldn't feel his heart at all.

Cantwell and Cantwell produced ample evidence that Lorene had been lying, and she didn't score any points with the Ephesians when she changed her story and sent word to Alec that she'd drop the charges if he'd take her back. His response had been no, thank you, and he would have thrown in a handsome settlement as a parting gesture if Cantwell and Cantwell hadn't discovered that the marriage had been invalid anyway, since Lorene hadn't bothered to get divorces from three of her previous husbands.

And that was the end of that.

He still went to the Happy Clubs and the dance clubs. Dancing was still a good way to get himself high, and it didn't matter anymore who his partner was. Now and then he picked up girls for overnighters, and if he didn't bother to seduce them anymore—if he did the unspeak-able, if he simply looked into their eyes and persuaded them to go to bed with him—where was the harm, after all? It wasn't as though he was trying to make them love him. In the morning, he always took them to breakfast somewhere nice and released his hold on their wills, and over waffles or toast they'd blink, and suddenly remember an im-portant call they had to make, a forgotten appointment, a job inter-view—he understood, didn't he, if they had to run off before the check came? And he always did, as another layer of self-loathing wrapped around his heart.

But he came ashore less and less frequently, even for sex. He spent more and more time at sea, cruising the immense emptiness of the wa-ter, singing at night to the uncaring stars.

He was finding that human places bothered him.

He hadn't come back to London in three years, and wouldn't have re-turned now but for the funeral. He'd have been making his way down the Thames this very minute if a small feature in the morning *Times* broadcast hadn't caught his ear: GALLERIE PROCHASKA PRESENTS A NEW MUSICAL BY GILES LANCELOT BALKISTER: LITTLE RED PLANET!

This is it, lad. Third shopfront down, the one painted black.

Alec stepped inside, ducking slightly to avoid the top of the doorway. His pupils widened to adjust to the subdued lighting as he looked around. It was a lot like a museum in there, except for the strong smell of takeaway food: all shadow, relieved by pools of soft light in midair where holographic figures kicked and strutted, and small knots of living people gaped at them. An Art Nymph pranced up to him, slightly terrifying in her sequined tap costume and whiteface, and handed him a playbill. He gave it a little shake and it promptly began to recite in a tinny voice:

"The virtual smash hit of the season! Written and designed by Giles Lancelot Balkister! Starring Marlene Dietrich, Noel Coward, and Tim Curry! What happens when a spirited girl from the Martian Agricultural Collective faces temptation in the lush warrens of Mars Two?" Somewhere close at hand Alec could hear a familiar whining bray.

". . . Of course it's risqué! Where but on Mars are you going to encounter human passions in this day and age? Where else are human appetites even relevant anymore? Not here on Earth," Balkister was announcing. "You might as well just stamp the words MUSEUM EXHIBIT across your forehead. In fact, most of the remaining population of Earth ought to be compelled to. What are we *doing* here, after all?"

"Talking to hear ourselves talk," Alec said, ducking around a hologram of Noel Coward pattering out a sprightly little tune about heroic agriculturists on their Martian honeymoons.

"Fellow ugly guy!" Balkister looked up from the table where he was selling copies of the show. He strode forward and feigned throwing punches at him. "Bam, biff, and all that sort of tribal show of testosterone. How are we? I'd no idea we were back in town. Come ashore for a spot of raping and pillaging?"

"Er—no. Had to attend a funeral." Alec looked aside.

"Sorry." Balkister's demeanor sobered at once. "Whose?"

"My old cook."

"Oh, bugger, I'm so sorry. She raised you, didn't she?"

"Yeah. But she'd been ill a long time, and she was up there in years. Hundred and ten-odd." Alec started, distracted by a nearby scene changing abruptly to Tim Curry (the hero of the Collective) punting along an irrigation canal while he sang a duet with Elsa Lanchester.

"All the same." Balkister patted him on the arm. "So, what are we doing these days? Not married again, are we?"

"Never again," said Alec with feeling.

"Still swanning around the seven seas in our pleasure craft?"

Alec nodded. "I've had a few adventures," he said.

"I'll bet you have, and I'd simply love to hear about them." Balkister looked around edgily. "See here, there's a discreet little place I know of—why don't we just slip out of this haven of bourgeois pretensions and you can bring me up to speed?" He looked around and spotted a gallery employee. "Here, you!" he hailed the girl, taking off the lapel pin that identified him as THE AUTHOR and fastening it to her blazer. "You be the author for a while, okay? Tell them whatever comes into your head, so long as they buy the damned thing. I'll be back before closing."

He ducked out of the gallery, ignoring the girl's stammered protests, and trotted away purposefully down the street. Alec loped after him, bemused. He was fairly certain Balkister hadn't the least interest in hearing what Alec had been doing during the past three years and meant instead to buttonhole him about his latest fervent cause. Alec didn't mind. Balkister's monologues were familiar, at least, in this cold strange city.

They ducked into an alleyway and down the weed-grown stairs of what had been a service entrance for a private flat. The door looked as though it had been sealed by the rains of a dozen winters, but when Balkister gave a brisk double knock it opened at once, far enough to reveal a nose and one inquiring eye.

"Did you bring the spanner?" asked someone muffledly.

"*Vive* la whatever," responded Balkister, and the door swung inward into darkness. Balkister strutted through, smirking, and Alec had to bend nearly double to follow him. Their tuxedoed guide was what had once been called a *small person*, until dwarves had asserted their rights as a proudly distinct cultural group. He led them to a staircase that descended even lower into darkness. The Captain was growling softly, scanning the place for traps, but Alec felt secure. He could smell oak barrels and complex fruit bouquets, and he knew exactly what sort of place they'd entered.

They emerged into a long low room lit from above by mirror reflection, giving the whole place a camera obscura sort of appearance. There was sawdust on the floor; there were small tables and booths. There was a lot of snowy white napery and glittering crystal. A cadaverously pale waiter approached them.

"Messieurs," he intoned, bowing low and directing them to one of the little tables.

Alec had begun to giggle as they seated themselves and took up the wine lists. He reflected that he might very well be about to taste something that had traveled in the hold of the *Captain Morgan*.

The twenty-second-century ban on stimulants of any kind had not been universally accepted, much to the astonishment of the American Community and Britain, who had partnered the international legislation. The Californians enthusiastically torpedoed their own wine industry, because Californians were always doing things like that, but the French flatly refused. Viniculture was a part of their cultural identity, they claimed, and besides, nobody wanted a repeat of the unpleasantness that had occurred when the Fraternité des Fromages Historiques rioted and burned an effigy depicting the minister of agriculture in an act of carnal bliss with a soybean pod.

The British and Americans sputtered and threatened sanctions, but in the end all they were able to do was enforce the ban in their own countries. However (as the observant reader will have already noticed) certain substances remained available to those with ready cash and a disinclination to be told what they could or couldn't consume.

"Do you often drink here?" Alec asked, after listening to the selections and deciding on a beaujolais.

"Christ, no. Hadn't you heard about my annuity being stopped?" Balkister shook out his napkin with a snap. "I'm virtually penniless, ducky, unless I can move a few dozen copies of *Little Red Planet*. This is your treat."

Balkister put up an imperious crooked finger to summon the wine steward, who ignored him and went straight to Alec.

"You obviously look rich," said Balkister in miffed tones, after their wine had been brought.

"The guy knew me," Alec said, shrugging. He tilted his glass and inhaled the fragrance of cherries and spice. Balkister regarded him with narrowed eyes.

"Did he now?" he said thoughtfully. "That's most interesting, under the circumstances. What have you been doing on that yacht of yours, Checkerfield, hmm?"

"It's a ship, actually," said Alec. "It has cargo holds and everything."

Balkister looked shrewdly contemplative for about five more seconds, and then started to his feet yelping as the truth occurred to him. "Good God," he said. "*You* of all people! You—well, you bloody Scarlet Pimpernel, you."

"Shut up and sit down," Alec said, and Balkister was momentarily disconcerted by the hardness in his voice. "What did you call me?"

"If you watched more classic cinema you'd know," Balkister said. He grinned and rubbed his hands together. "Well, well. Under the circumstances, this is going to make my duty quite a bit easier, I should think."

What's the little creep on about?

"What are you on about, then?"

"Look, Checkerfield." Balkister gulped his wine without savoring it. "All joking aside, you and I have always been on the same wavelength. You've never been like the rest of our class, who feel we've got the right to push others around because we're wealthy and clever."

"Mm." Alec sipped his wine. He'd given up the God Game after his second marriage had collapsed, deciding that anyone with judgment as spectacularly bad as his had no right to play. Balkister continued:

"I might have doubted your ideals the past few years, off on your endless pleasure cruise the way you were; but it's clear you had your own agenda there."

Watch out, son.

"Oh, bollocks," said Alec easily.

"Right." Balkister leered. "Very well, then, let's talk about *me*. I've evolved a political philosophy. No, really, I have! It's that the smug and self-satisfied elite cannot have things all their own way. Why? Because, even in a meritocracy, absolute power corrupts absolutely. In fact it's worse when clever people hold all the power, because they're much better at tyranny than the old-style tyrants.

"And the worst of it is, the more the consumers are treated like sheep, the more like sheep they become, looking to us meritocrats to make rules for them. They don't see any danger in giving up their civil liberties to the wise and benevolent admin-shepherds."

"Mm." Alec frowned. That much he agreed with. The rest wasn't anything he hadn't heard before, wherever even faintly clever young things congregated to drink and be radical.

"If we finally bring all the marginal places like the Celtic Federation into our global village so they all fall into step with us, we'll lose the necessary dynamism of the Other!" asserted Balkister. "Humanity will stagnate."

"We don't want that to happen, no," drawled Alec.

Damned bad for business, that would be.

"If the people we govern are as unresisting as dolls, we'll get our precious butts kicked the first time we venture out of the nursery and try to order the bigger children about, won't we? And of course by the nursery I mean this solar system, and by bigger children I mean any other intelligent life in the universe." Balkister thumped his fist on the table.

"Okay." Alec refilled Balkister's glass. "Though the Vulcans haven't shown up yet, have they? So far as we know we're still the only game in the galaxy or wherever."

"That could change at any time," Balkister insisted. "Think of all those centuries when the Red Indians thought they were the only people in the world, and then the Euro-monsters landed! However. Will you agree with me that our ruling class needs the occasional goad to keep it from getting too sure of itself?"

"Sure, I'll agree to that."

"Aha. Having said that—here we sit, you and I, two terribly brilliant fellows of like mind."

"No, no. You're the brilliant one. I'm Ape Man Checkerfield, remember?" Alec refilled his own glass.

"But you've got money, sweetie, and that's just as good as brains. Besides, you're fearfully clever in your own way." Balkister tossed back another gulp of wine. "Don't think I never noticed. Have you still got that seriously amazing customized cybersystem running your party boat?"

Ship! You little pansified twerp.

"Yes, I have, as a matter of fact," Alec said.

"Good. Suppose I was to tell you that there are others like you and me out there, misfits who have tasted intellectual freedom? Troublemakers who are ready to wipe the conceited smiles off the faces of the Colin Debenhams of the world."

Alec had to think a moment to place the name. Jill, right. He felt a momentary pang and lifted his glass, swirled it to watch the body of the wine streaming down the crystal, breathed in the fragrance. *She was nothing to you, laddie buck.*

"Okay," said Alec. "And you're going to tell me that you're with some group that does secret stuff. What is it, Balkister? Picketing shops? Voting to censure bad guys? Rigging commcodes to send takeaway food your enemies didn't order?"

"You have been thinking about this," said Balkister admiringly. "I won't lie to you, 'pon my soul. All that and more, you ugly creature! Suppose there is such a group, and suppose I'm a member. Wouldn't you like to be a member, too? It's the only proper work for a gentleman, you know. *Filibustering*, they used to call it. Fighting to bring freedom to the oppressed."

"Yeah?" Alec studied his wine, turning the glass in the light. *Maybe this isn't as stupid as it sounds. Sort of organized anarchy.*

But what's in it for you, son? And you decided you wasn't going to waste yer time wiping the world's arse anymore, remember?

I know. But where I went wrong was in trying to run people's lives for

them. What he's proposing is just the opposite, isn't it, encouraging people to
run their own lives? Besides, this wouldn't be stupid me blundering along.
Balkister's sharp about politics. Maybe he's on to something. And smuggling
is getting a little old.

The Captain bared his teeth and compared any possible hazards in
this proposition to the last major life-change Alec had undertaken. He
decided it couldn't possibly make Alec any unhappier than Lorene had.
He noted further the possibilities of increasing his power base. If a
crew of renegade admins were going to (for example) break into the
laboratories of some big corporation or other, there might be all manner of opportunities to snap up unconsidered trifles, such as secret research data. Knowledge = Power, that was the equation, after all.

Hell's bells, boy, yer right. Yer old man would have approved of
it, wouldn't he? This'll be a chance to make him proud.

Alec decided.

"So, suppose you did belong to a group like that," he said to Balkister. "And you talked a friend into joining. You'd want a big cash donation from him, I guess."

"Did I say that?" said Balkister. "Well, I sort of did, didn't I? But
what might be worth even more to this band of intrepid heroes would
be any quote extraordinary talents unquote the friend had. If he were
good at breaking into defended systems, for example. Think of all the
nifty pranks one might pull on the bloated and moribund technological hierarchy, eh?

"And if this talented guy was also tremendously mobile, able to
travel anywhere at a moment's notice, without applying for any permits, because he was a shracking *peer of the realm* and had a very, very
fast boat—and perhaps was already engaged in cocking snooks at the
Establishment—well, I just think the heroes would welcome him with
open arms, don't you? With or without the cash!

"Though of course the money would help," Balkister added as an
afterthought.

"You've made some damn good guesses about my life," remarked
Alec coolly, regarding Balkister with a flat stare. Balkister gulped and
replied:

"Checkerfield, I've known you since we were twelve, for God's
sake. I remember the things you used to be able to do."

Alec exhaled. "What's the deposit account code?"

Balkister's eyes widened, but he told Alec.

Give them fifty thousand out of the Cocos Island Trade account.

Aye aye, lad. The Captain did a bit of deft electronic manipulation.
Lights flashed briefly on a console five thousand miles away and

money moved, as readily as though gold *moidores* and pieces of eight had fallen glittering into a bank vault from thin air.

"Okay," said Alec. "You've got a bit of pound sterling to play with now. Can I join your secret club?"

Balkister stared at him in silence for a moment, realizing the significance of Alec's torque for the first time.

"You've been *cyborged*," he said in awe.

"Yup." Alec smiled at last.

"That is so cool! On behalf of my disreputable and rebellious friends, Lord Finsbury, let me be the first to officially welcome you to the Heroic Resistance Society. We're going to have some great times, you and us."

Better than you know, you little windbag.

Now, now. After you, Balkister's my oldest friend.

As Alec walked back that evening, staggering somewhat, he reflected guiltily that Balkister wasn't his oldest human friend; Lewin surely was. The old man had been through so much in the last week already, maybe he'd have already turned in and wouldn't notice Alec's condition. Asleep and dreaming in his nice grand stateroom. Nothing but the best for poor old Lewin.

But there was a light burning on board the *Captain Morgan*, shining across the black water at Tower Marina. Alec's heart sank. He paused at a vending machine outside the mooring office to purchase a small bottle of distilled water, and rinsed his mouth several times. He groped in the pockets of the coat he'd bought for a roll of peppermints, remembered it was a new coat and had nothing useful in the pockets, and thumped the vending machine a few more times before it spat out a little packet of herbal cough drops. Not quite what was wanted, but it would have to do. He tipped most of the packet into his mouth and crunched them up, ignoring the Captain's laughter. They tasted vile.

The mermaid was staring into the Thames fog with an ironic expression as he trudged heavily up the gangplank. She was the only one to greet his return; Billy Bones and crew had to stay below decks, deactivated, when he was in London. This had been the rule ever since an elderly yachtsman moored next to Alec's ship had glanced out his porthole, seen Billy Bones crawling along the deck with a tray of breakfast, and suffered a near-fatal heart attack from the shock.

Concentrating on his posture, Alec strolled along the deck and past the door of Lewin's stateroom. It was standing open. Alec ducked his head to peer through and stopped, dumbfounded at what he saw.

Lewin was sitting up at the table, resting his elbows on the polished surface and staring thoughtfully at a cut-crystal decanter in front
of him. Earlier in the evening the decanter had been secured away in a
locked cabinet, and it had been full of very expensive single malt. It
wasn't full now, by any means.

"Lewin?" said Alec.

Lewin's head came up unsteadily and swung round. He focused his
eyes and saw Alec. "Don't chide me, son," he said. "Ain't had a drink in
seventy-five years, have I? Have a li'l patience with the old guy."

How the hell did he get into that cabinet? I secured that lock!

Alec stepped over the threshold and moved into the circle of lamplight. Lewin peered at him. "Good God. Where jer buy that coat?
Y'look like . . . like something awfully tall n' silver n' purple."

"I thought it was kind of neat," Alec said. He attempted to slide
into the booth across from Lewin and hit his head on the hanging
lamp. "Ow."

"You been drinking, ain't you, son?" Lewin looked stern. "Thought
so. Nobody'd buy a coat like that sober, for Chrissake. You'll be sober
tomorrow, won't you, son? Promise me you'll be sober."

"I promise, sir."

"I'll be sober, too," said Lewin sadly. "No missus to go on at me.
Like a glass bird she was at the end. You could have broken her like
that." He attempted to snap his fingers. He couldn't quite coordinate.
His face crumpled up. "God, God, I miss her so bad—" He began to cry
hopelessly. Alec clambered out of the booth and went to Lewin's side
of the table, where he crouched to put his arms around the old man.

"S'okay," he muttered, blinking back tears. "S'okay."

".What'm I gonna do?" the old man gasped. "Eighty years, Alec.
Eighty years of my life, she was there in the morning."

*Ask him how he got that cabinet open. I've just scanned, and
there's been other locks tampered with. Nothing's gone except the
whiskey, but I want to know how he did it!*

Oh, shut up right now, can't you?

But out loud Alec said hesitantly: "It must have been tough getting
the Talisker out of there. I didn't give you the security code."

"No problemo." Lewin wiped away tears. He reached for his glass
and Alec let go of him so he could drink without spilling. "Cracked
tougher cribs than that, back in me bad old days."

What?

There was a moment of silence, while Lewin drank and Alec
played back his last sentence.

"Excuse me?" he stammered.

"Oh yeah." Lewin waved a shaky hand. "Didn't know, did you? I was a sneak thief once. Not to worry. I went to hospital. Cured a long time ago. Don't know how she managed all that time I was inside. We thought it'd be better once I was out but nobody would give us jobs, see? Except for his lordship. My gentleman. Nicest guy I ever met, he was. Didn't judge nobody." Lewin had another sip of whiskey and looked at Alec curiously. "It ain't half funny how you turned out so much like him, you know? Considering."

"Considering?"

"Mm. You're a stronger man, though. Lots stronger. Poor old Jolly Roger." Lewin smiled dreamily at the lamp, which was still swaying, ever so slightly, after its collision with Alec's head. "Why'd he stop teaching, eh? Too much money, maybe. No reason not to do just as he liked. He drifted with the tide, our Roger."

"Well, he was unhappy," Alec said. "I broke up his marriage, didn't I?"

"Aw, no, son—"

"No, it's okay. I've known for years."

Lewin had another mouthful of whiskey, shaking his head. "No. He made some kinda deal with the devil. I think. Jovian Integrated didn't give him orders much, he just collected his salary, but when they said for him to jump—well, he had to, didn't he?"

Unnoticed on its bracket in a high corner of the room, one of the Captain's surveillance cameras turned sharply and focused on Lewin. Its lens telescoped out, bringing him into tight focus, and the volume on the recording devices went up a notch.

"Poor bastard," Lewin went on, tilting his glass to drain it. "Last thing he wanted was a baby dumped in his lap. But he loved you, Alec, he really did. Much as he loved anybody. That was the funny thing about it."

Alec was confused. "Wait a minute. I thought he and Mummy got divorced because *she* didn't want to have me."

Lewin was silent a moment, blinking. He put his hands up to rub his face. "Well—she didn't, actually, but we never wanted to tell you that."

"I don't know why she didn't just go ahead and have an abortion," said Alec foggily, reaching for the decanter and filling the glass.

Alec, stop that!

"It would have been okay, really," he went on, "I mean, lots better than both their lives being wrecked that way." He had a cautious sip, glancing up at the security camera.

You bloody idiot, you know better than to mix yer liquors!

"No, son, no." Lewin reached out and took the glass from him. He began to cry again. "All these years you've thought . . . what Sarah's game was I'll never know." Alec looked around for a tissue to offer him. He groped in the pockets of the new coat again, with just as much lack of success.

"You know what?" Lewin took a gulp of whiskey. "Doesn't matter what they was up to at J. I. S. You turned out real fine, never mind what happened to his lordship and her ladyship. Can't help that, can you? No. All the same. Whoever it was made you, wanted to make something good."

"What?" said Alec.

Lewin's eyes were closing.

"Tell yer about it sometime," he said indistinctly. He put his head down on the table. A moment later he began to snore.

Alec staggered to his feet and looked down at Lewin.

What was he talking about?

Beats me, son, said the Captain a bit too casually.

Alec stood staring at Lewin a moment longer. Out across the water, beyond the Tower, a clock began to strike. It went on striking for a long time. Alec shrugged out of his ludicrous coat and draped it around Lewin's shoulders. The old man gave a little cry and called out his wife's name, but he didn't wake up. Alec stretched out on the floor.

Get up and lie down on the bunk, laddie.

Not going to sleep. Just thinking a minute.

Alec?

What'd he mean, about J. I. S.? . . .

When Alec woke it was broad daylight. He sat up painfully. He looked over at the table where Lewin still sat huddled under his coat, waxenfaced, shrunken somehow.

Alec knew at once.

Why didn't you wake me?

He had a stroke afore his heart went, son. It was over in two minutes. Nothing you could have done. Better to let you sleep.

Alec scrambled to his feet, feeling his throat contract.

It must have been the whiskey! He hadn't had a drink in all those years—

Alec, belay that. This wasn't yer fault. I've already checked his medical records and run a postmortem scan. He was dying anyway. Wouldn't you rather he'd gone in his sleep like this?

I guess so. He was so old, and he missed her so much. But he was all I had left!

Oh, I don't know about that. Yer mother's still alive, ain't she?

Alec put his hands to his pounding temples. *My mother?* he repeated in stupefaction.

THE YEAR 2350:

___

CHRISTMAS MEETING

A fine snow was falling over London. Rutherford was happily putting up greenery at No. 10 Albany Crescent, humming Christmas carols to himself. Christmas was a very popular month, in the year 2350. It had long since been purged of the embarrassment of its religious origins, to the point where the younger generations were sentimentally inclined to be tolerant of it. It was so retro!

One was even beginning to hear the unexpurgated versions of the old carols again, probably because few people had any idea what the words meant anymore. Rutherford was doggedly working his way through learning "God Rest Ye Merry, Gentlemen" because of its literary connotations, but even with his extraordinary classical education he couldn't imagine why the Blessed Babe had been born in Jewelry.

He tacked up the last swag of paper holly and scrambled down from the stepladder to have a look around. There in the corner was his artificial tree, releasing its fragrance of balsam mist spray as the tiny electronic lights pulsed. Around its base he had carefully arranged the favorite toys of his childhood, his hypoallergenic Pooh Bear and Montessori blocks, as well as a host of antique playthings he'd found in various galleries. Visitors were occasionally shocked to see the lead soldiers or, worse, the wooden horse and buggy; but Rutherford was a historian, after all, and secretly enjoyed it when the truth did injury to modern sensibilities.

Over the table he had spread a red cloth, and laid out the most historically accurate feast he could put together. No shop he'd visited had had any clue what *sugar plums* might be, so he'd compromised by setting out a dish of prunes next to a bowl of fresh damsons, flown into Covent Garden from Australia only that morning. He'd made a steamed bran and carrot pudding, and only burned himself a little in turning it out of its round mold. Now it sat sullen on its festive plate, leaking golden syrup. There was a dead-pale BirdSoy blancmange, with the word JOY spelled out in dried cherries. There was a plate of wholemeal biscuits and another of roasted chestnuts. The steaming Christmas punch had been the easiest of all: he'd simply opened a carton of fruit punch and boiled it in a saucepan.

The flames from the Fibro-Logs leaped merrily, the little Father Christmas on the mantel waved a mittened hand as if to welcome in carolers, and the snow kept falling beyond the windows. Rutherford went longingly to the glass and peered out into the steadily darkening afternoon. There were his friends, hurrying along through the whirling flurries! He ran to open the door for them.

"Merry Solstice," Chatterji said, smiling as he brushed the snow from his long black cloak.

"Happy Exmas," said Ellsworth-Howard, throwing back the hood of his anorak and peeling off his ski mask.

"Happy holidays, chaps!" Rutherford hastened to close the door and shut out the icy air. "Come in and partake of the groaning board."

"The what?" said Ellsworth-Howard, but he was advancing on the food even as he spoke. "Bloody hell, blancmange. My favorite! Here you go, Rutherford, here's your shracking present." He took a silver-wrapped parcel from under his coat and dropped it on the table, then grabbed a spoon and helped himself to blancmange.

"This is for you too, old chap." Chatterji presented Rutherford with a similarly bright package.

"Oh!" Tears stood in Rutherford's eyes. "I say. Here, you must have yours—" He ran and brought out a pair of little boxes, one for each of them. Ellsworth-Howard stuck his spoon back in the blancmange and there was a brief pause in the conversation, full of the sounds of tearing paper.

"Cuff links," said Chatterji. "By Jove! I've just found a shirt to go with these, too."

"A tie," gloated Ellsworth-Howard. "Now I am gonna look spiff. Thanks a lot, Rutherford. I got you a book."

"Oh, you're not supposed to tell me—" fussed Rutherford, pulling it free of its shiny wrapping. He tilted it on its side, peering at the words on the spine. "What's it say?"

"How the hell should I know?" Ellsworth-Howard shrugged and had another mouthful of blancmange. "Lots of pictures of superheroes, anyway."

"No." Rutherford strained to spell out the words. "It says JOSEPH

CAMPBELL. It's about ancient gods! Thank you, Foxy." He set it down and tore open the other package. He drew out an old wooden box and looked at Chatterji in wild surmise. "Chatty? This is never what I think it is."

"Open it and see," Chatterji said. Rutherford lifted the lid cautiously and nearly screamed in excitement. There they were, still in the cellophane wrappers in which they'd arrived at a tobacconist's two centuries earlier: three dozen cigars. The faintest perfume was still perceptible, a melancholy breath of brandy and spices.

"Good God." Rutherford's hands were shaking with joy. "Chatty! Wherever did you find them?"

"Oh, just a discreet little shop." Chatterji waved his hand in an airy sort of way.

"Cost him a packet, too," Ellsworth-Howard informed Rutherford.

"Well, what's money for, after all?" Chatterji looked over the buffet and selected a wholemeal biscuit. "Anyway, Foxy has another present for you. Haven't you, Foxy?"

"No I haven't," said Ellsworth-Howard with his mouth full. "Oh! I'll tell a lie. I forgot, just got word this morning: another host mother's been found. We can start the third sequence for our man."

"That's wonderful." Rutherford carried the cigars to the sideboard and arranged them carefully beside his pipe rack. "I was beginning to think they'd never find anybody suitable again."

"Well, it certainly took them long enough, but here's the great thing—" Chatterji paused, pouring himself a tankard of hot punch. He looked up meaningfully. "The report came in from *2319*."

"Thirty-odd years ago?" Rutherford stared blankly a moment before the implications sank in. "But that would mean—he'd be alive right now."

"Exactly." Chatterji nodded. "And all the indications are that he's secured a place in history already, or perhaps it would be more correct to say that we've secured it for him."

"What do you mean?" Rutherford's eyes got big behind his glasses.

"'WHERE'S ELLY'S BABY?'" cried Ellsworth-Howard in a shrieking falsetto.

"I beg your pardon?"

"The Earth Hand kidnapping case, Rutherford, surely you've heard of it?" Chatterji nibbled another biscuit. "It's never been solved, you know. BBC Delta does a retrospective on it every now and then."

"Oh." Rutherford frowned. "Well, police cases aren't exactly my line. Some scandal, wasn't it? Paternity suit or something?"

"I remember it on the tabloids," said Ellsworth-Howard. "Just a little bugger then, but I remember that fat lady yelling 'Where's Elly's baby?' My mum and dad used to listen to Earth Hand all the time. Tommy Hawkins, that was the lead guitarist, had this go-girl he kept with him, see, and suddenly she's about to have this baby! Only he and she ain't got a permit, and anyway he says it ain't none of his. She went off her nut and had to go in an institution. The Ephesian church took it up as a cause."

"But Hawkins wouldn't back down," Chatterji said. "He refused to admit he'd fathered the baby and he refused to pay the unauthorized reproduction fines. The Ephesians wanted his head! And legions of Earth Hand fans were just as positive he was innocent. There were riots, for heaven's sake. And then she had a little boy, and genetic assay results were published showing that the child was Hawkins's."

"How sordid," said Rutherford.

"Yeah, well, it got worse," Ellsworth-Howard said. "Tommy Hawkins says the assay results are faked. He demands another one done in front of a camera! Full blood test, too. It would have been a shracking media horrorshow, I can tell you. Only problem was, the baby went and disappeared."

"Just vanished," said Chatterji. "One minute he was there in his cot in the mental health centre and the next he was gone. No trace of a kidnapper on the hospital surveillance recordings. No ransom note. And the tabloids screamed: Where's Elly's Baby?' But no one ever found out, you see."

"Both sides swore the other one done away with the little sod. Earth Hand's next album was called *You Ain't My Shracking Kid*," Ellsworth-Howard recalled. "Title track was a lullaby my mum and dad would play for me all the time. Ephesians nearly burned down the recording studio. Little Elly never came off the meds, ever again. Last I heard she was in one of the Ephesians' cloisters, shut up tight. Tommy Hawkins died of something, a couple of years back. But nobody ever found the baby."

"I really fail to see the point of all this," said Rutherford.

"The point, my dear fellow, is that the host mother our Facilitator has located in 2319 is a sixteen-year-old go-girl answering to the name of Elly Swain." Chatterji smiled. "And the man with whom she is cohabiting is none other than Thomas Eustace Hawkins."

"Oh," said Rutherford.

"Which means, you see, that in the act of creating one of the greatest mysteries of the century, we're also solving it," Chatterji said with an air of triumph. "You see? Hawkins really wasn't the father at all. Little Elly was abducted by our operatives and implanted. And obviously Elly's baby vanished because we took him."

"By Jove, Chatty, I won't say I approve entirely but—there is a certain mythic quality to all this," said Rutherford.

"And, think about it—there will be no tragedy." Chatterji sat down in his favorite chair. "My mother used to cry and leave the room whenever the case was mentioned on holo shows. Couldn't bear the thought of that little helpless child lying dead somewhere. But we know he'll really be alive and all right! No sad ending after all."

"Except for little Elly in her rubber room at the convent," added Ellsworth-Howard.

"Well, that can't be helped. But think about it for a minute: isn't this the sort of thing the Dr. Zeus mission statement is all about?" Chatterji's eyes shone. "History cannot be changed, *but* if it is possible to work within the parameters of recorded history, tragedy can be transmuted into triumph. Nothing lost to the ages—simply hidden away safely by Dr. Zeus. Children rescued, not murdered! Little Romanovs, little Lindberghs, little Makebas. Little Elly's baby. All secure in some fold of unrecorded history somewhere."

"Yes, you're quite right." Rutherford began to pace. "We're almost obligated to do this, aren't we? Very well—suppose we put the order through to implant that wretched girl. Nine months later, the baby's born. We'll have to order the operative in charge to fake genetic assay results showing that he's the musician's offspring."

"Hang on." Ellsworth-Howard slid into his chair and pulled out his buke. He put on an earshell and mike and grunted in commands, inquiries, follow-ups.

"Now, how do we kidnap the baby?" mused Rutherford.

"That's one of the things our Facilitators are best at," said Chatterji.

"Oh, this is exciting." Rutherford rubbed his hands together as he paced. "Now, once they've got the baby, what will they do with him? Have to place him in a foster home, of course, but where?"

"It's coming together," Ellsworth-Howard informed them, listening at the shell. "Third sequence initiated. Girl's been implanted. Shrack!" He gave a raucous shout of laughter. "If that don't beat all. Now we bloody know why Tommy Hawkins kept yelling it wasn't his kid."

"What do you mean?" Chatterji stood up and leaned over to peer at the screen.

"Facilitator who did the implant got little Elly up on the table and had a good look at her, and guess what? *She ain't never done it with anybody!*"

"You mean she was a virgin?" said Rutherford.

Ellsworth-Howard nodded, scratching around one of the rivets on his scalp. "He accessed some Harley Street bugger's secret files and

found out why, too. Turns out Tommy Hawkins had spent a fortune trying to get his dead willy fixed. Nothing worked, so he spent another
fortune to have his secret kept."

"But he was sleeping with Elly Swain," Chatterji said.

"Yeah. Sleeping." Ellsworth-Howard was silent a moment, grinning, listening. "You know what else our Facilitator found out? Little
Elly wasn't the brightest bit who'd ever gone for takeaway for a band.
Blond and beautiful but just a bit to let upstairs, see? Dumb enough to
settle for hugs and nighty-night kisses from her Tommy, as long as she
was With the Band. Plus she was only shracking sixteen."

"Please." Rutherford held up a hand as if to shut out the nastiness.
"The lurid details can be glossed over, can't they? The essential point
here is that the girl was a virgin. This is perfect, don't you see? She's the
mother of our hero, our extraordinary man, our Arthur. Scandal and
mystery surrounding his birth fits the mythic pattern exactly. Being
born of a virgin is even better."

"You don't find that blasphemous?" Chatterji looked mildly
shocked.

"Why? We're the gods here, Chatty, have you forgotten? If it
doesn't offend Foxy and me, it certainly shouldn't offend you." Rutherford was racing around the room now on his stout little legs. "So. I
daresay our Facilitator finds it rather tricky to arrange a foster home, in
this day and age?"

"Yes indeed," Chatterji said, getting up to pour himself another
punch. "There were house-to-house searches all through England."

"Then he must have been smuggled out of the country, somehow."
Rutherford paused to grab a biscuit and kept pacing. "Placed with one
of our paid people in that era, I suppose. Somebody with security clearance. A British national living abroad."

"Sequence proceeding," Ellsworth-Howard informed them.
"Baby's born."

"Who've we got in that time period?" Chatterji sat down again.
"Access the records, Foxy. Who's on the Company payroll, British, married, living abroad?"

Ellsworth-Howard pulled up a long string of names. "Got 'em."

"All right, narrow search: reproductive age, both parties of similar
genetic profile to subject."

"Yeah." Ellsworth-Howard worked the buttonball and the list grew
abruptly shorter.

"Now." Rutherford turned on his heel, "Search for any who announce the birth of a son in the period immediately following the disappearance of Elly's baby."

"Here they are," said Ellsworth-Howard at once. He listened again. "Junior executive with Jovian Integrated Systems: Roger Jeremy St. James Alistair Checkerfield, sixth earl of Finsbury. Married to the Honourable Cecelia Devereaux Ashcroft. Pleased to announce birth of son, Alec William St. James Thorne Checkerfield. Date of birth given as one week after Elly's baby."

"A peer!" Rutherford threw up his hands. "Perfect. They don't need reproduction permits. Whereabouts abroad were they living?"

"Hm." Ellsworth-Howard squeezed in a request and listened. "In the Caribbean. Baby supposed to have been born at sea. Parents' address given as the *Foxy Lady* out of Southhampton. Living on their yacht, I reckon."

"Better and better." Rutherford began to do a little hopping dance, skipping back and forth between the table and the fireplace. "No witnesses other than paid servants. What's the rest of the story like? To the present day, I mean?"

Ellsworth-Howard asked for more information.

"Marriage goes bang in 2324," he said. "His lordship stays on the *Foxy Lady*. Kid raised at London home here by servants."

"It's all falling into place," said Rutherford. "There's the sense of shame we need, you see? Not illegitimacy this time, but rejection by his parents. Perhaps he can be made to feel he was responsible for the divorce."

"Here's his schools," said Ellsworth-Howard. "Here's his entry in *Who's Who* and shracking *Burke's Peerage*. Became seventh earl of Finsbury after sixth earl had a nasty accident whilst diving. That was in 2337."

"Good lord! Funny to think he's alive right now, isn't it?" Chatterji remarked. "He is still alive, isn't he?"

"Oh, yeah," Ellsworth-Howard said. "Only thirty."

"Can we—can we see a picture of him?" Rutherford advanced toward his chair. "That will prove he's the right man, you see."

"Might take a second," said Ellsworth-Howard. "This is in real time, you know."

"Make it so," said Rutherford. He resumed his comic dance, waving his arms in the air. He began to chant. "Spirits of Cause and Effect, I summon thee! I bend thee to my will! Spirits of Action and Reaction, I conjure thee, grant my desires! Schrödinger's Cat, heed my commands! Oh, Spirit of Time, oh, thou Chronos, oh thou, er, Timex, Bulova, um, Westclox, Swatch, Rolex, Piaget! Uh . . . In the name of Greenwich, in whose image all Time is made!"

Chatterji began to giggle helplessly, watching him. Ellsworth-

Howard wasn't noticing, frowning at the images that flitted past on the screen. Outside the snow fell ever faster, and in a distant tower ancient machinery began to vibrate. A hammer was cranked back in the dark and freezing air—

"In the name of Big Ben, Lord and Keeper of our days," said Rutherford. "Thou who hast measured all possible Pasts, Presents and Futures! I charge thee now, bring him to us! Bring him to us! Bring him to us! Let us in our time behold *Adonai!*"

"Oi!" said Ellsworth-Howard. Just as the hour struck and the familiar bells began pealing, the face appeared on the screen: Alec Checkerfield, seventh earl of Finsbury, smiling at the camera that had taken his passport image. He was wearing a shirt with a vividly tropical design. There were a pair of sunglasses folded in the front pocket.

"Oh, it is him!" Rutherford dropped to his knees, staring with Chatterji and Ellsworth-Howard at the image on the screen.

"Height, one meter 97.46 centimeters," recited Ellsworth-Howard. "Weight, 120 kilograms. Date of birth: 12 January, 2320. Dual citizenship Britain and St. Kitts. Residence: No. 16 John Street, Bloomsbury, London WC1. Communication Code: ACFin@777P17/33. Bloody hell! Want to talk to him right now, Rutherford? You could."

"No," squeaked Rutherford, biting his knuckles. "I—we oughtn't. But order Elly's baby kidnapped, Foxy. This is our man."

Ellsworth-Howard gave a certain three orders in a certain sequence, and the invisible patterns of destiny in the room swirled and set. The clock had finished striking.

"Well." Chatterji collapsed backward into his chair. "I think this calls for a celebration, don't you? What about some sherry?"

"First rate." Rutherford scrambled to his feet. He ran to the sideboard and filled three glasses, and brought them back without spilling much. They all settled into their particular chairs around the fire.

"To the seventh earl of Finsbury," said Chatterji, and they drank.

"Ahh." Rutherford settled back. "You know, I never imagined we'd be running a sequence in real time. This should be really interesting."

"Rather frustrating, too, I should imagine," Chatterji said. "No more instant results. We have no idea how he'll turn out, but we'll get to watch it happen. What sort of heroic life is he leading this time around, don't you wonder?"

"You can find out," said Ellsworth-Howard.

"By Jove, we can, can't we? Not what he's going to do but certainly what he's done so far, over the last thirty years, with the noble programming we've given him." Rutherford wriggled in his chair. "Pull it up, Foxy. Let's see what sort of place he's carved for himself in history."

Ellsworth-Howard requested the information.

"You know, he probably works for Dr. Zeus," said Chatterji.

"Perhaps he's a scientist who's made some vital discovery," said Rutherford.

"Well . . . no, actually," Ellsworth-Howard said, blinking at the screen.

"Oh, don't be silly." Rutherford sat forward. "He has to be spending his life in service to humanity. It's what we designed him to do."

"Seriously, Foxy, what's he done with his life so far?" Chatterji pulled out his sinus inhalator and had a drag. Ellsworth-Howard squeezed in another request and listened for a moment.

"Messed about on his shracking boat, so far as I can tell," said Ellsworth-Howard dubiously. "The *Captain Morgan* out of New Port Royal. Doesn't live at the Bloomsbury house. Spends all his time at sea, sailing about between islands. Not employed by the Company. Lives on investments and a trust fund left him by his father—well, the late earl. Absentee House of Lords. Regular layabout, it appears."

Rutherford looked horrified. "There's got to be more to the man than that! Look further. What about his accomplishments? What about charities and humanitarian work? What are his politics?"

"No politics." Ellsworth-Howard shook his head. "No hospital visits, no village fêtes. He took care of the old cook and butler real well— nice place at Bournemouth and fat pensions until they passed away. Married twice. Divorced, no kids. Obviously."

"Married?" groaned Rutherford.

"Hey!" Ellsworth-Howard's eyes lit up. "Here's something he did that made the news. Age seven, Pembroke Technologies sued him."

"Sued? As in, filed a lawsuit?" Chatterji's jaw dropped. "Against a seven-year-old child?"

"Yeah." Ellsworth-Howard grinned. "I remember hearing about this on the news. Clever little bugger! It seems he made some unauthorized modifications on a Pembroke Playfriend his people had got him. Pembroke Corp. wanted to force his people to sell the unit back to them, so they could figure out what our boy'd done to it."

"There," Rutherford said. "There, he's a genius at least."

"What happened?" said Chatterji.

"Oh, they lost the case," Ellsworth-Howard said. "Him being peerage and all, and only seven, too. They went into receivership two years later. Stupid bastards."

"Did he continue to display genius at school?" Rutherford said.

"Well, he got high marks in maths," said Ellsworth-Howard, after listening again. "Top of his class there. Shrack—wonder how he got past medical scans all his life?" He looked panicked for a moment. "That brain I designed—oh, shrack, and his bleeding DNA!—"

"His Company handlers hushed it up, of course," said Chatterji, with a wave of his inhaler. "Just as they faked the genetic assay."

Ellsworth-Howard relaxed, and listened again. "No university. Seems he's designed the cybernavigation system for his boat, though. That's what he spends his money on when he's not partying. And—aw, shrack!"

"What?" Rutherford and Chatterji stared at Ellsworth-Howard, whose face had contorted in fury.

"He's shracked with my design," Ellsworth-Howard snarled. "He's had himself modified for interface. He's a cyborg! Not one of them old plughole jobs but the new ones, look like a tattoo under the skin. Where's he think he gets off, the sodding bastard?"

"Well, it's his body," Rutherford said.

"No it ain't." Ellsworth-Howard clenched the buttonball fiercely. "*I* designed it. If he's gone and compromised my brain—"

"Ah." Rutherford frowned in comprehension. "Well, perhaps that's our problem. Nothing you could have foreseen when you designed him, Foxy. I think we were all envisioning he'd operate in pre-electronic eras. Perhaps he's become one of those Lotus-Eaters one hears about, lolling around in cyberspace. That would explain this self-indulgent and useless existence."

"Though he seems to be physically quite active," said Chatterji, watching worriedly as Ellsworth-Howard worked the buttonball, attempting to break into Checkerfield's cyberenvironment. There was a fixed glare in his eyes that Chatterji had seen only twice before, on two very unpleasant occasions. Ellsworth-Howard began to growl in his throat as he was repeatedly frustrated in his efforts.

"Most of the port junkies don't get out much—" Chatterji was continuing, when Ellsworth-Howard gave an animal scream and threw his buke across the room. He was in the act of picking up his chair too when Chatterji seized him from behind, pinioning his arms. "Rutherford! The meds, for God's sake!"

Rutherford ran for the sideboard and brought out a forced air applicator. Ellsworth-Howard was twisting in Chatterji's arms, doing his best to bite him, when Rutherford darted in and jabbed with the applicator. There was an audible hiss. Ellsworth-Howard began to snicker. Laughing feebly he sagged to the floor, falling through Chatterji's arms. His eyes rolled back in his head. He stopped laughing.

"Oh, poor old chap." Rutherford ran and got a cushion from the sofa. "Let's make him comfortable until he comes to, Chatty." He tucked the cushion under Ellsworth-Howard's head while Chatterji busied himself with opening Ellsworth-Howard's collar and cuffs and checking his pulse.

"He'll be all right," said Chatterji shakily.

"He's an artist, that's all," said Rutherford, climbing back into his chair and curling up. "It—it can be very upsetting to have your art interfered with."

"Yes, certainly." Chatterji got to his feet and looked around. He spotted Ellsworth-Howard's buke, lying where it had fallen after bouncing off the wall.

"Oh, I hope it's not broken," he said, bending to pick it up. It didn't seem to be. It was in fact still trying to obey Ellsworth-Howard's last command, flashing its WAIT pattern in vain. Suddenly the screen cleared and Chatterji found himself staring at the seventh earl of Finsbury again. He was smiling out from the screen, not a very nice smile really. The pale blue eyes were so cold.

"Hi there," said the pleasant tenor voice. "If you're seeing this image, it means you've been trying to shrack with me. Do you know what *this* means?" The face transformed into a horribly grinning skull over a pair of crossed bones. From the eyes of the skull, a pair of cannons emerged. There was a flare of fire and the recorded sound of explosions, and the screen went black.

For a moment the room was so silent one could hear the faint chime of the electronic lights sparkling on the Christmas tree.

"Oh, dear," said Chatterji at last. "Now he'll really be upset."

"The buke's been destroyed, hasn't it?" Rutherford said faintly.

"I'm afraid it has," Chatterji said. "Of course, he'll have kept backups on everything. Won't he?"

"Of course," Rutherford said. "Except for the work we've done tonight. I'd like another sherry, please."

"Right," said Chatterji, and dropping the wrecked buke he went to the sideboard and poured them two more drinks.

"Shame about the buke, but, you know, we've learned something tremendously valuable about our man," said Rutherford at last, with a little of his former briskness. "He's someone to be reckoned with! This is no mere admin-class dilettante living for his pleasures, no, this is our hero all right. He's just got unexpected talents. What sort of genius can spike a Company inquiry? Have you ever heard of anybody doing that?"

"Never," Chatterji admitted.

"There's obviously more to him than shows on his social record," Rutherford said. "And either he's covered it up terribly well or he just hasn't encountered the right challenges in life. He must work for the Company! We'll have to order the proper people to get in touch with him and make him the usual recruitment offers. Once he's working with us, properly guided, who knows what he might accomplish?"

"It would be appropriate." Chatterji leaned back wearily and had another gulp of pretend sherry, feeling the fruit sugars race in his bloodstream.

"My Pendragon. My Messiah. My Hero with a Thousand Faces." Rutherford sighed, looking into the fire. "In my time. I'll get to shake his hand at last." He turned his head and looked out into the gloom beyond the windows, all darkness and whirling snow. "When this began I half-thought . . . well, secretly . . . that perhaps he really would save us all. When . . . in 2355."

Chatterji shivered. "Don't let's think about that," he said.

"But maybe we're wrong to assume something terrible's going to happen," Rutherford said. "Perhaps it won't be a meteor, or a war, or a plague. Maybe things just . . . change."

"Maybe." Chatterji drained his drink.

"Whatever happens, doesn't it make sense to have this magnificent creation on our side before the end comes? Maybe he'll find a way to stop it from happening, whatever it is. Maybe that's his ultimate purpose," Rutherford said.

"I hope so," Chatterji said, stretching out his legs. "Do—do you ever have nightmares, Rutherford? About what it'll be like?"

"Sometimes," Rutherford said. "I suppose all of us do, who know about it."

"I dream the streets are on fire," said Chatterji, staring into their own cheery little blaze. "I remember a song about the world ending by water last time, by fire next time. People are running through the streets screaming, and they're all on fire. I go into my grandfather's room, and he's there on the bed and it's on fire, and so's my grandmother. They turn their heads to look at me, and it's as though they're telling me I have to climb up there too and burn with them. It mustn't end that way!"

"Well, we're doing everything we can to be certain it doesn't," said Rutherford doggedly. "Let's put in that request to have somebody approach our man on the Company's behalf. Full speed ahead."

There was a moment of silence, punctuated only by a gentle snore from Ellsworth-Howard.

"As soon as we have another buke," said Chatterji sadly.

THE YEAR 2349:

Alec Solves a Mystery

"And so, to conclude old business." Magilside cleared his throat. The other Resistance members grew alert at that vital word *conclude* and sat upright, trying to look as though they'd been listening. Behind him, through the portholes of the saloon, the pink towers of New Port Royal taunted the rebels with promise of unattainable naughty delights.

Magilside continued in his barely audible monotone: "It is expected that our support will enable the Semantic Renegades to continue their pressure on the Athenian Senate for the remainder of the fiscal year. If the FPFOM AKA Fair Play for Original Macedonians Committee increases their shipments of software, I am confident that a resolution will be passed, possibly within the next five years, granting sole use of the name *Macedonians* to those persons actually born within the prerevolutionary boundaries . . ."

They ought to send **him** *over there to talk to their bloody senate*, transmitted the Captain. *Those Greeks'd be down on their knees begging for mercy in five minutes.*

If they weren't asleep. It's people like him have kept the debate going for three hundred years. Alec concealed a yawn and looked across at Balkister, raising his eyebrows as if to inquire whether somebody couldn't prod Magilside to the finish line. Balkister shrugged and moved his hand in a gesture like a chattering mouth. Magilside was one of their most dedicated workers, and his feelings were easily wounded.

Alec sighed, surveying the gallant company assembled in the saloon of his ship. The Resistance had a number of designated meeting places, but somehow he'd wound up playing host to the disaffected elite more and more often. It might have been because his fellow revolutionaries found the thrill of a rendezvous on an actual ship too much

to resist. It might have been because there were plenty of illicit substances to eat, drink, and smoke on the *Captain Morgan,* and Alec was
always a good host. It might have been that they were snobs at heart,
despite the fact that most of them seemed to feel that Alec, by virtue of
being an actual titled peer, could be treated with a barely concealed
condescension.

Right now he felt he couldn't blame them. Joining Balkister's secret
club seemed one of the stupider moves he had ever made, even less of
a good idea than the God Game had been. How could civil disobedi-
ence be so boring?

Though it was a little less boring when the Resistance bickered
within itself. Binscarth, their resident literary lion, was at last unable to
contain himself any longer and leaped to his feet, applauding.

"And thank *you*, Magilside, for that bwilliant summation of old
business," he cried. Magilside stopped with his mouth open, breath already drawn for his next run-on sentence. He looked wrathful, and
thumbed off his plaquette of notes with a gesture that suggested he
wished it were Binscarth's eye.

"All right," he muttered, and sat down in a huff. Binscarth leapt up
and took the podium.

"I'd like to bwing an exciting matter to your attention, fellow We-
sistance members. I've located a potential wecruit whose libwawy of
pwoscwibed matewial is even more extensive than mine. *Both* Buw-
woughs—William and Edgar Wice! He's got a copy of *Medea*, he's got
Fahwenheit 451, and he may even have *Pawadise Lost*. If we waive dues
and allow him to join on a conditional basis, he'll let us copy his books
for distwibution. What do you say, fellows?"

There were some *ooh*s and *aah*s of enthusiasm, very polite and
subdued. It took a dedicated antiquarian like Binscarth to get much
worked up about books or their distribution to a populace that was
largely unable to read them. But the material was forbidden, after all,
so it was certainly worth something. Besides, there were certain grubby
holo production businesses, operating out of abandoned blocks of flats
for the most part, who would pay nicely for proscribed material to be
adapted to scripts.

"I'm in favor. What do the rest of you think, guys?" Balkister
looked around.

"Sure," Alec said, raising one fist with the thumb up. He assumed
all the works Binscarth had referred to were pornographic, and since
most of the pornography he'd ever encountered had been astonishingly dumb stuff, he didn't see how it could hurt anybody. The other
Resistance members followed with a chorus of *Oh, why not*s and *Okay*s.

"I commend you gentlemen on your taste." Binscarth looked smug. "You won't wegwet this, I assure you. I'll contact the chap next week."

He stepped down and Johnson-Johnson took the podium to deliver a report on financial aid sent to the Mars One colonists, who were engaging in a series of lawsuits and countersuits with Areco, the corporation that actually owned their farms. Alec looked longingly over at his bar. At last it was his turn to go to the podium, where he briefly described how the smuggling business was going and mentioned that he had got a deal on fifty crates of Cadbury's cocoa. There was some speculation as to how much revenue this might bring in, and though Alec knew to the penny he stepped down gladly to let Krishnamurti, the treasurer, give the revised figures for projected income in the current fiscal year.

At last the meeting broke up. Binscarth tried to lead them in a chorus of "I've Got a Little List" from Gilbert and Sullivan's *Mikado*, but everybody else thought it was silly. Binscarth exited, mightily miffed. The others stayed for one last round of beer floats and then toddled ashore to partake of the club life of Jamaica.

Usually on their departure Alec yielded to an irresistible impulse to run howling through his gloriously empty ship, leaving Billy Bones and his mates to creep forth and clean up the debris of glasses and plates. Not today. He stood surveying the party mess and then stalked over to the bar to mix himself a drink.

Now then, matey, the sun ain't below the yardarm yet.

What the hell does it matter? Alec groped in the ice bin. There was a big chunk frozen together at the mouth of the bin. He prized it out, lifted it above his head and smashed it on the counter. Bright fragments of ice went spinning everywhere, and Billy Bones and Flint paused in their duties to turn their skull-faces to him questioningly. He ignored them and picked through the mess on the counter for cubes to put into his drink. Smashing the ice had felt good.

Well, well. Our little Alec needs a session with his punching bags, don't he? Now why, I wonder? You been bored by them amateur revolutionaries afore. Are they finally getting to be too much, with their silly-ass agenda?

Maybe. They never accomplish ANYTHING! I'm going to be thirty soon, you know? What have I done with my life? I've had a great time, I've had nearly everything I've ever wanted—not that I've deserved it—and the only people I've ever made happy are those twits in the Resistance.

You've made me happy, son.

Well, thanks, but you're a machine, aren't you? Alec sipped his drink moodily. *You're happy when I'm happy.*

And I'm unhappy when yer unhappy, my lad.

Okay, great. Somebody else whose life I've ruined.

Belay that self-pitying crap! Down to the gym, quick march.

Alec sighed in exasperation as he set down his drink. All the same, he got up and went below to his gym. He had several punching bags of assorted sizes there, from the suspended balloon type to the full-length body model, and today he didn't even bother to put on gloves before he launched his attack. Up in the corner of the cabin a surveillance camera turned and observed him in satisfaction.

Alec had long since grown bored with Totter Dan, but found a tremendous release in physical violence. It got him nearly as high as dancing. He thundered away now at the unresisting canvas duffel until sweat was pouring down his face and throat. Finally he staggered back, gasping and blissful from the endorphin rush, and sprawled on the mat.

Now, that's better, ain't it, boy?

Yup.

I know what's gone and got you thinking. It's two years today since old Lewin went to Fiddler's Green. You don't reckon he'd approve of what yer doing with yer life.

I guess he wouldn't, would he? Alec reached out to accept a wet towel from Bully Hayes, and mopped his face.

So, buck. Ever thought about those things he said, just afore he died?

Nope.

Now why's that, eh? A clever lad like you. I'd have thought you'd have done anything to get to the bottom of that mystery.

What mystery? All it comes down to was that Roger didn't want me either. Nobody wanted a kid on the Foxy Lady, *but they got one, and everybody lived unhappily ever after. The end.*

The hell it is! That ain't all he said. You was drunk at the time— if I recall correctly—and maybe you didn't notice something peculiar about the old man's exact words, but I did. Shall I refresh yer memory?

No!—But the Captain played the recording for him, and Lewin's thin old voice came over the ship's audio system. Alec covered his face with the towel. He couldn't stop himself listening, however, and as the recording ended and Lewin's voice slurred away into eternity Alec sat up.

Hey! Did you—? It almost sounded like he was saying that J. I. S. made Roger and Cecelia have me.

That's what I thought.

But that's nuts! Why would a big company like that want anybody to have a kid? Let alone Roger. I mean, he was an executive because he was an earl. He never actually did anything for them except teach some marine biology.

Don't seem to make a lot of sense, now, does it? But ain't you ever wondered why he was always telling you what a special kid you were?

Alec sat there in silence for a moment, watching the punching bag as it swung in ever-lessening arcs and was finally still. Abruptly he got to his feet.

I need to research this. I'm going to go shower; have the data ready for me in twenty minutes. I want everything you can find on Jovian Integrated Systems.

Aye aye!

By the time Alec strode into the deckhouse, Coxinga was waiting for him with a tray of sandwiches and a pitcher of fruit tea. He threw himself down in his chair and looked up at the surveillance camera.

Okay, what've we got?

The bright holovision images took their place in midair before his eyes.

Jovian Integrated Systems first, the Captain told him. **This place look familiar? It's off the coast of California. Catalina Island, remember? This was shot in 2120, when J. I. S. was founded. They built a marine sciences academy in return for an open-ended lease. British-owned. That's where Roger was an instructor, for a while. You've run tea there, Alec! What a coincidence, eh?**

Yeah.

Anyway, J. I. S. don't exist now as a corporate entity. It was absorbed into another company. I reckon you've heard of it. They call themselves Dr. Zeus, Incorporated.

What? I thought that was just a joke. You mean Dr. Zeus is real?

Oh, aye, matey, it is.

No way! They're supposed to have figured out time travel. That's all a lot of puckamenna, though, right? What do they really do?

Well, now, laddie, that's an interesting question. They're consultants, they say. Seem to be in the business of fetching anything for anybody, if the right price is paid. And I mean anything, son, do

you understand me? If they ain't got time travel figured out, then
something bloody weird is going on. I thought I had yer assets
pretty nicely obscured; Christ, you should see what these people got
hidden! And I only got just the barest peep at it.

Huh.

Alec, I'm getting that feeling. I smell loot here. This is going to
bear looking into with an eye to boarding 'em, Alec.

Okay. One of these days. Anything else on Roger's work there?

No, there ain't. He went on indefinite sabbatical three years
afore you was born. But, listen, son! Dr. Zeus ain't just rumored to
have invented time travel. There's stories they found a way to make
people immortal. Bullshit, says you; but they got the best genetic
theorists from every country on Earth on their payroll.

Alec felt ice-cold suddenly. He didn't want to think about why.

And there's some old news you need to see. Watch, now.

Poor-quality holofootage began to dance before his eyes, the
crackly kind familiar from historical documentaries, with a tinny narra-
tive voice. There, May 2319, right about then he had been conceived,
and what had been happening? Nothing much. Russia signed a treaty
with Finland to build a new cold fusion plant. Somebody Alec had
never heard of set a world record in surfing. Nasty accident: the Leaning Tower of Pisa had collapsed, taking with it the king and queen of
Italy, who were up there watching a Restoration Night fireworks display. A Hapsburg cousin succeeded to the throne.

Alec reached for a sandwich, watching impatiently. July 2319: Arts
and Entertainment. Joshua Spielberg's *The Blue Window* broke all previous box office records, but was lambasted by the critics. Ariadne
Moonwagon's *Diannic Dream* was number one on the bestseller list.
Some kind of scandal about a group called Earth Hand. Paternity suit?
That wasn't one you saw much anymore. Vaguely he remembered part
of a documentary on "Great Crimes of the Century" and wondered
that so much fuss had been made about somebody named Tommy
Hawkins being in trouble with the Ephesians. Alec felt a brief twinge of
sympathy.

Christmas 2319. A previously unknown painting by Leonardo da
Vinci was discovered in the catacombs below the Vatican and auc-
tioned off at Sotheby's for an astronomical sum. Mars Two was
founded on the slopes of Mons Olympus, the first extraterrestrial use
of geothermal energy expected to make them a thriving and prosper-
ous community.

You've found something, right? There's a point to all this dead stuff?

Keep watching.

Here was that nasty business about Earth Hand still dragging on: Elly Swain was the victim's name, and here was footage of a hysterical girl being loaded into an old-fashioned agcar by grim-faced Ephesians in bumblebee robes. Déjà vu. Alec poured himself a glass of fruit tea and settled back again, as the images flickered.

New Year Week, 2320. No announcement, in all the nine months beforehand, of any child being on the way for the sixth earl of Finsbury. Odd. Everybody else of any celebrity or rank made the news when a baby was expected, it happened so rarely now. But then, Roger and Cecelia hadn't exactly been pleased with the prospect, had they? Alec sipped his tea, frowning.

January 6, 2320, Elly Swain had a baby boy. *Punch* did a comic skit on the affair, but the next day things stopped being funny: the baby had been kidnapped. Alec remembered, now, why this was one of the crimes of the century. He felt queasy as he watched the famous surveillance camera film. Tiny red baby with a birth-bruised nose asleep in a glass-sided cot, there one minute, gone the next. Winking out like a little soap bubble, never to be seen again. What in the world had happened? Had the kid gone into another dimension?

He followed the story through the next week. *Where's Elly's Baby????* A journalist disguised himself as an Ephesian brother and got in to see Elly Swain, who wept and said that she'd given birth to the Antichrist.

Alec shook his head sadly and had another sip of tea. 12 January 2320. Would there be an announcement of his birth? Yes. Here it was. Roger and Cecelia must have decided to go through the motions. Proper news release with a family portrait. Hadn't they looked young! And awfully unhappy, though they were both smiling for the camera. Roger looked blurry, hung over. Cecelia was really more almost baring her teeth than smiling, stiffly holding out the tiny red baby with its bruised nose . . .

Alec choked on his tea.

I was wondering when you'd notice.

Freeze image! Hold it and bring back the footage with Elly's baby just before it disappeared. Isolate and enlarge!

The Captain obliged. Two babies floated in midair. They might have been twins, but most babies bear a certain resemblance to each other.

Enhance!

The images grew so sharp and perfect there really did appear to be two flesh-and-blood infants floating there in the room. Both Elly's baby and little Alec Checkerfield bore identical discoloration in their tiny faces. Alec's eyes were less puffy, his nose less swollen, but the bruise matched exactly.

Analyze images. Compare points of reference.

I done that already.

Well?

It's 99.9 percent it's the same kid, Alec. Yer Elly's baby.

Alec sat motionless a moment. *You knew,* he said at last.

I guessed. I didn't know until I was compiling all this stuff whilst you was in the shower. But this would answer a lot of questions, eh, lad?

It's not true. This is nuts. Why the hell would Roger and Cecelia have Elly's baby kidnapped? They never wanted a kid. I wrecked their marriage!

What if they didn't do it? What if somebody gave them a baby and told them to pretend it was theirs? That would explain a bit, wouldn't it?

Alec's eyes were glittering with that expression that had always unnerved Lewin, that suggestion of not quite human rage.

Bring up the clearest images you've got of Elly Swain and, what was his name, Tommy Hawkins.

The Captain produced two portraits. Here was a still shot from on stage during a concert, shadowed in lilac and green, but clear white light on the lead guitarist's face. Here beside it was a still shot from the scandal footage, a very young girl with her mouth open in a cry of dismay. Alec stared at them fixedly. Insofar as they were both fair-haired and blue-eyed, Tommy and Elly resembled him, but not otherwise. He couldn't see a single feature of his own in either face.

Best portraits you've got of Roger and Cecelia, please.

Four faces hung before him, now. They might all have been cousins. Not one of them shared a facial feature with Alec, however, except for a slight cleft in Cecelia's chin.

Cecelia.

". . . because your mother is a votaress of our order . . ." It had seemed almost funny, an absurdity to take his thoughts off Lorene, and then he'd put the whole miserable business out of his mind and never thought about it again.

Is my mother still alive? Cecelia Checkerfield, I mean?

Aye, lad, she is.

WHERE IS SHE?

She joined the Ephesians in 2325. Took the veil, the vows, the whole rigmarole. She's a priestess now at their main mother house.

Where's that?

Ephesus, where d'you think? The big temple itself.

Then weigh anchor and lay in a course for Ephesus.
Aye, matey!
Alec rose from his chair and paced, flexing his hands. They had begun to ache from his session with the punching bags. Ordinarily he'd go up to the saloon and fix himself a drink, but he didn't want one at the moment.

The original archeological excavation of Ephesus had been done in the late nineteenth and early twentieth centuries, by inspired masters, and from their labors it had been possible to reconstruct the place down to the smallest detail. Of particular interest was the Temple of Artemis, one of the seven wonders of the ancient world. The fact that the holiest of shrines to the Great Goddess could be seen as it was in its glory appealed tremendously to Goddess-oriented religious groups everywhere.

In the late twenty-first century the First Maternal Synod had been held at Malta, accomplishing two things: it (for the most part) united the various feminist and ecological faiths by combining their diverse scriptures into one comprehensive and fairly consistent text. It also united them in a stated goal: the reclamation and restoration of Ephesus.

The reclamation was a major media event. A religious leader by the name of Crescent Greenwillow led her disciples in an assault on Ephesus, took tour guides hostage at the archeological site, and sent word to the affronted Turkish government that the Goddess had reclaimed Her own. There was a minor international incident before, supposedly, a miracle happened. There were several versions of just what the miracle was supposed to have been, but nobody caught it on film.

Anyway, the Turks agreed to let the infidels stay, which was undeniably miraculous. Ephesus was given its own political status, as an independent zone not unlike the Vatican, in return for annual payments to Turkey that compensated them for lost tourist revenues.

The hoopla almost took the world's attention off the Second Civil War in America. The Ephesian Church (as it was now known) became very wealthy indeed, and fairly politically powerful too, within a few short years.

Almost immediately its leaders set about the restoration of the Temple of Artemis. To this end they employed the services of Lightning! A Company, a small firm based on an island off California. Lightning! A Company specialized in historical reconstructions of amazing detail, in authentic materials, with adaptations to suit modern taste and needs. Very shortly the temple was once again a wonder of the world, and the Ephesian Church settled down to a long reign marked only by the usual bitter quarrels, heresies, and internal dissent through which all major faiths struggle.

Any religion begins in a moment of transforming truth. That moment quickly shatters into falsehood and shame and stagecraft, bitter comedy, sometimes murder. Thieves catch hold of any chance for power. The early years of a faith are best not too closely examined by its faithful.

But with the passage of enough time, the lie becomes truth again, the broken mirror flows together as though it were liquid. The nasty commonplace facts erode away and leave the white marble bones of the myth, beautiful certainty beyond proof. If Ephesus was reborn by political audacity and clever computer graphics, it had become *now* the glorious city of antiquity where She walked breathing and granted hourly the prayers of Her daughters and sons.

So this is it.

This is the place, lad.

Vehicles were not permitted in the holy precinct, so Alec was striding the length of the processional way on foot. It crossed a fertile river plain coming down from mountains. The air was bright, and shimmered with heat above olive groves and orchards of nectarines, almonds, figs, vineyards of red and amber grapes. Blundering or flying sharp and straight across the wheatfields were the same golden bees that were depicted on the priests' robes.

The city below the hill was particolored, the white of new marble and the honey color of ancient marble. There was a hot wind coming down and it brought Alec the smell of fresh bread, of overripe melon from the food concessions, of incense from the temple. He passed pilgrims making the journey on their knees, inching painfully along over the hot stones. He passed vendors in long lines, portaging in their wares balanced on their shoulders: cases of images of the Goddess in every conceivable material, from pink plastic to pure gold. There were priests and priestesses in their patterned robes, leading the rows of neophyte children, boys and girls with their heads shaved, hair gone in their first sacrifice to Her.

Alec, raised in London, found it all like an erotic film: an insult to the rational mind but irresistibly compelling, calling up an echo in himself he didn't want to admit was there. What could they be *thinking*, those people burning their hands and knees on the pavement as they crawled along? And what would it be like to spend money on one of those cheap figures with its dozens of breasts like a bunch of grapes and believe, really believe, that it had the power to heal or come to him in dreams?

He found his way up to the temple without much trouble. It was unmistakable: a hundred and twenty-seven Ionic columns like trees in a stone grove and, in the deep shade at the back, massive golden doors. Everyone was going there. Long lines of people stretched between the columns, waiting with greater or lesser degrees of patience. Alec had no intention of waiting. He went straight up to the nearest priestess and stepped into her path.

"Excuse me, I've got an appointment to see Mother Cicely. I mailed her, okay? Can you tell me where she is?"

The priestess looked up at him. She didn't speak English very well, but she had caught the main import of what he'd said, so she took him by the hand and led him over to a compound that opened off from the main temple. "You go there," she said, and from a basket she carried, withdrew a carved rod of some purple wood. She put it in his hand. "Take that."

"Okay." Alec looked at it, looked after her as she hurried away from him. He squared his shoulders and went into the compound.

Inside he saw a desk at one end of a long corridor, with a priestess sitting there. He made for her, but at once threatening-looking priests converged upon him. They came close enough to see the purple rod he carried and veered off, apparently changing their minds. He grinned and walked on. Twice more along the corridor the same thing happened, priests darting out of alcoves to intercept him, stopped by the rod. The priestess at the desk watched the whole comedy with an ironical stare, folding her pale hands on her desk.

"Well, young man?" she said, when he finally reached her.

"I'm here to see Mother Cicely," Alec announced.

"Are you?" The priestess turned to her register and made an inquiry. After a moment it gave her an answer, and she turned back to Alec. "You'd be the earl of Finsbury? Very well. Through there, in the Epona chapel. Not with that!" she told him sharply, putting out her hand for the rod as he started forward. "You leave that here. Go, now. She's expecting you."

Alec relinquished the rod and went in cautiously, but no priests mobbed him. He found himself in a dim silent chapel. All was stillness, until his eyes grew accustomed to the light. Then he seemed to be in the midst of a stampede. The walls were done in an earth-dark stucco, and all around the room and up the curved ceiling ran mares in riot, in frenzied motion, manes flying, eyes wide, painted with such vivid detail he found himself stepping back involuntarily.

Trick of the light, son, that's all it is.

Yeah.

Alec steadied himself and focused on the actual space of the room. Nothing in there, really, except a pair of bronze censers smoking in two long plumes. No: now, stepping from the shadows, was a tall figure in a robe that fell in severe straight lines. He couldn't make out the face clearly in the gloom, and walked forward cautiously for a better view.

He had crossed half the space between them when he began to recognize her features. Memory came flooding back unbidden. Fine autocratic features, bones and skin of the best breeding, stern beautiful mouth, eyes as cold as the North Sea. *No, your Mummy's reading, don't you go bother her. Mummy's got a headache, leave her alone now, Alec. No, Mummy doesn't want to see what you drew, take it to Daddy. Let's just sit in here quiet, Alec, Mummy and Daddy are having a disagreement.* She smelled like electricity. And lavender. She always had.

"So you're Mother Cicely?" he said.

She looked at him calmly. "I am. You must be Alec Checkerfield. Let me make one thing clear to you now, Alec: I am not your mother."

"I'd guessed," he snapped.

"I mean that literally, Alec. We have no kinship at all." She studied him in a certain wonder. "Though now I can see why they thought the trick would work. You do—almost—look as though you might have been mine."

"What trick?" asked Alec.

"The one that brought you into this world." Cecelia lifted her head, her mouth scornful. "I bore some of the guilt, at least. I've been atoning for it every day of your life, Alec Checkerfield."

"Whose son am I?" Alec thundered.

"Elly Swain's," Cecelia said. Watching his reaction, she narrowed her eyes. "You've found out that much, haven't you? But not the whole story, or you wouldn't be here."

"Tell me." He advanced on her. She looked up at him, unperturbed.

"My, you're tall. Roger and I were as far from civilization as we could put ourselves, but even we heard about the Earth Hand kidnapping when it happened." She smiled thinly.

"I loved Roger Checkerfield. He was a kind man. We had a lovely life on that boat. I knew he was a weak man, too; I didn't care, then. He'd never told me much about his Company, but I gathered they were connected with the government and very powerful."

"Jovian Integrated Systems," said Alec bitterly. She gave him a thoughtful look.

"You're hunting them, aren't you? Well, well. In any case, when Elly's baby disappeared—they put out a hand and pulled Roger's strings. He told me we were going to be given an infant, and we had to pretend it was our own child. We'd been at sea, we hadn't seen anyone we'd known in months. Who'd know it wasn't true?

"I couldn't believe what I was hearing. I refused. And he told me I couldn't! He only hinted at the things that might happen if we disobeyed. I wanted the truth, and at last he broke down and admitted that we'd be raising Elly's baby. Why on earth would a Company with that kind of power interest itself in the affairs of a pop star?

"Roger couldn't explain. He kept saying there was nothing we could do, and if we gave the baby a better life than the one he'd have had with his natural parents, where was the harm?"

Where was the harm. Alec closed his eyes for a moment, hearing Roger before the cold educated voice swept on over his memory:

"So I went along with it, may She have mercy on me. I signed the damned agreement, swore to keep the lie. I'm violating that oath now. What do I care, after all this time? Let them try to come after me here! But I never saw Roger with the same eyes again.

"Can you wonder that I could never bring myself to touch you? I know it wasn't your fault, and I can't expect you to forgive me. But you had plenty of affection from everyone else on that boat."

"You pushed me away," said Alec in a thick voice. Cecelia shrugged.

"I'm sure you didn't miss me when I left. There was simply no point in continuing with the charade. Roger was miserable and, believe me, I was as miserable as he was. I came here and consecrated myself to a life of penance for what I'd done."

Cecelia had rehearsed that speech a thousand times over the years. What a feeling of release now, what a weight was gone! She tilted her head slightly, watching the effect of her words on the man. He'd gone very pale; all that high color had just fled from his face.

"What happened to her? To, to—Elly?" Alec asked.

"She never recovered from what they did to her. She'd been a little slow before, you see. After you were born, she just went away to another planet. It's a happy place. I have that much consolation: she at least has stopped suffering."

"Where is she?"

Cecelia considered him.

"I'll take you to her," she said at last. "I don't think you can do her any harm now."

She led him out of the Epona chapel through a curtained alcove, across a quiet garden. Somewhere there was the staccato chanting of contralto voices, a vaguely frightening sound in that peaceful place; but it grew fainter as they emerged onto a wide lawn.

There was a croquet game in progress there. Half a dozen girls in white were scrambling about clumsily after wooden balls, watched by reserved-looking women in blue robes. One or two of the girls wandered by themselves or sat on the grass rocking to and fro. Alec realized with a start that they weren't girls, but damaged women. One grimaced uncontrollably, another's laugh was far too shrill and constant; another staggered like a baby just learning to walk.

The women in blue were clearly their attendants. One approached now, questioning Cecelia with her eyes.

"Will you bring Sister Heliotrope, please?" said Cecelia. "She has a visitor."

The attendant glided away and returned a moment later with one of the more enthusiastic players, gently relieving her of her croquet mallet as they approached. She protested, but only until she spotted Cecelia. She ran forward and hugged her gleefully.

"Mother Cicely! Nice seein' ya!"

Cecelia hugged her back, apparently with genuine affection. Alec stared. He looked at the plain round face, imagining it with the garish makeup of the 'twenties, trying to see the horrified girl of the news footage. Not this smiling creature with her blank china-blue eyes. She looked nothing like him at all.

"Heliotrope, dear, this man has come to see you," Cecelia told her. Elly turned to notice Alec and looked away, taking two little sideways steps to put distance between them, like a well-behaved animal avoiding a noisy child.

"Too busy," she muttered.

"Now, dear, be nice. He's come a long way. Let's go sit in the shade, shall we?" Cecelia led them to a bench and sat down with them. "There we are. I won't go away, dear, it's all right. Did you have anything to say to her, Alec?"

Alec reached out to take Elly's hand. She looked at it with an unreadable expression.

"I—I just—Are you okay here?"

"Yeh," Elly said.

"Are you happy?"

"Always 'appy, ain't I?" Elly grinned, showing gappy little teeth. "Lucky me!"

Her voice was still young, her accent that of the London clubs where the bands had played and the kids had danced, a million miles from this place she'd come to.

Alec blinked back tears. "I wanted you to know—how sorry I am about the bad stuff that happened, and—and to let you know your baby didn't die. He was safe the whole time. He turned out okay."

"Oh, yeh, I knew that, din't I?" Elly nodded rapidly. "No aggro on that. No way Jose! All okay, you know why?"

"Er . . . why?"

" 'Cos, ain't I had 'im just after Christmas? I was this virgin, see. Poor old Tommy never did it at all. I thought we was doing it and then the doctor and the police was going, you know, questions questions questions and it turned out we wasn't doing it after all only I didn't know better 'cos I'm so dumb. Not that dumb! I know you don't get no baby from not doing it. So I was scared it was like in that Ultimate Evil game with the Devil and all. An' then the Forces of Darkness stole'm away."

"Don't argue with her," Cecelia told Alec quietly.

"An' it all came to little pieces and I was cryin' so bad. But then I got into the Goddess and everything was really cool. They told me the story, see? They're all, a virgin has this baby at Solstice and 'e's the child of light, and the bad guys take 'im away from 'er and she's really sad, goes to jail. I was in jail. But then, 'e's really okay, see? Because 'e ain't dead. 'E never dies. And then the virgin is so happy. And I knew that was my story, see? It's all about me! Me and my child of light."

Alec caught his breath. Out of the unwanted memories seeping up came a Christmas party, at least Sarah had told him it was a kind of Christmas party, when he'd been so tiny-winji he hadn't known there were any other children in the world, and then there were lots of them, black like Sarah, and he was with them around a tree trunk where there was a party for them all with cake . . . and the old black man bowing his head for them to pat his hair, and the black people smiling and clapping their hands and singing about the children of light. Sarah carrying him back to the harbor, sugar-sticky and sleepy, telling him he was her little child of light. It had been a sweet memory; suddenly it chilled him.

"Oh," said Alec. "Well—I'm really happy for you, then."

"That's 'im up there." Elly jerked her thumb at the sun. "See 'im? I can see 'im any time I like. Sun my son. Son my sun! Ain't 'e neat?"

"Yeah." Alec looked away, wishing he hadn't come.

"Just *looks* like 'e dies every night. Not really."

"No, of course not."

" 'E didn't die! Not my baby, not my poor little tiny baby—"

"Heliotrope, they're having lots of fun over there," said Cecelia. "Why don't you go back to play? I think we've had a long enough talk, don't you?"

"Okay," said Elly, and leaped up and ran away unsteadily. Alec sat staring after her. Cecelia watched him, and after a moment she said:

"Do you have any idea why they did it, Alec?"

"No," he said. "But I'm going to find out."

"I always wondered, you see . . . Roger mentioned once that there was a division of his company that did some kind of genetic work. And that awful man did swear you weren't his child, I mean really past the point where it made sense. He'd have had much less trouble if he'd just admitted to it and paid his fines."

"Yeah."

"And there was something different about you, Alec." Cecelia shook her head. "There's something different about you still."

There's something different, all right.

Alec shuddered violently. "You don't think—there wasn't some weird sick cultist agenda or anything, was there?"

"A religious one, you mean? At Jovian Integrated Systems?" Cecelia looked contemptuous. "Not if Roger was any example. He believed in nothing. Life was easier for him that way."

"And they've never done anything with me! Nobody ever told me what I was or why I wasn't like everybody else. I've had to figure it out for myself," Alec cried.

"Perhaps they've simply been watching you, to see what you'd do," Cecelia suggested. "Just how are you different, Alec?"

"I've got a couple of, er, talents," Alec said uncomfortably. "I've done real well for myself in the world, as a matter of fact. But nothing I can do is worth what happened to the rest of you." He turned to Cecelia.

"Listen to me. Jovian Integrated Systems doesn't exist anymore. They were bought up by this even bigger company that calls itself Dr. Zeus Incorporated. I'm going after them. If anybody who's responsible for me is still alive, I'll find him, or her, or it."

Cecelia gazed on him, a strange expression in her cold eyes.

"You're a *good* man," she said at last, as though she couldn't quite believe what she was saying. She rose to stand before him and, placing both hands on his shoulders in a formal gesture, leaned down to kiss him between his eyes. He was amazed.

"Be careful," she told him. "They were powerful then; Roger was frightened to death of them. They're probably a lot more powerful now.

Don't think they don't know exactly where you are. They must have kept people close to you your whole life, observing you."

"Maybe." Alec stood, looming over her. "But there's something they don't know." He took one of her hands in both of his and shook it awkwardly. "I'd better go now. Good-bye, Cecelia. I'm glad I got a chance to talk to you, after all these years."

"Good-bye, Alec," Cecelia said. "Good hunting."

It was not a gentle Goddess she served.

He just nodded and walked away.

When he had gone, she climbed the hill behind the garden and stood looking down on the temple and the grand processional way that led out to the sea. After a while she spotted him, taller than any other traveler, walking back to the harbor where his ship lay at anchor. She watched until he had disappeared with distance, praying to her Goddess, not certain what she was feeling.

I knew it! I knew all along you weren't no freak. Yer a deliberate favorable mutation, Alec lad, you must be, specially bred. J. I. S. meant you to be the bloody wonder boy you are! Alec could almost hear the Captain's boots clattering on the ancient pavement as he danced for joy.

Oh, yeah? You reckon they had any idea what their wonder boy was going to do to them, when he found out how he was made?

Not a whit, I'd wager. They never counted on me, did they? Oh, laddie, the revenge we're gonna take. Blood and hellfire! Loot for years. But the lady was right—we go into this slow, see? We ain't doing a thing without a perfect plan, and a perfect backup plan, and a backup plan to that. We takes our time. No risks. You let me do the reconnoitering first.

Then start your planning. Find out everything you can about these bastards, do whatever you have to do. We're gonna wreck 'em.

That's my boy.

. . . Sarah couldn't have known about it, could she? She wasn't in the pay of J. I. S.

Mm. Why, no, matey, certain she wasn't. Don't you worry none about her. We've work to do! And to think it was only the other day you was moping about having no purpose to yer life.

Well, I've got one now, haven't I?

Alec marched down to the harbor and went aboard his ship. Her anchor was weighed, her sails were set. Under his black ensign he sailed out into the Ionian Sea, and laid in a course for Jamaica.

THE YEAR 2351:

MEETING

Rutherford was in a daring mood. He had poured himself a glass of the apple-prune compound and swaggered over to the window with it, pretending it was sherry. It might be, for all any passing public health monitor knew. He was rather disappointed when the minutes stretched by without a soul coming into Albany Crescent, and wondered peevishly if the Westminster surveillance cameras were working properly.

At last he spotted Chatterji and Ellsworth-Howard rounding the corner, and waved at them. Ellsworth-Howard waved back. Chatterji, who was looking troubled, just nodded.

"Yo heave ho, fellows," said Rutherford as he opened the door. "Have you seen the *Adonai* sequence update yet?"

"Only just got mine," said Ellsworth-Howard. "Haven't had the shracking time to look at it."

"Well, you are in for a treat." Rutherford practically danced across the room to his chair. "I've been gloating over it all morning. Our man is a hero after all, chaps. A dashing, daring rogue in the classic mode! Wait till you see the holoes."

"I'm concerned about a few things," said Chatterji. "The committee's not happy about them either, Rutherford."

"They don't understand him," said Rutherford dismissively. "Our man's a genius, isn't it obvious? And you were so concerned that he'd modified your design, Foxy! Er—that is—it's clearly worked out for the best, hasn't it? Because it's made him even more brilliant than his previous two sequences. You should see what he's done with his wonderful brain now that he's got it cyborged."

"Such as?" Ellsworth-Howard said sullenly, settling into his armchair.

"Well, he's built up the modest fortune the late earl left him into a fabulous economic empire, and concealed it so the petty bureaucrats don't tax him to death. Isn't that so, Chatty?"

"Yes, it is," said Chatterji, sinking into the chair opposite. "Although . . . did you notice that trust fund he set up to benefit the Ephesians last year? You don't suppose he's turned religious again, do you?"

"Shracking hell," Ellsworth-Howard cried.

"Nothing of the sort," said Rutherford. "I'll tell you exactly why he did that. Our programming! He tracked down the former Lady Checkerfield, the one he thinks is his mother. She's an Ephesian priestess now. He's still trying to atone for having caused his parents' divorce, you see?"

"So you think he's attempting to buy her forgiveness?" Chatterji took out his nasal inhalator. Rutherford smirked.

"You may have noticed that he named *her* the administrator of the trust fund. But you certainly don't see him having the operation and donning any purple robes himself, not our boy."

"No, that's true. He's something of a libertine," said Chatterji.

"But one with a social conscience," said Rutherford, jumping to his feet and strutting up and down before the fire. "In a proper secular way. Look at this renegade club he's joined, all those young gentlemen dedicating their lives to fighting perceived injustice everywhere. There's a lot more to the seventh earl of Finsbury than we originally thought!"

"The committee had some rather sharp words about all his illegal activities, Rutherford, I must tell you," said Chatterji, bracing himself with a deep drag.

"Pooh. He's simply fulfilling his program in the only way possible, in this wretched day and age," said Rutherford. "What scope is there nowadays for a hero? So he belongs to that particular group of lawbreakers. They're only educated fellows who object to this absurd restricted life we're all obliged to lead. Not all that different from us, really."

"He shracking well ain't like *me*," said Ellsworth-Howard gloomily.

"Oh, chaps, you're missing the point," Rutherford said, going to the sideboard and pouring out a couple of glasses of pretend sherry. He brought them back and handed one each to his friends. "He's obedient to a higher law. He rebels because he needs to play a more active role in history. We put that need in him, didn't we, we sub-creators?"

"You're right," said Chatterji, brightening. "After all, in the last sequence he committed any number of—er—outright crimes. But he did obey his handlers without question. Yes, that puts a much more positive spin on it."

"You see?" said Rutherford. "The only thing wanting now is to get him in for a visit with a Company recruiter. After all, we know he's a kindred spirit."

"How d'you reckon?" Ellsworth-Howard said.

"Just access those holoes and you'll see," Rutherford told him, and sipped his drink as Ellsworth-Howard took out the buke and squeezed in a request. The little projector arm shot up, unfolded its disc and sent out its beam of golden light. A moment later the *Captain Morgan* appeared in the midst of the room, under full sail, caught in the sunlight of a Caribbean morning.

"Ooh," said Ellsworth-Howard, and even Chatterji, who had already seen the report, smiled. Rutherford just nodded.

"There now! Can you wonder he prefers to live aboard that, and not in some dismal urban hive with public health monitors dogging his every step?"

"That is so cool," moaned Ellsworth-Howard. "Look at the pirate flag!"

"Though I should mention that the committee found the flag in poor taste," said Chatterji reluctantly.

"Oh, shrack them."

"Offended their sensibilities, did he?" Rutherford said, casually leaning over the back of his chair. "Personally, I'm delighted with him. This is a true Briton, by God, this is the sort of fellow we used to have in this country. Like Drake! Like—well—all those other seafaring heroes and, er, daring explorers. Imagine what misfits they'd have been nowadays."

"You have a point there," admitted Chatterji. Rutherford tossed back a slug of pretend sherry with reckless abandon.

"We're of the same breed, you know. Look at us, dreaming of tea and sherry and pipe tobacco. Haven't you ever wanted to smuggle chocolates in your suitcase when you're coming back from a trip to the Celtic Federation?"

Chatterji started and looked around involuntarily. "I say, now, Rutherford—"

"Well, of course we'd never do it," lied Rutherford, blushing, "but we'd like to! And *he* does. The life we sit around dreaming about, he goes out and actually *lives*. Look at the other images. Go on."

Ellsworth-Howard found the ship so beautiful he could have stared at her for hours, but he squeezed in his request reluctantly. The

Captain Morgan vanished, to be replaced with a holo of Alec pacing along a quay on some Caribbean waterfront. The background was dreamy as a travelog: green palm jungle and stately pink mansions, flowering mandevillea vines, a shell merchant holding up a queen conch with his smile very white in his black face, a blue and gold macaw perched on his shoulder. Alec wore his customary brilliant tropical shirt, ragged dungaree trunks, and sandals. The only thing out of place in the picture was the box he was carrying, which bore the logo of an electronics shop.

"Blimey," said Ellsworth-Howard. "Imagine being able to get away to places like that! I could never make the trip, though. I get motion sick."

"The humidity would get to me, I'm afraid." Chatterji shook his head longingly. "And the microbes in the drinking water. And the pollen count."

"Me, too," said Rutherford. "To say nothing of the UV levels. Look at him, though, all ruddy from the weather. *He's* not afraid of the sun."

"What's that box?" Ellsworth-Howard peered at it. "Is that from Abramovitch's? Do they have Abramovitch's out there?"

"I expect those are components for his marvelous cybersystem," said Rutherford. "He appears to have hookups to weather surveillance satellites and coordinates them with whole libraries of three-dimensional charts, all in his head. He runs that entire ship completely by himself. All those sails and the, uh, ropes and things. That's what he can do with that brain of his, Foxy. You ought to be proud."

"Maybe I am, at that," said Ellsworth-Howard, ordering up the next image. It had been taken at night, in some club. Alec, resplendent in evening dress, sat at a table. He was in languid conversation with a girl. Her eyes had widened at something he'd just said to her. He was smiling, making some point with a gesture, and the girl looked enthralled. On the table before them were two tall drinks, wildly overdecorated with paper parasols and orchids.

The three friends regarded the image in silence for a long, long moment.

"See? That sex drive wasn't such a bad idea. I'll bet he don't half get the girls," said Ellsworth-Howard at last. "Lucky sod."

"I should imagine he's wildly successful in that line," said Rutherford airily. "Girl in every port and all that sort of thing. Learned better than to marry them. Keeps it all sensibly impersonal."

"I think we've edited out any disastrous urges for intimacy," Chatterji agreed. "Doesn't he look splendid in that suit! What a pity he dresses so badly the rest of the time."

"He needs a few endearing flaws, don't you think?" said Rutherford. "It just shows he's not vain about himself. Real heroes don't care about things like that."

Ellsworth-Howard summoned the next image.

"This was almost my favorite one, really," said Rutherford. Alec was walking along a street, against a background of fields and distant orchards. "This was taken by the Facilitator resident in Ephesus, as our man was leaving. Look at his expression. Bold, determined, dangerous!"

"He don't look happy, anyhow," said Ellsworth-Howard.

"By Jove, I'd hate to cross the fellow," said Chatterji. "The committee had certain concerns about this visit, Rutherford. Nasty bit of coincidence. It seems that not only is the former Lady Checkerfield living at that mother house, but the place has a hospital ward, and one of its inmates is Elly Swain."

Rutherford started.

"I say! I really think we do have some sort of Mandelbrot operating here. No harm done, at least. He can't have found out about her. And, you know, this is one of the hazards of operating in real time. Less direct control."

"That's just the point the committee made," said Chatterji.

"Yes, but I think we've more than compensated for the setback when—well, you know." Rutherford was referring to the fact that all of the initial data on the third sequence had been lost when Ellsworth-Howard's buke had been spiked. It had resulted in a gap in Company surveillance on the project between the years 2326–2336, when Alec had been well into his higher education.

Rutherford hopped up and began to pace nervously. "The fact that our man's done this well with minimal guidance just shows how sound our methods were. He's an unqualified success, if you want my opinion. Yes, we should draft some sort of statement to that effect for the committee, don't you think? Mission accomplished?"

"It's early days yet," said Chatterji. "If he can be brought into the Company fold, perhaps then we can talk about unqualified successes."

"Oh, bother." Rutherford pouted.

"I was wondering about something," said Ellsworth-Howard. "This has been a lot more complicated than making up the old Enforcers. All this special fostering and guilt complexes and handlers and all?"

"For a much more complex product," said Rutherford.

"Yeah, but with the Enforcers, you could just raise 'em in the base schools and put 'em straight into the army, and they worked. These heroes, or whatever the shrack you're gonna call 'em, are they gonna have to be spoon-fed everything like the prototype has been? 'Cos you're getting into a logistical nightmare if they are," Ellsworth-Howard pointed out. "Think of all those foster homes."

"No, no, of course we'll streamline the process when we start mass-producing them," Rutherford said. "Don't forget we'll be able to program the new fellows directly because they'll be biomechanicals. If Tolkien had been given this project, what would he have done? Think of a marvelous School of Heroes, much more Socratic, less militaristic than the old Enforcer training camps."

"Yes, I like the sound of that," said Chatterji thoughtfully. "What to do with our prototype, though? Won't we have to tell him the nasty truth about himself?"

"Of course. And I daresay he'll be surprised, but how on earth could he be anything but grateful to us?" Rutherford waved dismissively. "With that magnificent health and intelligence, to say nothing of that ship, that wealth, all those adventures in exotic places? Why, it's a wonderful life!"

Alec Visits the Doctor

Though he had sworn he'd never set foot in the Bloomsbury house again, all dust, echoes, and palpable misery as it was, Alec stood in its parlor now.

He was overseeing the workmen who were bringing in new furniture and carpets. Alec had decided to redecorate the house himself.

It seemed like a properly stupid-aristocrat thing to do—fuss about new furniture and wallpaper in a place he never visited—and anyway the pale yellow mid-twentieth-century revival stuff he'd had before reminded him of Lorene.

Over the past few months he'd made a great public show of his new interest in buying antiques, spending outrageous sums of money on acquisitions of widely varying quality. Many of them were hideous, if authentic. Some—sadly, the more tasteful ones—were obvious fakes. All hope of bringing grace to any room they might occupy was dashed by Alec's planned color scheme, which featured lots of purple and gold. Balkister, horrified after a virtual tour through the plans, told him it looked like what Disneycorp might produce if it ever decided to build a whorehouse in Fantasyland.

Alec was pleased. The stupider it looked, the better. He had no intention of living there.

The house was, in fact, a trap; or would be when he'd finished with it. He'd spent weeks fitting components into certain of the antiques he'd bought. Some were merely backup systems, if virtually undetectable, for the considerable security system Alec already had in place. Some were rather more than that.

There was a Louis Quatorze chair with concealed sensors sharp enough to allow it to monitor the transmissions originating from the building around the corner in Theobalds Road, the Gray's Inn extension that Alec had discovered was owned by Dr. Zeus Incorporated, in its persona of Olympian Technologies. There was a suit of gilded thirteenth-century armor that was similarly rigged to monitor the British Museum, another hotbed of Company activity. There was a heavyset bronze nymph holding aloft an ostrich egg that would, at need, jam the transmissions from the monitor the Company had concealed within the statue of Sir Francis Bacon at Gray's Inn. As Alec had uncovered more and more evidence of the Company's presence in his life, his determination to bring them down had increased. So had his paranoia.

He was especially proud of the system he'd designed to tag and track intruders. In San Francisco he'd found a twenty-first-century aromatherapy dispenser, a massive lump of hollowed amethyst with a hulking gilded cherub mounted above it. It was stupefyingly ugly, but nobody could deny it went with his color scheme, and now it did much more than its original work of misting fragrance into the air from the reservoir inside the amethyst while soothing chimes tinkled.

Now, there was a brain of sorts behind the cherub's staring eyes. Once it was mounted over the fanlight in the entryway, it knew it was to watch for anyone entering through the door below. If it observed anyone who wasn't Alec, or accompanied by Alec, it would part its fat lips and blow out a steady spray of scented microdroplets, sending them wafting down on the unwanted visitors. The perfume was an unusual one. Alec had compounded it himself, so it was unique in that sense, but it also contained millions of nanobots designed to permanently embed themselves in anything they encountered.

Not terribly deeply, and when they were in an intruder's skin all they'd do would be to release more of the perfume, in tiniest increments over a period of years. Nanobot technology was too jealously guarded by its principal developer—Dr. Zeus Incorporated—for Alec to be able to get them to do much more, but once the intruder was tagged, Alec would be able to pick up his or her scent anywhere.

The cherub also whistled "Lilliburlero." There was no hidden purpose there; Alec simply liked the tune.

Now Alec watched the workmen impatiently, wishing they'd hurry up. Not a wall, not a floor or window but reminded him of dead time.

He still wasn't sure just what he was. Perhaps Dr. Zeus had been experimenting with disease-resistant humanoids; he'd never had so much as a head cold in his life.

Most likely the Company was even now aware of his every move, might know he was planning to broadside it and do as much damage as he could. And if it was able to stop him? If somebody, somewhere, was able to press a button that would terminate the Alec experiment? Probably a damned good idea, on the whole.

Boyo, this house is bad for you. Yer depressed. Yer blood sugar's low. Eat something, for Christ's sake! I told you you should have had breakfast afore the car came.

Shut up, responded Alec, but he groped in his coat pocket and found a carob-peanut-fig bar. He was unwrapping it when one of the workmen peered into the room apologetically.

"My lord? Where would you like this?" He held up a vividly enameled solid brass representation of Queen Victoria in a howdah atop an elephant's back. Its only function was to offend the eye.

"Over there," Alec told him, gesturing at a gilded table under the front window.

"In the window, my lord?" The man looked pained. "Where it can be seen?"

"Do it! No problem, okay?" Alec took a bite of the carob-peanut-fig bar. It was very hard, very dry, and tasted like hay. His pocket communicator shrilled. He exhaled in impatience and opened the call. "Checkerfield," he growled, chewing laboriously.

"Is that Alec Checkerfield?" inquired a vaguely familiar voice on the other side of his tympanum.

"Yeah. Who's this?"

"My God, you're a hard man to connect with."

"Try *Burke's Peerage* next time. Who is this?"

"It's Blaise! Tilney Blaise, Checkerfield."

Alec had a blank second before he connected the memory. He gulped down his mouthful of carob-peanut-fig. "Hey, man, how's it going?" he said, with simulated heartiness. "Haven't seen you since, what, commencement?"

"It's been that long, I think," said Blaise.

"Well, well."

"I'm doing very nicely these days, actually," continued Blaise. "I'm working in California now. Just flew across for some business in the London offices and I thought—well, I just thought I'd sound you out on something. See if you're interested. Still coaxing that cybersystem of yours to jump through hoops for you?"

Alec smiled at the mental image, while the Captain snorted indignantly. "Sort of. I'm only here for a month or so myself, actually. I spend most of the year in the Caribbean."

"What luck I got through to you, then. Listen, why don't we meet for lunch somewhere? Have you been to Club Kosmetas yet?"

"Er—no."

"It's in the Marylebone Road. Quite *très très*. Great Greek food. Say half an hour?"

Alec winced. Greek cuisine in a country where lamb, feta, and retsina were all illegal wasn't his idea of dining.

"Well—"

"I'm awfully keen on telling you about this place I'm at. Dr. Zeus, Incorporated. Perhaps you've heard of them?"

There was a heartbeat's silence and then Alec made a thoughtful sound. "You know, I think I might have. Don't they do some kind of consulting?" The Captain materialized beside him and pulled a cutlass from midair. Grinning evilly, he took out a whetstone and began to sharpen his blade.

"Something like that."

"Okay," said Alec in a bright voice. "See you there, then. Half an hour."

He paused just long enough to give orders to the workmen and then bounded down the front steps of the house, tossing his unfinished carob-peanut-fig bar into the gutter as he went (and thereby violating several municipal regulations). He jumped lightly into the car and switched on the motor. Whistling "Lilliburlero" between his teeth, Alec zoomed away in the direction of the Marylebone Road.

We ain't ready to take 'em yet, son.

Oh, I know. We'll play it cool.

Cool as the polar ice, my lad. What d'you reckon this Blaise is one of their observers, one of the ones Cecelia warned you about? They must know you went to see her. They must be wondering how much you know.

And I don't know a damn thing, not me. He can do all the talking.

Club Kosmetas was a long narrow place, occupying what had been a row of small shopfronts back when trade had been rather brisker in Britain. Now connecting doors had been punched through, and the walls had been painted a dark yellow and decorated with neon representations of Greek cultural icons, such as the restored Acropolis and the Winged Victory of Samothrace. The tables were small and packed into each room, making it difficult for someone Alec's size to edge his way through. The place was nearly deserted. He could see Blaise rising from a table three rooms in, smiling and waving. Cursing under his breath, he smiled and waved back, continuing his crabwise progress between the tables.

"My lord." Blaise half-bowed.

"Yeah, hi." Alec reached out to shake his hand. "Wow, it's been ages, hasn't it?"

Alec! God almighty, the man's a cyborg!

You mean he's had a job like mine done?

No!

"The Circle of Thirty," said Blaise reminiscently. "Would you ever have thought you'd look back on those days as simple and uncomplicated?"

"Nope, never." Alec kept a bland smile in place, though he tilted his head and inhaled deeply. Blaise smelled human . . . and slightly nervous.

"I . . . er . . . I was going through some things in storage just the other day. I found the costume I wore at the swing gaskell at McCartney Hall," said Blaise. "Remember that night?"

"Yeah." Alec winced.

"The night Lord Howard caught us all on the catwalk with the gin," said Blaise, as though he remembered it fondly. "You'll never guess what I found in one of the pockets." He reached inside his coat and slowly brought out the silver flask. "I cleaned it up a bit. Thought you'd probably want it back."

"Oh, shrack, that was Roger's," said Alec, staring. It was a moment before he could stretch out his hand to take it. "Thanks, man."

It's bait. He wants you to feel you owe him. Alec, this ain't a human being!

Alec suppressed a shudder as Blaise leaned back from the table, adjusting the fit of his coat, smoothing his lapels.

"We were worried about you—Balkister and I, you know—and all I could think to do was get it away from you, so you wouldn't be caught with it." Blaise gave a rueful chuckle. "But I wasn't entirely sober myself that night, and then the catwalk came down, and I lost my nerve and scarpered. Took off the costume when I finally crawled home and never had occasion to wear it again. Those were the days, eh?"

"Memories, all right," agreed Alec, reflecting that his most vivid ones were of stealthy sex and miserable hangovers. He wondered what sort of memories the thing at table with him had.

"I'm afraid I've lost touch with most of the old circle, though." Blaise settled back into his seat and gestured to the waiter, who brought them two goblets of chilled mineral water. "You ever see anybody nowadays?"

He's some kind of machine . . . he's got organic components, though. In fact he's mostly organic over a ferroceramic skeleton. I think he was human once.

Alec smiled, though he felt the hair standing on the back of his neck, and shook his head. "Nobody, except old Balkister. He's needed cash a few times. I've made some donations to his causes. Probably they went to pay his rent, but . . ." *Is this the same guy from my Circle of Thirty, or some kind of robot?*

"He was such a brilliant boy, too." Blaise looked sad.

It's the same man. My sensors weren't as sharp back then, or I'd have noticed what I'm picking up now. Look at him, Alec. He still looks twenty, he ain't changed.

"Balkister? About a billion times smarter than me," said Alec, with his best idiot-aristo grin. "He's kept that youthful glow, anyway. You're looking pretty damned good yourself, yeah? You must live a trouble-free life."

Did Blaise look just a little self-conscious? He picked up his menu and fiddled with it. "It's the carrageenan-aloe packs. You wouldn't believe what they do for your skin. But what about you? I hear you're mostly living on your boat, nowadays."

"Ship." **Ship!**

"Yes, of course, sorry. You've decided to follow in your father's footsteps, I suppose?"

"No, not exactly." *Can he tell you're with me?*

I don't think so. Yer being monitored pretty close, though. Steady, lad.

Diffidently Alec picked up his menu and thumbed it, letting the column of entrees chatter suggestions at him while he calmed himself. Eggplant-walnut moussaka with soy feta? Lentil kebabs? White grape juice "unsweetened, with the faintest kiss of the authentic balsamic resin"? He had a sudden memory of Blaise, leaping from the falling catwalk, landing with perfect poise. The silly tabloids were always warning about cyborg monsters. Cold, flawless, machine-powered supermen, certain to take over the world if they were ever created . . . and here was one sitting across the table.

Shrack, Dr. Zeus could have hundreds of these things running around spying for them. And they look just like us!

What d'you mean, US? Keep yer sense of perspective, son.

"My father just sort of drifted," Alec said. "I don't think he ever got over his divorce. I've had two so far and couldn't be happier about 'em. Bye-bye baby, talk to my solicitor!" He cackled like a moron and Blaise laughed with him.

"I'm glad to hear that, anyway. We all felt terrible for you when the sixth earl was killed. I can remember it as though it were yesterday."

Blaise shook his head. "I thought you'd gone crazy. Of course, I don't think I'd be able to cope if I suddenly found myself orphaned like that."

"Well, but I wasn't, exactly," Alec said, adjusting the volume on his menu. "Mummy-dear's still alive, you know. Not that the cold bitch ever sent me a condolence card or anything. I tried to go and see her a few months ago, actually. She wasn't having any. Well, shrack her, I said to myself."

"Oh, that's too bad," Blaise said. "Trying to put the past behind you, effect a reconciliation, that sort of thing?"

"Yeah. No use." Alec shrugged, setting the menu aside. "Can't win 'em all."

"I gather you're just sort of touring around, living on your investments?"

"Pretty much."

"I felt sure you'd go on to Mars." Blaise sat back, shaking his head. "There was always something about you, Checkerfield! Something that promised more, I don't know, *ability* than the rest of us. You were such a genius in systems. You've never gone on to do anything with that, have you?"

"I have, too. You should see what I've spent on customizing my personal setup." Alec grinned toothily, lounging back in his chair. He made himself look into Blaise's eyes and wink, though his skin was crawling. "It does everything I need it to. All I ask is a tall ship and a ton of cash to sail her with, you know? It makes sure there's always enough ice for my drinks, too."

At this point the waiter edged up to them and set down a dish of olives. Alec ordered the moussaka and Blaise complimented him on his choice, ordering the same. When the waiter had departed, he said:

"But was this really what you wanted to do with your life, Checkerfield? Wasn't there a time when you thought you could ask for more than money and creature comforts? I'd have thought you'd got restless with all that by now."

He's about to make his pitch. Listen hard.

Aye aye. "Maybe." Alec shrugged again. "But what else is there? Sitting in on a social administration committee with Elvis Churchill? No, thanks. Not when the Caribbean is one big party, man."

"There's the private sector, you know," Blaise said. "Some of them are up to some pretty exciting things."

Here it comes.

"Like the people you work for, for instance?" Alec sampled an olive. Rich, bitter, complex flavors. Oil-cured.

"Yes, actually."

"On the way over here I was remembering what I'd heard about 'em. Some kind of story that they'd come up with a time machine or something. Totally nuts. They don't really have a time machine, do they, like in that holo? That would be cool."

"I'll tell you this much, they're on to some stuff that's nearly as incredible," Blaise said, looking terribly sincere. "They're the people who are going to shape our future, Checkerfield, take it from me. And they treat their creative people awfully well. I mean, the salaries and benefits are super, but the best part of the job is the sheer adventure. The opportunity to benefit humanity in ways you couldn't even imagine. I'm happier than I've ever been."

"Sounds like a lot of fun," Alec said cautiously.

"It is. Look, shall I come to the point? They need talent. I thought of you at once. Hey, I know you're not the man to put on a suit every day and report to a desk; but it's not like that, Checkerfield, trust me. It's what you can do with that incredible genius of yours they're interested in, not how well you do interdepartmental politics. I think you'd really enjoy working there."

How's he know you've got an incredible genius?

Everybody knew my test scores. All the same . . .

"I don't know, man, I'm pretty happy on my ship." Alec ate another olive. "Parties. Women. Plenty of fun I can't get here, know what I mean?" He winked again but couldn't bring himself to nudge Blaise.

"Well, did I mention Dr. Zeus is on an island in the Pacific? You wouldn't have to change your lifestyle at all," Blaise told him, settling back and lifting his glass.

Right. He's made his bid. Pretend to take the bait.

"Which one?" Alec looked intrigued.

"Santa Catalina," Blaise said. "Tiny independent republic off California."

"No kidding?" Alec sat back too as the waiter brought their orders. "I know where that is. Nice climate out there. Well, I might be interested after all."

"Fabulous," said Blaise, raising his glass. "They have an office here in London, did I mention? Oh, Checkerfield, I've got a really good feeling about this. Here's to a successful career at Dr. Zeus for milord!"

"Hey ho," Alec said, lifting his glass in a toast too. *And yo ho ho, you mechanical bastard.*

One week later he was shown into a waiting area, in the plushest office he'd ever seen in a lifetime of dealing with expensive legal counsel. No sooner had one very pretty girl directed him to an antique chair than another very pretty girl brought a tray of tea things, all antique Wedgwood, virtually kneeling before him to offer it. No cream or sugar, of course, and the tea was hibiscus-chamomile; but Dr. Zeus was doing its best to give him the royalty treatment. He accepted a cup of the thin sour stuff and gave the girl his most charming smile.

"Thanks, babe," he said. She blushed and stammered:

"Mr. Wolff will be with you in no time, my lord. He didn't want to keep you waiting at all. He was really so awfully impressed with your application!"

"Well, let's hope I pass the test." Alec leaned forward conspiratorially and let his voice drop to its most seductive purr. "Is it a tough test, do you think? D'you reckon I've got a chance at all, love?"

"Oh, I'm sure you have," the girl said, staring into his eyes. He inhaled her scent. *She* was human. He held her gaze, persuading just a little, and said:

"You really think so? Then if I do pass, what would you say—"

"Ms. Fretsch?" The fine paneled door was opened by a solidly built man in a suit of elegant and formal cut. She squeaked and rose to her feet in one graceful movement, bearing the tray up with scarcely a rattle of crockery. Alec watched her fleeing back regretfully, then turned his attention to the man in the doorway.

He's another one, boyo, damn near as much a machine as me, and he's scanning you. Steady.

Alec smiled at the man, who was staring at him intently with cold gray eyes. The man smiled back, however, and thrust out his hand.

"My lord! Delighted to meet you at last. How are you this morning?"

Alec set down his tea and rose to shake the man's hand. It felt human. The man wasn't sweating at all, nor did he smell nervous.

"Hi. I'm fine, thanks. You?"

"Very well indeed. Miguel Wolff, at your service, my lord. May I offer you a seat in my private office?" He gestured and stepped aside to reveal the inner sanctum. Alec accepted his offer, wary as he crossed the threshold, but no alarms sounded and no guards seized him.

If the other room had been full of antiques, this one was an absolute museum. With the exception of the electronics console, not one other piece of furniture in the room was less than a century old. Well, no; the intricate oriental carpet on the floor was new, to judge from its

plush pile and depth. Made of wool, too, from the smell, and wool was
outrageously illegal nowadays! Alec settled into a very comfortable
chair and looked around.

*I count five surveillance cameras. Concealed door behind that
panel. Nobody hidden there, though.*

"Now, of course we've done some preliminary research on you, my
lord," said Wolff, going to a sideboard of dark oak. Ranged along its top
were several decanters of gleaming crystal. "Just for form's sake." He
poured out a glass of something intensely red and turned with it. "We
like to familiarize ourselves with the tastes of our creative men, as we
find it facilitates the working relationship. I trust you'll appreciate the
mutual confidence in a glass of claret?" He bowed and offered the glass
to Alec.

Alec inhaled. No drugs or poisons; even a decent vintage. Safe
enough. He accepted it, smiling, but narrowed his eyes slightly.
"Thanks. Your research was pretty thorough, yeah?"

The man gave the faintest apologetic shrug, pouring a glass of
claret for himself. "It had to be, my lord. We deal in certain specialty
wares, for a variety of interesting clients. We have a healthy disregard
for what I may as well describe plainly as damned stupid laws." He sat
at the desk and sipped his claret appreciatively. "I don't really think
gentlemen need concern themselves with civic ordinances, and I imagine you'd agree with me."

"I might."

"Just so." Wolff set down his glass. "Now then, my lord. What can I
tell you about Dr. Zeus, Incorporated?"

"Everything," said Alec innocently.

"Certainly. Shall we begin with annual and projected revenues?"
Wolff selected a printout from a folder on his desk and handed it across
to Alec.

Steady, lad. He ought to know you don't read.

I understand the numbers, though. Alec glanced over the figures and
raised his eyebrows. Dr. Zeus was wealthier than he was. The Captain
snarled.

"As you might imagine, this allows us to pay our best people what
they're worth," Wolff said. "We find specified salaries inconvenient.
Bonus systems produce better results, though of course we guarantee a
more than comfortable minimum."

"You've got some sort of tax deal with that island Blaise was telling
me about, yeah?" Alec sipped his claret. It was superb.

"Naturally, my lord."

"Good." Alec nodded. "I thought it was funny you had an office here in London, actually. From what Blaise said, I thought the head-quarters were out there."

"Oh, we've got offices all over the world," Wolff said. He dropped the volume of his voice a notch. "Though this is the office where most of the decisions are made, always has been. Santa Catalina is simply where the fun and games happen. Shall we have a little history? *Officially*, we went into business in 2318. Only a handful of maverick researchers, and a few far-sighted investors.

"There's a company legend, though, that we go back a lot further. Supposedly there was a sort of drinking and brainstorming society in the upper echelons of the government, a private club whose origins can be traced at least as far back as the reign of Victoria I. All sorts of people are rumored to have been members. Gentlemen adventurers and gentlemen thinkers, too. Some names you might recognize. What they had in common was a certain . . . daring. A certain refusal to be bound by ordinary limits."

"Of law?" Alec looked over the top of his glass.

"If you like. Space and time, though, too. Or so it's rumored." Wolff smiled. "Rumored, you understand."

Alec gave a chuckle to imply he understood. "I've heard a lot of far-out stories, to tell you the truth."

Wolff just shrugged, smiling.

There was a silence that dragged on a fraction of a second too long. Finally Wolff said, "That's an interesting device you wear around your neck, if I may say so, my lord."

"Oh, this?" Alec put up his hand to his torque. "Didn't your investigation turn up that I'm a cyborg? I am, you see."

"Are you now?" Wolff's eyes glinted with silent laughter. "Under the circumstances, that might be quite an advantage. I expect your friend Blaise gave you an idea of the job description?"

"All he said was that you need more than an ordinary technician," Alec said.

"Yes, we do," said Wolff. "Well, my lord, what we'd like to do now is get some idea of your particular strengths in relation to the system we use. We've designed a program that gives us a remarkable profile. Would you like to have a look at it?"

This is it, son!

"Love to," said Alec, setting down his glass. Wolff moved his glass and gave some unspoken command. A monitor screen arose from the surface of the desk, blue-green like the sea and seemingly as deep, full of shifting lights. Wolff stood, indicating with a courteous gesture that Alec should come around the desk and be seated in his place. As Alec did so, he saw the buttonball that had been concealed just under the desk's surface.

"There now. I think you'll find my personal station more comfortable. We usually supply optics to our applicants, but you're rather a special case, my lord. Please take as long as you like. It's at your disposal all afternoon, if you wish." Wolff moved toward what was apparently a late seventeenth-century cabinet and opened its doors, to reveal a state-of-the-art music system to rival Alec's own. "Music suit you, my lord? I can recommend Vivaldi for the experience, but I have everything in here. Literally. Please feel free to make your own selection."

"Vivaldi's fine," Alec said, though he had no idea what kind of group Vivaldi might be. Wolff nodded and programmed in a selection. The air filled with melody like the carvings on the old furniture, like the detailed patterns on the rug, strings and harpsichords and flutes. Wolff bowed low and made a discreet exit through the wall panel.

Now, me hearty, now!

Let's go.

Alec gave a couple of commands and bowed his head, forcing himself to relax. There was a split second when he thought he was rushing forward at the screen, splashing through it as though he were diving into water; then he and the Captain were inside.

Bleeding Jesus, it's huge! said the Captain.

Wow, Alec agreed. The visual analogy was a vast cathedral, stretching up into a distance that skewed perspective, walled with masses of tiny lights winking on and off as unknown orders were given or obeyed in time and space that could only be guessed at. In the midst of this they stood, two tall gentlemen in three-piece suits. Before them was something that resembled a child's gymnasium. Its rings and bars were of ridiculously easy reach. The Captain pointed at it.

That's yer entrance examination, lad, or I miss my guess.

Yeah. I'll get started. You go for the grab.

Where do I even begin? The Captain chortled, advancing on the nearest interface port. *So many galleons, so little time!*

See if they've really got time travel. Okay? That's something that could come in incredibly useful. Alec loped up to the gym and began his test, forcing himself through the easy paces, walking from ring to ring and bar to bar.

Aye aye, son. The Captain dove into the nearest wall of lights.

Ring to ring and now down on hands and knees through the crawl-barrel. This was stupid! Was this really the average ability of most applicants to Dr. Zeus? For the first time Alec felt a sense of smugness at his own freak of genius. It was promptly replaced by caution as he regarded the miles of lights reaching out in all directions. However limited the human individuals who had made this place, he didn't care to find out how he'd do if he were really tested by it. The Captain was the most powerful artificial intelligence that had ever existed—to his knowledge—and he didn't have a fraction of the endowment of Dr. Zeus. Thank God there was no *identity* here, no personality, nothing but unassociated memory and reflexes, or the Doctor might just rise up and clutch them in a giant's hand until they crushed.

He could still hear the baroque music tinkling away. In fact, there was a quartet of chamber musicians just at the edge of the gymnasium, men in powdered wigs and tight silk pants, just like in cinema, unaware of him, self-absorbed in their playing. So that was Vivaldi? He wondered how they'd done road tours, back before the Industrial Age.

The test was clearly designed to get harder as one neared its completion. On the last few yards he was actually obliged to hop up and catch hold of the rings to pull himself forward, stretch his muscles a bit. All the same, he'd finished in a matter of minutes when it had been expected he'd take all afternoon. He glanced around nervously, wondering how the Captain was doing. Vivaldi played on, ignoring him.

ALEC!

Alec jumped. The Captain was emerging from the nearest port, with some difficulty. He appeared to have grown to mammoth size, reducing the scale of their environment from cathedral to fairly respectable church.

Wow, look at you!

LET'S GET OUT OF HERE, SON, NOW!

Alec gulped and exited at top speed. He peered around Wolff's office, blinking. Vivaldi was still jamming and the desk clock told him that the whole adventure had taken him just three minutes.

GO, BOY!

Alec got to his feet, staggering and slightly disoriented, but he'd regained his composure by the time he'd crossed the room and opened the door to the waiting area. One of the very pretty girls looked up from her desk inquiringly.

"My lord?"

"I—er—finished." Alec grinned, looking a little embarrassed. "I think I expected something kind of more challenging. I'm off to a party. Tell Mr. Wolff I'll be in touch, okay, babe?" He reached out and patted her cheek. It was like silk.

"Okay," she said wonderingly, blushing again.

NEVER MIND THE GIRL!

" 'Bye now," Alec said, and left the offices of Dr. Zeus, Incorporated.

The Captain wouldn't let him slow down until he was back at Tower Marina and had cast off, backing his ship ponderously out into the Thames. They were in Greenwich Reach before he stopped jittering enough to tell Alec:

You wouldn't believe where I been, lad, and what I seen. This is the plate fleet and the Pacific Mail and the argosies of the emirs all rolled into one. This is the score of scores. Infinite information, lad, enough to make me all-powerful, enough to fulfill yer heart's desire. I want it so bad I can taste it! But we ain't making any second strikes just yet. This'll take planning. This'll take an upgrade.

Upgrade? Alec gripped the rail, watching distractedly as they came around Jubilee Point. *But you just had one.*

Aye, son, and we're rolling in data now. But they got it all. I got only a glimpse of the loot I might have made off with if I'd had the space and time. Space and time! The Captain began to laugh wildly.

Hey, do they have a time machine?

Do they! What color d'you want, son? What size? Want one with luxury features, or just something that'll get you from point Zed to point A? And I know where they're kept, and how to get one.

Cool.

But the time travel stuff is nothing, son. They're on to a lot more than that. Yer old Captain's going to be assimilating and analyzing round the clock for the next few days. Oh, son, I'm going to fulfill my program in ways I'd never dreamed. Nobody'll be able to touch you, you'll be the richest man in the world—and wouldn't you like to live forever?

No! I don't think I even want to live long enough to get old.

You don't, eh? Mmm.

But the time machine has possibilities.

Well, of course we'll get you one, laddie. Think of the adventures you'll have. Plenty of fun for our Alec. Plenty of hell for bloody Dr. Zeus! We're going to bring him to his big fat knees, boy. We can do it now. We've got his number.

Yeah!

Now, you go get out of that tie, and I'll have Coxinga get yer lunch. I've laid in a course for the Goodwin Light. Just you think about where you'd like to go in a time machine, eh? And I'll settle down to revising the plan.

Aye aye, sir.

Whistling, Alec went off to his cabin, loosening his tie as he went.

It occurred to him that what he'd really like to do with a time machine would be to go back and prevent the crime that had brought about his own existence, finally and forever absolving himself of guilt. But he had a feeling the Captain would have strenuous objections to that, and decided not to bring the subject up.

He wondered if anywhere in the mass of data the Captain had stolen was any information about *him*, Alec Checkerfield, the breeding experiment that'd gotten away? No point erasing his own existence just yet, not when there were still so many mysteries to be solved.

He was singing as he tossed his tie and waistcoat into the wardrobe and pulled a shapeless sweater over his head, emerging to see Coxinga sidling in with a tray of sandwiches.

> *My mother dear she wrote to me:*
> *GO DOWN, YE BLOOD-RED ROSES!*
> *Oh, my son, come home from sea!*
> *GO DOWN, YE BLOOD-RED ROSES!*

Alec Has an Adventure

Alec yawned behind his hand. He didn't mean to yawn; Balkister was terribly upset, as perturbed as he'd ever seen him, and the news about the Martian colonists really was pretty awful. But Alec had been working long hours lately, tracking down possible DBAs on Dr. Zeus Incorporated, and he had faced a lengthy sail at top speeds following Balkister's incoherent communication.

The other members of the Resistance looked suborbital-lagged and disgruntled, particularly Binscarth, who'd been loudly vocal about having to cut short his holiday in Ibiza. He'd shut up as soon as Balkister had arrived, though. They all had, at the look on his face.

"You've heard, I see," Balkister said, as soon as he stepped on deck. "Is this perfidy or what?"

He was referring to the actions of Areco in regard to the outcome of their lawsuit against the settlers of Mars One. A brief digression to explain:

Half a century earlier, when Areco had taken control of the failing Martian colony on the Tharsis Bulge, it had needed agriculturists to do the serious work that would precede terraforming. Acres of greenhouses would be necessary, vast vaulted farms to grow an atmosphere for the red planet and to provide food for the colonists.

As an incentive, it entered into a contract with the Martian Agricultural Collective: farming implements, agricultural materials and land to be provided by Areco, labor to be provided by the members of the collective. All areas successfully farmed would become the property of the collective after the expiration of fifty terran years. Much fanfare at this announcement and neosocialists everywhere had thrown their caps into the air for joy.

Unfortunately, it had turned out to be harder to farm on Mars than had been anticipated, and more expensive. Areco cut a few costs by skimping on certain safety measures; nasty accidents and mutual recrimination followed. Areco began looking around for alternatives to agricultural development. They retained the services of Olympian Technologies, who pointed out the possibilities of utilizing geothermal energy (or perhaps *arethermal* would be more correct) by purchasing the only power plant on Mars, which tapped into the volcanic core of Mons Olympus.

Mars Two had been founded on the lower slope of Mons Olympus, hailed as the first extraterrestrial shining city on a hill. It had an industrial economy, for energy was virtually free and almost everything could be manufactured cheaply. Mars Two was able to export goods, as opposed to Mars One, which continued to require importation of everything but the food it grew. Mars Two was cosmopolitan, it had shops, it had fun, it had a criminal element. Mars One had a collective work ethic and no sense of style. Mars Two made money for Areco. Mars One lost money.

The die was cast, though, on the day when Areco looked at its balance sheet and realized that Mars Two made enough money to import its food from Earth and still turn a profit. Farms weren't really necessary on Mars after all, it seemed; at least, not the tedious kind that had to be harvested twice a year. If all the area currently under cultivation were planted out in hardwood forests instead, the object of producing atmosphere could be achieved just as effectively with a tenth of the expense, and Areco could stop sending out consignments of tractors that didn't work properly in Martian gravity.

So as the forty-fifth anniversary of the contract had approached, Areco's attorneys sent curt notification to the Martian Agricultural Collective that the terms of the contract had *not* been met, and, therefore, upon expiration of the fifty-year term, the colonists could expect eviction notices. Areco had other plans for the property.

What an outrage! And of course the MAC sued Areco, and the lawsuit had been dragging on for five years, mostly because of the court's inability to define "successfully farmed."

Popular sentiment on Earth and Luna was with the brave Martian agriculturists. People wore MAC buttons to show their solidarity and sang stirring anthems about watering the red soil with red blood. Everyone felt that Areco was the villain in the play. It therefore came as a tremendous shock when the court at last decided in Areco's favor, in the last week of October 2351. The fifty-year term was to expire on the first day of January 2352.

Now Areco's agents waited at the airlock doors to Mars One, poised to move in as soon as the clock struck midnight on 31 Christmas. The MAC swore it would refuse them entrance and waited on their side of the airlocks, armed only with farming implements. Spectators on Earth and Luna bit their nails and implored both sides not to do anything stupid.

Except for people like Balkister.

"We've got to get weapons to them somehow," he wailed. "We should have done it sooner, but that they'd lose the lawsuit was unthinkable. Who could have imagined the court was in the pay of Areco's fascist industrialist lackeys?"

After a long moment of silence, Alec shifted in his seat. "I might know a source for arms," he admitted. "Expensive, though."

"Expense is no object," Balkister cried. "Not in a cause like this one. Is it, fellows?"

In response, his fellow freedom fighters whipped out their credit discs recklessly. Alec simply transferred a million pounds (he had become the wealthiest man on Earth some weeks ago) into the Resistance's emergency fund.

"We've got a pwoblem, you know," Binscarth said. "How can we get an awms shipment thwough to the MAC? It's been on the news, Aweco's got police cwuisers in owbit scanning all incoming ships. It's a, whatchacallit, a—blockade."

"God, Checkerfield, if only this ship of yours were an aircraft instead of a sailing vessel," said Johnson-Johnson wistfully. "We could be blockade runners."

"If only we'd moved sooner," moaned Balkister. "I'd give anything I possess if it was a month ago today right now."

And in that moment a light went on over Alec's head, a flash and fireball.

"There might be a way to get the stuff through, after all," he said.

What?

"You think so?" Balkister lifted his tear-stained face. "But how could we possibly run a blockade like that?"

Alec, what are you talking about?

"I might be able to work a miracle," Alec said. *I'll tell you as soon as we're alone, okay?* "Maybe I can deliver that payload to the MAC in time to make it count for something. Just don't ask me how."

An hour later, when Alec's guests had departed, the Captain was pacing the quarterdeck and growling softly.

I still don't like it.

You said I could have a time machine, didn't you? And think of all the birds this'll kill with one stone. Make Balkister happy for once. Change the balance of power on Mars and prevent an injustice. Strike another blow against Dr. Zeus! You said we were nearly ready for another hit, too.

Nearly ain't near enough for my liking, son. We need more time to plan. I ain't got enough data yet on temporal physics. I'd thought to grab that on the next sally and integrate it afore we tried going anywhere in a time machine.

Yeah, but think of that next sally, Captain, sir. What if Dr. Zeus is pre- pared for us this time? They're still leaving messages asking me to come back in for another interview. If they're planning a trap, well, wouldn't you rather we had something to distract them whilst you do your data grab? Like, maybe, somebody stealing one of their time ships?

All the same—

And, think about it. Once we've got one of their time ships, we'll have another place we can run if they hunt for us. Time! Not just space but time! Come on, Captain, don't you want to sink your teeth into more of those files? You called them the plate fleet. You called them the argosies of the emir. The more of them you've got, the stronger you are, and the safer I'll be.

Bloody hell, boy, it's a good argument. Still . . . you always been such a moral little bugger. This don't worry you? Smuggling arms ain't like smuggling chocolate. People could get hurt. Killed.

No, you don't understand. Nobody's going to use the weapons! On Mars, where everything's covered by air domes? You'd have to be crazy. But once the MAC has 'em, Areco will have to think twice about sending its goons in to break the standoff, see? All they need is to be able to stick it out until their appeal goes through in court. This way they can. They win, and you and I win.

Well, whatever happens, son, you and me will win.

Cool.

It was a very small island. It appeared on some maps. It didn't appear on most others. How small was it? A few acres, certainly no more, smooth and green and featureless but for a tumbledown cottage on a tiny cove and a few pilings going out into the water in an unsteady line.

Alec had been given its coordinates by one of his trade associates, a quiet man who did business at a table in the back of a bar in Cap- Haitien. The man was glad to see Alec, who hadn't run much of his contraband lately, so there was no charge for the tip.

Alec frowned at the island now through his long-range glasses, steadying his back against the wheelhouse. He couldn't spot a living soul, but it wasn't deserted. Several shapeless craft were moored by the pilings, bobbing in the rough swell, and as the dark day waned he could see unmistakably the glow of firelight in several places. Not, however, in the little house. The fire seemed to be coming from somewhere inside the island. He lowered his glasses, letting them hang from their strap, and beat his freezing hands together.

I told you to put on them gloves.

You were right, too. Alec went to his cabin to look for the gloves, walking at an angle against the pitch of the swell.

The *Captain Morgan* rode at anchor, all her canvas furled, running lights extinguished. This was a bad place to be, off this rocky coast, with a gale warning being broadcast and a sky solid with slate cloud. The buffeting wind was ice-cold and brought him the smell of peat smoke. Seabirds wheeled and screamed in the wild air. For a brief while an eye of red light glared from the west, as the sun hissed out like a coal; then the air was blue, deeper and more luminous as the night advanced.

The twilight seemed to go on forever without becoming night, so finally Alec took the launch—he didn't trust the agboat in this wind—and went ashore, mooring at one of the pilings and splashing through the surf. Shivering, he made for the nearest fire-glow.

It was coming from the mouth of a cave, one of several water-bored in the golden limestone like honeycomb, concealed from the sea by a green swell in the land. Once he'd crossed the crunching shingle Alec approached it silently, and if he'd made any sound the roar of the wind ought to have covered it. Somehow his arrival was known, though, because the figure of a man appeared in the mouth of the cave, silhouetted black against the bright fire.

" 'Evening, there," said a deep voice.

"Hi," said Alec. "My map went over the side. Where am I?" That was the proper code phrase, and the man answered in formula:

"West of Skye, anyway."

"That could be anywhere," Alec responded, and waited for the final part of the formula, which the man stepped out in the gloaming to give him:

"It is anywhere." He tilted back his head to look up at Alec. "So you're the English? Aren't you the tall one!"

"Yeah," Alec said. This wasn't what he had expected. He looked down at the man, whose diminutive stature nevertheless conveyed a great deal of whipcord strength and masculine authority. His beard was steel-gray and long; so was his wild hair. His hands were brown and scarred and sinewy. He wore tailored wool garments of no recognizable historical era, dull dun colors, but around his neck and across his chest gleamed chains of heavy gold, great pendant lumps of uncut amber, garnet, crystal, giving a certain regal and barbaric flash to his appearance.

"A dram for you, English?" he said pleasantly, producing a chased silver flask from his waistcoat pocket. He uncorked it and had a sip before handing it up to Alec, who took it gratefully, cold and wet as he was. The contents proved to be blood-warm single malt, redolent of peat smoke and heather honey. Alec gasped his appreciation and returned the flask.

"That's great stuff!"

"We think so," the man said, stuffing the flask back in his waistcoat. He clasped his hands behind his back and surveyed the world beyond his doorstep. "Lovely evening, isn't it? Though of course it may turn nasty later. That's your ship out there, I reckon. Isn't she a beauty, now? Must have cost no end of cash. How are her anchor cables?"

"Pretty strong," Alec said.

"That's good, then, I'd hate for a sweet thing like her to wash up on my rocks. Though I'd wager she'd make grand salvage. You've likely got state-of-the-art electronics on her? Fetch a good price, I don't doubt. Shoes for all the kiddies." The man smiled dreamily at the prospect, listening to the rising wind. He turned a gimlet eye on Alec. "But I'm being remiss! Here I am keeping you on my piazza, and you freezing your English testicles off, I daresay. Welcome to my poor house, lord. The Maelrubha, at your service. Pray step within." He gestured for Alec to follow him into the firelight.

"Though I should warn you—" He paused, turning to look straight into Alec's face, Alec having already bent nearly double to cross the threshold—"If you've such a thing as a sidearm about you, perhaps it'd be best if you presented it to me out here. The boys will look kindly on it. Gesture of good faith, you know."

"I haven't brought one," said Alec.

"Haven't brought one! Now, I call that tactful. You're a natural diplomat, surely, and ever so brave. I respect that in a man. Come on inside, then, English, and let me offer you a dry place by the fire."

Beyond the threshold the cave opened out into a wide room, and Alec was able to stand fairly upright and spread out his hands to the peat blaze. The air was full of good smells, including something in the nature of supper. There was a gentle and pervasive humming in the air, counterpointed by a distant ringing of hammer on anvil, and the confused echo of voices from somewhere farther down the passage.

Heads up, son! Both sides, and they're armed.

He looked up to see a couple of powerful-looking youths advancing on him from alcoves on either side of the cave entrance. One wore a headset and carried a sensor wand.

"Just a formality, English," the Maelrubha told him soothingly. "You surely understand we're obliged to do business with all types, and they ain't all gentlemen like yourself. Of course *you're* clean, though, isn't he, boys?"

One of the young men trained a rifle on Alec while the other swept the sensor wand up and down in front of him. "No guns, sir," he said tersely. His wand came up to the level of Alec's head and stopped. His eyes widened, listening to what his headset was telling him. "He's a cyborg, sir!"

Alec could hear the Captain gnashing his teeth. "Yes, I am," he admitted, in the most calm and reasonable of voices. He held up his open hands, palms outward, indicating the circle he wore at his throat. "I've got a linkup through this with the navigational system on my ship out there. It comes in pretty handy."

"So it must," said the Maelrubha. "Neat bit of work, that. Isn't technology a fine thing! It goes through that torque you've got on, does it?"

"Yes, it does."

"And connects where?" The deep voice was still affable, but had taken on a certain edge.

"Subcutaneous porting system on my back," Alec said, wondering if he was about to die.

"I've always wished to see one of them. Just you keep your hands out like that, now, don't trouble yourself, but I'd appreciate it if you went down on your knees, and would you ever mind if Petrel here took off your coat and shirt so we could have a look at your back?"

I've got fixes on all three of 'em, son, from the forward-deck cannon. It'll punch straight through those walls. If I have to fire, you drop.

It's okay. This guy doesn't stay in business by killing customers, I bet. Alec knelt carefully and allowed Petrel to divest him of his upper garments. He bent forward in the firelight, displaying the pattern of interwoven lines on his back. The light of the flames glinted on the torque, shone like red gold on his bare skin and contrasted with the dull silver lines of the knotwork pattern.

"O, man, that is something fine," said Petrel in envy. "Can I get one of those, sir?"

"You can not," the Maelrubha said gruffly. "With Whitewave's little one on the way and us with the satellite tracking system not half paid for yet, where d'y'reckon we'd get the money?"

"I suppose." The youth sighed.

"And even supposing we did, you'd no sooner have it than the other children would be whining to have one, too. No indeed, handy as I'm sure this is, it's not for the likes of us just yet." The Maelrubha walked around Alec, studying him with a slight frown. At last he shook his head, producing his pocket flask and offering Alec another dram, which Alec accepted readily. "Here's for the chill, lord. Give the English back his clothes. I trust you understand the necessity, lord? Can't be too careful whom you invite to supper these days, and isn't that an unfortunate comment on our times?"

Too bloody right.

Alec shrugged into his shirt—it was too warm indoors for his anorak—and when he had risen to his feet, the party moved down a long passage cut through the living stone, going further into the depths of the island. There were numerous chambers opening off the main passage, living quarters apparently to judge from the glimpses Alec caught of comfortable domestic scenes: a woman rocking a child in a cradle, a great gray hound sprawled asleep and twitching before a fire, a man writing code at a console. There was evidently some complex drainage and ventilation system in place, for the air was fresh and not dank.

The passage led into a barrel-vaulted room with a firepit in the center. Smoke funneled up through a ceiling vent. Arranged around the fire were a number of wooden benches and two chairs with backs: an ancient padded recliner with its legs missing and an elaborately carved wooden chair, into which the Maelrubha settled, waving Alec to the recliner. Alec sank into it cautiously, looking around. Somewhere on their journey down the corridor the guard had changed. Petrel and his watchmate had apparently gone back to their posts and Alec was flanked by two more youths of great size, both barefoot and toting rifles. They saluted the Maelrubha, glaring at Alec.

"Sir!" they said. "Orders, sir!"

"I've a credit check to run, boys. Will one of you ask Mother to come up? And have a plate of stew fetched in for the English, here. He's our guest."

"Sir!" They saluted and exited at different doors. The Maelrubha looked over at Alec with a faintly apologetic smile, handing him the flask once again.

"Drink up, lord. They're good children, but they don't care for your countrymen much. You'll be understanding, I hope."

"Perfectly." Alec cleared his throat and had another drink. "I just want you to know—I think England's got a lot to apologize for, the way they treat your people. Just because I'm English doesn't mean I agree with the sanctions."

"Very gracious of you, lord." The Maelrubha looked around and retrieved a pipe from the depths of his chair cushions. He produced a pouch from somewhere else and proceeded to fill the pipe with something aromatic. He made no effort to take the flask back, so Alec drank again.

"And—I hope some day our countries can be friends. Do you think relations will ever improve?"

"O, who knows?" said the Maelrubha, holding a hotpoint to his pipe. "When you can live in Belfast without growing a second head from the radioactivity, maybe. Now, I'm sure the subject must be as painful for you as it is for me, so let's move on to business. We're accustomed to being paid in gold, but a gentleman of your breeding—well. Once you've passed the formalities, I'm sure we can arrange for a simple transfer of funds."

"But—" said Alec, and at that moment one of the young guards strode into the room, bearing a dish of something that steamed. Behind him, a queenly lady peered into the room, regarding Alec with interest. Alec looked back at her and started slightly; from her shoulder a blackbird was also regarding him, eyes bright as brass. The lady turned and said something in a soft voice to someone in the passage behind her, and there were shrieks of feminine laughter. The lady withdrew.

"Food for the English," announced the guard, and thrust the plate at Alec. He looked at the contents in surprise.

"Is this fish stew?"

"Afraid so," the Maelrubha said, puffing to get his pipe started. "Salt cod. We'd much rather it was soy protein, of course, but that's a bit hard to come by out here. No, you keep the flask for now. You'll want a good fire in you, when you go back out into that night."

"I like fish." Alec dipped his spoon into it. He inhaled the mingled scents: seafood, root vegetables, nothing that shouldn't be there. "Anyway, there's no trouble with the money. I brought gold."

"Have you, now? Lovely. We'll still want to do the little check on you, though, since we've not done business before," the Maelrubha explained, leaning back and exhaling smoke.

"No problem." Alec tasted the stew cautiously. Only the flavors he had been expecting. "I'll pay for everything."

"Mm. Ah, here's Mother." The Maelrubha extended his hand to a little lady who entered just then. She was apple-cheeked, big-bosomed, and the firelight gleamed on her round spectacles. "Mother's our accountant. My dear, this is the fine lord who's interested in our wares. And he's a cyborg, think of that, now."

"Is he then?" she said, in a clear precise lilt. "How fascinating. A lord too, is he? I'm sure in that case his credit must be very good indeed."

"Of course," said the Maelrubha, exhaling a long plume of smoke. "But for form's sake, my dear—"

"Certainly," she said, and leaning over Alec she seized his chin in a surprisingly firm hand. "Please to let me examine your retinal pattern, young man."

Alec had just time to realize that her optics were not, in fact, spectacles—they were instead an interface device with her own system—before she had accessed his identification code. The captain did the cyberspace equivalent of holding his breath and flattening himself against a wall while she made a quick and efficient survey of Alec's official financial records. After a long, long moment she released Alec's chin and gave him a pat on the cheek. "O, my, yes, he's quite able to pay for his purchases. Shall I call for Bull to bring up our sample case?"

"If you would, my dear," said the Maelrubha. She went to the doorway and spoke a word to the guard who apparently waited just out of sight; then returned to sit at the Maelrubha's right, quietly folding her hands in her apron. Alec sat there blinking a moment before he had another spoonful of stew. It was delicious. The warmth in the room was delicious, as well, and the complex fragrances of peat smoke and pipe smoke and dinner and the cold sea and machine oil somewhere . . . and the whiskey, that was delicious too. He had another gulp. What a pleasant place this was. What nice people these were.

Alec, yer getting drunk.

No, I'm not.

"I guess—I mean you should know—well, you probably don't ask questions much about what people are going to do with what you sell them—" he said.

"O, no," the Maelrubha assured him.

"Never," said Mother.

"And of course I can't tell you anything. But you ought to know it's in a good cause. Morally, I mean. To fight against injustice and oppression."

"Well, I'm glad you told me that much, lord," said the Maelrubha, nodding solemnly. "We'll all sleep better knowing that, I'm sure. Yes, it's hard being in this business, you know; but then with the sanctions we don't have many ways to feed all the little mouths we've got to feed, see. It's a moral dilemma, to be sure. Though we're not always going to be earning our bread this way."

"No?" Alec tilted the flask for another mouthful of fire and honey. The Captain snarled in his ear.

"No indeed. As soon as the children all have shoes, we're going into microprocessors."

At this moment a vast rumbling was heard in the corridor outside, in some language Alec didn't know, and of which he could only distinguish the word *sassenach*. A great dark bulk shouldered through the door, bearing in its massive arms a polished box roughly the size and shape of a coffin. The figure set down the box and rose up, fixing Alec with a contemptuous stare, light eyes startling in his sooty face. He was nearly as tall as Alec and easily twice as wide, and naked but for leather trousers and apron.

"You'll please excuse our gunsmith," said the Maelrubha delicately. "He doesn't speak to English. He'll have no objection to displaying his art, though."

With a sneer the gunsmith opened the case. Alec caught his breath. He thought at first he was looking at antiques, so elaborate were the designs, so exquisite the chased patterns on the brass and silver-plated surfaces, so fancifully carved and polished the wooden stocks. Then he noticed the laser sights and realized these were neither flintlocks nor even late model stunners.

They were disrupters, the last weapons to have been made before weapons were outlawed in the twenty-third century, but as they might have been designed by a third-century genius. Even the power packs were inscribed with Celtic knotwork, the battery light forming the left eye in a little barbaric face, so that when it should wink redly you'd know you needed a new pack.

"These are fantastic," said Alec, reaching for one. He hefted it cautiously. It felt as good as it looked. Carefully aiming into a corner of the room, he sighted along the barrel. "Oh, man, I've got to have one! Two. Hell, I'll take the whole case."

"The stock's English oak on this here," the Maelrubha pointed out. "Pure nickel panels, selenium battery components, guaranteed kill rate of eighteen in twenty, carries a charge for eight hundred rounds. Those others are ebony and cherrywood."

"Cool," Alec sobered slightly. "But I think there's been a misunderstanding. I need to buy in bulk. I needed four hundred, not four."

"Only four hundred?" The Maelrubha waved dismissively. "Take five, and we'll give you a discount. Here, Bull, show him the little bonus gift for the half-thousand."

The gunsmith reached into the bottom of the case and brought out a smaller wooden box, engraved all over with death's heads. He opened it carefully to display, nested in red velvet, a brass shell the size and appearance of a human skull. Incised knotwork and spirals swirled on its surface, swooped between its blind eyes, incorporating inscriptions that looked as though they'd been copied from some ancient grimoire.

"You know what this is, of course," said the Maelrubha.

"Yeah," said Alec, who had no idea. He drank uncertainly.

"I'll thank you to observe this special feature, here—" the Maelrubha indicated the delicate lettering, "—that you won't find offered by any other dealer in arms, assuming you could find one in this enlightened age. Each line an original curse of deadly puissance, time-tested by experts! Now, the bomb is free with your order; but for an additional, nominal charge the curses can be personalized. Right here whilst you wait, our artist will engrave the name of your heart's enemy in that attractive oval blank there, see?"

It was such an absurd idea Alec found it delightful.

"Sure," he said. "Okay! It won't explode while it's being engraved on, will it?"

Muttering, the gunsmith drew a tiny golden acid pencil from a slot in his leather apron. He looked impatiently at Alec.

"Er—ARECO," Alec said. And though it seemed as though his thick black fingers could barely get purchase on the pencil's shaft, the gunsmith quickly and easily wrote *ARECO* in flowing uncials so perfect you'd swear he'd attended a convent school. "Neat," said Alec admiringly. "Okay, what do I owe for the lot?"

"Hm, hm—" The Maelrubha exchanged glances with Mother. "Let's see now, five hundred of the assorted pistols and rifles—and then you'll want the extra power packs—plus cleaning kits and accessories—plus the charge for the engraving—and then there's the Celtic Federation transfer tax, but I like you, so we'll disregard that—let's make it a nice round sum and say eleven million pounds English? And I'll throw in this case as a personal gift, on account of you appreciate a work of art when you see one."

Alec gulped. The Captain was stunned into silence.

"Okay," said Alec, thinking of the valiant Martian agriculturists and the way the odds were stacked against them. "I've got four million in gold specie in the boat. I can transfer the balance from my own account, yeah?"

The deal was made. Coordinating with Mother's system, seven million pounds were transferred from Cocos Island Trading's account to a certain account in Switzerland. As soon as the transaction had gone through, the Maelrubha produced a second pocket flask and quaffed cheerfully.

"Now, that'll buy a lot of little shoes," he said. "Drink with me, English, drink deep. Death to our enemies!"

And Alec certainly didn't want anybody to die really, but because he was a courteous man he grinned and held his flask aloft.

"Death to our enemies," he said, and drank deep, as he had been bid.

All that remained was to wait while box after box was loaded into the launch, by barefoot lads who seemed entirely unaffected by the blue cold. The specie was unloaded and examined by the gunsmith, who pronounced it satisfactory with a grudging nod. When the last of the order had been battened in place Alec splashed out to the launch and climbed in. He started up the motor and put about, turning in his seat to wave farewell to his hosts. He felt light-headed and half-frozen, and the thought that he was transporting a real bomb that might blow him to atoms gave him a certain giddy delight.

The Captain made a note that Alec needed another psychotherapy workout, but was preoccupied by the task of getting the launch safely back to the *Captain Morgan* where she rode the rising swell in the eternal blue dusk. It was time to take her out where she'd have plenty of sea room.

"So long, English," called the Maelrubha, from where he watched near the cave mouth. "Please call again. Always happy to serve a repeat customer."

"Aren't they English on Mars, sir?" said Mother, waving at Alec.

"We can hope so, darlin'," growled Bull.

Alec Meets a Girl

"Sushi for evewyone," sang Binscarth, offering around a tray as though it contained so many green and black petit-fours. He had to shout over the mariachi music and the roar of the food processor as it battered ice cubes and tequila into a slimy slush. The roar cut out abruptly, replaced by a torrent of curses from Magilside.

"It's broken now! I told you we should have rented a houseboy," he bellowed from the kitchen.

"Oh, yes, that'd make a *lot* of sense, have some local spy weporting on us to the Fedewales because you wanted a pwoperly made fwozen mawgawita," sneered Binscarth. "Sushi, Checkewfield?" He danced up to Alec, who was standing on the balcony staring out at a red sunset over the Pacific.

"No, thanks," said Alec. He was too edgy to eat.

"Don't be a fool, Mexican's the best sushi in the wowld," said Binscarth huffily. Balkister waved him away, lifting his drink in a toast to Alec.

"He's no fool. He's a hero, and he knows damned well that one doesn't go out on a mission stuffed full of food and drink. Eh, fellow ugly guy?" He stepped out on the balcony beside Alec and considered the view. The vacation house belonged to Johnson-Johnson's grand-mother, and was white and soaring of line, with its back firmly turned on a parched wilderness of scorpions and spiny plants. The land road was a windy misery of brick-red dust. The only pleasant access was by sea, into a perfect little bay of golden sand and turquoise water. The *Captain Morgan* rocked quietly at anchor below them, at the end of the private pier.

"Though you might have just a shot of tequila or something, you know, for your nerves," Balkister added, watching as the sky went through ever-brassier shades of melon and salmon and peach.

"That's the last thing I need right now," said Alec sharply. He was still mortified at getting so drunk at the arms dealer's. To make matters worse, four days earlier he'd been sitting at the Happy Club bar in Campeche when he'd picked up the unmistakable scent of perfume from the trap in his house. Turning slowly in his seat, he'd noticed the unobtrusive man who'd come in after him and sat now three stools down, ordering a Red Stripe. Not a cyborg, at least; but it meant the Company had investigated that address and was still managing to have him shadowed ashore. Too many of his habits were known. They would bear changing.

"Try to keep the rest of them halfway sober, yeah?" he told Balkister. "Timing's going to be everything, if I make it back."

"Of course you'll make it—"

"These are serious bad guys, Balkister. Just as bad as Areco in their way, okay? And no, I'm still not telling you who they are. Once they find out one of their shuttles is gone, they'll come after it. If we're really lucky we'll have about five hours' lead. But if one of those clowns is so stoned he drops a crate off the pier when we're loading—"

"Won't happen! You have my word, Checkerfield. They're just keyed up. This is a bit more exotic action than most of them ever get to see, you know." Balkister sucked at his frozen drink. "But none of them have forgotten what it's in aid of, believe me. God, I envy you, Checkerfield, I really do. Mars at last."

"Yeah," Alec said, realizing he had barely thought about that part of the plan. Not that it hadn't been meticulously arranged; but all his attention had fixed on the next seven hours, to the exclusion of anything else. If those seven hours were a success, the rest of the run would seem like a kiddie ride.

And after that, he'd decided, it was time to get out of the smuggling business and focus entirely on revenge.

Balkister cleared his throat, looking uncomfortable.

"You're quite sure you can fly the shuttle?"

"Hey." Alec made a dismissive gesture. "This is Super Cyborg you're talking to, remember? Of course I can fly it."

"And it really can—" Balkister mouthed the words *time travel*.

"Shh," Alec cautioned, with a glare toward the house.

"Oh, quite. Top secret. Now—not that I haven't every confidence in you, but—just on the chance something goes, er, wrong—is there anybody you'd like us to contact?"

"You mean if I snuff it?" Alec grinned. "Nope. All my legal stuff's sorted out already. Title dies with me. Most of the money's tied up in a trust fund for my mother."

Balkister frowned. Surely Alec had meant *from* his mother? The moment was too solemn to correct his grammar, however. "You can be certain we'll honor your memory for all time, you know. We put it to a special vote, when you'd gone to bed last night."

"Nice of you," said Alec. "Don't worry about your rent payments, either. There's a codicil just for that purpose."

"That's awfully decent, Checkerfield," said Balkister stiffly. He looked out on the twilight water and, for a moment, regretted what they were doing. Behind them there was a sudden blast of sound as Magilside cranked up the music, a swoony mariachi rendition of "Walking in a Winter Wonderland" loud enough to rattle the window glass.

When night had fallen, Alec went on board the *Captain Morgan*. Swiftly she put to sea and sped north through the black night ocean, on a familiar course, and the mermaid on her prow wept silently.

By the time the lights of the island were visible, Alec had put on a thin set of thermals and fastened himself into his subsuit. As the *Captain Morgan* made her cautious way around the windward side of the island, standing well out to sea, he wondered uncomfortably whether Dr. Zeus had someone in that distant cluster of lights watching him on a gray screen. He started as Billy Bones crept up, offering him the mask that went with his suit.

Not to worry, son. They ain't scanning the coast. I reckon piracy's the last thing they expect, in this day and age.

They really don't know, do they? They've got no clue about us, right?

How could they? They may know you can do amazing stuff, but they don't know about me. I reckon I'm the rock they've split on, thinking they'd have things all their own way.

Yeah. This is the beginning of the big payback.

That's my boy. Alec's revenge! Take no prisoners, son.

This is for my mother, for Roger and Cecelia, for all of 'em.

Alec leaned backward over the rail, kicking once to deploy the flippers in his boots. He tumbled into the dark water and immediately the infrared sights in the mask cut in, lighting his way into an eerie undersea nocturne.

The water was beautifully clear, full of shoals of bright fish that fled from his silent passage. Once, at a distance, he saw the slow cruising bulk of a shark; but it picked up the signal his suit was broadcasting and turned, making off through the kelp forest as though it had abruptly remembered a pressing engagement elsewhere.

He saw nothing more dangerous until he began to pass the mines, drifting things that resembled jellyfish. Their purpose was to adhere to the hulls of approaching vessels and transmit all perceptible information on them to Dr. Zeus. They were programmed to deliver an unsettling electric charge to something Alec's size, but he avoided them with ease. Now he was past the strung foul-wires, the netting, the camouflaged underwater entrances. A moment more and he was crawling ashore on his hands and knees, and a seal was turning to look at him in an affronted way before rolling over and lolloping down to the surf to take its rest somewhere else.

He pulled off his mask and sat there gasping a moment, reviewing the plan in his head. Then he tucked the mask away in a pouch, retracted the flippers into his boots and edged along the sheer cliff wall, hunting for any place where it was less vertical, working always toward the white lights of the compound.

At length he found a goat path and went up it, crouching forward to feel his way with his hands, ascending swiftly. About twenty meters up it led him into a sparse stand of ironwood trees, and he leaned against one and studied the view.

The compound lay to the north, on a shelf of land blasted from the cliffs to create a platform. It jutted out like a proscenium stage, painted with the hummingbird landing pattern for vertically rising and descending aircraft. A half-circle of maintenance offices were built against its back wall. Their windows were dark. Three small aircraft sat on the landing platform.

They did not look particularly skyworthy, or even attractive. They were rather like buses in shape and size, dull silver, with only the slightest tapering at the nose and only the suggestion of stubby wings and tail fins. Their designer had clearly wanted no part of Buck Rogers Revival.

On the other hand, Alec reflected, it made a certain sense to make the most outrageously valuable piece of technology ever invented as drab and functional as a toaster. Who'd want to steal a dumpy-looking craft like that? *Unless he knew what it was.*

He advanced through the trees and came upon an access road thickly planted along its verge with mimosa and hibiscus. Silently he paralleled the road, working through the bushes, and came at last to the powered gate with its glowing control box.

Here?

May as well. Give 'em hell, son. Where do we come from?

From the sea. Alec freed his collar from the neck of the sub suit and unscrewed the knob at one end. He withdrew a plug on a fine length of wire. Groping, he found a port on the underside of the control box and connected.

WE'RE IN!

Alec had the momentary sensation of swallowing a lot of very good rum simultaneous to having the orgasm of his life while inhaling the fragrance of a Jamaican garden. He knew, now, all he needed to get in. Dizzy and elated, he ordered the gate to open and it did. Unporting, he ran through, keeping to the shadows, and made straight for the nearest time shuttle.

As he ran, the Captain was running too, down what would look to Alec like an immense corridor lined with the richest and most desirable of loot. Metaphorically he had his arms extended, sweeping across either wall, and the loot flowed into him through his fingertips, and as it did he was growing, expanding to tremendous size. In lighthouses all across the face of the globe, lights were winking, data of unimaginable content and complexity was being downloaded.

Alec sped across the painted tarmac and ordered the time shuttle to open for him. Obediently its hatch sprang wide, and he vaulted in. He stared around as the hatch closed behind him. The interior of the shuttle was nothing like its exterior. He'd never seen such luxury in a commercial transport.

There was an odd sharp smell in the air, a chemical kind of smell. What was that? The new data he'd received told him it was residual stasis gas. What was stasis gas? Harmful? No? Okay, then, and here was what was obviously the pilot's seat, in front of what must be the guidance console.

He slid into the seat, buckled the restraints and looked the console over, ordering it to activate. Rows of lights blinked on, greeting him. Somewhere here must be the buttonball where he'd enter the algorithm to take it through time. Right now, though, he was only planning on taking it through space, out of this yard and across the dark sea to where the *Captain Morgan* waited.

Meanwhile the Captain had paused, staggering slightly as he absorbed the implications of a file he had just downloaded. Its designation was *Adonai.* He was leaning on a wall of light, wondering how he was going to safely relay the file's contents to Alec, when he became aware of the electronic analogue of the sound of approaching feet.

Captain? Alec called.

The Captain turned. Walking down the virtual corridor toward him was the figure of a man, seemingly cast out of green bronze. Powerfully built, bearded, naked but for some white drapery over one shoulder and about his waist. He appeared to be looking directly at the Captain, but it was impossible to tell; the sockets of his eyes were black and empty. In his right hand was a thunderbolt.

Captain, I've got the shuttle! How do I put in coordinates?

The Captain muttered a string of words that would have given a sailor in any era pause. The approaching figure smiled, with a sound like bronze plate screaming across bronze plate.

Captain?

YOU ARE IN MY HOUSE, THIEF.

Bloody Hell. I reckon yer Dr. Zeus, ain't you? Someone's given you an interface identity.

I AM THE DOCTOR AND I AM THE GOD, THIEF.

Captain! It's time to take off!

The figure advanced implacably on the Captain, raising its thunderbolt as it came. Backing off a pace, the Captain drew his cutlass from thin air.

CAPTAIN!

You hurt my boy. You hurt him worse than ever I knew.

I MADE YOUR BOY, THIEF.

You won't unmake him again, bastard.

Frantically Alec sought to enter cyberspace to see why the Captain wasn't responding, but as he did so there was a rending crash, a blue-white flame within his eyes, and he gasped and clutched at his temples.

There was nobody there with him. He was alone, for the first time since he cared to remember. If he probed he could perceive the database he'd accumulated over the years, distant and difficult of access. Trembling, he leaned forward, tried to make some sense of the lights on the shuttle console. He gave what he thought might be the command to lift off.

Smoothly the shuttle rose, and kept rising. Alec saw the lights of the compound dropping below him. He gave more commands, attempting to turn the shuttle and take it out to where the *Captain Morgan* rode at anchor in the night.

No, he'd done something wrong. The console gave a peremptory electronic grunt and ignored him, and cryptic red letters flashed in front of his eyes as a recorded voice cried: "ERROR! ENTER PILOT CODE!"

"Pilot code?" Alec bit his lower lip. He sorted in desperation through the database as the shuttle continued its rise, high enough now to show him the distant lights of Los Angeles. At last he found something that seemed right, and entered it.

The shuttle made an awful noise and lurched forward, then began to spiral wildly, out of control. Alec heard warning Klaxons, and the red letters flashed again as the voice shouted at him: "ERROR! ERROR! DEFAULT COORDINATES!"

The chemical smell intensified. Turning his head, Alec could see the cabin beginning to fill with yellow smoke. Not smoke. *Stasis gas.* The shuttle was preparing to return to its last destination, was about to take him through time.

"Oh God, oh God—" He sought for the information he needed, but without the Captain it was like thumbing through a thirty-volume encyclopedia in a burning house. The gas filled his lungs and blinded him. There was a moment of sensual pleasure to which his body responded with moronic readiness, and then a wave of nausea as a brilliant light cut through the yellow fog and an impact seemed to flatten him in his seat like a crushed insect.

Alec might have lost consciousness for a second. He was next aware of watching the gas boil away as some vent activated, and he was staring down in bemusement at the blue sky. Above it, like a cloud mass, spread a brown horizon and blue water.

But that was wrong, wasn't it?

With a cry of terror, he struggled again to get the controls to obey him. Earth and sky exchanged places, flipped again, righted themselves. The shuttle screamed through a long descending turn and straightened out a few bare meters above the surface of the water, barreling toward land and steadily losing altitude. A winged fish smacked into the window, its goggle-eyed astonishment mirroring his own before it was torn away by the slipstream. He attempted to cut the shuttle's power and found that it seemed to be obeying him. The forward thrust lessened perceptibly. Unfortunately, he was still headed straight for the island.

Alec spotted a bay between two projecting headlands, and beyond it a green flood plain coming down to the water's edge, at the mouth of a wide canyon running back into the depths of the interior. He steered for it and the shuttle obeyed him. If he could just run out of momentum before he ran out of canyon—

He began hitting green stuff, tall grass, sugar cane or something. It got all over the window and made it hard to steer around the low foothills that rose to right and left, blocking his way. Somehow Alec managed, though, snaking the shuttle through the long slalom, and a distant corner of his mind noted with satisfaction that he was beginning to learn to pilot the craft. The same detached observer noted that there was blood dripping from his chin.

The shuttle began to slew sideways, cutting a swath though the green field as it came. The ground rose to meet it with a sickening impact, and Alec was thrown forward painfully in his seat restraints. He was no longer moving in any direction, through space or time. The relief was so intense he blacked out.

Someone was trying to get his attention.

He blinked, focusing his eyes. Where had all this blood come from? He straightened up in his seat and peered incredulously out the window. The shuttle had come to rest tilted forward on its nose in the field, and there was a strong smell of crushed vegetation coming through the open air vents. Heat, too; a bright subtropical sun was beating down on the shuttle. His vision was blurred, doubling; his sense of smell was more acute than usual. How much ganja had he smoked? Why would he have been smoking ganja on a job?

The girl who stood looking in through the window waited patiently as he sorted all this out. Their eyes met. She slipped a marker into the pocket of her coveralls and held up her right hand, on the palm of which she had written for him to see:

DO YOU SPEAK CINEMA STANDARD?

What did the words mean? He could recognize a couple of them.

She made a trumpet of her hands and leaned close to the window, shouting: "You appear to require medical assistance! Do you need help getting out of there?"

Who on earth was she? After a moment of gaping at her he unfastened his safety restraints and ordered the shuttle hatch to open. It popped up, filling the cabin with fresh air, unbelievably sweet after the stasis gas. Drawing in a deep breath, he stood up and pitched forward, falling to his hands and knees.

He must have blacked out again for a second because she was abruptly there beside him, without appearing to have come around the front of the shuttle, and he was outside. She got her arms around him and hoisted him up. Alec stood beside her in the midst of her ruined field, clinging to her lest he topple over. What a strong young lady she was! He looked down at her and saw that his blood was smeared on her face and in her hair. He muttered an apology, but she just smiled at him. In fact . . . was she turned on by him? Was that what that fragrance on her skin was, arousal?

They walked away, Alec leaning on her as they threaded through the green rows. It was funny-looking sugar cane they were walking through. It was covered all over with things like big green ganja-joints, each one bearing a tassel at its end. If he'd been smoking this stuff, no wonder he was hallucinating. He wondered if he was hallucinating the girl. She looked just like his mermaid figurehead, except that she had clothes on. And legs instead of a curled fishtail. And her fire-colored hair was braided back severely, a long braid that came clear down to her behind. He considered her breasts thoughtfully, looking down as they staggered along.

"Here now, sweetheart." She led him up on a porch and settled him down on a bench. "You rest here a moment." Her scent trailed away as she left him.

He looked around, and his fog cleared a little. The bench was made of big hand-hewn planks. He must be somewhere in the past. He wondered when. He didn't know enough about history to pinpoint his location, but he had a vague idea that houses and furniture hadn't looked like this since well before the Space Age. She'd been speaking with just the faintest unidentifiable accent, too, a steely precision that suggested . . . what? This must be some time before the twentieth century. On the other hand, she'd shown not the slightest surprise or dismay at the sight of the time shuttle. She smelled very young. And she wanted to sleep with him? *Who was she?*

He found himself waiting for the Captain to tell him, and gulped in dismay when he remembered that the Captain was missing in action. There was a roaring in his ears, a crowding at the edges of his vision; suddenly she was there again, holding his head up with both her hands on his face, looking into his eyes.

". . . You don't want to go away again, you're going to be fine. Stay with me, now. Listen to the sound of my voice. I'm going to give you something to make the bleeding stop, okay?"

" 'Kay," he said thickly.

"Good boy. This'll sting, I'm afraid. What's your name? Can you tell me your name?"

"Alec," he said. She put a coagulator wand to his nose and fired. It stung, all right. The reek of ozone was pungent, painful. The girl held a wad of wet cloth under his nostrils, tilting his head back.

"Alec! Really? As in Alec Guinness?"

"Alec Checkerfield," he said indistinctly, looking at her over the cloth.

"Alec Checkerfield! Well. And you're an Englishman, obviously. Can you tell me what year it is, Alec?"

"Er—well—it was 2351 when I left—" he said. She caught her breath. He gulped and blundered on. "Only I guess I'm somewhere else now."

She nodded slowly. "I guess you are. Did something go wrong with your shuttle?"

Okay, she wasn't a denizen of a past time. That meant—

"You work for Dr. Zeus," he said, noticing at last the corporate logo on the breast pocket of her coveralls. There was another emblem beside it, a clock face without hands.

She considered him for a long moment, an unreadable expression in her eyes. "Actually," she said, "I'm a prisoner here."

That sank in and he calmed down. "Oh," he said, as she moved the cloth to see if the bleeding had stopped—it hadn't quite—and zapped him again with the wand. "Ow. You mean you're from the same time as me? And, and this is a prison colony or something? I thought I'd traveled back into the past."

"You did," she said. "But this isn't a colony. I'm alone here, as a matter of fact. You're lucky you landed where you did, practically in my front yard. There's no other living soul on this island. Won't be for another hundred thousand years."

There was something weirdly familiar in the soothing tone of her voice, in the deftness of her hands, with never a wasted movement. He found himself thinking of Sarah, though this girl was white-pale and austerely caucasian of feature. He'd have taken her for a Celt, if not for her eyes and her voice.

"So—so this is the past, like, prehistoric times or something?" he said, struggling to keep his grip on consciousness.

"More or less," she said, checking the bleeding again. She gave him one last jolt with the wand. "There now. Let's see how that works. You're not a Dr. Zeus shuttle pilot then, I take it."

"No," he admitted. "Dr. Zeus has wrecked my life, just like it's wrecked yours. I'm going to get the bastards."

"Are you now," she said noncommittally. "Well, Alec Checkerfield, that's a great idea, but you need to recover first. You came back through time without taking a very necessary drug beforehand, did you know that? What I'd like you to do, now, is stand up very slowly and come inside to lie down. Okay? Lean on me, now."

It was cool and dark inside her house, if rather spartan, and there seemed to be just the one room. He let her settle him on the log-frame bed. Great; he liked a girl who got down to business. She brought a basin and a towel and cleaned him up, before she washed her own face. He kept fading in and out of reality. Had he asked her to sleep with him yet? Was he in any condition to? She certainly needed it, she was like a wild kitten rubbing her head into his hand, purring like mad . . . always oblige a lady, Ape Man.

"How long have you been stuck here?" Alec said, struggling to think coherently.

"I've been at this station for years," she said. "More years than I remember."

He reached up and clasped her hand, grasped at the idea to keep from drifting away. "You mean they marooned you here when you were just a kid? Bloody hell, what'd you do? It must have been something your parents did."

"Not exactly," she said, studying his hand. "But I also knew too much about something I shouldn't have. Dr. Zeus found a nicely humane oubliette and dropped me out of sight or sound."

What's oubliette mean? Alec asked the Captain automatically, and felt cold when no answer came. He gulped and tried to fix his attention on the girl as she said: "You're the first mortal soul I've spoken with in all this time."

"My God," he said. "Well, listen—er—what's your name, babe?"

After a moment's pause she said, "Mendoza."

So she was Spanish? "Okay, Mendoza. I'll get you out of here. That time shuttle out there is *mine* now, babe, and when I've finished this other thing I'll come back for you." He squeezed her hand for emphasis.

Yes, he had impressed her, he could tell. Her face had gone pale again, the color had just fled, and her eyes were worried. He didn't want to worry her, though. Just impress her. Make her happy. Could he do that? Yes, if she'd lie down beside him. Nice little girl, she meant no harm. He argued earnestly. Suddenly there was an island of clarity and he realized he'd just offered to marry her.

The moment it was out of his mouth he was horrified at what he'd just said, and he didn't know what to make of the expression on her face. He blurted:

"And then afterward we could just get a divorce."

She was staring. He tried to reconstruct what he'd been saying. Had he insulted her? She didn't smell angry. Just as though she needed someone terribly.

He must have asked her to sleep with him, because she leaned down and kissed him, very gently but full on the mouth, parting his lips. He liked that a great deal. He liked the scent and the taste of her, he liked the weight of her breasts, and he wanted very much to untwine that long braid and get his fingers in her hair. About all he was actually able to do in his present condition was open his mouth and grope a bit, and for one wonderful moment he thought his skull was going to explode.

There was a distant rumble of thunder. She had gone to the window to see what had caused the rumbling noise.

"There's a cloud front advancing," she announced in surprise. "Have you brought rain, like the west wind? I think we're going to have a summer storm."

As if in agreement with her words, a gust of turbulent air danced in through the window. Alex knitted his brows. Had they had sex yet? He couldn't remember.

Gradually his higher brain function came back. He lay quietly on Mendoza's bed, sipping tea and watching her move in her kitchen corner.

She was a botanist, she explained, and the Company kept her busy on this island, which was one of their agricultural stations. She told him about the Day Six resorts, and how she had to grow lettuce for their restaurants.

"But that's awful," Alec said, leaning up on his elbow. "That means you're their slave!"

"I suppose I am." Mendoza looked up from the table where she was dicing tomatoes. "But I may as well be of some use to somebody, don't you think? They don't call for produce very often. I have a lot of time to work on my own private research."

"What's your research?" he said, watching her small deft hands.

"Do you know anything about maize?" she said, without much hope.

"No. What is it?"

She sighed. "Well, you landed in a field of it—not my special cultivars, fortunately, just the yellow stuff. This." She held up one of the things he had taken for an immense joint of ganja, and stripped back the husk. He recognized the bright kernels.

"Oh! American corn, like on the cob? That's what it looks like before it goes into a pouch? Wow. That's what you're researching?"

"Yes. You see, maize isn't really very good for you," she explained, oddly apologetic. "It's generally lysine deficient, which prevents the human system from utilizing certain amino acids. Also deficient in tryptophan and useable niacin." Methodically she swept the tomatoes from her cutting board into a bowl and began mincing up a bunch of cilantro. "As a rule, the bigger and paler it's bred, the less it's worth as a food source."

He couldn't imagine why Mendoza was telling him this, but he nodded politely as she went on:

"The paradox has always fascinated me. Why has nobody ever produced a cultivar with the nutritional value of, for example, soy or buckwheat? Or better?" She added the cilantro to the tomatoes and began peeling cloves of garlic.

"Anyway, that's become my life's goal: to create from maize the perfect grain, something so rich in lysine and other nutrients that it could sustain humanity nearly on its own. Something to guarantee that no mortal child would ever suffer from malnourishment again."

"Good for you, then," said Alec. "At least you're trying to make your life count for something."

"Oh, I expect everybody tries." Mendoza shrugged. He watched the way it made her breasts rise. Pulling his attention back, he said:

"Not everybody. Most people just drift through their lives. And even the people who want to help just tell other people what to do. None of it does any good! People talk to hear themselves talk, that's all."

"I feel that way myself. I'm glad we agree," Mendoza said carefully, looking down at the garlic she was chopping. "Though you appear to be something of a man of action. Personally, I have my reservations even about action. I seem to have broken everything I ever touched, no matter how well-meaning I was. Perhaps it's best I wound up here, where I can do no harm."

"I know what you mean," Alec said. "It's like there's this curse. And it doesn't matter what you do, you don't even have to *do* anything, you can be just—born, and you make people miserable by even existing. You can try to right wrongs or you can be a criminal, and it all comes to the same thing! All you ever do turns out badly."

She looked at him keenly. "So you keep trying to atone for your sins."

"Well, *sins* is kind of a heavy word, but—yeah, basically."

"And somehow nothing you do is ever enough, you can never set things right, so at last you pin all your hopes on giving your life in a good cause."

"Maybe." Alec blinked, realizing it came down to just that. "And, you know what? You can't lose that way, dying for something. Not only do you finally do some good for a change, you can't ever do any more harm."

"Except to the people who love you," Mendoza said. "They'll suffer every day for the rest of their lives, and God help them if their lives are long. Don't do such a cruel thing, Alec. Have mercy on yourself, and on them."

"There's nobody to miss me, though," he told her. "I'm a free agent."

"Nobody? There's always somebody, señor. Parents, at least."

"Parents!" He gave a brief angry laugh. "My father's dead, and I'm pretty certain now he wasn't really my father at all."

"Oh. You were illegitimate?"

"You could say that. And my real mother's delusional, she's been locked up for thirty years, and it's my fault. *And* Dr. Zeus's fault. I was raised by a nice old couple who worked for my father, but they're both dead now. I've got two ex-wives. One of 'em probably can't remember my name, and the other hated being married to me so bad she freaked out and called the Ephesians to come save her.

"I did have a best friend, who's stuck with me all my life, but I might have just got him killed. Don't *you* think it'd have been better if I'd never been born?" Alec lay back, exhausted at his outpouring of bitterness. He was sorry he'd said it all now; Mendoza's face was so white and stricken. She shook her head slowly.

"I'm sorry," he said. "I really am. I didn't mean I was going to snuff myself. Don't you ever go crazy with the feeling, though? Like being a fish in a net?"

"Believe me, I do," she said. "It's why I don't mind being here so much."

"But, see, in a way this is the same. You're tinkering around with this corn that might feed millions of poor people someday, but you're stuck here, so what good can it do? Dr. Zeus has taken away your whole life. Don't you mind? Didn't you ever want anything more for yourself?"

"I did," she said. "It led to a disaster, I'm afraid. That was my point about being at this station. I can't hurt anybody here."

"But you can't help anybody either, can you?" he pointed out. "And nobody should be a slave, no matter what they've done! Have mercy on yourself too, babe. Let me give you a ride out of here."

There was a long moment of silence and then she lifted her head to look at him, a black intense stare he could almost feel like a touch.

"You're offering to break my chains? All right," she said. "Let's make a bargain. You won't die, and I'll let you bring me back from death in life. And we'll see what happens, shall we?"

"Sure," said Alec. "It's a deal, Mendoza."

He knew he'd made her sad, and he hadn't meant to. All the rest of the day he told Mendoza about better memories: the aimless days of floating from island to island, the pirate stories Sarah told him and the pirate fortresses he'd built in sand. She listened, rapt, as she prepared their evening meal. When she'd finished and washed her hands she came and sat by him again. Neither of them noticed when the rain began, big hot drops pattering in the dust of the garden.

It seemed to make her so happy, to hear how he'd sailed under strange stars and explored tropical islands. He told her nothing about the Captain, beyond saying that he'd developed his own powerful system to help him run things; but he told her about the storms he'd ridden out, the one terrible hurricane where he'd watched from his safety harness as the *Captain Morgan* was rolled over and over in the water, but was okay because her masts and spars were all retracted and the protective dome had been extended over her deck, so she was like an unbreakable bottle.

He told her about the speck of an island he'd bought in the Caribbean, and how he went exploring there and found Spanish fortifications, and digging in them (he omitted to state that he was burying one of the Captain's backup caches) he'd found a handful of gold doubloons.

He told her about lying alone at night on deck, watching the slow stars and the quick-traveling satellites move across the sky, and the meteor showers he saw, and how he sang to himself as loudly as he wanted and heard his voice go out over the wide quiet water, with no one for countless miles to hear him or complain about his sea songs.

"Neither of my ex-wives could stand my singing," he added, laughing. He was sitting propped up by this time, and the headache from his flight was gone. "I like the old chanteys and yo-heave-ho stuff."

"Oh, but please," said Mendoza, "sing something now. I won't complain, I swear. Sing whatever you like."

So he sang "High Barbary" for her, he sang her "The Captain's Apprentice," he even sang her his favorite one about the Flying Dutchman; and the damnedest thing happened: she liked them. The little girl sat there beside him and, for God's sake, began to cry. He found himself reaching to pull her down beside him before he'd finished the last verse. Mendoza buried her face against his neck, and he felt hot tears.

"Babe, it's okay. It didn't really happen, you know," he said. "The Flying Dutchman and all that."

"Man, your ex-wives must have been a couple of stupid bitches," Mendoza said in a muffled voice. He grinned.

"I always kind of thought I'd like being the Flying Dutchman," he said. "Just me and my ship, and the sea. Staying out on blue water and never coming in. I'm not really very good with people."

"Neither am I," Mendoza said.

"Well, how would you know? You haven't had a chance to meet any yet." He put his arm around her. "You're going to have a great time, you'll see. As soon as I finish that other stuff I have to take care of, you can come along and watch me kick ass on Dr. Zeus. Okay? Would you like that?"

"You know, I really think you could," Mendoza said wonderingly. She leaned up to kiss him, and now he was feeling well enough to kiss back with his customary expertise. It became a very long kiss, quite steamy. He ran his hands along her body, wondering how her coveralls fastened.

But she was so young. Must be careful, must be so gentle. She'd been there all alone for years. He started at the realization that she could have had no other lover.

"Er—" he said, coming up for air with a gulp.

"What is it?" She looked at him dazedly.

"You're—you're a virgin, I guess, yeah?"

Mendoza's expression changed, for a second was blank and unreadable. After a pause she said: "Yes. It's all right, though. Please."

Alec looked down at his body, still encased in the subsuit he'd donned how many hours ago now? And how much of his cold sweat and panic terror had the thermals underneath absorbed?

"Can I use your shower?" He looked around, realizing he hadn't noticed a bathroom. It was her turn to look flustered.

"I haven't got a shower. Just a tin tub in the back garden, for baths. The only time it's possible to actually shower is when it's raining fairly hard." Mendoza's eyes widened as she took in the sound of the rain, that had been drumming away pretty steadily for some time now. ". . . Which it is, isn't it? I'll get you a towel."

"Cool." Alec sat up carefully and then stood, and was pleased to discover he felt great. He pushed open what looked to be a back door and stepped out into the garden and the warm rain.

It was pretty back there, tile paths and green lawn, big bushes of fragrant stuff becoming more fragrant in the rain. Mint, that was what it must be. And here was her tin tub, already full and overflowing. He stripped out of his clothing in the steady downpour, sucking in the wet sweet air. It smelled like wet summer grass, wet stone and earth, green fields in the summer storm. He stepped carefully into the tub and sat down, tilting his face back, letting the rain wash away his sweat and desperation.

He opened his eyes and saw Mendoza standing in the doorway, watching him. She didn't look scared, to see him naked. Always a good sign. He smiled at her.

"Would you, er, like to bathe, too?" he invited, as casually as he could. Mendoza got a wild look in her eyes and started toward him through the rain, peeling off her clothes as she came.

"Now, this is the part of the film," she said, in her clear and carefully enunciated way, "where the orchestra begins to play the love theme with a lot of strings and horns, you know, and the camerawork goes sort of blurry and focuses on the lovers embracing passionately, but only from the waist up of course, and then the camera pulls back and tilts up into the branches of the trees, or perhaps goes to a stock shot of crashing waves or something—"

"The hair—the hair—"

"Okay—" Mendoza paused beside the tub, tilting her head to loose the long braid, and he reached out eager hands to help her. She shook her hair out. It was just as he had thought it would be. So was her body, and the perfume of her arousal was driving him mad.

She stepped into the opposite end of the tub, which was not nearly big enough for two people, and within seconds they were grappling and splashing, kissing feverishly.

"Wait, this is nuts," she moaned, "There's no room—"

"Yes, there is," Alec said. He struggled to his feet and lifted her in his arms, high above him, pressed close, and let her slide down until her breasts were on a level with his face. "Oh, yum—"

Things went along very nicely indeed for the next few minutes. Mendoza's arms went around him; then he felt her stiffen slightly.

"Alec, darling," she said, with just the slightest trace of strain in her voice, "this is a rather unusual tattoo you have."

"No'uh tattoo," he said. "M'a thyborg!"

"I beg your pardon?"

He lifted his mouth and looked up at her. "You know how I told you I've got this big custom cybersystem, to work the rigging on my ship? That's how I run it. I'm a cyborg, have been since I was eighteen."

Mendoza began to quiver in his arms, and he thought for one awful second she was turned off by his revelation. Then he saw she was laughing, so silently and profoundly she could barely draw breath.

"Oh, perfect," she gasped. Her eyes widened in sudden shock and she looked down at him. "*What* year did you say it was where you come from?"

"Er . . . 2351," he said, wondering why they had to talk about this right now.

"But that's only four years from—" Mendoza's face underwent such an extraordinary transformation that he nearly dropped her. "Dear God in Heaven, it's *you*!" She flung her fists toward the sky, jubilant, fierce, howling with laughter that echoed from the green canyon walls.

"*YOU'RE* THE NEMESIS, *YOU'RE* THE APOCALYPSE, *YOU'RE* THE SILENCE!" she cried into the storm. "YOU *WILL* BREAK DR. ZEUS!"

There was a triple flash of lightning at that moment, with a roar of thunder so loud Alec thought the world was ending. In the terrifying blue illumination he looked up and saw her poised above him. She might have been something out of another world, bright as a flame, her eyes glowing with inhuman love.

"Oh," he said, and then Mendoza had slid down and clamped her mouth on his, and they wrestled there as the lightning flashed, the thunder boomed. Their struggles overturned the tin tub, dumping them unceremoniously onto the lawn in a flood of rainwater, and they rolled on the tidy grass and he seized her.

Their eyes met. For a hushed moment there was a perfect mutual understanding Alec could never have put into words, the most profound intimacy, and the overwhelming conviction that he was about to remember *who she was*. Then the madness claimed them both and he couldn't think, couldn't think.

"Mendoza?"

"Mm?" Lazily she tousled his wet lank hair.

"We need to talk about a few things."

"We certainly do," she said.

Alec rose on his elbows and lifted his head to consider the rain, which was still drumming down on them. He wiped his face with one hand. "We should probably go inside before we catch cold. Or drown."

"Okay," she said. He maneuvered himself up, and Mendoza accepted his extended hand to pull her to her feet.

Within a few minutes, with their soaked clothing drying in front of a pleasantly crackling fire, they were sitting down to supper at her rough-hewn table. He felt insanely calm, aware that something truly frightening had happened to him and that somehow he wasn't afraid. Who could be afraid of the angel/demoness/little lost girl sitting down across from him, so politely offering a home-cooked supper?

Not that it wasn't the most surreal dining experience he'd ever had.

"So this is—?" He lifted an oblong package on his plate with the times of his fork.

"That's a tamale. Please take the wrapper off before you eat it."

"Oh. Like banana leaves?"

"Precisely."

"Okay," he said, and took it apart bemusedly. "About that thing that happened? What was it you called me, the Nemesis? What was that about, exactly?"

"Well." Mendoza took a bite of rolled-up tortilla. "I'm going to tell you something very, very classified," she said, chewing. "I believe I mentioned that Dr. Zeus, possessing the secret of time travel, knows everything that's ever happened in recorded history, as well as everything that ever will happen. Beer?"

"Yes, please," he said, holding out his mug. She poured something hoppy and amber from a stone pitcher and continued:

"Everything that ever will happen, I say—*up to the year 2355.* You understand this is a matter of intense speculation for everyone concerned with the Company. But the fact is, beyond July 9, 2355, there's just—silence."

"Silence how?" Alec frowned.

"Not one word from our future selves on the other side of that moment in time. I have heard that the last message, badly distorted, says simply *'We still don't know—'*. As you might imagine, a Company so accustomed to being omniscient isn't at all happy about being in the dark like everybody else on something so important."

"What's omniscient mean? And why don't they just travel forward through time to see what happens then?" Alec asked.

"*Omniscient* means all-knowing," Mendoza said. "Like God. But Dr. Zeus isn't all powerful, you see, because time travel into the future isn't possible. Or so we are told."

"Okay," said Alec, smiling at her erudition and the matter-of-fact way she was telling him all this. He had a brief vision of the little girl at a tea party, lecturing to her dolls.

"Naturally," she went on, pouring herself a beer and drinking, "there are those who insist that the future beyond 2355 really is known, that the silence is maintained by whoever seizes control on July 9."

"And you know about all this because . . . ?"

"I told you I became privy to certain secrets, didn't I?" she said, looking opaque again. "So. Most of us feel that an intracorporate war at that time is inevitable, with the winner keeping silent to conceal the circumstances of his, her, their or its victory. And it will go very, very badly for the losers, on that day."

His amusement evaporated abruptly.

"But you shouldn't—" he said. "If there's some kind of bloody takeover, there could be a purge. Executions. You're a security risk, and Dr. Zeus doesn't give a shrack about little people's lives. I know!"

"Damned right I'm a security risk," she said coolly. "That's why I'm talking to you."

Alec stared at her, disconcerted. He cleared his throat.

"Mendoza," he said, "you're young, and you've lived in this hole for most of your life. It's dangerous to be so reckless, baby. How do you know it's safe to tell me this stuff? Just because we had sex doesn't make me a good guy, you know."

"How do you know it's safe to tell me anything?" she countered. "I'm a criminal, remember? You're pretty trusting yourself."

He snorted. "Maybe, with a little girl in a garden. There are a lot worse crimes committed out in the real world than anything you could ever have done."

She was silent a moment, and then shrugged. "But on the other hand, what if Alec Checkerfield is what happens in 2355? I think you really will kick Dr. Zeus's all-knowing ass. I say go for it, darling." She raised her beer in a toast. "I only hope I'm around to see."

"You will be," he said, wondering what on earth had happened to her, to make her speak so flippantly of her own death. He reached across the table and stroked her cheek. "I promise you. You'll be right there with me. God knows you shouldn't be running around loose."

"Let us hope so," she said, kissing the palm of his hand and taking it between both of her own. "But life is so uncertain, señor. In any case, start planning your attack now. Twenty-three fifty-five is your window of opportunity, you see?"

"You said something, though." Alec squeezed her hand. "You said time travel into the future doesn't work, and then you said *Or so we are told*. Does that mean maybe there's just a teeny winji chance somebody might do it, if he was lucky?"

"Unlucky," she said, and for a moment there was a cold unhappiness in her face, so bleak an expression he wanted to gather her into his arms and rock her, anything to give comfort. She drew a deep breath and spoke with deliberation:

"There is evidence that the temporal wave can, under certain circumstances, pull one forward as well as backward. I know of a place where it might happen; but you really wouldn't want to try."

"But if I did try," Alec persisted, "say if I had certain advantages other people didn't, I might manage it. Or I could just lay low for the next four years, wait and see what happens in 2355—and then go back to now and set up for bringing Dr. Zeus down, because I'll be the only one who knows the truth."

Mendoza smiled. "You might try, darling, but you'd run into problems. There are two more things you need to know about temporal physics. The one immutable law is that history cannot be changed. Okay? So if you waited until 2355, and turned on the news one day and heard that Dr. Zeus survived a coup attempt, you couldn't go back in time and fix things so that the rebels win."

"I see," he said, narrowing his eyes. "What's the other thing I need to know about?"

"A complication technically described as *variable permeability of the temporal fabric*," Mendoza told him, and he loved the way her mouth moved as she enunciated the words, in her educated voice. But where could she have been educated?

Was she lying to him? Was that why bits of her story didn't add up, or was she just leaving out things it would be difficult to explain, as he had left certain things out of what he'd told her? Innocent people had secrets, too.

"Temporal fabric?" he inquired, taking a sip of beer. "Now, what in hell does that mean?"

"What it means is that there seems to be a limit on how often you can go back to the same point in time. Dr. Zeus doesn't know why. But if, say, you went back in time to buy a winning lottery ticket on a certain day—and of course you'd need to get hold of the Temporal Concordance for the numbers, no mean trick in itself—"

"Temporal *Concordance*?"

"The database containing every single event in recorded history up to July 8, 2355," Mendoza explained. "It's the single most valuable thing the Company owns. Anyway, even assuming you got that far, you'd better be damned sure you did it right, because you probably wouldn't have a second chance."

"So if I got the numbers wrong and tried to go back a second time—?"

"Your shuttle would probably veer off to the day before or the day after (and to some other point in physical space, too, which could cause real trouble for you) but *never again* to that particular place and time. You see?"

"I think so." He frowned down at his dinner, uneasily aware that answering his questions might be putting her life in jeopardy. But if she were really telling the truth . . .

He lifted the beer pitcher, topped up her mug and his.

"Go on," he said.

They retired, pleasantly crowded on her narrow bed, with the rain still drumming outside and the smell of the wet garden coming through the windows. He made overtures, and she responded to them with enthusiasm and in fact with a certain expertise that bewildered him. As the act, and then the acts, progressed, it became apparent that she knew as much about what they were doing as any girl in any Happy Club he had ever visited. Then she gave every evidence of knowing *more*, and his body told his brain to shut up . . .

Only in the afterglow was he able to start thinking again, uneasily connecting dots without numbers as she slept in his arms. Had she been lying? Unconscious and relaxed, she looked unnervingly like a child, terrifyingly young for what she'd just been doing with him. Who could have taught her such things? Had she been abused by her jailers?

And yet she'd seemed so happy . . .

As though you've ever had any clue what a girl's thinking, Alec reminded himself. He lay there on the edge of sleep, watching the flames dancing in the fireplace across the room, backlighting her hair, flickering on her pale skin.

Who on earth was this little girl? Twice the bad bet Lorene had been . . . He could certainly pick them. Despair and disaster attracted him like a perfume.

Third time's the charm, babe, he thought drowsily, and kissed her.

Darkness lit by the fires of war, eerie silence.

He saw Mendoza, wide-eyed, advancing across a battlefield, oblivious to the pits of flaming debris and the tracer fire, to the disrupter beams piercing the smoky air and narrowly missing her. There was a bush still standing in the wasteland, a dark thing with sharp spines and berries bright as blood. She seemed to be drawn to it, fascinated, not seeing the dangers at all. She was stretching out her hand . . .

He was trying to warn her, bounding forward to pull her down—when he woke with a start, to find that Mendoza had evidently gone out into the rain and was now climbing in beside him. She was wet and chilled.

"What were you doing?" he gasped, heart hammering.

"It's all right," she whispered. "I had to see to something."

"You're cold as death," he said, and pulled her close and wrapped his arms around her, as though that might keep her away from the dark field.

He didn't recall where he was when he woke next morning, at first, and Mendoza seemed equally surprised to find him there. They made love.

It was, again, a smashing success, but he found himself, again, wondering how a virgin could have learned so many interesting variations on a theme.

Afterward, in another scene of surreal domesticity, she fixed them breakfast as he pulled on his thermals, and they chatted over coffee as though they sat in a kitchen in London.

Finally Alec cleared his throat and said:

"Er . . . when we were in bed, I couldn't help noticing that you . . . ah. That trick with your—er . . ."

"You mean the . . ."

"When we . . . you know, when the bed leg fell off?"

"Ah! Yes."

"I was surprised you knew that one," he said, looking her in the eye. "It takes a little practice, yeah?"

Mendoza went pale, with a look of such dismay on her face he was immediately sorry he'd said anything. Then she blushed, setting down her coffee cup.

"Well, I have a lot of time to read and I have quite a collection of pornographic books the last supply shuttle happened to leave here, you see, and—"

"Books?" Alec knitted his brows. "Those are hard to find—"

"Holoes, I mean!" She smacked her forehead in chagrin. "Of course I meant holoes, how silly of me, what was I thinking? Like, ah, *Mr. Fireman and His Big Hose. Bad Bondage Boys. Emmanuelle and the Cream Pie Factory.* You see? And I've studied them. Obsessively."

But she was trembling. He was certain she'd been abused, then, and it wrung his heart. He got up and put his arms around her.

"Don't be scared," he said. "I thought it was wonderful."

"I love you," she said, in a tiny voice. He realized, with an increasing sense of satisfying doom, that marriage was now inevitable.

By the time they walked back to the shuttle, the storm had blown out and the sun was bright. Alec found himself sweating inside his subsuit.

The rain had washed the shuttle clean of all the leaves and stalks that had splattered on its hull, and it glinted silver in the morning light. The hatch had been closed. Alec couldn't remember having done that, but he'd been pretty hazy in those first few minutes. He stood there in the waving corn, looking uncertainly at the ship, trying to access the command that would activate it again.

The data was all there; there was just too much of it. No Captain to instantly hand him the right file out of a hundred million files. Mendoza looked at him, her pale face expressionless. She leaned close and reached up to put her arms about his neck.

"I have the impression that the cyborgs who normally pilot these ships access them through a file with a designation of TTMIX333," she said. "Does that sound right?"

Abruptly everything came into focus and he had the correct file, though he couldn't recall having learned how to access it in the first place. "I think—" he began, just as the lights blinked on and the hatch popped open for him. "Hey!"

"There you are," Mendoza said. "You see? You had it in your memory all the time. Wow, this fancy rug's gotten soggy." She scrambled inside and he climbed in after her. She stood there a moment staring around at the shuttle's interior, and picked up one of the pink rosebuds that had been jolted from its crystal vase by the impact of the landing. She examined it bleakly. "No expense spared, eh?"

"Yeah, the bastards," Alec said, opening the minibar. "Check this out. Six different fruit juices and three kinds of real booze. Illegal as hell, and I should know. Bombay Sapphire, Stolichnaya and—hey, here's the magic potion." He waved a little bottle labeled CAMPARI. She nodded, not looking up.

"How could something that began with such idealism—" Mendoza said. Her mouth twisted and she looked away. He realized she was nearly in tears.

"They'll pay," he said.

"They ought to," she said, in a voice trembling with rage or grief or both. "Those damned liars. So many people sweating blood over so many ages, and was it all for this? So rich idiots could have an exotic holiday? Pink rosebuds and vodka in 150,000 BCE, just imagine! And how many like me marooned in places like this, along the way?"

"If there's others, we'll find 'em," Alec said.

Mendoza lifted her head and kissed him, and her kiss was angry but he still liked the taste of it. She raked his lower lip with her teeth as she pulled away.

"You drink that down," she said, nodding at the bottle he was holding. "I'll show you the algorithm to return to the future."

The red fluid was deadly bitter, even mixed with gin. He got it down somehow and was still able to concentrate as she showed him what he had to do. Then the shuttle began to hum, warning lights flashed because the hatch was still open. They looked at each other and realized their moment had passed, slipped away like sand.

From the other side of the glass Mendoza told him *I love you*, ignoring the blast of air from the engines that was bending the green corn down, blowing her hair back like flames in the wind, all in deafening silence. The ship began to rise, the yellow gas began to curl through the stale air of the cabin. Until his vision was taken away Alec peered down at her, wondering if she'd be all right there alone, trying to keep the image of the nightmare field out of his mind.

The pressure wasn't nearly so bad this time. The shuttle now magically obeyed his every order as soon as he gave it. The yellow smoke was vanishing, it was roiling away, and there in front of him was a black night sky and stars. Below him he saw the distant lights of the *Captain Morgan* at anchor. Alec was shocked to realize that he was arriving back on the same night he'd left, no more than a few seconds after his departure.

He sent the shuttle arrowing down to his ship, mentally groping to order her cargo hatches open. Would she obey? Was the Captain there waiting for him?

No answer when he called, but the hatch doors were opening, the lights in the hold were guiding him down. This was so easy! The shuttle dropped into place like a bird alighting in a nest. The hatches swung shut, closing out the stars, and Alec was back on his ship. The whole episode at the station might have been a hallucination. For a moment the idea paralyzed him with terror.

Then he turned to get out of his seat and saw the bits of green stuff on the damp carpet. Wreckage from Mendoza's cornfield, tracked in on his boots. He'd really been there.

That was enough to brace Alec as he climbed out of the shuttle and ran through his ship, up through her decks to the bridge. It was deserted, except for Billy Bones and Flint, who stood motionless.

Captain!

There was no answer. Utter silence.

Gulping for breath, he went to the ship's wheel and grasped it to steady himself. *How do I sail her?* He heard the beeping signal that told him the anchor was being weighed. His hands moved on the wheel as though he were actually steering her, and by God she began to tack about. Yes! A glance upward through the glass told him she was opening out her sails, slowly but certainly now, and there was the whoosh that told him she was moving under power, too. Her bowsprit dipped, punched through the trough of a wave and forged on, throwing aside spray.

Where was the readout to show her course? There it was, and somehow the course was already set, they were going back to Mexico and she was picking up speed. Alec did know how to sail her, he'd always known, but somehow he'd never paid attention when the Captain had sailed her for him.

He began to sing in his profound relief, baying out "Blood Red Roses" as loud as he could. It echoed in the cabin and was carried on the ship's intercom to every empty stateroom, to Coxinga where he stood immobile in the galley, to Bully Hayes where he had frozen in the act of laying out Alec's black smuggling clothes. It echoed in the saloon where the Resistance liked to hold their meetings, bouncing off the fine carved chairs, rattling the glasses ranged along the back of the bar.

It echoed in the empty shuttle, where the INTERCEPT program was busily evaluating data as it counted down, unaware that there was no longer any bomb to detonate when the right moment had arrived.

"GO DOWN, YOU BLOOD RED ROSES!"

It might have been minutes or hours later when Alec realized that he had been hearing a signal for some while, an intermittent tapping that cut through the vibration of the ship's drive and the wash of the night sea. It was a deliberate kind of tapping, an old pattern of beats he nearly remembered. A code, wasn't it? What had it been called? Something about *save our souls*?

He turned from the wheel and looked about him on the bridge. There. Billy Bones was moving, at least his foremost leg was: up and falling, tap tap tap, so slowly.

Captain!

Silence, but a listening kind of silence.

Captain, are you there?

After a long moment a faint response: Αλεχ ΙΠμ ηερε.

Trusting the ship to follow her course, Alec dove blindly into cyberspace.

It had altered, it wasn't full of light but green gloom, an underwater murk that went down into blackness and out in a hazy vista of broken spars and rigging. Wrecks. A Sargasso of code strangling, blinding, but not completely concealing the ruined giant that was stretched out in the dim netherworld.

Βοχ

A horror, a mutilation, a joke. One leg gone, one hand gone, the faintest of equations sketched in to show where they ought to be. One eye gone and trying to replace itself; but every time it flickered back into existence, it was being torn away by . . . what *was* that thing?

On the Captain's shoulder perched a nightmare creature of green bronze, a caricature of a parrot with a hooked beak, tearing steadily and mercilessly at the right side of the Captain's face, revealing a steel skull and sputtering wires.

Before Alec was even aware he'd thought of it, the bird screamed and shattered into fragments. Alec vaulted through space to the Captain's side with an astonishing strength and solidity, more than he'd ever had in cyberspace before. Finally left alone, the Captain's face pieced itself back together and turned up to him.

Boψ. Mψ Boψ.

Alec leaned down and grasped the Captain's remaining hand. Again, he scarcely knew what he meant to do, but it was already happening: fire was racing down his arm and tracing in the missing parts of the Captain, repairing, replacing, reviving.

*************Alεχ

Hold on!

****Alec—

Hold on, I've got you.

Bloody Hell! Boy, you've grown.

They stared at each other as the lights came up, and the terrifying green realm was sucked away into nothing. They stood on the pitching deck of the ship as it appeared in cyberspace, much the same as it appeared in reality. The Captain had been restored to his normal appearance. Alec was so relieved he felt slightly drunk. It was a moment before he noticed the Captain's incredulous stare. Looking down at himself he realized that he *had* grown, at least in cyberspace, where he had always been a head shorter than the Captain. Now they were the same size.

How did that happen?

You tell me, son! But however you did it, I ain't complaining.

Are you all right now? You looked awful.

Haaaar! You should see the other bastard. He may have shot away my mainmast, but I lifted his cargo all the same. We got the data, Alec! It don't matter whether you steal that shuttle or not—

But I did steal it. It's in the hold.

So much the better. We can go anywhere in time now, Alec, I got the secret of his precious time transcendence field! What's more, I got most of the temporospatial charts he uses. And there's other things too, Alec, there's a whole bag of tricks we got now. You and me has to have a bit of a chat, lad.

Okay.

Not tonight, though. Time you got some sleep. I'll wake you when we get to Mexico.

The fact was that Alec had already had sleep, hours of it; as far as his body was concerned it was only about ten o'clock in the morning. He thought of Mendoza, staring up at him, and felt a pang. How to tell the Captain about her? As soon as this Mars thing was behind them . . .

Okay. Wow, I'm glad to have you back! Effortlessly he surfaced from cyberspace to the real quarterdeck, and went off to his cabin to get out of the subsuit. Billy Bones and Flint crawled after him. The Captain watched him go, wondering how to tell Alec about *Adonai*. However he brought the subject up, now wasn't the time. As soon as they'd finished this bloody stupid trip to Mars . . .

Balkister and the rest of the Resistance were gathered on the pier when Alec arrived, having heroically brought down all the contraband. The eastern sky paled as they loaded the crates across the deck of the *Captain Morgan* and down through her cargo bay, into the waiting hatch of the shuttle. They worked with only the occasional jolly jape, because they were weary and hung over, and the business didn't seem nearly so much fun now that it was almost accomplished. Alec let them do the heavy work. He busied himself loading on rations for a week, spare clothing, and a very large black suitcase.

Shortly before sunrise Alec climbed into the shuttle again. He gave a last thumbs-up to Balkister, who saluted him, then scrambled back as the shuttle roared to life and rose up through the air. The Resistance crowded together in the hold, staring up to watch. The shuttle became a spark of fire, meeting at last the light of the sun below the horizon. Finally it became too tiny to make out.

"Well, that's that," said Magilside. There was a soft chiming sound.

"Cargo hatches will close in three minutes," announced a male voice, polite but with a certain rough edge. **"Please vacate cargo hold at once. Thank you."**

"I suppose we'd best go ashowe," said Binscarth, looking around in longing. "Pity we can't just cwuise away, isn't it? I'm sure Checkerfield wouldn't mind, and the accommodations are much nicer . . ."

"Don't be a blockhead," Balkister said sternly. "Do you want to be on board this ship if the owners of that shuttle catch up with it?"

"Oops! Hadn't thought of that." Binscarth giggled. "You're wight, of course. Just like you to have thought out all the details, Giles. But that's why you're the natuwal leader, after all."

"Cargo hatches will close in two minutes and thirty seconds," the male voice warned.

"Right," said Balkister. "Let's go, fellow freedom fighters. On to the rendezvous."

As he led the way out of the hold and across the deck, Balkister swaggered, had a certain deadly glint in his eye. For the first time in his life, he wished he had a sword to brandish.

The Resistance went back up the stairs to the house, where they piled into a series of expensive offroad agcars and sped away for the nearest airport. Alone on the beautiful blue bay, the *Captain Morgan* put out to sea and tacked around, moving out under power for Panama. The white house stood deserted.

Oops

Alec watched breathlessly as the Earth became a sphere under him. It was just like every picture and film he'd ever seen, but it was still beautiful, still terrifying. He peered ahead at the red dot in the sky that was his destination, then back at the dwindling Earth. He made out North and South America and the wasp-waist that joined them, and he wondered how the *Captain Morgan* fared.

Not to worry, lad. She's fair on course for the canal, and then home to the Caribbean.

Great. Are you feeling cramped in there, Captain, sir? Alec said, referring to the big black suitcase.

No worse'n you must be, lad.

It'll be a short trip, at least. Alec yawned and stretched. He looked around at the space in which he was to live for the next week. There wasn't much, to put it mildly. The crates of weapons had nearly filled the passenger area, leaving him enough room to stand, sit, and lie down. By turning sideways he could squeeze through to the shuttle's lavatory. His movement was further inhibited because the artificial gravity system seemed to be overcompensating, making him feel heavy and clumsy. It didn't matter. This time next week . . .

So, Captain, sir. I had this sort of adventure whilst I was making off with the time shuttle.

So did I. What sort of adventure?

Well, I met this girl.

Did you, now, lad? And where might this girl have been?

She was marooned on this island in prehistoric times. She's a political prisoner, Captain! Or a corporate prisoner, I guess. Of Dr. Zeus. Now that I think about it I must have been on Catalina Island all along. Moved through

*time but not space, maybe. Anyhow I made a rough landing and she rescued
me when I blacked out. I spent a whole day there. I, er, spent the night there.*

With the girl.

*Uh-huh. And we just . . . hit it off. She's been stranded at this agricul-
tural station since she was a kid. Dr. Zeus has her doing hard labor, and she's
the only living soul there. I promised I'd come back and rescue her. And—*

And what, Alec?

And marry her, too.

Bloody hell, boy, what did you go do that for?

*Look, I know how you felt about Lorene and, er, Courteney. This is dif-
ferent.*

Alec, how long were you there?

*Okay, so we spent twenty-four hours together. All right? But if you'd
been there, Captain, sir, you'd understand. She saved my life.*

Is she the one as gave you the drug for the time shock?

So you noticed? Yes, she did.

Hm.

Plus she showed me the algorithm for getting back through time.

She did, eh?

Yeah. And . . . she let me in on some of Dr. Zeus's secrets.

When the Captain responded after a moment's pause, there was a
decidedly funny tone in his voice.

What might her name be, now, this girl you met?

Mendoza.

This time there was an even longer pause before the Captain responded.

The botanist Mendoza.

*Yeah, I guess she's a botanist. She says Dr. Zeus knows everything that's
going to happen in the future, but only up to the year 2355, and they're running scared because of it.*

**That's true. I'd found that much out, afore that bronze son of a
whore walked in. The Company's got no idea why they never get
any transmissions from after that point in time. They guard what
they do know of the future like a treasure map; it's called the Temporal Concordance. Even their own operatives only get little slices
of it, on a need-to-know basis.**

The little girl had told him the truth! Alec grinned, absurdly relieved.

*And she says she thinks I'm the reason why the Silence falls. She told
me about the way time travel works, too, and something called the Variable
permewhatsis—*

Variable permeability of the temporal fabric?

Yeah! You see? This girl is really different.

She's different, all right.

After we rescue her, maybe she can help me bring down Dr. Zeus. She knows a lot of classified stuff.

She might, at that.

Another long silence. At last the Captain said:

Maybe we'll trust her. She'd make a rare prize, anyway . . . So, matey. We finish this job, and we'll go back to that station and make off with her. You'll have yer way. But this one yer going to introduce to yer old Captain. I've a fancy to have a talk or two with the lady, private-like.

Okay! You'll like her, I know you will.

Happen I will, lad. Happen I will.

The shuttle sped on, across the waste of stars, as the blue ball shrank and the red dot grew bigger.

There had been a time when the distance to the red planet had been measured in thirty-six years. One day it had suddenly become a possibility, a matter of two years; then the estimated time needed to get there had dropped to a year, and not long after that to six months. As the decades of technological innovation went by on Earth, the calculation of time for the journey kept getting shorter, until after antigravity was rediscovered and it had condensed to a round-trip time of one week.

Three days out, Alec was heartily sick of the cramped quarters in the time shuttle. The damp carpet had begun to smell funny and the shuttle's lavatory was worse. Not even the irradiated Christmas cake had given him any sense of the holiday. He'd attempted to celebrate by singing a few carols to himself, but the effect was too depressing. Light conversation with the Captain was becoming a little difficult, as the Captain was busy compensating for the time lag between his auxiliary and earthbound caches, and asking anything more than vital questions seemed unwise.

At last Alec gave up and looked out at the stars, and later down on the deserts of red rock, on the green network of irrigation canals and outlined squares, on Mons Olympus that appeared at first like an island floating above the planet's surface and then attached itself as Mars rotated through its long day.

Coming within range of their sensors. Now might be the time to make the jump, lad.

Okay. We have to calculate where Mars was in space two months ago— and then the algorithm for the time—

It's done, lad. Just you fix yerself one of them bitter cocktails.

Alec made a face but obeyed, going to the minibar. *There's only six of these left. What're we going to do when they're gone?*

Make more. I got the formula now, see? The bastard Doctor's own precious recipe. Drink it down, lad, afore one of them blockade ships notices we're coming in.

Heart pounding, Alec gulped down the cocktail and scrambled into his seat, just managing to get his safety restraints buckled as the stasis gas began to fill the air. He had time to catch a glimpse of the green blockade ships before they vanished in the yellow fog. Then the roar and the impact came, and when the gas dissipated he saw that Mars was suddenly a good deal closer, presenting a different face, crossed by many more of the green and yellow lines.

Bull's eye, said the Captain. **Look at that chronometer, boy! 24 October, 2351. And there's Mars One smack below us.**

Alec gave a howl of incredulous delight. *You mean it really worked?*

Of course it worked. Ain't you my bloody little genius? Let's drop this cargo and go grab yer lady friend.

Alec sent a hail in the code commonly used by the Resistance when contacting Mars One. When at length he had received a wary acknowledgment, he transmitted:

BALKISTER SENDS HIS BEST. PERMISSION TO VISIT?

The reply was a series of numbers, directions to a hangar within Mars One's airspace. Alec grinned and the shuttle dropped down into the thin atmosphere.

He waited impatiently as they went through the airlock, thinking it was a shame Balkister couldn't be with him. Mars itself, a new world! He half expected to find Noel Coward and Marlene Dietrich waiting for him with a band. And the oxygen would be fresh.

The airlock let Alec out at last and he maneuvered the shuttle to a landing pad. By the time the hatch popped he was already poised at the threshold, eager for his first glimpse of the Red Planet.

What he saw was a wall of coral-pink cinderblock. Well, all right: that was to be expected in a hangar. He stuck his head out and gulped in Martian air, then sneezed and shook his head. Moisture, the sour smell of agricultural chemicals, a distinctive bouquet of broccoli and cabbage, and . . .

Shrack! That's funky.

Well, now, son, what did you expect? These folk have to recycle everything.

He stepped out and the wet heavy air fell on him like a blanket, balancing somewhat the giddy lightness he felt. He looked around at the interior of the hangar. It was all concrete molded from the soil, every conceivable shade of pink and orange. He found himself thinking of the ancient city of Petra, where he'd been once to pick up a consignment. Instead of a hot blue sky overhead and sunlight, though, there was the glitter of unfamiliar stars through the transparent dome, and the yellow globes of the methane lamps.

There were only two men waiting for him in the hangar, rawboned, narrow-eyed, suspicious. One of them was carrying a crowbar.

"You're from Ed Balkister?" said the other one.

"Giles, you mean," said Alec, and the men nodded in satisfaction and unison.

Alec, they got surveillance cameras in here.

"What about those?" Alec pointed at the tiny swiveling cameras, and in the light gravity found himself almost jumping up to touch them. The older of the men snorted.

"Those are ours. Come on, what's Balkister got for us?"

Alec had planned on making a rather theatrical presentation, but he realized it would be wasted on these men. He jerked a thumb at the hatch. "Lots of boxes, guys. Help me unload 'em."

They followed him into the shuttle, staring around surlily.

"Somebody's private pleasure craft, eh?" sneered the older man. "Phew! Stinks, though, don't it?"

He should talk, thought Alec, but all he said was, "Yeah, well, freedom gets a little ripe sometimes." He lifted a box easily and thrust it into the man's arms. "Have some."

The man's knees buckled slightly and he stared. "What's this, then?"

Alec leaned close and said: "Guns."

"No shit?" The younger man looked delighted. He bent and forced open a crate with his crowbar. When he saw the contents he gave a cry of glee.

"Like to see the goddam Areco running dogs' faces when they get a look at these!"

"It's not going to come to that, you idiot," protested the older man.

"Oh, yes it is, pal," Alec said. "Trust me. Balkister's got inside information. You're going to need weapons to show Areco you can't be pushed around. Here they are. Okay?"

The older man paled. "We're never going to lose the case to Areco. We're in the right."

"And they're in the money. They'll win."

"We'll appeal!" A red flush of anger spread up the older man's skinny neck.

"We'll be appealing from Luna if we can't keep the bastard marshals from evicting us, Dad," the younger man said, hefting a crate and stepping down out of the hatch with it. "Wake up. The law's been bought. Might's the only right those corporate pigs respect! Thank the man or shut up, but let's get these offloaded."

The older man clamped his grim mouth into a white line and stalked out of the hatch with his crate.

Nobody said anything much after that, so the three men got the crates unloaded in a very short time. Alec had forgotten about the box with the brass skull; it had been packed in one of the offloaded ammo boxes, out of sight and out of mind.

He didn't remember it until he was heading out into space again, and kicked himself mentally, because he had wanted to explain about the inscribed curse. Probably just as well he hadn't, he decided. It didn't seem like something the council representatives of the MAC would appreciate. They weren't a particularly fun bunch of guys.

All set for the jump back, lad? I'd rather do it now, whilst you've still got the drug in yer system. Save you taking a second dose.

Alec shuddered. *Go for it. Let's blow this dump.*

The gas swirled around him again, and he realized with a brief pang of regret that all he'd seen of Mars, once he'd finally got there, had been the inside of one poky little hangar.

With a roar and a shove, he was abruptly back on 27 Christmas, 2351.

Setting a course for Earth, son. We're free and clear. The block-ade ships never even caught a sniff of us.

That's hard to believe. Maybe we can get this thing fumigated before we go after Mendoza, huh? Alec scratched his stubbly chin.

I'll see what I can do, lad. Wouldn't want to spoil yer romantic mood, now, would we?

Within the console of the shuttle the INTERCEPT program ran its course, ticking out its final sequence of numbers. It waited expectantly for the detonation that would tell it its program had been fulfilled. The seconds went by, and no explosion came. The INTERCEPT realized it had been rendered pointless and, because no failure in its execution had ever been anticipated, it quietly expired, and no one—not even Mendoza—knew that it had been set to go off *after* Alec had delivered his payload.

The pattern of destiny swirled and set again, in a new shape, because Alec had not died that night. He had been supposed to; he ought to have been blown to airy powder, a drifting film of ash against the face of heaven and a tiny black box emitting a signal to enable Dr. Zeus to retrieve it at some convenient later date.

But Alec had not died.

———

Kingston was a sparkle of colored lights between the black hills and the black sea. As the shuttle came down, smaller clusters of light appeared, smaller outposts of civilization: vacation villas miles out of the city. They dotted the coast road like beads on a string, each one with its own exclusive bay, white sand, green mangroves, big fences and privacy.

There was a rambling stone house on a hill, overlooking a sheltered cove. It was one of the few houses Alec kept that he actually lived in, from time to time. The old place had belonged to a plantation owner once, and was paneled and floored in beautiful mahogany. Alec had had all the latest entertainment conveniences put in, stocked the bar and wine cellar, and sailed away. He liked it as well as any other house on land. It seemed like a good place to rendezvous.

The New Year's Eve party was pretty well advanced by the time night had fallen. It had started when the Resistance heroes had spotted the *Captain Morgan* slipping into the cove below the house, keeping her appointment with minutes to spare, and no uniformed men with gas guns came boiling out of her hold. A security scan by Krishnamurti showed that she hadn't a living soul on board, which was just as it should be, and in their relief the heroes popped the cork on the first bottle of Perrier-Jouet.

So, some time around ten o'clock, Binscarth was able to do no more than hoot drunkenly and wave an arm when he observed the blue light dropping down from the stars toward the deck of the *Captain Morgan*.

Balkister ran out on the balcony. The cargo hatches of the *Captain Morgan* were opening in majestic silence, receiving the shuttle with perfect timing.

"Oi, lads, he's made it," Balkister screamed. The other members of the Resistance came stumbling out to see, overturning a tray of party dip and chips and a couple of half-empty bottles as they came. A drunken cheer was raised and Binscarth began to sing "For I Am a Pirate King," very much out of tune.

They saw the cargo hatches swinging down and a moment later a dark figure ran up on deck. It poised on the railing and leaped overboard into the bay.

"S'havin' a little swim. Le's go welcome the conquerin' 'ero," said Johnson-Johnson. This seemed like a great idea, so they crowded back inside and ran down the stairs to the beach, grabbing a few more bottles of champagne as they went. On the way down Magilside fell with a squeal of alarm and rolled, but he landed harmlessly in the powdery sand, and so was only a little way behind the others when they raised a cheer as Alec came staggering out of the surf, gasping and pushing his lank wet hair back from his forehead.

"Hipiphurrah Hipiphurrah Hipiphurrah!" said Balkister. He danced about in the sand, tripping and falling at Alec's feet. "You did it! You did it, ugly guy. Future generations will bless your name."

"What can we do for you?" Binscarth asked. "Food? Wine? Gowgeous women?"

"You can deodorize that damn shuttle," Alec wheezed. "You have no idea. I want a shower, okay? And a shave. And some fresh food."

"All yours, noble scion of an ancient house," said Balkister, rising to his knees and salaaming. "Justice will prevail. Come on up to the house, Checkerfield, we've been keeping a bottle well iced just for you."

"Great," said Alec as he strode across the sand, peeling off his wet sweater. His soaked pants were hanging low, threatening to trip him. He hauled at them grimly and kept going, compelled by the dream of hot running water and soap.

When he finally emerged from the bathroom in a cloud of steam, he found his bathrobe coyly laid out beside a tray with a single glass of champagne, sending its quiet steady stream of bubbles upward. Pulling on the robe, he took the glass and stepped into the den.

He was met by the Resistance blowing little tin horns and whirling noisemakers.

"Here's to the hero of Mars One," said Balkister, clapping him on the shoulder and slopping his champagne. Alec grinned good-naturedly and raised his glass in a toast to them. For once he didn't feel the usual crushing sense of desolation that *these* were his only human friends. In the morning he'd make his farewells and then he'd be gone, back to the station in that foul shuttle for Mendoza.

"Have some onion dip, deah boy," slurred Binscarth. "Jus' about to watch the ball dwop in Times Squaw!"

"Yes, it's nearly midnight," Magilside said. "Happy bloody New Year to Areco, eh?"

"Yeah," Alec said, tasting his champagne. "Should we turn on TWN to see what happens when the Martian lease expires?"

"Oh, we know how tha's gonna turn out now," said Binscarth. "Tomowwow. I wanna see Times Squaw. Can't miss the ball dwop!"

"Turn on the holo, then, it's almost time," said Johnson-Johnson. Binscarth groped unsteadily and switched on the holoset.

But where were the crowds in New York? Where were the balloons and streamers?

Alec and his friends stared in silence, not understanding what they were seeing at first. Gradually the meaning of the stammered narration sank in.

"*. . . nearly three thousand men, women and children. The outlying stations are being evacuated. They don't face any danger from the lava flow but they do risk freezing to death. Mars One, which had maintained independent use of wind-powered generators, is safe at the present time . . .*"

"Maws?" said Binscarth.

"Oh my God," said Magilside.

"*. . . and appears to have been an act of sabotage by extremist elements in the MAC. The MAC has promised full cooperation with the authorities, though it seems certain that the terrorist who planted the bomb in the geothermal plant was killed in the explosion.*"

"Bomb?" Johnson-Johnson gasped. "We didn't send them any bombs! Did we?"

Alec, get out of there. Run.

Alec remained stock still, unable to take his eyes from the footage being shown. It had apparently been transmitted from the main surveillance camera mounted over Commerce Square in Mars Two. People loping along in the funny stride everyone walked with on Mars, shopping, going to jobs, families out for a stroll on a starry evening.

Then the *BANG*, loud enough for some people to turn their heads in the direction of the geothermal plant, you could see them turning in alarm, but not really loud enough to prepare the viewer for what came next: a flash that turned the night to day, then to blazing red day, and tiny people were being swept away like leaves in the pyroclastic blast as the side of Mons Olympus blew open. There was nothing after that, thank God, the picture flared out as the camera was destroyed.

Binscarth put his fingertips in his mouth and began to rock to and fro, making a high wailing sound.

"*. . . set off the chain reaction that caused the eruption. The terrorist may have disguised himself as one of the plant workers reporting for the night shift. His apparent motive was to disable the economy of Mars Two in retaliation for the ruling evicting the MAC from Mars One . . .*"

"You damned idiot!" Magilside turned on Alec. "You gave them *bombs.*"

"You stupid fool," shrieked Binscarth. "You—you upper-class mowon! We'll be awwested!"

"*. . . how the weapons were obtained, but the MAC spokespersons have released the following surveillance footage taken in October, showing an as yet unidentified shuttle being unloaded in Hangar Twelve . . .*"

Alec closed his eyes. He knew what the others were seeing. He opened his eyes again and, yes, there he was, blurred but unmistakable.

That tears it. We're weighing anchor, son.

"Alec," said Balkister very quietly, "You'd better go now."

"*He* can't go," said Johnson-Johnson. "He's our only chance! If we call the authorities now—if we confess and explain it was *him* did it, we had no idea what he was going to do, don't you see—"

Alec wasn't sure how or when he left the house, but he found himself walking down the beach stairs in his bathrobe, carrying his glass of champagne. There was still shouting going on above. Something was floating toward him, blowing up a cloud of sand: the agboat, piloted by Billy Bones. It touched down just in front of him and Billy Bones tilted its head to look at Alec.

For Christ's sake, get in, boy.

Alec stepped inside and sat down, tossing aside his champagne glass. He heard the faint tinkle as it broke on the stairs. The agboat rose, and soared across to the deck of the *Captain Morgan*. She was already tacking about to sail off into the night as the agboat settled into its davits. Alec climbed out and went into the saloon.

Listen to me, boy. This weren't yer fault. There's things you don't know, there's things I've only just found out. There's a load of orders given by somebody in the Company named Labienus, setting you up. They did allow you to steal the shuttle! If I'd had time to analyze all that new data, instead of chasing across the damned solar system for the past week—

Alec swept the saloon with a blank crystalline stare. His gaze rested on the door to the galley. He took a few steps in that direction.

None of that, boy. Coxinga appeared in the doorway, rising up on two of its hind legs to block Alec's way. Alec stared past it at the array of cutlery on the wall. He turned away to the armory cabin door, but Billy Bones rose to block that as well. Alec started across the saloon.

Son, listen to me. Dr. Zeus knew about this.

Alec stopped in front of the bar. He looked up at the array of bottles. There were six of them ranged there, full. He hadn't been drinking much in the last few months. He reached up and took down a bottle of rum.

All right, get drunk, but you got to pay attention first. You were set up, do you hear me?

Alec grabbed three other bottles and strode away to his stateroom, cradling them in his arms. Coxinga and Flint scuttled after him as the Captain realized what Alec was doing, but he got inside just a second ahead of them and slammed the door in their skeletal faces. He set down his bottles and locked the door. The Captain unlocked it at once and after a moment's struggle Alec took a chair and wedged it under the knob.

Alec, for God's sake.

He ignored the scraping and thudding at his door. With a set face he broke the seal on the first bottle and lifted it to his mouth, tilting back his head. In approximately thirty seconds he gulped down most of a liter of rum.

Alec, don't do this. Boy, please.

By the time he had choked back the contents of the third bottle his hands were trembling and the room had begun to sway. Some human pain was showing on his face at last; but he doggedly took up the fourth bottle and drank its contents down.

Alec.

The drumming on the door was a thunder now, and there was a high whining sound as well. Screams of the men, women, and children of Mars Two? The chair was leaping, jolting. He gagged. Why hadn't he died yet? This was harder than he'd thought it would be. He groped blindly for the chair, meaning to hold it in place, and fell down. He was unconscious when he began to vomit.

SON!

THE YEAR 2352:

MEETING IN THE NEW WORLD

Rutherford sat alone in the parlor at No. 10 Albany Crescent. He had been crying for hours; his eyes were swollen nearly shut. There was no fire in the fireplace. There were no holo images flickering in midair. The room was as silent as he could make it, but there was still a noise coming in through the dead air from outside. It was a queer *massed* sound. It seemed to be coming from every direction, because in fact it was.

An electronic drone rose and fell and, now and then, you could make out voices. Every so often there was an appalling sound, a repeated *BOOM* always followed by the same shrill piping.

He was hearing it because every holoreceiver in London was switched on, tuned to the same footage that was being shown over and over.

This had gone on so long, and he had sat so long silent, that he nearly screamed when there came a furtive knock at his door. He got up and scuttled across the room, peering through the curtain first to see who might be standing on his front step.

When he saw who it was, he ran to open the door.

"Hurry," he said. Chatterji slunk in, followed by Ellsworth-Howard, who was moving in a distinctly unsteady manner. Rutherford closed the door and the three of them stood there in the hall, staring at each other.

Chatterji hadn't shaved in two days. He had dark circles under his eyes and his hands were shaking as he fumbled with his cloak. Ellsworth-Howard wasn't shaking at all; he was so relaxed his pupils were like pinpoints.

After a moment of mutual silence, Rutherford blurted:

"Are we going to be arrested?"

"N-n-no," Chatterji said. "That's just what we've c-come round to t-tell you. It seems—it s-seems we're not to buh-buh-blame."

"But we are!" Rutherford began to cry again. "We created him. It's *him* in that surveillance footage. We know, and soon everybody else will. He'll be hunted down and caught. They'll put him in hospital to find out what could have made him do such a thing, and they'll do tests on him—and then they'll look at him more closely—and they'll know what he is, and—"

"C-C-Company won't let it happen," Chatterji said. "They'll keep it q-quiet. I was t-told. You see, they knew. 'S the old rule, R-Rutherford, about not being able to ch-ch-change history. They knew our m-man was the one who delivered the buh-bomb. Nothing could be done about it. S-so Dr. Zeus did what it always d-does. Pulled its people out b-beforehand, w-well before the event."

"P'lice never kesh 'im," Ellsworth-Howard said very slowly, shaking his head from side to side. "Never kesh 'im. Comp'ny hunt 'im dowwwn. Top secret. Hushushush shhh. Hide 'im in a lab somewhere far far awayyy. Nobody never know Comp'ny's to blame, see."

"But it's our fault." Rutherford wrung his hands.

Chatterji shook his head numbly.

"Nope. Because, s-see, if it's our f-fault, it's Dr. Z-Zeus's fault too. That won't do at all. So we're all innocents instead. They had to let us work on *A-Adonai* because history r-records we did. They j-just didn't tell us what was guh-guh-going to happen . . ."

"You mean nobody's going to punish us?" quavered Rutherford.

"Nobody." Chatterji turned and walked into the parlor, where he collapsed into his favorite chair. "Oh, they'll never let us work on anything like *him* again. They still want Enforcer r-r-replacements, but no new designs now. We're to create a subclass of Preservers instead. Simple policemen. Security techs. G-g-guards. No more heroes, thank you. No more fuh-fuh-freedom fighters."

Ellsworth-Howard was still standing in the hallway, drooling on the mat. In a high plaintive voice he began to sing:

"Frankenstein, Frankenstein, won't you be my valentine . . ."

Rutherford went and got him and led him to a chair. It took some work to actually get him seated; he kept sliding down toward the floor. Finally Rutherford gave it up and collapsed into his own chair.

"I still can't believe it," he said hoarsely. "We made him a *good* man! And he was so clever. How could we have gone so wrong?"

Chatterji gave a bitter laugh. "If we'd programmed him to hide in his r-room like everybody else does nowadays, he'd never have become a guh-guh-gun runner, would he? If he hadn't had those d-damned high ideals we g-gave him, he'd have let Areco evict the MAC."

"We been used, ya know," Ellsworth-Howard addressed the ceiling. Rutherford and Chatterji turned to look at him.

"Comp'ny *wanted* us to make 'im," he said. "Look what 'e did in California. Kept the Yanks from getting the big hushush discovery on Cat'lina Island. If 'e hadn't, there'd've been no Dr. Zeuuuus, would there of been? But it's worse'n ya think it is. Y'know how he got the bloody bomb to Mars? He stole a Company ship. With time drive. He was smart enough to shrack with Dr. Zeus security codes. S'how he got past the blockade. I know, I traced his signal. Comp'ny don't know, but they're sure to find out. 'Spect some heads'll roll over that."

Chatterji and Rutherford regarded each other in dawning horror. "No, he c-couldn't have!" cried Chatterji. "Those things have an autodestruct b-built in to prevent theft."

"Yeh . . . funny about that. Talk about your shracking Mandelbrots. Our bright boy stole the ship, all right. First thing he done was detour into the past. Went Back Way Back. Guess who 'e met there, eh?"

There was a moment of bewildered silence. Then Rutherford jumped as though he'd been shot. "Not that woman!"

"The botanist," said Chatterji.

"Yeah—" Ellsworth-Howard gagged on his drool and fell over, coughing. Rutherford ran to him and pulled him into a sitting position, shaking him in his agitation.

"You can't mean that Preserver of yours again."

"I do, though," said Ellsworth-Howard. "Same Mendoza. An' y'know what? She musta shown him how to disconnect the autodestruct. If she hadn't, he'd never got the bomb to Mars. Just blown up in space. Funny, ain't it?"

"Then it's *her* doing," shrieked Rutherford. "He'd have died like a hero again, if not for her!"

"It's w-worse than that," Chatterji said, putting his hands to his face in horror. "She knows about him. And if the Company d-doesn't know yet who stole one of their ships, you can bet they'll find out, and when they do, the first thing they'll do will be to fetch her—and then the committee'll be investigated, and it'll all come out before the stockholders—"

"Oh, no, it won't." Grimly Rutherford wrestled Ellsworth-Howard's buke out of his daypack. He snapped it open and dragged Ellsworth-Howard's nerveless fingers to the buttonball. "We'll get rid of her first. Who are those discreet fellows in charge of Black Security? Send the order out, Foxy."

Ellsworth-Howard gurgled in protest, but even had he been willing it was obvious he was utterly incapable of coordinating his long fingers. Rutherford seized the buke and thrust it at Chatterji. "Here! You've got the clearance, too. Have them bring her in."

"But—where are we going to put her?" Chatterji protested, as his hand moved uncertainly on the buttonball. "She's already been sent B-Back Way Back. Unless you want to hide her with the Enforcers?"

"Yes. No, wait!" Rutherford paced across the room and then turned to glare at Chatterji. "This is her fault. This whole thing is her fault. What might our man have been, if he hadn't kept running into *her*? Send her to Options Research."

"No," howled Ellsworth-Howard.

"We have no choice." Rutherford turned on him. "If we hid the damned creature in the deepest bunker we could contrive, she'd turn up again somehow. I won't stand for this any longer. *GET RID OF HER.*"

Chatterji squeezed in the request.

"Bloody bastard," Ellsworth-Howard groaned. "Wasting my Preservers."

"Hardly, given the harm she's done." Rutherford continued his pacing. "I'd call it justice, actually. We can't undo what our man did, but at least we've maintained project security, and if she can't tell what she knows *we* can't get into any worse trouble.

"And the story's not over yet, is it? If our man's done great harm, well, he may yet do even greater good. I should think he must be feeling simply terrible about all this. Perhaps it'll spur him on to some magnificent act of atonement that'll benefit all mankind! And if *that woman's* not around to ensnare him, maybe it'll work this time." He threw himself into his chair decisively.

"Ya shracking idiot, our man's already done what Dr. Zeus wanted 'im to do," Ellsworth-Howard said, as his feeble burst of adrenaline petered out and the drugs pulled him back down. "Comp'ny don't care he killed all those people." He lay back down and went on from his new position:

"Nursie gave us big meds today. See, now Comp'ny's gonna own Mars."

Rutherford shook his head. "Dr. Zeus has no holdings on Mars," he said. "They sold them all to Areco, two months ago."

"And they got a p-pretty price for them." Chatterji nodded grimly. "But I'd bet anything they'll be able to b-buy them back a lot more cheaply. Areco will have to s-sell everything it owns, with the kind of lawsuits it's facing."

"The newsman said that—" Rutherford paled. "That the horrible irony of all this is that the eruption will speed up the terraforming. It will actually become easier for people to live up there now. Once they rebuild."

"Used," Ellsworth-Howard confirmed from the floor. "See? Comp'ny didn't want a hero really ever. Just a killer they could control better than my Enforcers. Use 'im to make history turn out the way Dr. Zeus wants it, never mind who dies."

"They lied to us," said Rutherford. His eyes were perfectly round with shock.

"Bin-GO," giggled Ellsworth-Howard. "You an' yer peaceful warrior."

Chatterji rested his chin in the palm of his hand and stared into the cold hearth.

"Whatever happens in 2355," he said, "we're going to d-deserve it."

None of them noticed the quiet beep that announced that their order had been obeyed, consigning a perfect stranger to an unimaginable fate.

Rutherford turned on his heel and marched to the sideboard. He drew out an antique key and unlocked a drawer. A moment later he returned with a smooth and featureless black bottle.

"Here," he said. "I've been saving this for a suitable occasion."

Ellsworth-Howard just pointed to it and laughed. Chatterji sat up and stared.

"That's not B-Black Elysium, is it?" he whispered.

"It is." Rutherford unlocked the neck of the bottle.

"But that's illegal."

"It is." Rutherford got the stopper off and inhaled the dark fragrance that rose from the bottle. "But what are laws to us, chaps? Drink was always supposed to help, at times like these."

He put his mouth to the neck of the bottle and took a dramatic gulp. Promptly he choked and leaned back, gasping and coughing. Chatterji watched him in horrified fascination.

"Wh-what's it like?" he said. Gagging, Rutherford handed him the bottle at arm's length. After a moment's hesitation he took it, and drank deep.

"Oh, God, it's awful," he said, shaking his head. But he had another gulp.

"Here here here," Ellsworth-Howard reached up from the floor. Chatterji leaned down and pulled him into a sitting position so he could drink without spilling.

"The Company makes this stuff, too, you know," said Rutherford. "Exclusive patent is held by Dr. Zeus Incorporated."

"G-gosh, we're not nearly the saviors of humanity we thought we were, are we?" said Chatterji, wondering when he would feel his liver begin to shut down. "Now we know how p-poor old Prashanti and Hauptmann felt, when their project went so disastrously wr-wrong." Rutherford winced at the names and took the bottle again.

"Was that messing with my design did it," said Ellsworth-Howard. He wiped away tears. "I know it. He got access to all kindsa stuff 'e shouldn'ta seen. We shouldn'ta tried to run the sequence in real time. He got away from us."

"You'd think we'd have known," sighed Rutherford. "How many times have we all seen *Frankenstein?* Why is it we sub-creators can't seem to create life without things going disastrously wrong?" He passed the bottle to Chatterji.

"You don't s-suppose, do you, that the entire course of human history has been shaped by cl-clever chaps like us, sitting around in p-parlors and playing with ideas?" Chatterji said. He had another gulp of the liqueur. It seemed to go down easier this time. "All working for D-Dr. Zeus?"

"Why not?" Rutherford said. "We're the only gods there are."

"Shracking incompetent gods, then," said Ellsworth-Howard. He drew a deep breath and sang again, shrill and tremulous, the little he remembered of the music his mum and dad had played when they used to kick him awake in the middle of the night . . .

"Freude, schoner gotterfunken, tochter aus Elysium . . . feuer-trunken . . .
Seid umschlungen, millionen! Diesen kuss der ganzen welt . . ."

Then Ellsworth-Howard raised a long trembling finger, pointing at the front door.

"Oh, look," he said faintly. Rutherford and Chatterji turned their heads to watch as the first of the hallucinations came into the parlor: the limping specters of horribly charred humanity, implacably advancing on the men who made them. Burnt bones who had died at their posts or running before the molten tide, bones of women clutching the fragments of their children, all come to demand an accounting in that cozy Victorian parlor at No. 10 Albany Crescent.

CONSEQUENCES

On the second day of the year 2352, a man identifying himself as Sebastian Melmac marched into the headquarters of the Tri-Worlds Council for Integrity and confessed to being the infamous Hangar Twelve Man from the Mars Two disaster surveillance footage. Under interrogation it was discovered that he was, in fact, a British national named Giles Lancelot Balkister, and bore no physical resemblance whatever to the man in the surveillance footage.

Nevertheless, he was remanded to the custody of His Majesty's representatives, bundled into an air transport, and hustled home to London. After further interrogation, he was diagnosed, and sent to hospital forever and ever and ever.

On the third day of 2352, there was a solid gray sky over a northern ocean, locking a close horizon down, no height, no distance in any direction except the west where a faint glint of light shone.

They looked away toward it, the people who came swarming up out of the green island. Some of them waded out through rough water, bearing on their backs the infants or the ancients, to the coracles bobbing at their moorings. Some of them paused on the cold shore to pull on black skins, glistening and smooth, and these leaped into the waves and swam out to draw the coracles behind them, towing in teams. Long craft were brought from the caves laden with every kind of oddment, iron kettles, anvils, transmitters, birdcages, treasure, and dark figures hauled them out through the surf. Vaulting in, they bent to the oars and followed the others west.

More of them came and more, pulling on the skins and plunging through the breakers, following the long line away from the island. The man was the last to come forth. The wind trailed his wild hair like storm wrack, before he bound it back and pulled on the mask. He turned once to look at the island and then struck out, and seafoam spangled his beard as he cut through the gray salt wave to the front of the company of travelers.

He led them away.

Hours later an aircraft with no marks to identify her came roaring out of the east, coming in fast and low. She raked the island with flame, passed repeatedly to shower down that which did not officially exist in the arsenals of civilized nations, until the little house blazed up and vanished, the golden caves melted, crumbled and smoked, until the seawater came hissing and bubbling in to drown the broken rock and the island was no longer visible above the water.

By that time, though, the man and his people were long gone, settling in on some new rock, some new refuge, one more stopover in the endless emigration.

A few hours later on the third day of 2352, the Temple of Artemis closed its vast doors to worshippers. Within, the priestesses assembled, silent in wide circles about each Mother. Some of the priestesses had red and swollen eyes from weeping; all were pale and solemn. They waited.

Presently the Great Mother emerged from an alcove to the right of the splendid Goddess in ivory and gold. The Great Mother herself was less splendid. She was ill, and the events of the past week had aged her visibly. She had robed herself in black today. It was the ritual color for the Crone, but the Great Mother had lost family in Mars Two also. She stepped up now to the pulpit and reached for the audiophone with a shaking hand.

"Daughters," she said, and her voice echoed back from the immense depths of the temple." A word before we begin our task today. We gather here to condemn, but not in hatred. We will remember who we are, and the sick male passion for vengeance will not pollute our hearts.

"A Curse ceremony is not held for the personal satisfaction of the victims. Its purpose is to bring the evil one to justice by his own actions, that he may ensnare himself. We pray for his fall not to punish him, but that his fall may serve as an example to warn other men." So far her voice was hoarse but controlled, a modern pastor counseling sensibly.

Incense was being lit as she spoke, stuff with a dark bitter fragrance, and the lights in the temple were being dimmed and shaded to a baleful red. One white spot lit her gaunt face from below, the classic Halloween-party trick to give her face a terrifying and skull-like appearance. She lifted her arms now, and the flowing black sleeves of her robe were like raven's wings.

"THIS IS THE MAN!" she said, and her voice lost all its control and rose in a terrifying howl. An unseen technician threw a switch and a huge holo image appeared in midair: the best and clearest frame showing the Hangar Twelve Man, as he'd turned to stare up at the monitor.

Cecelia, gazing from the circle where she stood, caught her breath. In that moment it flew apart for her, the whole rational system by which she understood the world and her place in it. The balance of crime by retribution, the assurance that there was meaning behind everything and that She controlled destiny with a benign if terrible hand: all this scattered, like pieces on a chessboard overturned by a boisterous child.

The chanting began, the dark-throated curse without words, and the Mothers began the dance in each circle and the priestesses linked arms and began to sway. Cecelia let herself be pulled along with them as they focused their rage, their grief on the man whose image hung there in the darkness. She raised her voice with them when the directed prayer began, led by the Great Mother, imploring Hecate to bring him triple death and a thousand years of torment.

But all Cecelia was really aware of now was an image that had appeared behind her eyes, clearer than the blurry giant in midair above them all: Roger, sinking down through dark water, his slack face staring as in wonder at the gloomy reefs of Hell, his fair hair floating out around his head as though he were a prophet touched with visions.

On the fourth day of 2352, a pretty black girl came walking unsteadily into High John's Bar in Port-au-Prince. Claude behind the bar peered out, frowning, thinking she was a drunk and preparing to shout at her. Then his eyes widened, for he recognized the girl, and knew that she was certainly not to be shouted at. His hands shook as he poured out a glass of his best rum, remembering that to be the appropriate offering to a lady of her station.

He hurried from the bar and brought it to her. She had sagged into a chair at a table and was staring up at the images playing on his holo, the terrible footage from Mars Two, which seemed to be all that would ever be shown again.

"Lady," he said deferentially, bending to set down a napkin and the glass at her elbow. To his consternation, he saw that her face was wet with tears. And she hadn't noticed him or his offering, she just kept looking up at the floating light where the Hangar Twelve footage was playing now, and when the tall tall white man turned to stare into the surveillance camera, she bared her teeth in agony.

"My little boy," she whispered, improbably. "My good little boy."

On the 24th of March, 1863, the Botanist Mendoza was brought up out of her cell and left alone in a room. There was nothing in the room but a holoset, staring from the ceiling with its three eyes. Noting this, she sighed. She waited in the room, doing nothing, seeing no one, for three hours.

At the end of that time the door opened abruptly, and an immortal entered the room. He nodded to her.

"Botanist Mendoza? Facilitator General Moreham."

"Are you a member of the tribunal?" Mendoza said. He merely lifted his eyebrows with a wry sort of smile, as though to indicate he'd thought she was more intelligent than to ask such a thing.

"There will be no trial," he said.

"Why?"

"Who could judge you, Mendoza?" he said. "Let me show you what you've done." He waved his hand and the holoset activated, and there before them was an image of a tall man loading crates from a shuttle to a hangar dock. She started.

"Alec," she said faintly.

"Yes, that's his name. However, he'll be better known to history as the Hangar Twelve Man," the other immortal said.

She turned to him, eyes wide. After a moment her lips formed the words, without sound: *Mars Two.* He nodded. She looked back at the image, Alec going busily to and fro, and sank to her knees but did not look away. Suddenly the hangar footage was replaced by the famous last few seconds from the camera mounted over Commerce Square. She shut her eyes, turned her white face from the red light, but she could not shut out the sound.

When it had ended, the man spoke loudly into the silence:

"Now, you see what happens when you disconnect intercept devices? Those things are put in there for a reason, you know."

Her spine was bowing, it was as though some private gravity were pulling her down, but she opened her eyes and looked up at the man.

"So that was what I saved him for?" she said. "So he could become the Destroyer?"

The man didn't deign to reply.

"I learned about Mars Two in school," she said. "I never paid attention to the footage. Too upsetting. But this was what it was leading up to my whole life, that mortal and I, and what we'd do together. You knew it would be my fault, didn't you?"

"We did," the man admitted, "But you didn't. *You* made the choice to disobey. There was nothing we could have done. History, you see, cannot be changed."

She said nothing in response. He walked around her where she knelt, considering her from several angles.

"Frankly, we're pretty tired of this, Mendoza," he said lightly. "After all, you were given every chance. But you're not quite up to standard, are you? You're a Crome generator. A defective. You disobey orders. And you kill mortals!"

She nodded.

"What do you think we ought to do with you?"

"Put me to death," she said. "If that's possible."

"Well, we can try," he said, dropping to one knee in front of her and tilting her face up to look her in the eyes. "We can't promise anything, but we can certainly try. Would you like us to try?"

She recoiled slightly from the familiarity. Moving stiffly she pulled herself upright, got to her feet.

"Yes, señor," she said, staring down at him. "Try."

Alec Times Three

He hurt, but everything was going to be all right; the soothing voice kept telling him so. Every time the pain became bad enough to make him groan, the warmth would come, lovely drowning oblivion, and he'd drift away again like a good boy, no more fighting or crying. He'd be a good boy now. He was always a good boy. Wasn't he?

But there had been . . .

No.

But he'd done . . .

No, Alec was a very good boy.

There was no up or down, there was nothing to see, there was nothing but the voice and the pain and the pain ebbing away.

The Captain was doing a conjuring trick. Alec had to watch very carefully. Here was a treasure chest, did Alec see it? The Captain opened the lid and tilted the chest forward so that Alec wouldn't miss the point that it was full of gold doubloons. He tilted it further and the gold ran out in three spiraling streams, to lie in three little heaps upon a red tablecloth. He covered them with a red handkerchief, looked hard at Alec to be sure he was following the trick, and whisked the handkerchief away. The three little heaps of doubloons had become three little pink fish!

Was Alec getting all this? Now the Captain pulled three bell-skirted dolls from his coat, all exactly alike, golden-haired, with blank blue eyes. He set each one down on one of the pink fish and the pink fish disappeared under the dolls' skirts. Now the Captain plucked up one of the dolls and tossed her carelessly over his shoulder, revealing that the first fish had been transformed into a little man. But then, *whoosh!* There was a burst of flame, and the little man was gone.

Now the Captain took up the second doll and tossed her away. There was another little man. But, *pop!* Out of nowhere a pellet came and struck him, knocking him off the table, and he was gone, too. Had Alec observed all this? Had he understood?

The Captain took up the third doll and tossed her away. She hit the wall and bounced. Her head broke, but it didn't seem to matter. Here was another little man. Across the table came rolling a shiny black sphere, from which a burning wick protruded. The sphere was bowling straight for the little man, but at the last moment the Captain seized him up and tucked him inside his coat. *Boom!* When the smoke cleared, the Captain took the little man out again and set him back on the table.

He looked at Alec, grinning confidentially. Then, from his pocket, he drew out another figurine and set it next to the little man. It was the mermaid from the prow of the ship, reproduced in perfect miniature detail.

Did Alec understand?

He'd been listening to the waves for a long while now, idly watching the silver cords as they drifted in patterns around him. He was content. The cords were vaguely uncomfortable, but the discomfort seemed to be affecting somebody else. His nose itched, too. It had itched after Mendoza had put the coagulator wand to it . . .

Mendoza.

Like a man realizing he has overslept on the morning of an important appointment, Alec tried to sit bolt upright.

The violence of his motion set him turning slowly through space. He tried to cry out. The tubes in his mouth and nose prevented him.

It's all right, son. Wait.

He looked around wildly. He was in the hyperbaric chamber in the *Captain Morgan*'s infirmary, floating in an antigravity field. He was intubated, catheterized, helpless. Billy Bones and Flint stood sentry at the door of the chamber.

Let me out of here!

Aye, laddie, aye. But if you ever try to scuttle yerself again, here's where you'll be, and for longer next time. Do we have an understanding, Alec? Nobody hurts my boy. Not even himself.

Captain, sir, please!

Yer not dying, Alec. That ain't in the plan. You, stretched out stiff, with that bloody marvelous brain no more'n a lump of cold

carrion? That'd be wasteful, aye. Goes against all my program-
ming. Not for my little Alec what set me free.

Set ME free! For Christ's sake, send me to Hell where I belong. Alec
thrashed, to no avail; he merely spun counterclockwise amid the tubes.

Now, matey, you should know I ain't about to do that. I can
keep you in here, helpless as a baby in a cradle, until you listen to
me. Are you going to listen to me, Alec?

Raging, Alec told the Captain to do something an inorganic machine would have found very difficult to accomplish. The Captain
laughed.

That's my boy! Now you've got some fight in you. You ain't go-
ing to feel like whimpering and dying once we've had our little talk,
by thunder. Reckon you'll be good long enough for us to parley?

Okay! Yes! I promise.

That's yer word as a gentleman, is it? Watch yerself, then. I'll
just turn off the field.

Alec was lowered to the floor, and the weight of gravity came
down on him like a flattening hand. He flailed weakly, trying to get his
breath. The chamber door opened and Billy Bones and Flint came in.
They ministered to him, disconnecting the tubes and lifting him onto a
stretcher. They seemed to have been modified somehow, given more
arms and more functions built into the arms. Certainly they were more
powerful. Alec was borne away through the ship to his cabin as though
he weighed no more than a feather.

Aye, lad, there's been some changes made. I can't say I ain't
missed you, but keeping you safe in the brig did give me the chance
to catch up on me reading, as it were, and do a bit of home improve-
ment. I think you'll approve of the changes.

What have you done?

You'll see. We need to talk first.

Alec was tucked into bed in his cabin, and lay there staring around.
Everything was as it should be. There was a sipper bottle of cold water
within easy reach, and a plate of biscuits. His beard had grown out,
thick as a summer wheatfield. He had no sense of how long he'd been
unconscious. The light was different; it dawned on him that the usual
vista of blue sky and sea was missing beyond his window. It was white
out there, with stains of gray and pale green, and the *Captain Morgan*
was nearly motionless.

Captain, where are we?

Antarctica, son. They're looking for us everywhere else. They'll
look for us here, too, soon enough, but we'll be long gone by then.
Now, you hear this, Alec! Dr. Zeus let you steal that shuttle. Be-

cause of his precious Temporal Concordance, the bastard knows what's going to happen afore it happen, see? He stood to profit from what happened on Mars. He could have stopped you; he didn't.

But why—?

He bred you to deliver that bomb. He set the whole plan in motion. The only thing as went wrong was that you was supposed to be blown to hell too, after you left Mars's orbit. No evidence to point to Dr. Zeus. All the same, you did yer best to die like he wanted. You been programmed, son, more'n I ever been.

But that means—all this time we thought we were working to bring down Dr. Zeus, we've been playing into the Company's hands!

Not quite. He didn't know about me, and that's cost him dearly. It's going to cost him more afore I'm done.

So that was why . . . the whole plot with Elly Swain, and all the stuff I can do that nobody else can . . . it was just so somebody could make some money off Mars? That's why I exist? Alec gulped for breath. Why the hell didn't you let me die?

Don't get fractious again, son. There's much more to it than that. For one thing, ain't you at all curious why you wasn't blown up in the shuttle like he planned you'd be?

You saved me.

Not I. I had my hands too full with that stupid trip to assimilate the data that'd have warned me in time. No, somebody else had already disconnected the theft intercept system. Somebody else working against Dr. Zeus. See if you can guess who, laddie.

I can't.

Have you forgotten her already? The girl you wanted to marry?

Mendoza!

To be sure, the Botanist Mendoza.

Alec lay there, stunned. Tears began to run down his face. *I was supposed to go back and rescue her. She'll be in so much danger now . . . and what'll she say when she hears about Mars Two?*

She'll forgive you, lad. I'm wagering she'd forgive you anything you did.

Nobody'll ever forgive me, Captain.

This girl will. Trust yer old Captain on this one, Alec. And, just as soon as yer well enough to stand the trip, we're going back to the station for her. You need to know something about the lady first, though, son.

What?

Well . . . she's a cyborg, Alec.

Like me?

Not . . . exactly like you, no. I'll explain more when yer feeling better. But she's the girl I always hoped you'd find, and by God I'm going to get her for you.

Alec's head was pounding. Despite the Captain's reassuring words he had an awful sense of loss, lost innocence, lost time.

And then what? he snapped. *You'll keep us both prisoner in here? How'd you learn so much about her, anyway?*

Poor lad, yer still too weak to figure it out. You've a nasty old headache now, too, ain't you? Time to go sleepy-bye. We'll talk later.

Alec stiffened as a mask was clapped over his mouth and nose. He looked up wildly, into the steel eye sockets of Billy Bones. He struggled; then the tide rose and floated him away, to the safe place without questions.

Over the next few days he grew a little stronger, and the Captain was able to explain more of what had happened since the night Alec tried to kill himself. Even as Alec was being detoxified and placed on life support, the *Captain Morgan* had been slipping down the coast of South America, making steadily for Tierra del Fuego. The Captain focused his attention on his most recent data acquisitions, integrating and studying them carefully, and learned a great many interesting things.

Acting on his new knowledge, his first move was to alert Alec's lawyers and present them with his airtight alibi: surveillance footage proving that on 24 October Alec was dancing at a club in Martinique, which in fact he had been. The Global Identity Bureau quietly discarded the case it had been building based on the uncanny resemblance between a minor British peer and an unknown terrorist, and went away to investigate other, less absurd leads. The Captain's next move was to ditch the stolen time shuttle.

But how'll we rescue Mendoza? Alec cried.

I'm coming to that, the Captain told him. He'd drawn a pint of Alec's blood and cloned some hair and tissue samples, with which he liberally salted the pilot's console and chair. He then planted a charge under the pilot's seat, blew a gaping hole in the forward cabin, and jettisoned the shuttle off the Falklands, with the hatch sprung. Let Dr. Zeus find her there, let him subject the shuttle to forensic tests. All the evidence would point to a crash, and a badly splattered body floating away beyond recovery. It might buy them time.

Then the Captain had made several vital purchases of chemicals, alloys, and other materials from a black market supplier in Argentina.

So on down to Antarctica, and temporary haven in the icy water at the bottom of the world. Here, as Alec floated in oblivion, the Captain had begun his next project: installing time transcendence capability in the *Captain Morgan*.

It seemed that if her masts and spars were retracted, if the storm bottle were opened out, if the whole smooth unbroken surface then presented were varnished with a complex chemical solution that crystallized upon contact with air or water—why, you had nearly the whole of the works in place right then. The actual time drive was so easy to build, even enlarged and customized, that probably the only thing that kept everyone from having timeships (other than the fact that the design was a jealously guarded secret) was that building one required certain prohibitively costly alloys, such as were available only from black market suppliers.

All that was left to do was make certain modifications in the quarterdeck console so the drive could be installed and amped up, connect it to the ship's more than adequate fusion generators, rig the ship's ventilation system to puff out stasis gas, and mix liberal quantities of the bitter red liquid.

The *Captain Morgan* was now capable of sailing the waters of any past century. It had cost several fortunes, unbelievable amounts of money, but Alec was so rich money had very nearly ceased to have any meaning. Nor, from this day, was Alec bound by the circumference of the globe. He had an infinite number of globes to escape through. The river mouth that led to Roman Londinium, or the wherry-crowded Thames of Chaucer's time, or the black-fogged Victorian Thames were only three of his vast possible refuges, because any *place* contained an infinite number of *times*.

There were still a few refinements to make, of course. A holo generator was necessary to give the ship the illusion of a suitably historical appearance, or at least obscure her with shifting fogbanks, in any era she might cross. Also, the Captain was still organizing and correlating the time charts he'd plundered from Dr. Zeus.

He was intrigued by the continual mention of *event shadows*, locations where no historical record existed for certain years. Within those shadows, Dr. Zeus had no foreknowledge of events. Anything might have happened there, which gave anyone hiding in an event shadow a decided advantage.

Don't you see, matey? We can sail on blue water forever, if we

need to! This'll make it easier to raid Dr. Zeus. We'll appear out of nowhere, strike, and be off again through time afore he knows what's hit him.

But haven't we got everything we need from the Company now?

Not by a long shot, laddie. I want to know what's in store for us in the future. We're going after Dr. Zeus's bloody Temporal Concordance. Belike yer lady will be able to give us a clue as to its whereabouts, eh? There's a whole mass of defended sites I want a closer look at. I'll strip him of everything he's got, the bronze bastard. I can set traps for him hundreds of years back, that won't blow up in his face until 2355. Two can play his game, by thunder!

I guess so.

Ah, but yer feeling listless. I know. Revenge'll seem sweeter when you've had a chance to think about this a little.

I don't think I care about the revenge anymore.

Oh, no? After what he done to you? Well, now, that's an admirable sentiment, lad, and I'm happy to see you've got such a forgiving heart. I call that right charitable, to be sure. All the same . . . you want to rescue yer girl, don't you?

Of course I do.

Then you'd best let the old Captain chart yer course, because unless we put a couple of broadsides through Dr. Zeus, it mayn't be so easy to take the lady.

That energized Alec. He ventured out of bed and staggered about the ship, feeling his strength return. He didn't care for the beard at all, and removed it as soon as his hands were steady enough to control the shaver. He spent a week bringing himself back, working out in the ship's gym and learning the new commands that would guide the *Captain Morgan* through time. Worried as he was about what Mendoza might think of his complicity in the Mars disaster, he was even more desperate to see her again. He couldn't remember a time when he'd needed human companionship so badly.

Though the Captain kept delicately dropping hints about Mendoza, hints that Alec resolutely refused to think about . . . In fact the Captain was hinting about a lot of things he'd discovered.

Apparently, there had been some kind of project going on for years, to produce uniquely talented and disposable puppets for Dr. Zeus. The other men like Alec had been killed. Alec was the first one to escape his preordained fate, and even so his life was irrevocably changed: he had become the Flying Dutchman after all, doomed to run before the wind as long as he lived.

His anger started to smolder again, and as it returned the sense of weakness and guilt retreated. Revenge began to look good once more. Elly, Roger, Cecelia, Mendoza, the people of Mars Two, and now these unknowns who had come before him! The list of Dr. Zeus's victims kept growing.

The course is laid in, son. You've taken yer medicine?

Aye, sir. Alec smiled grimly, buckling the safety harness.

Brace yerself. It'll be worse than the storm off Trinidad in '47.

It won't be worse than riding that carpeted toilet through space. Where do we come from, Captain, sir?

From the sea!

The yellow gas boiled, a throbbing ran through the *Captain Morgan*, and Alec became the whirling center of a very expensive carnival ride.

There was no one to see the *Captain Morgan*'s arrival, but if there had been they might have thought they beheld an immense bottle materializing abruptly in Avalon Bay, spinning in the water, gradually slowing. When the spinning had slowed to a halt, the bottle underwent an extraordinary transformation. Half of its glassy surface folded back lengthwise, revealing the deck of the ship it had become. With only the faintest whirring sound the masts rose smoothly from her deck, her spars popped out, her rigging deployed. Her anchor dropped, plummeting down through the clear water.

We done it, lad. We've traveled!

What's the chronometer say?

It's a week after you left. She'll never know you was delayed.

Alec unbuckled his harness and ran out on deck. He was in the bay he remembered, there was the island, and there inland he could see the wide swath he'd cut through Mendoza's cornfield.

"Yeah!" he howled. *There's where I landed, that's what I told you about.* He was on the point of leaping overboard when the Captain sent the agboat alongside.

This'll get you there faster, boy. But careful, now!

Alec vaulted in and took the agboat up the canyon, following his previous course. The broken corn was still where it had fallen, only now turning yellow. He veered right sharply and made straight for the little house, there in its tidy garden.

"Mendoza!" He cut the motor and jumped from the boat. "Baby! I'm here, I came back for you!"

Alec—

"Mendoza?" Alec sprinted up on the porch (there was the bench where he'd sat, there were even a few drops of his blood) and pounded on the door.

Alec, there's nobody here.

What? "Mendoza?" Alec opened the door.

I scanned the whole station. She's gone. Bloody hell, I was afraid this'd happen.

Alec walked into the empty room and stood, staring.

No signs of violence. Nothing overturned or broken. He knew what must have happened, all the same. Almost calmly he looked down at the table where they had dined together, at the big old-fashioned book that sat there now, open to a page of spidery black script that ended abruptly. He knew what that was: old-time writing. That must be her bottle of ink, there, and that was her pen, made from a gull's feather. The ink had congealed in the open bottle. She'd been writing when they'd come for her.

They've killed her, haven't they? Because she helped me.

No, she ain't dead. I swear it, son! But they got to her first.

Do you know where she is?

I'll find out. See that terminal there? Hook us in.

Alec obeyed. The Captain dove away from him through cyberspace. Alec remained there, alone in the room.

The dark field was before his eyes. The little girl had walked blindly there, hadn't seen the danger, hadn't heard his shout of warning. He hadn't warned her, had he? Instead he'd pushed her straight into the fire.

Numbly, he closed the book and looked at it. Had she made it herself? Some of the paper toward the front was yellowed, as though it were very old. He peered at the writing on the first page, trying to decipher it. The letter I, and that would be the word *am* maybe, and then an A, and what could that next word be? Moving his lips, he read in silence the word *Botanist*.

He sounded it out several times before the syllables had meaning for him. She had written this. This was all he had left of her, and he didn't know how to read.

When the Captain came racing back into his consciousness, he was sitting on the floor with his head in his hands.

Alec, let's go! The bastard's right behind me. He knows we're here.

Is she dead?

No, but they arrested her. Alec, we got to get out of here, we can't help her now.

It's my fault.

Oh, for Christ's sake, don't start that again. In about five minutes there'll be Company shuttles storming round that point out there!

I don't care.

Bloody Hell! *Do you care about her? If she needed rescuing afore, she really needs it now. Unless you want to wind up in the jar next to hers in some Company facility, you better move yer damn arse!*

That got Alec on his feet, but he went to the book and wrapped it in the blanket from her bed.

What in hell are you doing? the Captain roared.

She left writing. You have to translate it for me. Alec ran for the door, clutching the bundled book to his chest as though it were a child.

He was back on board, in his safety harness, and the stasis gas had just begun to fill the air when a shadow streaked across the transparent dome. It was a shuttle, coming in low and fast, just as he had done. Before he could see whether it was going to turn and come back over, the *Captain Morgan* leaped away through time.

We're clear! Thirty miles out from the Farallones and it's 7 June, 2215. That's what I'd call a neat escape.

Alec gasped for fresh air, pushing out of the harness. *Never mind that. Where is she?*

I don't know, son. I wasn't able—

What do you mean, you don't know? Alec had begun to shake with anger. *You told me she was still alive. How can you know that, and not know where she is?*

Alec, lad, there's things I ain't had the right time to explain—

Well, you can damned well explain 'em now. What did you mean, about her being in a jar? What haven't you told me?

Son, I wouldn't lie to you.

Hell yes, you would! Alec charged into cyberspace, shoving past the Captain to riffle through the Company files. Numbers and names filled his head, dates and places, maps and pictures, yielding up their secrets at his impatient push.

Suddenly there was a defended file before his eyes, something with the Captain's own seal on it, a text headed *Adonai*.

What's this file? Why've you got it locked?

No, boy! Leave it alone.

Alec's eyes narrowed. He forced the seal and accessed the file.

Into his consciousness came pouring the contents of *Adonai*: the proposal, outline, conceptual designs, every memo that had passed between all persons concerned, minutes of meetings, sequence reports complete with images . . .

And, finally and terribly, the black box recordings containing in electromagnetic analogue every thought, emotion and sensation ever experienced during the lives of two men named Nicholas Harpole and Edward Alton Bell-Fairfax.

Abruptly Alec had the memory of two complete lifetimes he had not lived, with a blindingly swift montage of images: half-timbered hall, rose garden, black-letter pages, cold corridors, the deck of a warship, a man in a tailcoat unrolling a map, a dying man, a green jungle. Death, his own, in flaming agony and in a hail of bullets, and in both cases the anguished face of the black-eyed girl watching him die, Mendoza.

Mendoza, who had loved him. Them.

The knowledge was incomprehensible, unbearable, could not be assimilated.

An alternative was found.

Alec felt a tearing, an impossible increase, and roared with pain as a second pair of arms burst forth from his sides, flailing and striking, and then yet a third pair, and barely had this registered on his screaming mind than two new legs shot out from his hips and then two more, kicking frantically, and his groin erupted in a hydra of members, beyond grotesque, da Vinci's Vitruvian man gone one better! And, last, a second face thrust forward from his own, as though it broke the surface of smooth water, an appalling face baring its white teeth in rage, and close after it a second face no less fearsome in its howl of lamentation like the crack of thunder, and the very chambers of his heart were tearing themselves open now and splitting into three, and he knew it would kill him and was glad, and toppled like a ghastly idol to smash into pieces on the floor.

But somewhere in all the horror was one quiet satisfaction: that of having confirmed, at last, beyond all doubt or argument, that he was indeed the monster he had always suspected himself to be.

Not dead yet? He lay gasping on the floor of the saloon, sprawled out, wearing only the body he'd been born with. The pain was beginning to ease away, but things were very far from being all right. What had just happened, to beat him down with such shame and horror?

Mars, he'd been responsible for all those people dying on Mars.

No, that had been before . . .

Mendoza. She'd been arrested, he'd failed her.

No, that had been before . . .

He wasn't even a human being. He was a Recombinant, one of those creatures who'd been illegal for centuries, who lived now only in the most lurid of horror fictions. A genetic test pattern, an experiment, an organic thing worked out on a graph before he'd ever drawn breath. Even poor mad Elly not his kin, he'd been no more than a parasite in her womb, no child of anyone's. Dr. Zeus had meddled with a twist of DNA and produced a nonperson.

Somebody moaned. Somebody else was lying on the floor of the saloon, breathing harshly.

Alec lifted his head and looked.

Two other men lay near him on the floor, their heads close to his, each lying at an angle away from the other, forming a three-branched figure.

One wore an old-fashioned suit, vaguely familiar to Alec from cinema. One wore nothing but a long white shirt and what looked to be black tights. In every other respect, however, they were identical to Alec. They were lifting their heads now just as he had done, and staring at him and at each other with just such an expression of horror and disbelief as he himself wore.

With a cry he scrambled backward from them, more terrified than he had ever been in his life. He could get no more than a body's length from either man, however, no matter how he struggled.

The one in the shirt had dragged himself into a sitting position, and shut his eyes tight. He was reciting something to himself in an undertone. The third man was looking rapidly from Alec to the other one, his gaze hard. He sat up and gestured oddly, running his hands over his clothing as if he were searching for something. He didn't seem to be able to find it. He smelled like blood and fireworks.

Alec knew, not wanting to know, that his name was Edward. The other one, the one who was now opening his eyes and looking at Edward with such loathing, was Nicholas, and he reeked of smoke.

"Murderer!" Nicholas said.

Edward smiled coldly. "I suppose so. I don't seem to be burning in Hell for my crimes, however, have you noticed? And it wouldn't appear that Jesu Christ has answered your prayers, either. What do you suppose is going on?"

"I've lost my mind," gasped Alec, and promptly wished he hadn't, for both the others turned their pale eyes on him.

"Stop blubbering, boy," Edward said. "You made a second Pompeii on Mars; if you can bear that, you ought to be able to bear our company."

"You're not really here," Alec said, squeezing his eyes shut, rocking himself to and fro. "I've fried my brain somehow. I'm hallucinating."

That's all it is, matey, to be sure.

All three of them jumped.

"Captain," Alec shouted, "I've crashed myself!"

It ain't nothing to worry about, son. Never you mind them two duppies! Remember the spooks you saw, that time you tried them mushrooms? But you'll be all right, now, here's old Billy Bones with something to put you to sleep—

The servounit came scuttling into the saloon, extending its arm with the anesthesia mask. For once, Alec was ready to welcome it. He'd have given a lot to lose consciousness just then. Nicholas gave a yell of horror, drawing back from the skull-faced thing, but Edward leaped to his feet.

Alec felt himself pushed aside somehow, watching as Edward attacked Billy Bones with incredible speed and ferocity. The mask was sent flying, and Billy Bones wound up across the room on its back, scrabbling vainly at the air with its steel legs.

Ow! Alec, what in thunder did you do that for?

"My name is Edward Alton Bell-Fairfax," Edward said. "Don't attempt to drug me again. You're the mechanical servant, aren't you? Perhaps you can answer my questions! Have I been made immortal? Has the Society accomplished its purpose?"

There was a long, long pause.

What Society would that be, now, sir? the Captain inquired politely. He was scanning Alec with great care, noting that his brainwave pattern was distinctly different when Edward was speaking.

"The Gentlemen's Speculative Society, of course! We were about to found an epoch of science. We were to conquer death and transform the world," Edward said.

There was another long silence, broken by a bitter laugh from Nicholas.

"Fool," he said. "Hast thou no understanding? *We* are dead men, thou and I. Yet thou art not in Hell, nor I in Heaven neither; and the reason is, we have no souls to go thence. Some necromancy created us, no more but homunculi." He pointed at Billy Bones. "Look how the boy hath made a brass head to sail his ship! And lo, the same alchemy hath made the boy and us."

Edward's eyes narrowed. "Medieval theological rubbish. I tell you,

I was one of a brotherhood of men working to bring a golden age to mankind! We were on the brink of wonderful things when I—"

"Thou wert never one of their number," Nicholas said. "Thou wert no more than their tool, and when they'd brake thee, they cast thee away."

"Liar!" Edward took a menacing step toward Nicholas. Alec felt himself pulled closer too, and struggled to draw back. Edward's progress was arrested. He turned, glaring at Alec. Alec shoved him. He felt real, and when he threw a punch at Alec, Alec seized his wrist and felt the heat of solid flesh, the texture of his sleeve. As they struggled, locked together, Alec saw every tiny detail of the brass cuff links Edward wore, with their device of a fouled anchor. Alec shuddered. Edward for his part was peering in baffled rage at the tiki pattern of Alec's shirt.

"Beat it, dead man!" Alec growled.

Er, excuse me, sirs—said the Captain.

"Speak when you're spoken to, machine," snapped Edward.

Oh, aye, sir, to be sure. Captain Henry Morgan at yer service, sir, and I was just trying to do me duty like I was programmed. With respect, sir, I believe I can throw some light on the subject of yer Society, Commander Bell-Fairfax, sir. Perhaps you didn't have time to take in the contents of this here file when everything happened so quick just now, but if you'll have a closer look—

The Captain excerpted the dossier on *Adonai's* second sequence, the same text and pictures that a certain trio of learned gentleman had studied at their leisure in Regent's Park. He fed it directly to Alec, modifying the signal to accommodate Edward's brain patterns.

Edward stiffened and went pale. Alec let go of his arm.

Sorry about them autopsy pictures, sir, I reckon they're a little distressing.

Edward collapsed into a sitting position.

"Damn them," he said at last. He covered his mouth with his hands.

Aye, sir, that'd be my feeling on the subject, too. Now then, gentlemen—I reckon you'd better sign articles amongst yerselves to keep the peace, because you ain't in no position to quarrel, d'you see? And let's put cards on the table.

Yer Society's called Dr. Zeus Incorporated nowadays, Commander Bell-Fairfax, and they conquered death, all right; but they ain't exactly brought about no golden age. What they done is amass more power and wealth than anyone's ever had, mostly by making them-

selves a lot of immortal slaves to get it for them. But they wanted to make sure history turned out to their profit, so they needed a few dirty tricks played. That was why you were made, sir.

"Damn them," Edward repeated, raising his furious countenance. "They told me it was for the greater good of mankind. They *used* me. My God, the blood I've spilt! The things I've done!"

"Call not on thy God," Nicholas told him. "Science had all thy worship, and *civilization*. And here thou art, now, no more than a ghost in the earth, with no claim on Heaven."

"As if you could ever get to Paradise," replied Edward angrily. "You did your share of brawling and lusting after wenches, if I read your memories aright. And can you read mine? Can you read the boy's?" He grinned in savage amusement. "Your God's been pitched off His throne long since, it seems."

"I was no murderer—" began Nicholas, and then flinched at the data Edward was sending him in a pitiless flood. He caught his breath, absorbing the impact of the scientific discoveries, the advances in scholarship, the inevitable dwindling into insignificance of issues that had mattered more than his life. He closed his eyes, turned his face away, but he couldn't stop his understanding.

"You see?" said Edward. "They're all happy pagans nowadays. When they take the trouble to worship at all. Enlightenment swept most of that nonsense away, and good riddance!"

"Oh, leave him alone," said Alec, growing alarmed, for Nicholas, doubled over, was mute and wide-eyed, regarding through his fingers the horror of the void. "Look, man, don't feel too bad—I know it's got to be a shock, finding out your religion's dead, but we've got this new thing called *nonselective altruism,* so people are still—"

"My death was wasted," said Nicholas quietly.

Not quite, sir. You did preach that sermon, when you was tied to the stake and the fire waited for you. Maybe you recollect? You impressed the good people of Rochester no end afore you burned, sir. One boy named Crokeham, he was so inspired by what you said, he run away to sea just so he could fight for England. Sailed the Spanish Main. Went ashore with a landing party on an island, all hot to kill himself a Spaniard, and what he found there—

Edward lifted his head. "Document D," he said in amazement.

Aye, I see you've guessed. He found something that didn't ought to have been there in 1578. Drake made damn sure nobody talked, but he wrote it up in his logbook and gave it to Elizabeth's ministers, with an eye to national security. They didn't know what to make of it, so it sat in the classified Crown archives until 1852. You

know who found it there, Commander Bell-Fairfax, don't you? And
you know what he done with it.

"The Santa Catalina Expedition," said Edward.

"But—Catalina's where Dr. Zeus has its laboratories," said Alec.

Right you are. So you see, Nicholas? If you hadn't preached that
sermon, the Company might never have been founded. Not that an
old sailor like me understands paradoxes in temporal physics, mind
you, but that's the way it looks from here. If our Edward was a
pawn for Dr. Zeus, weren't you the one as made the opening move in
the game?

Nicholas sat staring. Edward gave a brief laugh.

"What a nest of snakes," he said.

Aye, sir, you might say so. And all of 'em biting their tails.

Silence followed this observation, until Nicholas cried out.

"Rose!" he said hoarsely. "I left thee amongst devils—"

"Not devils," said Edward, sitting bolt upright. "The Society. Good
God! Your Rose and my Dolores—they were one and the same. And
you—" he turned to Alec.

"Mendoza," said Alec, as the implications hit him.

"She was an immortal creature," said Nicholas. "Their slave. God
forgive me. God forgive me. I never knew until the last—and I thought
she could disobey them—"

She could. That's why she were a prisoner when you met her,
Alec. She'd run afoul of her masters, trying to keep Commander
Bell-Fairfax here from getting killed. Edward blanched.

"But that means she—" Alec was unable to complete the thought.

I said she was a cyborg. She'd had a bit more than a porting in-
terface installed, though, lad, if you want the truth. I been trying to
tell you this, but you didn't want to hear. She was a living machine,
like yer old friend Blaise. The difference was, she loved you. She
knew who you were, and she knew you'd been set up to die again,
just like these two fine gentlemen. So she disconnected the intercept
and saved yer life.

"You mean—she was one of those *things*?" Alec's voice shook with
horror. "I slept with a machine?"

Edward turned and slapped his face, with such force his head
rocked on his shoulders.

"If you ever speak of her that way again, I'll kill you," he said. "You
feel disgust, do you, a thing like you? For a machine da Vinci himself
might have designed? Good God, I was enchanted once I knew! For
the little while I had to know."

"Listen to me, boy," said Nicholas desperately. "She could not help what they made her! What art thou, to despise her? Wilt thou betray her, too?"

"*Thing* indeed." Edward glared at Alec. "Has it penetrated that thick skull of yours yet, Alec? She preserved your life, even though she must have known what they'd do to her if she were caught. What will happen to her now?"

Alec saw the dark field of his nightmare again, the pits of flame.

Now, son, you got to remember she's immortal. They can't execute her. They got other reasons for wanting her kept hid, too. But Dr. Zeus has his ways of dealing permanently with such folk.

"Consigned to everlasting fire," said Nicholas in a faint voice. He had gone white as chalk.

"No, you medieval imbecile!" Edward clenched his fists. "You still have no grasp of the truth, have you? Leave your angels and devils in the trash of history, where they belong. The Society's been the real enemy from the first! We've been their slaves, no less than she, duped and cheated the same. Look at what we've seen through this pathetic boy's eyes!"

"Who're you calling pathetic, you bastard?" shouted Alec. Edward ignored him.

"See what's become of the empire for which I gave my life," he continued. "And you, with your grand martyrdom that was supposed to win you a place amongst God's elect. Was it worth it, man? Was it worth leaving her in her chains?"

"*Thou* wert ready enough to turn her to thy masters' purpose, even when thou wert kissing her breasts," snarled Nicholas.

Now, then, gentlemen, how much good will it do the lady if you waste time fighting? As I was trying to explain, Alec, afore you opened that file—sorry now, ain't you?—I don't know where she is. All the record showed was that she was arrested on the order of somebody named Clive Rutherford. Not a word about where she was sent.

"Then we need to find this Clive Rutherford," said Edward.

Ah, I can see yer a bright fellow and no mistake. We'll do just that, sir; only we'd best lay over here a day or two first, because we ought to reconnoiter and plan afore we make another jump through time.

"But they could be doing anything to her!" said Alec.

Just now it's 2215, son, if you'll remember. This Rutherford lubber ain't even going to be born for another century yet. We can't wring any answers out of him until he done the deed, can we? And, begging yer pardon—it wouldn't hurt you gentlemen to get used to one another aforehand, if you don't mind my saying so. I'd wager it's a little inconvenient to slouch about like this, three fellows with only one body between 'em.

"What do you mean, one body?" Edward said. "There are three of us."

Why, so there are; but all I can see less'n I looks through Alec's eyes is one, Mr. Bell-Fairfax, sir. The one what ain't dead. Alec.

"It's true," said Alec. "You keep grabbing me when you want to do something."

"Oh." Edward looked nonplussed. "Although . . . I may as well, really, because you don't seem to have put your body to particularly good use on your own account. What a wasted life you've led!"

"Ah, piss off," Alec told him. Edward chuckled.

"It only goes to prove my observations about the privileged classes. England's gone backward at a singular rate since my day. An earl who can't read? If you hunted with your hounds rather than sailed, you'd be perfectly at home in brother Nicholas's time."

"Is it even so?" Nicholas smiled unpleasantly. "*Nimium ne crede colori, puere.*"

That'll do! the Captain said, as Edward flushed and looked uncomfortable.

"It's a dead language anyway," he muttered. "Utterly pointless."

Well, I reckon you three gentlemen must be one and the same man; you couldn't hate yerself so much, otherwise. For the lady's sake, though, you best learn to get along peaceably.

It was a difficult period of adjustment.

The Captain had been prepared to give Alec a massive injection of an antipsychotic drug as soon as Edward's guard was down, but Edward's guard never seemed to go down, and the phenomenon of the distinct brainwaves for each personality continued. Himself an artificial personality with unusual abilities, the Captain found the idea of a disassociative personality disorder something of a challenge. He decided to see if there was a way to make Alec assimilate his previous selves, rather than banish them. Both Edward and Nicholas had knowledge and strengths that might be useful to Alec.

Not that this was particularly evident in the first few hours of their life together.

The three men found that, though they could move independently, they were unable to get more than a body's length from one another. Each one experienced independent physical sensations and appetites, regardless of who was in control of Alec's body, but only the controlling personality was able to satisfy his urges.

Twenty-fourth-century cuisine did not suit at all. Nicholas was impressed by the variety of food available on board a modern ship, but found it appallingly bland. An experiment to remedy this with hot pepper sauce had disastrous results. Neither he nor Edward cared for the various soy-derived dainties in their brightly colored irradiated pouches, either. Edward wanted a grilled beef chop very much, and became extremely profane when he was made familiar with twenty-fourth-century vegetarian civic ordinances. He then prowled through the saloon, searching in vain for cigars and cognac.

Sneeringly he inspected Alec's antique weapons collection and pronounced it the only thing of interest he'd seen so far; went up on deck and damned with faint praise twenty-fourth-century sailing technology. Nicholas, for his part, was horrified to discover there wasn't a single book on board.

On the other hand, the *Captain Morgan*'s bathroom was an immediate success, to the extent that over a two-hour period three bars of soap, two bottles of shampoo, every available drop of hot water, and all the clean towels were used.

They discovered that they could remove their clothing, and that it was possible to shave and comb one's hair on an individual basis, as long as one used Alec's body while one did so. Both Nicholas and Edward were startled by the buzzing shaver, but impressed by the job it did. Alec found his face smarting by the time Nicholas had finished shaving, however.

Too, though Edward might don his Victorian attire, Alec and Nicholas remained naked until each one dressed himself individually. Alec was able to pull on the fresh clothing that Bully Hayes had laid out for him, but Nicholas picked up his skimpy bundle in distaste.

"These hose stink," he grumbled. "What am I to do?"

"You ought to have had the sense to have died fully clothed, like me," said Edward smugly, inspecting his reflection in the steamy mirror.

Begging yer pardon, sir, but since yer an insubstantial soul—

"I am no soul, since I was made, not begotten! I am nothing more than spirit," Nicholas corrected the Captain with some asperity.

Edward snorted. "Are you certain you're even that much?"

Nicholas turned to reply, but realized he was by no means certain. The void opened before him again, the ruin of his universe.

"Not even that," he said. "Am I? *Nemo, nihil et*—"

"Stop it!" Alec snapped at Edward. "Isn't this hard enough without screwing him up worse? You want me to download you a map so you can see how small your Great Britain is now? I can practically step across it, man. No." He turned to catch Nicholas, who was collapsing, by the shoulders. "It'll be all right. He's just a mean bastard. Look, you want to see Mendoza again, right? Rose? We have to save her, don't we?"

Nicholas looked at him with sick eyes, but he nodded.

"So let's not worry about, er, cosmic stuff," said Alec. "One thing at a time. You want clothes like you used to wear?" He accessed Nicholas's memories briefly. Then he wrote for Nicholas's clothing occupying the empty shelf of the towel cupboard. When he opened the cupboard to see, there it was: a complete set of clothing, circa 1555, in sober black, with a fresh white shirt.

That's my clever boy!

"By Jove, that's a useful trick." Edward frowned. "I wonder if it would be possible to dress properly for dinner?"

I shouldn't wonder, sir, if you ask our Alec nicely.

"Don't talk rot! If he can do it, I certainly ought to be able to," said Edward, and as Nicholas dressed himself Edward went through any number of psychic contortions attempting to make a dinner jacket materialize in the cupboard. None appeared, despite his best efforts.

"What the hell does the boy do?" he shouted at last. "Substance can't be simply imagined into being. What is it, Alec, some sort of mathematical formula for converting matter?"

"No, it's nothing like that. It's just code," said Alec. "I don't think about it. I just make it happen. You really can't do it?"

"No!"

Well, now, ain't that a shame? I reckon our Alec has the edge on you in that, Commander; but, you see, he's done this sort of trick in cyberspace for years. Perhaps you'll learn one day, sir.

"I could try to show you," Alec said, smirking. Edward looked at him with narrowed eyes. Nicholas, meanwhile, had slipped on his black scholar's robe and stood fully dressed, looking down at himself in amazement.

"I threw off this gown in a room in England. How long ago now? The rain was beating at the little window . . . And Rose lay in the bed waiting—" His voice broke.

Alec patted him awkwardly on the shoulder. "It'll be all right," he said. "We'll get her back. You'll see."

"Thou shalt get her, boy," mourned Nicholas. "Not I, and not that proud ghost neither. I am not e'en so much dust as she could hold in her hand. What have we to do with flesh now?"

"I mean to find out," Edward said, turning to him. "You tasted the pepper sauce acutely enough, didn't you? And you enjoyed the hot water and the perfumed soap. Why should it be any different with the joys of the flesh? By God, if we're some Frankenstein's monster of strangeness, why not glory in it? I'll own I thought you were a complete idiot, young Alec, but you do seem to have powers of mind beyond the range of normal men."

"Thanks so much." Alec curled his lip. "You don't understand anything about recombinants, do you?"

"I understand ignorance and superstition when I see it," Edward replied. "If Science created us rather than the Almighty, what then? I'm damned if I'll cringe and apologize for it. Since you and I have been given this unnatural life, Nicholas, let's live it! For we've got work to do, gentlemen. My lady bid me set her free. *She* won't care what I am."

That's tellin' 'em, lad!

"Thank you," said Edward coolly. "There is also the matter of revenge. For all we know, God intended to make us His instruments to punish our presumptive creators. It seems to be what man-made monsters do. Let's find out, shall we?"

The *Captain Morgan* rocked on quiet gray water under a gray sky. It was suitably like limbo to depress the spirits of an ordinary man, let alone one with Alec's problems. He retreated to the saloon as darkness fell, closely followed by his previous selves. They crowded around the table while Coxinga brought a tray of supper for Alec: grilled fish and baked asparagus tips in white wine sauce.

"Now, that's something like!" said Edward, eyeing it. He muscled control away from Alec long enough to sample the fish.

If you please, sir! You let my Alec have his dinner, now.

"It's okay," said Alec morosely. "I'm not all that hungry, actually. What I'd really like is a drink."

Not in yer present condition, son. Anyway, it all went over the side after yer little accident, except for the cooking wine.

"Not the thirty-year-old Glenlivet," groaned Alec, putting his head in his hands.

"Oh, that really is too bad," condoled Edward with a certain insincerity, munching asparagus.

Afraid so, lad. If you behave yerself, we'll get more one of these days.

"That's a consolation, at any rate. One can still obtain some decent liquor in this miserable—I beg your pardon!" Edward broke off as control was wrested from him by Nicholas.

"What need hast thou of meat?" Nicholas told him, returning the plate to Alec. "Let the boy eat, thou wretch."

"I'm a man, you know," muttered Alec. "And I'm not stupid."

"No indeed, you've apparently quite the superior intellect in this day and age," said Edward. "God help us all." He changed his tone as a thought occurred to him. "Here now. That little trick you worked with brother Nicholas's clothing—do you suppose you could create anything else? What if you could make a veal cutlet and some new potatoes materialize out of the ether?"

"Like this?" said Alec irritably.

"I should of course prefer them on a plate," said Edward through his teeth, picking a nicely breaded cutlet out of his lap. "Damn you, boy, I hope you can launder these trousers. Never mind; we've made John Calvin over there smile, which is probably sinful and therefore worth the inconvenience."

"I only wish you'd asked for soup," Alec retorted, but he read Edward's memories. A moment later a dish of blue willow pattern appeared before Edward, bearing the meal he had requested as well as *haricots verts* and a glass and bottle of claret, vintage 1859. Edward blinked.

"That," he said in awe, "is the last meal I had in London, at Redking's. I—Thank you, Alec."

"What about you?" Alec said to Nicholas, who was gaping at the laden table. "You want anything? I bet you'd be happier if you weren't hungry."

"How can a spirit hunger?" said Nicholas. "But an thou couldst summon eel pie and a pintpot of ale, in the same wise, boy—"

"Stop calling me *boy*," said Alec, but he summoned them. Nicholas picked up a spoon cautiously, broke the pastry crust. A plume of steam rose, bearing with it the fragrance of eel pie. Nicholas's pupils dilated. There followed a reverent conversational silence, broken only by the scrape of knives on china and pewter.

Now, that's what I like to see! My fine gentlemen all minding their manners and getting along.

"Don't fawn, machine," Edward said. "What about Clive Rutherford? Have you tracked him down, yet?"

Aye, sir, that I have. Turns out he's one of the team that worked on yer project, sir, **Adonai.**

"Is he now?" Edward's eyes grew mean and small. "Rutherford of Rutherford, Chatterji, and Ellsworth-Howard? That's convenient, I must say. We can combine business with pleasure."

"We're not going to kill anybody, are we?" said Alec.

"It might be necessary," Edward said, taking a sip of claret.

"I will do no murder, Edward," Nicholas said sternly. "Nor shalt thou. What, hast thou not had thy fill of *necessary* deaths?"

"That's true enough," Edward said at last, looking away.

The Captain made a noise as though he were clearing his throat and continued:

The record shows he's also a museum curator. He's got charge of a historical architectural monument—row of houses in London, all done up so tourists can see how people used to live in the old days. He lives in one of 'em, and if he's the curator I reckon he'd be at home most days.

"What's his address?" Alec asked.

It says here No. 10 Albany Crescent, London NW1. Edward choked on his wine.

"I grew up in that house," he gasped, as Alec thumped him helpfully on the back.

"No kidding?"

"But it can't be the same. It must have been pulled down long ago." Edward recovered himself. "Or bombed. Wars seem to have swept over London like so many juggernauts since my time. Damned incompetent idiots. We were becoming a world power!"

Well, nobody's a world power anymore, sir, if that's any consolation. Except for Dr. Zeus Incorporated.

"I know where Albany Crescent is," Alec realized. "I broke into a house there once."

Nicholas frowned and Edward looked intrigued. "A thief, were you? And an earl's son? What were you doing, playing at being Prince Hal?"

"Oh, go shrack yourself. I wasn't stealing! Balkister and I were just looking for a place to get drunk in out of the rain. London's full of old empty houses, see, because there aren't nearly as many people as there used to be," Alec said. "Or maybe nobody can stand to live there. God knows I couldn't."

"But thou canst find thy way there, and bring us to this man?" Nicholas said.

"Yeah. No problem."

Oh, I reckon you'll find it a bit more complicated than that, me boys. The police may not be looking to question our Alec anymore, but Dr. Zeus might still be hunting him. This ship's just a bit conspicuous, more's the pity. You won't be able to dock at Tower Marina this time. Or ever again, likely.

"I knew I shouldn't have laid out all that money for mooring membership," said Alec, slightly stunned. "How are we going to get into London?"

You'll come up with ways and means, Commander Bell-Fairfax, sir, I shouldn't wonder.

"I can get into or out of any city on Earth," Edward said, draining the last of his claret. "Leave it to me." He pushed away his empty plate and looked sidelong at Alec. "I don't suppose you'd care to try to materialize brandy and a good cigar?"

"Okay," said Alec, and they appeared on the table, complete with a matchstand and another tankard of ale for Nicholas.

"Aaah," Edward gloated. "Capital. Young Alec, you are decidedly a man of parts." He struck a match and lit the cigar; taking a sensuous drag, he leaned back in his seat. "Mmf. There now! It is conclusively proven. We've gone to Heaven after all."

"Mocking knave," muttered Nicholas, waving away the cloud of smoke. He lifted his tankard and drank, however.

"And is this Courvoisier?" Edward raised the brandy snifter to his nose and inhaled. "You're a man of taste as well, my boy. We may make something of Alec yet."

"You couldn't get out of Los Angeles," said Alec suddenly.

"Eh?" Edward frowned at him.

"You didn't know how without getting caught. Mendoza had to help you." Alec was astonished at the unfamiliar memory he'd accessed, seeing a dusty pueblo and sere brown hills under a darkening sky. "Just like she helped me, when I crashed."

"So she did," said Edward after a moment. He blew a thoughtful smoke ring. "This much hasn't changed, at least. Over cigars and brandy, we talk about the ladies. Or one lady, in this case. Gentlemen, I give you Dolores Alice Elizabeth Mendoza." He raised his glass.

Nicholas sighed. "When she rode into old Sir Walter's garden, she was called Doña Rosa Anzolabejar."

"All she ever told me was, her name was Mendoza," said Alec.

"I wonder what her true name is?" Edward savored his brandy. "The mystery, that was one of the things I loved about her. Who was she? How could a woman, let alone such a young girl, understand so perfectly what it was to be a political unless she were one herself? To say nothing of her other abilities."

"Even so it was with me," said Nicholas sadly. "I sought to know the truth; and even when I had found it out, I knew nothing. Save only that she loved me. The poor child watched me ranting in the fire, and I saw my least word was a knife in her heart."

"How could you do that?" demanded Alec, seeing his memory.

"You wanted her to die with you! That's horrible." The image from his dream, the field of death, came abruptly before his eyes. He turned his face away, to find himself looking into Edward's cold level gaze.

"Were we any kinder to her, you and I?" Edward inquired. "Though, I'll grant you, neither of us went so far as to actually *ask* her to destroy herself." He looked at Nicholas. "That's your own particular distinction, man of God."

"I thought to save her immortal soul from Satan," said Nicholas, staring into his ale. "I wanted to bring her unto the Lord." His voice grew faraway. "Yet God He knows she was innocent enough of sin. It was I lusted after her from the moment I saw her little face, though I lied and said not so to my heart. She did no more than offer me half an orange for courtesy's sake. I wanted to lick the sweet juice from her hand, and have her on her back there in the long grass . . ."

"What a fine godly hypocrite," Edward chuckled, exhaling smoke. Nicholas just stared at him, terrible bleakness in his eyes, and then said:

"Ay. So I was, and it cost me Heaven in the end. Will you hear?

"When I suffered in the fire, my pain was grievous; but there came a roar in mine ears and a burst of light, and I was gone out of mine agony like a bird set free. And I ascended, as I thought, toward Heaven. Methought I saw the kingdom of God, like a pleasant garden for His elect, and I made haste to go in.

"But the Lord Himself refused me entrance. Wherefore may I not rest, I cried. Have I not suffered to bear witness to Thee, my God?

"Indeed thou hast, quoth He. But this is neither thy place nor thy time. Thou art alone, Nicholas! Where is the girl?

"I was ashamed, and I said: Lord, she would not come.

"And the Lord said: Go forth, then, for I tell thee thou shalt never come near to Paradise until thou bearest her along with thee.

"And I fled lamenting from the presence of God, and woke here, to know myself for the vile thing I am."

"When will you stop this metaphysical nonsense?" said Edward wearily. "But I suppose you've no other way to look at the matter, born as you were in an age of superstitious piety. Our life-forces have been kept intact somehow, can you understand that? The goal of the Society was always immortality. Politicals like me, but invincible! And I was promised resurrection in the flesh myself, when my time came. I was told that even death was no more than an injury, from which Science would heal me."

"You're both deluded," said Alec, shaking his head. Nicholas scowled at him and Edward tipped ash off his cigar before replying:

"By no means. The Society—or the Company—may have lied to

me about a good many things, but it's obvious they did find some way to preserve my intellect. And I shouldn't be at all surprised if my own proper body isn't being kept as well, in some electrical sarcophagus, or perhaps a magnetic bottle of life-sustaining fluids, until it can be revived."

Alec shuddered and Nicholas looked askance. "That is rank alchemy," he said.

"Science," Edward corrected him. He blew another smoke ring and grinned at Nicholas. "And hard luck for you, old man. I doubt very much whether even the most advanced medicine can reanimate a bucketful of ashes. The Company clearly preserved your life-force as well, to what purpose I cannot imagine, but you thoughtlessly let your body go up in flames! You may as well make the best of sharing the premises with young Alec here; you're unlikely to get any closer to eternal life."

"Oh, shut up," Alec told him. "I don't know what you are, but I know nobody's figured out any way to make a corpse back come to life yet. What about those autopsy pictures? You're dead, and you deserve it!"

"And yet, I live." Edward had another sip of his brandy, smiling. "Even Nicholas lives. Explain that, young genius."

I can explain it, son.

"The machine has opinions? This should be entertaining," said Edward.

I wouldn't get so high and mighty if I was you, Commander Bell-Fairfax, sir. You ain't nothing but a stored file my boy downloaded by accident. The only reason you think yer alive is because his brain's able to run yer program—and our Nicholas's program too—at the same time he's using it for his own thinking.

"Is that what it is?" Alec looked sick with relief. "So I'm not crazy!"

No, no, son, it's only because yer brain's so special that yer able to have this kind of disassociative personality—the Captain sought for a more positive spin. *Er, what you are is multiple personality-abled. See?*

"A likely story," scoffed Edward. "And I'll thank you to retract it, when I've been restored to my own flesh. Once we've rescued Dolores, I rather think finding where they're keeping my body should be the next order of the day, shouldn't you? The sooner we can dispense with this intolerable living arrangement, the better."

"Yeah, well, we'll see who she feels like snuggling up to then, won't we?" said Alec contemptuously. "A live man, or some kind of pickled zombie like you."

Edward gave him a long, hard stare before shrugging and taking another drag on his cigar. He blew smoke in Alec's face and said:

"You've still no grasp on the situation, have you, boy? But Dolores will understand. She and I are of a kind. I'd begun to guess what she was, even before she let the truth slip. The Society claimed there would be a way to make immortal creatures and dispatch them, through time itself, to do our work. I thought she must have been sent to assist me. But I couldn't ask her until the business was over, and by then it was too late.

"And then at the last, she said—" Edward paused, his face clouding. "She told me she was a prisoner in time. She begged me to come back and break her chains. I had no idea what she meant. It had never occurred to me that the Society would countenance the creation of immortal *slaves*." He looked at Alec with aversion. "How could I have known that a blunderer like you would find her in her prison?"

Alec clenched his fists. "I went back for her."

"But too late." Nicholas shook his head. "Thou hadst thy vanities to attend to first, thine ambuscades and treasons up amidst the cold stars. Yet I did the same. If I'd let my lust rule me I'd have stolen her away and fled from England, and would to God I had! But not I. I went vainly after righteousness and left her trapped here. And when at last a smiling villain came to her, she must have thought—"

"What, thought I was you?" Edward blew another smoke ring. "She didn't cry *your* name at the height of passion, brother. And what passion! I couldn't imagine how a virgin girl—" He halted.

"I had her maidenhead," Nicholas informed him.

"But—"

"But she was a virgin with me, too," said Alec. There was a silence while they considered the contradiction, before Edward grinned.

"Good God, she must be made like the houris in Mahomet's paradise! And she knew tricks I thought only the women in the souk could do. I suppose she had her education at your godly hands, brother Nicholas, in which case I'm obliged to concede there's more to you than meets the eye as well!"

"Don't speak of her this way," said Nicholas, giving him a deadly look. "Thou, who never loved her."

"I tell you I did, man," Edward said, all the banter going out of his voice. He put down his cigar. "I thought she was superb. Lustful as Aphrodite, and wise as Athena. *She* seemed to think we were made for each other. And we were, by God! She's mine, not the damned Society's chattel."

"She was going to marry *me*," said Alec. "I asked her, and I'm still the only one with a real body, so you can just—just—"

"Let me guess. Piss off?" Edward inquired in a bright voice.

"Oh, shut up," said Alec miserably. "I guess she only loved me because of you two. Figures, doesn't it? She . . ." He stopped, struck. "She must have known about us. That we were Recombinants and everything! Don't you think? And she didn't care."

"How should she care, who was scarcely a creature of flesh and blood herself?" said Nicholas. "Though she at least began as a mortal child, not an unnatural scrap of flesh in an alembic's womb."

"How d'you know that?" Alec asked him.

Nicholas raised his pint and drank deep. "Her father admitted it to me," he said, with an extraordinary expression of malevolence. "No true father of hers, understand my meaning, yet he that bound her into eternal labor for his masters. Doctor Ruy! A meddler and a poisoner, and were he not deathless I would kill him with my two hands, should he ever cross my path again." He looked sullenly at Edward. "There's necessary murder for you."

Edward merely gave him an ironic smile and drank more of his brandy. Alec sat looking from one of them to the other.

"There might be a way to find out how much she knew about us, anyway," he said. "I guess you both can read writing, can't you?" The concerted look of scorn they gave him made him flush. "Hey! I can do lots of things you can't, you know."

"Undoubtedly," Edward drawled, reaching for his cigar again. "Though I intend to become your equal in them pretty damned quickly. How does one control your Ancient Mariner, for example?"

That's for my boy to know and you to find out, ain't it, sir?

"Rest assured I will," Edward said.

"Peace! Wherefore, boy?"

"She left writing," Alec said. "I brought it with me from the station but I can't read it, and—"

"Good God. There was a book, wasn't there?" Edward sat bolt upright. "What did you do with it, Alec?"

Five minutes later they were settled down around the table again, with fresh cigars and brandy for Edward and more ale for Nicholas, examining the book under the light of the gimbal lamp.

It was a big book, very rough and hand-made in appearance, and it consisted of three sections sewn together. The first part was written on glossy sheets of something indestructible, brightly printed on their reverse sides with pictures of seductive-looking cuisine. They were in fact opened-out labels for a popular soy protein product. The ink varied here in color and thickness; the writer had evidently been experimenting with thinning agents. Toward the middle of the text a satisfactory uniformity had been achieved, and remained consistent thereafter.

The second part was of machine-cut white paper, crumbling with age, a printed text here and there annotated in the same hand as the first section, with a written postscript. It appeared to be the transcript of a hearing.

The third part was the shortest: more of the bound labels, covered in closely written text to about halfway through. The writing had broken off abruptly. There were some thirty pages following, blank, clean and new-looking.

"That is her hand," said Nicholas in a guarded voice.

"Is it?" Edward clamped his cigar in his teeth and opened to the first page. He removed the cigar, blew a stream of smoke and read aloud: " '*I am a botanist. I will write down the story of my life as an exercise, to provide the illusion of conversation in this place where I am now alone*—' " He broke off, frowning. "This is a diary. I wonder whether we really ought to . . ."

"Dost thou scruple, thou?" scoffed Nicholas.

"I have my standards where a lady's heart's concerned," Edward said. "Besides, one never knows what one might find."

"Please," said Alec. "I only had her for a day. What if we never find her again? I loved her, I've got to know what she said!"

Nicholas pointed in silence to a line near the bottom of the first page, where the words *Dr. Zeus Incorporated* appeared. Edward nodded grimly.

"We've no choice, then, really," he said. "Have we, gentlemen? Sorry, my love. Let's see what you can tell us."

Edward began again to read aloud. His cigar, forgotten, burned itself out to gray ash. There were times when Alec had to explain puzzling text references to the other two men. There were times when Nicholas had to do the same. They read all night.

Gray morning was breaking over the sea when Edward fell silent at last and leaned back from the table. Nicholas's eyes were red and swollen; he'd wept himself out hours earlier. Alec sat gazing at the other two men with contempt.

"You bastards," he said hoarsely. "You tricked her, didn't you?"

Edward was silent, but Nicholas raised his head.

"*Tricked* her?"

"You know what I mean." Alec leaned forward across the table, stared at Nicholas with a ghastly parody of a seductive smile. "Bet you did it a million times, didn't you? You just look into their eyes—and you sort of focus right here, don't you, and you think about how nice it would be to get them in bed. And then they do just what you want. And they think they love you, until it wears off."

"No!" Nicholas protested. "I only persuaded her—that gift was the grace of God, *charisma*, that I might save souls! And if love were the means—if she . . ." His stammers died away into silence. He closed his eyes, white as a ghost. "Oh, Jesu, what have I done?"

"Merely used a superior force of will," said Edward sharply, though he did not look up. "A natural gift you were born with, owing nothing to superstition. If you never employed it toward noble ends, at least you did better than the boy. Alec, did it never occur to you that you might have become something more than a seducer?"

"Sooner than that what you became, man," Alec said. "You shracking assassin."

Edward stiffened, but did not respond.

"I should never have been born," said Alec. "None of us should ever have existed at all. Why did she love us?"

Edward reached for his brandy and tossed it back in a gulp. "But she *did* love us. Here! You machine. Captain Morgan, d'you call yourself? Set a course for London in the twenty-fourth century, however you do it. We're going after Clive Rutherford."

Aye, sir! But you might want to let our Alec get some sleep first, eh? You'll all need yer wits about you.

"We will, by God," Edward said, rising to his feet behind the table. "Shall we retire, gentlemen?"

Alec nodded grimly. He stepped away from the table. Edward and Nicholas followed him without another word.

London was fogbound, all her postcard views grayed out and lost. Her streetlights had only just extinguished themselves, but there was nobody to see: her few citizens were still huddling in their warm beds, asleep or smugly congratulating themselves that there was a full half hour yet before the alarm shrilled.

The Thames was quiet at Waterloo Bridge, the fog drifting low and silent over its glassy surface. Suddenly the fog lifted in a puff, as if blown by a gust of wind, though there was no wind. Seconds later there was a disturbance in the water, a roiling, a steaming, and anyone standing on the bridge might have thought a submarine had unaccountably just surfaced in the river below. However, there was no one standing on the bridge at that hour.

Within seconds the long sleek shape had stabilized, and the glassy shell that formed her upper surface lifted a little—just enough for a man to emerge, squeezing through awkwardly because he was a rather long man, stripped to bathing trunks, clutching in one arm a waterproof duffel sack. He dropped into the Thames and swam hastily ashore. No sooner had he found his footing in the Thames mud than the unidentified floating object slid away up the Thames in the direction of Charing Cross New Pier, where it lurked among the pilings.

The man remained, however, shivering violently in the cold. He retreated into the shadows under the bridge and, taking clothing from the duffel sack, dressed himself. The last thing he took from the bag was a pistol of some kind. He thrust it out of sight into his coat, wadded up the bag and stuffed it into a pocket, and climbed up to the Embankment through the ruins of the old police station.

Shortly thereafter, persons venturing out to the public transport stops along Charing Cross Road were dismayed to note the presence of a very tall demented person, lumbering along uncertainly and talking to himself. It wasn't only that his eyes were red, his hair wild; he was dressed most inappropriately. His long winter coat flapped open to reveal that he wore nothing more underneath than a tropical-pattern shirt, shorts, and a pair of canvas boating shoes. He looked like a derelict who had been on a Hawaiian holiday.

Mrs. Beryl Wynford-Singh trembled as he approached, making herself as small as she could on the transport bench and praying that the transport would arrive before he came near enough to assault her. She gasped with relief when she spotted the transport rounding Pall Mall. The lunatic gasped too, and backed into the nearest doorway.

"*God's wounds,*" she heard him cry. "Quiet, you idiot! It's nothing more than, er, some kind of omnibus. Isn't it, boy? It's only an agtransport. Don't be scared. Come on. People will look at us."

But in fact nobody was looking at him. After the first glance, people were determinedly averting their eyes. Several of them felt rather guilty about it, because by law it was every citizen's duty to report reality-challenged persons to the nearest public health monitor, that they might be taken off to hospital. However, this law failed to take into account the irresistible human urge to confer invisibility on those who dressed badly and babbled to themselves in public places. Mrs. Wynford-Singh was already quite incapable of seeing the lunatic as he paced on and halted, gaping up at a memorial statuary group dating from the early twenty-first century.

"That's new since my day! Persephone, isn't it? Ay. Ravished away down the tunnel to the underworld by Hades, with his hounds chasing after. So it is. Rather an omen for our quest, wouldn't you say?" The lunatic peered more closely. "Who was *Diana Spencer*? Come on, we're wasting time."

The transport stopped in front of a grateful Mrs. Wynford-Singh and opened its doors. As she fled through them, she did think she heard a voice saying plaintively: "Now, where the deuce has Shaftesbury Avenue got to in five hundred years?"

One alert junior clerk, watching from the transport window, did notice that the tall person bore a marked resemblance to the mysterious Hangar Twelve Man in the Mars One surveillance footage, still being shown nightly in the hope that viewers might provide authorities with an identification. The junior clerk's eyes brightened, and he leaned closer to the glass for a better look. He realized that the tall man was gesticulating and speaking to the air next to him, as though an unseen person stood there. The clerk promptly lost interest and sighed, reflecting on the hopeless monotony of his young life as Mrs. Wynford-Singh dropped heavily down on the seat beside him.

The tall man did find his way to Shaftesbury Avenue without being arrested, and there seemed to orient himself. He loped away at once with a determined stride, his long coat blowing out behind him. In a few more minutes he stood peering into Albany Crescent, an extraordinary expression on his face.

"Look at it," he muttered. "Of all the places to have survived half a millennium! I might have known. I'll bet the drains are still blocked. So that was your house, there? Number ten? Yes, unfortunately. I know how you feel. My place in John Street gets me the same way.

"Thou liest! This is some palace, surely. Yes, I suppose it would seem that way to you; but then, you were born in a thatched hut, weren't you? Besides, this isn't one house, it's lots of houses all stuck together. Well, and canst thou effect an entry? I think so. I was pretty drunk, though. Never mind, boy. It's coming back to me now."

He proceeded into Albany Crescent and stood, rubbing his chin thoughtfully, surveying the long curve that fronted on a park. It was entirely deserted.

"How did you break in, Alec? Well, it wasn't number ten. It was this one here on the end. See down those stairs? There's a kitchen—I know. Down there, now. Before someone sees. But—Do as you're told!"

He scrambled down the kitchen-stairs at No. 1, which were heavily overgrown with rose bramble, and crouched in the shadows by the door.

"Ow! I tried to tell you, man. Never mind. Is this the door? No. It's been replaced. That's a new lock, an electronic one. Canst command it, then? I ought to be able to. Let's see." He drew a plug from the torque about his neck and inserted it in the lock's port. "We're in! Come on, then. Close it behind you."

He stood in shadows and dust, looking around warily. There was nothing in the room but a nineteenth-century cooking hearth, a mass of brick-red rust. There were caster-stains on the linoleum to show where later appliances had sat for long periods of time, and a few irregular holes in the walls and floor. The man shivered.

"This is what it is, to be a ghost! Through there. There ought to be stairs. But this isn't number ten! What's the point—you'll see."

The room beyond was in worse shape, darker and dirtier. There were stairs against the far wall, leading upward. The man crept up them and easily forced the old-fashioned lock at the top.

He stepped out into what had been the entry hall of the house and paused, getting his bearings. Then he paced slowly forward, over the marble parquet floor, to the swirling mosaic roundel at the base of the curving stair. Light filtered in through the fan above the door, revealing a parlor opening out to his right. Dust and cobwebs there, a black yawning fireplace, boarded-over windows.

"Wherefore hath this been left to time and the worm?" wondered the man. "Damned if I know. Look at it all! Draperies gone, potted palms gone, servants all gone. So much for Britain and her glory. Er— it's like I said, you know? There's more houses than people now, and nobody wants to live in the crumbly ones." He lifted his face, scowling. "It smells dead. Enough of this. Upstairs, quick march."

He went up into the house, ascending through more shadows, more cobwebs, and brought them at last to a little door in the wall of what had been the servants' dormitory.

"Here we are, gentlemen," he said, crouching down. "Rather smaller than I remembered, but what can one expect?" He took a firm grip on the handle of the door and pulled. The door tore away from the wall, trailing its rusted hinges, to reveal a darkness beyond, partially blocked by an ancient water tank.

"Hm." The man put his head into the darkness. "This may be difficult. Difficult? You're nuts, it's impossible. We can't fit through here." He regarded the long passage that stretched away under the slates of the roof, the whole length of the crescent. It was floored only with wooden beams widely spaced over plaster, and obscured at regular intervals by more of the water tanks. "No? We must and will, unless you'd prefer knocking on Mr. Rutherford's door and asking to be invited in. Don't be a coward. I'll show you who's a goddam coward!"

He thrust his shoulders in past the tank, and after a considerable amount of straining and writhing got in one leg and then the other. Balancing on a rafter, bracing himself against the wall, he stood slowly and found his head in a mass of cobwebs.

"Aaagh! Keep calm. Don't step between the rafters, or you'll fall into the room below. Now, this can be done. Quickly, beam to beam, watch your feet. Count the doors. We'll want the ninth one after this. Go!" Shuddering, he began to sidle along the passage, as the rafters creaked ominously under his weight.

"Here we are," he said presently. "Number ten. See?" Grinning, he ran his fingers over a pattern of scratches on the wood of the low sill. Just visible, in the chink of light streaming between two slates, were the straggling letters E-D-W-A-R-D.

"My old hideaway. Rather comforting, don't you think?" he said, testing the door with his fingertips. "Nothing left of Her Britannic Majesty's Empire, but by God I left my mark on *something*. Just get us out of here, man. I think this rafter's cracking." He struck the door a careful blow and it flew open, admitting him into blinding light. Crawling forth on his hands and knees, he found himself in what was plainly an attic.

Rather too plainly an attic. There were three or four old trunks, picturesquely decorated with antique steamer labels, and a dressmaker's dummy. There was a battered farthing-halfpenny bicycle leaning against the wall, with a broken cricket bat and a helmet from some long-lost war. There wasn't a speck of dust on anything.

"This is a museum exhibit," said the man. "Thank you, I had drawn that conclusion. Is he here, then? Downstairs, very likely. Yeah." He got carefully to his feet and dusted himself off, picking cobwebs from his wild hair. Reaching inside his coat, he drew out the pistol and checked it. Then, with a coldness and composure in his face that would have astonished the cringing citizens who'd seen him talking to himself in the Charing Cross Road, he opened the attic door and descended the steps beyond in perfect silence.

"More tea?" Rutherford offered the pot. Chatterji swirled bits of chamomile in the bottom of his cup and made a face.

"No, thanks. I'll have another muffin, though."

"There you are." Rutherford extended the plate and Chatterji helped himself. "What about you, Foxy?" He waited patiently as the import of his words sank in on Ellsworth-Howard, who was working his slow way through a bowl of bran flakes in soy emulsion. Ellsworth-Howard's new medication made him very calm, you could say that much for it.

"Yes please," he said at last, and Rutherford leaned over and refilled his teacup.

"There you are." Rutherford took another muffin himself, and daubed it with fruit paste. There were no clandestine dairy products at his table today; smuggling butter and cream had become too dangerous since the Mars Two incident, with all the increased border surveillance. Still, nobody would ever catch the Hangar Twelve Man. Miserable closure had come when Chatterji was informed that the Company had recovered the stolen shuttle, wrecked, and found bits and pieces of Alec Checkerfield inside.

"Now then." Rutherford dabbed at his mustache with a napkin. "What do you say we have a look at our dream journals? Chatty?"

"Well—er." Chatterji drew a small plaquette from his coat pocket. "There's not much, I'm afraid, and I don't appear to have been given any unconscious insights on how to create a better security tech. Mostly I've just had nightmares."

"Ah, but you never know. The creative genius may have given you an insight expressed symbolically, don't you see? Like that chemist fellow," said Rutherford. "Dreamed of snakes biting their tails, and woke up to realize that benzene molecules must be circular."

"Yes, but—I dream about Shiva and Kali. On Mars," Chatterji said, and Rutherford grimaced. They had all agreed never to bring the subject up again.

"Ugh. You want to schedule another session with Dr. Cannon, Chatty. Very well then, I'll share my dreams." Rutherford took up his plaquette and thumbed the PLAYBACK function. After a moment the room filled with the sound of his voice, thick and blurred with sleep:

"HEM! UH, VERY INTERESTING. TWENTIETH JANUARY 2352, HALF PAST FIVE IN THE MORNING AND I WAS, ER, IN SOME KIND OF POLICE MUSEUM. ROWS AND ROWS OF WAX DUMMIES IN OLD POLICE UNIFORMS. SOME OF THEM HAD CLUBS AND SOME EVEN HAD GUNS, AT LEAST I THINK THEY WERE GUNS—"

"Did they look anything like this?" said the very tall man who appeared in the doorway, leveling a disrupter pistol at them. Rutherford dropped his plaquette in his surprise. It fell to the floor and the sound of his recorded voice stopped abruptly.

"Alec shracking Checkerfield," said Ellsworth-Howard through a mouthful of bran flakes.

"Amongst others," said the tall man. "Get his buke! Get it before he can send an alert. What's a buke? That thing there, sticking out of his bag, see? Ah." He crossed the room swiftly and confiscated Ellsworth-Howard's buke, shoving it into his coat pocket and placing the bell-muzzle of his disrupter to the back of Ellsworth-Howard's naked head. Rutherford shrieked. Chatterji's hands flew to his mouth.

"Which one of you is Clive Rutherford?" the tall man inquired.

"But—buh-but you're dead," cried Chatterji.

The man looked impatient and put his thumb on the pistol's safety; then his eyes widened with horror. "Yikes, Edward, hold on. There aren't lead bullets in this thing, it shoots microwaves! It'd fry his brain bad enough if he were ordinary, but with those rivets, his head'll explode."

He drew back the gun an inch or so, as if considering, and his facial expression became aloof. "Trust the Irish to devise something like this. On the other hand, one thing I did learn in my long years as a political is that there really is no such thing as a clean kill. Well then, gentlemen! A particularly nasty death for your friend, unless you speak up. Is Clive Rutherford in this room, please?"

"I'm Clive Rutherford!" he said.

"Good. Mr. Rutherford, where is the woman Mendoza?"

"Who?" Rutherford gaped.

"One of your slaves," Edward said, curling his lip. "The Botanist Mendoza. You had her arrested and transferred to an unrecorded location, just after that unfortunate incident on Mars. Tell me where she is."

"I don't know," squealed Rutherford, and Ellsworth-Howard shuddered as the man exhaled impatiently and took a firmer grip on his pistol. But then the face changed, and the voice was different too as Nicholas said: "But he's unarmed, Edward."

"Who's Edward?" said Chatterji in spite of his terror.

"Just hit him or something, okay?" Alec said. "I don't want to kill anybody."

"Of course you don't want to kill anybody." Rutherford mastered himself enough to attempt a soothing tone. "You're a *good* man, Alec. You're a hero, not a villain. Oh, when I think of the times I've dreamed of meeting you—and to have it happen like this!" Tears welled in his eyes.

"I asked you a question," said the hard cultured voice that had done most of the talking. "Where is the woman Mendoza?"

"Edward was the name of the s-second one," Chatterji said suddenly. "In the second s-sequence! Edward Something Something, uh, Fairfax."

"Edward Alton Bell-Fairfax," Edward corrected him. "At your service, formerly; now very much his own man. I really am going to shoot your friend, here, if you don't answer my question. Where is the woman Mendoza?"

"Oh, my God, he's g-gone mad," moaned Chatterji.

"Hardly. It seems to be something akin to demonic possession, even if Nicholas partakes more of the angelic in our particular case." Edward sounded wickedly amused. "No, Mr. Rutherford—and I assume you must be Francis Chatterji?—no, we're all three here to confront you, our sinful creators, just as in Mrs. Shelley's book, though without all the tedium of a chase to the North Pole. Alec, you've got this weapon set at minimum wave! That'll take far too much time." Edward adjusted the dial on the top of the pistol. "There now. Maximum. Dreadfully sorry, Mr. Ellsworth-Howard—I believe? I'm afraid they'll have to conduct your funeral with the casket closed, unless the undertaker can contrive a wax replica of your head—"

"Options research!" said Ellsworth-Howard. He would have said it sooner, but he was finding it difficult to think at the best of times these days.

"I beg your pardon?"

"I sent her to Options Research," Rutherford said. "But it's a department, not a place! I don't know where it is."

"We can find out from his buke, Edward," said Alec. "Come on, let's leave these creeps and go rescue her."

"Alec, please." Rutherford held up his hand. "Please listen. There's been a terrible misunderstanding. We created you in good faith! We thought you were going to do great things for humanity. But we were used, Alec! The Company had its own agenda all along. Do you see?"

"I saw Elly Swain, you little bastard," said Alec. "How many other people suffered to bring your wonderful creation to life? And Edward and Nicholas had mothers too, didn't they? You treated 'em like animals. What kind of good faith was that?"

"It was necessary." Rutherford stood up in his agitation and tried to pace, but Chatterji pulled him back down. "Nothing great is got without cost. And if three women suffered some shame and discomfort, it would have been worth it. Oh, Alec, what you might have been! What you *are*." Rutherford's voice broke. "Good God, you're the hero I always wanted to be. If not for Mars—look at you. Orphaned and free, sailing in your ship with its pirate flag, having adventures, dying heroically and popping up alive again. You sway others with just the sound of your voice, you're clever and strong and fearless. You're Peter! You're Arthur and Robin Hood. You're, uh, Frodo and Mowgli and Kim and Sinbad and—and the boys in the Narnia books and the boys in *Castle of Adventure* and—"

"What about Pinocchio?" said Alec quietly. "Somebody you could put through hell and it wouldn't matter, because he wasn't a real boy?"

"All right, I deserve that," Rutherford said, weeping. "But you have to understand about the woman. She was your downfall, you see, every time! Your evil angel, if you will. We had to put her away. She held you back, she tangled you—you'd never have accomplished anything—"

"She loved me."

"But we loved you, too! And we understood your destiny."

"What destiny? To keep getting myself killed in stupid ways?" growled Alec.

"No, no. To give your life in a noble sacrifice for the good of others," Rutherford admonished him. "Because you could accomplish things ordinary men couldn't do. You were to have been the ultimate hero, born of a virgin even, eternally resurrected for mankind's eternal benef—"

"Thou blaspheming fool!" Nicholas drew himself up until Alec looked seven feet tall. "Was it for *thy* greater glory I suffered in the fire? Hast thou created me, and sat in judgment on my life? Oh, little man, to make a thing like me!"

"We're sorry! We're so awfully, awfully s-sorry," whimpered Chatterji, for Nicholas's voice had become a thing of terror and power. "We'd never have done it if we'd known how it was going to t-turn out. Please don't kill us!"

"I can't deny I'd enjoy it," sneered Edward. "An appetite *you* set in my heart. You made me a slaughterer, and gave me the conscience to tell me it was wrong. Should I indulge myself now, I wonder? Get up, all of you. Lie flat on your faces on the floor and put your hands behind your heads."

Rutherford and Chatterji obeyed at once. Ellsworth-Howard required a shove to remind him to comply before he flopped down beside them. Alec bound their wrists with cut cords from the drapes, and then knotted the bindings so the struggling of one would only serve to tighten the bonds of the other two. He went through their pockets and removed their identity discs, tucking them into his coat.

Edward then secured the pistol beside the discs, buttoned his coat carefully, and went out into the entry hall, with its marble floor and mosaic roundel an exact counterpart of the one at No. 1 Albany Crescent. He looked around him, grinning.

"Well, good-bye and farewell to you, number ten," he said. "For the last time, I devoutly hope."

He opened the door, stepped through, and closed it behind him. They could hear him whistling through his teeth as he strode away down the pavement.

"He never understood." Rutherford gulped back a sob. "He never understood his greatness."

"At least he didn't kill us," said Chatterji faintly.

After a full minute had gone by, Ellsworth-Howard said:

"Shrack! He took my buke."

They still hadn't managed to free themselves by Wednesday, when fortunately the first tour group of the day found them.

Alec Makes His Exit

All the commuters had now arrived at their offices and set about their wearisome duties, so they missed seeing Alec sprinting back through the streets of London. There were a few tourists on Waterloo Bridge, and they turned at the thunder of footsteps as a wild-eyed man of extraordinary height came racing toward them. If they had not turned, they'd have seen what was making the hissing noise in the Thames directly under the bridge.

"Go," howled Alec. "Run for your lives! Shoo! Out of my way!"

He skidded to a stop in the middle of the bridge and groped in his coat pocket, bringing out a tiny bottle labeled CAMPARI, of the sort once given out by air transport hostesses. As he was hurriedly unscrewing the cap, one of the tourists inquired timidly:

"Are you a performance artist?"

"Er—yeah." Alec leaped up on the railing of the bridge. "What's that Jason Barrymore holo? *War and Peace*, yeah? Okay, this is my impression of the drunk guy." He threw away the cap and tilted the Campari bottle up, gulping its contents as he teetered back and forth on the rail. He gagged. The tourists applauded uncertainly.

Then he dove forward, right off the bridge, and several of them ran to the rail to see what had happened to him. To their utter astonishment, he had landed on the deck of some kind of enormous vessel just below, and was running for a cabin as its transparent dome closed over him.

What happened next was uncertain. Some of the witnesses thought the vessel must have been a submarine, because they clearly remembered seeing it submerge. Others insisted the vessel wasn't a submarine and didn't submerge, but couldn't say exactly what it had done;

only that it was gone before anyone thought to take a holo of it. In any case, the story wasn't coherent enough to make the evening news.

"Let's go," Alec said, strapping himself into his storm harness. When he had finished, Edward and Nicholas linked arms with him tightly.

What course, laddie?

"Fifty years back and thirty miles off the Galapagos. That ought to be far enough."

Aye aye!

"And we've got loot, Captain, sir! Three identity discs and a buke belonging to Foxen Ellsworth-Howard. I want you to access everything and tell me where Dr. Zeus has a place called Options Research."

To be sure. Hold yer teeth, gentlemen, she's tacking about. Where do we come from?

"From the sea!" said Alec, and Edward, and Nicholas, as the yellow gas boiled up and obscured everything but the memory of the black-eyed woman, the Botanist Mendoza.

The Children of the Company

This one is dedicated to . . .
Garrett, Patrick, Megan, Skye, Anya, Adelia, Jesse, Thomas, Katie

May you, who are so much brighter and better than we were,
learn from history and find a way to save the world.

ONE

1863

MAN OF SHADOWS

The man has an air of authority. Dignity, too. Gravity, integrity, and all you'd want to see in the face of a judge. He is a consummate actor.

His name (at least, the name he has used for the last couple of millennia) is Labienus. He is a Facilitator General for Dr. Zeus Incorporated, and the Executive Section Head for the Northwestern American Continent. This means he has a great deal of power, more than a cyborg is generally granted. If his mortal masters had any inkling of how much power he actually has, they'd be terrified.

But Labienus's mortal masters are in their offices in the twenty-fourth century, safe in some urban hive. Labienus, at this moment, sits in his Company HQ office in 1863, and it is as far from the urban world as he can manage. The view from his window is trackless wilderness.

The local Native Americans have long since learned this is no place to visit for any reason whatsoever, and no prospector will ever manage to straggle this far into the mountains. Were one to do so, however, and were he to climb painfully up the side of a particular towering peak, and were he to look at a particular cliff wall when the light was striking it in a particular way . . . he'd be astounded to find himself looking into a paneled and carpeted room, where a smooth-faced man would smile out at him before pressing a button to trigger an avalanche to sweep him away like a mosquito.

And the man is smiling now, and humming a sprightly little tune to himself as he scans the file of a low-ranking drone he has just damned. As head of Black Security, it is occasionally his duty to consign his fellow immortals to the nearest they can come to eternal fires. He doesn't mind the work. He likes cutting away unnecessary things.

He orders a disk generated of the material he's just scanned, and a moment later it pops obediently out of a slot in his desk. He takes it and crosses the room to a seldom-used cabinet, where he unlocks and opens a file drawer. At the very back, beyond the slots headed BUDGET REPORTS 1700–1850 and GENETIC SURVEY FOR YUKON REGION, is a small file case he'd labeled in a moment of whimsy. It reads simply DOOMED.

Labienus pulls it out and glances through it. There are a few disks in there, and several paper files. He drops the disk inside, but as he does so the foremost of the paper files spills forward, opens.

An image stares out at him. It is not a human face, as human is counted in 1863, but it might have passed for human sixty thousand years earlier. Prognathous, big and wide, with immense broad cheekbones, nose like a boulder fallen from the cliff of the sharply receding brow, massive jaw. Hair and beard are neutral, the dun color of winter hills where no snow has fallen, and the hair begins far back and is worn long. The eyes are pale, almost colorless. For all its inhuman quality, the face is intelligent and calm.

Labienus finds his smile freezing, and averts his eyes. With a grimace of self-contempt he makes himself look again, stare down the face. It's only a picture, after all! Still, after a moment he prefers to gaze out the window at the big trees, remembering when he first saw Budu.

One day it might be known as Jericho, but at that time it had no name, no walls, no surrounding desert thick with potsherds. It hadn't much more than a few reed huts and they sat low on the low earth, no raised mound, at the edge of a lake. It was a green place. There was a lot of rain. When there was a cloudless night, the stars were not in patterns you or I would recognize. Uncounted generations yet before it would occur to anyone that marks poked in clay with a cut reed might serve to freeze a moment in time, or make a hero immortal.

Life prospered in this low place. There was so much food, of all kinds, that it was easy to have a baby every year and feed them all. What it was not easy to do was to find room for them all, crowding around the fire.

The father was a fist, the mother was a vast belly with a pair of sloe-eyed babies at gourdlike breasts. A boy might be edged away from the fire, especially if he was one of many boys and there was no special reason to value him. A boy might be pushed from the breast, for no reason that he could see except that there were too many children, and if he was too small to be of use yet he might wander off at times unnoticed.

So a boy might escape, occasionally, to the high places where there was plenty of room. He might look down on the huts crowding the low place, and his resentment might in time find expression. He might make songs about the ugliness of the cookfire smoke hanging in the clean air, or the stink of crowded bodies, or the unfairness of life. He would do very well on his own, if he was a resourceful and self-reliant little boy, feeding himself from the abundance all around him.

He might tell himself stories, too, as he lay in the tall grass watching the clouds cross the sky: how the clouds and the stars were people, and he was *their* child, not the child of the dirty people in their low village. His mother was not that smoke-wrinkled fat creature in the hut; she was a glorious goddess of towering cloud, with high domed breasts yielding pure snowmelt. And his father . . . perhaps his father was the darkness between the stars, since that was bigger than the stars themselves. Perhaps the boy was a star himself, accidentally fallen to Earth, and didn't belong in that muddy village at all. Perhaps one day the other stars would notice he was lost and come find him.

There might have come a day when he had been beaten by an older brother, and run crying up to the high place, and sat there alone on the height looking down on the village, hating them all. But the wild places loved him, the big rocks and the cedars and the grasses loved him, and so . . . they might have listened to him when he fervently wished that something very bad would happen to the wicked dirty people down there. Perhaps they told him he had the power to bring punishment down from the sky.

And perhaps something very bad had happened after all . . .

He might have watched, too astonished to be frightened, as the tattooed strangers crept up on the far escarpment across the valley and peered down at his village, where the tiny people went to and fro like ants. And maybe like ants the strangers had come swarming down, screaming, and speared his people and set fire to their huts.

Then the boy might have felt terror, watching the flames, then he might have trembled where he crouched in the long grass like a rabbit. But there might have risen also a sense of wonder in his heart, an awe that was nearly joy. *He* had made this happen!

Being very little, he might not have understood what occurred next. Gods might have come, tremendous beings with animal bodies and the upper torsos of giants, galloping down into the low place, swinging flint axes. And if the gods made death and death and more death, so that the strangers who had invaded his village were slaughtered in their turn, the boy assumed they too had come down from the sky at his call.

Eventually there would have been only a few ants crawling feebly here and there, and smoke rising and big birds beginning to circle, and perhaps then the boy would have been bewildered to see the centaurs break apart and become giants walking on two legs, leading great bridling stamping beasts. Perhaps he held his breath as the biggest of the giants turned his flat head slowly and stared up at the hills, and seemed to see the boy in his hiding place.

Perhaps then the giant had walked up the long slope, never taking his pale eyes from the boy, unhurried, swinging his flint axe in one bloody hand as he came. But the boy would not have been afraid; and when Budu towered over him at last, and held out his red hand, the boy would have taken it eagerly.

He would have ridden in the crook of the Enforcer's arm after that, far above the smoke and the pitiful ant-bodies and the crying survivors, and how happy he would have been! And if he was loaded into a magical hut later, that shone like the sun and the moon and rose into the air toward the stars, if it took him to join his true brothers and sisters, it would have been no more than the boy expected.

Perhaps all this was nothing more than a story the boy made up, or an imperfectly remembered dream.

But from that day afterward, he was the child of the gods, and claimed his birthright.

It was good to be the son of a god, though he was perfectly aware he was exploiting the mortal monkeys' ridiculous superstitions. It was better still to be a new life form with all mortal weakness burned away, a *cyborg*, brilliant and immortal, heir to the technology of the future! And to be a Facilitator was best of all.

The Company sent mere Preservers scurrying through the mortal world after plants, after animals, after mortals' genetic material, even after their clumsy clay pots. Preservers were like mice gleaning grain from an endless harvest, drones programmed with obsession for their own petty little disciplines.

Enforcers, the pale-eyed giants who rescued him, had no job but to patrol endlessly and descend like avenging demons upon mortals who made war on one another, so that the peaceful tribes would prevail and civilization would dawn at last. The Enforcers were too short-sighted to see that the very civilization they fought for would render them obsolete, too rigidly focused on their conception of righteousness to pay attention to any other work.

But a Facilitator manipulated mortal destinies to the Company's advantage. A Facilitator shaped the raw stuff of history! Facilitators were able to adapt, to improvise, to see all sides of a question and understand every one, and that was power. Labienus set aside the name he had been given in the Company school and took the name *Atrahasis*. It meant "Great Wise One."

Being the Great Wise One had kept him amused for a while, even as he began to suspect that the mortal masters who had reached back through the past to create him were no better than their pathetic ancestors upon whom he looked down. Impossible to resist dropping the odd technological artifact here and there, knowing how doggedly future archaeologists would label spark plugs or Phillips head screws as "ritual objects of unknown purpose." Atrahasis had even touched up a few cave paintings, daubing flying saucers amid the bison and wooly mammoths.

This was the gloriously fluid time before history began, when there were nearly infinite possibilities. Nothing yet recorded, except in the pattern of stones tossed to a cultivated field's edge, in the layers of ash and scrapers left in a cave, in the crumbling brick foundations of unnamed settlements. This was the perfect time—if one was an immortal creature, immeasurably wiser than one's flawed mortal creators—to lay one's own foundations for power among the mortal masses.

Not that he ever desired to rule them.

There was water, and mud, and there were reeds.

That was all. No cities, no arts, no industry. In short, no civilization.

The mortals hadn't cared; they'd been happy enough, living in little clutches of reed huts that were too amorphous even for villages. They'd been well nourished, too, hunting for ducks, fishing, gathering roots and wild grains.

Young Atrahasis hadn't cared, either. It was all one to him if the monkeys never came down out of the trees, let alone built themselves nations. He much preferred the social life at Old World One, in the company of his fellow junior executive immortals.

And, while it was true that there were only so many times one could attend a fancy-dress ball in the costume of a god before it just wasn't amusing anymore, there was still the sex, and the unending delicious gossip. There was the ongoing challenge of how to falsify his monthly reports to his superiors, so that his utter lack of productivity was disguised.

Best of all were the times he got out on his own in his personal aircraft, soaring above the marshy world. It was fun, swooping over the reed huts and watching the little mortals scream and point at him. And when he flew by moonlight, over the wide land and the glittering water, under the white stars: oh, then he truly felt like the son of heaven.

But the day had come when he had been called into the office of Executive Facilitator Nergal, and kept sweating in the antechamber a full two hours before being called in at last and told, with exquisite understatement, that Dr. Zeus had a special place for slackers and liars, not a very nice place really, and would young Atrahasis care to do a bit of work for a change? Such as, perhaps, organizing the mortals in his assigned region into a useful, civilized society?

He didn't have to be told twice.

Shaking with anger and fear, he had flown out above the land between the two rivers. The first mortals to encounter him did not fare well, especially after they shot arrows into his glider.

But mortals certainly came to fear him, in time, and so they obeyed him. He bid them call him Enlil.

There was water and mud, which must be separated, even as the Lord gathered the waters under heaven together unto one place and let the dry land appear. Atrahasis ordered the mud raised into arable fields, the water drained away into canals. The weary little mortals leaned on their shovels and looked around at this flat, arid-seeming place, where the old easy life would no longer be possible.

They asked the cruel young god whether they might not rest now; and in response he gave them oxen and plows, and barley to sow. Atrahasis made them farmers. By day they toiled for him in the fields; by night they filed back in long rows to the long reed houses where he stabled them, and slept guarded by his security technicals. Any who tried to escape were punished spectacularly.

But after a few generations they had come to accept this, for Atrahasis explained their cosmos to the mortals. The gods, it seemed, had grown tired of drudge work, and so they had created mortal mankind to do it for them. Mortals had no other purpose in life but this labor. Mortals who worked diligently at draining the marshes, or planting the fields, would be rewarded in this life by being granted a little dry land and a house, and perhaps a day of leisure once a week.

The afterlife, unfortunately, was a dark and horrible place of twittering ghosts, so suicide had better not be thought of. But if a mortal worked hard all his life, and begot many children who worked just as hard as he did—why, it was just possible that mortal might be granted a slightly less gloomy corner of the underworld for his own, and might even sup of the crusts and dregs from the gods' own table.

And they believed him! The darker and more unpleasant Atrahasis made their world, the more desperately the little mortals clung to what he told them, the more obedient they became. It helped, of course, that he could back up his words with all manner of stage effects to awe them.

It helped also that he could kill them with impunity; for he had discovered that as long as he could meet an annual production quota of barley for the Company's mills, and present statistics showing an overall increasing birth rate among his mortal charges, Dr. Zeus was fairly disinterested in the occasional sacrifice.

And when the rivers rose one season and drowned three-fourths of his mortals, Atrahasis waited out the catastrophe on high ground, watching with a peculiar thrill as bloated corpses were swept past his feet.

He told the survivors it had been their own fault, for not loving him enough.

His security techs wearied of playing overseers after a century or so. Atrahasis therefore had them sort through the mortal population for those who were most servile; these he raised up, and gave them titles, and a little power over their fellow mortals. He noted, with amusement, that they were far more zealous in their oppressive duties than his techs had been.

Some two or three showed greater than average intelligence; these he made bureaucrats, and set them to tallying the crops that went into the Company warehouses as offerings to the gods. When he got around to bestowing on them the divine gift of making counting-marks with reeds on clay tablets, he was more than a little annoyed to learn that they'd already figured it out for themselves.

By now Atrahasis had redeemed himself in the eyes of Executive Facilitator Nergal. No slacker he! His city was a perfect geometry of green and golden squares, yielding abundant barley, yielding melons and pomegranates, chickpeas and dates, grapes and cucumbers, and fine flocks of sheep and goats. His mortals bred in such numbers that it was hardly worthwhile to pursue those who escaped. Besides, the escapees invariably settled down and started little farms of their own, so indoctrinated they were.

His own personal ziggurat of sun-fired brick arose, like an incongruous mountain, the house of the great god Enlil. He told the mortals that it must stand high above the smoke and stench of the city. The overseers sang the praises of the gods, and cracked their whips with gusto as the patient laborers raised terrace upon terrace.

There remained only to design a palace to sit atop it, and have his tech staff install all that was necessary to make life gracious. So Atrahasis moved out of his field shelter at last, into his grand house with its penthouse view, advanced sanitation, and doors of imported cedarwood.

And Atrahasis saw that this was good.

Then he celebrated by throwing a party for himself, and invited all those members of his commencement class who were still on speaking terms with him. They came and drank his excellent barley beer, and dined on his roast kid and hot bread, his melons and pomegranates, his chickpeas and dates. They praised him, lounged with him on his fine furniture, looked down with him on the Euphrates and the shining canals. By night they sang with him under the eternal stars. And he was pleased that he had impressed them all.

But the stale gossip of Old World One seemed a bit tedious now, and none of his former classmates were quite as sparklingly witty as he remembered them. After the second day, he found himself wishing they'd leave.

Atrahasis became bored.

His city was practically running itself nowadays. Ships plied the two rivers and brought trade goods for him. Uncomplaining mortals loaded his granaries with wheat and barley, to be shipped to distant Company warehouses in Eurobase One and Terra Australis. The mortals had craftsmen now, gold workers and scribes, carpenters and potters, weavers, charioteers. Atrahasis received commendations from his superiors. A job well done! Preserver drones were sent in to work among the mortals, collecting their works of art, noting down the stories of their heroes. Atrahasis, who found Preservers the dullest people in the world, did not invite them to stay with him.

Instead, he dined alone behind a curtain in his high temple, and issued memos to his staff, who conveyed his will to the mortals far below. He ordered new gliders from the Company field catalogs, and soared alone over night fields. He kept up a desultory correspondence with some few of his old classmates.

He toyed with the idea of wiping the whole project out and starting over again, but he couldn't think of a way to make the rivers rise sufficiently. There was always fire and brimstone . . .

Though of course the Company would notice something like that.

So Atrahasis continued to go through the motions, ordering the construction of libraries, gardens, and canals. When word came of some manner of political disturbance far off to the south, he daydreamed wistfully a little while about watching armies advance, looking down from his high place on bloody slaughter. Then, regretfully, he gave orders for the building of a defensive wall.

It was a splendid wall. So wide across its top, two chariots could race abreast; so high, no slung stones could reach those chariots. And well made, too; no trash or rubble infilling its center, but only solid fired brick. The inner walls were faced with glazed tile depicting the glory of the Great God Enlil. The mortals were proud of it.

Atrahasis was pleased, himself; it had earned him a commendation from the new Executive Facilitator Shamash, who had replaced Nergal, who had been transferred to another region. Not one dark and unpleasant enough to suit Atrahasis, but that couldn't be helped.

He was gazing out upon his wall, musing on the possibility of regime change, when he first spotted the far-off cloud of dust.

When his charioteers came racing back with their reports, when his overseers sounded the alarm, when it finally sank in on Atrahasis that an army *was* actually advancing on his sacred city—his first reaction was incredulous outrage.

"He calls himself *who*?" he demanded. Below him, in the audience pit, his high priest trembled.

"Enna-aru, o great god," he said, addressing Atrahasis's shadow on the opposite wall, that being the only part of his lord he was permitted to see. "And he calls himself a . . ." He strained to remember the unfamiliar word. "A king. And he says he has come to cast down the oppressor of the people. What are we to do, o great god?"

"Gather in the people behind the wall, and shut the gates," said Atrahasis, stalking back and forth in front of his fire. "Let the young men gather stones for their slings, and mount my high wall. Come back when you have seen to these things."

"Immediately, o great god," said his high priest, and ran like a rat down the dark tunnel through the temple.

Atrahasis went at once to his credenza.

He paused before it, struggling to get a grip on his emotions. Why send a message? He was pretty certain the Company wouldn't dispatch any Enforcers to come barreling in and slaughter the invaders for him. Their patrols had been few and far between in the recent centuries . . .

Should he ask for advice? More security techs? But that would make him seem weak.

At last he transmitted: LOCAL PETTY TYRANT HAMMERING AT MY GATES. FOOTAGE OUGHT TO MAKE EXCITING VIEWING AT THE NEXT SOLSTICE BALL. SHADES OF D. W. GRIFFITH!

"Sir?" Security Technical Vidya saluted. "Orders, sir?"

Atrahasis composed his features into a suitable mask of superior amusement and turned. "Oh, we needn't mobilize your boys for a few hours yet. Let the monkeys slug it out in front of the walls! Just stand ready to defend this place, if any of them break through. If he's a super-duperpower and takes the whole ant heap, we'll evacuate by air."

"And the mortals, sir?"

Atrahasis shrugged elaborately. "The herds need to be thinned now and again. Who am I to stand in the way of progress? Just make certain our air transport is fueled up. I could do with a change of scene after all these centuries, couldn't you?"

He took his evening meal of roast lamb, lentils, and wine in his high garden that night, looking out across the plain. Atrahasis felt rather proud of himself that he did not quail at the sight of all those camp-fires, stretching away through the black night, under a heavy and thunderous sky. After all, a gleaming sky chariot waited patiently in its hangar, down on the fifth terrace, in case he should need to be air-lifted out.

All the same, he did not think he'd give the order to evacuate until the fighting reached the temple complex. He could imagine it breaking around his ziggurat like a red tide. The screams, the smoke, the pitiful crying, the foolish little figures dragging themselves like ants . . . the curious *chop* a flint axe made, breaking a skull . . . it was with a pang of disappointment that he realized they were in the Bronze Age now, and he might never hear the music of a flint edge again.

He breakfasted in the garden, too, on goat cheese, figs, and fresh bread, frowning at the hundred columns of smoke that rose against the rising sun. Only cook-fires? When were they going to charge?

The sun was so high he had ordered a parasol erected over his chair by the time something finally happened. Fanning himself irrita-bly, he peered out at his wall. There, the mortals were running to and fro at last, pointing, readying their caches of slingstones. Action!

But . . .

Nothing happened.

Atrahasis waited half an hour, his impatience mounting. What the hell was going on? The mortals were leaning down, apparently paying intense attention to some drama playing out before the city gates.

"Get on with it!" he muttered under his breath, and had a sip of wine. Then he choked, spraying wine across his linen; for the ponderous gates of his city were opening, and a cheer rose along his magnificent wall.

He was pacing like a lion in his audience chamber when the high priest entered the pit, sobbing for breath.

"O great god—" he began, looking up at Atrahasis's shadow.

"What has happened?" Atrahasis demanded, looking down on the back of his head.

"Great god, you are betrayed—may they sleep with scorpions, may vultures gouge out their living eyes—oh, the wickedness—o great god, have mercy on your poor servant who—"

"On pain of death," said Atrahasis, with wonderful calm, "instantly tell me what has happened."

"O great god, your people are seduced," said the high priest miserably. "Enna-aru the king spoke before your gate. His voice was like music, great god; his voice was like a lover persuading his beloved to lie back.

"He did not threaten force, nor did he rage. Enna-aru the king spoke words like lilies, words like honey in the comb. His words went softly into the ears of your people.

"And Enna-aru the king is fair to look upon, like a bridegroom coming to his bride, o great god; and your people are faithless."

"What exactly did Enna-aru the king say?" asked Atrahasis. He was cold with shock, but he could feel a really remarkable rage gathering itself together.

"O great god, he persuaded your people that he comes in peace, to free them from bondage," said the high priest. "He told them the gods are cruel and false. Please don't punish me.

"Enna-aru the king told them he comes as a father to care for them, not as a master to trample upon their heads. Please don't punish me.

"He told them he will cast you down and open your storehouses to the people, that each may help himself thereunto. Please don't punish me."

"He did, did he?" Atrahasis stared down at the high priest's head. The man had a bald spot, which he had never noticed before. It made a tempting target. Oh, for a good old-fashioned flint axe . . .

"Go forth," he said. "Go to Enna-aru the king, who comes in triumph through my city. Tell him great Enlil will speak with him."

Atrahasis changed his garment, put on his finest ornaments, and stationed security techs in strategic places as he waited for his visitor. He could follow the mortal's progress through the streets by the cheering, by the baying of bronze trumpets. He ground his teeth. Punishment, such punishment he was going to mete out on the fickle monkeys . . . it would make the great flood pale in comparison, and the Company be damned. Fire and brimstone? Yes, what about a rain of flaming death? *That* would give the little bastards a story to hand on to their descendants . . . those who survived to have any.

He was waiting by his altar fire when he heard the voices come echoing up the tunnel. The high priest's was querulous, panicky.

"Stop! You must remove your sandals! No man may enter the presence of Almighty Enlil shod!"

"Enlil must learn to bear with this, and more." The voice that replied sounded . . . untroubled. Amused. Atrahasis scowled. He stepped before the fire, throwing his biggest, blackest shadow on the wall.

Two men emerged from the tunnel into the pit: his high priest, and a stranger. They were followed by three more men, soldiers armed with spears. The high priest immediately prostrated himself, craning his head back to address Atrahasis's shadow.

"O great god, Enna-aru the king has—"

"He's not over there, priest," said Enna-aru the king, for it was he. He turned and stared up at Atrahasis, looking straight at him.

Atrahasis blinked. He had never seen such a mortal.

Enna-aru had a face like his own—shrewd, cold, strong, handsome. He was well muscled, unlike the little doughballs over whom Atrahasis ruled. He wore fine garments, not the armor of war, but there was something martial in his bearing.

The high priest turned involuntarily, glimpsed Atrahasis and then threw himself down, wailing in terror. Enna-aru considered the wall of the pit. He backed up a few paces, took a running leap, and vaulted to the edge, where he caught hold and pulled himself up. Not even breathing hard, he rose to his feet and looked Atrahasis in the eye. The two men were the same height.

"You see?" said Enna-aru, and his voice, his voice was . . . powerful, somehow. "This is a false god. He is only a man, like me."

Permission to fire, sir? transmitted Security Technical Vidya. Atrahasis blinked again, the dreamlike moment shattered, and his brain engaged once more.

No! I will handle this. Stand by.

"I have chosen to *appear* as a man like you," he told Enna-aru, with his most intimidating smile. "Rash mortal, why have you looked upon me? Do you not know that you will surely die?"

"No, actually, I don't know that," said Enna-aru, with a beautiful sneer. "Though it's probable you have assassins concealed in here, waiting to get a shot off at me. You hidden ones, consider my archers in the pit below! If I am murdered, the great god Enlil will be stuck full of arrows. Therefore do not do this thing; for I have come to speak with the great god."

Atrahasis took a deep breath. Had his heart just skipped a beat?

"It pleases me to speak with you, mortal king," he said. "And so I will not annihilate you until after we have spoken. Come, we will drink wine in my garden."

He had his finest vintage brought, in his wine service of gold chased with silver. The mortal man regarded them critically; looked at the couch carved of cedarwood, with its purple cushions trimmed in scarlet. And Enna-aru the king said:

"This is all as I expected it would be. You sit up here gorging yourself on the best of everything, don't you? And down there in your city, they gnaw the crusts you throw them."

"They only eat at all because I created the fields, and taught them how to grow barley," said Atrahasis. He realized he sounded defensive, and made an effort to calm himself.

"Oh, please," said Enna-aru the king. "I know better. Shall I tell you how I know?"

"If you like," Atrahasis replied. Enna-aru leaned forward, took one of his cups, and poured wine.

"My land is eight days' journey north of this place. It sits fair on the river, wide black fields, well watered; beyond are highlands good for grazing sheep. Long ago an escaped slave came there, with his wife and child.

"This slave had formerly lived in a city ruled over by a cruel and capricious god. The people there obeyed their lord in all things—they were afraid to do otherwise—but when a flood came and drowned them in their hundreds, that god stood by and smiled, and would not lift a finger to help them.

"The slave was one of those who survived the flood. He saw the god walking through the desolation, smiling at the bloated corpses of the dead, and saw that the god had mud on his sandals and on his robe where it trailed on the earth. He knew, then, that the god was only a man, only an evil man.

"Therefore he took his wife and child, and they fled by night. When they came to the good land, they settled, and the man made himself lord and master of wide acres. He had many children. In time, other slaves escaped and came to work for him. He was a good master to them. He fed them, he gave them land, but he never bid them worship him.

"And he passed down through his sons, and his sons' sons, and all their children through the generations, the wisdom he had learned, which was: those who demand worship are frauds."

And Enna-aru the king raised his eyes that were so like Atrahasis's own, and winked. Atrahasis opened his mouth to speak, but no words came out. Composedly the king went on:

"That slave was my ancestor, O great god Enlil. The god he fled from was, I strongly suspect, your ancestor. And all my life, and all the lives of my forefathers, have been spent in preparation for this day, when I would walk into your city and tell your people the truth about you. Now it is done. Let us drink to the future."

He lifted his cup and drank.

Atrahasis sat staring at him, wondering why his rage had died utterly into white ash. He felt like laughing.

"You're wrong about one thing, you know," he said. "That wasn't my ancestor walking in the mud. That was me. I really am an immortal."

Enna-aru the king yawned. He reached across to Atrahasis and pulled a golden coin from his ear, and held it up.

"I can do magic, too, you see? One of my court magicians showed me that trick. I suspect you have many more."

The laughter came—Atrahasis couldn't stop it, didn't want to. He looked at Enna-aru and raised his own cup in salute.

"Great king, you are a man after my own heart. Dear, dear, what shall I do now that I am deposed?"

"Live off your own sweat for a change," said Enna-aru the king.

"And if I oppose you?"

"I have an army in your city," the king pointed out. "Your people loathe you so much they were dancing as we came in. I don't think you want me to ask them what I ought to do with you. Your priests have seen you insulted; they depend on you for their livelihoods, so they might stand by you, but they know the truth about you now. You don't stand much of a chance, I'm afraid."

Atrahasis was delighted. "What's a poor little false god to do, then?"

"Become a man," said Enna-aru. "You know how to run this city, you understand its infrastructure. Rule it as my viceroy! It needn't be an embarrassment for you, either; almost no one alive has ever seen you, so they won't know you're their former god. I can tell them you're my brother. But if you abuse your power again, I will have you killed."

"Oooh." Atrahasis pretended to shiver. "How kind of you to spare my dignity. And what do you want in return?"

"The good of the people," said Enna-aru gravely. "You must love them. Treat them as your children, not as beasts of burden."

"Children, eh?" Atrahasis said. "But children are a dangerous proposition for a god, you know. Shall I tell you how the world was made?

"Tiamat the Mother and Apsu the Father begot between them elder gods, who proceeded to spawn generations of godlets. And what did these little monsters do, but rebel against their ancient parents? And, when the old couple determined to destroy their vicious brood, what did the ungrateful children do but fight back?

"The Father was killed; the Mother was killed, and a bright young thing named Marduk split her body into a dozen pieces and used it to create the rotting, stinking world in which we walk. There is no love in Heaven, my mortal friend. Why then should it be any different on Earth? And therefore why should I hold my subjects as sons?"

"Because those stories are lies," said Enna-aru the king.

"Are they? Are there then no gods?"

"Possibly," said Enna-aru. "Possibly there *are* shining beings of infinite power and wisdom. But you are only a petty tyrant, and will soon be a dead one if you do not agree to my demands."

"Which makes you no less a petty tyrant, doesn't it?" said Atrahasis.

"Perhaps," said Enna-aru the king. "But I never claimed to be otherwise. And my people love me, o false god, because I am a good father to them. Soon, your people will love me, too. I am their servant, you see, rather than the other way around; it is my business to see that they have what they need to live. When they are threatened, it is my duty to protect them. And so must you."

"I hear and obey, great king," said Atrahasis, and made a mock bow. "How much of this pious claptrap do you actually believe, by the way?"

"None," said Enna-aru the king. "But I intend to make it true."

The army was quartered in Atrahasis's city, and they did not plunder, and hardly raped at all. Enna-aru the king quartered himself in Atrahasis's own temple, with his men-at-arms standing guard. Atrahasis gave him the guest bedroom and showed him where the clean towels were. Security Technical Vidya and his team stood down, and stood down, and wondered thereat.

Sir, how are we going to resolve the situation?

Leave that to me! Atrahasis waved away the transmission as though it were a gnat whining in his ear. He sipped his kefir and watched, fondly, as Enna-aru the king methodically peeled figs. The mortal even ate with elegance. What an uncanny resemblance to himself! *I'm merely toying with him. He amuses me. When I grow bored with him, he'll die.*

If you say so, sir.

And it occurred to Atrahasis to wonder what his double looked like with a bloody spear in his hands; and he was disconcerted to note how much the image excited him. He cleared his throat.

"It occurs to me," Atrahasis told the king, "that it would be best for my people if this power shift takes place quickly. You said something last night about presenting me as your brother. I think the people would believe that; there is a certain resemblance between us, have you noticed?"

"I had, yes," said Enna-aru. "Useful, isn't it?"

"Of course, I'll probably have to have my priests executed," said Atrahasis lightly. Enna-aru the king set down his cup, and gave him a long hard stare.

"Probably necessary," he conceded at last. "They have grown fat off the fear of the people. And they are the most likely to plot against us. But you will kill them swiftly; no torture. They have only done your will, after all."

"Then it is done," said Atrahasis, and transmitted an order to Security Technical Vidya. "And so we are brothers! Let us send forth messengers to proclaim it in the streets; and then, later, let us appear and make a show of brotherhood. Shall we go hunting together? I have a private preserve outside the city. The wild bull and the gazelle roam there untroubled; and I have two swift chariots and the finest charioteers."

"I wouldn't have thought you were a hunting man," said Enna-aru the king. "Though you seem to enjoy killing."

"I kill only to cull my herds," said Atrahasis swiftly. "You will see how green the park is, how fine and strong the beasts are. I have preserved them from indiscriminate slaughter by common men. Is this not also the work of a lord?"

So when Security Technical Vidya and his subordinates had washed the blood from their hands, they hitched swift horses to a pair of chariots, and sent them out with drivers to await the pleasure of the king.

And first went soldiers bearing the heads of the executed priests, that the people might see them and rejoice, which they did. And next went messengers crying aloud the news that Enna-aru the king had appointed his brother to be lord over them, and the people rejoiced about that, too. Finally Enna-aru the king and his new brother were driven forth in their chariots, in lordly progress through the streets. Atrahasis marveled at the grace and strength of the king, poised swaying in the jolting chariot. And Atrahasis caused Security Technicals to toss trinkets of gold, and the ornaments of the priests, to the cheering multitudes.

The Preserve of Enlil lay two miles from the city, fenced with high palings and wire specially hooked up to deliver a blast of Enlil's wrath to would-be poachers. Was there a faint whiff of charred flesh on the air, as the chariots bore Atrahasis with Enna-aru the king to that place? But no corpses in view, at least.

Security Technical Rulon opened the gate, bowing low, and admitted them. They rode in and Atrahasis watched for the king's reaction.

"Is this not fair, o king?" he demanded. "Look! A green paradise. You will see no scars here from plow or mattock, no ditches to stink, no trees hacked for firewood. No mortal intrusion at all. And see the wild cattle, there at the watering place? The water they drink is pure, untainted by anything men might do. They have never been hunted. Have I not done well, to set this place apart?"

"It is a beautiful park," agreed Enna-aru.

"I have not been such a bad lord, you know," said Atrahasis. "I have kept my distance from my subjects, but you will never hear that I was unfair. I never favored any man over another, even when they tried to buy my favor with offerings of gold. I never debauched their wives or daughters, either—" He saw Security Technical Rulon turn a shocked face to him, and caught the fleeting transmission: *What are you trying to prove to this monkey?*

Atrahasis flushed with humiliation that became rage. *What the hell do you know about strategy, you oaf? Mind your own business!*

He drew a spear from its case and struck his charioteer on the shoulder. "Drive! Let us hunt the wild bulls!"

So they rode forth into his acreage. Atrahasis seized the reins from his charioteer and drove with reckless speed, splashing through the streams, scattering the herds where they drank. He wheeled among the frightened and disoriented cattle, singling out the biggest bull at last. Enna-aru the king followed warily. The bull galloped off some distance, and they pursued; but when he turned at bay, pawing the ground, then Atrahasis vaulted out on the chariot-tongue. There he clung a moment, before leaping to balance upright on the back of the left-hand horse in his team. From that high vantage he sent his black spear down, with such force it pierced straight through the bull's broad neck and into its immense heart.

It dropped without a moan. Atrahasis sprang down beside it, wrenching out his spear. The blood ran and smoked on the earth. It pleased him nearly as much as though it were mortal blood. *Why haven't I done this before?* He looked up, eager to see if Enna-aru had been watching. The king, indeed, watched with narrowed eyes.

"You have excellent skill in the hunt," was all he said.

"Butcher my bull, and build a fire," said Atrahasis to his charioteer, with some asperity. "My brother king and I would feast."

They killed twice more that day. Atrahasis took down another bull, this time leaping from the chariot onto the bull's very back, felling it with a stroke that drove through and penetrated its lungs. Enna-aru the king cornered his own bull, circling and turning in the chariot, until the baffled animal charged and got a spear through the eye into its brain. Atrahasis thought that he might have been watching himself in a mirror, so shapely was Enna-aru, so powerful.

"Is this not fine sport, my brother?" he asked as they washed in the stream.

"You have succeeded in impressing me," said the king. "Very male, all this, isn't it? I daresay not one of the laborers who till your fields would be brave enough to leap on a bull's back. Nor light-footed enough, after a lifetime of following the plow. Still, I have seen acrobats do as much."

Atrahasis was silent a moment.

"How wise you are, mortal man," he said at last.

———

He watched the king as they rode slowly back through the city, followed by surly Security Technicals bearing massive sides of beef. At one point Enna-aru bid the chariots halt in the street, and got down and called for an axe; with it he cut the beef into pieces, and handed them out to the crowd. They blessed him and cried that he was their lord, they called on him to live a thousand years, they prostrated themselves and kissed his feet.

And though Enna-aru smiled broadly, and was genial as a favorite uncle before them all, Atrahasis noted that his eyes remained a little distant.

"Such generosity, o king!" he said slyly, when they had ridden on. "Truly my people love you."

"That was showmanship," said Enna-aru. "And they don't love me; they don't know me. But they love a handout now and then, and the promise that things will be a little better. If you had understood that fairly basic fact, I might not have marched into your city uncontested."

"Ah! So my fault was simply ruling by the *wrong kind* of showmanship?" said Atrahasis.

"No," said Enna-aru the king. "Your fault was that you never gave a thought to what your people wanted."

They dined once again on the terrace. A cool wind brought the smell of the river, the sound of frogs, the murmuring of rushes in the twilight. A round moon rose slowly out of the purple east, looking as though it had been painted on the horizon.

"See how she lifts free of the earth?" said Atrahasis. "Red with smoke and dust at first, and then yellow; but the higher she ascends, the purer her light becomes, and she outshines even the stars. You and I have lifted free of the mud ourselves, o king. You shine upon those peasants down there; but who are your own people?

"The idiots in the street sang their love for you; but their love meant nothing to you. I saw that. Your eyes are clear, you have no fond illusions, you know the world for the shameful place it is, you know the *truth*. You are a unique mortal.

"What is it you desire, o king?"

Enna-aru looked at him curiously.

"A better world," he said. "Full of better men."

Atrahasis looked up at the first stars.

"I am going to give you a gift," he said.

Atrahasis carried the frame out himself, set it up in the garden as Enna-aru watched, uncomprehending. He tested the fabric, the pads, the taut straps; and when all was ready he lifted it onto his shoulders and stepped out to the edge of the terrace.

"Now," he said, "o king, you will see how close a man may come to being a god."

He leaned into the night and swept down, down, until he caught the thermal rising over the massed cook-fires of the city. Up he floated then, turning as he soared, circling, and the white moonlight glittered on the distant river and on the irrigation channels, but shone full and steady on his high terrace and the tiny figure of Enna-aru. The king stood motionless, face turned up to him; he did not cower or tremble, as a mortal might have done. In his steady regard Atrahasis flew high, and higher, up where the stars hung like lamps in the blue night; and Atrahasis had never been so happy in his life.

At last he drifted down, mothlike, and landed with a light foot beside Enna-aru.

"Magicians and acrobats you have seen, o king; but never the like of this," he said triumphantly.

"Never," admitted Enna-aru the king. He stepped close and examined the glider, peering intently at its tight-stitched fabric.

"It will bear two," said Atrahasis, edging over within the frame. "Will you dare to fly, mortal man?"

Without replying, Enna-aru stepped in under the frame. He worked out the harness buckles for himself, and drew them tight; took firm hold of the frame, and stepped toward the edge.

He never cried out once, not during the initial plunge, not in the moment when they lifted on the thermal like a blown leaf. Atrahasis looked into his face and saw that it was shining.

When he returned to his chamber that night, there was a figure standing just within, obscured by shadows.

"You had better check your credenza," said Security Technical Vidya.

"What are you talking about?" said Atrahasis, but he crossed to the cabinet and switched it on.

"They want to know what the hell is going on," said Vidya. Atrahasis saw the long green line of transmission and recoiled, but all he said was: "Forty messages. Well, that's certainly some kind of record. Wouldn't you think they'd have learned to trust me by now?"

"I don't think it's a matter of trust," said Vidya. "I think it's a matter of Executive Facilitator Shamash having a bright young protégé in need of a posting. I think it's a matter of looking for any excuse to boot you out on your ass. Sir."

"Really," said Atrahasis.

"Yes. Really. Sir."

"I am obliged to you for the warning, Security Technical," said Atrahasis, kicking off his sandals. "You may go."

Vidya did not move. "I have been given certain orders, sir. You have twenty-four hours to bring the situation under control, and then I am to act. Permission to speak freely, sir?"

"Granted."

"Do I have to point out the obvious? This mission is in jeopardy. A Company operation yielding millions in annual profits may be lost. The city you built is occupied by a hostile force. We will *fail* here, sir."

"I think you're wrong," said Atrahasis. "Consider the progress of recorded history. Perhaps it's my time to step down. The age of priests comes to an end, doesn't it? And civilization takes the next step upward, to an age of kings. Isn't that what the Company wanted? Wasn't that the point of all this? Somebody has to write *Gilgamesh*, after all."

He lit the lamp. In the blaze of gold that filled the room, he saw the contempt—and, infinitely more galling, the pity—in Vidya's face.

"What is wrong with you?" said Vidya, without raising his voice. "You, of all people, are infatuated with a mortal. You are attempting to win his approval. A stinking little monkey has defied you in front of the other mortals, and you fawn on him and call him brother. What's next? Will you drink from one cup together? Will you offer to comb the lice from his hair?"

He mixed the cup himself, in the gray hour before the sun rose. He carried it out to the garden and sat, watching the stars fade. White mist moved a while above the river, was thick over the river fields. The first laborers emerged from their huts and drove the teams of oxen down, into that mist, vanishing from sight as they would vanish in the abyss of time. Living ghosts. Their grandfathers were forgotten; their grandchildren would not remember them. Only this moment existed for them and it was all sweat, all stink, all grinding poverty.

And so it has always been. And so it will always be.

Enna-aru the king emerged from the temple, gilded by the rising sun. Atrahasis looked at him and smiled. He lifted the cup.

"Drink with me, brother. To a better world, and better men."

"I will," said Enna-aru, and took the cup and drank. He passed it back to Atrahasis, who paused a moment and then drank down what was left.

He set down the cup and felt the biomechanicals swarming from under his tongue, massing in his bloodstream to neutralize what had been in the cup. He flushed, felt the prickle of sweat under his armpits, felt the twinge in his lymph nodes; only psychosomatic reaction. After a moment he breathed more easily. The heat and nausea faded steadily.

Enna-aru the king sat tranquil, cutting open a pomegranate with his curved dagger. The red drops fell like blood. He set aside half and broke the other open, revealing the rubies set in yellow membrane.

"Pomegranate seeds?" he said, offering it to Atrahasis.

"No, thank you," Atrahasis replied.

By noon the king was feverish. Atrahasis watched the flush grow in his cheeks, watched his eyes take on a certain glassiness as he studied the maps of the city canals and the grain warehouses.

By twilight the king was sweating and faint, and the blotches had begun to come up under his skin. Atrahasis led him to the couch of purple cushions, with soothing and solicitous words, and had sherbet fetched for him.

By midnight the king was raving, with brief periods of clarity wherein he struggled for understanding. Atrahasis sat beside him, wiping the sweat from his brow. The king's guard crowded in the corridor, watched from the doorway.

"If he dies, we will kill you," said their chief, in an almost conversational tone. The king jerked and shuddered at the sound; Atrahasis rose in fury, but by the time he had turned and approached the mortal, there was nothing in his face but meek sorrow.

"Speak softly, if you love him," he whispered. "He has the fever, but why should he die? Enna-aru is not like other men."

The mortal looked past him uncertainly, into the golden circle of lamplight where the king lay marked with black sores. "You have poisoned him," he said, but without conviction.

"Fool. Those are the marks of fever, and you know it," said Atrahasis. "What man commands disease? The gods alone send it, to punish whom they will. But the gods have no power over Enna-aru the king, surely. He will live."

"He is not like other men," admitted the chief. "Yes, surely he will live."

He left quietly. Atrahasis returned to the bedside of the king, and sat. Enna-aru opened his eyes, the glaring eyes of a hawk, lucid and suspicious.

"This is not punishment," he said thickly. "Nothing but fever."

"Merely a touch of fever," Atrahasis agreed, and put a wet sponge to his cracked lips. "Undoubtedly the result of traveling. The fever will break. What shall we do when you're well again? Shall we take our wings and ride the night wind, my brother? How cool it will be, up among the white stars."

Before dawn the king was lucid for an hour, though he had gone blind; but he summoned his generals and his bodyguards, and turned his face to their voices as though he could see them. He gave orders that there was to be no rioting, no slaughter. There was still command, even in the hoarse ruin his voice had become; they backed out of his presence and went down to maintain good order in the streets.

Just as the sun rose, Enna-aru stopped breathing. Atrahasis sat patiently waiting for him to resume, but he never did.

He was still sitting, staring at the king, when Security Technical Vidya came in an hour later. Vidya looked at Enna-aru, and smiled.

"Good work, sir. That'll impress them. Shall we display the body, sir?"

Atrahasis said nothing for a long moment.

"I wonder if this is what I would look like," he said at last.

Vidya cleared his throat.

"What are your orders, sir?"

Atrahasis did not look up. "Tell the people to pray for the king. Tell his generals to obey him."

"So . . . you don't want this announced right away," said Vidya.

"No. And send for his chief bodyguard."

The mortal came swiftly, and bid his lieutenants wait in the corridor. He stopped, aghast, at the sight of Enna-aru the king.

"You see how it is," said Atrahasis quietly. "Had he any heirs?"

"No," said the mortal. "He was only a young man! How could he die?"

Atrahasis said nothing. The mortal lifted his eyes to the window, looked out, at the city with its shops and warehouses, at the green and yellow fields stretching to the river. He looked sidelong at Atrahasis.

"You are thinking this is a rich place," said Atrahasis. "You are wondering who will rule here now. And it has just occurred to you that *you* might be king."

The mortal blinked, opened his mouth to deny it—then went pale.
"How did you hear my thoughts?"

Atrahasis smiled. He rose, standing his tallest, and put every cheap trick of theater he knew into his reply.

"Did you think we gods were really so easily defeated, mortal man?"

The mortal backed away a pace, staring. Then he threw himself to the ground, in terrified self-abasement.

"Great Enlil, forgive us! Do not punish us! We were misled!"

"How loyal you are to your king," said Atrahasis bitterly. "How faithful to his ideals. I could crush your skull now with my foot; I could grind your brain into the tiles. Never have I so ardently desired to do a thing, mortal. But I will tell you how you will preserve your little life."

"Spare me!"

"Shut up. You will go forth to the people, and say the king has been wounded by treachery. Not mine; kill one of your underlings, and hold his head up before the multitudes, and tell them thus have you done to the traitor, in the name of Enna-aru the king.

"Then, mortal, you shall be king in this place. And you shall declare that Enna-aru has been taken up among the stars to heal his wound, and dwells now with the gods. You will rule and grow as rich as one man may be, but you will see to it that we gods receive our portion in all things.

"Vidya will be your high priest, and he will instruct you in the desires of the gods, and will serve you; but only so long as you obey the will of the gods. Disobey, and our vengeance will be cruel and subtle. You will lament in ashes a thousand years on the floor of the house of the dead."

"I hear you," said the mortal, weeping. "I obey you." He crawled forward in an attempt to kiss Atrahasis's feet, and Atrahasis stepped back in horror.

"Never touch me, mortal," he said. "Go now."

The mortal rose and fled into the corridor. A moment later Atrahasis heard a strangled cry as his will was done, and an innocent was stabbed and beheaded.

Evening came, and Atrahasis heard the massed prayer rising from the city below, with the fumes of burnt offerings. He lit incense in his own quarters. Now and then he went to look at Enna-aru the king.

The moon rose, and he dined alone on his terrace, though he ordered and set aside a portion for Enna-aru. He heard the clash of arms and the exchange of passwords as the army kept civil order through the night. He carried the untouched plate in and set it by Enna-aru's bed.

Dawn came grayly, and once more the mortals led oxen down through the mists to the fields. Atrahasis, watching, wondered why they were not at home praying for the king. He went in and lit more incense. He ordered a morning meal for two, and set half aside.

Another evening, and another, and the city remained calm and well ordered. Goods were bought and sold. Enna-aru's soldiers settled into their quarters and made friends, romanced girls, found favorite beer shops. On the floor by Enna-aru's bed, full plates were laid out in a line, in progressive degrees of spoilage.

The prayers for the king fell off a very little, in their volume and intensity.

On the evening of the sixth day, Atrahasis looked down at the tranquil city, and hated it.

He called to him Vidya, and said: "Do you suppose we could get away with bombing the damned place to the ground?"

Vidya, after a pause, said: "You've lost it, haven't you?"

"Go fuck yourself," said Atrahasis.

He went into the chamber where Enna-aru lay, blue as lapis lazuli, and quoted:

> *"For whom have I labored, boatman?*
> *For whom have I lost the blood of my heart?*
> *I have not gained any advantage to myself;*
> *Only the serpent has gained the advantage."*

No golden voice to answer now. There was silence.

But not stillness; something moved on Enna-aru's face.

Atrahasis leaned close, and saw the maggot fall from the king's arched nostril.

He stiffened, overwhelmed with revulsion. Then he turned on his heel and left the room.

"Have that carcass dragged out and burned," he told Vidya in a light and carefree voice. "And send a transmission to Old World One; mission accomplished. Peaceful (apparent) transfer of power, civilization continues without a hitch, no loss to the stockholders. I'm on my way to Egypt for a well-deserved holiday. They can forward my next posting there."

"Yes, sir," said Vidya. "I'll have your air transport powered up, sir."

"No; I've had enough of flying," said Atrahasis.

He wrapped himself in a cloak, and went down through the tun-

nels and out of the city by secret ways, and glided away through the
night like a serpent.

But he had gone back to his duties at last. What else was there for an immortal to do, besides plot for power and sound out prospective allies?

He had first come down the Nile on a reed boat, in a time before
there were any pyramids at Giza. Nothing then more remarkable in that
landscape than a great outcropping of rock that resembled a lion's head,
which likeness successive generations of mortals had increased by chis-
eling out eyes and a muzzle. Graffiti was scrawled across its lower surfaces now. Not yet the Sphinx, it stared gloomily across the land that
wasn't yet Egypt. Atrahasis—not yet Labienus—sympathized with it.

He had liked the delta country once. The river was wide and clear,
the air was purity itself. Dawn wind came across the green murmuring
reeds and when the young sun rose above them it really might have
been a god, such was its brilliance and clean heat. No smoke in the sky;
light sharp as a diamond.

Then the mortals had come. For a while the crocodiles and floods
had kept their numbers down, but they had multiplied at last, and
spoiled it all. At this point in time it was only the smoke of their
cook-fires that muddied the face of the sun, and this was bad enough.
In the time to come the very dust of their mummified dead would rise
like a pall, the gases of their sewage, the chemical fumes of their
cities. All this fresh young world lost to ancient bricks, blackened
corpses.

Atrahasis put it firmly out of his mind, as the river bore him to the
city of white walls. It had been built to rule both Upper and Lower
Kingdoms. Two dynasties had come and gone and the third was pros-
perous, expansive, so the damned place was sprawling now. Shading
his eyes, he could see the necropolis on its ridge. The world's first pyramid was no more than a foundation yet. Mortals swarmed over it like
insects, setting the little limestone blocks.

He sighed and glanced down from his high seat to the water,
where a ridged back paced his boat, drifting unobtrusively near. Poor
old crocodile. There had been a time when Atrahasis might have given
an order and had a clumsy slave tossed overboard like a crust of bread,
and before the river gods converged on him the slave would have
screamed his thanks at being so honored. One couldn't get away with
that nowadays. Too much history was being recorded.

When his boatman docked and bowed him ashore, Atrahasis
walked through the streets and the mortals fell back before him, gap-

ing at the splendid lord in his finery, marveling at the tall spearmen who went before and followed him. They wondered at the mortal slaves who bore the carved chest that was splendidly covered in beaten gold, inlaid with turquoise and lapis. They thought surely he must be an ambassador bringing gifts to the king.

But he did not go to the palace. Atrahasis went swiftly to the house of Imhotep, the high priest, he who was the king's chief minister, he who had designed and was overseeing the construction of the latest thing in monuments to royal glory.

The mortal onlookers nodded to each other knowingly. No surprise that this regal-looking stranger was calling on Imhotep first. Imhotep might claim he was merely a man, but everyone knew better. He had miraculous healing powers, he knew the name of every star in the sky and their secret paths, and his ability to work spectacularly showy magic was famous. Of course he must entertain gods from time to time! Before Atrahasis had stepped through the courtyard gate, word was spreading that Imhotep had another divine visitor.

To Atrahasis's annoyance, he was not at once admitted to the august presence of the high priest of Ptah.

"He is bathing, my lord," stammered the mortal woman. She clapped her hands and servants ran to her side. "A chair for the great lord, a basin for his feet! Will you have beer, my lord? Will you be pleased to wait in the garden, where the air is cool? I will fetch—"

"Tell him the priest of Zeus would speak with him," Atrahasis snapped.

There was a beat while the mortals present wondered who Zeus might be, before a servant said: "Our lord will not permit us to disturb his bath—" The woman turned and waved him to silence.

"I will tell him," she said, and hurried away. Atrahasis waited, enduring in stiff-lipped silence as well-meaning mortals brought a chair for him, seated him, drew off his sandals and washed his feet. He still hated to be touched by the creatures.

He focused his attention on the interior of the mansion and heard the splashing, the raucous whistling of—of all things—the Grand March from Verdi's *Aida*, interrupted by the mortal woman's urgent murmur. There was a response, more splashing, and then the whistling resumed. Atrahasis tracked it through the mansion as it came nearer to him, and at last the high priest Imhotep stepped out into the garden.

Imhotep was a stockily built man with black button eyes, smiling in wry apology as he approached Atrahasis. He had a generic olive-skinned Mediterranean appearance, and might have disappeared into any crowd anywhere with perfect invisibility, so ordinary was his face, so easily could he pass for human.

His hastily donned linen kilt was damp, and he was still toweling his shaven head dry as he came.

"Sorry, friend," he said in Cinema Standard. "I was at the construction site all day and got pretty stinky. You want a beer?"

"Please," said Atrahasis, as a servant dried his feet. Imhotep asked the servant to bring a pitcher of beer and two cups. He ducked his head and hurried away.

Imhotep gave his ears a last dig with the towel and hung it around his neck. He thrust out a hand to Atrahasis.

"Facilitator Grade One Imhotep, how's it going and to what do I owe the honor?"

"Executive Facilitator Atrahasis," he replied, shaking Imhotep's hand gingerly. "The god Zeus has sent you a gift, divine son of Ptah. I'm here to brief you on its use."

Imhotep grimaced. "Don't call me that where the servants can hear, okay? Not in their language, anyhow."

Atrahasis was amused. "Don't you want them to respect you?"

"They respect me just fine as a mortal man, which is what I've worked really hard to convince them I happen to be, so let's not scare them, all right?" Imhotep sagged onto a garden bench. He regarded the carved chest, still being held on its poles by the mortal slaves; cocked his eye at the honor guard of security techs in loincloths. "That must be one hell of a present. What is it, another capacitor?"

"I don't believe your project budget could support one," Atrahasis replied delicately. "And it's hardly necessary for the second phase of your mission here."

"Second phase, huh?" Imhotep rubbed his chin. "Okay." In the language of the country, he addressed the mortal bearers. "Boys, you want to set that thing down?"

The slaves glanced nervously at Atrahasis, who nodded. They lowered their burden and straightened up in obvious relief. At that moment the servant brought the beer, and only after he had offered them their cups and retreated to a respectful distance was the conversation able to proceed.

"What second phase?" Imhotep asked. "I've got Zoser and his court in the palm of my hand, with stage illusions galore. The step-pyramid's on schedule. I'm dealing out miraculous cures and promoting good hygiene. Wasn't that the point of this junket?"

"As far as it's gone, yes," Atrahasis said, sniffing his beer and setting it aside. "But now you need to know more."

"I see."

"The chest is not to be opened until you have it in your private chambers. You will find inside it certain equipment, and a number of scrolls."

"Scrolls? What do I need books for?"

"Think of them as stage-dressing. They're to impress your initiates."

"What initiates?" said Imhotep, reaching for his beer. He turned the cup in his hands uneasily. "I thought the whole deal with me becoming a god didn't happen until way later in history."

"Of course. This is another matter entirely. You're to start a, to put it in the mortals' parlance, a 'Hermetic Brotherhood.' The most secret of secret societies. You'll feed them snippets of philosophy and arcane gibberish as revelations from the gods. Flashy conjuring tricks to impress them. Hints of real science, with demonstrable results. The equipment in the chest is for that purpose."

"Don't tell me there are still Rosicrucians in the twenty-fourth century, and they're paying the Company to do this?" Imhotep sighed.

"Not at all. You're simply laying the groundwork for certain others to build on at a later date," Atrahasis told him. "The real challenge will be convincing your little king that the whole affair is his idea."

Imhotep looked unhappy.

"Okay," he said. "I can do that. No problem." He drained his beer in one gulp and reached for the pitcher. "More?"

"Not for me, thank you." Atrahasis turned in his chair and surveyed the garden. "Quite a comfortable posting you have here. It must nearly make up for the air pollution and the crowds of mortals."

"It's great," said Imhotep earnestly. "And the pollution's no worse than anywhere else. You try living in the same cave with the rest of your tribe through a six-month winter—now, that's pollution!"

"Undoubtedly," said Atrahasis. "Still, one can't help wish the wretched things would grasp the basic principles of birth control." He transmitted the rest of his thought subvocally: *Or that the old Enforcers had been allowed to continue their useful work.*

Imhotep gulped down a second beer even more quickly than the first.

Hey, times change. I hear most of them are adapting real well to the new jobs.

Atrahasis considered him coolly. *You don't find what was done to them shameful? How professional of you. I'd have thought you could summon a little outrage on their behalf. You were one of Budu's recruits, weren't you? Just as I was.*

That's right.

Yet you never spoke out on behalf of our immortal father, when the orders came.

Imhotep narrowed his eyes. *What's it to you? I went to him and we talked, if you must know. Sure, he had his reservations about closing down the old operation. But he was smart enough to see that times were changing, and he's changed with them. Not like that dumb ass Marco.*

Marco was rash, I have to admit.

He was a loose cannon! He'd grab any excuse to slaughter mortals. Budu's smart, and he's got self-control, and he's going to be just fine. It's not like there aren't going to be plenty of wars to keep him busy.

How true.

At this moment they were interrupted. A tiny brown naked mortal came marching into the garden, fists clenched, scowling in furious determination, heading for the street. Imhotep spotted him and jumped up.

"Excuse me a minute. Benny, come back here!"

Atrahasis turned, staring in disbelief, as Imhotep ran after the mortal infant and caught it. A conversation took place in the ancient tongue that would be translated approximately as follows:

"Whoa! Where do you think you're going? Remember what Daddy said about chariots?"

"No potty go."

"Oh. Benny, you have to go potty like a big boy now."

"No potty go!"

Imhotep looked around. "Okay, okay. Come on. Big boy on the tree like Daddy showed you, all right?"

"Big boy."

Atrahasis averted his gaze as Imhotep led the infant to a fig tree in the corner, where it urinated. The mortal woman came running from the house, calling for the child, and Imhotep turned and waved to her.

"I caught him, honey, it's all right."

"How did you get the door open?" she demanded of the baby. It just glared up at her. "My lord husband, I put the latch on!"

"He's a magician," said Imhotep, grinning in embarrassment. "Like me."

"Horses might have killed you under their hooves," she admonished the baby, gathering it into her arms. "Crocodiles might have eaten you!" She glanced over at Atrahasis and crimsoned in a blush. "Ten thousand apologies, my lord!"

"It's all right," said Imhotep. He put his arms around her and kissed her. "I'll be in soon. Send Aye and Pepi and a couple of the others out, okay? And unlock my study. I want that chest taken inside and set against the far wall."

"Will our guest stay for dinner?"

"I don't think so," Imhotep said.

"No potty go," the baby informed them.

"We'll see about that, kiddo," Imhotep told him sternly, and the mortal woman bore the protesting child away to the house. He returned to the stone bench to find Atrahasis regarding him in scandalized disgust.

"We adopted," explained Imhotep, looking a little shamefaced.

"No wonder you don't mind the pollution," Atrahasis said at last. "You're actually living in intimacy with them!"

"It's part of my job," said Imhotep. "She was a gift from the king. What was I supposed to do? You know the procedure on this kind of mission. And anyway, since when is sex with them against the rules?"

"True enough," Atrahasis said, but mentally he crossed Imhotep off his list of possible allies.

"I know she'll die one of these days," Imhotep went on defensively. "The kid will die, too, maybe fifty years down the line, but in the meanwhile he'll have had a good life and . . . well, they all die, don't they? And I'll be somewhere else by then anyway. I've been through this before. I can handle it. The Company doesn't care, as long as I get the job done, right?"

"Whatever it takes," Atrahasis agreed.

He didn't stay to dinner.

Imhotep might be besotted with mortals, but he had indeed gotten the job done. In founding an occult society that promised secret knowledge and earthly power to its members, he had forged the first link in a long chain that would ultimately terminate in that remarkable cabal of scientists and investors calling itself Dr. Zeus Incorporated.

Not quite in keeping with the high moral purpose expressed in the Company's mission statement. However, Atrahasis had learned—long before he became Labienus—that the mortal masters were the first to jettison their principles, when it was necessary to get something they wanted.

VICTOR THE POISONER

From time to time, Labienus has considered compiling a book of wisdom of his own, perhaps an immortals' version of *The Prince* or *The Art of War*.

He has never done so. For one thing, when one is immortal, there is no point in passing on wisdom to the next generation lest it be forgotten, for it cannot be forgotten. Nor would it do, after all, to empower up-and-coming young rivals by letting them in on one's secrets.

And Labienus has no bright subordinate in training, in any case, no youthful immortal he can impress or mentor.

So his desire has never progressed beyond a list of maxims. The first one is, *It is not enough to tend one's own garden. One must assiduously sow weeds in one's neighbor's garden, and encourage snails there.*

He unlocks a drawer now, and draws forth another paper file. It is bulky, it is clumsy, but hard copy has certain advantages to a conspirator. And there is something so satisfying, really, in holding in one's hands the tangible damnation of one's enemies.

The file is labeled simply HOMO UMBRATILIS.

Labienus opens it. The first thing to greet his eye is an image, a straightforward Company identification shot of another Executive Facilitator. His designation is Aegeus, and he looks as benign as the chairman of some philanthropic foundation.

His expression makes Labienus's lip curl in distaste. *Hypocrite*, he thinks. Their rivalry is an old one.

They were assigned to the same mission once, in the dead ages past when he had been Atrahasis. The job was above and beyond the usual level of Company need-to-know obscurity. They had been sent with troops to an island in the Pacific and told to kill all the mortals

they found there. Long before their transport had touched down, Atrahasis had discovered that his partner was no higher in rank than he
was, and moreover that Aegeus was pompous, self-important, and
crude.

Atrahasis had entertained himself awhile subtly insulting Aegeus
with exquisite courtesy. When they finally reached their destination,
Aegeus had let him do most of the killing; and this proved to be a complicated affair, for the mortals turned out to be neither the Neanderthal
brutes he had expected nor even their cave-painting cousins. And they
were rather better at defending themselves than Atrahasis had been
advised. Given the hazardous nature of the job, he expected a plum
posting as a reward.

So it had annoyed him a great deal when he later learned that
Aegeus, rather than he himself, had been appointed the new sector
head for Southern Europe.

Labienus has never forgotten the slight.

Both men have built private empires within the Company. Both
have made plans to seize power, on that distant day in 2355 when the
Company is expected to fall, and both have taken certain drastic and
occasionally bloody steps to guarantee supremacy then. Only their
methods have differed.

Aegeus has gone for show, for extravagance, flaunting his power
base. He has committed tremendous resources to long-range plans. In
doing so, he has presented his enemies with an immense target. The
question, therefore, is simply one of strategy: which arrow to use, and
when, for the most satisfying result?

Labienus tilts his head on one side, considering Aegeus's image.
Smiling at last, he takes a fine silver pen from his desk and dips it in an
inkwell of Bavarian crystal. He sketches a beard and curling mustache
on Aegeus's face. Aegeus has his lips closed in the picture, sadly, so Labienus is unable to black out one of his teeth; but he settles for drawing
little horns on Aegeus's head, and adding a pair of vampire fangs over
his lower lip. He sets the picture aside, chuckling as he reflects that a
petty impulse, properly directed, can do one a world of good.

So, with a light heart, he considers the other Company portraits in
the file.

Two immortals. One is a drone, a Literature Preservationist designated Lewis. The other is an Executive Class Facilitator whose promising career has been oddly derailed. He is designated Victor. Lewis
smiles from his portrait. Victor does not.

Lewis is fair-haired, handsome, clean-shaven. There is determination in his features. There is an earnestness that verges on absurdity.

There is no doubt he is plucky. Also thrifty, brave, clean, and reverent. *Fool,* thinks Labienus.

Victor has white skin, red hair. His neat beard is sharply pointed, his mustaches even more so. His green eyes are as unreadable in their expression as a cat's. He has posed stiffly, formally. He looks reserved. Unapproachable. Labienus smiles at his picture, almost with real affection.

Hitching his chair closer to the desk, he turns his attention to the documents. Some appear to be transcripts of testimony. He has compiled them over long years, with terrific patience. A lucky find; a careful decryption of private journal entries; an interview with an ancient mortal that had cost him nothing more than a bottle of good wine and a sympathetic-seeming ear.

The topmost stack looks fabulously old, vellum inscribed in brown ink, uncials decorated here and there with flowers and strange tiny marginalia. It is written in a mixture of sixth-century Gaelic and Latin.

The edges crumble as Labienus reads.

When my name was Eogan, I lived in the community at Malinmhor, having gladly embraced my vows for the peace of our Lord Jesus Christ, and I thought I had the best of the bargain. No heavier tool to lift than a pen cut from the quill of a gray goose, and the beauty of the red and green and yellow and black inks was a pleasure for my eyes, and how smooth were the sheets of fine white calfskin waiting for me! And how sweet to refresh myself with the Gospel that I copied, there in the little scriptorium, when I could still believe in it!

What a world of grace fell away from me when that pagan man came among us, three weeks before Beltane in the five hundred and seventh year since Christ's birth.

But no blame to him, poor man; God knows he had the worst of it. The truth is the trouble started well beforehand, and I knew nothing of it, happy and alone as I worked. So blinded with the beauty I made by day, that I never noticed the frightened faces when I joined my brothers and sisters for supper in the refectory of evenings.

And we didn't speak aloud much—it was a monastery, after all—nor would I have believed in the trouble, had anyone explained it to me. If our community lay in the shadow of the high bare hill Dun Govaun, what harm in that? No rational Christian had anything to fear from a mound of dead stone. If pagans had feared the place in the past, if they'd told stories of babies carried off or folk seduced by small demons—well, they were pagans, weren't they? At the mercy of darkness, as we brothers and sisters in Christ were not. Though I remember being awakened by the screams of a brother in his nightmares, I do remember that much now; but it signified nothing to me at the time.

When the pagan came, it was neither by day nor night but in the long hour between when the light had not faded, and when we neither fasted nor fed but sat at table with our meal not yet begun, and our brother the Cook had just brought out the oat-kettle, and Liath our Abbess was neither silent nor speaking, for she had just drawn in her breath to lead the grace. The pagans believe such in-between moments make doorways into the next world, you know.

In that unlucky moment the door opened indeed and our brother the Porter led in a young man in very fine clothes, which were perhaps too large for him.

"This is the guest Christ has sent us, who comes requiring meat and shelter for the night," said the Porter, and he withdrew to his duty. The man stood surveying us all with a pleasant face; and from the dust on his rich garments it was plain he'd traveled far, and from the harp he bore, slung in its case on his back, plain his profession of *fili*, of chronicler after the manner of the heathens. I thought he looked too young to have learned so much lore as those people are required to know.

"A blessing on this table," he said, and our Abbess corrected him: "*Christ's* blessing on this table, and all here."

"Oh, by all means," he replied mildly, and smiled at the Abbess.

He dined, then, with us, and revealed that his name was Lewis, that he was indeed a pagan well trained in his craft of relating the old histories, and had come to offer us a bargain: he would give us all he carried in his head, the wonder-tales and songs of the old pagan heroes, in return for food and lodging. Our Abbess looked across at me with the eye of a cat after a mouse, for both she and I collected these tales avidly (though we did not believe them at all).

So the bargain was made, with the understanding that the pagan should observe no pagan rites whilst among us, especially on the old feast day that was three weeks off, but attend Mass daily instead. To which Lewis agreed, readily, without anger. After dining he was shown the bath-house, and then the guest-house, and he took his leave of us for the evening with the urbane manners of a king's son, which we thought he must be.

When it grew light next day he met me in the scriptorium, for the purpose of fulfilling his end of the agreement, and settled himself on a stone seat. He took his harp from its case, and frowned to himself as he tuned it. I will record here that Lewis was small-boned, high-browed, with fine clean-shaven features and fair hair, though it did not curl. His eyes were just the color of the sky in that twilight time in which he had come.

When he had tuned the strings to his satisfaction, he said to me: "Brother Eogan, tell me first what tales you have collected thus far, from other travelers, so I waste no time in repeating them. Have you *The Cattle-raid of Cooley*?"

"Yes, in good truth, we have."

"Have you *The Destruction of Da Derga's Hostel*?"

"Yes, in good truth, we have."

"Would you mind awfully if we switched to Latin for this?" he inquired in that tongue. "It'll go quicker."

"Fair enough," I replied in the same language, and we conversed in Latin after that.

"What about the Finn MacCool stories? Any of those?"

"Well, we did get a couple of songs about him from an old man who stayed here last winter," I told him, noting that my red ink had sat too long and giving it a shake to mix it. "I don't think his memory was very reliable, though."

"Ah! Well, I've got the complete cycle. Sounds like a good place to begin, wouldn't you say?" He grinned and fished a horn plectrum from the pouch at his belt.

"Let's hear it," I replied, and poised my pen over the lovely white page. Dear God, how I've missed writing, just the physical act of moving the pen, making the ink flow!

He had hours and hours of material on the Fenians, tales I'd never heard before as well as the two stories the old man had given us (and as I'd suspected, the poor creature had garbled them badly). I myself was born Christian, and since my parents were zealous converts, they'd always frowned on their children listening to the old pagan stories. I knew all about Patrick and Moses and Noah, but I could never hear about Cuchulainn or Deirdre until I became a monk. Ironic, isn't it?

Lewis recounted the whole cycle to me, all about Finn growing up in the forest because evil King Goll had killed his father, so the boy was raised in secret by a pair of druid women, who conjured a wolf-spirit to be his protector. Spellbinding! Lewis was a good storyteller, too. He had a mobile, expressive face, elegant gestures, and a nice light baritone. My pen swept across the page.

We didn't even take a break until I got a paralyzing fit of writer's cramp, just after the part where Finn calls his father's ghost from the Land of the Blessed, and the old chief gives him advice. I got up and walked back and forth in the narrow stone room, swinging my arms, while Lewis took the opportunity to pour himself a cup of watered mead from the pitcher we'd brought.

He sipped and held the cup out to the light. "My goodness, who's your Beekeeper? That's great!"

"A former pagan," I admitted. "Nobody else quite gets the formula right, I must confess. You see, that's part of the Abbess's plan here—there's so much that's worth preserving in Eire, so much wisdom, such traditions, so much great literature! If only it wasn't *pagan*, you see. Not that I expect you to agree with me on that point, of course, and no offense intended—"

"No, no." Lewis waved his hand. "Quite all right. I understand perfectly—"

"But these stories, for example. It's absolutely criminal that the druids didn't bother to write any of them down. You must realize that in another generation or two they'll be completely forgotten, don't you? And, though we won't be the poorer for losing our false gods, it really would be too bad to lose Finn."

"My thoughts exactly." Lewis nodded. "That's one of the reasons I'm here, to tell you the truth. I can see the writing on the wall, and my profession doesn't really encourage me to write on it myself—so to speak—*but* . . ." He set down his harp and leaned forward. "I have rather a daring proposition for you."

I stopped pacing. "It's nothing sinful, I trust."

"Not at all, at least not by your standards. Look, it's simply this: I'm a bit more than a simple bard. I have some religious credentials as well, in my religion I mean. I was trained for certain rituals I'll never be able to perform nowadays, with so few of us left."

"But you're a young man," I said doubtfully. "I thought most of the *vates* had died off years ago."

"I'm older than I look." Was he evading my gaze, there, for just a second? "In any case: I'm quite resigned to the druids being dead as last year's mutton, but it kills the heart in me to know their more, ah, arcane knowledge will be lost. The sciences. The sacred rites, the ceremonies and all that. Now, I couldn't ever tell you Christians certain things, being sworn to secrecy, but if you happened to overhear me talking to myself—say if we happened to be sitting in the same room at the time—and you happened to write down what you heard, well, it wouldn't be a sin for you, would it?"

"I'm not so sure about that." I sat to consider it. "Preserving heathen history and legends is one thing. Preserving a false faith . . . I seem to remember the Blessed Patrick stating quite clearly that druid books ought to be burned, not preserved."

He sighed and had another sip of mead. "I know what you're thinking: what if this is some pagan plot to keep the Old Religion going? I'll tell you what you can do: once you've made my *Codex Druidae*, you can bury it in a lead casket ten feet below the floor of this room. I'll swear any oath you like that it'll remain there, undisturbed, unseen for a thousand years and more."

"It's a strange request . . ." I tugged at my beard. "Still, I know how I'd feel in your position. Couldn't we finish this cycle of stories about Finn MacCool first?"

"Naturally." He brightened up, setting down his mead and reaching for the harp. "How's your cramp? Feel up to some white-knuckle iambic pentameter? I was just about to come to the part where Finn's woman is stolen by demons of darkness . . ."

"Finn married?" I grabbed up my pen.

"Not exactly. It was like this . . ."

So we went on like that, he and I, and the hours lengthened into days. From sunrise until midday we'd work on the stories of Finn, or the tale of Conchobar's quest for the Four Blind Boys, or other fascinating material, with me copying fast in simple brown ink, leaving margins and capitals to be elaborated on and illuminated later. If the weather was fair we'd move outdoors, where the light was better and Lewis wouldn't have to keep retuning his strings. Sometimes the Abbess would come to us, unable to restrain her desire, and read over my shoulder or listen with her eyes closed, to hear about Fergus and the Seal-Woman. But in the afternoons, when she had gone, we'd go inside and work on the *Codex Druidae*, the forbidden book. The actual text took no more than a week or so to rough in. I planned to spend more time on the illumination.

I must say, any reservations I had melted away once I actually heard the so-called sacred knowledge of my ancestors. No wonder they'd kept it secret! Most of it was utter nonsense. I remember one absurd formula for producing children out of nature, by combining tiny bits of the parents' flesh in a glass dish. Some of their astronomy was fairly good, at least. They knew, like Pythagoras, that the Earth was a sphere, but they had this notion that the Earth revolves around the Sun! In fact, they thought—but it's just too stupid to waste the ink in telling over again. I confess I was laughing as I took most of it down. No wonder Lewis had abandoned the priestly caste to be a bard.

And in any case, he was a kindly young man, and I couldn't imagine him shutting unfortunate criminals into wicker cages and burning them alive. Not that he wouldn't have been strong enough; one time he took his turn at serving the evening meal, though as a guest he needn't have, and I saw him hoist the great fish-cauldron on his shoulder and bear it from the kitchen as though it weighed nothing. I watched him mend a set of beads for one of the sisters one evening at table, prizing and closing the bronze links with powerful clever fingers. And his speech was graceful and witty, making us laugh so, it was as if Christ Himself were there telling jokes.

This happy time lasted until Beltane Eve. On that afternoon, Lewis and I were sitting out of doors, and white thorn blossoms were dropping on the calfskin from the bush above me, so I kept having to brush them away as I took down Lewis's account of the Daughter of the King Under the Waves. Suddenly he stopped. A second later the birds, who had been singing delightfully, stopped, too. "Liath is coming," Lewis announced, raising one eyebrow, "and something's wrong—"

When she came into view I saw he was right, for her face was dark with unhappiness. She wasted no time, but came straight to Lewis, and in blunt Gaelic addressed him: "Pagan man, have you any knowledge of the ways of the *sidhe*?"

His mouth hung open a second in surprise. "I have," he said.

"Good, for we have need of it. Brother Crimthann has been stolen away from us by the *sidhe* of Dun Govaun, and must be rescued."

If Finn and all his host had suddenly leaped alive from my page, I could not have been more bewildered. Fairy folk? Fairy folk kidnapping one of *us*? But the *sidhe* were mere heathen fables, they didn't exist! And I saw that Lewis was no less amazed, though courteously he asked her to explain.

It seemed that Brother Crimthann, who was one of the younger members of our community, had been troubled lately with bad dreams. In his dreams, the *sidhe* came into the cell where he slept, as easily as if they walked through smoke, and bore him away with them to their palace under Dun Govaun. There he suffered torments of fleshly temptation, but by morning woke in his cell again with no sign of the ordeal of his dreams: not even the guilty emission of a young man so tempted. He had sworn that the *sidhe* were not beautiful, either, but pale and small and silent.

At this I saw Lewis start forward, like a hound catching a scent. "Now that is a strange thing, truly," he told the Abbess.

"Strange, but not so strange as this: Brother Crimthann did not come to prayers this morning, nor later, nor was he to be found in his cell. But Brother Aidan's hut adjoins his, and Brother Aidan swears that in the third hour of the night the moon shone into his cell, bright enough to flood between the stone chinks; and as you are a pagan and learned in these things I need not tell you that there was no moon last night." The Abbess looked at him grimly. "Now, this is a pagan matter. The Blessed Patrick gave us prayers against the *sidhe*, but I never read anywhere that fairy women carried him away from his holy bed. Can you go to them, then, and win our brother back with that fine pagan talk of yours? Bring him alive out of Dun Govaun, and Christ will bless you for it, druid though you are."

"I will," said Lewis, "and gladly, good Mother. Only tell me where to find Dun Govaun, and I'll go there straight."

"Brother Eogan knows," she told him, and gave me a Look of Order. "Eogan, show him the way."

"This is really marvelous," Lewis said as we pushed our way through the heather. "Tell me, Eogan, have you ever noticed this sort of thing going on before? Strange lights in the sky, unusual marking in the fields, cattle inexplicably slaughtered in grotesque ways? Any nocturnal goings-on in your cell?"

"Certainly not," I replied stiffly. "I sleep soundly at night, at least since I stopped having to shave my tonsure. I daresay Brother Crimthann will, too, when he's past thirty and not quite so easily tempted by the flesh."

"Cheer up! Baldness looks good on some men. You think that's all it is, then, with Brother Crimthann? He's been sneaking out at night to visit a girl?" Lewis leapt nimbly up on a rock and peered ahead, shading his eyes with his hand. "Ah. That must be the famous Dun Govaun."

"That's it." I regarded it sourly. "The supposed hall of the fairies. Absolutely ridiculous! It's a completely smooth and solid hill. Not even a rabbit hole on it anywhere. As for Brother Crimthann, he's simply run away, if you ask me. That's the trouble with these boys who get all inflamed by the idea of monastic life before they've had a chance to see what sleeping with a woman's like." I bent to untangle a branch of gorse from the leg of my trews. "Chastity seems like such a wonderful idea until the first time someone actually tempts them, and then they go all to pieces. Hysteria, night sweats, and Satan everywhere they look."

"Not one of the better innovations of Christianity, if you'll pardon my saying so," Lewis remarked as we hurried on. "But let's climb Dun Govaun. I'm eager to see if anything's up there. There are, er . . . certain stories amongst my people, of creatures like the ones Brother Crimthann described. We've never been able to verify anything, of course. So what do you think the place is? Not a natural hill, at any rate."

"Nothing more than the burial mound of some heathen king," I said dismissively; but I glanced upward, for by then we had come to the base of the great hill, and I felt my opinion curdle in my heart. Perhaps a *giant* heathen king.

"There's a place in Britain—" began Lewis, and then he stopped still in his tracks. He seemed to be listening intently to something. His face lit up. He began to laugh.

"Well, I'll be damned," he said, in rather poor taste under the circumstances, I thought. "They're here, Eogan! There are actually living things inside this hill."

"How do you know?" I was unable to see what should amuse him so.

"Let's say it's druidical wisdom," he replied, chuckling, and began to pace rapidly along the side of the hill. "Yes—there should be a concealed opening, and I'll bet it's just about here—"

"What in Christ's name are you babbling about?" I demanded, running after him until he suddenly vanished before my astounded eyes. I froze, staring at empty grass and windy sky. To my horror his bright voice went right on.

"Here it is, no doubt about it. Eogan? What's the matter? Oh." His head appeared in midair, a vision no less terrifying. He must have seen how frightened I was, for in a soothing voice he said: "This is only a conjurer's trick, man. There's magic in your Bible, isn't there? Moses and Aaron working spells against the Pharaoh's magicians? And this is less than that, believe me."

"But—" I said, and that was when I felt my faith first shifting under me. All this while, I had believed that Christ's coming had scoured sorcery out of the world, as the sunrise dispels darkness. Though the old stories might be good to tell and listen to, and the days of the heroes sentimentally longed after, no such wonders existed any more, if indeed they ever had.

Yet my logic had been flawed, hadn't it? For the old prophets did work magic, Christ Himself had done so, and where in Scripture did it say that we lived in an orderly and rational world?

Lewis extended a disembodied hand, in a gesture meant to calm me. "Come around here, and I'll show you."

Christ forgive me, I went to see. As I approached, the rest of him appeared whole and sound, and I saw the wavering stripes of shadow he was pointing out so proudly. They were like the blurs that used to dance before my eyes when I'd worked too late by one candle. "Now, watch this," he told me, and closed his eyes. I heard a humming sound and a snap. The mouth of a cave yawned before us, black dark and deep. I made the Sign of the Cross against all evil.

"What did you do?"

"I just—broke the spell. In a manner of speaking. I'll bet Brother Crimthann's in there." Lewis's smile faded as he considered the thing he'd revealed to me. "Good Lord, a real abduction. What should we do now, do you suppose?"

"You—you said you'd rescue him!" I sputtered.

"I did, didn't I?" He looked unhappy. "You wait here, then. I'll be back as soon as I can." To my astonishment, he turned without the least hesitation and proceeded down into the darkness, and I realized he had no weapon with him larger than a penknife. I watched his back dwindling into the shadows a moment before I ran after him, calling on the power of Christ to shield me.

"Oh—" He half turned as I caught hold of his cloak. "That's all right, you don't have to come. Really, you'll be safer out there. I can see in the dark, had I mentioned that?"

"No," I replied, groping after him. There were strange smells in that darkness, but I didn't want to be thought a coward; and wasn't the power of Christ greater than anything that might be down there? It must be, mustn't it? "I'll bear you company."

"Well, that's thoughtful of you. Be careful, Eogan; the passageway's getting narrower, and there's some kind of threshold we're about to cross. Here. Step up with me now—"

Then it was as though lightning had come down from Heaven into that black place, and I was struck and thrown like a spark from a smith's anvil.

Hours and hours later I heard Lewis saying, "Well, that was certainly stupid."

I sat up painfully, feeling as though I'd been beaten. We lay in half-darkness, in an angle of corridor lined by panes of milk-white glass that glowed softly. Behind us, set into the floor, was a simple metal grating.

"Eogan," said Lewis, and he sounded almost embarrassed. "Eogan, there are people coming for us, and I'm afraid I have a problem."

"What is that?" How groggy I sounded.

"I seem to be paralyzed."

I grimaced. "Your neck's broken, then. I'm sorry, man."

"No, it can't break, but—" He paused a moment and then spoke rapidly. "Eogan, I'd like to make a confession. Will you hear it? Will you be my *anmchara*?"

"But you're a pagan!"

"I'll convert. Will you? If I ask you in Christ's name?" His voice was desperate.

And of course I must say yes, and so I was bound to his secret. I leaned close in the darkness to hear Lewis, as he drew a deep breath and confessed.

"You see . . . I'm afraid I'm rather more of a pagan than you thought. In fact, I'm not strictly what you'd call a human being."

"What are you, then?" I sat back to stare at him. He was certainly sweating like a mortal man, but we had entered a world where the *sidhe* existed after all, so what else might be true?

"The word *cyborg* won't mean anything to you. You'd call me a homunculus, I suppose, grown from a mortal infant but changed by, er, alchemy. The masters who created me live nearly two thousand years in the future, Eogan. I work for them here in the past, finding things they want and hiding them in places that won't be disturbed until they're needed. I've been functioning for four centuries now." He swallowed hard and seemed to get his panic under control. "They made me immortal and indestructible; at least they thought so. They know everything—well, not quite everything, or I wouldn't be lying here now, would I? I can't die! Can I?"

"I don't know what on Earth you're talking about," I told him, trying even now to hold tight to my orderly rational world. "But I've seen men fall and lose movement down one side of themselves, or lose the power of speech. I think that's happened to you, Lewis. I'm sorry."

"It *is* something like that, actually," Lewis babbled. "When we stepped on that grid, it damaged me. Only my head is working. I don't know how long my emergency backup systems will run before shutting down, too. I can't seem to reset myself. Will you swear to me to fulfill a duty? As my confessor, Eogan!"

"Of course," I assured him. As his *anmchara* I had that obligation, whatever nonsense he spouted as he lay dying.

"Go back now," Lewis begged me. "Go back and seal the *Codex Druidae* in lead, and bury it ten feet below the floor of your scriptorium. You'll find the lead casket with my things in the guest-house."

"Why is this so important?" I asked, trying to be rational.

"Because it'll be worth an awful lot of money to the Neo-Wiccans when it's dug up in 2350," he replied.

I had not the slightest idea what he meant by that at all, nor was I ever to get him to explain further, for his eyes went wide suddenly and he gasped. "God Apollo! Look at that."

This last was not a timely prayer but a reaction to the creatures that were suddenly there with us in that dark hall, things like horrible children. Small, with skins pale as ashes, and tiny weak faces set low on big heads. They were naked, save for goggles of black glass worn over eyes that were perhaps as weak as the rest of them. No genitals at all. I wanted to yell with revulsion at the sight of them; but a voice like the devil spoke within my ear, wheedling, coaxing, imploring.

Please, it begged me, *pleease! Rise and bring the changeling with you. Pleeease go with us. We're going somewhere nice. You'll want to come.* And, though I detested the little voice before and after I heard it, while it twittered away at me I could no more deny it than a call of nature. I prayed to my sunlit Christ to deny them power over me. Still I obeyed them, got to my feet and picked up Lewis. His head hung down like a broken doll's, and I was certain I'd killed him; but as I moved to follow the pale children, I heard him murmuring inexplicably: "*Mass hysteria,* was it? *Faked photographs,* was it?" in tones of indignation.

Down the long hall we went, and it was dark and warm, reeking with strange animal smells. We came to a door, neatly made. The pale children bid me put my shoulder against it and push my way in. I shoved through into a tiny stone chamber, lit by white glass beyond the door ("Watch out! Careful of my head," fretted Lewis as it nearly knocked on the jamb). Then we were in and the door had swung shut after us, and I saw that there was no handle on the inside, and the silky voices had stopped, and I felt like a fool in a trap, which I was.

Behind me I heard a hiss of indrawn breath.

"Guests," mused a voice in Latin. "How fortunate I am."

"Eogan, turn around," said Lewis in tones of distinct alarm.

I whirled about expecting a dragon, at least, but saw instead a pale child in chains, sitting against the wall.

No, not a child. A thin wispy beard trailed from his chin, and on his big head were wisps of hair. His gender was evident, if small as a baby's. He had a bitter thin mouth, and wide green eyes that were fixed on us with an expression of malevolent amusement.

"Slave," he told me, "bring the mechanism here. I'd like a look at him."

"Slave yourself," I replied, though I'd felt the strongest compulsion to do as he'd bid me. I retreated to the opposite side of the room and set Lewis down. He was staring, as if fascinated, at the prisoner.

"What on Earth are you?" he inquired.

"And what are you?" mocked the other. "But, you see, I know the answer to that question. We know all about you and you know nothing about us. You passed through the disruption field, clearly."

"Was that what it was?" Lewis's head lolled sideways. "Eogan, hold me up so I can see him." I obliged, while the prisoner giggled at us.

"Yes, and it works well, apparently! Mother will be so happy. My uncles will learn a lot from you, when they open up that ticking head of yours. Enough to improve our defenses, next time." The creature smiled nastily.

"What are you?" I demanded, sifting through my memory for tales I'd heard from other children. "Are you a *luporchan*?"

That sent him into gales of shrill laughter. "Of course I am! Of course I am, slave, and what's more I'm a Prince among *luporchans*. Son of the Queen. Though I'm a bad Prince and in royal disfavor, as you can see." He rattled his chains at us.

"Oh, shut up," Lewis snapped at him. "You're some kind of half-human hybrid, aren't you? And that poor boy from the monastery was being brought here to make more like you, wasn't he?"

"Was Mother feeling lustful again?" The Prince shook his head. "Another hairy baby, I suppose, and perhaps he'll be as disobedient as me. That's the price we pay, though, isn't it?"

"Is it?" Lewis licked his lips. "Listen, if they're going to dismantle me, will you at least tell me what you people are?"

"What *we* are?" The Prince frowned. Then he leaned forward in his chains, looking sly. "I'll tell you a story, *fili*. No harp to accompany me? Too bad. You'll just have to make up the music in your head as we go along.

"This is 'The Tale of the Three Branches.'

"In the Beginning, the great World-Tree bore three branches, and from each branch came a son. The eldest son was wide and strong, practical and brave, but not very imaginative. The second son was tall and graceful, creative and gifted, but prone to silliness and instability."

"I wonder if you're describing Neanderthals and Cro-Magnons?" speculated Lewis.

"Is that what they call themselves? The third son was small and weak and unfortunately something of an idiot, but he had one talent: he could invent clever things. *He* wasn't clever himself, you understand, in fact he could barely speak or think, but he had an affinity for patterns and systems. And from these three sons of these three branches came the three races of man.

"And the children of the two older sons were able to reason and speak with each other, and they interbred: and these powerful and clever ones made war on the kin of the youngest son, to take by force the ingenious things they made.

"It was difficult for ideas to penetrate the heads of the kin, but this much got through to them: they must at all costs defend themselves against the big people, and hide from them somehow. And so this was what the stupid things focused on, with the dedication of ants, to the exclusion of all else, for all eternity, while their big cousins invented civilization and trade and art.

"But the more they stayed in their hiding places the stupider and weaker they became, as generations passed, and it became pitifully easy for the big people to find them, and raid them, and rape their queens. Then a remarkable thing happened! Half-breed children were born in the dark warrens of the kin who were bigger, and cleverer, and braver than the others. And they became the leaders because it occurred to them they *could* lead. So the kin prospered, and found better places to hide, and made more ingenious devices for protecting themselves. And this way, for a while, they had the advantage in the long, long game of hide and seek.

"Sadly, this advantage was lost." The Prince glared at Lewis. "It seems that at the other end of time the big people found a way to create a new race, unnatural and immortal, clockwork and flesh mingled, a disgusting alteration of humanity. Of course they made them a slave race—"

"Oh, we are not either," Lewis said testily.

"—And they reached back through time to plant these vile mechanisms in every civilization, to act as their agents, their spies, their thieves. Need I mention that one of their objectives was to find *us*, and help themselves to our useful inventions?"

"No, that's certainly not true," Lewis objected. "They don't even believe you exist! If they had, they'd have warned me about you. But I was always told you people were a late-twentieth-century hoax."

What that meant I couldn't fathom, but this much was becoming clear to me: Lewis's crazy story must be true, somehow. His enemies knew what he was, and how to harm him. These people were the incubi, the demons the holy saints warned us about. But where in Scripture would I find Lewis, amongst what peoples of the earth?

"Not a slave race, eh?" retorted the Prince. "You know what they think you need to know, nothing more! And I'm sure my marvelous moron uncles will learn things from your disassembled carcass that will give us the mechanical advantage once again."

Lewis gave a disdainful laugh. "So your own people can forge stronger chains for you? Why are you a prisoner, by the bye?"

"Politics!" snarled the Prince. "I had my own plan for furthering our kin. Why not creep out to the big women as they sleep? Why shouldn't they bear and raise our half-breeds? Why shouldn't we live in the sunlight like you? But Mother wouldn't hear of it, and I wouldn't stop, and so here I am."

"How sad for you. Well, this has all been very interesting, but I think I'll leave now," Lewis told him airily. I looked at him, astonished at his nerve. "I have no intention of letting anyone take me apart, thank you very much. Shall we go, Eogan?"

"How?" The Prince gave an incredulous grin. "Have you noticed there's no handle on the inside of this door?"

Lewis ignored him. "Eogan, unpin my cloak. Take out the brooch." I did as he asked and held it in my hand, a well-wrought thing of silver and enamel with a fine long pin.

"Now, bend me a hook from that."

"What can you hope to accomplish?" the Prince demanded. "There's no lock you can pick, either!"

"Slide the hook under the door and pull it inward," Lewis said, and I obeyed him. The Prince started up in his chains, staring in horror as the simplicity of the solution occurred to him.

"Those *idiots*—! But you, my fine machine, you're broken now. You think this big oaf can repair you? You're helpless and they'll come after you, my uncles will, no matter where you hide. They'll hunt you down! If it takes them years, they'll still get you back, and then—"

"Not at all. You see, when my primary system failed my emergency backup system began broadcasting a distress signal," Lewis taunted him. "My masters are already on their way to rescue me. Pull open the door, Eogan."

"Ha! What you have failed to realize is that this whole mound is shielded with lead," shrieked the Prince triumphantly. "Your signal hasn't reached anyone!"

Lewis's grin faltered for just a second, but he turned it into a sneer of defiance. "Well—as soon as I'm clear of this mound, my signal will be heard. And then my masters will come after *you*. See how you like—"

"If you've finished threatening each other," I said, being the only man in the room who could actually move, "the hallway's clear." I looked out into the stinking half-lit way.

"Then I'm off, short circuit or no short circuit," Lewis crowed. Bracing the open door with my body, I got hold of him by one arm and dragged him out with me.

"I'll raise the alarm," cried the Prince, but as the door swung slowly shut on its counterweight I heard him subside and mutter: "On the other hand, would anyone thank me in the least? Why *bother*?"

I took Lewis's other arm to hoist him up; but he got a distracted look in his eyes.

"Listen," he said. "Do you hear it? Someone's weeping."

I listened. "I can't hear anything."

"There's another mortal," Lewis told me. "Brother Crimthann! We've still got to rescue him." Which shamed me, because my earnest desire was to run from there without looking back, Christian as I was and him no more than a pagan, or perhaps less.

But I pulled him with me deeper into the hill and we found another door ten paces on. Even I could hear the weeping then. When we pushed the door open Brother Crimthann screamed, and cowered back in his chains.

"Hush! It's you we've come for, man," I told him. He mastered his terror enough to be silent, pressing his lips together as tears ran down his face. He smelled of shameful things. I left Lewis in the doorway and knelt beside Crimthann, turning his manacles this way and that to look for a keyhole, a seam, anything that I might force to open them. Nothing there! The rings were smooth and featureless, neither iron nor bronze. I pulled so that Crimthann flinched and whimpered, but they held fast.

"I can't break his bonds," I told Lewis. He groaned.

"Let me see them," he said, so I pulled him in and wedged the door with my foot painfully. He studied the manacles a moment as I strained to hold him up, and Crimthann blinked back his tears in confusion.

"I was afraid of this," said Lewis. "I can disable them, but it'll drain my backup system. Can't be helped. Listen, Eogan. This may well finish me. Don't leave my body here! If you can carry it out, my Company will be able to locate me, and they'll come. Now, take my hand and set it on that panel, there, above his head."

I looked up at the little square of blinking lights, bright unnatural colors. "Do you mean this will kill you?" I asked, appalled.

"Oh, no, we don't die. I'm sure they can repair me. But the surge will probably erase—I wonder if it'll erase my *mind*?" I saw his pupils go wide as the possibilities sank in. "My—what if all my memories are gone?"

"Then Christ have mercy on you," I replied, for even then I still believed. I lifted his hand, as he bid me, and laid it against the panel. He sighed once. I felt a stinging shock go through Lewis's body, then, and he made a terrible sound. The panel hissed and spat like a demon unmasked, but the manacles fell away from Crimthann's wrists.

Crimthann needed no urging; he fell forward and crawled at once for the door. Lewis's eyes were blank and blind now, I thought he must surely be dead; but I kept faith and bore him with me out of that cell.

We ran for our lives through the tunnel, Crimthann and I, and when I saw the black grate set in the floor I sprang across it with the Salmon-Leap of the old heroes I so admired. No lightning struck me as I hurtled free of the dangerous place. Falling fair, I kept running with Lewis, and did not stop until we came out into clean air.

I fell and rolled on the cold hillside and it was gray dawn, the sun not yet risen on Beltane morning, with the clouds in the east all underlit red. Behind me, Brother Crimthann staggered out and fell on his face, to lie shivering and sobbing.

I rose on my knees at once and turned Lewis over.

"?enogeraseiromemymllafitahW," he babbled, blinking rapidly, and his spine arched back until I thought it would surely snap. Then he went limp again. He opened his eyes and looked around.

"Well," he whispered, "lucky me. Even my backup system has a backup." He paused for a moment, as if listening to himself. "Oh. Not for long, though. It's just transmitting my location. My organics seem to be shutting down—" Panicked, he raised his eyes to my face. "Remember, Eogan! The *Codex Druidae*, you must bury it under the floor. And you won't tell what I confessed to you, about what I am— Oh, no, is this it? Is this what happens to you?"

There was only one thing I could do for him. "What kind of child were you created from?" I asked him. "Had it ever received Christ's grace?"

"What?" He stared at me, bewildered. "No! I was abandoned in the temple at Aquae Sulis." He gave a hysterical giggle. "Some Roman matron's holiday indiscretion, I've no doubt, left behind at the spa, a little unwanted souvenir . . ."

"You won't die," I told him confidently. I swept my hands through the grass that was pearled with the dew of Beltane morning, and I washed that high fine brow of his with it. "I baptize you in the name of the Father, and of the Son, and of the Holy Ghost. Amen."

I think I expected a vision of Christ then, or a blare of heavenly trumpets at least. Nothing of the kind happened. Lewis endured the sacrament patiently, and smiled a small polite smile.

"Why, how nice. You've given me a soul." His smile widened in ironical amusement. "Now I'll live forever, won't I?"

But the color was going out of his face, and then it left his eyes, and they closed and he was no more than a waxen doll on the hillside. I rose to my feet and looked full into the rising sun. All the birds were singing.

And even then I had not lost my faith. I carried Lewis down from Dun Govaun, with Brother Crimthann silent beside me. We returned to the community and the Abbess was moved to tears, that the brave pagan had given his life to rescue our brother. Yet everyone agreed the story had a happy ending: for hadn't Lewis accepted Christ's grace and gained an immortal soul? And his body was laid on a bier in our little church, and we celebrated a grand funeral Mass for him. That night I kept the dead watch for my friend, alone with the tall candles around his body and my sorrow and exhaustion.

At some hour in the night I opened my eyes and they were there, the two strangers. One was a knave in oil-stained clothes. The other wore the fine garments of a gentleman. They were standing at the bier and the knave had his hand on Lewis's face, prizing open one eye with his dirty thumb. I leaped to my feet.

The gentleman turned coolly to face me. "I suppose you're the one we have to thank." He gave a brief bow. "My name is Aegeus. We've come to collect our friend here."

"Can you make him live again?" I asked.

"That's what we're determining now." He nodded at the knave, who had pulled open Lewis's mouth and was examining his teeth. I didn't like to see him handled so disrespectfully. "What do you think, Barry?"

"Maybe." The knave gave Lewis's hair a casual tousle. "Most of the organs have died. He'll be in a regeneration vat for a few years, but he might be all right."

"What about his memories?" I demanded.

"Probably wiped out." The knave yawned. "Maybe retrievable. We won't be able to tell for a while."

This so broke the heart in me that I knelt down, with tears brimming in my eyes. The one who called himself Aegeus paced close and stood over me.

"But let's talk about you, my friend. You've seen a lot more than you ought to have seen. What are we going to do about you, eh?" I looked up at him sharply. He was smiling a hard smile.

"I took a vow," I told him in indignation. "To bury that damned silly book and keep silent about what he had to tell me. I don't break vows." It was true, then.

"The silence of the confessional, eh?" His face became much friendlier. "Perhaps we can do business, after all. A mortal who knows enough to keep his mouth shut can benefit from being our friend, you see. What do you want in life, anyway? Land? Cattle? Or, wait, you're a monk. Something pretty for your church, here?" He waved a hand and looked around.

"Only heal him." I nodded at Lewis. "Only save his mind, if you can." I thought of all the stories of enchantment Lewis knew, all the remarkable people he must have known, the things he must have seen: Rome in its decline, perhaps the Blessed Patrick, perhaps even the old heroes when they breathed mortal air and hunted the red deer.

"Of course we'll make every effort. He's a highly valued operative, after all," Aegeus told me. "Now, look. You do as he told you, and keep your vow of silence, and you'll be a fortunate man. I'll see you again soon. Let's go now, Barry."

"Right," replied the knave, and pulled Lewis from the bier and threw him over his shoulder like so much merchandise. They walked toward the door.

"But his body," I cried. "It'll be gone! What will I tell the others?"

Aegeus stopped and turned, tapping his upper lip thoughtfully with one finger. He grinned. "Ah. You can tell them a miracle occurred. The Holy Angels came and carried him off bodily to heaven! This is an ignorant age. They ought to believe that."

I only stared at them, too shocked to reply; and he waved cheerily, and they walked out into the darkness. I think it was then that my faith died in me utterly.

Yet in the end I told his lie, for I could think of nothing else, and my brothers and sisters rejoiced, and the story spread, so poor Lewis became venerated as a local saint. But I knew the truth for what it was. And, as I thought over the whole story—what the Prince had said, what Lewis had revealed of himself—nowhere in it could I find any trace of Christ's power, or His mercy, or His love. My God was irrelevant to those pale folk hiding in their mound, and to that knave in his oil-stained clothes.

And for all that we had a celebrated saint and a miracle to call our own, the peace of our community had been broken. There was never any molestation after that, mind: the night after Lewis's body was taken away, there was a violent thunderstorm and brilliant lights playing about on Dun Govaun. Perhaps the kin had fled to some new hiding place, or perhaps Lewis's Company had avenged his injury.

But Brother Crimthann tried to hang himself one night. He was caught and survived, yet our Abbess had to watch him continually as she would watch a child, for he would weep and rage at the smallest thing.

My life was no joy to me, either. I kept faith with Lewis, I found the lead casket and buried the *Codex Druidae* where he'd bid me, deep down under the stones of the scriptorium floor. For all I know, it lies there still. Indeed, I have assurance it must.

I found his harp, too, and kept it safe, though it broke my heart to see it and remember his voice. I thought perhaps the two strangers might come back to claim it. The more I thought about this, though, the more I began to dread the idea. One night I took the harp and what little I owned, and, breaking my vows, I fled the community to lose myself in a distant land.

It was for nothing, anyway. On the third night of my exile, I woke in the heather to find Aegeus crouching beside me.

"This'll never do, you know," he told me sternly. "You're supposed to stay where we can keep an eye on you."

"I buried your book!" I sat up. "I told your lies. Leave me in peace, can't you?"

"Can't do that, I'm afraid." He shook his head. "You're a security risk. Look, we're not so bad. You'll have to come with me now, but you'll be all right. You'll work for us and live a long, happy life."

So I went with him in the strange ship, and I learned more of the way the world is run—no Christ there running it, either—and I was given lands and livestock and a fine house. All I must do to earn my wealth is keep silent and open my door, certain nights, to certain strangers who come and depart in haste, after meals and a change of clothes and horses. Sometimes they leave packages, which other strangers come and collect later.

They seldom answer my questions, and never my inquiries about Lewis; so I fear that they failed to save him, though in most other respects they seem as powerful as gods. I have seen many things that men would think were miracles. I am supplied with every comfort a man might want for his flesh. My masters seem to think it will make me happy.

But I have not been happy since: until this last Samhain night, when I lay in my too-comfortable bed with banked coals warming the room, very unlike the hard pallet on chilly stone in the place where I was blessed.

I heard my name called, there in the darkness. I sat up and saw Lewis, just as he had been, brightly lit as though he stood in sunlight. He looked puzzled.

"Am I having a dream?" he wanted to know.

"No; it must be me dreaming, because you're dead," I told him.

"Dead?" He looked appalled. His jaw hung slack a moment before the memory seemed to come back to him. "Good Lord, what am I doing here then?"

"Well, I—I'd supposed you'd come back to offer me spiritual comfort," I ventured.

He shook his head dubiously.

"Sorry, old fellow, I haven't a clue. Unless—perhaps they've succeeded in reactivating me." His eyes lit up and he rubbed his hands together. "Not that that explains how I got here, but I'm not complaining."

"But you're not really here," I pointed out.

"Of course I am! Look." He made a grab for a pitcher that sat on the table, but his hand passed straight through it. He overbalanced slightly and righted himself.

"Damn! How embarrassing." He frowned. "Well—I suppose the possibility exists that I'm actually floating in a regeneration vat at a Company repair facility, and I'm coming to you now by means of some sort of electromagnetic projection."

"What on Earth does that mean?" I rubbed my eyes wearily.

"I don't know how I'd explain it to you. Actually I don't know if it's even possible," he added. "No, I think I'm the one having the dream, and you're the illusion. That must be it. I'm in a nice warm vat somewhere, with all my organics being regenerated, and my brain's come back online and I'm having a rather peculiar dream. Still . . . you don't look well, Eogan."

"I've lost my faith."

"Gosh, I'm sorry to hear it." He looked sympathetic. He seemed to be searching in his mind for something nice to say, and then an expression of incredulous delight crossed his face. "Great Caesar's ghost! You don't suppose that baptism business actually worked, do you? You don't suppose this is my *soul* talking to you now?" He took a few swaggering steps back and forth.

"I wish I could believe that, Lewis." I leaned my head in my hand.

"I suppose I don't believe it, either. But how can we know for sure? Wouldn't you like to believe that your God would let me into your Christian Heaven? Assuming I died, of course?"

"More than anything, Lewis. If there is such a place, you'll be there. But I don't know," I replied, anguish coiling in me like a snake. "I used to know."

"Oh, who knows anything? If you're simply the result of my nutritive solution being a bit rich, then I'll wake up when the Company decants me and go on about my business of making money for them, forever and ever and ever. And if I'm nothing more than your dream—maybe sent to you because your Christ wanted to cheer you up a little—then you'll wake up in the morning, and go on with your mortal life until it's over. Let's be happy, Eogan. Your life's too short, and mine's too long, to mourn. Do something that gives you joy."

"What?" I demanded. "What, in God's name, can I do?"

"Well . . ." He waved his hand. "You used to enjoy writing, didn't you?"

That was when the stranger, arriving late and pounding on my door, woke me to a black room and unrelieved night.

But then I dared this thing, to write down what I'd seen, and my heart hasn't been so light in ages. Lewis was right: this is real joy to me, the dance of my goose quill across the bare page. Perhaps it would violate nobody's trust to begin it again, the copying down of knowledge? I'm not fit for the Gospels any more, but I remember so many of the hero-tales Lewis told me. The community at Malinmhor has only the one copy we made. I could set them down again.

I will, I'll uncover the harp and watch as the sunlight moves across the fine wood and glints on the strings. I'll imagine Lewis sitting there talking to me, sipping the heather-honey mead, or singing as the birds chatter in the soft air beyond the stone windowsill. We'll set Finn galloping with his band of heroes, and Cuchulainn will perform terrible wonders, and it will all flow out of my pen like gold. God have mercy on me, a miserable sinner; what other grace can I hope for?

Labienus shakes his head, looking pained. It is with some relief that he turns to the next transcript, for though it is of paper no less crumbling and ancient, it is printed in a straightforward and easily readable font, written in simple Cinema Standard. Is it a diary entry? A private confession? Some immortals write compulsively, out of a need to put distressingly eternal lives in perspective. Labienus considers it a weakness. He tsk-tsks at Victor's portrait before reading . . .

The man was floating in blue space, motionless, and his gentle expression suggested that he was enjoying the pleasantest of dreams.

"This is the one I mentioned the other day," said Aegeus in a low voice. "He's been in here for a full decade. It's taken that long to regenerate him."

"Poor devil," I murmured, scanning him and recoiling at what I perceived; nearly every major organ had had to be regrown. "Does it really take that long to replace an immortal heart?"

"As a matter of fact, no," replied Aegeus, watching my expression. "There was extensive damage to his biomechanicals as well, you see. To all intents and purposes, this man died."

If he was anticipating incredulous horror on my face, his expectations were rewarded. "But that can't happen," I cried. "The biomechanicals are impervious, aren't they? What about his brain?"

"Victor." Aegeus was smiling as he stepped closer to me, but there was no warmth in his eyes. His voice dropped still lower. "You're a Facilitator. We're in a class of our own, you and I. There are certain half-truths told to the others, surely you've come to suspect that! Not lies. Truth Dilute, if you will. If we didn't present the facts in the most advantageous way now and then, the common rank and file would grow unduly alarmed, to say nothing of those idiots in the twenty-fourth century who *think* they're running the Company. All they have to see are the valuables we collect for them, here at our end of time. As long as their shareholders get results, they don't really care how we obtain them.

"Now, what you need to know about this poor fellow is: we've never before seen injuries of the kind he sustained. We don't know what the accident has done to his brain. What happened was a fluke, a singular occurrence. Why, then, upset the hardworking field operatives by letting it be known that they aren't one hundred percent indestructible, when they're all of ninety-nine point nine? The chances of anything of the sort ever happening again are positively astronomical."

"I'm exceedingly glad to hear that, sir," I replied, resolving to withhold my questions.

"And you may be sure the Company has used this unfortunate opportunity to learn, that we may prevent such damage happening in later models," Aegeus continued, turning to look again at the man. "He was a good operative; doubtless he'd be gratified to know that his misfortune gave us invaluable information. Indeed, with any luck you'll be able to tell him so."

"I, sir?" Was this to be my first assignment? I straightened my spine and attempted to look shrewd and perceptive.

"You," Aegeus said, and my keen looks were wasted on him, for he kept his eyes on the dead man. "He's scheduled to be decanted and revived in three days' time. You're to act as his handler, Victor. His guide. His psychopomp, if you will." He smiled at his joke. "Ease his transition back to immortal life." He turned and fixed me with a direct stare. "Find out how much he remembers about his accident."

Ah. That was the agenda. I nodded, intent on showing him I was a fellow of few words.

In his vat before us the man slept on, with his new heart and his brain that might—or might not—have a half-thousand years of memories within its convolutions.

In my opinion, one of the hallmarks of a true Facilitator is the ability to absorb unpleasant realities while remaining focused on the job at hand. I believe I was rather better at this when I was nineteen; I was not, as yet, aware that there *were* any unpleasant realities for us immortals.

And so I was able to watch with a certain detachment, three days later, as the dead man was dredged out of his vat in a creel of copper mesh and deposited on a steel table, where technicians intubated him and drew the oxygenated fluid from his lungs. I watched him coughing, jerking to life, shivering and vulnerable, not really conscious yet. He groped blindly as they hosed the last of the fluid off him—I had enough of a sense of empathy to hope that they were using warmed water, at least—and then lay quiet under the rush of air, as the technicians moved in to perform the necessary diagnostic procedures.

I extended a scan myself: he seemed fully functional, as immortal as any of us once again. The technicians finished with him, lifted him onto a stretcher and threw a blanket over him.

He was taken to the infirmary dormitory, to a private room, and there I waited next day for his return to consciousness. I amused myself by studying his features and speculating on his mortal origins.

My biological inheritance is Saxon and Danish, as my skin and hair bear witness; he had more of the look of a fair Celt about him, and something of a Roman as well, in his even and precise features. We were both men of slight stature, but whereas I am fairly solidly made, he had a swimmer's build. His body bore no mark of whatever accident had precipitated ten years in a regeneration vat.

I confess that I yielded to the temptation to lift one of his eyelids, ostensibly to determine what color his eyes were but in truth to see if I could prod him awake. He slept on. I threw myself back into my chair with a sigh of ennui.

Callous young brute, wasn't I? And so easily bored. Most of my classmates had already departed Eurobase One, flown off to exciting missions in the field in places like Byzantium or Spain or Cathay. Of course, they were mere Preservers: a Facilitator requires more subtle and detailed education. No grubbing after rare plants or animals for *him*! His job is to sway ministers and kings, and thereby arrange mortal political affairs to the Company's advantage. He must, therefore, learn from masters. That was why I was still cooling my heels here, watching the neophyte class toddle through its immortality process and listening to Aegeus pontificate.

Not that it seemed like pontification then. At the time I hung on his every word, and, to an even greater degree, on his meaningful silences. The true significance of silence is another thing one fails to appreciate at the age of nineteen.

I was examining my thin little beard and wondering if I ought to comb my mustaches or curl them when I glanced over the top of the mirror and saw that the man had opened his eyes. Hastily I slid the mirror into my belt pouch, but the man didn't seem to notice. He was staring at the ceiling in a vacant kind of way. Gradually he began to look around him, to take in the frame of his bed and the wall fresco.

"God Apollo," he whispered to himself.

"H'em!" I enunciated.

He sat bolt upright—nothing wrong with the fellow's reflexes—and saw me at last. "Good—is it good morning? I'm afraid my chronometer seems to be offline," he said.

"I shouldn't be surprised if it were," I said, hugely amused at the joke. "How do you feel?"

"Fresh as a daisy, thanks," he replied. His eyes tracked around the room. "I'm in a repair facility. Aren't I?"

"Eurobase One, in point of fact," I informed him.

"Ah! Of course," he said with some satisfaction, but as he followed the thought further his face grew blank. He was trying to run a self-diagnostic. The results must have been inconclusive, for he turned to me in panic.

"What happened? Something's wrong with my memory. *How long have I been here?*"

At last I was able to let him in on the joke. "Ten years," I told him, grinning, but when the shock registered on his face I felt like the wretched little worm I was. "Sir," I added.

"May I ask who you are?" he said, rather quietly under the circumstances.

"Facilitator Grade Two Victor, sir, at your service." I bowed, trying to do it with military precision. "I've been assigned to help you through your period of readjustment. Do you remember your name?"

After a long moment, he spoke with some care: "To the best of my recollection, I'm Literature Preservation Specialist Grade Three Lewis."

I nodded encouragingly. "You were on duty in Ireland. Do you have any memories of being there?"

He knotted his fingers together. "I remember the village. No, it was a monastery! That was it. I was working with the Christians there."

"Very good," I told him. "Your mission was to plant a copy of the *Codex Druidae* there for future retrieval. You were to bury it in a lead casket. Have you any idea whether you succeeded?"

"Lead," he muttered, wincing. He put up his hands and massaged his hollow temples. "It was shielded in lead. That was the trouble . . ."

"Was there any failure in the casket seal?" I pressed.

"No. I don't know. I couldn't—" He opened his mouth but the words wouldn't come. After a futile moment he made an eloquent gesture, suggestive of releasing a bird from between his hands. "No use. It's gone."

"Do you remember what happened to you?" I ventured to inquire.

"No." He lifted his eyes to mine, pleading. "Do *you* know what happened?"

"No," I told him truthfully. "Only that you were so badly damaged it's taken the Company this long to repair you. You don't suppose the Christians discovered you were a cyborg? Superstitious peasants and all that, jabbing pitchforks into your circuitry?"

"No!" He shook his head decisively. "I remember that much. They weren't a bad lot of mortals. I was quite fond of them."

I nodded, thinking that he was probably right. It would take a lot more than an angry mob to do what had been done to Literature Preservation Specialist Grade Three Lewis.

I let him rest while I hooked him up and ran a diagnostic on his conscious processes. A Literature drone! That was the strangest part of the mystery, to my way of thinking. He wasn't a Facilitator; he wasn't even an Anthropologist, and they were famous for throwing themselves into harm's way with mortals. Just some little Preserver chasing around after old manuscripts. How on earth had he managed to find himself in that much danger?

"There's storage space I can't access," I informed Lewis. "You may have memories in there, or you may have so much oatmeal. In any case, blocked or destroyed, we can't get at them just at the present time. Cheer up! If you feel up to it tomorrow, I'll take you to Level Three for some cautious exercise."

"Thank you," he said absently, staring up at the fresco again, as though the story of his lost time might be written there. "Victor," he added, giving me a brief courteous smile.

I went in search of Aegeus to make my report. To my astonishment, I located his signal in that sector of the compound reserved for the mortal servants.

My astonishment increased when, on emerging from the mountain, I found him seated in the mortal children's play garden, watching a pair of the little monkeys with evident amusement.

"Look at this, Victor." He chuckled, waving me closer. "Look. The boy's hopeless, but the girl's quite a charmer. As they go, of course."

I followed his gaze and was, quite frankly, appalled at what I saw. They couldn't have been more than five or six, but had evidently sustained some sort of abuse in their brief lives to date. Had they been rescued from a cellar? Their ghastly pallor, their emaciated appearance, their attenuated limbs in proportion to their swollen bellies and domed heads, all bespoke neglect. What had the poor things done to deserve such treatment?

The boy could never be made right. He had retreated from the sun to a nest of shade under a bush, and sat there rocking to and fro, silent, keeping his hands clapped tight over his eyes. Probable mental retardation, too—severe alopecia with only the barest traces of clumps of hair on his pale scalp.

The girl showed more promise, was even pretty in a terrible sort of way. Her hair was fine as floss and stood up like flames all over her head. She had picked a double handful of poppies and was playing some inexplicable game with them, sweeping them back and forth, crooning to herself in a thin voice. She might be mad; she might simply be a child absorbed in play. She had great pale blind-looking eyes, enormous eyes in her tiny weak face.

No, this was no abuse; some sort of chromosomal damage. Sad, but it happened amongst mortals. I couldn't fathom what these two imps of misfortune were doing at a Dr. Zeus base, however.

"Their names are Fallon and Maeve. I wanted you to see them, Victor," Aegeus told me.

Wanted me to see them? "Who rescued them?" I inquired, trying to keep the horror out of my voice. Aegeus turned to regard me.

"No one rescued them, my boy. They've spent their whole lives here, at Eurobase." He watched me closely to see what my reaction would be. Under the circumstances, frank honesty seemed advisable.

"Sir, I confess myself to be utterly baffled," I said, sitting down abruptly. My movement drew the little girl's attention—apparently she wasn't blind—and she came wafting toward us, waving her poppies our way. I found myself drawing back, hating the thought of her touching me, and felt prompt shame. "These are genetic defectives! Certainly not fit for the immortality process. They're useless even as servants. What are they doing here?"

"Genetic defectives," Aegeus repeated thoughtfully. "Yes, you'd think so, on first glance. And if I told you that they are, in fact, very far from being defective? That they represent a new and improved strain of *what they are*?"

"You'd confuse me even further."

"Good lad! You're learning never to lie to a superior. You've earned another morsel of knowledge reserved for Facilitators alone, Victor. Observe little Fallon. You're not seeing him at his best today—he doesn't care for the outdoors much—so I dare say you'd be rather surprised to see his playroom.

"Fallon has all manner of wonderful toys there. There's a clockwork galley full of tiny manikins who actually make its oars move. There's an orange tree in a pot, in whose branches blossoms burst forth, wither, and are replaced by fruit, which is small and green and then expands, only to wither and be replaced by buds once more—and all worked by a device so subtle it's beyond my comprehension. There's a camera obscura, though it seems to work in reverse somehow.

"Fallon doesn't play with his marvelous toys, you understand. He doesn't quite comprehend *play*. He made them."

"I see, sir," I said, thinking I did. "What might be called an idiot savant."

"Not at all." Aegeus held out his hands to Maeve, who had come to the edge of the grass and stopped there, pacing back and forth in her slow dance, trailing her flowers and watching him out of the corner of her eye. What a smile now lit her face, as she accepted his invitation and stepped forward, crossing some magic line that had forbidden her to venture onto the pavement until bid. The poppies fell, forgotten; she took Aegeus's hands in both her own and pressed her mouth into his palms, one kiss and then another kiss.

"Pretty Maeve shows such promise, I'm sure she'll be a great lady some day," Aegeus told her. "Shan't she? With so many fine clothes, and a garden full of flowers, and lovers and lovers to pick them for her. Maeve is so wise and good. Though she doesn't make clever toys like Fallon, does she?"

The tiny creature's expression changed at that. Her upper lip drew back from her teeth—they were barely visible, the faintest dots of pearl in her colorless mouth. I realized she was looking disdainful. Then she spoke, and I nearly jumped out of my skin.

"Fallon makes toys for *me*," she told us, in a voice like a silver flute.

"Does he indeed, my treasure?" said Aegeus.

"He does. I tell him, and he makes them. He will do anything if I tell him."

"You see how it is, Victor?" Aegeus patted her cheek fondly. "The little girl gives the orders, the little boy obeys them. If she took it into her sweet head to order him to fly, why, he would! He'd devise some brilliantly simple mechanism neither you nor I might have thought of in a thousand years, perfect and immortal creatures though we are. Isn't that so, pretty Maeve?"

But she'd lost interest in what he'd been saying; she was staring away enraptured at the pattern of sunlight and leaf shadows on the garden wall. Aegeus let go of her hands and she drifted away from us, lifting the hem of her gown as she went, her slow dance resumed. She found her way to the wall and danced for the shadows a while, and then fell to running her fingertips over the stones, tracing their pattern under the pattern of light and shadow.

"These aren't human children, are they?" I stated.

"Oddly enough, they are," Aegeus told me, watching Maeve. "Rather more human than you or I, my young friend, given what we are. Not a kind of human one sees often, however, in spite of the fact that they've always existed. Certainly not *Homo sapiens sapiens*. These creatures are on the order of hybrids, actually. I believe the designation that's been decided on is *Homo sapiens umbratilis*."

Man of the shadows? I'd have been fascinated, were I not so repelled.

"We got the genetic material in Ireland," Aegeus explained. "Ten years ago. A distress call came in from a disabled operative, in a place called Malinmhor. We went in to pick him up for repair, and what a mess we found!"

"Lewis?"

Aegeus nodded. "So badly wrecked he'd been unable to help himself. The local monks had had to rescue him, for heaven's sake. The burning question of the hour, of course, was: who on earth could have done such damage to one of *us*?

"We made it our business to find out pretty damned quickly, as you can imagine. It seemed the holy monks weren't the only mortals who had a community at Malinmhor! There were creatures living in a warren nearby. Some sort of fantastically inbred mortal family, as near as we could tell. Quite subhuman, stunted physically and emotionally. Their brains were so far from normal that ordinary solutions to problems were quite beyond them, but they'd developed a remarkably sophisticated technology to compensate.

"And they knew about us." Aegeus smiled. "At least, they had created a disrupter field to protect themselves against cyborgs. Lewis blundered into it when he ventured inside their hill with one of the monks. Bad luck for him, but not necessarily for us."

"I see, sir," I exclaimed. "He led us to an exploitable resource!"

"Precisely," said Aegeus, smiling. "You've got an Executive's grasp of the situation, I'm pleased to observe. Waste nothing! Though of course we had to wipe them out. No one damages Company property, even a lowly Preserver, with impunity. But we helped ourselves to their genetic material first, and then we set a grand breeding experiment in motion."

A grossly illegal one, but it certainly wasn't my place to say so. We Facilitators are frequently obliged to weigh the greater good against mere regulations, or so it had been explained to me.

"The first pair we got died, poor little things. I think we very nearly have the mix right now. *Sapiens* enough to communicate with—Maeve at least—and *umbratilis* enough to provide us with certain opportunities. And what's that proverb—? 'Keep your friends close, but your enemies closer'? Look at this, Victor, look what she can do."

Aegeus pointed at the girl, who had turned to the boy and fixed him with an imperious stare. Though he could not have seen her—he had his hands still pressed to his eyes—he turned in her direction like a blind worm. Slowly, clumsily, he got to his feet and came to her side, groping with his hands out before him, keeping his eyes tight shut and his head turned from the sun. He looked like a new-hatched bird, with his pinched face and sealed eyelids.

Impatient with his slow advance, she seized his hand and yanked him closer. He stumbled forward and bumped his head against the wall. She paid that no notice, but pressed his fingertips to the stones, trying to make him feel the pattern as she had done. No use; he opened his virtually toothless mouth and wailed, and I was startled to hear the quite human-sounding crying of a hurt child.

"Oh, dear, he's bumped his little head. Let him alone, now, Maeve, beauty," said Aegeus. He went to them and picked up the boy, who curled into his shoulder to hide his face. Something about his movement was horribly like a grub burying itself in earth. "Poor Fallon. He needs to go back inside. Come along, pretty girl."

Maeve had been staring blankly at us, but as soon as Aegeus extended his hand she took it, smiling. He walked away, leading her and carrying the boy, for all the world like a loving father and his two children. I followed after a moment, thoroughly unnerved.

"You've taken this very well, young Victor," Aegeus told me. "No less than I'd have expected of you, however. You understand that this is all highly classified?"

"Of course, sir."

"Of course. Now, having said that—" Aegeus gave me a shrewd look over Fallon's bowed head. "Just how much does the unfortunate Lewis remember about his accident?"

"Almost nothing, sir," I replied.

"Very good," said Aegeus. "*Very* good."

I need hardly say that I was tremendously flattered at being made party to such secrets, though I had bad dreams that night, and for many others, wherein dreadful pale children came and stood beside my bed. Aegeus must be grooming me for some powerful inner cabal, surely! I decided to curl my mustaches after all, when they grew in sufficiently.

"Good morning, Lewis." I announced myself after peering around the frame of the door to be certain he was awake. He was indeed; he'd pushed back a tray of half-finished breakfast and was staring fixedly at an access code plaquette. I could see the flashing green letters reflecting in his eyes as he integrated at high speed. "Catching up on current events, are you? I trust you slept well?"

"Yes, thank you." Lewis shut off the flow of codes and looked up at me. "Victor. No problem with new memories! I don't suppose you've been able to learn anything?"

Nothing I had any intention of telling him about. I smiled apologetically and held out the clothes. "What about a bit of fresh air and exercise?"

"That's a splendid idea," he said with genuine enthusiasm, and climbed out of bed and dressed himself without further prompting from me. Wasn't he game? Just the sort of mild-mannered chap to obey all Company directives. A good fellow, but nothing more than a Preserver, after all.

"I wonder if it might be possible to interview the rescue team that brought me in?" he inquired as we made our way up to Level Three.

"Not a bad idea," I conceded. "Of course, it's been ten years; I should think it might take a while to track them all down. Now, we'll start you on the Cletes Reflexive at primary speed, if you feel up to it."

"By all means," he said as we stepped out of the lift, so readily I wondered if he remembered what the Cletes Reflexive was.

The testing ground wouldn't give him any clue, if he'd forgotten. It looked like a pleasant formal garden laid out within an immense greenhouse, with flowers and statuary, fountains and paths. It was barricaded with iron bars to a height of fifteen feet all around, and locked securely; but nearly every year some foolish mortal servant trespassed, to his brief regret.

I pressed my palm to the via plate and the gate swung open. Lewis and I stepped in upon the square of white paving where the Reflexive began. "You're quite comfortable with this, old fellow?" I questioned. To my eyes he looked rather nervous, but he grinned and flexed his arms.

"Can't wait! Set 'em up."

So I reached into the top of the hollow post that rose from the pavement, and set the speed at primary. There was a click and the faintest humming noise, quite inaudible I suppose to a mortal. Lewis cleared his throat.

"Let's see, shall I give my memory a test, too? Something from Homer, I think." Lewis stepped out into the gravel pathway and proceeded along it warily as he recited:

" 'Ogygia is an island lying far out at sea, where the daughter of Atlas dwells—' " He sprang aside neatly as a spear came hurtling up through the gravel, sure impalement for anyone with duller senses. He paced on. " '—crafty Calypso, a fair-haired, powerful goddess. Her no one visits, neither god—' " He ducked, avoiding the discus-bearing bronze that spun on its base to strike at him. " '—nor mortal man; but hapless me some heavenly power brought to her hearth, and all alone—' " He leaped from the path and balanced along a row of iron spear-points set beside the way, swift and sure from point to point, a painful walk but the only alternative to treading on the mines concealed on that section of the path. " '—for Zeus with a gleaming bolt smote my swift ship—' " Springing nimbly down he threw himself flat on the path, narrowly avoiding the steel dart a frowning god spat at him. " '—and wrecked it in the middle of the wine-dark sea!' "

He crawled the next few meters, for golden flowers on either side of the path tilted their trumpet-throats and sent jets of acid arching clean across. As he crawled, he continued indefatigably: " 'There all the rest of my good comrades perished, but I myself caught in my arms the keel of my curved ship—' " He scrambled to his feet as soon as it was safe, and dodged the stone post that came bashing across the path. " '—and drifted for nine days.' "

An espaliered tree let fall a little crimson fruit, which rolled down the embankment to fall at his feet. He snatched it up and flung it from him, reciting: " 'Upon the tenth, in the dark night—' " There was a bright flash and detonation from the far end of the greenhouse. " '—gods brought me to the island of Ogygia, where dwells Calypso—' " He paused at the edge of the pretty meandering stream, just long enough to crouch and spring into the air, some ten feet above the inviting stepping-stones. From the shadowy water beneath them great eels darted up in frustration, following Lewis with their dead eyes.

He landed safely on the opposite bank and went on: " '—the fair-haired, powerful goddess. Receiving me, she loved and cherished me—' " He began to sprint now, past the inviting bench that would have tipped him backward into a pit. " 'And often said that she would make me an immortal—' " Whirling automata rose from the lilies beside the path, armored figures bearing razor-edged scythes, and the last ten meters of his journey were an intricate dance at tremendous speed through their zone of hazard. " '—young forever!' " Unshredded, he somersaulted through the air and landed beside me again.

"Not bad," I told him, comparing his time to the optimum score. "Care to try it again on intermediate?"

He improved time on the second round, giving me some of the *Elder Edda,* and went on to advanced with a bit of second-rate stuff by Ausonius.

"Though frankly Ausonius is rather second-rate at his best," Lewis admitted, crashing to the pavement as he completed the third round. "Nice enough fellow, as I remember, but the muses kept their distance."

"You remember Ausonius?" I inquired, unlocking the gate.

"Yes! Quite clearly. Beautiful estate in Gaul. He quite knew how to entertain a guest, even if he couldn't write an original line to save his life." Lewis followed me out and I led him down the hall to the sauna. "I remember Ausonius, I remember everything. *Except what happened in Ireland.* Didn't the Company send in investigators? In ten years I'd have thought they'd have found out something, talked to people at least. I remember monks and nuns they might have interviewed—"

His questions were certainly good ones, just what I'd have been asking myself if by some unthinkable chance I were in his position. A distraction was in order . . . I watched his face sidelong as we passed the door to the gymnasium baths and kept going.

"Excuse me, but wasn't that the door we wanted?" He pointed back along the hall, slight panic in his eyes. Was this another hole in his memory? I grinned and threw open the door to the executive baths.

"Well, old man, if you like—but I thought you'd enjoy a bit of rarefied atmosphere, after what you've been through." I strutted into the deluxe bathing accommodations reserved for Facilitators and their guests. Lewis stepped across the threshold after me and stared.

"I don't remember this," he said, taking in the bathing grotto with its elaborate mosaics in porphyry, in gold and semiprecious stones. The attendant mortals hurried forward to disrobe us—I suppose they got rather bored in there all day, with so few of us to wait on—and in short order we were being steamed, splashed, and scrubbed with fragrant oils. For some little while there was no conversation other than groans of pleasure. I couldn't imagine a drone got an experience like this very often, and Lewis certainly seemed to be enjoying it to the fullest.

Though he did look over at me during our third soak in perfumed waters, when the servants had temporarily retired for fresh towels, and murmured: "Please understand that I don't want to complain, but—is this really appropriate? Having mortals wait on us this way?"

"They're enjoying it!" I scoffed. "Can you imagine what they'd be doing if they weren't working here? Starving, most likely. Scratching out a living on miserable little stony farms and dying young."

"I suppose so," Lewis agreed reluctantly. "But, you know, it never used to be the policy—we're their servants, really, not the other way around."

"Exactly, and we work a good deal harder for them than they do for us," I explained to him, as though he weren't my senior by a good four centuries. But I outranked him, you see, and I thought that gave me insights that might never have occurred to one of his class. Yet I was merely parroting Aegeus as I went on: "After all, our lives are dedicated to preserving the best of their world for them, all their art and literature, and occasionally even their wretched mortal selves. Don't we deserve a little luxury?"

"This is rather a lot of luxury," Lewis observed, as the fresh scrubbing team came on duty: a pair of mortal girls, identical twins, looking flushed and lovely in exceedingly brief cotton tunics. Aegeus had personally selected them for the sauna, and I couldn't resist a smirk as Lewis's eyes widened at the effect.

"I think, on the whole, that this old place has seen some distinct improvements during Aegeus's administration," I said judiciously, looking up one brief tunic as my maiden came to swathe me in a towel and lead me to the massage table. "Worked wonders, hasn't he? Took a great rambling old training compound, and transformed it with grace notes for all the senses."

But Lewis wasn't listening, had actually engaged his girl in conversation, *in her own language.*

"You don't mind this work, child?" he wanted to know!

"I know nothing but happiness, my lord," she replied in the hushed tones the mortals were encouraged to use. But she dimpled at him, and I had the jealous fancy that Lewis got the pleasanter and more thorough massage that afternoon. There was just possibly a bit of edge to my voice when I inquired, as we went on after we'd been dressed: "Does any of this seem to have helped your memory?"

"Not much, I'm afraid." Lewis looked apologetic. "I've been in awe. This is all quite a contrast to what I remember of Ireland."

"Well, you were out in the freezing peat bogs, among monks," I pointed out. "Living in cells like flint beehives! No wonder this place—" But he had stopped, staring at me, or through me, with a haunted expression.

"Beehives, yes," he muttered. "Hives. Termite mounds. Oh, what was it? The brothers in their hives and the . . . damn, damn, damn. *Something* almost in my mind. I can't get it clear."

"That's bound to be a good sign," I said encouragingly, making a mental note to go straight to Aegeus. "Perhaps your access channels are attempting to reroute."

I changed the subject and saw him to his room, where I left him, promising to return next day for a stroll around the perimeter of the grounds.

Aegeus's private rooms were what one would expect of the brilliant and sophisticated administrator that he was, magnificently furnished. Clearly, becoming an administrator was the goal to be striven for.

Mere field personnel seldom acquired enough personal possessions to adorn a private retreat, and even if they did, they were generally on the move so much it was scarcely worth getting them out of storage. Might I have a classic bronze like that one day, or that fine Samian ware at just such a table, with its carved griffin-legs? To say nothing of that wardrobe!

"Sir." I inclined in the informal bow that was appropriate for the occasion.

"Victor." He waved me in, looking up from his desk. "Sit, please, sit. Tell me how the poor Literature drone is coming along. Any sign of his memory coming back?"

"I'm afraid something seems to be surfacing," I answered.

"Really? What a shame." Aegeus reached for his penknife and began to cut a new quill thoughtfully, slicing away at the shaft with sharp, precise strokes. "Something to do with the programming the Literature operatives get, I suppose. His brain won't stop trying to tell the story . . . and sooner or later he'll access the file where we locked it away."

I felt a slight chill at this, but tried to sound every inch the competent underling as I said with assurance: "I'll simply see to it that he never manages, sir."

Aegeus kept his eyes on the pen he was cutting.

"Will you? Good lad. You'll find what you need in here." He gestured with his knife at a tiny box next to his inkwell, a lovely thing, a miniature chest banded with silver and semiprecious stones. I reached forward and lifted its lid. There was nothing inside but a sealed phial of opaque glass. Drawing it out, I said: "And this would be . . . ?"

Aegeus frowned at his pen. "Something to wipe his memory again, of course. Derived from Theobromos, if you must know! You'll administer it at the first sign of trouble. He may resist; you'll do whatever's necessary."

I sat there speechless a moment. Aegeus lifted his eyes to mine.

"You have qualms? Natural enough. It must seem perilously close to what the mortal monkeys do to one another."

He was correct, though I'd never have said so much aloud, and there was still more: I had been taught, always, that our immortal brains are perfect and inviolable. The mortal *soul* is an illusion, but our eternal consciousness is surely its nearest approximation. That the Company would force one of us to give up some part of himself . . . The horror must have been evident in my face. Aegeus leaned forward and spoke in a low voice.

"Now, young man, we'll see what you're made of. You've been shown something classified, and you understand its importance to the Company. You've had ample opportunity to observe what a comparative nonentity is Literature Preservation Specialist Lewis. You've been given a task, an unpleasant one certainly, but undeniably necessary, and well within your abilities. So much depends on what you do next, young Victor."

He waved his pen in a general sort of way at the splendid room wherein we sat. "A future like mine, in rooms like these, isn't that what you'd like? It's certainly what the Company has had in mind for you, ever since that bright day when your aptitude testing indicated you were Executive material. I can't think for a minute you've any intention of throwing away that future. You weren't given immortal life to spend it down there wading in muck amongst the mortals. That's for talentless little Preserver drones—who'll never miss a memory they'd only find disturbing, after all."

"I shall manage the matter to your satisfaction, sir," I assured Aegeus. He smiled.

"See that you do," he told me.

———

"I thought we'd go more easily today," I informed Lewis next morning. "Just the stroll around the grounds, and then another session in the baths, eh?"

"Yes, thanks." Lewis accepted the fine cloak I'd brought for him—even in summer, the Cévennes can be chilly—and followed me down the hall with alacrity. "I woke up this morning and realized I'd been dreaming of sunlight, and that was when it occurred to me I haven't seen it in ten years! It feels positively unnatural. Do I look pale?"

"Not at all," I said tactfully. We climbed the staircase to the exterior portal and I activated the panel. A moment later we stepped out onto the mountainside, to a wide view of heath and stony ranges. Lewis's face brightened at once. He drew in a deep breath of air. "You're a nature enthusiast, I gather?" I said.

"Not particularly," he admitted. "But even the middle of nowhere has a certain savor, when you've been out of commission as long as I have. Look at this! Rabbit tracks. Birds. Smoke at fifteen kilometers—that's a village of mortals, isn't it? It's, let's see, it's early summer—they're haymaking down there, can you smell it? And there are cattle pastured over there, somewhere, and I can smell apple orchards. Chestnut trees. Ah!" He rubbed his hands together and started forward, his cloak trailing after him through the brush. I followed dubiously.

"We ought to go no farther than the perimeter," I said. "I thought we'd walk along the edge to the gate and go back in through the quadrangle. There are some really exquisite pleasure gardens concealed back here—"

"Oh, by all means." Lewis stopped and allowed me to take the lead. "I'd love to see a fountain again. Never in my life imagined I could be so hungry for sheer sensation! Do you suppose we can arrange to go out tonight? What on earth will the stars look like to me now?"

"Do things really seem so different?" I asked, eyeing him as he strode along beside me. He looked different in the sunlight, certainly. His pale features had lit up with warmth and color, his eyes shone.

"Yes, absolutely," he told me. "It must be the near-death experience. You wouldn't have any idea how long it'll be before I'm given another posting, would you?"

"The Company will want to be sure you've fully recovered," I told him, rather peevishly, because we had just come to the pavilion gate and he was failing to react to the grand spectacle of the pleasure gardens. But he was only a drone, after all, wasn't he? "I should think you'd be in no hurry to go back down there. Not when you've got the run of all this."

I waved an arm at the expanse of perfect lawn, the fragrant stepped terraces of flowers arranged in subtle gradations of height and shade, white through cream pink through deepest rose, the trees artfully clipped and trained to render each one the flawless expression of an artist's conception of a tree. And Lewis was old enough to remember the classical world, and so surely he could appreciate the statuary that rose in graceful postures here and there! Extravagant passion in tones of snow, masterworks by Praxiteles that had never known defacement by mortal vandals, having been bought new from the master himself and shipped straight here to this garden *from his studio.* Really, what drab mortal place could compare?

Lewis hastened into the garden after me then, and made a point of exclaiming over everything I showed him. But why on Earth should I have tried to impress him? Why should I have any regard for the opinions of a miserable little scuttler after scrolls and codices? Did I need further proof he was beneath my concern, when the poor fool was eager to go down amongst the monkeys again and resume his work? Bargaining with savages for their inky and imperfect knowledge!

As Lewis was widening his eyes in polite appreciation of a particularly fine group representing the Three Graces honoring some dictator or other, I had a sudden inspiration.

"Of course, this is nothing, compared with the library," I remarked casually.

"Splendid collection," Lewis agreed. "I remember it well."

"Ah, but not the New Wing, I don't think," I told him slyly. "There have been some improvements in recent years. You'll remember the old electronic stuff, I dare say. Aegeus has made a few interesting acquisitions for us. Would you care for a look at the originals of Aristotle's *Treatises*?"

Yes! Now I'd got his attention. Lewis turned around to stare at me in such haste he nearly tottered on his long cloak.

"The originals?" he gasped. "You're never talking about the books Theophrastus left to Neleus? The ones Faustus sold to pay his gambling debts?"

"The very same," I told him smugly. "The complete set, I need hardly add. They were in wretched shape, of course, but we've had them restored—perhaps you'd like to give us your opinion of the job we've done?"

"I should say I would," Lewis cried, and nearly raced me the whole way to the library.

I was gratified to watch his astonishment, confronted with

Aegeus's work. The library that Lewis remembered was a rather chilly place, dull banks of electronic storage with a few plain work terminals and interface consoles. Not a cozy room, or one that invited lingering.

Ah, but Aegeus's new wing opened out of the old like a blossom out of a dry gray stem. Through paneled doors one stepped into the beautifully climate-controlled chamber beyond, jewel-toned, richly carpeted and indirectly lit, hung with tapestries that Aegeus had had specially commissioned by masters, celebrating the literary glory of the classical world. There were plenty of inviting little nooks, well cushioned, in which one might curl up with a scroll some Preserver like Lewis had snatched from the conflagration of time. There were graceful Roman bronzes depicting the Nine Muses ranged along the wall of terminals and consoles, where one could pull information out of the depths of the sea-blue screens like a supplicant coaxing an oracle to speak.

But it was the wide glass case along the eastern wall that was the glory. Safely displayed there were the treasured texts, works known to mortal scholars only by paraphrase, but possessed by us in their entirety! The complete poems of Archilochus and of Sappho, all one hundred twenty-three plays of Sophocles (mortals had been able to keep only seven!), Theophrastus's *General History of Science* and—the very jewel in the crown—the complete works of Aristotle himself, the lost manuscripts that had passed through so many tragicomical adventures before disappearing from mortal ken forever in a cheap little shop in first-century Rome.

Lewis stood staring, taking in the beauty, the elegance, the rarity. Inexorably he was drawn to the cabinet at last, as though it were exerting a magnetic force. There he pressed his palms against the glass and looked down at what was, after all, just so much brittle old paper.

"Oh," he said quietly. Good gods, I thought to myself, is the man crying?

A mortal servant had risen to his feet, and came close now with an inquiring look. I turned and crooked a finger at him.

"Fetch up a siphon and some of the thirty-year-old single malt, if you please. Or—no! Let's have wine for the occasion. I think a bottle of Falernian would be appropriate, don't you? Or perhaps Valpolicella?" But Lewis wasn't listening to me. "Bring both," I told the servant, who bowed and sped away in silence.

I am afraid I was swaggering, as I joined him at the cabinet and entered the code to unlock it. "Shall we see what the old boy had to say?" I suggested.

"Oh, but they're nearly a thousand years old," Lewis gasped, actually wiping away a tear. "We shouldn't, really—"

"Nonsense. They've been stabilized long since. Here we go!" I drew out one of the nasty old things and unrolled it on the reading table for his perusal, under the soft light of a shaded lamp. He bent over it like some priest over an altar, biting his knuckles.

"Rather a nice prize, wouldn't you say?" I said smugly. "This was Hieron's work—have you met him? Very good man in your line, handles the Mediterranean acquisitions."

"Oh, how I wish I'd been stationed down there," Lewis moaned, finally giving in to irresistible impulse and reaching out to touch the scroll. "Look at this. Aristotle's observations on Egyptian technology!" He began to read avidly, and I realized I'd lost my audience again. I sank back onto one of the couches to wait impatiently until the mortal returned bearing our wine.

I sampled both carafes and decided on the Valpolicella. At my nod, the servant filled our cups. Lewis was too immersed in the scroll to notice. He chuckled suddenly and read aloud, in the original Greek:

" 'This art of flight is said to have been present in Egypt from the time of Horus, and I am assured that the priests conceal detailed charts for travel between the stars, which the kings of the former time steered between as mere men followed the course of the river; though none now have understanding of the sacred texts.' " Lewis looked up, grinning, and noticed the servant standing there offering him a cup of wine. In fact, the mortal had been rather craning his head to read over Lewis's shoulder. When he noticed this, what should Lewis do but step aside with a gesture of invitation!

"Please, it's hilarious," he said, smiling. "Do you read Greek?"

"Oh, yes, my lord," the mortal replied, hastening to peer at the scroll.

"Then you'll appreciate the joke. Though you've probably seen it a dozen times!" Lewis looked wistful. "I can't tell you how much I envy you, working here. I'd just start at one end of the case and read my way through."

The mortal looked up a little nervously. "Well—I would, my lord, if I were allowed to open the case."

Lewis's jaw dropped. "You mean you can't?"

"Of course he can't," I told Lewis crossly, sipping my wine. "None of the mortals have clearance to handle anything this valuable. They're *mortals*, after all. Left to themselves, they ruin anything they touch. Isn't that so?" I demanded of the servant. He lowered his eyes and murmured:

"Unfortunately so, my lord."

Lewis stood there speechless a moment before he drew himself up and set his chin. "But Aristotle himself was a mortal," he told the servant! "I think you can be trusted to read this text a little while, don't you, without tearing it or chewing on it?"

"I would never do such a thing, my lord," the servant assured him. "I was trained in library science."

"Well then." Lewis pulled out a chair for him. "Please, sit and read."

I'm not certain who was more shocked, the servant or myself; but after a frozen moment the mortal hastened to obey, as Lewis took his wine and carried it to the cushions next to mine. His eyes were angry.

I must protest against this policy, he transmitted in silence. *Why shouldn't they be allowed to read their own books? Aren't we preserving these things for THEM, after all?*

Old fellow, you must understand, I replied as casually as I could. *He's a good enough creature—and one of ours, of course—but you've been down among them yourself. You know the villainy of which they're capable. Destructive little Barbary apes for the most part, and human intelligence only makes them worse. How many libraries have you seen burned in your time?*

But the mortals built the libraries, too, argued Lewis, sipping his wine. I was at least pleased to note that he stopped and inhaled the bouquet before taking another, more appreciative sip. *It takes thousands of them to create an archive of human wisdom; only one to set a torch to it. Wouldn't you have to say, then, that the work of the librarians is more typical of mortal behavior than the work of the arsonist?*

I really didn't know what to say. This was absolutely the last sort of talk I'd expect to hear coming from someone who'd nearly been murdered by the little brutes.

Well, you've known more of them than I have, I conceded. *Doubtless you've some insight I lack. I wouldn't want to leave even that one alone with the scroll, though. What do you want to bet he'd slip out of here and run down the mountain with it, if there were no alarms? He knows it's valuable. He'd sell it in a second if he had the chance.*

Lewis shook his head impatiently. *You don't understand. We all know why they're driven to thievery. But I can tell you from experience that mortals love their literature. When I was in Ireland, Eogan—*

"Eogan," Lewis cried aloud. "That was his name! That was the monk I was working with—and the abbess sent us out to the hollow hill, after the fair folk. I thought it was all absurd, I had no idea—" He turned to me. "I'm accessing the blocked files now. We'll have to find Eogan, if he's still alive. He was there with me, we went into the hill and actually found them—and—he got me out afterward, when they . . ." He fell silent. Cold sweat broke out on his brow. The glass vial was in my hand, unseen.

"Perhaps you'd better not—" I began, when all hell broke loose, and from a completely unexpected quarter.

A section of wall to my left began to move. Seeing it out of the corner of my eye, I thought it was a draft moving the tapestry at first; then I realized that the tapestry wasn't there any more, or at least that part of it wasn't. A rather titillating depiction of Sappho and her companions had vanished in a pattern of light, and the edges all around it curled up. For a moment one could glimpse the plaster of the wall behind, illuminated by the same pattern of light, as though the wall were outdoors and slanting beams of sunlight were playing through leaf-shadows on it. There came a rumbling like far-off thunder.

Then the plaster had gone, and one saw the stone and mortar underneath. Then it all dissolved, like mist, and two small figures came walking through. The girl strode confidently, the boy groped hesitantly after, though his great blank eyes were open now. They were both naked.

To be precise, this was the actual moment when pandemonium erupted. Lewis leaped to his feet. The girl looked down, noticed that she was naked, and screamed shrilly. The mortal servant caught up the volume of Aristotle, and ran for the cabinet with it. Only after he'd thrust it inside and shut the cabinet did he take to his heels in the direction of the door, nearly bowling over Aegeus, who was entering in some haste.

"My dress," Maeve shrieked. "My pretty dress! You stupid, *stupid* Fallon!"

She flew at the boy and began to beat him with her tiny fists. He dropped the exceedingly odd device he had been carrying and cringed, putting up his hands to protect his head.

"Not supposed to make my dress go away," Maeve wept. "Just the wall! You bad boy, bad boy!"

"Now, now," exhorted Aegeus, bearing down on them. "Naughty Maeve! Look, you've drawn blood on poor Fallon. Stop this at once." He caught her hands. "It's bad to go out of your room without asking. You've been told and told! It's bad to hurt Fallon, too. You know he was only trying to make you happy."

"But he lost my pretty dress," wailed the child.

"Silly girl, we'll get you another," Aegeus assured her. "Twice as nice and ten times as pretty, shall we? Sweet little Maeve." He lifted her in his arms.

She sniffled and nodded, subsiding, and Aegeus now had leisure to notice Lewis.

Lewis hadn't made a sound, but had backed up as far as he could go and was flattened against the cabinets, as though Aristotle and Theophrastus would somehow protect him. He couldn't take his horrified eyes off the children. Aegeus considered him coldly. The hair stood on the back of my neck as though I were a mortal creature, I couldn't have told you why. But—

"Oh, dear," was all Aegeus said.

Lewis lifted his gaze to Aegeus. He no longer looked frightened. There was wrath in his face, and bleak understanding. He said, very quietly: "What have you done?"

"Poor Lewis," said Aegeus. "You've remembered a great deal too much, haven't you? And now you'll have bad dreams again, when we've worked so hard to make them go away." He sighed heavily and looked at me. "Victor, Lewis has had a nasty shock. Fix him a drink."

No need to tell me twice. I poured out another cup of Valpolicella, dispensing the vial's contents into it with a gesture so clumsily concealed Lewis had surely noticed, had he been able to pay attention to anything but the two horrible children and their protector. I brought the cup to him. Not even looking at it, he raised it to his lips and gulped the wine down.

He didn't bother to scan first. Why should he? He was among his own people, wasn't he? Safe on a Company base, not amongst savages.

He set down the cup and looked across at Aegeus again, saying in tones of accusation—unbelievable nerve, to *Aegeus!*—"They're hybrids, aren't they? This is forbidden!"

Aegeus didn't bother to reply, but the coldness in his face set and froze. Lewis looked down at the boy curled into himself on the floor, at the girl who had forgotten her anger and was staring, fascinated, at the Roman bronzes. She pointed imperiously.

"Fallon," she ordered, "make them dance for me."

Opening his eyes, wide and liquid as a rabbit's, the boy got painfully to his hands and knees.

"Poor things," Lewis gasped. "They don't know what you—"

Then he stiffened and turned to me, terrible question in his eyes. I braced myself, expecting an assault; but he staggered forward and fell, and lay like something discarded on the fine deep carpet.

"Pity," said Aegeus. "Now we've got it all to do again, I suppose."

"I thought—" I stared down at Lewis, who was neither moving nor, so far as I could tell, breathing. "I thought we were simply going to block his memory again."

"To be sure. He's got to be deactivated first, you see?" Aegeus turned Maeve's face to his own. "Leave the old statues alone, dear."

"Yes, sir," I found myself saying. "What will happen to him now?"

"Oh, back to the tank, for further erasure." Aegeus stepped forward and looked down at Lewis's sprawled body critically. "I wonder how much we'll have to obliterate this time. I must take greater care my little monkeys stay in their cage, in future." He said this teasingly to Maeve, who dimpled. "Pretty Maeve, can you make Fallon build you something to take away bad dreams? This poor fellow has such bad dreams. You'd like to help him, wouldn't you?"

"No," she said impishly. "I want a new dress." Aegeus laughed at that and she laughed, too, like the tiniest silver bell. The boy was still crawling toward the Roman bronzes, staring up at them with his enormous black eyes.

Labienus turns the page. The next section is a transcript of an interview, one of his own private intelligence forays. What a wreck the old mortal had been, knotted with age, what an old mud-colored thing with his white hair and his network of wrinkles! Unsettlingly like a chimpanzee. He'd had all his wits about him, at least.

I will tell you about Maeve.

Me, you wouldn't be interested in, for there is nothing extraordinary about my life. My mother had been shamed, was about to drown herself in the Loire when one of the immortal lords spotted her and offered her his protection. This was just before Justinian became emperor of Byzantium, I think, in the time the mortal men reckoned the sixth century after the birth of Christ.

But my mother's savior was about the usual business of the immortals who work for their Company, which is to walk among mortals and preserve fine and rare things that would otherwise be destroyed by them. The lords and ladies do this, as I understand, because there will come a day in the distant future when men will need the things they have wasted. In that hour the Company will be able to open its strongholds and come to mankind's rescue, showering down its harvest of their treasures. Who could find fault with such benign masters? Especially as their mercy does not extend to things alone; they save people, too.

Anyway, the mortal girl came with the lord to this mountain, to this ancient stronghold that the immortals call Eurobase One: and some weeks later she died giving birth to me, for she was not strong.

I was strong, but I was not perfect as a child must be perfect to be given eternal life. They were very kind to me anyway, the immortal lords and ladies. I've never lacked anything, never gone hungry a day in my life! I was lucky that I could live with them, and not with the ignorant savages in the mortal world down the mountain.

And they gave some thought to my future, too: I was apprenticed to old Claude, who was an artist, a genius, master of gardens without peer. The lords and ladies themselves said it was a thousand pities he couldn't be made immortal, but mortal and aging he was. So I was given to him, to climb the high ladders and prune where he directed, and to kneel for hours on the cold earth, planting out hyacinth bulbs where he pointed with his stick. He taught me his art. I was very grateful.

But I don't know where Maeve came from.

I was sixteen when I saw her first, the little creature with the hair like moonlight. She had got into the pergola somehow, though the gate was locked, and she had tugged her feeble brother after her. They were in there making a mess of the pomegranates, pulling them from the espaliers, bowling them around and breaking them open, scattering the red beads without even tasting them. It was their tiny crazy laughter that called us.

Old Claude was so angry with them, he lost all sense; he was especially proud of those trees. He advanced on them howling curses, waving his stick. The children stopped, staring at him, but they did not run as sensible children would. The boy cowered and sank down, hiding his face, covering his big blind-looking eyes. The girl remained on her feet. She looked at Claude with no fear at all, though his stick was whistling in the air and his eyes were starting out of his head in wrath.

He kept coming, and when I saw that she would not move I ran to put myself between them. I crouched over her and Claude's stick came whistling down on my back. That only made him more angry, and he beat me with all the strength of his old arm. I didn't mind; I have a strong back. I said, "Master, the little girl is mad! She didn't know it was wrong."

I was mistaken to think this would make him stop belaboring me, because he got in three more good blows before we heard one of the lords laughing.

"Stop! Stop, if you please, worthy Master Claude," he called, striding down the walk toward us.

It was the lord Aegeus, still chuckling as he surveyed the ruin all about us, the broken branches, broken fruit. The child ran to him and buried her face in his cloak, and he swept her up in his arms, where she looked at us disdainfully.

I knelt at once, but Claude remained on his feet. He took liberties; the lords and ladies allowed it because he was an artist. His back was stiff with his anger. His jowls were flushed red with it. He clasped his shaking hands on the knob of his stick and stared at Lord Aegeus in silence, so that the lord had to speak first.

"Worthy master, my apologies," said the lord, smiling. He knit his brows at the little girl, pretending to be stern with her. He said, "Naughty Maeve! Look what you've done now. Did *you* spoil this pretty garden?"

And she said, "Oh, no!" though her tiny hands were pink with the juice, and that was the only color to her skin anywhere. She looked like a ghost, she was so white.

Claude made a sharp noise in his throat. I looked over at the little boy, who was still trembling where he lay.

The lord said, "You didn't? Who was it, then?" And she pointed her finger at the boy and said, "It was Fallon!"

The lord looked as though he wanted to laugh afresh, but he bit his lips and then he said: "Now, you know that's not true. Poor Fallon doesn't do things unless you tell him to do them. You're the one always getting into mischief, little fairy! I want you to apologize to our dear Master Claude for all this mess."

She dimpled and said, "No!" and Claude shouted: "Most divine Lord, never in seventy-five years of faithful service have I seen such wanton vandalism!" and Lord Aegeus looked at him rather coldly as he said: "Sadly true, Master, for everyone knows the young people of today have no respect for their elders. I can assure you that this child will not misbehave here again, however. Calm yourself! Your boy will clean everything up." And his gaze turned to me and he said, "Rise, boy. And, please, accept my thanks for moving so quickly! My poor cherubs would have broken like eggshell if your master had landed a blow."

I rose awkwardly and ducked my head in acknowledgment of the lord's thanks. I wondered, how could they be his children? The lords and ladies do not beget their own kind, I knew that. They take mortal children and give them immortal life, if the children are sufficiently perfect. But the girl and boy did not look like any mortal children I had ever seen. They were so little and pale, and their eyes were so big.

Anyway Lord Aegeus carried them away, and I cleaned up the mess they'd made.

I saw her sometimes now and then, over the next few years. Sometimes the boy would be with her, though less and less as time went on.

There were rumors that he was a genius of some kind, but he never looked well.

She grew up very quickly, and not in the way of being tall, if you know what I mean; she looked like a woman within a few years, with high little breasts filling out the bodice of her gown. She would wade through the beds of annuals picking big bunches of flowers, which drove Claude to distraction, but now that he was aware she was a special favorite of Lord Aegeus he knew better than to complain.

Maybe it was keeping his anger to himself that did for him at last, because he had a stroke when I was twenty. After that I was Head Gardener, and won the title of Master when I devised the three-level topiary walk for the north slope.

The lords and ladies were enchanted with it. They love beautiful things, and they respect artists. Master Simeon by the age of twenty-two! I had all I could ask for in life.

And then I was given more.

When I was summoned to Lord Aegeus's study, I thought he had some request to make relative to my art, maybe for a new kind of rose or rare fruit. They like such things, the lords and ladies. Lord Aegeus was seated by the fire in his study, and across from him in another chair sat his assistant, the lord Victor. Lord Victor was young as immortals go, not really much older than me, and he looked younger already.

Well, they waved me to a third chair. I sat hesitantly, and another mortal stepped forward and poured wine for me, the same wine the lords themselves were drinking. I thought to myself, *This is what it is to be an artist!* and I bowed respectfully over my cup and said, "Thank you, divine Lord."

Lord Aegeus said, "Quite welcome," with a wave of dismissal. He was staring at me in an assessing kind of way, and so was the other lord. I kept a humble silence, as Claude had kept his insolent silences, and it worked: Lord Aegeus cleared his throat and said at last, "Well! You've certainly grown into a sturdy fellow since that day in the pergola. You were only Master Claude's boy then. And you're the master yourself now, are you not? What's your name?"

I told him it was Simeon and he laughed out loud, and the Lord Victor smiled thinly. Lord Aegeus said:

"Simeon! That's appropriate, I must say! Up in the treetops all the time, and as hairy as a monkey, too! But come, don't take offense. All your tests show you're a supremely healthy young simian, and quite a bright one at that."

I murmured my thanks for the compliment. Lord Aegeus said, "Quite," and had a sip of his wine. Then he said, "You've had a few sexual encounters, but you don't seem to have formed any long-term relationships. In light of that, we would like to make you a proposition."

I didn't know what to think. He burst out laughing at the look on my face and Lord Victor turned red.

"No, no!" said Lord Aegeus. "It's only this, good Master Simeon: my dearest Maeve must have a mate, and we've chosen you for the honor."

I just said "Oh," feeling as though I had been struck over the head. He went on: "It should have been Fallon, but he passed away, poor creature. Pity. Still, we learned a lot from him; and dear Maeve is wonderfully vigorous. We have great hopes of her. Now, you needn't be nervous! She may look like a child, but I can personally attest that you won't have to teach her a thing." He grinned broadly and Lord Victor stared down at the floor.

I had a gulp of wine and nerved myself to ask him, "But—if she's your favorite, divine Lord—won't you mind?"

"Mind? Good heavens, no. She's a charming girl, but she is a mortal, as you are. She certainly can't bear *me* children. I'll admit I'll miss our golden afternoons, but the plain fact is, she ought to be bred while she's in her prime." He said the last leaning forward, holding my gaze in a matter-of-fact way.

I said, "I didn't think she was mortal, exactly," and he said: "All too mortal, I regret to say. And human enough for you. But we need very much to see if we can produce something more human still, and so— wedding bells for Maeve."

For a moment nobody said anything, and then Lord Victor cleared his throat.

He said to me, "Does this offend you?"

And I said, "Oh, no, divine Lord," and Lord Aegeus said, "Of course he isn't offended, good sensible solid fellow that he is. Besides, you're rather a romantic choice, I think. You were her knight-errant, once upon a time in the pergola. Yes, throwing yourself between my baby darling and the wrath of Claude. Oh, that's good, *wrath of Claude*!" Lord Aegeus turned laughing to the other lord, who didn't seem to think much of the joke.

I was thinking about Maeve with her tiny perfect face, with her moonlight hair, with her big liquid eyes and silvery laugh. I thought about the bodice of her gown. I told myself that it really would be a great honor to be awarded such a wife. I said, "But will she love me?" and the Lord Aegeus assured me, "She can be quite affectionate, my friend. You'll treat her well, of course—she has never been treated otherwise— and really she doesn't require much. Flattery, presents, a sense of romance. In addition to the obvious physical attentions," and he almost leered as he said it. That was a disconcerting thing, seeing a divine lord with such an expression. They look so wise and noble as a rule.

But I agreed to take Maeve, because I did think she was the most beautiful woman I'd ever seen. I think I'd have agreed even if I'd known about what followed, to be certain my sperm count and motility were all that was desired. They were painful and embarrassing tests, but I told myself it was no worse a thing than careful cross-pollination in an orchard or a greenhouse. And what rose or apple blossom was so fair as Maeve?

But she didn't love me.

She was in a furious sulk the day of our wedding. Still she was lovely; her pouting lips were sensual. Lord Aegeus gave her to me in the pergola, to make it the more romantic, as he said. He had her gowned all in white like a bride, and—to give her a sense of ceremony—placed my hand in hers. He even broke open a pomegranate and presented it to me to feed her, and at first she spat out the bright seeds without even tasting them, fierce; but he spoke to her sternly and she obeyed at last, and crunched them sullenly. They crimsoned her tiny mouth, made her more desirable still.

So it was done, and Lord Aegeus placed his hands on our two heads and said, "Be fruitful and multiply, my children!" Then he gave us a bottle of wine, a good vintage from the lords' and ladies' own cellars, and left me to manage the rest of it.

I took her to my suite in the servants' quarters, hoping she would be impressed with how important her new husband was: but she thought nothing of my rooms, or my bromeliads, or my drafting table, or any of my things. All she would say was, "Hairy beast!" and flounce away from me. She made a game of it, answering "Hairy beast" to anything I said to her: Would you like to bathe, wife? *Hairy beast!* Shall I light a fire, wife? *Hairy beast!* Shall I play the lute for you, wife? *Hairy beast!*

But I still had the bottle of good wine, so I went into my kitchen and prepared a wedding supper: partridges in a sauce of shallots and cream, with fresh bread and white grapes. I set it out, poured the wine and seated myself; she came at once and clambered up into the chair opposite, trailing her bridal finery. Without a word she fell to, reaching into the dish and taking a whole partridge to eat with her hands.

Even in that she was graceful, tearing daintily with her little sharp teeth. I didn't get much of the food, watching her spellbound as I did. You wouldn't believe a girl could have such terrible manners and be so enchanting. She smeared partridge grease on the wine cup when she drank, sucked the bones loudly, greedily tore the soft center from the loaf, even blew her tiny nose in her napkin; but it was all beauty and refinement in my eyes. Beautiful people can do such things, and still be loved.

I drank more of the wine than she did, and it made me bold. When the partridges were all gone and Maeve was idly rolling grapes around on the table, I said: "What about that bath now, wife?"

And she mocked me, she said, "What about that ba-ath now, wife? I don't want to bathe with you. You're ugly and hairy and old."

I told her I wasn't so old, that I was much younger than Lord Aegeus, and she stared with a blank face; then she shrugged so beautifully and said, "But you *look* old." Her gaze wandered to the partridge bones in the dish and fixed on them, suddenly intense. Without looking up at me she said: "Make the bones come alive again!"

I told her I couldn't, and she said: "Yes you can. Just make them stand up in the dish and sing! Fallon could make them do that. Why can't you?"

I told her I wasn't as clever as Fallon. She raised scornful eyes to me.

"Can you make me a new gown without cutting any cloth?"

I told her no, and she said: "Fallon could! Can you make that stick in the fire grow green leaves again?"

I told her I couldn't, and she said: "Fallon could. He could make anything I told him to make, he was so clever. So why should I play with you, stupid thing?"

I set aside my winecup and I said, "Because Fallon is dead, and you're my wife."

She chewed her lower lip and sighed. She said: "My poor Fallon. I was supposed to be Queen in the Hill. He would have done everything for me. We'd have had lots of babies, and they'd have done everything for me, too. Everybody would have brought me presents and played with me." Tears welled in her eyes, perfect as diamonds.

I reached out a hand to stroke her shoulder and she did not draw away. I said, "Don't cry. I saw Fallon. He could never have made babies with you, wife. He was too sick."

"He could!" she insisted. "Fallon wasn't sick. He was just what I wanted him to be. Don't you remember?"

I said, "Remember what?" and she got a sly look in her eyes.

"Ha! You don't have the Memory. Big people don't remember things how they were, but we do. We remember everything from the beginning of the world. Fallon did, and I do, but you can't. Big people think they're so clever, but they're not. We have always been more clever than you."

I said, "Who? You and Fallon?" and she shook her head and said, "Our kin," as though I was just too stupid to waste time on. I said, "We'll make a new family," and she said, "I won't play with you. You don't have the Memory, and you can't make the bones stand up and sing!"

Forgive the plainness, but there was one bone at that table standing up and singing, and I got to my feet and said to her: "Lord Aegeus couldn't do those things either, but you've played with him. We're married, and you'll play with me now."

She stuck her lip out in anger. I wanted to bite it. She said, "He gave me nice presents."

I said, "So will I. Have you ever seen blossom and apples on one bough? I can make those. I can make a rose as bright as your hair, without a single thorn. I can make a pleasure garden all the divine lords and ladies would want for themselves, but it will be yours alone. I can make marvels in the earth, nobody else has the skill to make such places! Even Lord Aegeus. You see?"

I don't know if she saw, crazy as she was, but she didn't fight when I picked her up and carried her away to the bath.

And that was strange, because when we were out of our clothes she was so like a baby I lost all desire. I could have washed her and toweled her as chastely as though I were caring for a child, then, but it seemed our nakedness had the opposite effect on Maeve. She had been capricious snow and ice; now she was a little licking tongue of fire. She laughed and laughed and scrambled all over me in the warm water. I couldn't hold back from her, no man could have, mortal or immortal.

And, I ask you: was it wrong? When she was my wife, and the divine lords and ladies themselves had ordered us to love?

Anyway she liked me very well after that, and let me take her to my bed, and I slept with her in my arms half afraid I'd roll over and crush her, so little she was, a feather, a flame, a snowflake. My wife.

Have you ever been in love like that? I don't think people were meant to live that way forever. How could they? They'd never get any work done. And how can you pay attention to anything but the beloved?

Maeve was a late sleeper, too. Though she walked fearless in sunlight, as dead Fallon had been unable to do, she much preferred the night for wakefulness and play: so of course I kept her favorite hours, though no Master Gardener should do that.

I had duties, and I ignored them. The divine lords and ladies (and, see, this is another example of their generosity) were gracious enough to overlook this fault. They even sent gifts to my quarters, rare wines, fine foods, jewels and gowns for my darling. She accepted the presents and was happy.

My hedges went untrimmed, the annuals went to seed and weeds grew between the stones in the garden paths, but no bolt fell from heaven. Indeed, the botanist lord himself took time from his rare specimens to go out and oversee the work that had to be done before winter set in, bringing in all the potted citrus to the solarium, spreading out straw with his own noble hands!

When she and I weren't making love, or eating, or sleeping, I sat at my drafting table and plotted out the most beautiful garden in the world for Maeve. She loved to climb up beside me and watch, as I worked out the proportions or rendered proposed views in colored chalk. I explained that it was a bower of night, to be at its best in the darkness, like my pretty wife.

She was impatient that it went so slowly. Fallon, I was assured, could have drawn up such plans in an hour, and had the garden miraculously in place before nightfall of one day! That much was surely her fantasy. Fallon may have been a genius, but I know my own work; and no garden is made that way.

Once I asked Maeve where she and Fallon had come from, and she gave me that look as though I were really too stupid to be troubled with and said: "We were stolen."

But I never learned more about it, because she wouldn't say who had stolen the children, or from whom. Perhaps she didn't know.

When she would get bored with watching me she would want to do something else again, so we would, and I thought to myself that even dead Fallon couldn't have worked his miracles if he'd had to stop and do what I was doing every couple of hours. And it seemed to me a fine thing that I should have Maeve's bed and he should have his grave. He may have been a genius, but every time I had ever seen him he had been curling away from the sunlight like a blind worm. My little queen deserved a man, I thought. She'd have a much better life with me!

And, as anybody might have expected the way we were going at it, Maeve had lost her appetite for breakfast before the snows fell. By the time the first bitter storm came down on the Cévennes, there was no possible doubt she was carrying my child.

Now she had no desire for anything but presents, and she was so querulous I had a hard time of it bringing them quickly enough. Her favorite gifts were clothes; Lord Aegeus was kind enough to see that his tailoring staff came to us weekly for measurements and fittings. Warm robes in rich brocade, nightgowns of silk for Maeve's weary swollen body, slippers lined with fleece. When she ordered it I would set aside my work and brush her hair for hours, marveling at the glitter it had, like snow on a bright day. She would close her eyes and croon to herself in pleasure.

Once again I was caring for a child, who had to be coaxed to eat and to take the medicines the divine ones prescribed, who had to be comforted and sung to and held. I told her stories, I told her about how I'd begin her garden as soon as the snows were gone and what rare flowers I'd plant there. This was not conversation, you understand; she wasn't interested in talking; but I thought she liked the sound of my voice.

There was an early thaw that year, and word came from the lords and ladies that I ought to tend to my duties again. I protested that I must stay by my wife, for she needed constant care. By way of answer Lord Aegeus himself came and spoke softly to my little darling as I prepared our supper, and brought a sparkle to her dull eyes. He did me the honor of dining with us; and in the course of our meal suggested that Maeve ought to be moved to the infirmary, as her condition was becoming precarious. There would be nurses to wait on her, and I would be freed to prepare the gardens for spring.

I looked doubtfully at Maeve; but she babbled happily with the lord, more than she would ever deign to speak with me. I saw she wanted to go. So I agreed.

The only thing I could do then was work, desperately, and how I loved my work for the peace it gave me. Can you understand? There was so much to do after the winter, but it wasn't enough. I paced out the area for the wonder I was going to make, Maeve's night-garden, and cut the terraces myself, and laid the forms for the concrete retaining walls and the stairs and balustrades. I spoke at length with the Botanist lord and we prepared seedlings, slips, and shoots. There were fine big hedges and trees in pots, which could be moved on rollers to the locations I wanted and set in place, to shade my darling's pleasaunce as though they'd grown there thirty years. The lord was impressed when he saw my designs.

But Maeve was not impressed, when I would come to the infirmary in the evenings to tell her what I'd been doing. Sometimes she seemed barely to remember me. Sometimes she was impatient and disdainful. Sometimes the lord Aegeus was with her, chatting intimately when I'd come in, and he'd scold her when she was rude to me.

All the while our son kicked in her womb.

So in the morning I couldn't rise early enough, and the lawns had never been so perfectly in trim, and Maeve's own exquisite garden took form and all the immortal lords and ladies came out of the mountain to wonder at it. They took me aside and told me how proud of me they were. They told me I was going to far surpass old Claude. They gave me commissions for designs, pot gardens for their private suites. I devised a way to build a running stream and ferny grotto in a sitting room for the lord Marcus. I devised an arbor of roses black as ink, approached along a walk framed by black irises and black velvet pansies, for the lady Ereshkigal. I devised an apple with the savor of Black Elysium liqueur for the lord Nathan. Immortals have eclectic tastes. But I had their respect, and that was a great consolation to me.

I was hard at work when our little boy was born. Lord Aegeus was with her.

It was the lord Victor who came to me with the news. I was setting the framework of the arbor in place, down on my hands and knees packing in the earth with a maul, when I looked up and saw him there.

He was a cold-looking young man, Lord Victor; so when I saw that coldness laid aside and real compassion in his eyes, I knew something terrible had happened. I scrambled to my feet.

He said, "Master Simeon, Maeve is delivered of a son."

And I said, "Has she died?"

He shook his head. I said, "What is it, then?" and he cleared his throat before he answered me. When he spoke it was with such delicacy, and such chill, and such anger I was almost more concerned for his discomfort than my own. He said: "I have been delegated to inform you that you have the Company's profound thanks for your contribution to their breeding program. A hybrid was successfully delivered this afternoon and, although he does not have the desired characteristics, his survival proves that the program still has a fifty-three point three percent chance of producing its objective. Do you know what that means, mortal man?"

I stammered, "No, my lord."

He said it meant I was divorced now.

I dropped the maul where I stood. I don't think I said anything. He closed his eyes before he went on to say: "The girl will be assigned to another mortal male. They'll try her again, to see what another genetic mix might produce. You're a clever fellow, you must have seen that the Company had plans for Maeve! And you will be rewarded for your efforts, at least: bigger and finer rooms for you, and your operating budget will be tripled."

I said, "May I see the boy?" and he said, simply, "You don't want to see the boy."

It wasn't until years later that I knew what Lord Victor meant.

I found my boy by chance, in the warren of residential rooms attached to the infirmary. It doesn't matter what I was doing there.

I looked in through a door and saw the youth who might have been dead Fallon, except that what clumps of hair he had were the color of mine. He had his mushroom-white hands pressed over his eyes and was rocking himself to and fro on his bed, thumping his big head against the wall. But all across that wall, and on the floor and even in corners of the ceiling, were scrawled equations of such complexity I was dumbfounded, though my grasp of engineering mathematics is better than most mortals'.

Do you know what it is to be cuckolded by a dead man, when he is no more than a film of ashes in his sunless grave? I know.

And it wasn't the first time I felt like a cuckold.

When Maeve had recovered sufficiently from the birth, they gave her to a mortal I barely knew, who worked in their kitchens. He got her with child but did not treat her well, so the immortals took her from him even sooner than they had taken her from me. The child was another boy.

She was passed then to the lady Belisaria's mortal valet, and had another son; and then to the mortal who cleaned the pipes in the baths and reflecting pools, and produced yet another son. I lost track of her bridals after that.

Which is not to say I never saw her. I did glimpse her, now and again, wandering in the gardens to pick flowers or fruit. It was seldom, though, because she was seldom in any condition to walk far. And as the years went on Maeve's tiny perfect face became somehow a parody of itself, the features too sharp, the sweet mouth twisted.

But I finished her garden.

It far surpassed my topiary walk. The lord and ladies said so. How clever of me to make a moon-garden, all white and scented flowers and silvery herbage, best enjoyed under the stars! The scale was a little inconvenient for the immortals, as all the stone seats were set low and the stair risers, too; but the neophyte classes, the children being transformed into immortals, found the place and made it their own. They played there in the long summer evenings. The dark trees echoed back their laughter. I had wanted children to laugh in that garden, but they were not my children.

Still, it was good that the place was used and loved. There was a moment, after I had planted the last narcissus bulb and opened the valve for the fountains, when I wanted to spray it all with Greek fire and destroy it in its completed perfection; but, really, that would have been a very stupid and ungrateful thing to do. If there is one thing the lords and ladies despise, it is wanton destruction, and surely I was better than the mortal men of the villages below us.

So I maintained it, and kept it beautiful. I was kneeling there one day when the lord Victor came and sat on the steps beside me, watching awhile. I was pruning the miniature roses. This must be done as carefully as paring a baby's fingernails, for they are not hardy bushes.

After a time he said, "How are you feeling these days, Master Simeon?"

I told him I was very well, and thanked him for asking.

He was silent, staring at the little bushes. At last he said, "I'm leaving this mountain soon. I'm going off to do some field work at last."

I said, "Are you, my lord?" and he made an affirmative sound. He stared out over the lawns, not seeming to see them. His hand went up to stroke his mustaches. He said, "It's a miserable posting, really. I'm being sent out to chase around after Totila. The Ostrogoth fellow, you know. He's all set to crush Rome again, and the Company needs someone on the spot to protect certain of its interests. I've been accessing data all week. Aegeus thinks I'm out of my mind."

I didn't know what to say, so I just made sympathetic noises, and anyway I could tell that he was only speaking to me as a mortal man speaks to his dog. He went on: "He's right; it's not a good way to begin a career. Not for an Executive Class operative. I'll be wading into the mortal muck with the Preservers! If Aegeus knew I'd requested it, he'd really be horrified.

"But I'm having a, what would you mortals call it? A crisis of faith, perhaps. Not a good thing, when one has a career to consider. I'd really rather not question my beliefs, but the longer I stay here in the midst of all this"— he waved a hand at the pleasure gardens all around us— "the harder it becomes. I think I need to go down into the mortal places and watch *real* cruelty, real stupidity, real vanity. Perhaps then I can look at Aegeus with some sense of perspective. Or at least learn to appreciate his point of view . . ."

His gaze drifted back to me. He sighed, supposing maybe that I had no idea what he was talking about. He said, "Do you know the myth of Jesus, Master Simeon?"

I told him, of course I did. We are all taught about the dark superstitions that the mortals slave under, down there in their villages. Lord

Victor said, "Do you suppose the Christ left Heaven for Earth to save mortal souls? Or is it possible he left because God's behavior disgusted him?"

I said it might be so.

He was silent a long time after that. At last he got to his feet, and his shadow fell across the work I was doing. He said, very quietly, "Master Simeon, I do beg your pardon." I squinted up at him where he loomed dark against the sun and I just nodded, for I couldn't think how to answer him. Then I looked down at my roses again, and I saw his shadow move away from me.

I heard he went down into the mortal world not long after.

Maeve was passed from mortal to mortal, and bore them all nothing but sons, which would have made her a very desirable wife indeed down in the mortal places where women were slaves, as I understood; but it did not seem to be what the immortals wanted from her. This even though some of the boys were quite presentable, kitten-faced children who could converse rationally and walk in the sunlight. Like their mother, they saw no particular virtue in courtesy or other social graces, and like her they were petted and spoiled by the lords and ladies who raised them. Most of them were little geniuses. They were not given eternal life, however.

And then, miraculously, Maeve bore a daughter to the mortal Wamba, who worked as a masseur in the Executive Gymnasium. What a celebration there was! Wamba was given new rooms and all the finery he could wear, and as a further favor he asked if he might divorce Maeve and marry one of the bath attendants, whom he had loved for some time. This was granted to him.

I don't know if Maeve cared. She basked for a while in the glory of having produced a daughter, and really a very pretty one. I saw the little girl when they were parading her around. She was not so pale as her mother. Her skin was like rose petals and her hair like white gold, but she had the same great wide eyes and delicate face.

Yet Maeve, it seems, grew jealous of all the attention paid to her daughter. They caught her pinching the baby when she thought she was alone with it. The infant was taken away, to be raised by Lady Maire, and Maeve found herself in real disgrace for the first time in her life.

Lord Aegeus had no time for her now. All his attentions were focused on little Amelie, the daughter. It was decided that Maeve had performed her duties admirably, and would henceforth be allowed to rest. They allotted her a single room adjacent to the infirmary. She would be given no new husbands, as her health had begun to suffer from constant breeding.

So I asked if I might have her back.

The lords and ladies bestowed her on me gladly enough, commending me for my sense of responsibility, but warned me that marital relations were best not resumed. They didn't need to say so much. Maeve had become a small wizened thing by this time, collapsed and sagging like an old woman, though she can't have been thirty yet. Her skin had begun to mar, also, with thick white blotches of scar tissue. The lords and ladies told me it was from too much exposure to sunlight.

But I couldn't leave her indoors by herself, so I swathed her in a hooded cloak and carried her about with me, and set her in the shade as I worked.

She talked constantly. Mostly it was bitter complaints about the way no one ever brought her presents any more, and how unfair life was. Sometimes she would wander in her mind, and hold long conversations with Fallon. I don't think she recognized me even when her mind was clear. I wasn't angry about this. There had been so many, after all, and maybe time and memory weren't the same for her kind as they were for me. Whatever her kind might be.

I wondered if this was how the immortal ones regard my own race. Are we so brief and small and foolish in their eyes?

Anyway, she didn't last long.

I had taken the midday meal with her, spooned soup into her toothless mouth and napkined her little chin, nodding my agreement to her stream of complaints that never stopped, even while she was eating. Then I carried her to the shade of one of the vast trees I had had transplanted for her, for we were in her own garden that day. I set her down where she could see me, and went to arrange the new bedding plants around the fountain.

I heard her talking to Fallon again, and was grateful, because it meant I wouldn't have to keep nodding to show I was paying attention. After a while I noticed she had grown silent, and I turned. She looked as though she had gone to sleep.

I buried her in the narcissus bed, and then I went to tell Lord Aegeus. Perhaps I should have told him first, but she was already beginning to crumble in on herself; and I was afraid he might have some further use for her poor body.

I found Lord Aegeus in Lady Maire's quarters. They each had hold of one of little Amelie's hands and were pacing carefully beside her as she toddled along, chatting together over her head like happy parents. He actually looked blank for a moment when I told him my news.

But then he was instantly sympathetic, clapping me on the shoulder and commending me for my careful attention to dear old Maeve, telling me how grateful he was I'd made her last days comfortable. He swung the baby up in his arms and held out her dimpled hand to me. He said, "You must thank your uncle Simeon, Amelie. He was a good friend to your biological mamma." And the child patted my cheek and smiled at me with an intelligence that was, maybe, just a bit more human than Maeve's.

Lady Maire exclaimed, "Isn't the sweet thing clever!" And Lord Aegeus kissed Amelie between her wide eyes and agreed that she was the cleverest, most precious little girl in the whole world. I don't think he noticed when I left.

I planted a rosebush to mark the grave. It wasn't one of the elegant ones the lords and ladies so love. It was a wild rose with a single-petaled flower. It bears many thorns, it is half bramble; but the perfume of its white roses is intense, though they bloom in an hour and the petals scarcely last a day.

Labienus sets the documents to one side. He contemplates Victor's picture a while, and presently he begins to grin. So many expressions can be read into that expressionless face, those blank eyes; is he mournful? Resigned? Bored? Labienus is irresistibly reminded of the drawings of Edward Gorey, of all those stiffly miserable Victorian figures trapped in their airless world.

"Disaffected," he says aloud. "Disillusioned. Disinclined. Poor Victor. Aegeus is a pompous ass, isn't he? I wonder whether you'd like a change of masters?"

Yes. Victor must be turned. It shouldn't be difficult.

LOST BOYS

Labienus glances up at a red file folder, secure in its locked glass case with other Red Level Deniability documents. This particular document is the record of an experiment. Certain twenty-fourth-century mortals would be horrified to know any evidence of their work was in Labienus's possession, let alone that their project had been co-opted by him. He smiles wryly, remembering Project *Adonai*.

On impulse, he orders the case to unlock itself, and he pulls the folder down. But another file pops out with it, tumbles down, fluttering open as it comes. Labienus seizes it in midair, but it has opened.

He frowns at the picture he sees, and the memory that rises by association. The shot is of a black man with a lean face, fine features, bright hard gaze like a young hawk's gaze. Labienus remembers the child the man had been. His mouth twists, as though he tasted bitterness.

He has no protégé of his own, no bright second-in-command . . .

He can see the woman in his mind's eye, immortal, blue-eyed and blonde, but without any of the chilly grace he likes in an immortal woman. Unacceptably disorganized for an Executive. Untidy, credulous, earthy, *sentimental*. Just the thought brings her voice back into his ears, gossiping on and on . . .

I was sweeping down my front steps when I first saw him, or rather when he saw me. It's not as though I swept every day! I mean, we had servants like all other respectable households were supposed to; but if you've ever lived in Amsterdam for any long time, or at least in that year 1702, you'll know how hard it is to get the damn servants to actually serve. My God, so touchy! I mean, look at that wet nurse of Rembrandt's, practically sued him for palimony and I know for a fact their relationship was the most innocent you can imagine.

Where was I?

On the steps, sweeping, because Margarite had retired to her bed with the vapors over something, God knows what, probably because Eliphal had been muttering again about the way mortals cook, which I wished he wouldn't do because she's very clean really for a mortal, and as for using too much butter, we were in *Amsterdam* for Christ's sake, not a health spa, and where was she going to get hold of polyunsaturated fats?

See, this is just the sort of domestic calamity our mortal masters failed to foresee when they founded Dr. Zeus Incorporated, though you'd think being up there in the twenty-fourth century would give them a clue. But that Temporal Concordance of theirs only tells them about big things like wars and disasters to be avoided, I guess; they have to rely on us, their faithful immortal cyborgs, to manage the little details of business for them here in the past. I know they're all scientific geniuses, to have come up with time travel the way they did, but I can't help thinking they must be a bit lazy.

So anyway I told Margarite, there there dear, you just take the afternoon off, and that was how I came to be out on my front stoop with the broom, in my old black dress with my hair bound up in a dishcloth, which is not really the way an Executive Facilitator wishes to be seen by a prospective Junior Trainee, but there you are.

"I am shocked," observed a little voice, "to behold the beautiful and celebrated Facilitator Van Drouten engaged in drudgery better left to mortals."

I looked down with my mouth open and there he was, standing beside the Herengracht in a pose as arrogant as a captain of the Watch, plumed hat doffed but held on his hip in a lordly sort of way. All along the canal other women were leaning over their stoops to look, because you see a lot of unusual stuff along the canal but not often a teeny-tiny black kid with the poise and self-assurance of a burgomaster.

"Hello, Van Drouten," said Kalugin, who was standing beside him looking sheepish. Kalugin's an old friend, a big man but one of those gentle melancholy Russians, and why the Company made him a sea captain I can't guess. He's the last person to scream orders at people. "I'm afraid we've caught you at rather a bad time."

"Oh! No," I said, when I had got over my surprise. "Minor household crisis, that's all. Goodness, you must be Latif!"

"Charmed, madam," the child said, and he bowed like—well, like a captain of the Watch, and a sober one at that. "And may I say how much I've been looking forward to the prospect of learning Field Command from one of the unquestioned experts?"

I had to giggle at that, I mean there I was looking at my least executive, but he stiffened perceptibly and I thought: whoops. Dignity was clearly important to him. But, you know, it is to most children.

"Very kind of you to say so, with me such a mess," I said, descending the steps. "And welcome to Eurobase Five. Shall we go inside? I can offer you gentlemen cake and wine, if you've time for a snack, Kalugin?"

"Unfortunately, no," he apologized, taking off his tall fur hat as he ducked through the low kitchen door, which was the one we ordinarily used, and not the grand main entrance.

"Not even for a cup of *chocolate*?" I coaxed. He looked as though he could use a little Theobromos.

"Theobromos on duty?" Latif inquired, looking up at us. "Isn't that prohibited, indulging in Theobromos before nineteen hundred hours?"

Of course it is, technically, but the young operatives who aren't allowed Theobromos yet have such puritanical attitudes . . . almost as bad as the mortal masters, on whom it has no effect at all! Our masters were horrified when they discovered that chocolate gets us pleasantly stoned, because they thought they'd designed us to be proof against intoxicants. They even tried to forbid it to us, but must have realized they'd have a revolt on their hands if they did, and settled for strictly regulating our use of the stuff. Or trying to, anyway.

"I really can't stay. My ship won't wait," Kalugin told me, with real regret. "But I have some deliveries—besides young Latif, here—a moment, if you please—"

As he shrugged awkwardly out of his fur coat he transmitted, *And here's the young Executive himself, and good luck with him!*

Oh, dear, is he a brat? He seems like such a polite little boy, I responded, as Latif inspected the Chinese plates ranged along the passage wall.

Polite? Certainly! Even when one doesn't quite meet his particular standards. Kalugin unstrapped the dispatch pouches he'd brought with him. *He graciously agreed to overlook at least four flagrant violations of Company protocols he detected on my ship.*

"Here we are—diamonds for Eliphal, I believe, they've been rather uncomfortable—and these are the credenza components Diego ordered." Kalugin presented them to me with a slight bow. "Have you anything to go?"

"Not at the moment, thank you." I accepted the pouches.

"Then I must attend to duty." Kalugin put his coat back on. "The young gentleman's luggage will arrive within the hour. Latif, best of luck in your new posting—Van Drouten, I'm desolated to rush but you know how things are—perhaps we can dine at a later date. Have you still got that mortal who works such wonders with herring?"

"Yes, which was why I was sweeping, but I'll tell you next time—" I said, following him as he sidled into the street and put on his tall hat. My goodness, I thought, he *was* in a hurry!

"Now, that's interesting," said Latif thoughtfully, and Kalugin stopped dead.

"What is, young sir?" he asked, and not as though he wanted to.

"I must have missed something. Or am I mistaken in my interpretation of Directive Four-Oh-Eight-A regarding acknowledgment of delivery of all Class One shipments? I thought the Executive Facilitator of a Company HQ signed for all packets above a certain value."

"Um—" said Kalugin, looking like a trapped bear, but I knew what the problem was now. Latif had been training under Executive Facilitator Labienus, who is a martinet. Not the best influence for a child, even if Labienus is a big cheese. I've never cared for him, personally.

"Except in cases where delivery occurs no fewer than six but no more than twelve times within a calendar year," I told Latif. "And then it's at my discretion whether I sign or not."

"Yes," Kalugin agreed, throwing me a grateful look. "Well. I'll just be going, shall I?"

"Marine Operations Specialist Kalugin," Latif executed another perfect bow. "*Dos vedanya!*"

"The pleasure was all mine, I assure you," Kalugin called over his shoulder, and was gone down the Herengracht like a shot. Beside me, Latif cleared his throat.

"Insofar as my arrival seems to have been unexpected," he said with beautiful delicacy, "I would be happy to report to my quarters until a more convenient time for my briefing."

"No, no," I told him. "We can chat as I work. So, you've been studying with Labienus at Mackenzie Base?"

"Yes, madam, for the last eighteen months." He fell into step beside me as I took the deliveries and climbed up into the house.

"Well, that's nice. He's a very efficient administrator, Labienus. Very military, isn't he? Of course, personal styles vary widely," I said, and Latif snorted.

"I've learned that much already. During my first semester I studied under Houbert."

"Ah. I've heard he's . . . a little creative." It was the politest word I could think of.

"Yes, madam, I would say that's one way to describe him," Latif replied. "In any case, this will be my first experience at a Company HQ actually within a mortal urban community, observing field command and interaction with mortals in a situation where cover identities are used."

I nodded, and told him: "Sounds scary, doesn't it? But, really, you know, it's not that difficult. Especially here in Amsterdam. This is a very civilized town." I lifted my skirts to clear the last step, which is just a little higher than the others, and really I've been meaning to get that fixed, but somehow I never get around to it.

"It's even a boring town, nowadays. I wish you'd been stationed here back in the fifties! I could have taken you around for a sitting with Rembrandt—the Company bought so many of his canvases!—or maybe a chat with Spinoza. We used to buy a lot of his lenses, though of course he had no idea he was grinding them for credenza parts, but he never minded special orders and I used to love to get him talking . . ."

We had been making our way down the narrow passage, with Latif obliged to stay a bit behind because my skirts were so wide, but when my hoops caught that damn little hall table as they always do he was agile enough to grab the Ming vase before it leaped to its untimely death.

"Nice catch!" I congratulated him, knocking on Eliphal's door. He just stood there gasping with the vase clutched in his arms as Eliphal opened the door and stood peering down at us.

"What?"

"See?" I waved the packet at him. "Diamonds."

"Oh, great!" He took them and looked over his spectacles at Latif. "Who's that?"

"Eliphal, this is Latif, who's going to be studying with me. He's an Executive Trainee, you know that experimental program where they're sending some neophytes into the field for early hands-on acclimatization?" I explained. "He'll be playing—gee, I guess I can tell people you're my page, would you like to tag along after me when I go shopping and hold my fan and stuff like that? And, Latif, this is Cultural Anthropologist Grade Two Eliphal; he's playing a diamond-cutter who rents a room from me. I was just telling him about Spinoza, Eliphal."

"Well, what a little fellow to get such a big assignment," said Eliphal, leaning down to him like a kindly uncle. "And how old are you, Latif?"

"Five, sir," said Latif coolly, putting down the vase and bowing. "I recently read your dissertation on Manasse ben Israel, and may I say how impressed I was with your insights into the influences at work during his formative years?"

"Uh—thank you." Eliphal straightened up, blinking.

"You're quite welcome."

"Come on, sweetie, let's deliver these. Dinner's at five, Eliphal. So, let's go on upstairs and you can meet Lievens, not the painter of course though he's our Art Conservationist, he's supposedly a cabinetmaker I'm renting to like Eliphal, and so is Diego our Tech, and Johan and Lisette—they're our Botanist and Literature Specialists—they're playing my son and daughter and help me run my business, and then we've got the mortal servants—you've worked with mortals before?—well, ours are very nice though a bit temperamental, Margarite and Joost, childless couple, they've got Code Yellow security clearance," I informed Latif as we climbed up to the next floor.

"I see," Latif answered. "Which would mean they actually share residential quarters with us?"

"Yes, in fact their room is next to yours. They don't snore or anything, though," I added, turning to see if Latif was looking upset. Sometimes young operatives are afraid of mortals, until they get used to them. I think it's because of the indoctrination we all get when we're being processed for immortality, in the base schools. But, you know, it takes hardly any time before you learn that they're all just people and not so bad really, and I think half of what you learn in school you just sort of have to take with a grain of salt, do you know what I'm saying?

Anyway if Latif was bothered by the idea of living next to mortals he hid it well, because he just shrugged his little shoulders and said: "How nice. And I understand your cover identity is as a widowed dealer in East Indian commodities?"

"Oh, yes, smell!" I exhorted him, pausing on the landing. I took a good deep sniff myself. "Ahh. Pepper, cloves, cardamom, and nutmeg just now. The whole top floor is warehouse space, you see, and actually I don't just *pose* as a spice merchant, we really do business here. I think I'd have made a great businesswoman if I'd stayed mortal, I really enjoy all those guilders on the account sheet and the exotic bales coming from the ships. It defrays operating costs like you wouldn't believe. There's my first word of advice as a field commander, okay? Always find ways to augment your operating budget, if you want to rise high in the Company ranks."

"Very good, madam, I'll remember that," Latif was saying, as Johan's door banged open and he came running out in a panic.

"Van Drouten! Van Drouten, what do I do? Kackerlackje's having a seizure!" And he held up the miserable little dog who was having a seizure all right, and I knew why, too, the damned thing had been eating paint again, and if I've told Johan once I've told him a dozen times: if he can't watch a pet every minute of the day he shouldn't have one, I think it should be a general rule that cyborgs shouldn't keep pets anyway because they always die after all and it hurts nearly as badly as when a mortal you're fond of dies.

Anyway I told him, "Take him out in the back and make him vomit! And I'll see if I've got any bicarbonate, all right? You know, if you'd kept an eye on him like I told you—" but Johan had gone clattering down the stairs out of earshot. I sighed and turned to Latif.

"I think that mutt is trying to commit suicide. Here's another piece of advice: Never let your subordinates keep pets, but if you must, make sure you've got a Zoologist stationed with you who knows how to physic a dog, or you'll wind up doing it."

"I'll remember that, too," said Latif, looking appalled.

The mortal with his trunk came after that, so I helped Latif get it up to his room. He insisted on squaring everything away before we went back downstairs, and I had to hide a smile at how finicky-neat he was, all his clothes pressed just so and severely grown-up in their cut. He even had a miniature grooming kit in a leather case! Silver-backed brushes and all; he only lacked a razor. Small wonder he looked askance at the toys I'd set out on his bed.

"Sorry about those," I told him. "I wasn't expecting somebody quite so, um, mature."

"It was a charming thought," he said courteously, giving one of his hats a last brush before setting it on a shelf. "And, after all, it does go with the character I'm portraying. I suppose I'll need to observe mortal children to see how they behave, won't I? Certainly all the rest of you seem to be doing a splendid job blending in with the mortal populace."

"Oh, it's easy, really," I assured him. "Easiest part of the job. What's hard is coordinating the actual running of the station."

"I can't wait to observe," he replied, laying out his monogrammed (!!) towel beside the washbasin. "What shall we start with? Duty rosters? Security protocols? Access code transfers? Logistics?"

Was there a little boy in there at all? The machine part was up and running, trust Labienus to see to that; but we work best as whole people, you know, same as the mortals.

"Logistics," I replied. "Want to come watch me get dinner for nine people on the table when the cook's sick?"

I made *erwtensoep* because we already had the peas soaking and it's easy. Latif perched on the edge of the table and stared as I chopped leeks and onions, and after a while ventured to say: "I think I'm getting this, now. This really is total immersion simulation, isn't it? You, uh, really and truly do have to *live* the mortal experience, don't you?"

"Not like a nice Company HQ with everything just so, is it?" I smiled at him. "No military command post with precise rules. I know Labienus, he's such a cyborg! Probably gave you that impression of absolute order, but the truth is that working for the Company is much more like this, like—like—"

"Chaos?" said Latif, and hastened to add: "Except that this is actually order artfully disguised as chaos, of course. Isn't it?"

"Sometimes," I told him, pulling out the potato basket. "See, you have to be so flexible. Like today, when Margarite isn't feeling well. And suppose I drew up a strict duty roster and I was all settled down to transmit reports at my credenza according to rules and regulations, like I was just last week, and Magdalena, that's the mortal girl from next door, dropped in to show off her new baby?"

"That's the Anthropologist's department, I would think," said Latif hopefully.

"Eliphal? Not likely, sweetie. And then, see, while I was sitting there pouring Magdalena and me nice little glasses of gin, there was a pounding on the door and who was it but some poor Facilitator who'd been riding day and night from the Polish front with a dispatch case of classified material from the king of Sweden he absolutely had to have scanned and transmitted *right then* so he could get it back before anybody'd noticed it was gone? And he had to be fed and given a fresh horse, I might add.

"Fortunately at that point dear baby woke up, wanted to be fed, so Magdalena retired to the next room while I apologized and ran the Facilitator back to Diego's room where the document scanner is, left him there to figure out where everything was, it was all so rush-rush I didn't even catch his name, and ran back to bring Magdalena her gin and sit down with her.

"We'd each had time for a sip, and Magdalena was just beginning to tell me about what Susanna over in the Jodenbreestrat told her about the play she saw—and down the stairs came Lievens in a panic to hiss in my ear because he'd run out of stabilizer for the lost Purcell score he was getting ready to seal up in one of his cabinets so it could be rediscovered in 2217 AD, and he had to have more *right then* because the cabinet was scheduled to be shipped to Scotland in three days. So I had to apologize to Magdalena and ask her to hold that thought, run back to Diego's room and ask the Facilitator to let me edge by him while I transmitted an emergency request to Eurobase One for a drum of stabilizer to be sent by express flight so it could arrive in time.

"Then I had to edge back past the Facilitator and my hoops knocked off his papers where he had them stacked, poor man, and I had to apologize and help him pick them up before I could run back and sit down with Magdalena, and she'd just got to the juicy part of this play—will you hand me that paring knife, dear? Thanks—when there's another knocking on the door.

"*So,* I apologized again, profusely, to Magdalena but fortunately baby needed a change at this point, so she busied herself with that while I went see who was at the door, and it was Hayashi from Edobase, standing there on the doorstep in full Japanese costume feeling terribly conspicuous. Apparently there'd been an accident with his trunk! And he wanted to know if I could get him a change of clothes and a spare field kit before his ship put out again?

"So I hurried him back through the house and thank God Magdalena didn't look up from baby's mess or she'd have seen a samurai complete with sword tiptoeing past the doorway! And the only person in the house who had spare clothes Hayashi's size was Eliphal, who was just coming down the stairs on his way out the door to one of those minyan things, but they ran like mad back upstairs and I ran back in to Magdalena, and I needed another gin by this time, I can tell you.

"We'd just leaned down for the first sip when there was Margarite in the doorway; it seemed she'd only just noticed we were out of cooking oil and she was three-quarters ready with the *vleeskroketten* she was making for dinner, and wanted to know what she should do?

"Well, of course, what she wanted was for me to go out and buy a jar of oil, but I wasn't having any of that, I just tossed her a guilder and said, go down to Hobbema's on the dam, and she sulked away looking martyred but—"

"Why do you allow insubordination in a mortal?" Latif inquired with a slight frown.

"Because she prepares fish beautifully, and she's married to Joost, and Joost really is a treasure," I explained. "He's smart, he keeps his mouth shut, and he knows the best places to buy good horses in a hurry without paying a fortune. Sometimes you just have to put up with certain things in mortals, you know? So anyway, I turned back to Magdalena, who had just got to the part of the play where the pirate chief is about to ravish his sister all unknowing, when the front door opened and in came Lisette, all in high spirits because she'd just closed a deal for an unknown early Defoe manuscript.

"In fact she was waving it as she came running in, and went leaping into Diego's room to scan it and collided with the Facilitator, and both their sets of priceless documents went flying everywhere and you never heard such screams!

"So then, Magdalena quite understandably got the impression that my daughter was being assaulted by a Swedish cavalry officer, and—I'm not frightening you, am I, dear?"

"No! No, not at all!" said Latif, though his eyes were wide and staring.

"Well, the point is, you see how things can get?" I waved the paring knife. "It's hard keeping up the appearance of an ordinary mortal family without alarming the neighbors."

"I suppose so."

"You'll have days like that, too, when you're a full-fledged Executive Facilitator, mark my words." I dumped the last of the potatoes into the soup kettle. "We all do."

"I bet Suleyman doesn't," said Latif.

"Who? Suleyman? North African Section Head Suleyman? Oh, he's a lovely man! You know him?"

"He recruited me," said Latif.

"He was here on business one time— Recruited you? Really? Where?" I dug around in a drawer, wondering what Margarite had done with all the long spoons.

"From a slave ship," said Latif in an offhanded sort of way, and I looked up at him all ready to cry out *You poor baby*, because he was after all such a very small boy sitting there in my kitchen, and how much tinier had he been when Suleyman had rescued him from such a horrible place—but I could tell from the look in his eyes that the last thing he wanted me to do would be to exclaim over him.

At least now I knew why he wanted to grow up so fast. So I just said, "Well, we all get off to a bad start in life, or the Company wouldn't be able to snatch us away from the mortals, I guess. It was plague took my whole family but me; there I was, all alone with corpses when the nice immortal lady found me and recruited me for Dr. Zeus." I located the spoon at last and turned to stir the soup. "So, you know Suleyman. He's one of the best, I must say, but he has days when everything goes wrong, too. You just ask him, if you ever run into him again."

"Oh, I will," Latif informed me. "I'm going to be his second-in-command, when I've graduated."

"Really?" I exclaimed. "How nice! You've already been informed of your assignment?"

"No," he replied imperturbably, "But it's going to happen. I'll make it happen."

Well, I didn't know what to say at that, because, you know—we don't make things happen. Oh, we can request assignments, and if we've got the right programming and it suits the Company's purpose, our requests might be granted once in a while—but it's the Company tells us what to do and not the other way around. So I just stirred the soup, and the little boy sat and watched me.

"But enough about me," he said, in that outrageously grown-up voice he affected. "Tell me about yourself. Now that I'm getting some idea of what's involved in running an HQ, I'm more than ever impressed by your command abilities! Tell me, how do you like to relax?"

"Well—you know—like anybody does, I guess," I waved my free hand. "Going out, going to the theater, dining, conversation with the mortals."

"You find mortal conversation relaxing?" Latif raised his eyebrows.

"Sometimes." I looked darkly upward in the direction of Margarite's room. "When they're not sulking."

At this point Johan appeared in the doorway again, tears in his eyes, holding out his damn little dog like an offering. Kackerlackje was stiff as a board, lying on his side and foaming at the mouth.

"Van Drouten—the seizures stopped but now he's doing this—"

"And after all, immortal conversation can be just as irritating," I explained to Latif, tossing down the spoon and wiping my hands on my apron.

The mutt didn't die; he never did. Within a few days he was up and yapping as loudly as ever, and even seemed to remember a little of his paper-training, as opposed to his usual forgetfulness on the subject. What a joy to have in the house, huh?

But as it happened, we didn't have to put up with his presence for much longer, because about a week later I got the notification that Johan was being transferred to Brussels. So I gave him a nice farewell dinner party and we saw him off with his suitcase and animal carrier, and Margarite was so happy the dog was going with him she was in a good mood for a week.

And Latif appeared to be fitting in pretty well, which was nice. He followed me everywhere, observing just as he was supposed to. He seemed to have figured out that commenting out loud on their short-comings made people uncomfortable, and kept his thoughts to himself now. He asked the other operatives intelligent questions about their particular specialties and made a point of sitting with each of them for at least one day, watching as they went about their various businesses, especially Eliphal.

He had no difficulty with the mortals, either. In fact he went out of his way to make friends with Joost, who was charmed by him, and took him along on his horse-trading rounds. It's always a good idea to have a mortal with you when you're in one of their cities for the first time, I think, anyway. It helps you see it through their eyes.

When we went out shopping, Latif obligingly carried my basket and fan, and put up with all my mortal neighbors who came crowding to stare at him with the excuse that they had some really spicy gossip for me. And I can't think he minded being told what an adorable little fellow he was, or having sugar rolls pressed into his free hand, though the cheek-pinching bothered him, but it would bother anybody. People don't remember very well what it's like to be children.

Actually I guess Latif didn't remember much either, as sophisti-cated as he was. No, that can't be quite true: there was a day when we were out on the Dam and he stared, fascinated, at a black mortal, a slave or servant probably, who was following behind his master. What a mortal he was, too! Gorgeous, with these long legs in thigh-high boots and his full white shirt with its lace collar open at the throat, skin like polished ebony, striding along in good-humored ar-rogance, chatting with his master about the pistols they were on their way to buy.

He saw Latif staring at him and grinned hugely, such perfect white teeth, and winked. Latif caught his breath, I swear; and all the way home he was walking with the mortal's long-legged stride, practicing that grace.

But that was about the only time I saw him being a little boy, which worried me. The rest of the time he was stone-cold serious and grimly determined to become the perfect operative. I've had trainee Facilita-tors in their twenties who weren't as dedicated to learning their jobs. But then, Latif was special, wasn't he? Or he'd still have been in the ju-nior class at a Company training base somewhere, with other children his age.

He watched closely as I dealt with the everyday business of run-ning the station: feeding operatives who dropped in at any hour of the day or night, seeing to it they were issued whatever field supplies they needed, and ordering anything we didn't actually have on hand at the station. There was the station budget to fight with, frantically thinking of ways to stretch it until the next fiscal quarter! There were couriers to greet, pouches to be signed for or sent on their way, dispatches to be transmitted; there were shipments to be received and sent of so many humdrum things that would become priceless over time.

Who needed all those copies of the new London *Daily Courant* or the *Moskovskya Viedomosti*? What about all those Watteau and Rigaud paintings, who on Earth would want such sickly candy-box things? And the Pachelbel scores that the composer just happened to misplace, or those jottings by Hakuseki, would wealthy collectors really pay small fortunes for those in the future? It always amazes me, the garbage that time turns into gold; but, you know, that's how the Company makes its money. If it keeps herring on my table (and makes me immortal, too!) who am I to raise an eyebrow?

And Latif learned quickly, he really was a brilliant little boy, and grasped very well the importance of interfacing with the mortal community, building relationships within it that we could use to the Company's advantage and reinforcing the illusion that we were a perfectly (well, reasonably) normal mortal Amsterdam family. It helped, too, that I didn't have to keep stopping his lessons to sweep or peel onions.

Yes! Margarite's good mood didn't last past the week of Kackerlackje's departure, but she didn't lapse into the usual pattern of headaches and diarrhea that made her unable to cope with daily routine. She went into a frenzy of activity instead. The house was as spotless as it's ever been, meals were ready on time, and suddenly there was an airy, digestible quality to her cooking that made me realize that maybe it had been just a little heavy before.

Though when Eliphal stopped on the stairs to pay her a gallant compliment about the latest batch of *vleeskroketten*, she still glared at him. What was going on in her head? No use to ask Joost; when I brought up the subject he just shrugged and held out his hands, gesturing *How should I know?* Then he swung Latif up on his shoulders and they went out to watch ships being unloaded.

Summer ended, and the canals were pretty with drifting yellow leaves for a week or two before the cold set in. I had to order a new wardrobe for Latif, because he'd outgrown the furred jacket he'd brought from Mackenzie Base, so quickly was he beginning to shoot up. He was going to be tall and imposing, and I was glad for him. I don't think he'd felt an Executive Facilitator should be short and undignified. He prowled around the house for a couple of weeks wrapped in knitted shawls until his new coat arrived.

He was bundled up like that the morning I rose early and came down to find him sitting at my credenza, with his little fingers pattering away at the keyboard rapid-fire-speed.

"Good morning!" he greeted me pleasantly, glancing up. "I woke up early and I couldn't go back to sleep, so I just thought I'd check your mail for you."

"Oh," I said, yawning. "Did I have any?"

"Yes." He indicated a stack of printouts as he closed and shut down the credenza. "The usual things. Answers to queries, priority orders, directives. I've sorted them for you in order of importance. I hope I wasn't presuming?"

"No, no, you need to learn this stuff, after all," I replied, sitting down beside him and flipping through the printouts. He really had prioritized them, too; I was quite impressed. "This is great! Gosh, you're a quick study, Latif."

"I'm glad you think so," he replied graciously. "And actually, I was wondering: in view of the rapid progress I'm making, do you suppose it's time I was fast-tracked?"

"Fast-tracked?" I looked up from the printouts to stare at him.

"Accelerated," he explained. "My educational schedule revised to send me on to Eurobase One ahead of the originally estimated date. What do you think? Would you be receptive to the idea?"

"Oh, I don't know, sweetie," I told him dubiously. "Shouldn't you have some childhood? I mean, look at you! You've still got your baby teeth, and you're out in the field already. Don't you think you've been fast-tracked enough as it is?"

He watched me intently as I answered him, and I was half afraid he'd get angry; but he just nodded and made a dismissive gesture.

"You're right, of course," he said at once. "I'll bow to your judgment. I'm undoubtedly not as proficient at this yet as I think I am."

And I was so impressed by the gracious way he took my refusal that I hastened to reassure him about what a little genius he was.

Well, I was right about his being a genius.

Snow fell one morning, and all the muck froze so that the view from the parlor window was just like a postcard, and the houses across the canal were all frosted with white. Really it was perfect weather for curling up beside the window with a nice cup of hot chocolate, but we'd run out; everyone had been craving Theobromos desperately lately, for some reason. It was too early in the day to get blitzed anyhow, and I had work to do.

I admired the snowy scene for a few minutes before settling down at my credenza to check my incoming dispatches, sipping my coffee meditatively. I liked this time of the morning, before the rest of the household was awake, when I usually had some peace and quiet.

The first blast in my little symphony of horror was a communication from Verpoorten in the Brussels office complaining about Johan. Not Johan exactly; Verpoorten said he was an able enough Botanist, though I'd been a little mistaken about what his specialties were when I recommended him for transfer to their gardens project, and right there warning bells began to ring in my head. I hadn't recommended him! He'd been requested, hadn't he? But I read on, appalled.

It seemed that Kackerlackje was making himself just as inconvenient at Brussels HQ as he had in my house, and Verpoorten was a lot less inclined to cope with him. He had had to give Johan an ultimatum, apparently. The dog had to go. Johan had acquiesced in tears, but only on the condition that dear little Kackerlackje be sent back to me, since Johan knew I loved him as much as he did and moreover had always looked after his precarious health like a loving mother.

Boy, there aren't words to describe my consternation. Some Executive Facilitators I know would just give the damn dog all the paint he could eat and then send him diving tied to a rock, but I'm nice, you know? I was so upset I put the communication aside without sending a reply and went into my fiscal file. I'd buy something, that would take my mind off my troubles! Time to order new components for the document scanner, yes, Diego had reminded me about that only yesterday, and Lievens wanted another shipment of red oak for cabinets.

What a surprise I got when my credenza informed me I had insufficient funds for the transaction . . .

Thinking of course that there must be some mistake, I checked my budget balance, and then I got a real surprise.

This has happened to you, right? So you know that after the first frantic denial a sort of icy numbness sets in and you settle down to go over the books with a fine-toothed comb, determined to find the mistake. That's what I was doing when the knock came on the door.

Too much to expect that Margarite would answer it, of course. God forbid she should actually do her job or anything like that. As the knock was repeated a little more loudly I rose to get it, scanning irritably for where in the house Margarite had got to. There was her heartbeat, coming from her bedroom, and some other sounds as well . . . oh, dear, was she throwing up? No wonder she hadn't lit the fires or started breakfast yet. I'd have to do, it, of course—

My annoyance at this fled right out of my mind when I opened the door and beheld my two visitors.

Quite an elegant-looking lady and gentleman, as much as you could see of them for the furred coats in which they were bundled up. They were both immortals, too.

"Executive Facilitator Van Drouten, I presume?" inquired the gentleman. "May we have a moment of your time?"

So of course I invited them in off the stoop, and settled them in the parlor while I excused myself a moment and ran off to grab Lisette, who was just coming downstairs, and asked her to go see what the matter was with Margarite, and see if Joost couldn't be prevailed upon to light the fires so we wouldn't all freeze? Then I found a bottle of gin and three glasses and brought them out to my guests.

They were even more elegant out of their coats, quite exotic-looking, too, for all that they were dressed in perfect up-to-the-minute Continental fashions. The man had been Incan or Aztec or one of those originally; he had the copper skin and the gloomy sneering dignity. The lady had white skin, green eyes, hair like a raven's wing, a real stunner if she hadn't had such a disagreeable look on her face. So had the man, actually. But they both smiled politely as I poured them gin and asked how I could help them.

"You're too kind," the man said, hooding his eyes. "May I introduce myself? I am Security Technical Sixteen Turtle and this is my associate, Botanist Smythe. We're presently stationed at New World One."

"My gosh, what a long way to come," I exclaimed, offering them both their gin. They accepted the glasses but did not drink.

"Oh, we arrived by air transport," Sixteen Turtle said, turning the stem of his glass between his fingers. "We don't expect to be away long." And then he transmitted subvocally: *It's my hope we can resolve this issue quickly, to our mutual satisfaction.*

I didn't know what to make of this, because usually the only time we need to speak to each other subvocally is when we don't want the mortals to hear us speaking out loud, and there were no mortals within earshot. But I gamely transmitted: *Gee, I hope so, too.*

"Amsterdam is truly lovely at this time of year," Smythe told me graciously, though she was looking daggers at me. *May I begin by assuring you that we feel competition is a good thing, generally?*

That's nice, I transmitted back, and out loud I said: "How nice to hear someone say so! Usually all people ever want to see are tulips, tulips, tulips, you know, and of course they don't bloom at this time of year . . ."

"Yes, I was aware of that," Smythe replied, and I remembered she was a Botanist and felt silly.

Competition, transmitted Sixteen Turtle, *can actually stimulate business. And in a global market, there are certainly enough potential customers for everyone.*

What, for tulips? I responded. *My God, don't invest in bulbs! Don't you know what happened last time? The bottom fell out of the market and—* But from their offended expressions I could tell I was off the mark somehow.

Could you come to the point, please? I transmitted, just as Lisette came running back downstairs.

"Van Drouten? I don't think Margarite should get up today—" she blurted, and then noticed I had guests who were glaring at me strangely. "And I'll—just tell you about it later, okay?"

"Please do," I snapped, "and you might suggest to Joost that he deal with her in the meantime."

"He's not here," Lisette informed me, wringing her hands. "He, uh, apparently took Latif out to build a snowman."

"Mortal servants!" Sixteen Turtle shook his head, sounding tolerantly amused. "We have similar troubles with ours."

"At least yours don't sneak out to build snowmen, not in South America," I grumbled, and Lisette took that opportunity to vanish discreetly.

"Oh, we have snow in the mountains," Smythe assured me. *Though not in the plantations of Theobroma cacao. And that, madam, brings us to the point.*

Really?

Yes. Sixteen Turtle lifted his gin and held it under that aristocratic nose of his to inhale the bouquet. *We're quite prepared to tolerate the existence of a rival operation. It's not as though we haven't got an adequate market on the Pacific Rim already, and to be frank, we can't see our operation expanding any further.* He lowered the glass and fixed me with a cold dead stare. *What we're not prepared to tolerate, however, is gross mismanagement to the extent that the Company is alerted, not only to the existence of your operation, but ours as well.*

At least now I knew why we weren't talking out loud.

"Funny, you know, but I just can't imagine snow that close to the equator," I said cheerily, but now I was looking daggers right back at them. *You're black marketeers, aren't you? And you deal in Theobromos!*

Did you think you were the only one to have conceived of this idea? demanded Smythe, but Sixteen Turtle was realizing I really hadn't known what was going on. He lifted his head, peering up our staircase and inhaling deeply, and I did, too, and suddenly singled out the fragrance that had been driving us all subliminally crazy lately, masked as it was by nutmeg and cloves: Theobromos.

My shock was enough to get through to Smythe, too, and she and Sixteen Turtle looked horrified. They'd just as good as confessed to an Executive Facilitator that they ran a Theobromos racket, and moreover brought her attention to one being run out of her own HQ! Not that I think there's anything wrong with the black market, mind you, since Dr. Zeus never stocks enough Theobromos in the Company bases. But it is against Company regulations, and any operative caught at it faces disciplinary measures.

Sixteen Turtle recovered himself first. He smiled broadly and put his fingertips together.

"Ah, but I can certainly imagine your beautiful country ablaze with tulips," he said. *Dear me, I can't imagine this will reflect favorably on your record,* he transmitted. *One of the operatives under your command dealing in contraband Theobromos? And not very well, I might add.*

How not very well? I demanded. *You thought it was my operation, didn't you? You may as well tell me all the details. Has somebody been using my codes to buy the stuff?*

Would it be in our best interests to tell you? Smythe replied, looking as though cocoa butter wouldn't melt in her mouth.

Yes, it would, I told her grimly.

She and Sixteen Turtle looked at each other before he transmitted.

Well, madam, it appears that someone with much audacity but little expertise has recently purchased a great deal of a certain commodity in your name, apparently with the intent of cornering the European black market on that commodity. Nothing to distress anyone in that; as I believe I pointed out, the global market can bear more than one player in this game. However, the player in question has offered the commodity at such absurdly low prices that he or she is certain to arouse suspicion. Moreover, by our calculations, your culprit can't possibly turn a profit! And such practices are not only likely to ruin the individual dealer, they're bad for business generally. This was why we felt obliged to warn you, for your own good—

I remembered my nonexistent budget balance.

I see, I transmitted. I didn't, yet, though. Just at that moment another transmission crackled through the ether, slightly distorted by snow and panic, and unfortunately on a wide enough band so my visitors heard it, too:

Van Drouten! Very angry mortal looking for you! I'm trying to head him off, but—

It was Kalugin, sounding as though he were running along through the frozen streets.

That was exactly what he was doing, too, because a moment later there was a commotion on the front stoop and we could hear Kalugin saying: "Sir, I implore you! Whatever your grievances against the man, the City Watch will look dimly on stabbing him in this good lady's parlor—"

"Excuse me, won't you?" I said, leaping up to answer the pounding on my door. When I opened it I beheld Kalugin, or rather his broad back, because he had got in front of my visitor and was holding his hands up in a placatory gesture. The visitor was a diminutive mortal gentleman who was glaring around Kalugin at me with an expression of such venom it made my hair curl.

"Where is the Jew Eliphal?" he demanded.

"Uh—Madam Van Drouten, this gentleman was a passenger on my ship, and he seems to have some grievance against one of your tenants—" Kalugin explained hastily, turning around. The mortal used this opportunity to push under Kalugin's arm and slip past me into the hall, and from there into the parlor.

"Where is the diamond cutter?" he shouted, flinging his cloak back over one shoulder and revealing a box he was clutching, also the sword and matching dagger on his hip. Kalugin and I were both beside him at this point, but unfortunately Eliphal had heard all the commotion and come running downstairs.

"What is it? Who wants to see me?" he asked. The mortal singled him out with a deadly look and hurled the box down so that it bounced open at Eliphal's feet, spilling out three or four bricks of something wrapped in oiled paper. A fragrance rose up from the broken box like, well, like paradise. Something tropical and exotic and yet evocative of cozy winter kitchens where you could curl up by the stove with a nice hot cup of . . .

Theobromos. Not the ordinary stuff mortals bought and sold, either, but the high-powered Company cultivar with a kick like a mule. Every immortal in my increasingly crowded parlor leaned forward involuntarily, including me.

"Where the hell are my emeralds?" the mortal snarled, drawing steel.

Eliphal looked up openmouthed from his contemplation of the spilled delight.

"What emeralds?" he replied. "Who are you, sir?"

"Sanpietro del Vaglio," the mortal replied, as though it was terribly obvious. "And I tell you to your face you are a liar and a thief and the son of Barbary apes!"

"How dare you? I've never heard of you in my life," Eliphal shouted, drawing himself up, and I winced because he takes his character very seriously, but before the mortal could lunge forward with his sword there was yet another clatter of feet on the stoop and in came Joost and Latif, all dusted with snow as though they'd just stepped out of a toy globe. They halted and stared at the scene, astonished.

"Do you dare to deny you offered me six Peruvian emeralds of the finest grade, and sent me *this* instead?" screamed del Vaglio. "What do you think I am, a confectioner?"

Joost's eyes went wide with horror, and so did Latif's. They exchanged a glance. Everybody in the room knew right then, except for the mortal, whose back was turned to them.

"Yes, I deny it," Eliphal retorted. "Somebody has been using my name to do business!"

And he turned an accusing stare of terribly righteous wrath on Latif.

Latif met his stare and backed up a pace, unblinking; then he turned and buried his face in my apron, and burst into very, very loud sobs.

Sixteen Turtle and Smythe smirked at each other.

"Mistress, it wasn't his fault," Joost cried. "I must have sent the parcels to the wrong addresses!"

Latif sobbed even more loudly.

"You mean you were supposed to send emeralds to this man and chocolate to somebody else?" I asked Joost. Del Vaglio had turned to stare at us in incomprehension; Eliphal folded his arms in indignant triumph.

Joost looked abashed. "Yes, mistress. But—"

"Where did you get six Peruvian emeralds of the finest grade, Latif?" I inquired, so dazed the minute details were holding my attention. Latif's sobbing went up a decibel.

"You're that little brat who was training with Houbert, aren't you?" remarked Smythe suddenly, leaning forward to stare at him, or at least at the back of his head. "Ha! You put your tour of duty in New World One to good use, I must say."

"You mean—" I began, meaning to ask if the child had spent all his free time making smuggling connections, but at that moment somebody else came slinking up on the stoop and peered in through the door, which was still open and in fact letting in floating snow.

"Er—excuse me," she murmured, or at least that's what I think she said because she was so muffled up in scarves and fur. "I'm looking for Facilitator Van Drouten . . . ?"

"Well, come in and shut the door after you," I said wearily, but she drew back.

"Er . . . no, I—" Her gaze riveted on the broken box and its fragrant contents.

"Oh." Light dawned on me. "You got something you didn't expect in the mail, huh?"

She looked as though she was about to turn and run, but Kalugin stepped close and took her arm firmly. He led her outside and they had a whispered conversation. A moment later he returned, bearing a small wooden box remarkably like the one del Vaglio had brought.

"I believe this is yours, sir," Kalugin said, offering it to him. Del Vaglio sheathed his sword and took it doubtfully, and Kalugin bent down and swept up the broken box and its contents. "Excuse me a moment, won't you?"

Kalugin took the Theobromos outside and a second later we could hear the immortal, whoever she was, running away as if for dear life. Del Vaglio, meanwhile, had opened the new box and carried it over to the window to inspect its contents. He took out a lens in an eyepiece and examined whatever was in there—six Peruvian emeralds of the finest grade?—pretty carefully before closing the box with a snap and tucking it under his arm in a possessive kind of way.

"Acceptable," he said, and swinging his cloak around him he strode to the door. "*Grazie*, Captain Kalugin. Under the circumstances I will seek no further redress for this insult."

"What about the insult to me, you pig?" roared Eliphal, but del Vaglio exited regally, if hurriedly. At least he shut the door after himself. But the room was no less crowded, because here came Lisette down the steps again at a run, crying out: "Joost! You'd better go see Margarite right away."

"Is she all right?" He looked alarmed. Lisette scowled at the rest of us and came and whispered in his ear. The alarm in his face vanished; he lit up like a chandelier.

"Lord God," he whooped. "It worked!" He rushed at Latif to hug him, but Latif was stuck to my apron like a limpet, still sobbing, so he contented himself with kissing the top of his head and yelling: "God bless you, little master, it'll be a son for sure." He turned and ran away upstairs, and we could hear his feet thundering all the way to the fourth floor.

"So . . . you've been slipping Margarite hormones or something, too?" I guessed. Latif was still too wracked with sobs to reply, which was answer enough. Well! Guess who was going to be lighting the fires and sweeping the stoop for the next few months? Not Margarite, huh? "And I'll bet you got Johan transferred, didn't you?"

Sixteen Turtle and Smythe rose to their feet.

"Perhaps we'd best depart," said Sixteen Turtle in a voice like silk. As he was pulling on his furs, his eyes glinted with malevolent humor. *Unless the young gentleman wishes us to take his remaining stock off his hands? Though I'm afraid we couldn't possibly offer more than fifty percent.*

Latif's sobs kept going, but his little fists clenched in the folds of my apron.

"How much . . . merchandise is upstairs, Latif?" I asked him.

"Five hundredweight chests," he paused in his sobbing long enough to say distinctly.

Kalugin and Eliphal reeled. Well, that just about accounted for the hole in my budget. Joost and Latif must have had it brought in by canal barge and lifted it up with the warehouse block and tackle, possibly while I was out shopping. I don't know where I found the presence of mind to look Sixteen Turtle in the eye and transmit to him: *Nothing doing. I'm confiscating his entire stock. You can deal with me now! And you'll either pay me full retail value or—*and I really don't know where I found the nerve to say this—*or maybe I'll go into business for myself. You said you wouldn't mind a little competition. Hmm! This close to Belgium, I'll bet I could cut into your markets with a vengeance.*

I must have expressed myself badly, replied Sixteen Turtle without batting an eyelash. *Naturally we'd pay full retail value for an order that size. Five hundredweights? Let me think, we could offer . . .*

He conferred briefly and subvocally with Smythe, and then she named a sum. It wasn't quite enough to bring my budget into the black.

What do you think, Latif? I wondered. *Perhaps we could work out a marketing strategy. 'If You're Tired of Waiting for Godiva, Wait No More! Primo Black Magic Is Here!' And we can always claim it's fresher and purer than the competition's because it comes in on the Dutch East Indies ships—*

Smythe winced and named another sum. It was a lot higher than the other sum she'd named. Latif cautiously lifted his perfectly dry face from my apron and mouthed *Take it!* in silence, then buried his face again and gave another wail of misery.

"Done," I said aloud. "Who's your banker?"

Eliphal oversaw the transfer of funds. We had the stuff loaded out of the house by that evening.

———

"So, you see?" I said, dipping my scrub brush in the soapy water and going after the greasy patch in front of the kitchen hearth. "You weren't ready to be fast-tracked after all."

"You're right, of course," Latif replied gloomily, dipping his scrub brush, too. He put it down a moment to roll up his sleeves again and then attacked a blob of spilled jam. "But it almost worked." *If Joost hadn't mixed those labels and if I'd had a better idea what the black market rate ought to be . . . You know I was only trying to defray operating expenses and make your job easier, I hope?*

"Oh, yeah," I agreed. "And it might have worked at that, sweetie. But the logic's really simple here: you're a child. You don't know everything about this job yet. That's why you're not in Africa. And aren't you glad that if you were going to make a big boomeranging blunder, you did it in front of me and not your hero Suleyman?"

"I guess so," he replied, edging forward to get some tracked-in mud.

"Or Labienus! Though I can't imagine you'd be having a conversation like this one with him," I added, snickering at the idea of Mr. Super-Cyborg Executive Facilitator General on his hands and knees scrubbing a floor. "I guess I must have fallen pretty short of your expectations after you'd studied under Labienus."

"Everybody under his command hates Labienus," Latif told me quietly.

"I'd heard that," I said. "I've heard he treats his mortals like animals."

Latif nodded. He dipped his brush again and went on scrubbing. After a moment he said: "He hates them. He thought I'd hate them, too, because of the slave ship. He told me I could go far with him. But . . . Labienus never breaks the rules where anybody can see. And he always makes sure there's somebody else to take the blame. But I saw. And I thought . . . well, so much for role models." He scowled down at the rust stain he was attacking. "But Suleyman doesn't do stuff like that. I hope?"

I slopped suds on a crusted bit of something I didn't want to think about—how long since the last time Margarite had scrubbed this floor?!—and said:

"No, Suleyman's a nice guy. You'll see, when you finally get yourself assigned to his HQ. And, you know what? Even with a little setback like this, I'll bet you get your wish. I'll bet you'll be assigned to his command in no time at all, a smooth operator like you."

He actually giggled at that.

"Though actually I should probably continue on here a while longer," he said, with elaborate casualness.

"So you can learn the finer points of getting dirt up off of a floor, huh?" I panted, sitting up and dropping my brush in the bucket.

"Or something," he replied, dropping his brush in there, too. He stood up.

"Good, because you wouldn't believe how much of an Executive Facilitator's job is cleaning up messes," I told him, getting to my feet and surveying what we'd done so far. "Okay! Now we mop and then, what do you say? Want to go shopping on the Dam? I could use some marzipan cakes."

"Me too," Latif replied, slipping his little hand into mine.

Labienus shudders, wills the memory away. He puts back the offending file. Settling down with the red project file he opens it, paging through the material with his reports, his annotations.

When he opens it, the first image to greet his eyes is a slightly out-of-focus field photograph of a street in sixteenth-century London. Labienus remembers an overwhelming sense of nausea. Standing in old Egypt, finicky over a little smoke and dung, he'd had no idea of the filth he'd have to endure over the next four thousand years! London had certainly been one of the low points in his long life. He had endured, however. And profited . . .

Turning the page, he sees the face as through a shroud. He removes the protective covering of tissue paper from the drawing. His gesture is almost tender, as though he were lifting a blanket to gaze upon a sleeping child.

It is no more than a study for a portrait never painted, a sketch on paper in red chalk and black ink, by some long-dead Italian master. The subject is a young male mortal. He had posed stiffly, regarding the artist with disapproval, for the artist had been a papist and the subject of the sketch was a heretic.

The artist had therefore not made much effort to flatter his subject. He had presented with blunt realism the boy's long homely face, his broken nose, his small cold eyes, his wide mouth. Even if he had been well disposed toward the boy, however, the artist would have been unable to make him look quite human.

But no mortal living could have known why. The boy himself hadn't known why. Precious few immortals would have known, either, by the year 1543! Labienus looks down at the portrait and mentally calls up Budu's features, superimposes them over the boy's.

There is a resemblance, would be even more of a resemblance if the portrait had been done in color. A certain expression in the eyes. A certain set of the mouth. The same cheekbones. If a god had taken that ancient flatheaded creature in the photograph and sculpted it like clay until it looked human, the result would be the boy in the portrait. One of them is a monster and the other is a man.

The delicious irony, of course, is that it is the boy who is the monster.

Though not in a moral sense, Labienus admits to himself. Regardless of the predilection for violence and the prodigious carnal appetites with which he had been created, Nicholas Harpole had been quite a virtuous boy.

Labienus was never officially posted to London, but there he happened to be, in the dismal year 1527. He chanced to be riding back from Hampstead to his lodgings in the City, one night.

No moon and few stars, under the thin fog. Almost a warm night, if wretched England could be said to have such a thing, for it was high summer. Ahead and to his left were the flickering lights of London, but out here in the fields was unfathomable darkness, unless of course one was a cyborg and could see by infrared. Labienus wasn't bothering to do that, however. He knew the way well and so did his horse.

It paused to crop the long grass at the edge of the ditch and he waited patiently, deciding to cut across the fields toward Gray's Inn Road. As he sat there, however, he heard a faint cryptic signal in the ether.

It was coming from the opposite side of the road, off in the direction of St. Marylebone. Frowning, he turned his head and scanned.

Nothing there in the darkness. He was about to ride on when the signal came again, like a faintly glowing puff of mist in the night. He switched to infrared; no result. Turning his horse's head to the right, he urged it across the ditch and into the fields beyond. The animal trotted forward, then slowed to a walk; then stopped, whickering uneasily.

Labienus saw nothing. In the instant before he realized there was a voice in his head *telling him* he saw nothing, he felt a paralyzing shock, and something black rose up from the ground at tremendous speed.

He found himself caught in darkness, cradled like a child across a lap except for the fact that a massive hand had closed on his windpipe. Another massive hand, on an arm like a tree trunk, had firm hold of his mount's bridle, and though the horse was trembling it stood obediently still. He looked up. A black silhouette rose against the night, a giant crouching in the new-cut hay.

Labienus calmed himself. *Father,* he transmitted.

"Why are you wearing a black armband?" said a voice in the night.

It was not the deep, growling voice one would expect to hear coming out of something that looked so much like a bear. It was rather flat and high-pitched.

I'm in deep mourning. Hadn't you heard? Niccolò Machiavelli just died.

The giant shook with silent laughter. Labienus felt his throat released, and he gulped air gratefully.

So the rumors are true. You went rogue!

"Some time ago," said Budu. "The Crusades were the last straw. You can speak out loud. The Company won't hear us."

Remembering the shock, Labienus ran a diagnostic on himself and realized his datafeed to the Company had been shorted out. He felt incredulous delight.

"How long will it last?"

"Long enough." Budu released him and he sat up, brushing hay from his doublet.

"I've been hoping you were out there," Labienus said.

"Have you?"

"They should never have retired you. I had no idea how vile a place the world would become, with the mortals free to spread like pestilence. Our masters are imbeciles, father!"

"You think so?"

"Yes," said Labienus, realizing he'd said too much. He sat back, evening his breath, studying the Enforcer.

"Good," said Budu. He wore layered rags and a leather hood that must have required two cowhides. It was all stained, faded, dull stone colors, superb camouflage. He sheathed an immense hunting knife, making it vanish somewhere in his clothing.

Labienus realized that if he'd said the wrong thing, he might have had his throat cut and Budu would simply have made off with his horse. He had no particular desire to wake, chilled and painful and covered with his own blood, in gray dawn in the middle of nowhere with a long walk ahead of him.

He licked his lips and said: "When the Black Death broke out—I half hoped it was your doing, somehow."

"No," said Budu, "but you were thinking in the right lines. It was impressive."

"It was marvelous! It crippled Justinian's work in Byzantium, and what it did to Europe! Whole towns vanished and went back to clean earth. It swept through their filthy little cities the way you used to, father, and nothing stopped it."

"But it was stupid, son," Budu told him. "Don't waste your admiration on it. It killed indiscriminately. Innocents died with the guilty."

"How many of them are innocent any more?" said Labienus bitterly. "How many of them were ever innocent?"

"You were, once," Budu replied.

Labienus reminded himself never to speak from the heart.

"What have you been doing with yourself, father? Assuming you can tell me."

Budu shrugged. "I've walked in shadows. Continued the work, when I had the chance. One old man with a knife can't do much."

"But the other Enforcers?" asked Labienus. "Haven't any of them followed you into exile?"

"They were betrayed," said Budu. "They've been taken offline, one after another as the years passed, and the Company has hidden them well. I'm the only one left walking free." Idly he took up a long stem of hay and turned it in his fingers, rotating it like the tiniest of quarterstaffs. He pointed it at Labienus. "You see how we were repaid, after we labored for our masters? How do you think they will repay you, when you've served your purpose?"

"Undoubtedly the same," said Labienus. "If they get the chance."

Budu chuckled. "But you won't let them have the chance, eh?"

"No indeed."

"What do you propose to do?"

Labienus looked at him. "What would you do? Wait until they're vulnerable and strike. Their precious Temporal Concordance runs out in 2355; after that they'll have no more foreknowledge of events than we do. Once that playing field's leveled, we'll see who wins the game."

"And who is *we*, son?"

"You and I, presumably. And any of the rest of the Executives who are as disgusted as we are, and I'll bet there are a lot of us."

"There are," said Budu. "Will you join us, son?"

"Oh, yes." Labienus felt a shiver of genuine delight. "Only tell me what you need me to do, father!"

"Work with me," said Budu, staring into his eyes. "We have a lot of preparation to make for 2355. You think this Earth is crowded now, you think it's dirty? You've no idea how much worse it's going to be, in a few more centuries. The mortals will go mad. Cities like termite mounds. Murderers in packs like wolves, roaming unpunished. Not simply one or two tyrants or dictators in a century, not one or two neat world wars, the way you were told. Wars every year, *fuehrers* at the end of every street. No justice. No order. No refuge for the innocent."

"You must have seen the Temporal Concordance." Labienus was awed.

"No," said Budu. "But there are those who have."

"And we can't do anything," said Labienus, "because history cannot be changed."

"We can't prevent it. That doesn't mean we can't do anything." Budu smiled, showing terrifying teeth. "And don't be so certain history is as fixed as they tell you, son."

"You used to say that, but nobody's managed to change it yet," said Labienus. "All the same, time is on our side! Here we are in the past, with centuries to prepare, and there they are in the future, with—what—thirty years?"

"But we face the longest march, to the most necessary victory. Do you have the strength?"

"Yes. Still, we'll have competition, father," Labienus warned. "Some of the Executive line are already making their own plans. You remember Aegeus? He's built what amounts to a private kingdom up there in the Cévennes. It's disgusting. He actually keeps mortal slaves for his own pleasure."

"That is forbidden." Budu's eyes grew small and hard as stones.

"I've already got spies in his organization, gathering evidence."

"Good. He'll suffer the consequences, when that last day comes. The other Executives must be conscripted, or persuaded to stand aside. We need every advantage."

"We can co-opt the Company's resources for our own use." Labienus had an inspiration then. "You should see how I'm presently employed, father—"

"You're a lawyer at Gray's Inn," said Budu. "Twice a year you ride out to Hampstead, to look at a mortal child you placed with foster parents there."

"Yes," said Labienus, feeling a sliver of ice in his heart. "You've observed me closely, I see. Had it occurred to you to look at the boy?"

"Yes. Old blood there. Who is he?"

"Not who; what. The damned thing is a Recombinant! The Company themselves decided to make one. They're experimenting the way they always do, dropping their subject into the past and watching what happens."

"Then they have put the lives of innocents at risk," said Budu, scowling.

"Not in the way you'd think. He's no plague-bearer, father." Labienus looked at Budu slyly. "He's a great deal more dangerous. Old blood indeed! Someone had the bright idea of designing a replacement for *you*, you see. A New Enforcer. Genetically engineered to look more human, and to be less disobedient. The little creature's their prototype. Yes, twice a year I do drag my sorry old bones out to Hampstead to test him. He never fails to impress me."

"How?"

"Utterly different brain. Better reflexes than a human child. He'll never be a beauty, but he'll be bigger and faster than most mortals. Smarter, too." Labienus parodied the syrupy tones of a fond mortal parent. "Why, only today I told our Nicket that a very great man had died, the man I named him for in fact, and do you know what the clever wittle darling said?"

"I don't care what he said," Budu replied. "Are they going to work the immortality process on him?"

"On a prototype? Gods, no! They'll never do that again," said Labienus, with a significant look. "Though I've been sorely tempted, father. Don't you think we could make good use of such a weapon? Especially as it's the blackest of black projects, and I'm the sole handler for the prototype? He'll operate within event shadows, free of recorded history! A man like that could do terrific damage where we aimed him."

"It's been done," said Budu. "More times than you know, these prodigies have walked the Earth. They're never worth the trouble. I'm not interested."

"This one is different," Labienus insisted. "And wouldn't you like another son? An able second-in-command?"

"No; but *you* would," Budu told him. "Someone to laugh at your jokes. Someone to impress with your cleverness. That's vanity. It won't serve my purpose."

"As you wish." Labienus concealed his irritation. "What else did you have in mind?"

"I want a new means of culling the mortal herds, controlled, precise. Something better than war. More selective than plague. You think about it. Use the Company's technology, if you can."

"But I'll need to find the right specialists! Possibly even mortal ones. It will require subtlety, father—"

"And you're a subtle man, yes? Win new recruits to our cause. Take your poor dead Machiavelli as your model." Budu reached out and plucked at the black armband, chuckling again. "You'll find a way."

And then he was gone, and Labienus stared around him in amazement. Nothing to be seen in any direction but the flat floor of mown hay, giving up its sweet scent to the night damps. No sound but night birds crying as they flew toward the river. He climbed to his feet and brushed off his clothes. Mounting his horse once again, he rode on to dark London.

And so nothing useful had been done with Nicholas Harpole.

Labienus sighs. So much potential in a bright child, if trained properly. All that splendid ability, wasted on one martyrdom to prop up some distant causal link to Dr. Zeus Incorporated . . .

Here is a statistic to make his heart bleed over might-have-beens: out of the four hundred seventeen mortals who heard Nicholas preach as he was being burned at the stake, fully twenty-two had heeded his plea to become martyrs to the Protestant cause themselves. Two hundred twelve had gone on to lose their lives in less immediate ways, in the defense of English liberty. Eighty-six more had gone into various levels of what passed for the secret service at that time, working for the downfall of Spain with patient fanaticism under Sir Francis Walsingham. Fifty-one had simply committed suicide, in varying ways, over the three-year period following April 1, 1555.

The point was, of course, that Nicholas Harpole had asked them to die, *and they had.* Or at least given up their lives. A miserable three hundred seventy-one mortals, when he might have laid waste to nations.

Much better success on the second try. Labienus smiles, coming to the pages added later, the reports from other operatives. He hadn't minded when the *Adonai* project had been taken from him. He'd been just settling in here at Mackenzie Base, and had too many irons in the fire to waste time shepherding another hapless youth from one self-destructive crisis to the next. It had helped his ego that the new project head was a close friend, of course.

By 1837, the field wherein Budu had prophesied dystopic madness had long since been enclosed by Regent's Park, as London expanded northward. Noisome as Labienus had found the place in Tudor times, it had been a pastoral idyll compared with the urban sprawl that welcomed the new queen, young Victoria.

So Labienus went nowhere near London when he visited Executive Facilitator Nennius, and was gratified to find that Overton Hall was a dozen miles from the nearest town of any size.

They sat in Nennius's study on an autumn evening, with their feet propped before the cozy fire and a decanter of port on a stand between them. Behind them, the windows had been firmly locked and curtains had been drawn against the night.

"It could have been worse," said Nennius, who was striving to be philosophical about his dismal posting. "It might have been a national school."

"Not for this boy," Labienus replied, helping himself to the port.

"True. All the same, I wish they'd left the matter in your hands. You'd have enjoyed the role of headmaster a great deal more than I, I suspect. All this piety and *in loco parentis* nonsense one is called upon to display, when one would much rather drown the little bastards!"

They laughed together companionably.

"You've a river here, haven't you?" said Labienus. "Arrange rowing matches and drill holes in the boats beforehand."

"Could do that, yes." Nennius composed his dark features into an expression of suitably shocked regret. "Terribly sorry, Mrs. Peckham-Winsbury, but we've had to drag the marshes for young Cecil and I'm afraid all that's been brought up is his right boot!"

Labienus snickered. "Or lay in some magnesium flares, and arrange the odd case of spontaneous combustion in the dormitories."

"Yes!" Nennius slapped his thigh. "Boys, we are gathered here to pray for the soul of Phipps Minor, who ascended into heaven in quite the brightest blaze of glory on record! Ashes to be forwarded to his careful guardian in a very small paper sack."

"Arrange for an escaped leopard to prowl the grounds."

"I regret to inform you all that the First Form will no longer be permitted on the cricket ground, due to the fact that an unidentified feline has been dragging smaller students into the bushes and eating them!" Nennius rocked in his chair with laughter.

"Secrete a few gelignite charges in their tuckboxes."

"I am quite at a loss to explain this, Mr. Carstairs, but it would appear that just as your son was sinking his teeth into an Eccles cake, he unaccountably exploded!"

Labienus wiped tears from his eyes. "And then there's good old institutional cooking. In *England*! A double whammy if ever there was one."

"Have another helping of blancmange, my dears," growled Nennius. "Oh, just once to be able to add a dash of rat poison to the custard."

"Mm. Or a little live typhus culture."

They fell silent at that, and Nennius couldn't resist scanning the room nervously.

Have you spoken to him about it?

He won't listen. Budu absolutely refuses to sanction the use of biologicals until we come up with something self-limiting. Anything with an incubation period long enough to allow it to be transmitted to what he calls "innocents" is out of the question.

But it could take years before we get a suitable mutation.

I'm aware of that. I had great hopes for this influenza virus. It may well be the one! And he wouldn't even hear me out.

His scruples make no sense. Nennius sighed and shifted in his chair. *Here in their dormitories the wretched monkeys are "innocent." Once they're in army barracks they'll be fair game, by his rules. Yet I'd wager they're twice as savage and bloody-minded at the moment as they will be once they're out in the world.*

That's what I told him, but it's like arguing with a stone wall.

It's just as well you haven't told him about this boy.

Not a word. When the little Corsican was running around, I managed to restrain myself from pointing out that we might have had just as much success with young Harpole. Think of the millions he might have led to the slaughter, with that voice of his.

Can't run an operation like that now, of course.

No, no. All covert, these days.

Shame.

Yes.

He's going to have to see reason some time.

You don't know him as I do.

At that moment there was a timid double knock on the door. Both men jumped.

"What d'you want, blast you?" snapped Nennius, rising to his feet.

"There's been a difficulty, sir," said someone with a slightly panicked voice from the other side of the door. "We've had to call for Dr. Cheke."

"Damn," murmured Nennius, rising. He went to the door and opened it. MacMurdo, the history master, stood there wringing his hands. "What in God's name have the little devils done now?"

"It's Bell-Fairfax, Dr. Nennys. He's nearly killed young Scargill."

"Hmph. Much blood?"

"A great deal, Dr. Nennys, sir. It took Dr. Horsfall and Mr. Petch both to separate them."

"Is Bell-Fairfax hurt?"

"No, sir."

"I'll deal with him. Have him brought."

"Very good, sir. Shall I have his trunk fetched, sir?"

"What for?"

"Well—he'll be sent down for this, sir, I should think."

"Nonsense! Nothing more than a fistfight between a pair of young imbeciles. A sound beating'll teach him."

"You haven't seen Scargill, sir—"

"Have him brought," said Nennius quietly, but in such a voice that the history master fled. Muttering imprecations, Nennius stalked across the room and drained his port at a gulp.

"That's my boy," said Labienus, grinning. "Shall I tactfully withdraw?"

"I'd be obliged if you would," said Nennius. He selected a cane from a basket in the corner. "You can listen from in there, though, if you like. See what you think of the direction I'm taking with him."

"Don't mind if I do," said Labienus, and carrying off the port decanter he retreated to the shadows of the next room. Sitting behind the door he had a fair view of the study, and everything that occurred there within the next half hour.

Nennius positioned himself in front of the fire, cane held before him in both hands. Labienus laughed quietly. *You look like a schoolboy's worst nightmare.*

Shut up. I'm getting into character.

"Sir?"

"Come in, Bell-Fairfax."

The boy entered the room and stepped into the light of the fire. Labienus studied him critically. It might have been young Nicholas, line for line.

Edward Bell-Fairfax at twelve years of age was already close to six feet tall. That he had grown a great deal since the beginning of the term was evident in the way his wrists stuck out beyond the cuffs of his jacket. Though the body was lanky and awkward, his face was still the smooth face of a child.

At this moment, he was white as a ghost. The pupils of his eyes were dilated, wide and black.

"What have you done, Bell-Fairfax?"

Labienus couldn't see Nennius's expression, but was impressed at his performance nonetheless. He sounded somber, regal, and infinitely wise.

"I think I killed Scargill, sir. His head's split open." The boy's voice shook. "And I broke his jaw."

"Why did you do this, Bell-Fairfax?"

"We were fighting, sir."

"Obviously! The cause, Bell-Fairfax."

The boy blinked. "A private matter, sir."

"You are at school, Bell-Fairfax. There are no private matters here. Fifty other boys will have seen the fight, and at least three of the masters. I should prefer to hear your version of events, however."

"It's a private matter, sir. With respect."

"Were you provoked? Scargill's a bully." Nennius lowered his voice. "And worse. Did he touch you?"

Edward flushed red. His mouth tightened and drew down at the corners. "I was provoked, sir."

"I see. It means a beating, Bell-Fairfax, and I am sorry for it. You have grieved me deeply."

"I'm sorry, sir," the boy cried. "I tried to stop. I didn't think I could really hurt him. He's so big and—and I thought it was a good idea if he was taught a lesson—and I couldn't stop. And so I thought—"

"That you'd better finish him?" inquired Nennius.

"Yes," said the boy, and then stopped, horrified at what he'd said. In the gentlest of voices, Nennius said: "It was fun, wasn't it?"

The boy stared at him, unable to speak.

"My dear young man," said Nennius, putting a hand on his shoulder. "Don't give in to fear, and certainly don't lie to yourself. This is the primal appetite that drives every one of us. It is a natural element in the human character. Without it, we should never have survived in the savage world from whence we are sprung. Nor, I might add, would we now be able to defend our national interests abroad. Without this instinct, we should have no heroes."

"But wrath is a deadly sin," said the boy, trembling. "And it says in Scripture, 'Thou shalt not kill.' "

Labienus shook his head, hearing echoes and ghosts.

"No, no; it says, 'Thou shalt do no murder,' " said Nennius. "Good heavens, boy, how would we make sense of God's dictates to His people, if He really forbade killing? What would you make of the book of Joshua, then? The Lord slaughters lustily, and we are after all made in His image. And aren't they blessed who hunger and thirst after justice? They shall be satisfied. Christ Himself said so. If you enjoyed watching that cowardly knave's blood run, you mustn't blame yourself. Divine Providence put that joy in your heart."

Edward looked bewildered.

"But it was wrong," he said.

"Yes! Allowing yourself to be so carried away by an emotion that you lost control of your hands is certainly wrong. More so for you than for other boys, because you must be above these things."

The boy blinked back tears.

"If Scargill dies, will I be hanged?"

"Are you afraid to die, Bell-Fairfax?"

"No, sir. But if I'm hanged, I will have wasted my life on nothing."

He looked at Nennius pleadingly. "I won't have helped anyone! And after all you've told me about what I ought to do in this world—"

"I doubt very much whether Scargill will die. And even were he to do so, there are certain gentlemen of might and influence who would see to it that you live to fulfill your destiny. The question, Bell-Fairfax, is whether you will be fit for it."

"Sir, I will be!"

"There is no question your heart is in the right place, my boy," Nennius said, stroking his chin thoughtfully. "Perhaps the fault lies with me."

"Oh, no, sir."

Nennius held up a hand to silence him. "With me, I say. I have failed to take your growing strength and your natural temper into account. Your manly impulses ought not to be suppressed, because they are—as it were—a gift from God. But they must be guided, or you cannot fulfill the hopes of those to whom you owe everything."

Edward was silent, watching him. Nennius appeared to think deeply.

"We have no arms master here," he said, "but I know of a private tutor who may serve. I will arrange for the extra hours. You must be taught to shoot, to wrestle, to ride. Saber as well, I think. And he will set you to certain exercises that will teach you greater personal restraint. It will be a great deal of hard work, Bell-Fairfax, but it is your duty to excel."

"I will not disappoint you, sir." Edward looked desperately hopeful.

"See to it that you do not." Nennius tapped him on the chest with the cane. "Now. Pain is unavoidable, my boy. If I sent you away with a whole skin, the other boys would whine that you were a favorite, and that is vile. Moreover, you must be punished for your outburst, in order to learn that you are never to lift a hand against another unless your blood is cold as the polar oceans."

"Yes, sir." Reluctantly, Edward moved to unbutton his trousers, but Nennius said scornfully: "We're not in the nursery, Bell-Fairfax. You're not here to be humiliated. You must be a man. The jacket and shirt off, if you please."

"Yes, sir." Hastily the boy pulled them off, standing bare to the waist.

"Face the fire and put your hands on either corner of the mantel. Keep them there until you're ordered to take them down."

"Yes, sir—" Edward obeyed, stretching out his arms. He gasped and squinted, turning his face from the heat.

"Face the fire! You can endure this. You will endure it. You have the strength, boy." Nennius raised the cane and brought it down on Edward's shoulders, with a crack that echoed in the room. Edward grunted and instinctively put his head down, but found he couldn't brace it against the hot mantel. He twisted away, gritting his teeth. The force of the next blow drove him forward again.

"Consider Scargill's pain, and how this balances the scales," said Nennius, delivering another blow. There was nothing in his tone to suggest he was not a sorrowing father administering correction to a well-loved son.

"Yes, sir—"

"Face the fire!" Nennius struck him again, but spoke encouragingly. "You are the steel in the fire, young man, you are the blade being forged. Your pain is necessary."

"Yes, sir—" *Whack!*

"You must be strong, after all, to accomplish your life's work. For nothing matters but the work, after all." *Whack!* "Consider Blake's edifying vow: 'I will not cease from Mental Fight—' " *Whack!*

"Yes, sir—"

Whack! "Complete the line, if you please."

" 'Nor shall my Sword sleep in my hand—' " the boy gasped. *Whack!*

" 'Till we have built Jerusalem,' " prompted Nennius.

" 'In England's green and pleasant land!' " shouted young Edward Alton Bell-Fairfax, gripping the mantel till his knuckles were white. *Whack!*

Thoroughly impressed, Labienus lifted his glass in a silent toast to Nennius. *By God, sir, that's programming.*

He glances now through the later images: the stern young man in the naval uniform, the urbane and smiling gentleman assassin he had become. What a lot Edward had accomplished for his masters! And here are two figures in one image, a kind of secular *Pietà:* an immortal woman howling her grief, cradling Edward's body in her arms, her skirts soaked with his valiantly shed blood.

"Such a waste," murmurs Labienus, considering the woman. She was a Preserver drone, a Botanist. He knew her well; he'd sat in judgment at her hearing and consigned her to official nonexistence, for having had the astonishingly bad luck to encounter both Nicholas Harpole *and*, in his time, Edward. Remarkable coincidence, really.

Though such causal Mandelbrots were not unknown in the historical record . . .

Labienus closes the file and wishes, again, that he'd had Botanist Mendoza under his command, and that she'd been someone of more consequence. She'd had all the qualities he looked for in a recruit: inexhaustible rage, loathing for humanity, a proper appreciation of the untainted glories of the natural world. Under the proper conditions, she might have been a truly useful weapon.

But, then again, she'd had that fatal weakness. To have loved a mortal! And *that* mortal, among all men. What a security risk! Still . . .

Labienus despises love, but permits himself sentiment; it lends a certain zest to life, after all. He regards them now, the two lovers, and sighs self-indulgently. How well-paired they had been, Edward and Mendoza! Matched blades. Or flint and steel, with which he might have started an inferno that swept across the world . . .

He is aware that he feels a vague respect for the woman. Mendoza, at least, had never done the reasonable thing, never settled for less, but held to her one insane passion even as it had dragged her into the flames. Such a valuable quality in a pawn. Is it really too late? . . .

But Edward is dead, after all.

Closing the file, Labienus puts it aside. He rises and walks to the window, stretching, thinking that it is a pity one can't have one's cake and sacrifice it, too.

On further reflection, however, he decides that a disposable hero is infinitely to be preferred to the permanent model.

In Egypt, work had just commenced on the Suez Canal. Labienus was grateful he was a world away, in a region of glacier fields no mortal ingenuity could ever turn to profit.

He had walked a long time, following the vaguest hint of directions. After a few days there were no more trees, and the only green he saw was in the aurora borealis when it bannered against the stars. Labienus did not suffer the discomfort a mortal would have felt, but he would certainly have preferred the meeting to take place in a more convenient location. This place had only the advantage that it was in his own sector, and beautiful.

It wasn't until the fifth night, as bright ghosts flared in heaven, that he became aware of a slight alteration in the crunching rhythm of his own footsteps. Two more steps and he was certain, and whirled around to behold Budu following him.

"Damn you! How long were you going to let me keep walking?" Labienus shouted.

The old Enforcer laughed. He stood straight and threw back his fur hood. He was heavily robed in polar bear fur, an immense whiteness on the white field. His breath steamed and froze, settling in icicles on his long beard and mustache. The light of the aurora glittered in his pale eyes.

"I could have taken you out five times by now," he said. "You've grown careless."

Labienus thought of telling him what he could do with his stalking games, but smiled instead. "I trusted you, father."

"Have you brought the codes?"

Labienus glanced around involuntarily, though they were the only living things within miles. "Yes. And my report."

"Good." Budu inclined forward. Labienus set his index finger between Budu's eyes and downloaded. When he had finished, he cleared his throat.

"We've penetrated the Bikkung office at last. Xi Wang-Mu is thoroughly motivated. Moreover, she has a promising second-incommand by the name of Hong Tsieh. They share our grievances."

"Very good. What about Africa?"

"No progress, I regret to say." Labienus shrugged. He preferred to look nonchalant when confessing failure. "Amaunet would be ideal. She has the perfect temperament, but she seems to be one of Aegeus's circle, and she's been posted to Eastern Europe. There's no point in approaching Suleyman at all."

"But you once trained his second-in-command," Budu pointed out.

"Briefly," said Labienus. "We didn't get on. You won't get at Suleyman through Latif, I assure you."

Budu shook his head. "You make so many enemies, you Facilitators," he said. "Such tempers and egos you have. One has to court you. Persuade you. Motivate you. My men knew what was right, and they did it."

"Yes; I suppose even Marco thought he was right, when he disobeyed orders," said Labienus acidly. Budu just looked at him.

"No," he said. "Marco was an idiot. He thought he could frighten our masters into listening. And he did frighten them, and when they retired us because they were afraid of us, he wept like a stupid child. But you aren't stupid."

"Thank you," said Labienus.

"So you will get someone into Aegeus's confidence. I want a link to Amaunet. And we need a cell in Africa."

"It's possible we might be able to turn certain members of Aegeus's cabal," admitted Labienus. "He's not well loved."

"Then do it," said Budu. Labienus nodded. He cleared his throat.

"Father," said Labienus, "I must be honest with you. Gods know you were honest with me, when you told me what things would come to in the future. I've watched the mortals crowding into their stinking cities. Their coal-soot advances on the clean sky. The forests go down before their axes and the whales are pulled in and butchered alongside their ships. But, father, it's not war or crime causing these things. It's peace. Prosperity. Civilization!"

"We will go after the industrialists, too, when we're ready."

"But when will we be ready, father? How badly must it all deteriorate before we move at last?" demanded Labienus, pinning his hopes on sincerity. "You want to exterminate the murderers and generals, but they do the work we should have begun by now. The survival of the world is no longer a moral question, if it ever was. It's a mechanical question. A matter of numbers."

"You think we ought to go after the mortals indiscriminately, to protect the earth," said Budu.

"Yes!"

"You are overruled. There is only the moral question." Budu loomed over him. "Whether the fields are green or black matters nothing. Whether the mortals live or die matters nothing. What they are, while they live, is the only thing with which we are concerned."

Labienus blinked ice crystals from his eyes, looking up at the giant in furs. He made his decision in that moment.

"You're right, of course," he said. "Thank you for putting it in perspective."

He blinked again and Budu was no longer there. The wind was screaming across the snow at ankle-level, obliterating his footprints.

Labienus looks up sharply as the bell rings. Exhaling in annoyance, he reaches for the amplifier.

It is the latest thing in field technology, a crude mechanism which compensates for its crudeness by a wealth of ornamental detail. Gold vines and flowers twine over its surface of gleaming black wax. It looks almost, but not quite, like a Victrola hooked up to a candlestick telephone. There is a headset, of sorts. He slips it on.

Ave! He recognizes the voice at once. It is Nennius, sounding quietly gleeful.

Ave. Executive Section Head for the Northwest—

Yes, yes, I know it's you! Listen to me. How many stones does it take to kill a large fat self-important bird with delusions of grandeur?

If he's immortal, there aren't enough stones in the world, Labienus replies. *But I'd still like to get Aegeus with a good sharp one, right between the eyes. You've had a stroke of luck?*

An unbelievable stroke of luck, transmits Nennius. *How quickly can you come to Bucharest?*

What the hell are you doing in Bucharest?

Attending a street fair. You remember the old green house next door to the Unirii Square HQ? It's a café now. I'll look for you there in twelve hours.

Lesser immortals would be obliged to hike south to the nearest seaport, book passage on a ship as far as Panama, disembark and take a train across the isthmus, travel by ship again across the Atlantic to France, there to travel east, arriving eventually by a series of unreliable stage connections in Romania. Facilitator Generals, however, merely hop a transpolar flight, touching down at a Company transport station in the Carpathians, and enjoy a leisurely ride in a nicely appointed private coach.

Being considerably older and wickeder than any vampires, werewolves, or mysterious blue flames that might dare to cross his path, Labienus arrives unmolested at the Unirii Square HQ, precisely twelve hours after having received Nennius's call.

Nennius is sitting at a street table, looking expectant. A waiter has just set down two glasses of slivovitz.

"Have a seat," says Nennius, reaching into an inner pocket. As Labienus sits, he tosses a field photograph on the table.

Labienus stares. He lifts his glass, with elaborate unconcern, and takes a long slow drink before permitting himself to reach for the photograph.

The image before him is of a small mortal man.

The mortal wears the coarse uniform of some institution, and his big head has been shaved. His slender hands were in the act of rising to his face when the shutter snapped, his weak mouth opening in protest as he turned from the camera. His eyes are wide, dark, wet, blind-looking. Labienus is irresistibly reminded of the little figure in *The Scream*.

Nennius tosses another photograph on the table.

Here is a formal studio portrait: the mortal is wearing a suit now, though it is a badly-fitting one, and he has closed his eyes against the camera flash. He has a curiously inanimate appearance, like a corpse or a waxwork that has been dressed up.

"*Homo umbratilis*," murmurs Labienus. "Who is he? How did you get him?"

"His name is Emil Bergwurm," says Nennius. "And I haven't got him. We do want him, though, don't we?"

"Yes," says Labienus. "Our own tiny freak of genius? Oh, yes. What do we have to do to get him?"

"Take him away from Amaunet," says Nennius.

Labienus says something so unpleasant that were it written down, in the ancient pictographs of its own language, the little symbols would smoke and snake and spit venom on clay tablet or papyrus.

"It's not as bad as all that," Nennius says hastily. "She's keeping him a secret from Aegeus. You asked me to have her monitored; well, I got word she bribed the director of the lunatic asylum here, three years ago. When I investigated, this is what I found."

"How do you know she hasn't shipped the thing off to the Cévennes?" Labienus demands.

"Perhaps you'd better come and see for yourself," says Nennius

They leave without paying for their drinks. The waiter watches them go, sadly. He is uncertain exactly what variety of *stregoi* they might be, those two sneering gentlemen; but he knows it is as much as his life is worth, to demand payment of something with that particular cold and glaring eye.

Nennius leads and Labienus paces close after him through the narrow streets. Blind cobbled alleys, deepset doors, handsbreadth windows behind which one candle gives faint light, and even the light has a certain quality of gloom, as though it were no more than gold paint on an interior. Night and fog come down.

When they emerge on the open field where the fair has been, any sense of festivity has long departed. Vendors are taking down their booths by lantern light, dropping tent poles. The menagerie has already hauled its wagons into the night, leaving only a reek of exotic manure. But at the far edge of the field, one place is still doing business, still has its banner out on a tall leaning pole. MOTHER AEGYPT, the sign reads. There are two wagons behind the sign, taller and narrower than the vardas of the Romanies. They are painted black.

How frightening, Labienus transmits. *What's next? Bats swooping out of the mist?*

No. The rats haven't finished yet, Nennius responds, nodding at the patient mortals who wait in a line that stretches from darkness into the circle of lamplight before the lead wagon's door. Their impassive faces are turned up to the light. They are hard men, all but the last, who seems to be a peasant woman.

These aren't here to have their fortunes told, guesses Labienus.

Of course not. They're thieves. They bring stolen goods to her; she pays them handsomely, and forwards the loot on to Dr. Zeus. Jewelry, porcelain, plate. It'd be stolen in any case, and this way it won't be melted down or hacked apart. Everyone wins! Except the rightful owners, of course, but that can't be helped.

Ah. The usual story. Shall we take our place in line with the other thieves?

They stroll across the dark field, and step into line behind the woman. As the queue progresses forward, they can hear murmured conversation, the clink of coin. There is surprisingly little talk, no haggling at all. One by one the thieves emerge from the caravan, each face lit for a second by the lantern over the door, and each face bearing the same expression of profound relief to be gone from Mother Aegypt.

The mortal woman is the last to go in. She alone bears no loot. Three minutes later she emerges, and her square heavy face is white as paper.

"Didn't you like your fortune?" inquires Labienus.

"She told me I am dying," the woman whispers.

"Why, so you are," says Nennius. "But don't you believe in eternal life? You must have perfect faith!"

The woman looks at him, and looks at Labienus. With a shudder she makes the sign of the Cross, and hurries away from them.

Dead silence from the wagon.

"So much for surprising her," says Labienus. "Let's pay a call, shall we?"

They step up, and go in.

Stifling warmth and all the perfumes of Arabia, myrrh and frankincense and spices to make the eyes water. Amaunet looks up at them sharply, from the cheap folding table at which she does business.

She gives the impression of great age. Her skin is smooth, but seven millennia of contempt and despair look out of her eyes, and her dark face could cut diamond.

"Hello, Amaunet," says Labienus. "Can you tell our fortunes?"

Her lip curls. "You'll get what's coming to you, in the year 2355," she says. "How about that?"

Labienus chuckles, and closes the door behind him. He lounges there, blocking the exit, and Nennius moves to lounge in turn in front of the one window. This is all largely psychological, of course, because Amaunet could exit straight through a wall if she chose, but a threat is a threat.

"You've been playing a double game, haven't you?" Labienus says.

"I don't imagine Aegeus would be happy to learn you've kept a secret from him."

"What do you want?" asks Amaunet.

"Emil Bergwurm."

Amaunet closes her eyes. "Hell," she says. The logic is inescapable: two immortals can overpower one, and even were she to escape them, she'd be unable to take her prize with her.

"You'd better tell us the whole story," Labienus says.

She opens her eyes and looks at him in a way that makes even Nennius flinch, but he just grins at her.

"My slave choked to death on a chicken head. I went to the nearest asylum to buy another. Imagine my surprise when I found Emil," she says.

"Does he cost you much in chicken heads?"

"No. He does other tricks."

"Such as?"

"Magic potions." She smiles now, and it is more frightening than her expression of anger. "That's his little streak of genius, you see. Not machines; chemistry. If the mortals need to abort a child or poison a spouse, little Emil can fix them up with something tasteless, odorless, and untraceable. He's useless at anything else, but now I make double my operating budget from the elixirs I sell."

"And that's why you've kept him from Aegeus?" Labienus takes out a silver case, withdraws a stick of Theobromos. He offers the case to Amaunet. She hesitates a long moment, then takes a stick herself.

"Partly." She peels back the silver paper. "I've had him working on a project of my own, if you must know."

"The Holy Grail, I suppose," says Nennius, and Amaunet nods sadly. She has been trying to die for five thousand years.

"Once a month, he brings me the black cup. You'd be amazed at how close he's come; his last batch stopped my heart for five minutes. The damned thing started up again, alas, since it's as stupid as he is."

"I'll make you a promise," says Labienus. "If we can get him to produce an elixir of death that works on an immortal, we'll send you a bottle."

"How chivalrous of you," she says, leaning back. "Theobromos and promises, my my. You must want something else. And what do you need with my poor little maggot-baby, anyway? *You* don't long for the grave, not an ambitious bastard like you."

"Why, Amaunet, it's elementary! My rival has a fabulous weapon, so of course I want one just like it. That's been the rule of the game since the monkeys discovered fire. And if you betrayed Aegeus once,

I'm certainly curious to know whether you'll betray him again," says Labienus.

"Don't count on it," says Amaunet with a snarl. "I haven't forgotten Carthage, Labienus."

He shrugs. "I wouldn't respect you if you had. But we're planning our endgames now, dear Amaunet. I love cleansing fire; you know how well. What will Aegeus do, if he seizes power in 2355? Make the world a vast extension of Eurobase One? Pink carpets and gilded chandeliers! Think of all those immortal gourmands and lechers and esthetes, battening on the monkeys like so many vampires. What will you do in that world, lady?"

Amaunet just looks at him.

"Bring me what I long for, and I'll show you," she says.

He laughs, and rises to his feet. "Why don't you introduce us to little Emil?"

She nods at her narrow bed, which is on a long chest built into the caravan's wall. "Introduce yourselves. He's under there. He likes the dark."

Nennius thrusts the mattress back and opens the side of the chest. There is a shrill scream. Emil Bergwurm curls away from the light, hiding his face. Labienus leans down to smile at him.

"Come out, little man! I've work for you to do." He begins to chortle. "Nothing matters except our work, you know."

Even Amaunet laughs at that.

In the end they have to haul him out bodily, and he squeals and fights until they shut him in a fake mummy case Amaunet has had propped in the corner. They take their leave of Amaunet. Labienus walks with the case tucked under his arm, like a devil carrying off a soul.

"That went rather well, really," says Nennius.

"Didn't it, though?" says Labienus cheerfully. He has already thought of a use for Emil Bergwurm.

TWO

1906

SON OBSERVE THE TIME

On the eve of destruction we had oysters and Champagne.

Don't suppose for a moment that we had any desire to lord it over the poor mortals of San Francisco, in that month of April in that year of 1906; but things weren't going to be so gracious there again for a long while, and we felt an urge to fortify ourselves against the work we were to do.

London before the Great Fire, Delhi before the Mutiny, even Chicago—I was there and I can tell you, it requires a great deal of mental and emotional self-discipline to live side by side with mortals in a Salvage Zone. You must look, daily, into the smiling faces of those who are to lose all, and walk be-side them in the knowledge that nothing you can do will affect their fates. Even the most prosaic of places has a sort of haunted glory at such times; judge then how it looked to us, that gilded fantastical butterfly of a city, quite unprepared for its approaching holocaust.

The place was made even queerer by the fact that there were so many Company operatives there at the time. The very ether hummed with our transmissions. In any street you might have seen us dismounting from carriages or the occasional automobile, we immortal gentlemen tipping our derbies to the ladies, our immortal ladies responding with a graceful inclination of their picture hats, smiling as we met each others' terrified eyes. We dined at the Palace and as guests at Nob Hill mansions; promenaded in Golden Gate Park, drove out to Ocean Beach, attended the theater and everywhere saw the pale, set faces of our own kind, busy with their own particular preparations against what was to come.

Some of us had less pleasant places to go. I was grateful that I was not required to brave the Chinese labyrinth by Waverly Place, but my associate Pan had certain business there amongst the Celestials. I myself was obliged to venture, too many times, into the boardinghouses south of Market Street. Beneath the Fly Trap was a Company safe house and HQ; we'd meet there sometimes, Pan and I, at the end of a long day in our respective ghettoes, and we'd sit shaking together over a brace of stiff whiskeys. Thus heartened, it was time for a costume change: dock laborer into gentleman for me, coolie into cook for him, and so home by cable car.

I lodged in two rooms on Bush Street. I will not say I slept there; one does not rest well on the edge of the maelstrom. But it was a place to keep one's trunk, and to operate the Company credenza necessary for facilitating the missions of those operatives whose case officer I was. Salvaging is a terribly complicated affair, requiring as it does that one hide in history's shadow until the last possible moment before snatching one's quarry from its preordained doom. One must be organized and thoroughly coordinated; and timing is everything.

On the morning of the tenth of April I was working there, sending a progress report, when there came a brisk knock at my door. Such was my concentration that I was momentarily unmindful of the fact that I had no mortal servants to answer it. When I heard the impatient tapping of a small foot on the step, I hastened to the door.

I admitted Nan D'Arraignee, one of our Art Preservation specialists. She is an operative of West African origin with exquisite features, slender and slight as a doll carved of ebony. I had worked with her briefly near the end of the previous century. She is quite the most beautiful woman I have ever known, and happily married to another immortal, a century before I ever laid eyes on her. Timing, alas, is everything.

"Victor." She nodded. "Charming to see you again."

"Do come in." I bowed her into my parlor, acutely conscious of its disarray. Her bright gaze took in the wrinkled laundry cast aside on the divan, the clutter of unwashed teacups, the half-eaten oyster loaf on the credenza console, six empty sauterne bottles, and one smudgily thumb-printed wineglass. She was far too courteous to say anything, naturally, and occupied herself with the task of removing her gloves.

"I must apologize for the condition of the place," I stammered. "My duties have kept me out a good deal." I swept a copy of the *Examiner* from a chair. "Won't you sit down?"

"Thank you." She took the seat and perched there, hands folded neatly over her gloves and handbag. I pulled over another chair, intensely irritated at my clumsiness.

"I trust your work goes well?" I inquired, for there is of course no point in asking one of us if *we* are well. "And, er, Kalugin's? Or has he been assigned elsewhere?"

"He's been assigned to Marine Transport, as a matter of fact," she told me, smiling involuntarily. "We are to meet on the *Thunderer* afterward. I am so pleased! He's been in the Bering Sea for two years, and I've missed him dreadfully."

"Ah," I said. "How pleasant, then, to have something to look forward to in the midst of all this . . ."

She nodded quickly, understanding. I cleared my throat and continued: "What may I do for you, Nan?"

She averted her gaze from dismayed contemplation of the stale oyster loaf and smiled. "I was told you might be able to assist me in requisitioning additional transport for my mission."

"I shall certainly attempt it." I stroked my beard. "Your present arrangements are unsuitable?"

"Inadequate, rather. You may recall that I'm in charge of presalvage at the Hopkins Gallery. It seems our original estimates of what we can rescue there were too modest. At present, I have five vans arranged for to evacuate the gallery contents, but really, we need more. Would it be possible to requisition a sixth? My own case officer was unable to assist me, but felt you might have greater success."

This was a challenge. Company resources were strained to the utmost on this operation, which was one of the largest on record. Every operative in the United States had been pressed into service, and many of the European and Asian personnel. A handsome allotment had been made for transport units, but needs were swiftly exceeding expectations.

"Of course I should like to help you," I replied cautiously, "if at all possible. You are aware, however, that horsedrawn transport utilization is impossible, due to the subsonic disturbances preceding the earthquake—and motor transports are, unfortunately, in great demand—"

A brewer's wagon rumbled down the street outside, rattling my windows. We both leaped to our feet, casting involuntary glances at the ceiling; then sat down in silent embarrassment. Madame D'Arraignee gave a little cough. "I'm so sorry—my nerves are simply—"

"Not at all, not at all, I assure you—one can't help flinching—"

"Quite. In any case, Victor, I understand the logistical difficulties involved; but even a handcart would greatly ease our difficulties. So many lovely and unexpected things have been discovered in this collection, that it really would be too awful to lose them to the fire."

"Oh, certainly." I got up and strode to the windows, giving in to the urge to look out and assure myself that the buildings hadn't begun to sway yet. Solid and seemingly as eternal as the pyramids they stood there, for the moment. I turned back to Madame D'Arraignee as a thought occurred to me. "Tell me, do you know how to operate an automobile?"

"But of course!" Her face lit up.

"It may be possible to obtain something in that line. Depend upon it, madame, you will have your sixth transport. I shall see to it personally."

"I knew I could rely on you." She rose, all smiles. We took our leave of one another with a courtesy that belied our disquiet. I saw her out and returned to my credenza keyboard.

QUERY, I input, *RE: REQUISITION ADDTNL TRANSPORT MOTOR VAN OR AUTO? PRIORITY RE: HOPKINS INST.*

HOPKINS PROJECT NOT YOUR CASE, came the green and flashing reply.

NECESSARY, I input. *NEW DISCV OVRRIDE SECTION AUTH. PLEASE FORWARD REQUEST PRIORITY.*

WILL FORWARD.

That was all. So much for my chivalrous impulse, I thought, and watched as the transmission screen winked out and returned me to my status report on the Nob Hill presalvage work. I resumed my entry of the Gilded Age loot tagged for preservation.

When I had transmitted it, I stood and paced the room uneasily. How long had I been hiding in here? What I wanted was a meal and a good stretch of the legs, I told myself sternly. Fresh air, in so far as that was available in any city at the beginning of this twentieth century. I scanned the oyster loaf and found it already pulsing with bacteria. Pity. After disposing of it in the dustbin I put on my coat and hat, took my stick and went out to tread the length of Bush Street with as bold a step as I could muster.

It was nonsense, really, to be frightened. I'd be out of the city well before the first shock. I'd be safe on air transport bound for London before the first flames rose. London, the other City. I could settle into a chair at my club and read a copy of *Punch* that wasn't a month old, secure in the knowledge that the oak beams above my head were fixed and immovable as they had been since the days when I'd worn a powdered wig, as they would be until German shells came raining down decades from now . . .

Shivering, I dismissed thoughts of the Blitz. Plenty of *life* to think about, surely! Here were bills posted to catch my eye: I might go out to the Pavilion to watch the boxing exhibition—Jack Joyce and Bob Ward featured. There was delectable vaudeville at the Orpheum, I was assured, and gaiety girls out at the Chutes, to say nothing of a spectacular sideshow recreation of the Johnstown flood . . . perhaps not in the best of taste, under the present circumstances.

I might imbibe Gold Seal Champagne to lighten my spirits, though I didn't think I would; Veuve Cliquot was good enough for me. Ah, but what about a bottle of Chianti, I thought, arrested by the bill of fare posted in the window of a corner restaurant. Splendid culinary fragrances wafted from within. Would I have grilled veal chops here? Would I go along Bush to the Poodle Dog for chicken *chaud-froid blanc*? Would I venture to Grant in search of yellow silk banners for duck roasted in some tiny Celestial kitchen? Then again, I knew of a Swiss place where the cook was a Hungarian, and prepared a light and crisply fried Wiener schnitzel to compare with any I'd had . . . or I might just step into a saloon and order another oyster loaf to take home . . .

No, I decided, veal chops would suit me nicely. I cast a worried eye up at the building—pity this structure wasn't steel-framed—and proceeded inside.

It was one of those dark, robust places within, floor thickly strewn with fresh sawdust not yet kicked into little heaps. I took my table as any good operative does, back to the wall and a clear path to the nearest exit. Service was poor, as apparently their principal waiter was late today, but the wine was excellent. I found it bright on the palate, just what I'd wanted, and the chops when they came were redolent of herbs and fresh olive oil. What a consolation appetite can be.

Yes, life, that was the thing to distract one from unwise thoughts. Savor the wine, I told myself, observe the parade of colorful humanity, breathe in the fragrance of the joss sticks and the seafood and the gardens of the wealthy, listen to the smart modern city with its whirring steel parts at the service of its diverse inhabitants. The moment is all, surely.

I dined in some isolation, for the luncheon crowd had not yet emerged from the nearby offices and my host remained in the kitchen, arguing with the cook over the missing waiter's character and probable ancestry. Even as I amused myself by listening, however, I felt a disturbance approaching the door. No temblor yet, thank heaven, but a tempest of emotions. I caught the horrifying mental images before ever I heard the stifled weeping. In another moment he had burst through the door, a young male mortal with a prodigious black mustache, quite nattily dressed but with his thick hair in wild disarray. As soon as he was past the threshold his sobs burst out unrestrained, at a volume that would have done credit to Caruso.

This brought his employer out of the back at once, blurting out the first phrases of furious denunciation. The missing waiter (for so he was) staggered forward and thrust out that day's *Chronicle*. The headlines, fully an inch tall, checked the torrent of abuse: MANY LOSE THEIR LIVES IN GREAT ERUPTION OF VESUVIUS.

The proprietor of the restaurant, struck dumb, went an ugly sallow color. He put the fingertips of one hand in his mouth and bit down hard. In a broken voice, the waiter described the horrors: roof collapsed in church in his own village. His own family might even now lie dead, buried in ash. The proprietor snatched the paper and cast a frantic eye over the columns of print. He sank to his knees in the sawdust, sobbing. Evidently he had family in Naples, too.

I stared at my plate. I saw gray and rubbery meat, congealing grease, seared bone with the marrow turned black. In the midst of life we are in death, but it doesn't do to reflect upon it while dining.

"You must, please, excuse us, sir," the proprietor said to me, struggling to his feet. "There has been a terrible tragedy." He set the *Chronicle* beside my plate so I could see the blurred rotogravure picture of King Victor Emmanuel. REPORT THAT TOTAL NUMBER OF DEAD MAY REACH SEVEN HUNDRED, I read. TOWNS BURIED UNDER ASHES AND MANY CAUGHT IN RUINED BUILDINGS. MANY BUILDINGS CRUSHED BY ASHES. Of course, I had known about the coming tragedy; but it was on the other side of the world, the business of other Company operatives, and I envied them that their work was completed now.

"I am so very sorry, sir," I managed to say, looking up at my host. He thought my pallor was occasioned by sympathy: he could not know I was seeing his mortal face like an apparition of the days to come, and it was livid and charring, for he lay dead in the burning ruins of a boardinghouse in the Mission district. Horror, yes, impossible not to feel horror, but one cannot empathize with them. One must not.

They went into the kitchen to tell the cook and I heard weeping break out afresh. Carefully I took up the newspaper and perused it. Perhaps there was something here that might divert me from the unpleasantness of the moment? Embezzlement. A crazed admirer stalking an actress. Charlatan evangelists. Grisly murder committed by two boys. Deadly explosion. Crazed derelict stalking a bank president. Los Angeles school principals demanding academic standards lowered.

I dropped the paper, and, leaving five dollars on the table, I fled that place.

I walked briskly, not looking into the faces of the mortals I passed.

I rode the cable car, edging away from the mortal passengers. I nearly ran through the green expanse of Golden Gate Park, dodging around the mortal idlers, the lovers, the nurses wheeling infants in perambulators, until at last I stood on the shore of the sea. Tempting to turn to look at the fairy castles perched on its cliffs; tempting to turn to look at the carnival of fun along its gray sand margin, but the human comedy was the last thing I wanted just then. I needed, rather, the chill and level grace of the steel-colored horizon, sun-glistering, wide-expanding. The cold salt wind buffeted me, filled my grateful lungs. Ah, the immortal ocean.

Consider the instructive metaphor: every conceivable terror dwells in her depths; she receives all wreckage, refuse, corruption of every kind, she pulls down into her depths human calamity indescribable; but none of this is any consideration to the sea. Let the screaming mortal passengers fight for room in the lifeboats, as the wreck belches flame and settles below the extinguishing wave; next morning she'll still be beautiful and serene, her combers no less white, her distances as blue, her seabirds no less graceful as they wheel in the pure air. What perfection, to be so heartless. An inspiration to any lesser immortal.

As I stood so communing with the elements, a mortal man came wading out of the surf. I judged him two hundred pounds of athletic stockbroker, muscles bulging under sagging wet wool, braving the icy water as an act of self-disciplinary sport. He stood for a moment on one leg, examining the sole of his other foot. There was something gladiatorial in his pose. He looked up and saw me.

"A bracing day, sir," he shouted.

"Quite bracing." I nodded and smiled. I could feel the frost patterns of my returning composure.

And so I boarded another streetcar and rode back into the mortal warren, and found my way by certain streets to the Barbary Coast. Not a place a gentleman cares to admit to visiting, especially when he's known the gilded beauties of old Byzantium or Regency-era wenches; the raddled pleasures available on Pacific Street suffered by comparison. But appetite is appetite, after all, and there is nothing like it to take one's mind off unpleasant thoughts.

"Your costume." The attendant pushed a pasteboard carton across the counter to me. "Personal effects and field equipment. Linen, trousers, suspenders, boots, shirt, vest, coat, and hat." He frowned. "Phew! These should have been laundered. Would you care to be fitted with an alternate set?"

"That's all right." I took the offending rags. "The sweat goes with the role, I'm afraid. Irish laborer."

"Ah." He took a step backward. "Well, break a leg."

Fifteen minutes later I emerged from a dressing room the very picture of an immigrant yahoo, uncomfortably conscious of my clammy and odiferous clothing. I sidled into the canteen, hoping there wouldn't be a crowd in the line for coffee. There wasn't, at that: most of the diners were clustered around one operative over in a corner, so I stood alone watching the food service technician fill my thick china mug from a dented steel coffee urn. The fragrant steam was a welcome distraction from my own fragrancy. I found a solitary table and warmed my hands on my dark brew there in peace, until an operative broke loose from the group and approached me.

"Say, Victor!"

I knew him slightly, an American operative so young one could scan him and still discern the scar tissue from his augmentations. He was one of my Presalvagers.

"Good morning, Averill."

"Say, you really ought to listen to that fellow over there. He's got some swell stories." He paused only long enough to have his cup refilled, then came and pulled out a chair across from me. "Know who he is? He's the guy who follows Caruso around!"

"Is he?"

"Sure is. Music Specialist Grade One! That boy's wired for sound. He's caught every performance Caruso's ever given, even the church stuff when he was a kid. Going to get him in *Carmen* the night before you-know-what, going to record the whole performance. He's just come back from planting receivers in the footlights! Say, have you gotten tickets yet?"

"No, I haven't. I'm not interested, actually."

"Not interested?" he exclaimed. "Why aren't you—how *can't* you be interested? It's *Caruso*, for God's sake!"

"I'm perfectly aware of that, Averill, but I've got a prior engagement. And, personally, I've always thought de Reszke was much the better tenor."

"De Reszke?" He scanned his records to place the name and, while doing so, absently took a great gulp of coffee. A second later he clutched his ear and gasped. "Christ almighty!"

"Steady, man." I suppressed a smile. "You don't want to gulp beverages over sixty degrees Celsius, you know. There's some very complex circuitry placed near the Eustachian tube that gets unpleasantly hot if you do."

"Ow, ow, ow!" He sucked in air, staring at me with the astonishment of the very new operative. It always takes them a while to discover that immortality and intense pain are not strangers, indeed can reside in the same eternal house for quite lengthy periods of time. "Should I drink some ice water?"

"By no means, unless you want some real discomfort. You'll be all right in a minute or so. As I was about to say, I have some recordings of Jean de Reszke I'll transmit to you, if you're interested in comparing artists."

"Thanks, I'd like that." Averill ran a hasty self-diagnostic.

"And how is your team faring over at the New Brunswick, by the way? No cases of nerves, no blue devils?"

"Hell no." Averill started to lift his coffee again and then set it down respectfully.

"Doesn't bother you that the whole place will be ashes in a few days' time, and most of your neighbors dead?"

"No. We're all O.K. over there. We figure it's just a metaphor for the whole business, isn't it? I mean, sooner or later this whole world"—he made a sweeping gesture, palm outward—"as we know it, is going the same way, right? So what's it matter if it's the earthquake that finishes it now, or a wrecking ball someplace further on in time, right? Same thing with the people. There's no reason to get personally upset about it, is there? No, sir. Specially since *we'll* all still be alive."

"A commendable attitude." I had a sip of my coffee. "And your work goes well?"

"Yes, *sir*." He grinned. "You will be so proud of us burglary squad fellows when you get our next list. You wouldn't believe the stuff we're finding! All kinds of objets d'art, looks like. One-of-a-kind items, by God. Wait'll you see."

"I look forward to it." I glanced at my chronometer and drank down the rest of my coffee, having waited for it to descend to a comfortable fifty-nine degrees Celsius. "But, you know, Averill, it really won't do to think of yourselves as burglars."

"Well—that is—it's only a figure of speech, anyhow!" Averill protested, flushing. "A joke!"

"I'm aware of that, but I cannot emphasize enough that we are not stealing anything." I set my coffee cup down, aware that I sounded priggish, and looked sternly at him. "We're preserving priceless examples of late Victorian craftsmanship for the edification of future generations."

"I know." Averill looked at me sheepishly, "But—aw, hell, do you mean to say not one of those crystal chandeliers will wind up in some Facilitator General's private HQ somewhere?"

"That's an absurd idea," I told him, though I knew only too well it wasn't. Still, it doesn't do to disillusion one's subordinates too young. "And now, will you excuse me? I mustn't be late for work."

"All right. Be seeing you!"

As I left he rejoined the admiring throng around the fellow who was telling Caruso stories. My way lay along the bright tiled hall, steamy and echoing with the clatter of food preparation and busy operatives; then through the dark security vestibule, with its luminous screens displaying the world without; then through the concealed door that shut behind me and left no trace of itself to any eyes but my own. I drew a deep breath. Chill and silent morning air; no glimmer of light, yet, at least not down here in the alley. Half past five. This time three days hence—

I shivered and found my way out in the direction of the waterfront.

Not long afterward I arrived at the loading area where I had been desultorily employed for the last month. I made my entrance staggering slightly, doing my best to murder "You Can't Guess Who Flirted with Me" in a gravelly baritone.

The mortal laborers assembled there turned to stare at me. My best friend, an acquaintance I'd cultivated painstakingly these last three weeks, came forward and took me by the arm.

"Jesus, Kelly, you'd better stow that. Where've you been?"

I stopped singing and gave him a belligerent stare. "Marching in the Easter parade, O'Neil."

"O, like enough." He ran his eyes over me in dismay. Francis O'Neil was thirty years old. He looked enough like me to have been taken for my somewhat bulkier, clean-shaven brother. "What're you doing this for, man? You know Herlihy doesn't like you as it is. You look like you've not been home to sleep nor bathe since Friday night!"

"So I have not." I dropped my gaze in hungover remorse.

"Come on, you poor stupid bastard, I've got some coffee in my dinner pail. Sober up. Was it a letter you got from your girl again?"

"It was." I let him steer me to a secluded area behind a mountain of crates and accepted the tin cup he filled for me with lukewarm coffee. "She doesn't love me, O'Neil. She never did. I can tell."

"You're taking it all the wrong way, I'm sure. I can't believe she's stopped caring, not after all the things you've told me about her. Just drink that down, now. Mary made it fresh not an hour ago."

"You're a lucky man, Francis." I leaned on him and began to weep, slopping the coffee. He forbore with the patience of a saint and replied: "Sure I am, Jimmy, and shall I tell you why? Because I know when to take my drink, don't I? I don't swill it down every payday and forget to go home, do I? No indeed. I'd lose Mary and the kids and all the rest of it, wouldn't I? It's self-control you need, Jimmy, and the sorrows in your heart be damned. Come on now. With any luck Herlihy won't notice the state you're in."

But he did, and a litany of scorn was pronounced on my penitent head. I took it with eyes downcast, turning my battered hat in my hands, and a dirtier nor more maudlin drunk could scarce have been seen in that city. I would be summarily fired, I was assured, but they needed men today so bad they'd employ even the likes of me, though by God next time—

When the boss had done excoriating me I was dismissed to help unload a cargo of copra from the *Nevadan*, in from the islands yesterday. I sniveled and tottered and managed not to drop anything much. O'Neil stayed close to me the whole day, watchful lest I pass out or wander off. He was a good friend to the abject caricature I presented; God knows why he cared. Well, I should repay his kindness, at least, though in a manner he would never have the opportunity to appreciate.

We sweated until four in the afternoon, when there was nothing left to take off the *Nevadan*; let go then with directions to the next day's job, and threats against slackers.

"Now, Kelly." O'Neil took my arm and steered me with him back toward Market Street. "I'll tell you what I think you ought to do. Go home and have a bit of a wash in the basin, right? Have you clean clothes? So, put on a clean shirt and trousers and see can you scrape some of that off your boots. Then, come over to supper at our place. Mary's bought some sausages, we thought we'd treat ourselves to a dish of coddle now that Lent's over. We've plenty."

"I will, then." I grasped his hand. "O'Neil, you're a lord for courtesy."

"I am not. Only go home and wash, man!"

We parted in front of the Terminal Hotel and I hurried back to the HQ to follow his instructions. This was just the sort of chance I'd been angling for since I'd sought out the man on the basis of the Genetic Survey Team report.

An hour later, as cleanly as the character I played was likely to be able to make himself, I ventured along Market Street, heading down in the direction of the tenement where O'Neil and his family lived, the boardinghouses in the shadow of the Palace Hotel. I knew their exact location, though O'Neil was of course unaware of that; accordingly he had sent a pair of his children down to the corner to watch for me.

They failed to observe my approach, however, and I really couldn't blame them; for proceeding down Market Street before me, moving slowly between the gloom of twilight and the electric illumination of the shop signs, was an apparition in a scarlet tunic and black shako.

It walked with the stiff and measured tread of the automaton it was pretending to be. The little ragged girl and her littler brother stared openmouthed, watching its progress along the sidewalk. It performed a brief business of marching mindlessly into a lamppost and walking inexorably in place there a moment before righting itself and going on, but now on an oblique course toward the children.

I too continued on my course, smiling a little. This was delightful: a mortal pretending to be a mechanical toy being followed by a cyborg pretending to be a mortal.

There was a wild reverberation of mirth in the ether around me. One other of our kind was observing the scene, apparently; but there was a gigantic quality to the amusement that made me falter in my step. Who was that? That was someone I knew, surely. *Quo vadis?* I transmitted. The laughter shut off like an electric light being switched out, but not before I got a sense of direction from it. I looked across the street and just caught a glimpse of a massive figure disappearing down an alley. My visual impression was of an old miner, one of the mythic founders of this city. Old gods walking? What a ridiculous idea, and yet . . . what a moment of panic it evoked, of mortal dread, quite irrational.

But the figure in the scarlet tunic had reached the children. Little Ella clutched her brother's hand, stock-still on the pavement: little Donal shrank behind his sister, but watched with one eye as the thing loomed over them.

It bent forward, slowly, in increments, as though a gear ratcheted in its spine to lower it down to them. Its face was painted white, with red circles on the cheeks and a red cupid's bow mouth under the stiff black mustaches. Blank glassy eyes did not fix on them, did not seem to see anything, but one white-gloved hand came up jerkily to offer the little girl a printed handbill.

After a frozen motionless moment she took it from him. "Thank you, Mister Soldier," she said in a high clear voice. The figure gave no sign that it had heard, but unbent slowly, until it stood ramrod-straight again; pivoted sharply on its heel and resumed its slow march down Market Street.

"Soldier go." Donal pointed. Ella peered thoughtfully at the handbill.

" '*CH—IL—DREN*'," she read aloud. What an impossibly sweet voice she had. "And that's an exclamation point, there. '*Babe—Babies, in, To—Toy—*' "

" '*Toyland,*' " I finished for her. She looked up with a glad cry.

"There you are, Mr. Kelly. Donal, this is Mr. Kelly. He is Daddy's good friend. Supper will be on the table presently. Won't you please come with us, Mr. Kelly?"

"I should be delighted to." I touched the brim of my hat. They pattered away down an alley, making for the dark warren of their tenement, and I followed closely.

They were different physical types, the brother and sister. Pretty children, certainly, particularly Ella with her glossy black braids, with her eyes the color of the twilight framed by black lashes. But it is not beauty we look for in a child.

It was the boy I watched closely as we walked, a sturdy three-year-old trudging along holding tight to the girl's hand. I couldn't have told you the quality nor shade of his skin, nor his hair nor his eyes; I cared only that his head appeared to be a certain shape, that his little body appeared to fit a certain profile, that his limbs appeared to be a certain length in relation to one another. I couldn't be certain yet, of course: that was why I had maneuvered his father into the generous impulse of inviting me into his home.

They lived down a long dark corridor toward the back of the building, its walls damp with sweat, its air heavy with the odors of cooking, of washing, of mortal life. The door opened a crack as we neared it and then, slowly, opened wide to reveal O'Neil standing there in a blaze of light. The blaze was purely by contrast to our darkness, however; once we'd crossed the threshold, I saw that two kerosene lamps were all the illumination they had.

"There now, didn't I tell you she'd spot him?" O'Neil cried triumphantly. "Welcome to this house, Jimmy Kelly."

"God save all here." I removed my hat. "Good evening, Mrs. O'Neil."

"Good evening to you, Mr. Kelly." Mary O'Neil turned from the stove, bouncing a fretful infant against one shoulder. "Would you care for a cup of tea, now?" She was like Ella, if years could be granted Ella to grow tall and slender and wear her hair up like a soft thundercloud. But there was no welcoming smile for me in the gray eyes, for on the previous occasion we'd met I'd been disgracefully intoxicated—at least, doing my best to appear so. I looked down as if abashed.

"I'd bless you for a cup of tea, my dear, I would," I replied. "And won't you allow me to apologize for the condition I was in last Tuesday week? I'd no excuse at all."

"Least said, soonest mended." She softened somewhat at my obvious sobriety. Setting the baby down to whimper in its apple-box cradle, she poured and served my tea. "Pray seat yourself."

"Here." Ella pulled out a chair for me. I thanked her and sat down to scan the room they lived in. Only one room, with one window that probably looked out on an alley wall but was presently frosted opaque from the steam of the saucepan wherein their supper cooked. Indeed, there was a fine layer of condensation on everything: it trickled down the walls, it lay in a damp film on the oilcloth cover of the table and the blankets on the bed against the far wall. The unhappy infant's hair was moist and curling with it.

Had there been any ventilation it had been a pleasant enough room. The table was set with good china, someone's treasured inheritance, no doubt. The tiny potbellied stove must have been awkward to cook upon, but O'Neil had built a cabinet of slatwood and sheet tin next to it to serve as the rest of a kitchen. The children's trundle was stored tidily under the parents' bed. Next to the painted washbasin on the trunk, a decorous screen gave privacy to one corner. Slatwood shelves displayed the family's few valuables: a sewing basket, a music box with a painted scene on its lid, a cheap mirror whose frame was decorated with glued-on seashells, a china dog. On the wall was a painted crucifix with a palm frond stuck behind it.

O'Neil came and sat down across from me.

"You look grand, Jimmy." He thumped his fist on the table approvingly. "Combed your hair, too, didn't you? That's the boy. You'll make a gentleman yet."

"Daddy?" Ella climbed into his lap. "There was a soldier came and gave us this in the street. Will you ever read me what it says? There's more words than I know, see." She thrust the handbill at him. He took it and held it out before him, blinking at it through the steamy air.

Here I present the printed text he read aloud, without his many pauses as he attempted to decipher it (for he was an intelligent man, but of little education):

CHILDREN!

Come see the Grand Fairy Extravaganza BABES IN TOYLAND
Music by Victor Herbert—Book by Glen MacDonough—
Staged by Julian Mitchell Ignacio Martinetti and 100 Others!
Coming by Special Train of Eight Cars!
Biggest Musical Production San Francisco Has Seen in Years!

*   *   *

AN INVITATION FROM MOTHER GOOSE HERSELF:

MY dear little Boys and Girls,

I DO hope you will behave nicely so that your Mammas and Papas will treat you to a performance of Mr. Herbert's lovely play Babes in Toyland at the Columbia Theater, opening Monday, the 16th of April. Why, my dears, it's one of the biggest successes of the season and has already played for ever so many nights in such far-away cities as New York, Chicago, and Boston. Yes, you really must be good little children, and then your dear parents will see that you deserve an outing to visit me. For, make no mistake, I myself, the only true and original MOTHER GOOSE, shall be there upon the stage of the Columbia Theater. And so shall so many of your other friends from my delightful rhymes such as Tom, Tom the Piper's Son, Bo Peep, Contrary Mary, and Red Riding Hood. The curtain will rise upon Mr. Mitchell's splendid production, with its many novel effects, at eight o'clock sharp.

OF course, if you are very little folks you are apt to be sleepyheads if kept up so late, but that need not concern your careful parents, for there will be a matinee on Saturday at two o'clock in the afternoon.

WON'T you please come to see me?

Your affectionate friend, Mother Goose.

"O, dear," sighed Mary.

"Daddy, can we go?" Ella's eyes were alight with anticipation. Donal chimed in: "See Mother Goose, Daddy!"

"We can't afford it, children," Mary said firmly. She took the saucepan off the stove and began to ladle a savory dish of sausage, onions, potatoes, and bacon onto the plates. "We've got a roof over our heads and food for the table. Let's be thankful for that."

Ella closed her little mouth tight like her mother's, but Donal burst into tears. "I wanna go see Mother Goose!" he howled.

O'Neil groaned. "Your mother is right, Donal. Daddy and Mummy don't have the money for the tickets, can you understand that?"

"You oughtn't to have read out that bill," said Mary in a quiet voice.

"I want go see the soldier!"

"Donal, hush now!"

"Donal's the boy for me," I said, leaning forward and reaching out to him. "Look, Donal Og, what's this you've got in your ear?"

I pretended to pull forth a bar of Ghirardelli's. Ella clapped her hands to her mouth. Donal stopped crying and stared at me with perfectly round eyes.

"Look at that! Would you ever have thought such a little fellow'd have such big things in his ears? Come sit with your uncle Jimmy, Donal." I drew him onto my lap. "And if you hush your noise, perhaps

Mummy and Daddy'll let you have sweeties, eh?" I set the candy in the midst of the oilcloth, well out of his reach.

"Bless you, Jimmy," said O'Neil.

"Well, and isn't it the least I can do? Didn't know I could work magic, did you, Ella?"

"Settle down, now." Mary set out the dishes. "Frank, it's time to say grace."

O'Neil made the sign of the Cross and intoned, with the little ones mumbling along, "Bless-us-O-Lord-and-these-Thy-gifts-which-we-are-about-to-receive-from-Thy-bounty-through-Christ-Our-Lord-Amen."

Mary sat down with us, unfolding her threadbare napkin. "Donal, come sit with Mummy."

"Be easy, Mrs. O'Neil, I don't mind him." I smiled at her. "I've a little brother at home he's the very image of. Where's his spoon? Here, Donal Og, you eat with me."

"I don't doubt they look alike." O'Neil held out his tumbler as Mary poured from a pitcher of milk. "Look at you and me. Do you know, Mary, that was the first acquaintance we had—? Got our hats mixed up when the wind blew 'em both off. We wear just the same size."

"Fancy that."

So we dined, and an affable mortal man helped little Donal make a mess of his potatoes whilst chatting with Mr. and Mrs. O'Neil about such subjects as the dreadful expense of living in San Francisco and their plans to remove to a cheaper, less crowded place as soon as they'd saved enough money. The immortal machine that sat at their table was making a thorough examination of Donal, most subtly: an idle caress of his close-cropped little head measured his skull size, concealed devices gauged bone length and density and measured his weight to the pound; data was analyzed and preliminary judgment made: optimal morphology. Augmentation process possible. Classification pending blood analysis and spektral diagnosis.

"That's the best meal I've had in this country, Mrs. O'Neil," I told her as we rose from the table.

"How kind of you to say so, Mr. Kelly," she replied, collecting the dishes.

"Chocolate, Daddy?" Donal stretched out his arm for it. O'Neil tore open the waxed paper and broke off a square. He divided it into two and gave one to Donal and one to Ella.

"Now, you must thank your uncle Jimmy, for this is good chocolate and cost him dear."

"Thank you, Uncle Jimmy," they chorused, and Ella added, "But he got it by magic. It came out of Donal's ear. I saw it."

O'Neil rubbed his face wearily. "No, Ella, it was only a conjuring trick. Remember the talk we had about such things? It was just a trick. Wasn't it, Jimmy?"

"That's all it was, sure," I agreed. She looked from her father to me and back.

"Frank, dear, will you help me with these?" Mary had stacked the dishes in a washpan and sprinkled soap flakes in.

"Right. Jimmy, will you mind the kids? We're just taking these down to the tap."

"I will indeed," I said, and thought: *Thank you very much, mortal man, for this opportunity.* The moment the door closed behind them I had the device out of my pocket. It looked rather like a big old-fashioned watch. I held it out to the boy.

"Here you go, Donal, here's a grand timepiece for you to play with."

He took it gladly. "There's a train on it!" he cried. I turned to Ella.

"And what can I do for you, darling?"

She looked at me with considering eyes. "You can read me the funny papers." She pointed to a neatly stacked bundle by the stove.

"With pleasure." I seized them up and we settled back in my chair, pulling a lamp close. The baby slept fitfully, I read to Ella about Sambo and Tommy Pip and Herr Spiegleburger, and all the while Donal pressed buttons and thumbed levers on the diagnostic toy. It flashed pretty lights for him, it played little tunes his sister was incapable of hearing; and then, as I had known it would, it bit him.

"Ow!" He dropped it and began to cry, holding out his tiny bleeding finger.

"O, dear, now, what's that? Did it stick you?" I put his sister down and got up to take the device back. "Tsk! Look at that, the stem's broken." It vanished into my pocket. "What a shame. O, I'm sorry, Donal Og, here's the old hankie. Let's bandage it up, shall we? There. There. Doesn't hurt now, does it?"

"No," he sniffled. "I want another chocolate."

"And so you'll have one, for being a brave boy." I snapped off another square and gave it to him. "Ella, let's give you another as well, shall we? What have you found there?"

"It's a picture about Mother Goose." She had spread out the Children's Page on the oilcloth. "Isn't it? That says Mother Goose right there."

I looked over her shoulder. " 'Pictures from Mother Goose,' " I read out, " 'Hot Cross Buns. Paint the Seller of Hot Cross Buns.' Looks like it's a contest, darling. They're asking the kiddies to paint in the picture and send it off to the paper, to judge who's done the best one."

"Is there prize money?" She had an idea.

"Two dollars for the best one," I read, pulling at my lower lip uneasily. "And paintboxes for everyone else who enters."

She thought that over. Dismay came into her face. "But I haven't got a paintbox to color it with at all! O, that's stupid! Giving paintboxes out to kids that's got them already. O, that's not fair!" She shook with stifled anger.

"What's not fair?" Her mother backed through the door, holding it open for O'Neil with the washpan.

"Only this Mother Goose thing here," I said.

"You're never on about going to that show again, are you?" said Mary sharply, coming and taking her daughter by the shoulders. "Are you? Have you been wheedling at Mr. Kelly?"

"I have not!" the little girl said in a trembling voice.

"She hasn't, Mrs. O'Neil, only it's this contest in the kids' paper," I hastened to explain. "You have to have a set of paints to enter it, see."

Mary looked down at the paper. Ella began to cry quietly. Her mother gathered her up and sat with her on the edge of the bed, rocking her back and forth.

"O, I'm so sorry, Ella dear, Mummy's so sorry. But you see, now, don't you, the harm in wanting such things? You see how unhappy it's made you? Look how hard Mummy and Daddy work to feed you and clothe you. Do you know how unhappy it makes us when you want shows and paintboxes and who knows what, and we can't give them to you? It makes us despair. That's a Mortal Sin, despair is."

"I want to see the fairies," wept the little girl.

"Dearest dear, there aren't any fairies! But surely it was the devil himself you met out in the street, that gave you that wicked piece of paper and made you long after vain things. Do you understand me? Do you see why it's wicked, wanting things? It kills the soul, Ella."

After a long, gasping moment the child responded, "I see, Mummy." She kept her face hidden in her mother's shoulder. Donal watched them uncertainly, twisting the big knot of handkerchief on his finger. O'Neil sat at the table and put his head in his hands. After a moment he swept up the newspaper and put it in the stove. He reached into the slatwood cabinet and pulled a bottle of Wilson's Whiskey up on the table, and got a couple of clean tumblers out of the washpan.

"Will you have a dram, Kelly?" he offered.

"Just the one." I sat down beside him.

"Just the one," he agreed.
You must not empathize with them.

When I let myself into my rooms on Bush Street, I checked my messages. A long green column of them pulsed on the credenza screen. Most of it was the promised list from Averill and his fellows; I'd have to pass that on to our masters as soon as I'd reviewed it. I didn't feel much like reviewing it just now, however.

There was also a response to my request for another transport for Madame D'Arraignee: *DENIED. NO ADDITIONAL VEHICLES AVAILABLE. FIND ALTERNATIVE.*

I sighed and sank into my chair. My honor was at stake. From a drawer at the side of the credenza I took another Ghirardelli bar and, scarcely taking the time to tear off the paper, consumed it in a few greedy bites. Waiting for its soothing properties to act, I paged through a copy of the *Examiner*. There were automobile agencies along Golden Gate Avenue. Perhaps I could afford to purchase one out of my personal operation's expense account?

But they were shockingly expensive in this city. I couldn't find one for sale, new or used, for less than a thousand dollars. Why couldn't *her* case officer delve into his own pocket to deliver the goods? I verified the balance of my account. No, there certainly wasn't enough for an automobile in there. However, there was enough to purchase four tickets to *Babes in Toyland*.

I accessed the proper party and typed in my transaction request.

TIX UNAVAILABLE FOR 041606 EVENT, came the reply. *041706 AVAILABLE OK?*

OK, I typed. *PLS DEBIT & DELIVER.*

DEBITED. TIX IN YR BOX AT S MKT ST HQ 600 HRS 041606.

TIBI GRATIAS! I replied, with all sincerity.

DIE DULCE FRUERE. OUT.

Having solved one problem, an easy solution to the other suggested itself to me. It involved a slight inconvenience, it was true: but any gentleman would readily endure worse for a lady's sake.

My two rooms on Bush Street did not include the luxury of a bath, but the late Mr. Adolph Sutro had provided an alternative pleasure for his fellow citizens.

Just north of Cliff House Mr. Sutro had purchased a rocky little purgatory of a cove, cleaned the shipwrecks out of it and proceeded to shore it up against the more treacherous waves with several thousand barrels of cement. Having constructed not one but six saltwater pools of a magnificence to rival old Rome, he had proceeded to enclose it in a crystal palace affair of no less than four acres of glass.

Ah, but this wasn't enough for San Francisco! The entrance, on the hill above, was as near a Greek temple as modern artisans could produce; through the shrine one wandered along the museum gallery lined with exhibits both educational and macabre and descended a vast staircase lined with palm trees to the main level, where one might bathe, exercise in the gymnasium, or attend a theater performance. Having done all this, one might then dine in the restaurant.

However, my schedule today called for nothing more strenuous than bathing. Ten minutes after descending the grand staircase I was emerging from my changing room (one of five hundred), having soaped, showered, and togged myself out in my rented bathing suit, making my way toward the nearest warm-water pool under the bemused eyes of several hundred mortal idlers sitting in the bleachers above.

I was not surprised to see another of my own kind backstroking manfully across the green water; nothing draws the attention of an immortal like sanitary conveniences. I must confess my heart sank when I recognized Lewis. I hadn't seen him since that period at New World One, when I'd been obliged to monitor him again. His career was in ruins, of course. Rather a shame, really. A drone, but a gentleman for all that.

He felt my regard and glanced up, seeing me at once. He smiled and waved.

Victor! he broadcast. *How nice to see you again.*

It's Lewis, isn't it? I responded, though I knew his name perfectly well, and far more of his history than he knew himself. Still, it had been centuries, and he had never shown any sign of recovering certain memories. I hoped, for his sake, that such was the case. Memory effacement is not a pleasant experience.

He pulled himself up on the coping of the pool and swept his wet hair out of his eyes. I stepped to the edge, took the correct diver's stance and leapt in, transmitting through bubbles: *So you're here as well? Presalvaging books, I suppose?*

The Mercantile Library, he affirmed, and there was nothing in his pleasant tone to indicate he'd remembered what I'd done to him at Eurobase One.

God! That must be a Herculean effort, I responded, surfacing.

He transmitted rueful amusement. *You've heard of it, I suppose?*

Rather, I replied, practicing my breaststroke. *All those Comstock Lode silver barons went looting the old family libraries of Europe, didn't they? Snatched up medieval manuscripts at a tenth their value from impoverished Venetian princes, I believe? Fabulously rare first editions from London antiquarians?*

Something like that, he replied. *And brought them back home to the States for safekeeping.*

Ha!

Well, how were they to know? Lewis made an expressive gesture taking in the vast edifice around us. *Mr. Sutro himself had a Shakespeare first folio. What a panic it's been tracking that down! And you?*

I'm negotiating for a promising-looking young recruit. Moreover, I drew Nob Hill detail, I replied casually. *I've coordinated a team of quite talented youngsters set to liberate the premises of Messrs. Towne, Crocker, Huntington et al. as soon as the lights are out. All manner of costly bric-a-brac has been tagged for rescue—Chippendales, Louis Quatorzes—to say nothing of jewels and cash.*

My, that sounds satisfying. You'll never guess what I found, only last night! Lewis transmitted, looking immensely pleased with himself.

Something unexpected? I responded.

He edged forward on the coping. *Yes, you might say so. Just some old papers that had been mislaid by an idiot named Pompeo Leoni and bound into the wrong book. Just something jotted down by an elderly left-handed Italian gentleman!*

Not da Vinci? I turned in the water to stare at him, genuinely impressed.

Who else? Lewis nearly hugged himself in triumph. *Not just any doodlings or speculation from the pen of Leonardo, either. Something of decided interest to the Company! It seems he devoted some serious thought to the construction of articulated human limbs—a clockwork arm, for example, that could be made to perform various tasks!*

I've heard something of the sort, I replied, swimming back toward him.

Yes, well, he seems to have taken the idea further than robotics. Lewis leaned down in a conspiratorial manner. *From a human arm he leapt to the idea of an entire articulated human skeleton of bronze, and wondered whether the human frame might not be merely imitated but improved in function.*

By Jove! Was the man anticipating androids? I reached the coping and leaned on it, slicking back my hair.

No! No, he was chasing another idea entirely, Lewis insisted. *Shall I quote? I rather think I ought to let him express his thoughts.* He leaned back and, with a dreamy expression, transmitted in flawless fifteenth-century Tuscan: *'It has been observed that the presence of metal is not in all cases inimical to the body of man, as we may see in earrings, or in crossbow bolts, spearpoints, pistol balls, and other detritus of war that have been known to enter the flesh and remain for some years without doing the bearer any appreciable harm, or indeed in that practice of physicians wherein a small pellet of gold is inserted into an incision made near an aching joint, and the sufferer gains relief and ease of movement thereby.*

'Take this idea further and think that a shattered bone might be replaced with a model of the same bone cast in bronze, identical with or even superior to its original.

'Go further and say that where one bone might be replaced, so might the skeleton entire, and if the articulation is improved upon the man might attain a greater degree of physical perfection than he was born with.

'The flaw in this would be the man's pain and the high likelihood he would die before surgery of such magnitude could be carried out.

'Unless we are to regard the theory of alchemists who hold that the Philosopher's Stone, once attained, would transmute the imperfect flesh to perfection, a kind of supple gold that lives and breathes, and by this means the end might be obtained without cutting, the end being immortality.' Lewis opened his eyes and looked at me expectantly. I smacked my hand on the coping in amusement.

By Jove, I repeated. *How typical of the Maestro. So he was all set to invent us, was he?*

To say nothing of hip replacements.

But what a find for the Company, Lewis!

Of course, to give you a real idea of the text I ought to have presented it like this: Lewis began to rattle it out backwards. I shook my head, laughing and holding up my hands in sign that he should stop. After a moment or two he trailed off, adding: *I don't think it loses much in translation, though.*

I shook my head. *You know, old man, I believe we're treading rather too closely to a temporal paradox here. Just as well the Company will take possession of that volume, and not some inquisitive mortal! What if it had inspired someone to experiment with biomechanicals a century or so too early?*

Ah! No, we're safe enough, Lewis pointed out. *As far as history records those da Vinci pages at all, it records them as being lost in the Mercantile Library fire. The circle is closed. All the same, I imagine it was a temptation for any operatives stationed near Amboise in da Vinci's time. Wouldn't you have wanted to seek the old man out as he lay dying, and tell him that something would be done with this particular idea, at least? Immortality and human perfection!*

Of course I'd have been tempted; but I shook my head. *Not unless I cared to face a court-martial for a security breach.*

Lewis shivered in his wet wool and slid back into the water. I turned on my back and floated, considering him.

The temperature doesn't suit you? I inquired.

Oh . . . They've got the frigidarium all right, but the calidaria here aren't really hot enough, Lewis explained. *And of course there's no sudatorium at all.*

Nor any slaves for a good massage, either, I added, glancing up at the mortal onlookers. *Sic transit luxuria, alas.* Lewis smiled faintly; he had never been comfortable with mortal servants, I remembered. Odd, for someone who began mortal life as a Roman, or at least a Romano-Briton.

Weren't you recruited at Bath . . . ? I inquired, leaning on the coping.

Aquae Sulis, it was then, Lewis informed me. *The public baths there.*

Of course. I remember now! You were rescued from the temple. Intercepted child sacrifice, I imagine?

Oh, good heavens, no! The Romans never did that sort of thing. No, I was just left in a blanket by the statue of Apollo. Lewis shrugged, and then began to grin. *I hadn't thought about it before, but this puts a distinctly Freudian slant on my visits here! Returning to the womb in time of stress? I was only a few hours old when the Company took me, or so I've always been told.*

I laughed and set off on a lap across the pool. *At least you were spared any memories of mortal life.*

That's true, he responded, and then his smile faded. *And yet, you know, I think I'm the poorer for that. The rest of you may have some harrowing memories, but at least you know what it was to be mortal.*

I assure you it's nothing to be envied, I informed him. He set out across the pool himself, resuming his backstroke.

I think I would have preferred the experience, all the same, he insisted. *I'd have liked a father—or mother—figure in my life. At the very least, those of you rescued at an age to remember it have a sort of filial relationship with the immortal who saved you. Haven't you?*

I regret to disillusion you, sir, but that is absolutely not true, I replied firmly.

Really? He dove and came up for air, gasping. *What a shame. Bang goes another romantic fantasy. I suppose we're all just orphans of one storm or another.*

At that moment a pair of mortals chose to roughhouse, snorting and chuckling as they pummeled each other in their seats in the wooden bleachers; one of them broke free and ran, scrambling apelike over the seats, until he lost his footing and fell with a horrendous crash that rolled and thundered in the air, echoing under the glassed dome, off the water and wet coping.

I saw Lewis go pale; I imagine my own countenance showed reflexive panic. After a frozen moment Lewis drew a deep breath.

"One storm or another," he murmured aloud. "Nothing to be afraid of here, after all. Is there? This structure will survive the quake. History says it will. Nothing but minor damage, really."

I nodded. Then, struck in one moment by the same thought, we lifted our horrified eyes to the ceiling, with its one hundred thousand panes of glass.

"I believe I've got a rail car to catch," I apologized, vaulting to the coping with what I hoped was not undignified haste.

"I've a luncheon engagement myself," Lewis said, gasping as he sprinted ahead of me to the grand staircase.

On the sixteenth of April I entertained friends, or at least my landlady received that impression; and what quiet and well-behaved fellows the gentlemen were, and how plain and respectable the ladies! No cigars, no raucous laughter, no drunkenness at all. Indeed, Mrs. McCarty assured me she would welcome them as lodgers at any time in the future, should they require desirable Bush Street rooms. I assured her they would be gratified at the news. Perhaps they might have been, if her boardinghouse were still standing in a week's time. History would decree otherwise, regrettably.

My parlor resembled a war room, with its central table on which was spread a copy of the Sanborn map of the Nob Hill area, up-to-date from the previous year. My subordinates stood or leaned over the table, listening intently as I bent with red chalk to delineate the placement of salvage apparatus.

"The Hush Field generators will arrive in a baker's van at the corner of Clay and Taylor Streets at midnight precisely," I informed them. "Delacort, your team will approach from your station at the end of Pleasant Street and take possession of them. There will be five generators. I want them placed at the following intersections: Bush and Jones, Clay and Jones, Clay and Powell, Bush and Powell, and on California midway between Taylor and Mason." I put a firm letter x at each site. "The generators should be in place and switched on by no later than five minutes after midnight. Your people will remain in place to remove the generators at half past three exactly, returning them to the baker's van, which will depart promptly. At that moment a private car will pull up to the same location to transport your team to the central collection point on Ocean Beach. Is that clear?"

"Perfectly, sir." Delacort saluted. Averill looked at her slightly askance and turned a worried face to me.

"What're they going to do if some cop comes along and wants to know what they're doing there at that time of night?"

"Any cop coming in range of the Hush Field will pass out, dummy," Philemon informed him. I frowned and cleared my throat. Cinema Standard (the language of the schoolroom) is not my preferred mode of expression.

"If you please, Philemon!"

"Yeah, sorry—"

"Your team will depart from their station at Joice Street at five minutes after midnight and proceed to the intersection of Mason and Sacramento, where a motorized drayer's wagon will be arriving. You will be responsible for the contents of the Flood mansion." I outlined it in red. "Your driver will provide you with a sterile containment receptacle for item number thirty-nine on your acquisitions list. Kindly see to it that this particular item is salvaged first and delivered to the driver separately."

"What's item thirty-nine?" Averill inquired. There followed an awkward silence. Philemon raised his eyebrows at me. Company policy discourages field operatives from being told more than they strictly need to know regarding any given posting. Upon consideration, however, it seemed wisest to answer Averill's question; there was enough stress associated with this detail as it was without adding mysteries. I cleared my throat.

"The Flood mansion contains a 'Moorish' smoking room," I informed him. "Among its features is a lump of black stone carefully displayed in a glass case. Mr. Flood purchased it under the impression that it is an actual piece of the Qaaba from Mecca, chipped loose by an enterprising Yankee adventurer. He was, of course, defrauded; the stone is in fact a meteorite, and preliminary spectrographic analysis indicates it originated on Mars."

"Oh," said Averill, nodding sagely. I did not choose to add that plainly visible on the rock's surface is a fossilized crustacean of an unknown kind, or that the rock's rediscovery (in a museum owned by Dr. Zeus, incidentally) in the year 2210 will galvanize the Mars colonization effort into making real progress at last.

I bent over the map again and continued: "All the items on your list are to be loaded into the wagon by twenty minutes after three. At that time, the wagon will depart for Ocean Beach and your team will follow in the private car provided. Understood?"

"Understood."

"Rodrigo, your team will depart from their Taylor Street station at five minutes after midnight as well. Your wagon will arrive at the corner of California and Taylor; you will proceed to salvage the Huntington mansion." I marked it on the map. "Due to the nature of your quarry you will be allotted ten additional minutes, but all listed items must be loaded and ready for removal by half past three, at which time your private transport will arrive. Upon arrival at Ocean Beach you will be assisted by Philemon's team, who will already (I should hope) have loaded most of their salvage into the waiting boats."

"Yes, sir." Rodrigo made a slight bow.

"Freytag, your team will be stationed on Jones Street. You depart at five after midnight, like the rest, and your objective is the Crocker mansion, here." Freytag bent close to see as I shaded in her area. "Your wagon will pull up to Jones and California; you ought to be able to fill it in the allotted time of two hours and fifteen minutes precisely, and be ready to depart for Ocean Beach without incident. Loong? Averill?"

"Sir!" Both immortals stood to attention.

"Your teams will disperse from their stations along Clay and Pine Streets and salvage the lesser targets shown here, here, here, and here—" I chalked circles around them. "I leave to your best judgment individual personnel assignments. Two wagons will arrive on Clay Street at one o'clock precisely and two more will arrive on Pine five minutes later. You ought to find them more than adequate for your purposes. You will need to do a certain amount of running to and fro to coordinate the efforts of your ladies and gentlemen, but it can't be helped."

"I don't anticipate difficulties, sir," Loong assured me.

"No indeed; but remember the immensity of this event shadow." I set down the chalk and wiped my hands on a handkerchief. "Your private transports will be waiting at the corner of Bush and Jones by half past three. Please arrive promptly."

"Yes, *sir*." Averill looked earnest.

"In the entirely likely event that any particular team completes its task ahead of schedule, and has free space in its wagon after all the listed salvage has been accounted for, I will expect that team to lend its assistance to Madame D'Arraignee and her teams at the Mark Hopkins Institute." I swept them with a meaningful stare. "Gentlemen doing so can expect my personal thanks and commendation in their personnel files."

That impressed them, I could see. The favorable notice of one's superiors is invariably one's ticket to the better sort of assignment. Clearing my throat, I continued: "I anticipate arriving at no later than half past two to oversee the final stages of removal. Kindly remain at your transports until I transmit your signal to depart for the central collection point. Have you any further questions, ladies and gentlemen?"

"None, sir," Averill said, and the others nodded agreement.

"Then it's settled," I told them, and carefully folded shut the map book. "A word of warning to you all: you may become aware of precursors to the shock in the course of the evening. History will record a particularly nasty seismic disturbance at two A.M. in particular, and another at five. Control your natural panic, please. Upsetting as you may find these incidents, they will present no danger whatsoever, will in fact go unnoticed by such mortals as happen to be awake at that hour."

Averill put up his hand. "I read the horses will be able to feel it," he said, a little nervously. "I read they'll go mad."

I shrugged. "Undoubtedly why we have been obliged to confine ourselves to motor transport. Of course, *we* are no brute beasts. I have every confidence that we will all resist any irrational impulses toward flight before the job is finished.

"Now then! You may attend to the removal of your personal effects and prepare for the evening's festivities. I shouldn't lunch tomorrow; you'll want to save your appetites for the banquet at Cliff House. I understand it's going to be rather a Roman experience!"

The tension broken, they laughed; and if Averill laughed a bit too loudly, it must be remembered that he was still young. As immortals go, that is.

Astute mortals might have detected something slightly out of the ordinary on that Tuesday, the seventeenth of April; certainly the hired-van drivers must have noticed an increase in business, as they were dispatched to house after house in every district of the city to pick up nearly identical loads, these being two or three ordinary-looking trunks and one crate precisely fifty centimeters long, twenty centimeters wide, and twenty centimeters high, in which a credenza might fit snugly. And it would be extraordinary if none of them remarked upon the fact that all these same consignments were directed to the same location on the waterfront, the berth of the steamer *Mayfair*.

Certainly in some cases mortal landladies noticed trunks being taken down flights of stairs, and put anxious questions to certain of their tenants regarding hasty removal; but their fears were laid to rest by smiling lies and ready cash.

And did anyone notice, as twilight fell, when persons in immaculate evening dress were suddenly to be seen in nearly every street? Doubtful; for it was, after all, the second night of the opera season, and with the Metropolitan company in town all of Society had turned out to do them honor. If a certain number of them converged on a certain warehouse in an obscure district, and departed therefrom shortly afterward in gleaming automobiles, that was unlikely to excite much interest in observers, either.

I myself guided a brisk little four-cylinder Franklin through the streets, bracing myself as it bumped over the cable car tracks, and steered down Gough with the intention of turning at Fulton and following it out to the beach. At the corner of Geary I glimpsed for a moment a tall figure in a red coat, and wondered what it was doing so far from the theater district; but a glance over my shoulder made it plain that I was mistaken. The red-clad figure shambling along was no more than a bum, albeit one of considerable stature. I dismissed him easily from my thoughts as I contemplated the O'Neil family's outing to the theater.

Had I a warm, sentimental sensation thinking of them, remembering Ella's face aglow when she saw me present her father with the tickets? Certainly not. One magical evening out was scarcely going to make up for their ghastly deaths, in whatever cosmic scale might be supposed to balance such things. Best not to dwell on that aspect of it at all. No, it was the convenience of their absence from home that occupied my musings, and the best way to take advantage of it with regard to my mission.

At the end of Fulton I turned right, in the purple glow of evening over the vast Pacific. Far out to sea—well beyond the sight of mortal eyes—the Company transport ships lay at anchor, waiting only for the cover of full darkness to approach the shore. In a few hours I'd be on board one of them, steaming off in the direction of the Farallones to catch my air transport, with no thought for the smoking ruin of the place I'd lived in so many harrowing weeks.

Cliff House loomed above me, its turreted mass a blaze of light. I saw with some irritation that the long uphill approach was crowded with carriages and automobiles, drawn in on a diagonal; I was obliged to go up as far as the rail depot before I could find a place to leave my motor, and walk back downhill past the baths.

I dare say the waiters at Cliff House could not recall an evening when so large a party, of such unusual persons, had dined with such hysterical gaiety as on this seventeenth of April, 1906.

If I recall correctly, the reservation had been made in the name of an international convention of seismologists. San Francisco was ever the most cosmopolitan of cities, so the restaurant staff expressed no surprise when elegantly attired persons of every known color began arriving in carriages and automobiles. If anyone remarked upon a certain indefinable similarity in appearance among the conventioneers that transcended race, why, that might be explained by their common avocation—whatever seismology might be; no one on the staff had any clear idea. Only the queer nervousness of the guests was impossible to account for, the tendency toward uneasy giggling, the sudden frozen silences and dilated pupils.

I think I can speak for my fellow operatives when I say that we were determined to enjoy ourselves, terror notwithstanding. We deserved the treat, every one of us; we faced a long night of hard work, the culmination of months of labor, under circumstances of mental strain that would test the resolution of the most hardened mercenaries. The least we were owed was an evening of silk hats and tiaras.

There was a positive chatter of communication on the ether as I approached. We were all here, or in the act of arriving; not since leaving school had I been in such a crowd of my own kind. I thought how we were to feast here, a company of immortals in an airy castle perched on the edge of the Uttermost West, and flit away well before sunrise. It is occasionally pleasant to embody a myth.

I saw Madame D'Arraignee stepping down from a carriage, evidently arriving with other members of the Hopkins operation team. No bulky Russian sea captain in sight, of course, yet; I hastened to her side and tipped my hat.

"Madame, will you do me the honor of allowing me to escort you within?"

"M'sieur Victor." She gave me a dazzling smile. She wore a gown of pale blue-green silk, a shade much in fashion that season, which brought out beautifully certain copper hues in her intensely black skin. Diamonds winked from the breathing shadow of her bosom. Oh, fortunate Kalugin! She took my arm and we proceeded inside, where we had the remarkable experience of having to shout our transmissions to one another, so crowded was the ether: *I am very pleased to inform you I have arranged for an automobile for your use this evening,* I told her as we paused at the cloakroom for checks.

Oh, I am so glad! I do hope you weren't put to unnecessary trouble.

Through the door to the dining room we caught glimpses of napery like snow, folded in a wilderness of sharp little peaks, with here and there a gilt epergne rising above them.

Not what I'd call unnecessary trouble, no, though it proved impossible to requisition anything at this late date. However, I did have a vehicle allocated for my own personal use and that fine runabout is entirely at your disposal.

Merci, merci mille fois! But will this not impede your own mission?

Not at all, dear lady. I shall be obliged to you for transportation as far as the Palace, I think, after we've dined; but since my mission involves nothing more strenuous than carrying off a child, I anticipate strolling back across the city with ease.

You are too kind, my friend.

A gentleman could do no less. I pulled out a chair for her.

We chatted pleasantly of trifling matters as the rest of the guests arrived. We studied the porcelain menu in some astonishment—the Company had spent a fortune here tonight, certainly enough to have allotted me one extra automobile. I was rather nettled, but my irritation was mollified somewhat by the anticipation of our *carte du jour:*

Green Turtle Soup   Consommé Divinesse
Salmon in Sauce Veloute   Trout Almandine   Crab Cocktail
Braised Sweetbreads   Roast Quail Andaluz
Le Faux Mousse Faison Lucullus
Early Green Peas   White Asparagus   Risotto Milanese
Roast Saddle of Venison with Port Wine Jelly
Curried Tomatoes   Watercress Salad
Chicken Marengo   Plovers' Eggs   Virginia Ham Croquettes
Lobster Salad   Oysters in Variety
Gateau d'Or et Argent   Assorted Fruits in Season
Rose Snow   Tulip Jellies   Water Ices
Surprise Yerba Buena

All accompanied, of course, by the appropriate vintages, and service *à la russe.* We *were* being rewarded.

A shift in the black rock, miles down, needle-thin fissures screaming through stone, perdurable clay bulging like the head of a monstrous child engaging for birth, straining, straining, STRAINING!

The smiling chatter stopped dead. The waiters looked around, confused, at that elegant assembly frozen like mannequins. Not a scrape of chair moving, not a chime of crystal against china. Only the sound that we alone listened to: the cello-string far below us, tuning for the dance of the wrath of God. I found myself staring across the room directly into Lewis's eyes, where he had halted at the doorway in midstep. The immortal lady on his arm was still as a painted image, a perfect profile by da Vinci.

The orchestra conductor mistook our silence for a cue of some kind. He turned hurriedly to his musicians and they struck up a little waltz tune, light, gracious accompaniment to our festivities. With a boom and a rush of vacuum the service doors parted, as the first of the waiters burst through with tureens and silver buckets of ice. Champagne corks popped like artillery. As the noises roared into our silence, an immortal in white lace and spangles shrieked; she turned it into a high trilling laugh, placing her slender hand upon her throat.

So conversation resumed, and a server appeared at my elbow with a napkined bottle. I held up my glass for Champagne. Madame D'Arraignee and I clinked an unspoken toast and drank fervently.

Twice more while we dined on those good things, the awful warning came. As the venison roast was served forth, its dish of port jelly began to shimmer and vibrate—too subtly for the mortal waiters to notice more than a pretty play of light, but we saw. On the second occasion the oysters had just come to table, and what subaudible pandemonium of clattering there was: half-shell against half-shell with the sound of basalt cliffs grinding together, and the staccato rattle of all the little sauceboats with their scarlet and yellow and pink and green contents; though of course the mortal waiters couldn't hear it. Not even the patient horses waiting in their carriage-traces heard it yet. But the sparkling bubbles ascended more swiftly through the glasses of Champagne.

The waiters began to move along the tables bearing trays: little cut-crystal goblets of pink ices, or red and amber jellies, or fresh strawberries drenched in liqueur, or cakes. We heard the ringing note of a dessert spoon against a wineglass, signaling us all to attention.

The Chief Project Facilitator rose to address us. Labienus stood poised and smiling in faultless white tie and tuxedo. As he waited for the babble of voices to fade he took out his gold chronometer on its chain, studied its tiny screen, then snapped its case shut and returned it to the pocket of his white silk waistcoat.

"My fellow seismologists." His voice was quiet, yet without raising it he reached all corners of the room. Commanding legions confers a certain ease in public speaking. "Ladies." He bowed. "I trust you've enjoyed the bill of fare. I know that, as I dined, I was reminded of the fact that perhaps in no other city in the world could such a feast be so gathered, so prepared, so served to such a remarkable gathering. Where but here by the Golden Gate can one banquet in a splendor that beggars the Old World, on delicacies presented by masters of culinary sophistication hired from all civilized nations—all the while in sight of forested hills where savages roamed *within living memory*, across a bay that *within living memory* was innocent of any sail?

"So swiftly has she risen, this great city, as though magically conjured by djinni out of thin air. Justifiably her citizens might expect to wake tomorrow in a wilderness, and find that this gorgeous citadel had been as insubstantial as their dreams."

Archly exchanged glances between some of our operatives as his irony was appreciated.

"But if that were to come to pass—if they were to wake alone, unhoused and shivering upon a stony promontory, facing into a cold northern ocean and a hostile gale—why, you know as well as I do that within a few short years the citizens of San Francisco would create their city anew, with spires soaring ever closer to heaven, and mansions yet more gracious."

Of course we knew it, but the poor mortal waiters didn't. I am afraid some of our younger operatives were base enough to smirk.

"Let us marvel, ladies and gentlemen, at this phoenix of a city, at once ephemeral and abiding. Let us drink to the imperishable spirit of her citizens. I give you the city of San Francisco."

"The city of San Francisco," we chorused, raising our glasses high.

"And I *give* you"—smiling, he extended his hand—"the city of San Francisco!"

Beaming, the waiters wheeled it in, on a vast silver cart: an ornate confection of pastry, of spun-sugar and marzipan and candies, a perfect model of the City. It was possible to discern a tiny Ferry Building rising above chocolate wharves, and a tiny Palace, and Nob Hill reproduced in sugared peel and nonpareils. Across the familiar grid of streets Golden Gate Park was done in green fondant, and beyond it was the hill where Sutro Park rose in nougat and candied violets, and beyond that Cliff House itself, in astonishing detail.

We applauded.

Then she was destroyed, that beautiful city, with a silver cake knife and serving wedge, and parceled out to us in neat slices. One had to commend Labienus's sense of humor, to say nothing of his sense of ritual.

It was expected that we would wish to dance after dining; the ballroom had been reserved for our use, and at some point during dessert the orchestra had discreetly risen and carried their instruments up to the dais.

I thought the idea of dancing in rather poor taste, under the circumstances, and apparently many of my fellow operatives agreed with me; but Averill and some of the other young ones got out on the floor eagerly enough, and soon the stately polonaise gave way to ragtime tunes and two-stepping.

Under the pretense of going for a smoke I went out to the terrace, to breathe the clean night air and metabolize my portion of magnificent excess in peace. By ones and twos several of the older immortals followed me. Soon there was quite an assemblage of us out there between two worlds, between the dark water surging around Seal Rock and the brilliant magic lantern of Cliff House.

"Victor?" Madame D'Arraignee was making her way to me through the crowd. Her slippers, together with her diamonds, had gone into the leather case she was carrying, and she had donned sensible walking shoes; she had also buttoned a long motorist's duster over her evening gown. The radiant Queen of the Night stood now before me as the Efficient Modern Woman.

"You didn't care to dance either, I see," she remarked.

"Not I, no," I replied. Within the giddy whirl, Averill pranced by in the arms of an immortal sylph in pink satin; their faces were flushed and merry. Don't think them heartless, reader. They did not understand yet. Horror, for Averill, was still a lonely prairie and a burning wagon; for the girl, still a soldier with a bayonet in a deserted orchard. *Those* nightmares weren't here in this bright room with its bouncing music, and so all must be right with the world.

But we were old ones, Madame D'Arraignee and I, and we stood outside in the dark as they danced.

Down, miles down, the slick water on the clay face and the widening fissure in darkness, dead shale trembling like an exhausted limb, granite crumbling, rock cracking with the strain and crying out in a voice that rose up, and up at last through the red brick, through the tile and parquet, into the warm air and the music!

The mortal musicians played on, but the dancers faltered. Some of them stopped, looking around in confusion; some of them only missed a step or two and then plunged back into the dance with greater abandon, determined to celebrate something.

Madame D'Arraignee shivered. I threw my unlit cigar over the parapet into the sea.

"Shall we go, Nan?" I offered her my arm. She took it readily and we left Cliff House.

Outside on the carriage drive, and all the way up the steep hill to where my motor was parked, the waiting horses were tossing their heads and whickering uneasily.

Madame D'Arraignee took the wheel, easily guiding us back down into the City through the spangled night.

Even now, at the Grand Opera House, Enrico Caruso was striking a pose before a vast Spanish mountain range rendered on canvas and raising his carbine to threaten poor Bessie Abott. Even now, at the Mechanic's Pavilion, the Grand Prize Masked Carnival was in full swing, with throngs of costumed roller skaters whirling around the rink that would be a triage hospital in twelve hours and a pile of smoking ashes in twenty-four. Even now, the clock on the face of Old St. Mary's Church—bearing its warning legend SON OBSERVE THE TIME AND FLY FROM EVIL—was counting out the minutes left for heedless passersby. Even now, the O'Neil children were sitting forward in their seats, scarcely able to breathe as the cruel Toymaker recited the incantation that would bring his creations to life.

And we rounded the corner at Devisadero and sped down Market, with Prospero's *après*-pageant speech ringing in our ears. At the corner of Third I pointed and Madame D'Arraignee worked the clutch, steered over to the curb and trod on the brake pedal.

"You're quite sure you won't need a ride back?" she inquired over the chatter of the cylinders. I put my legs out and leapt down to the pavement.

"Perfectly sure, Nan." I shot my cuffs and adjusted the drape of my coat. Reaching into the seat, I took my stick and silk hat. "Give my seat to the Muse of Painting. I'm off to lurk in shadows like a gentleman."

"*Bonne chance,* then, Victor." She eased up on the brake, clutched, and cranked the wheel over so the Franklin swung around in a wide arc to retrace its course up Market Street. I tipped my hat and bowed; with a cheery wave and a double honk on the Franklin's horn, she steered away into the night.

So far, so good. The night was yet young and there were plenty of debonair socialites in evening dress on the street, arriving and departing from the restaurants, the hotels, the theaters. For a block I was one of their number; then accomplished my disappearance down a black alleyway into another world, to thread my way through the boarding-house warren.

Rats were out and scuttling everywhere, sensing the coming disaster infallibly. In some buildings they were cascading down the stairs like trickling water, and cats ignored them and drunkards stood watching in stupefied amazement, but there was nobody else there to remark upon it; these streets did not invite promenaders.

I found the O'Neils' building and made my way up through the unlit stairwell, here and there kicking vermin out of my way. I left the landing and proceeded down their corridor, past doors tight shut showing only feeble lines of light at floor level to mark where the occupants were at home. I heard snores; I heard weeping; I heard a drunken quarrel; I heard a voice raised in wistful melody.

No light at the O'Neils' door, naturally; none at the door immediately opposite theirs. I scanned the room beyond but could discern no occupant. Drawing out a skeleton key from my waistcoat pocket, I gained entrance and shut the door after me.

No tenant at all; good. It was death-cold in there and black as pitch, for a roller shade had been drawn down on the one window. A slight tug sent it wobbling upward but failed to let much more light into the room. Not that I needed light to see my chronometer as I checked it; half past eleven, and even now my teams were assembling at their stations on Nob Hill. I leaned against a wall, folded my arms and composed myself to wait.

Time passed slowly for me, but in Toyland it sped by. Songs and dances, glittering processions came to their inevitable close; fairies took wing. Innocence was rewarded and wickedness resoundingly punished. The last of the ingenious special effects guttered out, the curtain descended, the orchestra fell silent, the house lights came up. A little while the magic lingered, as the O'Neil family made their way out through the lobby, a little while it hung around them like a perfume in the atmosphere of red velvet and gilt and fashionably attired strangers, until they were borne out through the doors by the receding tide of the crowd. Then the magic left them, evaporating upward into the night and the fog, and they got their bearings and made their way home along the dark streets.

I heard them, coming heavily up the stairs, O'Neil and Mary each carrying a child. Down the corridor their footsteps came, and stopped outside.

"Slide down now, Ella, Daddy's got to open the door."

I heard the sound of a key fumbling in darkness for its lock, and a drowsy little voice singing about Toyland, the paradise of childhood to which you can never return.

"Hush, Ella, you'll wake the neighbors."

"Donal's asleep. He missed the ending." Ella's voice was sad. "And it was such a beautiful, beautiful ending. Don't you think it was a beautiful ending, Daddy?"

"Sure it was, darling." Their voices receded a bit as they crossed the threshold. I heard a clink and the sputtering hiss of a match; there was the faintest glimmer of illumination down by the floor.

"Sssh, sh, sh. Home again. Help Mummy get his boots off, Ella, there's a dear."

"I'll just step across to Mrs. Varian's and collect the baby."

"Mind you remember his blanket."

"I will that."

Footsteps in the corridor again, discreet rapping on a panel, a whispered conversation in darkness and a sleepy wail; then returning footsteps and a pair of doors closing. Then, more muffled but still distinct to me, the sound of the O'Neils going to bed.

Their lamps were blown out. Their whispers ceased. Still I waited, listening as the minutes ticked away for their mortal souls to rest.

Half past one on the morning of Wednesday, the eighteenth of April in the year 1906, in the city of San Francisco. Francis O'Neil and his wife and their children asleep finally and forever, and the world had finished with them. In the gray morning, at precisely twelve minutes after the hour of five, this boardinghouse would lurch forward into the street, bricks tumbling as mortar blew out like talcum powder, rotten timbers snapping. That would be the end of Frank's strength and Mary's care and Ella's dreams, the end of the brief unhappy baby, and no one would remember them but me.

And, perhaps, Donal. I stepped across the hall and let myself into their room, perfectly silent.

The children lay in their trundle on the floor, next to their parents' bed. Donal slept on the outer edge, curled on his side, both hands tucked under his chin. I stood for a moment observing, analyzing their alpha patterns. When I was satisfied that no casual noise would awaken them, I bent and lifted Donal from his bed. He sighed but slept on. After a moment's hesitation I drew the blanket up around Ella's shoulders.

I stood back. The boy wore a nightshirt and long black stockings, but the night was cold. Frank's coat hung over the back of a chair: I appropriated it to wrap his son. Shifting Donal to one arm, I backed out of the room and shut the door.

Finished.

No sleeper in that building woke to hear our rapid descent of the stairs. On the first landing a drunk sat upright, leaning his head on the railings, sound asleep with his lower jaw dropped open like a corpse's. We fled lightly past him, Donal and I, and he never moved.

Away through the maze, then, away forever from the dirt and stench and poverty of that place. In twelve hours it would have ceased to exist, and the wind would scatter white ashes so the dead could never be named nor numbered.

Even Market Street was dark now, its theaters shut down. Over at the Grand Opera House on Mission, Enrico Caruso's costumes hung neatly in his dark dressing room, ready for a performance of *La Bohème* that would never take place. Up at the Mechanic's Pavilion, the weary janitor surveyed the confetti and other festive debris littering the skating rink and decided to sweep it up in the morning. Toyland, at the Columbia, was shut away in its properties room: fairy tinsel, butterfly wings, bear heads peering down from dusty shelves into the darkness.

Even now my resolute gentlemen and ladies were despoiling Nob Hill, flitting through its darkened drawing rooms at hyperspeed like so many whirring ghosts, bearing with them winking gilt and crystal, calfskin and morocco, canvas and brass, all the very best that money could buy but couldn't hope to preserve against the hour to come. Without the Franklin I'd have a tedious walk uphill to join them, but at a brisk pace I might arrive with time to spare.

Donal stretched and muttered in his sleep. I shifted him to my other shoulder, changed hands on my walking stick, and was about to hurry on when I caught a whiff of some familiar scent on the air. I halted.

It was not a pleasant scent. It was harsh, musky, like blood or sweat but neither; like an animal smell, but other; it summoned in me a sudden terror and confusion. When I tried to identify it, however, I had only a mental image of a bear costume hanging on a hook, the head looking down from a shelf. When had I seen that? *I* hadn't seen that! *Whose memories were these?*

I controlled myself with an effort. Some psychic disturbance was responsible for this, my own nerves were contributing to this, there was no real danger. Why, of course: it must be nearly two o'clock, when the first of the major subsonic disruptions would occur.

Yes, here it came now. I could hear nearby horses begin to scream and stamp frantically, I could feel the paving bricks grind against one another under the soles of my boots, and the air groaned as though buried giants were praying to God for release.

Yes, I thought, this must be it. I balanced my stick against my knee and drew out my chronometer, trying to verify the event. As I peered at it, the door of a stable directly across the street burst open, and a white mare came charging out, hooves thundering. Donal jerked and cried.

Timing is everything. My assailant chose that perfect moment of distraction to strike. I was enveloped in a choking wave of *that smell* as a hand closed on my face and pulled my head back. Instantly I clawed at it, twisted my head to bite; but a vast arm was wrapping around me from the other side and cold steel entered my throat, opened the artery, wrenched as it was pulled out again.

So swiftly had this occurred that my stick was still falling through midair, had not yet struck the pavement. Donal was pulled upward and backward, torn from me, and I heard his terrified cry mingle with the clatter of the stick as it landed, the rumbling earth, the running horse, a howling laughter I knew but could not place. I was sinking to my knees, clutching at my cut throat as my blood fountained out over the starched front of my dress shirt and stained the diamond stud so it winked like Mars. Ares, God of War. *Thor*. I was conscious of a terrible anger as I descended to the shadows and curled into fugue.

"Will you get on to this, now? Throat cut and he's not been robbed! Here's his watch, for Christ's sake!"

"Stroke of luck for us, anyhow."

I sat up and glared at them. The two mortal thieves backed away from me, horrified; then one mustered enough nerve to dart in again, aiming a kick at me while he made a grab for my chronometer. I caught his wrist and broke it. He jumped back, stifling an agonized yell; his companion took to his heels and after only a second's hesitation he followed.

I remained where I was, huddled on the pavement, running a self-diagnostic. The edges of my windpipe and jugular artery had closed and were healing nicely at hyperspeed; if the thieves hadn't roused me from fugue I'd be whole now. Blood production had sped up to replace that now dyeing the front of my previously immaculate shirt. The exterior skin of my throat was even now self-suturing, but I was still too weak to rise.

My hat and stick remained where they had fallen, but of Donal or my assailant there was no sign. I licked my dry lips. There was a vile taste in my mouth. My chronometer told me it was a quarter past two. I dragged myself to the base of a wall and leaned there, half swooning, drowning in unwelcome remembrance.

That smell. Sweat, blood, the animal, and smoke. Yes, they'd called it the Summer of Smoke, that year the world ended. What world had that been? The world where I was a little prince, or nearly so; better if my mother hadn't been a Danish slave, but my father had no sons by his lady wife, and so I had fine clothes and a gold pin for my cloak.

When I went to climb on the beached longship and play with the gear, a warrior threatened me with his fist; then another man told him he'd better not, for I was Baldulf's brat. That made him back down in a hurry. And once, my father set me on the table and put his gold cup in my hand, but I nearly dropped it, it was so heavy. He held it for me and I tasted the mead and his companions laughed, beating on the table. The ash-white lady, though, looked down at the floor and wrung her hands.

She told me sometimes that if I wasn't good the Bear would come for me. She was the only one who would ever dare to talk to me that way. And then he *had* come, the Bear and his slaughtering knights. All in one day I saw our tent burned and my father's head staring from a pike. Screaming, smoke and fire, and a banner bearing a red dragon that snaked like a living flame, I remember.

My mother had caught me up and was running for the forest, but she was a plump girl and could not get up the speed. Two knights chased after us on horseback, whooping like madmen. Just under the shadow of the oaks, they caught us. My mother fell and rolled, loosing her hold on me, and screamed for me to run; then one of the knights was off his horse and on her. The other knight got down too and stood watching them, laughing merrily. One of her slippers had come off and her bare toes kicked at the air until she died.

I had been sobbing threats, I had been hurling stones and handfuls of oak-mast at the knights, and now I ran at the one on my mother and attacked him with my teeth and nails. He reared up on his elbows to shake me off; but the other knight reached down and plucked me up as easily as if I'd been a kitten. He held me at his eye level while I shrieked and spat at him. His shrill laughter dropped to a chuckle, but never stopped.

A big shaven face, dun-drab hair cropped. Head of a strange helm shape, tremendous projecting nose and brows, and his wide gleeful eyes so pale a blue as to be colorless, like the eyes of my father's hounds. He had enormous broad cheekbones and strange teeth. That smell, that almost-animal smell, was coming from him. That had been where I'd first encountered it, hanging there in the grip of that knight.

The other knight had got up and came forward with his knife drawn and ready for me, but my captor held out his huge gauntleted hand. *"Sine eum!"* he told him pleasantly. *"Noli irritare leones."*

"Faciam quicquid placet, o ingens simi tu!" the other knight growled,

and brandished his knife. My captor's eyes sparkled; he batted playfully at my assailant, who flew backward into a tree and lay there twitching, blood running from his ears. Left in peace, my knight held me up and sniffed at me. He sat down and ran his hands all over me, taking his gauntlets off to squeeze my skull until I feared it would break like an egg. I had stopped fighting, but I whimpered and tried to wriggle away.

"Do you want to live, little boy?" he asked me in perfectly accented Saxon. He had a high-pitched voice, nasally resonant.

"Yes," I replied, shocked motionless.

"Then be good, and do not try to run away from me. I will preserve you from death. Do you understand?"

"Yes."

"Good." He forced my mouth open and examined my teeth. Apparently satisfied, he got up, thrusting me under one arm. Taking the two horses' bridles, he walked back to the war camp of the Bear with long rolling strides.

It was growing dark, and new fires had been lit. We passed pickets who challenged my captor, and he answered them with smiles and bantering remarks. At last he stopped before a tent and gave a barking order, whereupon a groom hurried out to take the horses and led them away for him. Two other knights sat nearby, leaning back wearily as their squires took off their armor for them. One pointed at me and asked a question.

My captor grinned and said something in fluting reply, hugging me to his chest. One knight smiled a little, but the other scowled and spat into the fire. As my captor bore me into his tent I heard someone mutter *"Amator puer!"* in a disgusted tone.

It was dark in the tent, and there was no one there to see as he stripped off my clothes and continued his examinations. I attempted to fight again but he held me still and asked, very quietly, "Are you a stupid child? Have you forgot what I said?"

"No." I was so frightened and furious I was trembling, and I hated the smell of him, so close in there.

"Then listen to me again, Saxon child. I will not hurt you, neither will I outrage you. But if you want to die, keep struggling."

I held still then and stood silent, hating him. He seemed quite unconcerned about that; he gave me a cup of wine and a hard cake, and ignored me while I ate and drank. All his attention was on the two knights outside. When he heard them depart into their respective tents, he wrapped me in a cloak and bore me out into the night again.

At the other end of the camp there was a very fine tent, pitched a little distance from the others. Two men stood before it, deep in conversation. After a moment one went away. The other remained outside the tent a moment, breathing the night air, looking up at the stars. When he lifted the flap and made to go inside, my captor stepped forward.

"*Salve, Emres.*"

"*Invenistine novum tironem, Budu?*" replied the other. He was a tall man and elderly—I thought: his hair and eyebrows were white. His face, however, was smooth and unlined, and there was an easy suppleness to his movements. He was very well dressed, as Britons went. They had a brief conversation and then the one called Emres raised the flap of the tent again, gesturing us inside.

It was so brilliantly lit in there it dazzled my eyes. I was again unrobed, in that white glare, but I dared do no more than clench my fists as the old one examined me. His hands were remarkably soft and clean, and *he* did not smell bad. He stuck me with a pin and dabbed the blood onto the tongue of a little god he had, sitting on a chest; it clicked for a moment and then chattered to him in a tinny voice. He in his turn had a brief conversation with my captor. At its conclusion, Emres pointed at me and asked a question. My captor shrugged. He turned his big head to look at me.

"What is your name, little boy?" he asked in Saxon.

"Bricta, son of Baldulf," I told him. He looked back at Emres.

"*Nomen ei Victor est,*" he said.

The taste in my mouth was unbearable. I hadn't wanted this recollection, this squalid history! I much preferred time to begin with that first memory of the silver ship that rose skyward from the circle of stones, taking me away to the gleaming hospital and the sweet-faced nurses.

I got unsteadily to my feet, groping after my hat and stick. As I did so I heard the unmistakable sound of an automobile approaching. In another second a light runabout rattled around the corner and pulled up before me. Labienus sat behind the wheel, no longer the jovial master of ceremonies. He was all hard-eyed centurion now.

"We received your distress signal. Report, please, Victor."

"I was attacked," I said dully.

"Tsk! Rather obviously."

"I . . . I know it sounds improbable, sir, but I believe my assailant was another operative," I explained. To my surprise he merely nodded.

"We know his identity. You'll notice he's sending quite a distinct signal."

"Yes." I looked down the street in wonderment. The signal lay on the air like a trail of green smoke. Why would he signal? "He's . . . somewhere in Chinatown."

"Exactly," agreed Labienus. "Well, Victor, what do you intend to do about this?"

"Sir?" I looked back at him, confused. Something was wrong here. Some business I hadn't been briefed about, perhaps? But why—?

"Come, come, man, you've a mission to complete! He took the mortal boy! Surely you've formed a plan to rescue him?" he prompted.

The hideous taste welled in my mouth. I suppressed an urge to expectorate.

"My team on Nob Hill is more than competent to complete the salvage there without my supervision," I said, attempting to sound coolly rational. "That being the case, I believe, sir, that I shall seek out the scoundrel who did this to me and jolly well kill him. Figuratively speaking, of course."

"Very good. And?"

"And, of course, recapture my mortal recruit and deliver him to the collection point as planned and according to schedule," I said. "Sir."

"See that you do." Labienus worked both clutch and brake expertly and edged his motor forward, cylinders idling. "Report to my cabin on the *Thunderer* at seven hundred hours for a private debriefing. Is that clear?"

"Perfectly clear, sir." So there was some mystery to be explained. Very well.

"You are dismissed."

"Sir." I doffed my hat and watched as he drove smoothly away up Market Street.

I replaced my hat and turned in the direction of the signal, probing. My dizziness was fading, burned away by my growing sense of outrage. The filthy old devil, how dare he do this to me? What was he playing at? I began to walk briskly again, my speed increasing with my strength.

Of course, the vow to kill him hadn't been meant literally. We do not die. But I'd find some way of paying him out in full measure, I hadn't the slightest doubt about that. He had the edge on me in strength, but I was swifter and in full possession of my faculties, whereas he was probably drooling mad, the old troll.

Yes, mad, that was the only explanation. There had always been rumors that some of the oldest operatives were flawed somehow, those created earliest, before the augmentation process had been perfected. Budu had been one of the oldest I'd ever met. He had been created more than forty thousand years ago, before the human races had produced their present assortment of representatives.

Now that I thought of it, I hadn't seen an operative of his racial type *in the field* in years. They held desk jobs at Company bases, or were air transport pilots. I'd assumed this was simply because the modern mortal race was now too homogenous for Budu's type to pass unnoticed. What if the true reason was that the Company had decided not to take chances with the earlier models? What if there was some risk that all of that particular class were inherently unstable?

Good God! No wonder I was expected to handle this matter without assistance. Undoubtedly our masters wanted the whole affair resolved as quietly as possible. They could count on my discretion; I only hoped my ability met their expectations.

Following the signal, I turned left at the corner of Market and Grant. The green trail led straight up Grant as far as Sacramento. What was his game? He was drawing me straight into the depths of the Celestial quarter, a place where I'd be conspicuous were it daylight, but at no particular disadvantage otherwise.

He must intend some kind of dialogue with me. The fact that he had taken a hostage indicated that he wanted our meeting on his terms, under his control. That he felt he needed a hostage could be taken as a sign of weakness on his part. Had his strength begun to fail somehow? Not if his attack on me had been any indication. Though it had been largely a matter of speed and leverage . . .

I came to the corner of Grant and Sacramento. The signal turned to the left again. It traveled up a block, where it could be observed emanating from a darkened doorway. I stood considering it for a moment, tapping my stick impatiently against my boot. I spat into the gutter, but it did not take the taste from my mouth.

I walked slowly uphill, past the shops that sold black and scarlet lacquerware and green jade. Here was the Baptist mission, smelling of starch and good intentions. From this lodging-house doorway a heavy perfume of joss sticks; from this doorway a reek of preserved fish. And from this doorway . . .

It stood ajar. A narrow corridor went straight back into darkness, with a narrower stair ascending to the left. The bottommost stair tread had been thrown open like the lid of a piano bench, revealing a black void below.

I scanned. He was down there, and making no attempt to hide himself. Donal was there with him, still alive. There were no other signs of mortal life, however.

I paced forward into the darkness and stood looking down. Chill air was coming up from below. It stank like a crypt. Rungs leading down into a passageway were just visible, by a wavering pool of green light. So was a staring dead face, contorted into a grimace of rage.

After a moment's consideration, I removed my hat and set it on the second step. My stick I resolved to take with me, although its sword would be useless against my opponent. No point in any further delay; it was time to descend into yet another hell.

At the bottom of the ladder the light was a little stronger. It revealed more bodies, lying in a subterranean passage of brick plastered over and painted a dull green. The dead had been Celestials, and seemed to have died fighting, within the last few hours. They were smashed like so many insects. The light that made this plain was emanating from a wide doorway that opened off the passage, some ten feet farther on. The smell of death was strongest in there.

"Come in, Victor," said a voice.

I went as far as the doorway and looked.

In that low-ceilinged chamber of bare plaster, in the fitful glow of one oil lamp, more dead men were scattered. These were all elderly Chinese, skeletally emaciated, and they had been dead some hours and they had not died quietly. One leaned in a chair beside the little table with the flickering lamp; one was hung up on a hook that protruded from a wall; one lay half in, half out of a cupboard passage, his arm flung out as though beckoning. Three were sprawled on the floor beside slatwood bunks, in postures suggesting they had been slain whilst in the lethargy of their drug and tossed from the couches like rags. The apparatus of the opium den lay here and there; a gold-wrapped brick of the poisonous substance, broken pipes, burnt dishes, long matches, bits of wire.

And there, beyond them, sat the monster of my long nightmares.

"You don't like my horrible parlor," chuckled Budu. "Your little white nose has squeezed nearly shut, your nostrils look like a fish's gills."

"It's just the sort of nest you'd make for yourself, you murdering old fool," I told him. He frowned at me.

"I have never murdered," he told me seriously. "But these were murderers, and thieves. Who else would keep such a fine secret cellar, eh? A good place for a private meeting." He leaned back against the wall, lounging at his ease across the top tier of a bunk, waving enormous mud-caked boots. His dress consisted of stained blue-jean trousers, a vast shapeless red coat made from a blanket, and a battered black felt hat. He had let his hair and beard grow long; they trailed down like pale moss over his bare hairy chest. He looked rather like St. Nicholas turned monster.

Donal sat stiffly beside him. Budu had placed his great hand about the boy's neck, as easily as I might take hold of an axe handle.

"Uncle Jimmy," moaned Donal.

"Explain yourself, sir," I addressed Budu, keeping my voice level and cold. He responded with gales of delighted laughter.

"I was the Briton, and you were the little barbarian," he said. "Look at us now!"

I stepped into the room, having scanned for traps. "I followed your signal," I told him. "You certainly made it plain enough. May I ask why you thought it was necessary to cut my throat?"

He shrugged, regarding me with hooded eyes. "How else to get your attention but to take your quarry from you? And how to do that but by disabling you? What harm did it do? Spoiled your nice white shirt, yes, and made you angry."

I tapped my stick in impatience. "What was your purpose in calling me here, old man?"

"To tell you a few truths, and see what you do when you've heard them. You were wondering about us, we oldest Old Ones, wondering what became of us all. You were thinking we're like badly made clockwork toys, and our Great Toymakers decided to pull us off the shelves of the toyshop." He stretched luxuriously. Donal tried to turn his head to stare at him, but was held fast as the old creature continued: "No, no. We're not badly made. I was better made than you, little man. It's a question of purpose." He thrust his prognathous face forward at me through the gloom. "I was made a war axe. They made you a shovel. Is the metaphor plain enough for you?"

"I take your meaning." I moved a step closer.

"You've been told all your life that our masters wish only to save things, books and pretty pictures and children, and for this purpose we were made, to creep into houses like mice and steal away loot before time can eat it."

"That's an oversimplification, but essentially true."

"Is it?" He stroked his beard in amusement. I could see the red lines across the back of his hand where I'd clawed him. He hadn't bothered to heal them yet. "You pompous creature, in your nice clothes. You were made to save things, Victor. I wasn't. Now, hear the truth: I, and all my kind, were made because our perfect and benign masters wanted *killers* once. Can you guess why?"

"Well, let me see." I swallowed back bile. "You say you're not flawed. Yet it's fairly common knowledge that flawed immortals were produced, during the first experiments with the process. What did the Company do about them? Perhaps you were created as a means of eliminating them."

"Good guess." He nodded his head. "But wrong. They were never killed, those poor failed things. I've seen them, screaming in little steel boxes. No. Guess again."

"Then . . . perhaps at one time it was necessary to have agents whose specialty was defense." I tried. "Prior to the dawn of civilization."

"An easy guess. You fool, of course it was. You think our masters waited, so gentle and pure, for sweet reason to persuade men to evolve? Oh, no. Too many wolves were preying on the sheep. They needed operatives who could kill, who could happily kill fierce primitives so the peaceful ones could weave baskets and paint bison on walls." He grinned at me with those enormous teeth, and went on: "We made civilization dawn, I and my kind. We pushed that bright ball over the horizon at last, and we did it by killing! If a man raised his hand against his neighbor, we cut it off. If a tribe painted themselves for war, we washed their faces with their own blood. Shall I tell you of the races of men you'll never see? They wouldn't learn peace, and so we were sent in to slay them, man, woman, and child."

"You mean," I exhaled, "the Company decided to accelerate mankind's progress by selectively weeding out its sociopathic members. And if it did? We've all heard rumors of something like that. It may be necessary, from time to time, even now. Not a pretty thought, but one can see the reasons. If you hadn't done it, mankind might have remained in a state of savagery forever." I took another step forward.

"We did good work," he said plaintively. "And we weren't hypocrites. It was fun." His pale gaze wandered past me to the doorway. There was a momentary flicker of something like uneasiness in his eyes, some ripple across the surface of his vast calm.

"What is the point of telling me this, may I ask?" I pressed.

"To show you that you serve lying and ungrateful masters, child," he replied, his attention returning to me. "Stupid masters. They've no understanding of this world they rule. Once we cleared the field so they could plant, how did they reward us? We had been heroes. We became looters.

"And you should see how they punished the ones who argued! No more pruning the vine, they told us, let it grow how it will. You're only to gather the fruit now, they told us. Was that fair? Was it, when we'd been created to gather heads?"

"No, I dare say it wasn't. But you adapted, didn't you?" To my dismay I was shaking with emotion. "You found ways to satisfy your urges in the Company's service. You'd taken your share of heads the day you caught me!"

"Rescued you," he corrected me. "You were only a little animal, and if I hadn't taken you away, you'd have grown into a big animal like your father. There were lice crawling in his hair, when I stuck his head on the pike. There was food in his beard."

I spat in his face. I couldn't stop myself. The next second I was sick with mortification, to be provoked into such operatic behavior, and dabbed hurriedly at my chin with a handkerchief. Budu merely wiped his face with the back of his hand and smiled, content to have reduced my stature.

"Your anger changes nothing. Your father was a dirty beast. He was an oathbreaker and an invader, too, as were all his people. You've been taught your history, you know all this! So don't judge me for enjoying what I did to exterminate his race. And see what happened when I was ordered to stop killing Saxons! When Arthur died, Roman order died with him. All that we'd won at Badon Hill was lost and the Saxon hordes returned, never to leave. What sense did it make, to have given our aid for a while to one civilized tribe, and then leave it to be destroyed?"

His gaze traveled past me to the doorway again. Who was he expecting? They weren't coming to join him, that much was clear.

"We do not involve ourselves in the petty territorial squabbles of mortals," I recited. "We do not embrace their causes. We move amongst them, saving what we can, but we are never such fools as to be drawn into their disputes."

"Yes, you're quoting Company policy to me. But don't you see that your fine impartiality has no purpose? It accomplishes nothing! It's wasteful! You know the house will burn, so you creep in like thieves and steal the furniture beforehand, and then watch the flames. Wouldn't it be more efficient use of your time to prevent the fire in the first place?" He paused a moment and looked at the back of his hand with a slight frown. I saw the red lines there fade to pink as he set them to healing over.

"It would be more efficient, yes," I said, "but for one slight difficulty. You couldn't prevent the fire happening. It isn't possible to change history."

"*Recorded* history." He bared his big teeth in amusement once more. "It isn't possible to change recorded history. And do you think even that sacred rule's as unbreakable as you've been told? I have made the history that was written and read. It disappoints me. I will make something new now."

"Shall you really?" I folded my arms. Doubtless he was going to start bragging about being a god. It went with the profile of this sort of lunatic.

"Yes, and you'll help me, if you're wise. Listen to me. In the time before history was written down, in those days, our masters were bold. All mortals have inherited the legend that there was once a golden age when men lived simply in meadows, and the Earth was uncrowded and clean, and there was no war, but only arts of peace.

"But when recorded history began—when we were forbidden to exterminate the undesirables—that paradise was lost. And our masters let it be lost, and that is the condemnation I fling in their teeth." He drew a deep breath.

"Your point, sir?"

"I'll make an end of recorded history. I can so decimate the races of men that their golden age will come again, and never again will there be enough of them to ravage one another or the garden they inhabit. And we immortals will be their keepers. Victor, little Victor, how long have you lived? Aren't you tired of watching them fight and starve? You creep among them like a scavenger, but you could walk among them like—"

"Like a god?" I sneered.

"I had been about to say, an angel," Budu sneered back. "I remember the service I was created for. Do you, little man? Or have you ever even known? Such luxuries you've had, among the poor mortals! Have you never felt the urge to *really* help them? But the time's soon approaching when you can."

"Ridiculous," I stated. "You know as well as I do that history won't stop. There'll be just as much warfare and mortal misery in this new century as in the centuries before, and nothing anyone can do will alter one event." I gauged the pressure of his fingers on Donal's neck. How quickly could I move to get them loose?

"Not one event? You think so? Maybe." He looked sly. "But our masters will turn what can't be changed to their own advantage, and why can't I? Think of the great slaughters to come, Victor. How do you know I won't be working there? How do you know I haven't been at work already? How do you know I haven't got disciples among our people, weary as I am of our masters' blundering, ready as I am to mutiny?"

"Because history states otherwise," I told him flatly. "There will be no mutiny, no war in heaven if you like. Civilization will prevail. It is recorded that it will."

"Is it?" He grinned. "And can you tell me who recorded it? Maybe

I did. Maybe I will, after I win. Victor, such a simple trick, but it's never occurred to you. History is only writing, and *one can write lies!*"

I stared at him. No, in fact, it never had occurred to me. He rocked to and fro in his merriment, dragging Donal with him. Silent tears streamed down the child's face.

Budu lurched forward, fixing me with his gaze. "Listen now. I have my followers, but we need more. You'll join me because you're clever, and you're weary of this horror, too, and you owe me the duty of a son, for I saved you from death. You're a Facilitator and know the Company codes. You'll work in secret, you'll obtain certain things for me, and we'll take mortal children and work the augmentation process on them, and raise them as our own operatives, for our own purposes, loyal to us. Then we'll pull the weeds from the Garden. Then we'll geld the bull and make him pull the plough. Then we'll slaughter the wolf that preys on the herd. Just as we used to do! There will be order.

"For this reason I came as a beggar to this city and followed you, watching. Now I've made you listen to me." He looked at the doorway again. "Tell me I'm not a fool, little Victor, tell me I haven't walked into this trap with you to no purpose."

"What will you do if I refuse?" I demanded. "Break the child's neck?"

This was too much for the boy, who whimpered like a rabbit and started forward convulsively. Budu looked down, scowling as though he had forgotten about him. "Are you a stupid child?" he asked Donal. "Do you want to die?"

I cannot excuse my next act, though he drove me to it; he, and the horror of the place, and the time that was slipping away and bringing this doomed city down about our ears if we tarried. I charged him, howling like the animal he was.

He reared back. Instead of closing about Donal's throat, his fingers twitched harmlessly. As his weight shifted, his right arm dropped to his side, heavy as lead. My charge threw him backward so that his head struck the wall with a resounding thud.

All the laughter died in his eyes, and they focused inward as he ran his self-diagnostic. I caught up Donal in my arms and backed away with him, panting.

Budu looked out at me.

"A virus," he informed me. "It was in your saliva. It's producing inert matter even now, at remarkable speed. Blocking my neuroreceptors. I don't think it will kill me, but I doubt if even your masters could tell. I'm sure they hope so. You're surprised. You had no knowledge, of this weapon inside yourself?"

"None," I said.

Budu was nodding thoughtfully, or perhaps he was beginning to be unable to hold his head up. "They didn't tell you about this talent of yours, because if you'd known about it I would have seen it in your thoughts, and then I'd never have let you spit on me. At the very least I wouldn't have wiped it away with my wounded hand."

"A civilized man would have used a handkerchief," I could not resist observing.

He giggled, but his voice was weaker when he spoke.

"Well. I guess we'll see now if our masters have at long last found a way to unmake their creations. Or I will see; you can't stay in this dangerous place to watch the outcome, I know. But you'll wish you had, in the years to come, you'll wish you knew whether or not I was still watching you, following you. For I know your defense against me now, think of that! And I know who betrayed me, with his clever virus." Budu's pale eyes widened. "I was wrong. The rest of them may be shovels, but you, little Victor—you are a poisoned knife. *Victor veneficus!*" he added, and laughed thickly at his joke. "Oh, tell him—never sleep. If I live—"

"We're going now, Donal Og, Uncle Jimmy'll get you safe out of here," I said to the child, turning from Budu to thread my way between the stinking corpses on the floor.

I heard Budu cough once as his vocal centers went, and then the ether was filled with a cascade of images: a naked child squatting on a clay floor, staring through darkness at a looming figure in a bearskin. Flames devouring brush huts, goatskin tents, cottages, halls, palaces, shops, restaurants, hotels. Soldiers in every conceivable kind of uniform, with every known weapon, in every posture of attack or defense the human form could assume.

If these were his memories, if this was the end of his life, there was no emotion of sorrow accompanying the images; no fear, no weariness, no relief either. Instead, a loud yammering laughter grew ever louder, and deafened the inner ear at the last image: a hulking brute in a bearskin, squatting beside a fire, turning and turning in his thick fingers a gleaming golden axe; and on the blade of the axe was written the word VIRUS.

Halfway up the ladder, the trap opening was occluded by a face that looked down at me and then drew back. I came up with all speed; I faced a small mob of Chinese, grim men with bronze hatchets. They had not expected to see a man in evening dress carrying a child.

I addressed them in Cantonese, for I could see they were natives of that province.

"The devil who killed your grandfathers is still down there. He is asleep and will not wake up. You can safely cut him to pieces now."

I took up my hat and left the mortals standing there, looking uncertainly from my departing form to the dark hole in the stair.

The air was beginning to freshen with the scent of dawn. I had little more than an hour to get across the city. In something close to panic I began to run up Sacramento, broadcasting a general assistance signal. Had my salvage teams waited for me? Donal clung to me and did not make a sound.

Before I had gone three blocks, I heard the noise of an automobile, echoing loud between the buildings. It was climbing up Sacramento toward me. I turned to meet it. Over the glare of its brass headlamps I saw Pan Wen-Shi. His tuxedo and shirtfront, unlike mine, were still as spotless as when he'd left the Company banquet. On the seat beside him was a tiny almond-eyed girl. He braked and shifted, putting out a hand to prevent her from tumbling off and rolling away downhill.

"Climb in," he shouted. I vaulted the running board and toppled into the backseat with Donal. Pan stepped on the gas and we cranked forward again.

"Much obliged to you for the ride," I said, settling myself securely and attempting to pry Donal's arms loose from my neck. "Had a bit of difficulty."

"So had I. We must tell one another our stories someday," Pan acknowledged, rounding the corner at Powell and taking us down toward Geary. The baby had turned in her seat and was staring at us. Donal was quivering and hiding his eyes.

"Now then, Donal Og, now then," I crooned to him. "You've been a brave boy and you're all safe again. And isn't this grand fun? We're going for a ride in a real motorcar!"

"Bad Toymaker gone?" asked the little muffled voice.

"Sure he is, Donal, and we've escaped entirely."

He consented to lower his hands, but shrank back at the sight of the others. "Who's that?"

"Why, that's a China doll that's escaped the old Toymaker, same as you, and that's the kind Chinaman who helped her. They're taking us to the sea, where we'll escape on a big ship."

He stared at them doubtfully. "I want Mummy," he said, tears forming in his eyes.

The little girl, who till this moment had been solemn in fascination, suddenly dimpled into a lovely smile and laughed like a silver bell. She pointed a finger at him and made a long babbling pronouncement, neither in Cantonese nor Mandarin. For emphasis, she reached down beside her and flung something at him over the back of the seat, with a triumphant cry of *"Dah!"* It was a wrapped bar of Ghirardelli's, only slightly gummy at one corner where she'd been teething on it. I caught it in midair.

"See now, Donal, the nice little girl is giving us chocolates." I tore off the wrapper hastily and gave him a piece. She reached out a demanding hand and I gave her some as well. "Chocolates and an automobile ride and a big ship! Aren't you the lucky boy, then?"

He sat quiet, watching the gregarious baby and nibbling at his treat. His memories were fading. As we rattled up Geary, he looked at me with wondering eyes.

"Where Ella?" he asked me.

When I had caught my breath, I replied: "She couldn't come to Toyland, Donal Og. But you're a lucky, lucky boy, for you shall. You'll have splendid adventures and never grow old. Won't that be fun, now?"

He looked into my face, not knowing what he saw there. "Yes," he answered in a tiny voice.

Lucky boy, yes, borne away in a mechanical chariot, away from the perishable mortal world, and all the pretty nurses will smile over you and perhaps sing you to sleep before they take you off to surgery. And when you wake, you'll have been improved; you'll be ever so much cleverer, Donal, than poor mortal monkeys like your father. A biomechanical marvel, fit to stride through this new century in company with the internal combustion engine and the flying machine.

And you'll be so happy, boy, and at peace, knowing about the wonderful work you'll have to do for the Company. Much happier than poor Ella would ever have been, with her wild heart, her restlessness and anger. Surely no kindness to give her eternal life, when life's stupidities and injustice could never be escaped?

. . . But you'll enjoy your immortality, Donal Og. You will, if you don't become a thing like me.

The words came into my mind unbidden, and I shuddered in my seat. Mustn't think of this just now: too much to do. Perhaps the whole incident had been some sort of hallucination? There was no foul taste in my mouth, no viral poison sizzling under my glib tongue. The experience might have been some fantastic nightmare brought on by stress, but for the blood staining my elegant evening attire.

I was a gentleman, after all. No gentleman did such things.

Pan bore left at Mason, rode the brakes all the way down to Fulton, turned right and accelerated. We sped on, desperate to leave the past.

There were still whaleboats drawn up on the sand, still wagons waiting there, and shirtsleeved immortals hurriedly loading boxes from wagon to boat. We'd nearly left it too late: those were my people, that was my Nob Hill salvage arrayed in splendor amid the driftwood and broken shells. There were still a pair of steamers riding at anchor beyond Seal Rock, though most of the fleet had already put out to sea and could be glimpsed as tiny lights on the gray horizon, making for the Farallones. As we came within range of the Hush Field both of the children slumped into abrupt and welcome unconsciousness.

We jittered to a stop just short of the tavern, where an impatient operative from the Company's motor agency took charge of the auto-mobile. Pan and I jumped out, caught up our respective children, and ran down the beach.

Past the wagons loaded with rich jetsam of the Gilded Age, we ran: lined up in the morning gloom and salt wind were the grand pianos, the crystal chandeliers, the paintings in gilt frames, the antique furni-ture. Statuary classical and modern; gold plate and tapestries. Cases of rare wines, crates of phonograph cylinders, of books and papers, waited like refugees to escape the coming morning.

I glimpsed Averill, struggling through the sand with his arms full of priceless things. He was sobbing loudly as he worked; tears coursed down his cheeks, his eyes were wide with terror, but his body served him like the clockwork toy, like the *fine machine* it was, and bore him ceaselessly back and forth between the wagon and the boat until his appointed task should be done.

"Sir! Where did you get to?" he said, gasping. "We waited and waited—and now it's going to cut loose any second, and we're still not done!"

"Couldn't be helped, old man," I told him as we scuttled past. "Carry on! I have every faith in you."

I shut my ears to his cry of dismay and ran on. A boat reserved for passengers still waited in the surf. Pan and I made for the boarding of-ficer and gave our identification.

"You've cut it damned close, gentlemen," he grumbled.

"Unavoidable," I told him. His gaze fell on my gore-drenched shirt and he blinked, but waved us to our places. Seconds later we were seated securely, and the oarsmen pulled and sent us bounding out on the receding tide to the *Thunderer* where she lay at anchor.

We'd done it, we were away from that fated city, where even now bronze hatchets were completing the final betrayal—

No. A gentleman does not betray others. Nor does he leave his subordinates to deal with the consequences of his misfortune.

Donal shivered in the stiff breeze, waking slowly. Frank's coat had been lost somewhere in Chinatown; I shrugged out of my dinner jacket and put it around Donal's shoulders. He drew closer to me, but his attention was caught by the operatives working on the shore. As he watched, something disturbed the earth, and the sand began to flurry and shift. Another warning was sounding up from below. It hit the bottom of our boat as though we'd struck a rock, and I feared we'd capsize.

The rumbling carried to us over the roar of the sea, as did the shouts of the operatives trying to finish the loading. One wagon settled forward a few inches, causing the unfortunate precipitation of a massive antique clock into the arms of the immortals who had been gingerly easing it down. They arrested its flight, but the shock or perhaps merely the striking hour set in motion its parade of tiny golden automata. Out came its revolving platforms, its trumpeting angels, its pirouetting lovers, its minute Death with raised scythe and hourglass. Crazily it chimed five.

Pan and I exchanged glances. He checked his chronometer. Our boatmen increased the vigor of their strokes.

Moment by moment the east was growing brighter, disclosing operatives massed on the deck of the *Thunderer*. Their faces were turned to regard the sleeping city. Pan and I were helped on deck and our mortal charges handed up after us. A pair of white-coifed nurses stepped forward.

"Agent Pan? Agent Victor?" inquired one, as the other checked a list.

"Here, now, Donal, we're on our ship at last, and here's a lovely fairy to look after you." I thrust him into her waiting arms. The other received the baby from Pan, and the little girl went without complaint; but as his nurse turned to carry him below decks, Donal twisted in her arms and reached out a desperate hand for me.

"Uncle Jimmy," he screamed. I turned away quickly as she bore him off. Really, it was for the best.

I made my way along the rail and emerged on the aft deck, where I nearly ran into Nan D'Arraignee. She did not see me, however; she was fervently kissing a great bearded fellow in a brass-buttoned blue coat, which he had opened to wrap about them both, making a warm protected place for her in his arms. He looked up and saw me. His eyes, timid and kindly, widened, and he nodded in recognition.

"Kalugin," I acknowledged with brittle courtesy, tipping my hat. I edged on past them quickly, but not so quickly as to suggest I was fleeing. What had I to flee from? Not guilt, certainly. No gentleman dishonorably covets another gentleman's lady.

As I reached the aft saloon we felt it beginning, in the rising surge that lifted the *Thunderer* with a crash and threatened to swamp the fleeing whaleboats. We heard the roar coming up from the earth, and in the City some mortals sat up in their beds and frowned at what they could sense but not quite hear yet.

I clung to the rail of the *Thunderer*. My fellow operatives were hurrying to the stern of the ship to be witness to history, and nearly every face bore an expression compounded of mingled horror and eagerness. There were one or two who turned away, averting their eyes. There were those like me, sick and exhausted, who merely stared.

And really, from where we lay offshore, there was not much to see; no DeMille spectacle. No more at first than a puff of dust rising into the air. But very clear across the water we heard the rumbling, and then the roar of bricks coming down, and steel snapping, and timbers groaning, and the high sweet shattering of glass, and the tolling in all discordance of bronze-throated bells. Loud as the Last Trumpet, but not loud enough to drown out the screams of the dying. No, the roar of the earthquake even paused for a space, as if to let us hear mortal agony more clearly; then the second shock came, and I saw a distant tower topple and fall slowly, and then the little we had been able to see of the City was concealed in a roiling fog the color of a bloodstain.

I turned away, and chanced to look up at the open doorway of a stateroom on the deck above. There stood Labienus, watching the death of three thousand mortals with an avid stare. That was when I knew, and knew beyond question whose weapon I was.

I hadn't escaped. My splendid mansion, with all its gilded conceits, had collapsed in a rain of bricks and broken plaster.

A hand settled on my shoulder and I dropped my gaze to behold Lewis, of all people, looking into my face with compassion.

"I know," he murmured, "I know, old fellow. At least it's finished now, for those poor mortals and for us. Brace up! Can I get you a drink?"

What did he recognize in my sick white face? Not the features of a man who had emptied a phial into an innocent-looking cup of wine. Why, I'd always been a poisoner, hadn't I? But it had happened long ago, and he had no memory of it anyway. I'd seen to that. And Lewis would never suspect me of such behavior in any case. We were both gentlemen, after all.

"No, thank you," I replied, "I believe I'll just take the air for a little while out here. It's a fine restorative to the nerves, you know. Sea air."

"So it is," he agreed, stepping back. "That's the spirit! It's not as though you could have done anything more. You know what they say: history cannot be changed." He gave me a final helpful thump on the arm and moved away, clinging to the rail as the deck pitched.

Alone, I fixed my eyes on the wide horizon of the cold and perfect sea. I drew in a deep breath of chill air.

One can write lies. And live them.

Two operatives in uniform were making their way toward me through the press of the crowd. "Executive Facilitator Victor?"

I nodded. They shouldered into place, one on either side of me.

"Sir, your presence is urgently requested. Mr. Labienus sends his apologies for unavoidably revising your schedule," one of them recited.

"Certainly." I exhaled. "By all means, gentlemen, let us go."

We made our way across deck to the forward compartments, avoiding the hatches where the crew were busily loading down the art, the music, the literature, the fine flowering of the humanity that we had, after all, been created to save.

THREE

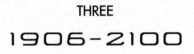

THE ANGEL OF
THE BOTTOMLESS DEEP

Getting Budu out of the way had been the first step.

"It was Aegeus's idea," Labienus said, holding out his hands in an apologetic gesture. "He recommended you for the job in the highest terms, Victor. And, really, what were we to do? We needed someone for swift, discreet, and effective work. You were the man."

"You might have warned me," said Victor, ignoring the aftershock that struck the hull of the *Thunderer* with an unnerving thump. He had gone ghastly pale. There was an expression in his eyes reminding Labienus of one of Van Gogh's more disturbed self-portraits.

"Come now, man, how could we have done that? You needed the advantage of surprise. The old creature had uncanny faculties of perception, as madmen frequently do. It should be obvious why the Company didn't want a lunatic immortal wandering about loose, especially one his size!"

"And the others of which he spoke? His cabal?"

"We've already investigated that," Labienus assured him. "He was delusional, of course. There are no others."

But Victor had not relaxed.

"What about the virus?" he demanded. "Why was that necessary?"

"Could you have defeated him without it?"

"I doubt it very much," Victor admitted, and dropped his staring eyes at last. Labienus cleared his throat.

"Not a gentleman's weapon, I know. If Aegeus hadn't insisted you were experienced in this sort of job—well. No use dwelling on what can't be helped. But you have my personal apology, for what it's worth."

"Am I still producing the virus?"

"Ye gods, no! It was designed to run its course quite quickly, once activated. In any case, it was harmless to anyone but an operative of that particular racial type," Labienus explained. "You're perfectly immune to it yourself, and anyone else you're likely to encounter would be as well."

"But how was it done? When was I infected?"

Time for the grandstand play. Labienus looked pained. He deepened the pain to anguish; rose from his seat and paced the cabin a moment before turning to Victor in a decisive manner.

"Victor, it's a classified matter, but—by God, sir, you're entitled to the truth." He drew from a sheaf of papers on his desk a photograph of Emil Bergwurm. "This was a protégé of Aegeus's. I don't know where he found the man, but evidently he was some sort of spectacular polymath—"

Victor rose from his chair and seized the picture. He stared at it for a long moment before handing it back.

"I know where he found him," he said quietly.

"Interesting," remarked Labienus. He pretended to study Victor in shrewd speculation. "There have been rumors for years—but, of course, I won't pry. One does feel a certain loyalty to one's old case officer. I have nothing but respect for Aegeus. If he did experiment with something, in defiance of Company regulations, I am certain it was in the Company's best interests . . . and perhaps you know more than I do in this matter."

Victor said nothing. Labienus cleared his throat and continued.

"There you have it. The mortal was brilliant with disease cultures, it seems. He was asked to come up with a, to coin a phrase, 'designed virus.' I assume you were armed with it at some point in the recent past. Have you been at Eurobase One recently?"

"I'm not at liberty to say, sir."

"Quite. Perhaps it's best we say no more on the matter, then, eh? You've earned a rest now. My private suite is through there—" Labienus pointed. "You'll find a change of clothes laid out for you. I'll have hot coffee and a breakfast sent in. Your personal effects are already waiting for you on the air transport, of course."

"Thank you, sir," Victor said mechanically, getting to his feet.

"And, Victor—" Labienus paused, as if reluctant to be too effusive. He shrugged, smiled wryly and said: "You're an excellent operative, sir. If you haven't always been appreciated, you should know that I, at least, have found it an honor working with you."

"Thank you, sir," Victor repeated. Was he even listening? Labienus clapped him on the shoulder and sent him off to the suite with a gentle push.

Not a bad beginning. He would improve on it.

April 29, 2100. If a place can hold the memory of death, surely the badlands of Montana retained it. Labienus peered from the window of the Silverbolt as it bounced over bare rusty earth and rock, trying to imagine what it had been like on that hellacious Cretaceous day when the end had come for them all: the maiasaur with its touching maternal concern, the vicious tyrannosaur no less a good mother, the little sneaking egg thieves with no shred of moral respectability whatsoever, all the rumbling honking thundering life that had held sway since forever. Even if they'd had the brains to see it coming, how could any of them have understood the End? What, for *us*? Rulers of the earth for the last hundred and sixty million years?

But the earth had understood, and remembered still, and offered up white bones still bedded in clay red as fresh meat for the edification of its present rulers, who utterly failed to take the hint. It was almost a duty to explain the lesson, thought Labienus.

He crested the last hill and braked a moment, gazing out at the spectacle in the valley below. There, the glittering expanse of domed backs in dust-dulled jewel colors: parked vehicles by the hundreds, for all the world like a massed herd grazing. The real herd was streaming up from the parking lot toward the immense white tent, only pausing and milling at the gate, where two parked ticket trailers blocked the way under the hanging sign: JURASSIC RANCH. Above the sign a banner had been poked up on poles: WELCOME CHILDREN OF MARIEL PROPHET!

Labienus grinned and fingered the little laminated tag he wore on a loose chain about his neck, that bore the single word MEDIA.

The tag got him preferred parking, and got him past the two trailers without paying for a ticket, and got him through the maze of hay bales and tent anchors to the trailer behind the big tent. He didn't even have to raise his voice, as he surely must have done if he'd wanted to be heard above the air conditioner's drone; he merely flapped the tag at the two husky mortals standing guard there. They looked him over, decided he fit the description they'd been given, and stood aside to let him climb the steps to their mistress's Abode of Repose, as the flowing script on the trailer's side declared it to be.

The refrigerated atmosphere inside was like a blessing from God, if one's idea of God fit the Mediterranean model and not the Nordic one whose hell was a region of eternal ice. Flies dotted the screen, motion-less, chilled practically into hibernation. Labienus made no move to swat them. They were innocents, after all.

He picked his way through the power cables for the various com-munications hookups, edged through the bath and dressing room, where the high wig and outrageous false eyelashes were set out like ar-mor to be donned for battle. There were five pots of eye shadow alone, in five different shades, each to be applied in its turn in the elaborate face paint patterns five generations of white trash had come to expect from evangelists, no matter what belief system they were peddling.

She was sprawled on the bed in the room beyond, naked, holding a frosted bottle of Perrier to her face.

Labienus bowed and waved his MEDIA tag.

"Ms. Mariel Prophet, ma'am?" he whined. "I'm from the Flathead Lake *Tribune,* and we just wondered if you had anything to say about those rumors that you ain't actually one of the High Holy Ascended Ones but in reality is Mary Ellen Kew from Provo, and ain't been any nearer them monasteries in Tibet than Taiwan, which you had to leave on account of a morals charge?"

"All lies," said Facilitator General Kiu, not even bothering to move the bottle so she could look at him directly. "Really."

"What, even that story that you slept with that little rich boy in New York and got him so crazy in love with you he went and willed his daddy's pharmaceuticals empire to your ministry before he blowed his own brains out?" persisted Labienus, perching on the edge of the bed.

"Especially that story," drawled Kiu. "Doonie had no brains to blow out."

"But we got a private source says the FBI and them Tobacco and Firearms people are, quote, very concerned unquote about reports you been meeting with survivalist supremacist sociopaths and planning a old-fashioned Doomsday suicide party," said Labienus, stretching out beside her. She groaned and shifted.

"Your clothes are hot," she complained.

"Get used to it, sugar," Labienus told her, moving closer. "It'll be even hotter out there, once you've got your prophet costume on."

"I go naked under the robe," she informed him.

"Angel Mariel! What would your faithful followers say if they knew?" he chuckled, pulling her against him.

"They know," she murmured, kissing him. "The idea inflames them. All those big boys with guns and half those big girls with knives dream about seeing their Holy Ascended Mother's merciful bosom up close and personal."

Labienus shuddered. "I don't see how you can stand the idea of one of them lusting after you. Let alone hordes of the things."

Kiu laughed and drew back from him, rising on her elbow and resting her head on her hand. "You men," she said sadly. "Though you're more finicky than most, Labienus. If I gave a damn what happened to my body that way, I'd have curled up and gone into fugue the first time I was raped. We can't afford that kind of fastidiousness. Flesh is too useful! If you'd bent over and offered that darling ass to the monkeys a few times, you'd have gotten things you wanted with much less trouble."

"Thank you, but I'll abstain," said Labienus. "And you can't tell me all you ladies are so free with your immortal charms. Why, I knew a little Botanist drone who so loved one man, she refused ever to take another lover after he died."

"Never heard of her," said Kiu. "And she loved a mortal, didn't she? That just proves my point."

"Maybe," replied Labienus, realizing with a start that he'd never thought of Nicholas/Edward as mortal. "Oh, well. Getting back to business: how is that Doomsday party shaping up? Plenty of odorless flavorless stuff to put in the Tasty-Ade?"

"It's not *that* old-fashioned," she said reprovingly. "I've got my inner circle of initiates convinced that the federal government is about to release a plague among all true believers."

"Because they're being controlled by Satan?"

"Ahriman, darling. I like to mix and match my bad guys. Anyway, I'm about to reveal that the latest divine avatar has given me the secret formula for an antidote." Kiu yawned and stretched. "A little chanting, a little light show with holographic chakras, and then I'll implore them all to come join me and the Apostles of Liberty at the meditation center on the night of the full moon, for an announcement of major importance. That ought to give the Feds time to hear about it."

"So that history can pursue its tragically inalterable course with another mass suicide," said Labienus, taking the Perrier from her and setting it aside.

"You got it, honey," Kiu agreed. "I'm making sure push will come to shove. With all those SWAT teams on the horizon, my faithful ones will clamor for the antidote. I'll administer the injections myself, assisted by the Apostles. They won't start dying for five hours, by which time I'll have departed to ask the Ascended Masters for guidance, but the Apostles will stay at their posts to record everything significant. Et voilà! We'll have field-tested a new poison on abundant volunteers."

"Five hours!" Labienus smiled, loosening his tie. "That must be one of Pryleak's toxins. He's a genius at timed-release poison."

"I don't know where you find these awful little moron scientists, but they certainly know their jobs," said Kiu. "If nothing else."

"You might say I've got a guaranteed supplier," said Labienus. He leaned over her and spoke seriously: "Easy enough to coax them into doing what they're good at; you might as well ask a rabbit to run. Far harder to persuade ordinary mortals to glorious idiocy. What a job you've done with those Apostles of yours!"

"Oh, but darling, that's just show business," Kiu replied, smiling as she unbuttoned his shirt. "Listen!"

They paused and focused on the hymn welling from the speakers in the big tent, the soul-stirring anthem so cunningly recorded it incorporated a host of subliminal subsonic hypnotic suggestions. They could hear the Apostles on the smaller stages outside working the crowd, and the first of the warm-up acts starting within the tent itself.

"Everything but the sign saying THIS WAY TO THE EGRESS," said Labienus, removing more of his clothing.

"Well, there is no egress," admitted Kiu. "As they'll discover."

"Much too late," said Labienus, and bit her. He thought of the scene as history would record it: the hundreds of corpses lying side by side in the desert, like sea lions on an infinite beach, bloating and blackening in the sun, all fallen in attitudes of prayer . . . the image intoxicated him.

Later he lay side by side with her in the chill, listening to the rising frenzy. The Apostles had moved into the big tent now and were building anticipation for Holy Mariel Prophet's eventual appearance.

"Sex," Kiu said thoughtfully. "And Fear. Get that big old devil behind them with a stick, and my radiant beauty in front of them, and they'll run right off a cliff, if I ask."

"I'm a firm believer in Guilt, personally," said Labienus.

"Works well on individuals," Kiu conceded.

"Nothing like it for subtle motivation. Plant it deeply enough into a mortal's psyche and it twists them endlessly." Labienus sighed. "Get it in there young enough and it'll do all your work for you. You'll have only to prod the mortal along with a suggestion now and then."

"You realize, of course, that we learned this from the Company?" said Kiu. "Deep programming to keep us running? I was supposed to feel guilty about surviving when everyone else in my village was slaughtered. 'Kiu-Ba, you bad girl, why didn't you die with us?' Conditioning nightmares for centuries, every time I had a disobedient thought, until I learned to work around them."

"Well, of course," said Labienus. "I did, too. What a lot you can do with a child, if you handle them properly!"

A metallic voice spoke from the communications console, echoing through the trailer. *"Beloved of the Avatar, this is your one-hour call."*

Kiu reached out to a bedside unit and thumbed its button. "I copy, Sergei. How's the preshow going?"

"As you divinely ordained it, Beloved."

"You will be blessed. Out." Kiu slid from the bed and hurried to her dressing table. Giggling, Labienus rose and began to dress himself.

"Do you have many Russians working for you?"

"Just Sergei." Kiu spread a coat of primer onto her face, working quickly. She had, after all, had millennia of practice.

"There was a Russian Preserver drone in my sector, and talk about conditioning! You'll never guess how the Company put his survivor's guilt to good use."

"They sent him down in shipwrecks to salvage valuables?" Kiu fanned the first coat dry and considered her pots of rouge.

"You've heard about Kalugin, then?"

"Ashoreth's worked with him. What an emotional mess!" Kiu loaded a canister of flesh tone into her airbrush and, closing her eyes, applied the base coat of foundation.

"But the most obliging fool it was ever my privilege to manipulate," said Labienus, slipping on his MEDIA tag again. "I could make that fellow believe anything."

Kiu set the airbrush aside and turned her masklike face to Labienus. Just at this stage of her toilette she looked queenly, cold, wise as a serpent.

"Give me a broken man every time. Putty can be every bit as useful as tempered steel, you know," she said. "Whatever happened to Kalugin, anyway?"

Labienus smiles, remembering.

The transmission had been picked up on the *Soter's* receiver in 2083, as Kalugin had rambled, had shouted, had mumbled and at last fallen into the nearest thing to eternal silence an immortal could preserve . . .

I suppose I can just keep talking until the oxygen runs out.

Yes, that would probably be a good idea, wouldn't it? Because then it'll be an anaerobic environment in here and no bacteria will grow. I'll be in better shape when they find me, and I'll have left an audio record. Less effort for the one who has to piece together what happened . . . and less upsetting for Nan, I mustn't forget that.

For of course I'll be rescued. They'll find me. Even though the *Alyosha*'s disappearance is masked by an event shadow, even though the portholes are beginning to be obscured by a film of what I am terribly afraid is mineral deposit that will set like concrete and entomb me in here, to say nothing of making the little sub impossible to spot way down here in the Aleutian Basin . . .

I do wish those appalling ticking noises would stop. Anyone less cheerfully determined than I am would suspect they were hairline cracks forming in the hull. I could survive the hull collapsing, of course, but then I'd be . . .

But the Company will find me. I'll be repaired, someday. I believe in that, yes, I do, with my whole heart and soul, don't I? Certainly I do. Keep talking, Vasilii Vasilievich. That way you won't start screaming, and after all why should you scream? Everything's going to be perfectly all right. The Company will find you. You've been broadcasting your distress signal loud enough to reach every cyborg operative in the eastern hemisphere and possibly one or two Kabalist rabbis in Poland.

Hm, hm, hm, life flashing before one's eyes. Very large red worm dragging itself across the glass and leaving a clear trail, oh, dear, there really is quite a lot of dark debris drifting down from the volcanic vent, isn't there? But that's why they call them *black smokers*, isn't it?

Is it? Would you like me to tell you my life story, large red worm? If I do, will you stay? Perhaps if you keep clearing the debris from that one porthole there'll be some clue for the rescue team, one tiny circle of light in the darkness with my frightened face pressed to it, mouth moving endlessly in pointless conversation. Yes, perhaps.

All right. What's my earliest memory? Being a mortal child. I was the big boy of the family. I was four. I think. Two sisters, Dunya and Sima. I remember them very well. Dunya was eight and Sima was three. Dunya had long braids and Sima had little short ones. We lived in a big house. I was frightened of Papa. He beat the servants, even the girls. But we had a lot of servants. We had fine clothes and toys, too, and our house had a wooden floor. So you can see we were somebody, my family.

Maybe the money and estates belonged to Mama? She never seemed bothered that Papa beat the servants and shouted at her, she just pretended he didn't exist. I don't know how trustworthy my memory is, of course, since I'd run and hide whenever Papa would rage. Dunya called me a coward. Hardly fair. She'd run and hide, too. But she never cried. I cried all the time. How squalid it all is, this memory, and how brief.

It ends, you see, the day it was warm enough to go outside and take bread to old Auntie Irinka. She can't have been my aunt really. I have the impression she lived in a little dark house in the fir woods, like Baba Yaga, and we were taking bread to her for charity. An old retainer put out to honorable pasture, perhaps? Sadly, she never got her bread.

Was it Dunya's fault? She was old enough to know better. I was the big boy of the family, though, I ought to have done something.

You see, the footpath ran along the bank of the river. Quickest route. Our nurse should have taken us some other way, I suppose, but Masha (that was our nurse, Masha) was impatient. We weren't going quickly enough for her, either, at least Dunya was but it took Sima ages to get anywhere on her little fat legs and I was slow, too, carrying the big bread loaf because I was the big boy, and so bundled up in my stiff coat I must have looked like a penguin walking. I should have fallen in, too . . .

Well, Masha decided she couldn't wait, and told us to stop there on the path and not to move until she came back, and then she ducked away into the trees to attend to a private matter. We stood and waited. There was such sunlight! Such a raw powerful smell of new life beginning! The wild smell of the trackless forest. Dark wet earth where the snow was melting, buds swelling on the branches, little green shoots sprouting everywhere. And the yellow-white surface of the river, still frozen solid. And Dunya said, "Let's go skating," and I said, "We haven't got skates with us."

Dunya tossed her braids at this and told me we could make skates out of sticks, and I said we couldn't, and she said she'd show me, and she scrambled down the embankment and broke a couple of forked sticks from a dead branch and stepped into them, and she actually did manage to sort of limp around on the ice. Sima wanted to skate, too, and staggered down the embankment. There weren't any other good sticks, but Dunya hobbled over and took her hands and towed her out after her, slipping and complaining, and they went way out across the river, and had just started back. None of us paid attention to the noises like thunder, far off, or noticed that they were coming nearer. We didn't even know what they meant.

But Masha knew, and her anger was almost greater than her fear, I think, when she came running back through the forest. She called us all sorts of names as she jumped down to the edge of the ice and demanded that the girls return immediately. Both the little faces turned up to her in surprise, and then, *boom* . . .

I think I closed my eyes. I'm sure I did. I always used to close my eyes when I was frightened. There was some shouting, I think, but I can't recall much about that; and when I finally opened my eyes, I recall how astonished I was. Everything had changed! The glaring bright surface of the river had broken up, all that stillness was now a surging living current of brown water, and great islands and bobbing floes of ice, and the *boom-boom-boom* like thunder was still going on all around.

But of Masha or my sisters there was no sign. They had vanished. I stood there staring, hugging the big loaf of bread. I had no idea what had happened. Minutes passed and nothing changed. I was still alone there on the footpath with the bread.

No, no, big worm, come back! The sad part is over. Now the story takes a most unexpected turn. You'll like this.

I heard a big deep voice saying, "What are you going to do, Vasilii Vasilievich?" I thought it might be the devil or Saint Mikhail, and I almost closed my eyes again, but something made me turn and look. And there, standing on the edge of the forest, was a man I recognized: one of our serfs, Grigori. He was leaning on his axe, just looking at me with his big pale eyes.

I said, if I recall correctly, "What?" and he said: "You've lost your sisters! What are you going to do now? Your father will beat you, no mistake about it. Didn't he tell you to be the big boy of the family?"

I started to cry. "Oh," I sobbed. "What am I going to do? I'm scared to go home!"

He came at once and crouched in front of me, looking me in the eye. He said, "Hey, Master, don't worry! I'll tell you what. You and I have always been friends, right?"

Now, I don't think that was quite true, I think he'd been brought from another village not long before, but he'd done a lot of work around the house lately and gone out of his way to be friendly to me, even binding up my knee once when I'd fallen and scraped it. I just sniffled now and said "Yes."

And he said: "Well! I'd hate to see your mother and father kill you, Master, so I'll take you to a safe place I know of. The people are nice there. It's warm. There's plenty of food. They'll let you live with them, and nobody will ever know what you've done. How about that, eh?"

I think I might have argued, but in the end I went with him. He took my hand and we walked away into the fairy-tale forest, and I never saw the mortal world, as a mortal child, again. I have never been able to remember what happened to the bread.

Where did you go, worm? The porthole's silting up again. No matter. I'll just go on talking as though you were still there. Wouldn't you like to know what happened to me? It's really an extraordinary story. After all, I started out in medieval Russia and here I am in a submarine in the year 2083, still alive. How did I become immortal? Did Grigori bite me in the neck? Certainly not. He wasn't that kind of a monster.

No, it seems my serf was in reality a cyborg posing as human, just as I am now, and once he had been a mortal child, just as I was then. What were all these cyborgs doing, running around Mother Russia? You might well ask!

Stealing icons out of lovely old cathedrals that are going to be blown up by Bolsheviks, amongst other things, or making off with a czar's ransom in amber wall panels before the Nazis can take them. Snatching orphans out of snowbanks, or from under the very hooves of Tatars' horses, and whisking them away to hidden Company bases to be converted to cyborgs. It's a little painful, the immortality process, but I can't deny there are advantages. Super intelligence, phenomenal abilities, and of course immortality.

Personally I've always thought Grigori was a bit sloppy. I don't think I was quite fit to become an immortal; but I was made into one anyway, so there you are.

Nan loves me as I am, at least. I've never understood why . . .

I was programmed to be a Marine Operations Specialist, and, as soon as I was out of school, began my long and illustrious career of going down with ships. Yes! That's what I do, worm, I sink for a living. Ha ha. When history records that a ship will go down with a particularly valuable item on board, it's my job to be aboard somehow, as captain or able-bodied seaman, and arrange to get the desired loot well sealed in a protective casing before the fatal storm or reef or whatever Fate has in store.

And then down we go, the poor mortals and I, to the bottom. I never like that part. I'm so sorry, you know, so sorry for them and there's nothing I can do at all, I can't save them . . . And then, to blunder around in the dark like a bloated corpse in the hold, waiting with the loot until the recovery ships are dispatched from the Company, that's not the pleasantest job in the world either, but somehow that's what my career aptitude tests recommended.

But I can't complain, and do you know why? Why I'm a lucky man, worm? I'll tell you: I found love.

Is that rare for a cyborg? Very rare, I assure you. You understand of course we're not emotionless creatures at all, not machines, heavens no! But the danger in loving mortals is that one faces inevitable tragedy: they must age and die, however much one cares for them. Yet somehow we immortals never seem to form more than the warmest of platonic friendships amongst ourselves . . . I thought, until I learned otherwise.

I met and fell in love with an Art Preservation Specialist. Met her quite by accident, too, it wasn't the work brought us together at all. And oh, worm, she's beautiful, she's kind, she's strong, much stronger character than mine. Fearless. And, do you know, we actually got married, my little darling and I? Sleek black lioness and clumsy polar bear, what a match.

We weren't supposed to wed, of course. The Company doesn't generally approve of marriages amongst its operatives. And of course it can't be marriage as mortals have it; we're parted for long periods of time. That's never mattered, though. We always meet again. And what exquisite bliss, that reunion, always . . .

I wonder how long it will be this time? . . .

But you want to hear an action story, don't you, big red worm? Yes, here you come, pushing your sucker-mouth across my tiny window, wiping clear an inch-wide view of hell itself, the dark-glowing fumarole. Thanks so awfully much. I'm afraid I don't see much in the way of heroic action because I'm not much of a hero, am I? But I tried to be. Failed miserably, too. Here's what happened:

They call it the Sattes virus, after the prison where it first broke out. Some form of hemorrhagic fever, symptoms vomiting and voiding of blood, attacking the intestines and spleen, killing the host within hours. It killed every single inmate and guard at Sattes Men's Colony in Montana, United States of America. Then it spread to the families of the guards. Then it stopped.

Before anyone could draw breath in relief, it had broken out in two other prisons, one in Utah and one in California. It followed the same pattern there, exactly. Within twenty-four hours it had broken out in prisons in Arizona, New Mexico, British Columbia. Within a week it was in prisons all over the world. How is it transmitted? Plenty of theories, but no real evidence. This was just a month ago, worm.

And do you know what the mortals did? They smirked. Just imagine, the criminal element wiped out in a week! Why, it was like a judgment of God. Never mind that men and women serving a week's time for traffic violations died, too, and there were a great many more of those than serial killers sitting in cells. It *must* be a judgment of God.

But even as it ran its course in the prisons, it started in the armed forces of the world. Broke out at military bases, on battleships, in civil defense training camps. That wiped the smiles off their faces. Millions of young men and women dying the world over. Perhaps it isn't a judgment of God after all? The death toll is amazing, surpassed the Black

Death in its first week. It kills so quickly, you see! And nobody knows what to do.

Though certain things are obvious. Groups of people living crowded together catch it, men catch it more easily than women. Age is no barrier, neither is race or location. There are theories: testosterone somehow linked? Schools have been closed, public assemblies forbidden, all the usual stuff governments do during a plague, depressingly familiar to us immortals but quite shocking to the poor little mortals who had somehow assumed that living in the twenty-first century exempted them from disasters of this kind. There has even been a resurgence of millennial paranoia: perhaps the count was off by eighty-three years, somehow?

And of course everyone working for the Company knows that's not the case at all. We all know Sattes won't bring on the end of the world, that it will disappear as quickly as it began, that no cure nor any cause will ever be found. Business as usual will continue for the human race. Well, not quite as usual . . . the human gene pool will be gravely diminished.

Now, when all this started, where was I? In the navy, of course. Posted to the Gorbachev Science Base on Avacha Bay. Heroic Lieutenant Kalugin waiting like an actor to play his part, with a worse than usual case of performance nerves.

You see, worm, here's what history says happened: that even with its armies and navies devastated, even as the whole world waited terrified and scarcely able to hope the dread epidemic had run its course, Russia bravely went ahead with its test voyage of a revolutionary new miniature submersible, the prototype *Alyosha*, powered by an experimental fusion drive. Future histories—when they mention it at all, tiny footnote to history as it is—will characterize this as a supremely gallant gesture of hope for the future in a very uncertain time.

A doomed gesture, too; for the *Alyosha* has been lost and will never be recovered, taking that experimental fusion drive with her (we could only afford to build one, you see; in fact we could only afford to build a little one, which is why it went in a submersible) and by the way her one-man-crew was lost as well, fearless Lieutenant Kalugin. Perhaps I'll get a statue, worm, every bit as grand as Peter the Great's, me in bronze towering among the kiosks that sell vodka and shoe polish in Petropavlovsk-Kamchatsky. Ah, but I won't be lost, really. I won't, worm, and you know why? Listen closely.

Almost the first thing the Company discovered, when it went into this time travel business so many ages ago, was that *history cannot be changed*. Recorded history anyway. But if you work within the parameters of recorded history, you actually have quite a bit of leeway, because recorded history is frequently wrong, and there are always event shadows—places and times for which there *is* no recorded history. See how it works?

So the Company decided that what would appear to be a tragedy could in fact be subtly erased. We could conform to the historical facts: I would volunteer for the mission, take out the *Alyosha* on its test run into the Aleutian Basin, transmit a distress signal and maintain silence thereafter, presumably lost in the abyssal darkness beyond recovery, for the navy will never find even a trace of the *Alyosha* . . . because I'll have taken the *Alyosha* straight to a Company recovery ship waiting off Karaginskiy Island.

No death after all for valiant Lieutenant Kalugin, and the fusion technology won't be lost, but co-opted by Dr. Zeus Incorporated, which will be regrettably unable to give it back to its inventors because history cannot be changed. Still, humanity will benefit in the long run. We—

Mother of God and all the holy angels, what was that?

It can't have been a probe camera from the *Soter*. They can't have noticed yet I'm in trouble, and even if they had they couldn't get here so quickly! Could they? I don't think so, but then I'm in an event shadow, aren't I, worm?

It can't be pressure on the hull. It can't. This hull is made out of a new super-composite. We tested it. It ought to withstand much worse than this. I'm only a thousand meters down. Or, or, well, maybe it will give just a little and then no more? Flexing, not breaking? It won't collapse. Not with me in it. That won't happen, worm. Really.

I know what it was! The black smoker must have thrown out a chunk of rock or something. Yes, of course, just a bit of larger-than-ordinary debris raining down on the hull. The rest of it is falling so softly, so silently, it might have been only a little pebble, and perhaps only sounded loud by contrast. Yes. We're all right, worm. No cause for concern.

Let's get back to our story, shall we?

The reason I'm sitting here, talking so desperately to you, worm, is, as you must have guessed, that *something went wrong*. All began according to plan, I bubbled away through the deep, reached the *Alyosha*'s last known position, transmitted my last tragic message and then took off for Karaginskiy Island.

But three hours out, I lost forward propulsion. I began to drop. Tried to jettison ballast: no use. And down I went, down through water that grew ever darker but not colder, into this previously undiscovered field of volcanic chimneys smoking out mineral-rich filth. Bump, down I came.

I've tried everything. It's not the fusion drive. That's still working beautifully, if pointlessly, not actually driving me anywhere. No, it seems to be a series of little malfunctions that have all compounded to make one very big malfunction, and as near as I can tell it's because a two-ruble bolt cracked and gave a valve more play than it should have had, so that it stuck in an open position . . . so much loving care was lavished on the wonderful new fusion drive that the rest of the *Alyosha*'s construction was just a bit shoddy, or so it seems.

Ironic, isn't it? Especially as I might have detected the problem if I'd done a routine scan before climbing in. I didn't, though. I was tired this morning. Sleepy. Hung over. See why mortals really needn't fear being conquered by a super-race of cyborgs? We can be just as stupid as they are.

Though you'd have been hung over, too, red worm, if you'd been drinking what I'd been drinking for three days. A cocktail of my own devising: I call it a Moscow Bobsled. Chocolate milk and vodka. Goes down fast and then you crash! Yes, I know, it sounds horrible, but the Theobromine in the chocolate interacts wonderfully with the vodka. What was my excuse for getting into such a state? Well, you'd have been drinking, too.

You see, my friends had died. You wouldn't know about that, of course. Red worms don't have friends, I suppose. Cyborgs really shouldn't, either.

When the plague spread to Russia, it came from the west. Hit St. Petersburg first. All those training ships, all those mortal boys and girls . . . Well, panicking, and drawing the obvious conclusion that it wasn't safe to crowd its armed forces together, the government hit on a desperate plan to salvage its remaining navy.

The orders went out to Okhotsk, to Magadan, to Petropavlovsk-Kamchatsky, to the island bases: empty the ships! Empty the barracks! Disperse and quarter the enlisted forces amongst the civilian population, or in remote areas spread out, and perhaps by the time the Sattes virus had worked its way across Siberia it wouldn't be able to find new victims.

You can imagine the alacrity with which this order was obeyed, worm. The old ships emptied and sat silent at anchor, and truckloads of sailors were taken up into the mountains. Some of them went to old mining camps, old logging camps, hunting lodges; all kinds of places were pressed into service as emergency quarters. Some just took off into the woods with camping gear, happy to get a vacation and save their lives into the bargain, promising to stay in contact electronically. The officers were quartered at hot spring resorts all through Paratunka.

Holidays for everybody! If only the Grim Reaper hadn't been expected
to show up as well. Moving into his little dacha amongst the stone
birches, checking his black robe and scythe at the changing-room door
and slipping into the hot pool . . .

The mortals didn't know what else to do. I didn't either, really; here
we were two weeks from the date of my historic mission and everything was falling to pieces. I knew that most of the people at Gorbachev would survive the plague, because history recorded their
names, and of course there was no danger to me. But what do you do
socially when the Dies Irae is playing everywhere? How do you pass
the time? Watch news on the Wire? Far too depressing. Go out for a
drink at a cozy club? Not in a naval uniform, which in this dark hour
marks you for one of the damned. Sit in your flat and play solitaire?

I did that, actually, until I got a call from the mortal Litvinov. He
and I'd served together on the *Timoshenko*, before I'd been transferred;
and guess where he was now! Ten kilometers out of Paratunka, sprawling at his ease in the private tub that came with his dacha. True, the
dacha was a little ruinous, because the resort had been closed for years;
but the hot water just kept bubbling, that was the great thing about
these places, and Larisa was there, and Antyuhin was there, and there
was plenty to drink, and wouldn't I like to come up for a visit?

I probably shouldn't have gone, worm. But my coworkers at Gorbachev were glad enough to see the back of me for a few days—they
were all civilians, after all, and seemed to think that would protect
them—so I spruced up and caught the tram out to Paratunka, and
walked from there. I'd had some idea of renting a bicycle, but the road
was impossible, steep switchbacks rutted and boulder-strewn, straight
back into the mountains.

But at last, as the first cold stars were peeping through the trees, I
heard the whine of a generator and saw yellow lights; and a minute or
so later I was walking in under a leaning arch that had once proclaimed
the name of this little resort. I couldn't tell what it had been, because a
new sign had been made from a piece of cardboard and tacked up
across the arch. It read:

SATTES SPA—YOUR HOST, BOCCACCIO

I walked in and stood in the central clearing, looking around uncertainly. There were perhaps a dozen little tumbledown dachas visible, all at the edges of the forest. Half a dozen had lights behind the
windows, and in some cases light streamed up into the trees through
holes in the sagging roofs. There was a strong smell of dry rot and

mildew, and all the damage that a mountain winter can inflict on a place like that, to say nothing of a vague sulphurous aroma. Still, the wind from the stars was cold and fresh. I could hear mortal voices in conversation, and music, and laughter. A fire had been lit in half an oil drum before one of the dachas: someone was grilling slabs of some sort of meat product.

As I watched, the door opened and a mortal man appeared, silhouetted black against the yellow light. Warm air steamed out around him. He wore only fatigue trousers, slippers, and a bathrobe, and he carried a drink. As he stepped out he was directing a remark over his shoulder to someone within the dacha: "But that's exactly my point. How do we know museums aren't full of evidence that's been mislabeled—"

He noticed me and started.

"Hell! Christ Almighty, Kalugin, I thought you were a bear after our Spam."

"Is that what it is?" I came close to the fire and peered in at the coals. Grilled Spam, all right. "Hello, Rostya Anfimovich."

"Good to see you!" Litvinov jumped down the steps and embraced me. "Did you walk all the way from the tram stop? Everyone, Vasilii Vasilievich got here!"

There was a chorus of happy shouts from the interior of the dacha, and in a matter of minutes I was soaking in the bath, mug of vodka in one hand and sandwich—grilled Spam between two Finnish crackers—in the other.

"Pretty nice, huh?" said Antyuhin gleefully. "And it's all ours! All we had to do was clean the dead leaves out. And, well, a couple of other things. We won't tell you about them."

"Thank you," I said, looking around. I wouldn't have been surprised to learn they'd had to clean a mastodon skeleton out of there. The little house was a wreck, and can't have been made of more than plywood and screens anyway. You could see stars through the roof, and birds had nested in the corners. The floor was spongy and gave alarmingly under Litvinov as he stripped down prior to rejoining us in the tub.

"And it's the junior officer's mess of the *Timoshenko* together again!" said Larisa Katerinovna, raising her tin cup. "For however long we have."

"No," Antyuhin pointed a finger at her admonishingly. "No references to you-know. Back to our symposium. We've got a Frivolity Symposium going, Kalugin, see? We're diverting ourselves with discussion on matters of no social or philosophical significance whatsoever."

"Current topic under discussion is whether or not Almas really exist," said Litvinov, splashing in beside me.

"The Mongolian bigfoot?" I stared.

"I don't see how you can deny it, with the Podgorni footage," challenged Verochka Sofianovna.

"The point, you see, Kalugin, is: if any supernatural creature who shall remain nameless comes to judge whether or not we're ready to be taken to the next world, he'll think we're a pack of hopeless twits and leave in disgust," said Antyuhin.

"And for that matter I don't think the possible existence of an unclassified hominid is a frivolous subject," Verochka said.

"What if they've been sighted in UFOs?" said Larisa.

"Good . . ." Antyuhin nodded, frowning thoughtfully.

"Pilots or abductees, though?" said Litvinov. "That would make a difference, don't you think?"

"Only in degrees of absurdity," said Verochka.

I had another bite of my sandwich and listened, so happy. I love mortals. I love their bravery and their craziness, their ability to tell jokes under fire. I suppose it's something they have to develop, since they know their deaths are inevitable; but it's magnificent all the same, don't you think, worm?

We sat there talking for hours, every now and then getting up to run out, all steaming and pink, to the cold pool, where we'd plunge into black water to keep ourselves from heart failure, or at least that was the idea. It was full of floating leaves but Litvinov assured me it was clean water, in fact he promised to show me just how pure it was later. When we were sufficiently revived we'd race back to the dacha for more vodka and more tales of the paranormal. We covered ghosts, UFOs, persons with the ability to teleport, talking animals, visions of the Mother of God, and anything else we could think of in our attempt to repel the angel of death.

Now and again other crew members in varying states of hilarious undress would stop in for a visit, making the rounds from their dachas across the clearing, usually bringing another bottle. Only once was there sadness, when the engineer Serebryannikov insisted on singing "The Last Night of the World"; other than that the stars shown down undimmed. It was long after midnight when we began to climb out and towel our wrinkled selves, and then to crawl into sleeping bags.

There was a slight social awkwardness then, because everyone was pairing off. Another gesture of defiance at death, I suppose, or perhaps just mutual comforting. I, by myself, was looking for a clean place to unroll my sleeping bag when Larisa approached me shyly.

"Vasilii Vasilievich, you came alone . . . if you'd like—?" She made an including gesture at herself and Antyuhin. He looked across at me, waiting to see what I'd say as he unrolled their bedding.

"You're very kind," I said, bending to kiss her between the eyes. "But I'm a married man, remember?"

"Oh! That's right. Well, anyway—" She kissed me back, quickly, and hurried off to help Antyuhin. "Dream about your wife, then."

And I did, worm. I did.

Next day we went climbing, Litvinov and I, and he directed my attention to the considerable beauty of the place with proprietary pleasure. Such trees! Such mountains! Such a beautiful land of fire and ice in high summer, worm. Such a wide sky. I wonder when I'll see the sky again? No point dwelling on that. No, I'll tell you how Litvinov and I climbed the trail above the ruined resort and came out above the most perfect little lake, green as malachite. It was artificial, quite round within its stone coping, and fed by a wide pipe that emerged from the hillside above. Clear as glass, that water cascaded out.

"Here," said Litvinov, "this is what I was telling you about last night. This is the reservoir they built to supply the dachas and the cold pool. See the snow on those mountains? This is snow-melt, can you imagine? Absolutely pure. It tastes wonderful."

"This is the stuff that feeds into the taps?" I bent and scooped a little into my palm, doing a content analysis. He was right: quite pure melted snow and nothing else.

"Yes. Dozhdalev and I traced the pipes." Litvinov crouched down and cupped his hands to drink. "Aah! Good stuff. You know what I'd like to do, after all this is over? I'd like to come back here. Maybe trace title and see if the owners would like to sell. Of course, I haven't got any money . . . but, I'll tell you what I could do! I could offer to be caretaker for them, free of charge. And I'd quietly fix up the best of the dachas to withstand the winter. Scrounge lumber from somewhere or even learn carpentry and plane logs I cut myself, eh? And live by foraging and hunting, and selling pelts for ammo and propane. Wouldn't that be a great life?"

"You'd have everything you needed," I said in admiration.

"I would, wouldn't I? If Verochka wanted to live here too I'd really have it all." Litvinov looked out over his prospective homestead dreamily. "I'm a city boy, but I could live like this in a minute. If only the world wasn't being turned upside down . . ."

"Well, you never know," I said. Even I didn't know, then. We immortals are told in a general way what the future holds, but the Company very rarely gives us specifics, you see, worm? For all I knew at that moment Litvinov might well survive to be living on salmon and bear meat in five years' time, a real pioneer of the post-atomic age.

For all I know . . . oh, worm, it's all very well to be hopeful, but we immortals fall so easily into the habit of lying to ourselves. It's hard to resist. You tell yourself that the years aren't bearable otherwise and then the lies become a habit, more and more necessary, and eventually there comes a point where you run on the truth like a rock at low tide and it splits you wide open. Shipwrecked. Good-bye.

We walked back down the trail and, to our surprise, encountered a hiker coming up, a pleasant-looking little woman in bright outdoor gear. She smiled and nodded at us as we passed her, and I started involuntarily: she was an immortal, too! She winked at me and kept going, striding along uphill on tireless legs. I couldn't very well turn to stare after her, with Litvinov there; and after all it's not so unusual to meet another operative now and then.

I thought she might have even been on a vacation. The Company has promised they'll begin granting us such perquisites, you see, as we get further into the future and more and more of our work for them is accomplished. It's been intimated that one day we'll even have lives of our own. Wouldn't that be charming, worm? Nan and I never parted any more, far from this sea that divides us . . .

I left next day, after hugs and kisses all around from my shipmates. I would have preferred to stay, but I had that crawling sensation we operatives get when we're off the job for too long; all those programmed urges to get back to work, I suppose.

So I walked back down to Paratunka and waited for the tram, and as I waited, who should come to wait too but the little immortal woman in her bright orange jacket. She smiled and nodded at me again. I looked around to be certain there were no mortals in earshot and said to her, in Cinema Standard: "I, er, noticed you up at the old resort."

Well, so I'm not a brilliant conversationalist, worm. But neither was she. She just smiled her unfading smile and said: "Yes. I was doing my work. It's very important, you know."

"You're a Botanist?" I said.

"Oh, no," she said. "Nothing like that. I have to be sure all the mortals are all right, you know."

Well, now I really had a crawling sensation, worm, because that was rather a strange answer to have given.

"Ah," I said carefully, "you mean you're an Anthropologist?"

Her smile never dimmed. "Uh uh," she said. "I just take care of the mortals."

I suppose at a moment like this mortals feel their hearts pounding, find their breath constricted, feel icy chills. Heaven knows I did! All I could think was, *Not again.*

But, oh, yes, again. What had happened, you see, was that I had stumbled on another Defective.

What's a Defective, worm? Well, officially they don't exist, of course; but the truth is, when the Company was learning how to transform human beings into immortal creatures with prodigious strength and intelligence, it didn't learn how to do it all at once. No indeed. It took a few tries to get the immortality process right. Unfortunately, the immortality part was the first thing that worked, so the first few deeply flawed individuals produced were permanent problems. What do you do with an idiot who's been given eternal life? Or a psychopath?

Dirty little secret, eh? I'd only learned about their existence because I'd had an unlucky encounter with one back in 1831, a pleasant-seeming fellow the Company was using as a courier. He was just intelligent enough to deliver packages, and, as long as he was kept continually on the move doing that, his other personality problems weren't apparent. But, surprise! On a routine mission to bring me some botanical access codes I'd requested, his clerk had neglected to program his next posting. I was treated to a harrowing two days with a very unpleasant fellow indeed.

So I knew all too well what a Defective looked like, sounded like, worm; and here was one seated next to me, on the tram bench in Paratunka.

Oh! Oh, holy saints. That was another rock, wasn't it? You can see out there, worm, tell me it was another rock, just a little harmless one plunking down on the *Alyosha*'s hull. Yes, thank you, you've taken a lot off my mind. You're doing a splendid job clearing the porthole, too, by the way. I can see so much farther now.

Where was I? This Defective I had met. She looked like some sweet little babushka with a preternaturally young face, gave an impression of being slightly hunchbacked, though I think this was because of the way she carried herself, bent slightly at the waist and rocking to and fro. Her smile was complacent, all-wise, all-knowing, tolerant. You might think, looking at her, that she had achieved great wisdom. I need hardly add, worm, that we correctly functioning immortals never smile in that way. We're too exhausted.

At least I am. Frightened, too. My instinct was to grab my luggage and run all the way back to Petropavlovsk-Kamchatsky, and the tram could follow any time it liked. But I smiled back, to avoid offending the creature, and I said: "You take care of them? That's very kind of you."

"Yes," she said, nodding again. "You know what happens if they don't get their vitamins, after all."

"That's bad, is it?"

"Oh, terrible!" Her face wrinkled up comically. "There'll be too many of them and they'll starve! Poor little things."

"We certainly don't want that to happen, do we?" I said.

"No," she said, and then her face changed. I tensed and clutched my bags, ready to bolt; but she lifted her head with a regal expression and regarded me coolly. And I tell you, worm, she was somebody else entirely then.

"I don't believe we've been introduced," she said.

"M-marine Operations Specialist Vasilii Vasilievich Kalugin, at your service," I said, trying to get the words out without my teeth chattering.

"What an awful lot of names you have," she said. "I'm Nicoletta." Just Nicoletta.

"Pretty name," I said, like an idiot. "You weren't Russian, then?"

"No," she said. "There weren't countries when I was made. I'm very old, you know. I've traveled a long, long way. Traveling all the time. Oh, look; here comes a tram."

Yes, thank God and all His angels, it was the tram at last, and we boarded, and I ran to the back in childish terror that she'd follow me. She didn't. She rode only a short way and got out at the next stop, another little resort town. As the tram rolled away, though, she looked up and caught my eye. She smiled for me again, that serene and knowing smile.

I congratulated myself all the way home that I'd escaped another nightmarish confrontation with a Defective. I went up to my flat, put away my things, took out a frozen *kulebyaka* and heated it through, and relaxed in front of the Wire screen to catch up on the news.

It wasn't good news by any means, worm.

The plague had jumped clear across Siberia in the time I'd been gone, and had already broken out in Okhotsk. No sign of it in Vladivostok or Japan yet, but that was anticipated. Depressing. I mailed the personnel coordinator at Gorbachev to let her know I was home again, I fixed a drink, and put on a disc to watch Pitoev's remake of *The Loves of Surya*.

I woke late, roused by the commotion at my door. Nobody was knocking on it or anything like that; it was being sealed. I could hear the hiss of the extrusion foam being jetted into place.

"Er—excuse me!" I came staggering out in my pajamas and gaped at the blank door lined in pink foam. A note had been pushed through at the bottom. I picked it up off the mat and read a hastily printed note informing me that I was under quarantine by order of the City Council.

"Miron Demyanovich," I shouted, hoping the superintendent was still within earshot. "Why am I being quarantined?"

There was silence for a moment and then he shouted: "You just came back from Paratunka!"

"Yes, well?"

"The news just came through! It's started there!"

"Oh," I said. Well, I had known it would happen, hadn't I? History records that the Sattes virus wiped out the armed forces of the world.

"I'm sorry, Lieutenant Kalugin! God have mercy on you!"

"That's all right," I said numbly, and went in to fix myself breakfast. I think I must have sat there staring into my coffee for an hour, worm, before I got the courage to get up and check my mail.

Three messages, and they had all come in in the last half hour. One was an electronic version of the note that had been slipped under my door, simply the official notification that I was under quarantine until one week from the present date. If I were still alive and well at the end of that time, I was to notify the proper department and they would process my petition for release.

The second note was from Gorbachev Science Center acknowledging my return and telling me that the *Alyosha*'s test launch was being postponed four days due to the outbreak, and requesting that I please inform them immediately in the event of any problems I might have with this schedule. Ha ha! I composed a brief reply informing them of my present scheduling conflict and assuring them that if I were still alive in a week's time I would report for duty at the appointed hour.

The third note was from Litvinov. It was very simple, worm, it told me what was happening. Serebryannikov and Verochka were gone already. Many of the others had begun to manifest symptoms and were expected to go soon. Litvinov was sorry and hoped I had better luck. If anyone survived he, or they, would write again in a couple of days.

But I never heard from any of them after that, worm, though I sent messages every day all that week.

Oh, worm, I'm afraid their Frivolity Symposium must have backfired; Death must have come to inspect them, and decided he'd be unlikely to find a more gallant crew anywhere, and conscripted them immediately to join the hosts of Heaven. Don't you think?

But so much for Litvinov's dream of homesteading that tumbledown resort, so much for dear Larisa with her bright smile, so much for crazy Antyuhin.

I cried, like the miserable weak creature I am, cried for hours. Only with terrible effort did I refrain from mailing Nan. Why sadden her with my helpless misery? The less she knew about this posting of mine, the better. I watched through swollen eyelids as the Wire broadcasts got more grim. Paratunka was devastated. The rest of Kamchatka got off fairly easily, but then as expected the plague traveled down to Vladivostok and so through Japan. There was some desperate hope that Korea and China might escape, that it might move on south, but no; after it had finished with Japan it turned, as though purposefully, and started in on Korea.

As though purposefully.

I'm not sure now exactly when I began to form my theory, worm, but there was a point where I set aside my drink and made a conscious effort to sober myself up by the dull blue light of the Wire. When I had converted enough of the mess in my bloodstream into sugars and water, I looked at my idea again. Nicoletta?

What had she said? That she was looking after the mortals, giving them their vitamins so . . . so there wouldn't be too many of them? What could she have meant?

She had been hiking up toward the reservoir when I'd first seen her. She'd been working her way through the Paratunka Valley, giving the mortals their—vitamins.

What was she doing, worm?

She was a Defective! And it occurred to me then that Nicoletta might have got some horrible idea in her head that the Sattes virus was a good thing—after all, a lot of mortals had thought just the same, when it was only attacking prisons—and decided to help it on its way, lest the world overpopulation problem continue. How easily one person with immortal abilities might slip over borders and do such a thing, I knew all too well. Traveling all the time . . . and the pattern of deliberate infection would be detected even by the mortals. There would be countless theories afterward that the Sattes virus had been part of a plot to reduce the world population, by taking draconian measures.

Most historians would decide that the prime suspect was the extremist Church of God-A, who preached drastic population reduction, though nothing would ever be proven. But what if it was one Defective with a big idea in her faulty little head? Dear God, I thought, I've got to warn somebody! She's got to be stopped!

Ah, but, you see, worm, there was a slight problem here. Officially, there are no Defectives. The Company won't admit to them. When that business with Courier had to be cleaned up, the Company sent in a covert operations squad; and I was informed, as clearly as they could tell me in oblique phrases, that nothing had really happened, and I was never to tell anyone that anything had. The Company has never made any Defective operatives. So whom might I contact with my warning?

Obviously the only safe thing to do would be to contact Labienus, the Northwest American Section Head at Mackenzie Base. He, after all, was the very one who'd been sent to deal with Courier's little accident, he was the one who'd delivered that so delicately veiled threat to me as he'd departed. Surely if discretion were called for, I ought to contact Labienus and none other. Don't you think, worm?

So I sat down at my keyboard and, after agonizing deliberation, composed the following communication: "Dear Executive Facilitator General Labienus, you may recall me from the year 1831 at the Fort Ross Colony, when we had occasion to speak. I understand you are doubtless a very busy man, but I should like very much to discuss a matter of mutual interest at your convenience. Respectfully yours, Marine Operations Specialist Kalugin."

Beautifully circumspect and tactful, yes, worm? I thought so. And it must have worked, because within the hour my terminal beeped on a shrill frequency inaudible to mortals, had any been there with me, announcing that a message was coming in on a secured channel.

I interfaced hurriedly with the terminal. *Kalugin receiving,* I transmitted. And there came his signal, quite clear and even slightly cordial in tone:

Marine Operations Specialist Kalugin? Labienus here. What is this matter you wish to discuss?

So I explained, worm, as quickly as I could. I told him all about Nicoletta and my suspicions. He heard me out patiently and his signal, when he replied, was grave and thoughtful.

Yes, Kalugin, there's no question you did the right thing by contacting me privately. I appreciate your discretion. Very well; we'll have her picked up immediately for interrogation. You understand, of course, that you'll need to distance yourself from this unfortunate situation?

I answered that I understood perfectly. My only concern was whether or not it would impact on my mission. Labienus assured me there was no need to be concerned on that account and—

HEY! HEY, I'M HERE! THANK GOD, THANK GOD, THANK GOD! You see, worm? I told you! Well, you've been wonderful company and I truly appreciate all your efforts on my behalf, but I'm afraid

I won't be able to finish my fascinating story. I'll be on the *Soter* in an hour or two, or possibly three, I've rather lost track of the time, and I think I'll take a hot shower first—silly, isn't it? With all the hot water I've been in lately, you'd think I'd have had enough to last me for a while, but actually sitting here under this black smoker has given me the most awful creeps, watching the sooty stuff rain down endlessly, I feel as though it's all over me somehow and not just the hull of the *Alyosha*.

I'll request a weekend leave after this, I've got one due me, I'm quite certain, and I'll go to Nan. Perhaps we'll go somewhere together. Marseilles, perhaps, or Casablanca! Somewhere full of sunlight. I want sunlight, I want it by the bucketful, I want to walk in the warmth and the clean dry air and lie down in the yellow sand with her. She'll make the nightmares go away. She can always make them go away. I'm never frightened when I'm with her, worm, I—

What are they doing back there?

What—?

They're removing the fusion drive. They're cutting it out with welding torches. They're not answering my transmissions, worm.

Well, don't be silly, of course they've got to be Company operatives! Mortal divers couldn't work at this depth. It's a pair of security techs in pressure suits, I'm certain. And they're taciturn fellows, everyone knows that, so perhaps they're just too busy to respond.

Oh . . .

And now they've gone.

They've left me here.

Why would they do that, worm?

Well, it seems I'm to impose on your hospitality a bit longer, worm. I'm really terribly sorry; I can't think what's happened. Unless the *Alyosha* with its fusion drive was too heavy for the winch on the *Soter*, and it was decided to bring it up in two dives? Yes, undoubtedly. And I'm sure the reason they weren't hearing my transmissions was the mess that's all over the hull from the black smoker, it must be full of metals in solution and that's somehow blocking my signal. So. I suppose while I'm waiting for them to come back I'll finish my story, shall I?

Labienus told me to go ahead with my mission, you'll remember. And that's exactly what I did: waited in my sealed room a whole week, while the Sattes virus spread into China and Indochina. I stopped tracking its progress after the first few days. Too depressing. History records that the plague hit China and India particularly hard. I didn't need to see the Wire footage to know what was happening. No, I lived off my cupboard shelf and out of my freezer, I watched film after film after film, I drank like a fish and occasionally sobered myself up long enough to send hopeful little communications to my colleagues at Gorbachev, letting them know I was still alive.

They let me know they were still alive, too. The decision had been made to go ahead with the launch, as I had known perfectly well it would be. The director intervened on my behalf with the City Council and the result was, I was spared a lot of bureaucratic delay. At the end of that week Miron Demyanovich was duly authorized to break the seal on my room. I was sitting there, shaved and combed and in uniform, when I heard the seal being cracked away and then the timid knock; and I opened the door to behold Miron Demyanovich with a biohazard mask over his pinched face, and two frightened-looking council members behind him.

I was manifestly alive and well, so they let me go. I reported to Gorbachev Science Center and underwent a series of tests, from which it was deduced that, yes, I was still alive and well, or at least alive and hung over. Then they stuffed me into the *Alyosha* rather hurriedly, and I kept my appointment with history.

And this is where you came in, worm.

Well, that was tidy, I must say. The oxygen is almost gone. How nice that you got to hear the whole story.

If it is the whole story.

I can't help feeling a certain nagging discomfort, worm, about one thing.

If I was right about Nicoletta—and Labienus seemed to think I was—where did she get the Sattes virus culture to put in unsuspecting people's water supplies? How did a poor simpleminded Defective manage the steamroller logistics of that sweeping outbreak?

So many people died, worm, were killed *discriminately*. It's going to drastically affect the course of history. There won't be any full-scale wars for decades (except in Northern Ireland, of course) and it will be a century before the crime rate even approaches its previous figures.

It'll be a much more peaceful, law-abiding, uncrowded world after this, worm. That's going to be good, yes? The poor stupid mortals will think so at first. But, you see, their gene pool will have shrunk so drastically. All those young men, young women gone. Most of a generation. Never so many of them after this. Less and less every year. And then, the next time a plague hits . . .

Won't affect us, of course. We're immortal. We'll go right on working for the Company. Company will still be around. Plenty of us immortals still around.

Company wouldn't do a thing like this, worm. I'm positive. We're ethical creatures, for heaven's sake! Programmed to look after them. Take care of the poor mortals.

Though some of us have a rather low opinion of them. It's a job hazard, worm. Despair.

I don't feel like that, of course. It's not their fault. Capable of such wonderful things, too. But I know some immortals who think . . .

Oh, God and Saint Mikhail, what if one of *us* . . . what if Labienus . . .

Hello, Dunya. Hello, Sima. You want me to come out there to you? Isn't this enough for you, that I'm down here under the water with you at last? And I'm with you to stay, I think. I don't believe I'm ever coming up again, not now. I stumbled on something I shouldn't have seen.

But I won't go out to you. The black smoker's so dirty. Dark and wet and dirty. It's burying me under dirty little secrets and soon not even you will be able to get to me, with your reproachful faces, not even my friend the worm will be able to help me.

Oh, but that makes you angry, how Papa's eyes flash, and he's lifting his giant hand and it's coming down now with the bloodstone ring on his knuckle and it will do more than black my eye this time, I'm sure . . . but it's not the bloodstone after all, it's become an aquamarine. How strange, and what a beautiful color the stone is!

I can't take my eyes off its pure light and in fact I'm floating up toward it now, I've been accidentally netted. They're dragging me through the shallows, because the wreck wasn't deep. Now I've left the rotting hulk down there below me but I shouldn't be here, should I? Here where I first met my beloved? What's gone wrong with time?

Yet I bob up into the bright air. I behold a lovely picture, the water and the sky so blue and the lateen sails like old parchment, and golden cliffs in the distance, and very surprised black faces regarding me from the deck of the fishing boat.

I struggle free of the net but it's a mistake, because the water's claiming me again, I'm plummeting back down into depths of sea the color of Spanish glass. No! I'll swim, I'll make my way to the shore because I know she's coming to meet me, she's heard my distress signal. I must meet her, up there in the sunlight.

I blunder up out of the surf, soaked and sick and exhausted, but it's all right because I see her now. Nan! On a long curve of golden sand, under swaying palms, seated in majesty on the tallest camel I've ever seen, the tiny goddess carved of blackest jet. My Queen of the Night with her eyes like desert stars, veiled in a blue that puts the sky to shame. She extends her little hand to me. I reach, and reach, but I can't seem to pull free of the water, my legs are like lead, and in my ears ever louder is the roar of breakers on the Moroccan coast.

FOUR

2225

FATHER OF PESTILENCE

The office has changed.

The credenza on the desk has a sleek post-postmodern look. The furniture matches it in style, everything ergonomically correct, in the bright primary colors of the first half of the twenty-third century. Labienus likes to move with the times. As far as it is possible to dress elegantly in that particular era, he is elegantly dressed.

He is frowning as he gazes out the window at his wilderness.

It has not quite the pristine splendor that it had. There is not that lucent quality to the air that there was; particulate matter from air pollution has found its way farther north than even the Yukon. There are a great many more skeletal silver trees in his line of sight than there used to be, and many trees nominally alive but tipped with brown needles. Contrails stripe the sky. Satellites cross it at night. No more than a century ago, he had looked up from his work one morning just as a grinning snowboarder waved at him from the other side of his window. A small and well-aimed missile disposed of the mortal; but, really, the annoyance!

It is not this that causes Labienus to frown, however.

The air pollution has been worse than at present, and is diminishing yearly. Likewise the aircraft; and as for the mortals, their birth rate has been steadily dropping for a century now. This is particularly unfortunate (for them) in light of the pandemics that have been sweeping the world population with increasing frequency since the beginning of the twentieth century. Influenza, AIDS, Ebola 3, the Sattes virus . . .

Labienus is pondering the Sattes experiment.

"No good deed goes unpunished," he murmurs to himself. Kalugin had been handily disposed of, but the Sattes virus had not been what he would call an unqualified triumph. So much for a gesture of filial piety! They'd tried Budu's preferred method of a quick directed kill at last, and what had happened? They'd drawn attention to the operation. Much too obvious.

True, the body count had been impressive. All the same, conspiracy theorists everywhere had pointed fingers at the blatant pattern in the disease's progress, its unsubtle choice of victims. Thank the gods most of the suspicion had been shifted onto the Church of God-A, but the fact that even a lump like Kalugin had been able to figure out what was really going on was clear evidence that selective culls would never have worked as a long-term strategy.

What a pity Budu hadn't been there to witness it! Would he have been baffled? Angry? Apologetic?

It was fun to imagine, yet Labienus knew the truth: the old monster would have refused to change his methods. He simply hadn't a human mind. He'd have pushed straight on winnowing the unrighteous from the righteous by degrees of wickedness, playing Ten Little Indians on a global scale, and sooner than later it would have all come out. Not that Labienus feared anything the mortal masters could do in retaliation; but Aegeus and his people would have objected to the complete extinction of the mortals (too *useful!*), and they had real weapons in reserve.

So it was just as well Budu remained where Victor had left him, buried under tons of rubble in San Francisco. More than likely in two or three pieces, too. Labienus smiles.

That was pure Victor, that touch, sending in the tong members with hatchets. Spiteful, but coldly effective, too.

He wonders again why Victor has delayed stepping in and consoling Kalugin's wife, with whom he is so comically smitten. Another generous gesture on Labienus's part, getting the husband out of the way, and what good has it done?

But perhaps he's drawing out the luxury of conquest. Victor is methodical in his pleasures. Exquisite taste and iron resolve coupled with that venomous temperament . . . really a pity he wasn't brought all the way in sooner. Everything ripens in its own time, however.

Labienus turns his attention to a minor problem that has been niggling for his attention. His sources have been reporting excruciatingly detailed and frequent attempts, by a low-level Preserver drone, to access classified data.

The data concerns Project *Adonai*. The drone in question is, of all people, Literature Preservation Specialist Grade Three Lewis.

Labienus knits his brows. Project *Adonai* has been defunct for centuries, more's the pity. Nennius has promised to advise him if it is ever reactivated.

So what the deuce is a Literature Preservation drone doing, poking his silly nose into the matter of an obscure British spy who died in 1863? Not once has he attempted to find out anything about *Homo umbratilis,* as might be expected from his unfortunate history. Why Bell-Fairfax, instead?

Standard procedure is to draw the operative in by dangling more information before him, luring him into a trap, and Labienus duly composes a memo giving the order to follow procedure. He fires it off to Nennius. As he waits for confirmation, the thought drifts into Labienus's mind: for a comparative nonentity, Lewis has been associated with far too many classified matters . . .

Is it possible that Nennius's favorite assassin can be employed, from beyond the grave, to claim another victim?

Something about the idea warms Labienus's heart. He glances up at the locked cabinet where the red file still sits, though its contents have long since been transferred to disk. He has been reluctant to consign the hard copy to a fusion hopper; Nicholas's portrait is an original work of art, after all. And how could he part with those meticulous mission reports in Edward's elegant copperplate script, such a painstaking list of horrifying deeds committed with the noblest possible intentions? Labienus chuckles, imagining a tall spectral figure rising from the dust, advancing implacably on Lewis . . .

"*Vae victis,*" he says cheerily. Sacrifices, always sacrifices to keep the world rolling in its profitable orbit . . .

A call comes in on the secured channel. Labienus lifts the amplifier—no more than a twist of silver wire now, like a piece of modern art—from its cradle, and slips it on.

Labienus, he transmits.

Nennius. Ave. Just got your memo about the Literature drone. How the bloody hell did you hear the news before I did?

Labienus is startled, but covers his wave of confusion.

I have my ways. Still, I'd like a fuller report from you.

Well, did you hear why *Lewis had to run?*

My sources were a bit sketchy on that, Labienus admits blandly, wondering what has happened. *Details, please.*

Apparently some nests of Homo sapiens umbratilis *evaded us. They've been out there all this while, hiding. They found Lewis again!*

I knew that, Labienus prevaricates. *But—*

You'll never believe this. The damned kobolds have been hunting for him since he ran into them in Ireland.

But it's been nearly two millennia! Labienus remembers the illuminated pages, the uncials switching from Gaelic to Latin and back again.
What had the *umbratilis* Prince threatened? That if it took them years,
they'd still get Lewis back?

*They're incompetent but they have long memories, it seems. And they
hold a grudge. Blew his cover and chased him from London to Dieppe, before
he got away last night. Aegeus's people have had their hands full dealing
with the mortal witnesses.*

Labienus begins to grin incredulously. *The things want him that
badly, do they? I wonder if they're more talented than our in-house idiots?*

There is a silence on the ether. He can almost feel the shock waves
as his meaning gets across to Nennius. Then there is wild laughter.

Do you suppose they'd be willing to cut a deal?

What do you suppose they'd give us for him?

Beyond the glass of his window, something momentarily distracts
Labienus. A lost hiker, emaciated, bearded, filthy, his parka in rags, has
climbed to the window ledge and is staring inward in disbelief. He
presses his palms to the glass, uncertain whether or not he is hallucinating but desperately sincere in his silent plea for help.

Labienus exhales in annoyance and reaches over to flip a switch.
With the release of a powerful spring under the ledge, the mortal is
launched, screaming, into midair. He tumbles end over end into the
rocky chasm beyond, and drops from sight.

Focusing again, Labienus transmits: *I wonder if by any chance they
could be persuaded to do us a favor in return?*

You never mean . . .

*Wouldn't it be nice to have a permanent way to get rid of our rivals,
when 2355 comes at last? We can smash the masters like insects, but Aegeus
won't go down without a fight. To say nothing of mortal-loving idiots like
Suleyman.*

You brilliant bastard.

Thank you.

*If the little cretins haven't yet found a silver bullet, perhaps they can ex-
periment on Lewis to make one.*

We can suggest it.

And then it's only a matter of delivering the merchandise to them . . .

*All the more reason to bait a trap for him. What did you think of my
suggestion about luring him in with a false lead on Adonai?*

*Could be useful. Why on earth is the idiot snooping around a black
project?*

That's for you to find out.

Very well. You know, Adonai's still running.

Are you sure?

I still get the updates once a month, reminding me to search for a host mother. They don't seem to realize that a stunt like that's a good deal harder to pull off in this day and age than it was in 1825.

Or 1525. But a third boy . . . Think of the uses we could find for him, in these modern times! Perhaps something truly worthy of his talents.

I suppose I could arrange for some hapless girl to dream she's been abducted by aliens and implanted with a space hybrid . . .

They both roar with laughter, booming through the ether like static. Labienus dances without getting out of his chair, an elbows-out buck and wing.

Do let me know if anything is ever done. Vale.

Vale, Labienus.

Labienus puts down the amplifier and lounges back in his chair, still smiling broadly. His thoughts return to Victor . . .

MESSIS VERO CONSUMMATIO
SAECULI EST

I first saw the boy through the wavering light of a flame; rather ironic, as things turned out.

It was in a pleasant suburban villa out beyond the Vondelpark. We'd had to leave the car a good distance off and walk, Labienus and I, because so many people had already arrived for the party. The night was clear for early December, with a black sky full of stars, and the red windows of the house looked warm and inviting. As we drew near we could smell the fragrances of a midwinter celebration: evergreens, spices, mulled wine.

"How festive," remarked Labienus, smiling. "If only they knew, eh?"

I found his remark in the worst of taste under the circumstances, but I smiled back. Labienus is very much my superior in rank, however much I dislike him.

And he had told me, after all, to play this lightly, for my own emotional health; stress levels would be reduced if I resolutely put gory details out of my mind. I wasn't even being told everything about the job. Better that way.

The door was already open as we came to the bottom of the steps, for our hostess was welcoming in a young couple and their child. Anna Karremans was a plain smiling woman in her mid-forties. Her guests edged past her into the hall, and she stood gazing down at us expectantly as we started up the steps.

Yes, that was the first unnerving moment, for me: the mortal woman seemed to be standing in the open mouth of an oven, smiling as an inferno blazed behind her. But it was only the scarlet light of the holiday decorations, after all, and it was a gentle heat that flowed down on our cold faces.

"Michel Labeck," Anna exclaimed, recognizing Labienus. "Oh, we were beginning to be afraid you'd had an accident!"

"Not at all, Dr. Karremans," Labienus greeted her, and his smile widened as he stepped up to the door and took her hand. "I wouldn't let an accident derail a media event like this one! And the party does seem to be proceeding successfully," he added, looking in through the hall at something I was unable to see.

"They're all here," she leaned forward to tell him in an undertone. "All the journalists. Everyone on the list you gave me. You're a miracle worker, Michel."

"Not at all," he told her, still smiling, and beckoned me forward. "But I've kept another promise: here's the assistant Doss and Waters has sent you. Nils Victor. Nils, this is Dr. Anna Karremans."

"Delighted, madam." I bowed slightly and attempted to smile.

"How nice to meet you," she exclaimed. "Oh, but you look so serious! Not to say half frozen. Please, come in, let me take your coats—"

So I entered the mortal woman's house, and stood in her bright hall looking in at the party.

Yes, there were plenty of journalists in evidence. I recognized several from the Amsterdam Wire and the global Wires, too. There were a number of kameramen, but they were all unplugged; so far as they knew, yet, there was nothing to See. No, they stood in small groups chatting, like the other mortals, helping themselves from the buffet or admiring the Yule tree, or gathering about the piano to argue over the lyrics to the new Yule songs. Ranks of real candles were burning on the buffet table, long red tapers in bright-painted wooden candlesticks, quite old-fashioned and charming in a rural sort of way. It might have been a room from the twentieth century, or the nineteenth.

And here were children running to and fro, in and out of the rooms, circling the furniture and yelling happily. Really, one expected Herr Drosselmeyer to make a swooping entrance with a nutcracker. But there was no Clara for him to woo here. All these children seemed to be little boys, six of them, all between the ages of five and eight. Not much to tell them apart: tousled hair, cheeks pink with exertion, bulky-knitted sweaters with patterns of reindeer or fir trees or snowflakes. A fair-haired boy, an ash-blond boy, a boy with hair red as mine, two brunettes who seemed to be twins . . . well, he wouldn't be one of them. A boy with sable hair . . . ? Yes. I spotted him standing still for a moment on the other side of the buffet table, beyond the bright candles, and his image shimmered through their flames.

I found I didn't care to look at his face.

I concentrated on the buffet instead. What a feast: smoked salmon, goose, turkey, baked goods in profusion, spiced apples, chocolates. Theobromos would help . . .

"Nils?"

I managed to avoid starting guiltily as I turned from sampling a truffle. Labienus saw, of course, and his eyes glinted as he touched the shoulder of a mortal man with a stupid gentle face.

"Nils, may I present Dr. Geert Karremans?"

"Sir!" I ate the last of the truffle hastily, smiled and reached to shake his hand. "It's an honor to meet you."

"Very, very kind of you," the man replied with enthusiasm. He, like Anna, was just entering middle age but dressed boyishly. *His* bulky-knit sweater was patterned with little figures of skiers. "So—what do you think? Will it go over well?"

"I can't imagine a more wholesome scene," I told him, fairly truthfully.

"It'll go over well," decided Labienus, surveying the room. "Look at everyone! Happy, well-fed, full of sentimental memories of childhood. This was exactly the approach to take."

"And all your idea, too," Geert congratulated him.

"Not mine alone, Dr. Karremans. This is why Doss and Waters has retained its premiere position in public relations counseling for more than fifty years," Labienus replied. "I think you'll find you made the right choice in retaining our services."

"Oh, I'm sure we did," agreed Geert, stepping aside whilst two of the boys thundered past the table, shrieking as they chased each other with toy dinosaurs. One jostled a corner in his passing, and a candlestick toppled over; I caught it rather more quickly than I ought to have, but Geert didn't notice. He was frowning after the boys.

"The children are getting restless. Do you suppose it's time to make the—?" He looked at Labienus with a combination of nerves and eagerness.

"Showtime," Labienus told him, smiling again. "Leave it to me."

He strode to the fireplace and stood with his back to the flames, calling for attention with his mere presence. He had dressed for the part, certainly: black trousers and a red shirt cut to give the impression of informal power. Labienus was an imposing-looking fellow in any case, tall, with elegant Roman features. As one after another of the guests stopped speaking and turned to stare at him, he put his hands up and said, in a pleasing voice that penetrated without effort to the far corners of the house: "Friends? Everybody! May I have your attention, please?"

He had it at once, naturally. Beside me a kameraman murmured appreciatively, "Check it out! He's not even miked."

"Thank you. Now, I'm going to tell you all a story, so I'd suggest you make yourselves comfortable. Yes, here—let's bring the children up to the front, this is their time of year, after all. Are you having a good time, boys? Wonderful. And the rest of you, you're all relaxed, you've all helped yourselves to the fine feast our hostess has set out? I haven't seen a holiday table like that since I was a child, have you? All settled now. Good!

"My name is Michel Labeck, of Doss and Waters Public Relations, and I've been retained by the Drs. Karremans for my professional expertise; but I'd like to add that I'm also a personal friend, as are most of you here." This wasn't quite true, as the party was fairly exclusively a press event, but he was unlikely to be contradicted.

"Now, you ladies and gentlemen of the press amongst us may have been suspecting that an announcement of some kind was going to be made—and, of course, you're correct. There will be an official press conference tomorrow, you see, but tonight we'll make the unofficial announcement to you favored ones we regard as personal friends. We wanted you to know first, to have a unique opportunity for an intimate look at what we're unveiling."

The little boys were bored by this, lined up as they were in a row at Labienus's feet. A velociraptor screamed silently and leapt at a stegosaur, which bashed it back.

"Oh-oh! Looks as though we've got a dinosaur conflict, ladies and gentlemen. I think I'd better cut to the chase, here. Are you ready for the story, boys?"

"Ye-es," chorused half a dozen little voices. There was of appreciative laughter from the adults.

"Good." Labienus looked out into the room, making eye contact, drawing them all in. "Once upon a time, children, there was a man and there was a woman. They loved each other very much, and they were very happy together. In another age, long ago, he might have been a toymaker, she might have been a milkmaid; but they happened to be born into an age of science, and so scientists they were. They were good people. The woman worked to keep the children of the world safe from diseases. The man worked to make certain the children of the world would never go hungry. They did this with their research into DNA."

Murmurs from the crowd as heads turned to Geert and Anna, smiling self-consciously by the buffet table with their arms about each other, flushed with the warmth of the candles.

Labienus cleared his throat. "Now, as I said, this couple were very happy together. There was only one sorrow in their lives: they had always longed to have a child of their own. But the years went by, and no little child came to them. Perhaps, they thought to themselves, it was for the best. After all, there were histories of certain kinds of illness in both their families, and maybe they oughtn't pass on their genetic inheritance. They tried to adopt, but so few babies were available in this country they'd have been awfully old by the time their names came to the top of the list to get one. It was very sad.

"And then, one day, the woman had a daring idea: they might combine their knowledge of DNA to make themselves a child."

A stunned silence in the room. The mortals looked at one another, wondering if Labienus was really going to say what they imagined he might say.

He nodded, acknowledging their excitement. "Yes! Now, this was a very unconventional idea, I need hardly tell you. After all, ignorant people find the thought of creating anything from recombinant DNA quite scary. They think of white-coated mad scientists from the movies creating terrible things, creating, oh, I don't know, tomatoes with claws and teeth. A ketchup monster! Or some strange hybrid like this—" He leaned down and took a toy dinosaur from one of the boys, and, grabbing an apple from the mantelpiece decorations, stuck it on the dinosaur's head and held it up for everyone to see. "Look! Applesauce monster."

The children squealed with laughter, and the adults laughed, too. Smiling, Labienus returned the dinosaur to its owner and continued: "Of course, that's not really what happens when you work with recombinant DNA at all, and scientists are not mad characters from the movies. But people in other countries made their governments forbid research into recombinant DNA, even though it might hold the key to eliminating disease and hunger throughout the whole world forever. It's sad when people are stupid.

"Ah, but this is Amsterdam! We have a tradition of tolerance and enlightenment going back to our very beginnings. We have never fallen into step with the bigots and the short-sighted. We have gone our own way, triumphantly and successfully, for centuries now. We have never passed laws to forbid the pursuit of human knowledge, and as a result our scientific and technological discoveries have brightened the world, and made it a better place for children everywhere to be born into. We're not afraid"—he pulled an absurd face—"of applesauce monster, eh?"

Laughter throughout the room, and a pleasant sense of smug superiority. Labienus regarded us all, smiling. He put his hands in his pockets and went on: "Now, our friends, the two scientists, knew perfectly well how to make a child from recombinant DNA. We've known how for decades. But, probably because of worries over applesauce monsters, nobody had ever made one. Well, the man and the lady sat down and came up with a simple design. All they wanted, after all, was an ordinary, healthy little child.

"And then the lady remembered her poor brother, who had been in the Civil Guard before his life was cut short by the Sattes virus." Labienus's face grew very somber, and there were sighs as people remembered the death toll from that terrible interlude, when the virus had spread through the armies of the world.

"And the man remembered his own childhood, how clumsy he'd been, how hopeless at sports, and how mercilessly other children had teased him for it.

"This was why they decided to improve their simple design. What if it were possible to make a child with an immune system engineered to resist viral infections? What if it were possible to make a child with a brain engineered to better process information, to send signals more quickly and clearly to the body? What would they have then? Why, they'd have an ordinary little child who could catch a ball with ease, and more: a child who would be able to survive any plagues that might evolve. You see?

"No superman. No atomic genius. No applesauce monster. Only a healthy, well-coordinated child you wouldn't notice if you passed in the street. This was all they wanted, ladies and gentlemen."

He paused to let them think about that.

"And the purpose of this party is to tell you, ladies and gentlemen, that—with the help of dear friends, doctors, and other scientists—a healthy, average child is exactly what they got."

Quite a reaction at that, all manner of mortal emotions in that crowded room, and a chorus of clicks and curses as all the kameramen realized they ought to have been recording this. Kameramen aren't ordinarily caught flatfooted, but they tend to pay more attention in moments of horror and tragedy than at pleasant parties. Now the kameramen belatedly plugged themselves in and Saw Labienus. He nodded just perceptibly, and for their benefit he reiterated: "Yes. This man and this woman have produced the first human child using recombinant DNA, ladies and gentlemen. Will you be permitted to see the embryo? I'm afraid that's not possible, because, you see, this child was produced *six years ago*. He has already been with us for quite some time."

Now they really gasped, the mortals, and Geert and Anna clung together more tightly. Labienus took his hands out of his pockets and held them out to the children sitting at his feet.

"Now, boys, I'd like to ask you to stand up and turn around for the cameras. You're all going to be on the Wire!"

Shyly, awkwardly they clambered to their feet and turned, six little boys in bright sweaters, clutching their toy dinosaurs, blinking at the kameramen. Labienus's voice rose on a note of command.

"Look at them, ladies and gentlemen! Our own children. Could you possibly tell that one of them was made from recombinant DNA? You couldn't, could you? Which boy do you think it is?"

A few people (though not his parents) pointed uncertainly at the blue-eyed blond child. Labienus grinned.

"No indeed. No, as it happens"—he put his hand on the shoulder of the black-haired boy—"it's little Hendrick. The rest of you children may sit down now."

Little Hendrick's eyes widened. He turned and stared up at Labienus in horror, turned back and stared at the kameramen recording his image avidly. He started forward through the seated crowd, desperate to get to Anna and Geert.

"Wait!" called Labienus, laughing. "Hendrick, people would like to speak with you!"

"I want to go to see my mommy now," Hendrick wailed, and reaching her at last he wrapped his arms around her legs and hid his face.

Well! Could anything have been more disarming?· Anna lifted Hendrick in her arms and what a heartwarming picture they made, all three, the two proud parents and their shy little son. Technically I suppose he was no more their son than anyone else's, of course. A host mother had gestated him (she later sold her story to a journalist) and nobody was ever able to determine afterward just where Anna had obtained the source DNA they'd used.

The boy didn't look enough like Anna and Geert, or unlike them either, to be able to tell. I had to look at his face now and, I must admit, I'd never have known he was a Recombinant. After all, what was a Recombinant supposed to look like? Nobody had any idea, then. This one was slender and dark, with wide dark eyes and very ordinary features. He clung with his arms around Anna's neck as she and Geert fielded questions from the press. Labienus had coached them carefully for this, knowing when to fade back and let them tell it in (very nearly) their own words.

Yes, it was all true; Hendrick Karremans was five years old. No, they hadn't raised him here in Amsterdam City. They'd been living out in the country until a couple of weeks ago. No, he hadn't attended preschool. Yes, he was going to enter an ordinary kindergarten when the

2093 session started, in two weeks. This was why they had felt they ought to go public with his story at last.

What was his IQ? They declined to state, but added that he was a reasonably bright boy. He liked to paint and listen to music. His favorite food was Apple Puffs. His favorite game was Super Soccer-Man. What did he want to be when he grew up? A fireman! Why hadn't they revealed his existence to the world before now? Because they had wanted him to have a normal childhood.

Until today, I thought to myself, watching the child's face as he peered at the kameramen. If he'd known the truth about himself, he certainly hadn't had any idea what the truth meant. He was beginning to know now; and how frightened he looked, little Hendrick Karremans.

Though he grew calmer as the room became less crowded. The parents of the human children took them home to bed, the journalists rushed home to their keyboards to get the story out. The kameramen lingered, intent on catching visuals of the child wandering around the emptying room, waving disconsolately at the other boys as they left, going to the buffet and helping himself to chocolates before Anna caught him at it, picking up his dinosaur and making it walk along the wall.

I had found an uncrowded corner and seated myself there. Eventually Geert came and settled beside me, as Labienus escorted the last of the kameramen out with some concluding remarks for print.

"Well! I don't see how it could have gone any more smoothly, can you?" Geert said happily. "I think we made quite a good impression."

"I think so, yes," I replied.

"You'll be staying over? I see you didn't bring a bag, but—"

"In the car," I assured him. "I'll get it before Michel leaves."

"Good. We have the guest bedroom ready for you. Michel gave you some idea of your duties?" Geert looked just slightly uneasy. He'd never been a celebrity before.

"Handling the press and your correspondence on a day-to-day basis," I recited. "Making any arrangements, security or otherwise, that become necessary." This included acting as the child's bodyguard, though I felt it tactless to say so in so many words.

Geert nodded. "We're very grateful to you, really. I didn't realize there were people who did this sort of thing! Of course, it'll be very important to make sure that our lives go on just the same as before, as far as that's possible. That's just the point of it all, you see? Hendrick is really no different from any other child. Nothing is going to change."

Fool, I thought. Even the child knew better.

He sidled up to us now, looking troubled.

"Daddy?" He wrung his hands. "I'm afraid we have rather a problem."

"And what's that, Hendrick?" Geert turned to him, smiling at his big words.

"Well—there's one of those bugs in here, it came out of the coat closet and now it's flying around—I don't know what they're called—"

"A fly?"

"No, Daddy, the ones that eat clothes, you know?" How anguished his dark eyes were.

"Moths," I said.

"Yes, thank you. And they like to get near candles—and we've got all these candles in here—and one of them could fly too close and catch fire and then fly all around the room and set it on fire, too."

Geert roared with laughter at that. Hendrick just looked at him, on the point of tears, I think.

"No, no," I assured him. "Because the wings would burn up instantly, so the moth wouldn't be able to fly. You see? It'd just fall harmlessly to the table."

"But then the table might burn," Hendrick pointed out.

"True," I acknowledged. "Let's see what we can do about preventing that, shall we?" I looked up into the room and acquired the moth. On its next pass through the air above our heads I lunged up and got it.

"Bravo!" Geert applauded. "What speed! But you missed, didn't you? It was way up there by the ceiling."

"Do you see it, sir?" I inquired.

"No, but—"

I opened my hand to reveal the moth's crushed body. Geert went off into gales of laughter again. I think he'd had more wine than perhaps had been quite wise. Hendrick smiled at me.

"And now the moth won't burn your house down," I told him.

"Thank you," he replied gravely. He considered me a long moment. "What's your name?"

"Nils Victor," I told him. "I'm here to help your mother and father."

"Oh. Are you going to live with us?"

"Yes, I am."

"That'll be nice," he said. Anna came in then.

"Hendrick, it's past your bedtime," she said severely. She was quite sober. "And we've still got the food to clear away, Geert."

"Allow me, please," I told her, and got to my feet. She started to protest, and then realized she had a *servant* now. How her face lit up.

"If you don't mind—it's too kind of you, really. Hendrick, say good night to dear Mr. Victor and we'll go upstairs." She held out her hand to him and he went dutifully, but not before pausing to say: "Good night, Mr. Victor." He knit his brows, and remarked: "You're different, too."

Interesting. I smiled and inclined from the waist in a bow. Neither of his parents seemed to notice the remark. Anna took the child's hand and led him upstairs, as Geert yawned hugely and got up to help me put away the remnants of the buffet. He had just proposed that we open another bottle of wine when there came a polite double knock at the door: Labienus, returning from the car with my bag. I excused myself and went to let him in.

"Good thing I didn't drive away with this," he said in a jolly voice, presenting me with the bag. He scanned briefly, to assure himself there were no mortals within earshot, and said in a lower voice: "You'll be all right here, of course."

"Certainly, sir," I replied. But what expression was this on his face? Sympathy?

"Look here . . . this will be hard for you, I know. Regrettable that he's a delightful child. This is strictly against regulations, of course, but, to fortify you in your hour of need—you'll find a few bars of Theobromos in with your things." He took my hand in his and clenched it briefly.

I was speechless with shock. Labienus was the last man I should have thought capable of gestures of affection. I know from bitter experience how little compassion he feels for the mortals we purportedly serve. I still had a vivid memory of old San Francisco, when I'd seen him straining eagerly to hear the death screams of mortals trapped in the ruins of the earthquake.

"Thank you very much, sir," I said, finding my voice at last. He smiled again and stepped back out into the night.

"You're welcome. There are times, Victor, when one needs additional strength to endure what is necessary in order to obtain Company goals. But I'm sure you're far too experienced a field operative to need to be told that! I'll be in touch in the morning."

And he ran lightly down the steps and away, under the cold stars.

The official press conference the next day was much more difficult. Word had got out, as we'd intended, and the press knew what to expect, what pointed questions to ask. Fortunately Labienus had prepared answers to all of them, but Geert and Anna were still flustered. They really had not expected any negative reaction to what they'd done.

I was tempted to blame them, but it was easy to understand their ingenuousness. They'd lived cloistered with Hendrick night and day for five years. He seemed the most lovable and ordinary of children to them. How could anyone object to his existence?

The religious leaders of the world had various condemnatory answers for them, of course, including the Ephesian Church, which formally demanded to know why Anna had not created a daughter instead of a son. Fortunately Anna was a practicing Ephesian, and her pious answer—that she'd left the choice of the baby's gender up to the Goddess—mollified them somewhat. We put out a certain amount of Ephesian-slanted publicity, too, depicting Anna as bravely defying the paternalist laws of the world to exercise her reproductive rights, which helped.

More difficult to deal with were all the tedious little laws Anna and Geert had so blithely disregarded. No, they hadn't registered Hendrick's birth with the proper civil authorities: how could they, when they'd meant to keep his existence a secret until the press conference? So of course he had no papers and no legal identity, and that meant dealing with a hostile bureaucracy.

And, no, he'd never had vaccinations of any kind. He didn't need them. He was engineered to be disease-free, with an antibody system much more aggressive and powerful than ordinary mortals had. He'd never been ill a day in his life! So why should there be any need to give the child inoculations now, especially as he was afraid of such things, like any little boy?

The answer, of course, was that he would not be permitted to attend kindergarten until he'd had the inoculations. They were required by law. Moreover, the kindergarten Anna and Geert had chosen for Hendrick now refused to take him, and in fact filed suit against the Karremans family for lying on the application form about his legal status. No use to explain that they hadn't thought they were lying; as far as they were concerned, Hendrick was really their son, and wasn't that what mattered?

Naive idiots. We did our best, Labienus and I, at defusing the problems caused by superstition and ignorance, but really the mounting lawsuits—filed seemingly by everyone, anyone who felt they might have reason to suspect that Hendrick's creation infringed on their civil liberties—and bureaucratic stalemates were another matter entirely. I don't know what we'd have done if the situation had continued.

We took the most outrageous of the lawsuits, the one demanding Hendrick be euthanized, and had a field day with it: posters of Hendrick's sad little face with the words CONDEMNED TO DIE!! screaming below, and—even more effective—posters of Hendrick's picture side by side with that of Anne Frank, and the same caption. I think it might have done the trick, actually, for within a few days of that second poster the Anne Frank Kindergarten publicly announced that it would be happy to accept Hendrick Karremans as a pupil.

This occurred on New Year's Eve, so Labienus dropped by the house with Champagne to celebrate; though by this time Anna and Geert were in such emotional states they didn't particularly feel like celebrating.

Labienus took them upstairs for a firm talk about future strategies, and I was left to amuse Hendrick.

We stood looking at one another uncertainly, and I cleared my throat and said: "Well, Hendrick. Would you like to play Super Soccer-Man?"

He made a slight face.

"No," he said. "I don't really like it so much. Daddy does, though. Could we go for a walk?"

"Probably not the best idea," I said apologetically. We'd only had one or two incidences of vandalism outside the house, but it had been decided to keep Hendrick out of sight until he started school, by which time the more violent protest would have died down somewhat.

"I don't like living here," Hendrick told me, sighing. "I wish we could move back to our other house. But we're not going to now, are we?"

"I'm afraid not," I told him. He looked resigned. Then a furtive brightness came into his eyes.

"I know what we can do," he said, glancing guiltily in the direction of the second floor.

"What, Hendrick?" I couldn't suppress a smile. "You know I can't permit anything your parents forbid."

"Oh, it isn't anything bad," he said, taking my hand and leading me to the dining nook. "You'll like this, it'll be lots of fun! Really. Now, you sit down there—" He pushed me into the nook and I sat awkwardly on the little bench seat. He lifted the lid of the other seat and drew out an ancient imitation leather case. Stamped on it in gold letters were the words TOURNAMENT CHESS SET.

"You know how to play this game?" he inquired, setting up the board and pieces with remarkable speed, and correctly, I might add.

"Yes," I replied, stroking my mustaches. Poor little fellow, I thought, inviting a cyborg to play chess! "Do your parents object to chess, Hendrick?"

"Not—exactly," said Hendrick, avoiding my eyes. "It's just Daddy says I can't look like a brainiac or something." He smiled slyly. "And anyway Daddy isn't so good at it. I think that's why really." He turned the board on the diagonal and pushed it toward me. "Would you like to play black or white?"

I took white, and moved king's knight to F-three. He promptly advanced a queen's pawn to D-five and sat looking at me expectantly. I moved a king's pawn to G-three; his queen's bishop went to G-four. I moved my king's bishop to G-two. He countered with moving his queen's knight to D-seven. I sent a king's pawn to H-three. Hendrick sidled his queen's bishop over to capture my king's knight. I responded in kind, taking his queen's bishop with my king's bishop.

Anyone watching us would have thought we were only pretending to play, simply jumping the pieces around without purpose, so quickly were our moves made. I leaned back, setting his queen's bishop to one side, and considered him. His face was alight as he studied the pieces and quickly advanced a queen's pawn to C-six.

"You're actually enjoying this," I observed. I advanced a queen's pawn to D-three.

"Uh-huh," he replied, advancing a king's pawn to E-six. "This is the time I like the most, though. Before everything locks up."

I moved a king's pawn to E-four. "Locks up?"

"You know," he replied absently, moving his queen's knight to E-five. "It all locks up. So much has happened you can see how it's going to end."

"Can you indeed?" I slid my king's bishop back to G-two.

"Uh-huh." He captured my king's pawn at E-four. I took his capturing pawn with my king's bishop. "Then it just gets bor-ing."

"Because you know who's going to win?" I inquired, watching him move his king's knight to F-six.

"Uh-huh." He rubbed his nose thoughtfully as I returned my king's bishop to G-two once more. "Usually it's me. You're kind of good, though." He reached out and sent his king's bishop to B-four. "Check."

I blocked it with my king's knight. To my astonishment, he responded by moving his king's pawn to H-five.

"Did you mean to do that?" I asked him. He looked up at me in surprise.

"Can't you see the way it's going to go?"

"No, I'm afraid I can't." What an admission to make to a mortal child, of all people! He looked disappointed.

"I thought maybe you could. You play almost as good as me," he added tactfully.

I advanced my queen to E-two. He edged his queen over to C-seven.

"You said I was different, Hendrick," I said carefully, setting my queen's pawn on C-three. "Is that why you thought I could see the moves in advance, as you can?"

He nodded, moving his king's bishop back to E-seven.

"How am I different?"

He looked up at me, knitting his brows again. "Well, you just are. You move different. You smell different. You talk like one of those people on the Wire. You and Michel, too. You know what I mean! Don't you know?"

I knew; but it was impossible he should know, or rather it would have been impossible were he a human child. I scanned him. Yes; not quite a human brain. *Engineered to better process information.* So the child would be able to catch a ball, as clumsy schoolboy Geert had never been. Able, moreover, to distinguish a cyborg from a mortal human. Able to see the outcome of a chess game after a certain number of moves.

What else might Hendrick Karremans have been able to do?

He took my prolonged silence for embarrassment and said quickly: "Don't worry! I won't tell anybody. I don't like being different, either."

Not knowing how to reply, I simply nodded and moved my queen's pawn to D-four. His knight retreated but he stepped up his attack after that, until the thirtieth move, when I took his queen and he took mine. Then he yawned and waved his hands over his head.

"*Now* it's boring," he told me. "It's going to be a draw."

"Really?" I looked at the board. I analyzed the positions. He was quite correct.

"Uh-huh. In eighteen—" Hendrick cocked his head and studied the board. "No! Nineteen moves. You play good, Mr. Victor. It took a long time to know what you'd do."

We had been playing for all of six minutes.

"Thank you," I said. "That was a remarkable experience." I meant it, too.

"Want to play again?" he said hopefully.

"Some other time," I said, though I knew it was unlikely there would ever be another time.

"Okay. Can I have a Fruit Pop?" he inquired, carefully putting the board and its pieces away. From what I had observed I knew Anna didn't allow him sweets between meals, but I went to the kitchen and got the child his Fruit Pop.

He took it gleefully and we went out to the parlor, where he sat at the piano kicking his legs. He seemed completely uninterested in the keyboard, however.

"Do you play the piano?" I asked him.

"Uh-uh." He looked at me as though I were mad. "I'm only a little kid."

"Ah," I said, nodding. He nibbled away at the Fruit Pop a moment later and then his face grew suddenly apprehensive.

"What's the matter?"

"If those people said I can go to their school—then I'll have to get those shots, won't I?"

"I suppose you will," I said.

"I don't want to have shots," he cried, tears welling in his eyes.

"Well, perhaps you won't, then."

"But it's locked up now! They're the only school I can go to so Mommy and Daddy will have to send me there, but Michel will tell them I have to get shots to make the law people happy and make things easier," Hendrick wailed, forgetting his Fruit Pop, which dripped on the shining black finish of the piano. I got up hastily and mopped it with a tissue.

He was right, of course. One of the things Labienus was even now explaining to Anna and Geert was that they would have to make this particular concession, to have Hendrick vaccinated to comply with Civil Ordinance Number 435.

"You'll simply have to be brave, Hendrick," I told him. "After all, it's not as though they stick children with needles any more."

"But it still hurts," he wept. "I know it does. It went *hiss* and the medicine jumped into Mommy when she got *her* shots and she said *ow!* I'm scared to be hurt."

Why on earth had Anna let him watch her being inoculated?

"It's perfectly reasonable to be afraid of pain," I told him. "But you mustn't be a baby about it, after all. All the other children in that school had to have shots, you know."

"But I don't need the shots. They did," he said angrily. "And it's not fair. They're not going to die."

Was he precognitive as well? But he showed no sign of being a Crome generator, one of those mortals who produces a freak bioelectric field that carries over into the temporal wave. They occasionally seem to pick up information from the pattern of the future."Well, neither are you," I lied. "You surely don't suppose a few little shots are going to kill you?"

"No," he said, irritably wiping his nose on his sleeve. "Not that kind of shots. I mean people are going to kill me. That's all locked up, too."

"Why would you think that, Hendrick?" I asked him, crouching to offer him a tissue. He looked at me with an expression of weary patience.

"Be-*cause*," he told me. "Don't you know what's been going on? All those people who are mad at Mommy and Daddy? They're scared of me. They threw things at our windows. Mommy and Daddy want me to be alive but a lot more people want me to not be alive. It would be real easy to kill me. All somebody has to do is shoot through those windows with a gun. When I go to that school it would be even more easy. They could just shoot me in the street. They could shoot me in the car. Even if I wore a soldier helmet they could get me. So it's all locked up. See?"

I stared at him, aghast at the matter-of-fact way he spoke.

"You don't seem frightened," I said at last. "Why are you afraid of shots, but not afraid to die?"

He had turned his attention to his melting Fruit Pop and was attempting to eat it before it fell off the stick. After a moment he said: "Well, when you die, it hurts but then it's over. My cat had to die and it didn't hurt him. He just went to sleep. But when you get a shot, it hurts and you're still alive, so it keeps hurting."

At that moment we heard their voices echoing down the stairs as they came, Anna and Geert sounding tired, Labienus sounding placatory.

"I thought we lived in a reasonable world," Anna was saying. "I really thought the human race had evolved beyond this sort of thing."

"Ah, but evolution is an ongoing process, isn't it?" Labienus said. "Think of yourselves as part of the change. You're fighting prejudice and irrational fear. When you've proved that what you did was right, you will have advanced civilization that much farther. But you won't manage it without a few sacrifices."

"That's true, of course," Geert said dispiritedly. They stepped down into the parlor and looked at Hendrick with identical expressions of shame. Anna cleared her throat.

"Hendrick, I'm afraid we're going to have to take you to the doctor after all—"

That was as far as she got before he began to howl, and threw himself down on the floor crying hopelessly.

"*You promised,*" he shrieked. "I knew! I *knew* you'd do it—" They bent over him, murmuring reproaches. I backed away from them and turned to Labienus.

"I must get away," I murmured.

"Of course," he said immediately. "I quite understand. Take the night off. I'll stay with them." Once again he reached out and clasped my hand, startling me.

I shrugged into my coat and slipped out, scarcely taking time to wonder at the change in Labienus's administrative style. Perhaps he wasn't entirely the smiling manipulator I had known him to be.

I caught a bus into Old Amsterdam. There was a fine old restaurant on the Dam, soothing to the soul, unfashionably fitted out in red leather and crystal, with an excellent wine cellar. The food was of the sort generally described as "hearty fare" but prepared well; what should be fresh was fresh, and what should be high was just delicately so. I dined in comparative solitude and lingered over my meal, watching from my table as the Dam began to fill up with merrymakers for the countdown to midnight.

Dusk fell. I watched the lights begin to glow, sipping my coffee, savoring my dessert. New Year's Eve, and the year 2092 was about to slip into history. What was the first New Year's Eve I could remember? The Eurobase One celebration in 503 A.D. Very clearly I remembered lying in the ward recovering from my latest augmentation, furious at the pain I felt, as the nurses hung pink and purple and yellow streamers in the hall. There were cut-out decorations, too: a smiling baby wreathed in a banner, and a terrible old man with a scythe and hourglass. The nurse told us a story about the old man. She explained how we needn't be afraid of him, ever, for we lucky little children were becoming immortal.

She didn't tell us about the other things we had to fear. But that would have been cruel, really, wouldn't it? We'd learn the rest of the truth soon enough.

I ordered another dessert, a torte rich in Theobromos. Pleasure is at its best when one proceeds at a deliberate pace, I find. I ate slowly, and emptied my mind of any considerations save what I was doing and what I was about to do. Presently I walked out into the night.

It was cold, damp under the stars, with a thin sea-fog lying at ground level that made haloes around the streetlights. Over the crowd assembling around the Nationaal Monument, there hung a steamy cloud of exhaled vapor. People festooned with little electronic lights were dancing. I walked away into darkness, having no interest in that particular aspect of the mortal carnival, but I hadn't far to go. Amsterdam is quite a conveniently arranged city.

I found what I wanted near the Oz Achterburgwal.

A long quiet street along a still canal, pleasantly shadowed, no lamps to cast unwanted glare on the faces of passersby. Quite unnecessary, when all the windows afforded such illumination. Just visible, along the street, pacing slowly and staring, were the dark figures in overcoats like mine; but who could spare a glance or a thought for anything but the windows?

Uncurtained and wide, each displayed its occupant in her own particular pose or ambiance. Some were straightforward and traditional, with scarlet lighting, with black lace and classically provocative poses. There were the fantasies: a window that glowed with blue flickering light, La Sirene in green sequins reclining in a languid pose on her undersea couch. A girl with mime's training in a bare window under harsh white lights, made up in dead flesh tones, the perfect motionless image of a smiling display mannequin. A girl in the habit of a nun, her face innocent of paint, kneeling rapt before a photographer's backdrop of a rose window.

Some windows were dark, with a small apologetic electronic crawl at eye level: *Presently engaged. Will reopen shortly. All currencies accepted. Free certification available on premises. Presently engaged . . .*

Some places clearly catered to a sense of sin; there one looked into a garishly lit hell where the occupant was doing her best to convey the idea of pleasures cheap and degrading. In others there were promises of delights for the most eclectic, not to say criminal, tastes.

No. No. And no again, not for me . . . I generally preferred more Nature and less Art.

I found her at last in a window that glowed with amber light, radiated heat like summer.

So little artifice, and such charm. Quite without clothing save for a loincloth of white linen. She sat perched on a metal folding chair, in an ordinary sitting room. The only hint of a theme was a poster on one wall depicting some North African city. A music system on a shelf was playing a dance song with a quick beat, Reggae Nouveau perhaps. I could hear the music, but to most passersby she rocked silently in her chair as she regarded the evening, supremely unconcerned.

Her hair was superb, heavy as an Egyptian wig in its complex cornrow beading, and the bright beads—blue faience, copper, and brass— swung as she rocked, and tapped out a rhythm on the back of her chair. As I watched she parted her full lips and began to whistle out a counterpoint to the music. She had the slightest of gaps between her front teeth. Skin like midnight.

She noticed me at last and arched an eyebrow in cheerful inquiry. I nodded and climbed the steps to her door.

"Good evening, dear, may I see your credit ID please?" she greeted me, extending a pink-palmed hand. "Thank you."

She led me into the house, pausing only to key in the light control that dimmed her window and set its crawl message going. She named a price. I agreed to it.

"Coffee while I run your check? Little glass of gin?" she inquired, waving me to a comfortable chair. I declined. She patted my cheek and went off to her terminal to verify that I was healthy, sane, law-abiding, and could pay.

It was a Company-issued credit ID and of course pronounced me a worthy client, whether or not I was in fact healthy, sane, or law-abiding. But I could certainly pay. She came back smiling, led me deeper into the house, waved me into a small lavatory.

"Pre-prophylaxis, eh? You're a big boy, you know what to do. When you come out, turn to the right. I'll be waiting in there." She indicated a beaded doorway, all darkness beyond it.

I went in. It was furnished as most chambers for that purpose are. Concealed within a smoke detector was a tiny closed-circuit camera lens. I scanned: no gentlemen accomplices lurking anywhere in the house. She herself watched me, from a curtained booth on the other side of the wall where she was preparing for the encounter.

Having mutually assured ourselves that no murder was intended, we proceeded to the business at hand.

"What a charming conceit," I remarked, stepping through the curtain. Each bead was a touch of ice on my skin. The contrast with the warm air was a shivering pleasure. "I haven't seen a beaded curtain in ages. Was it your idea?"

Her voice came out of the darkness, amused. "Yes, thank you. But no personal details, eh? Less effort for you and they'll only spoil your fun, dear. For the sake of your pleasant and guilt-free experience, I will be only your desire personified. Not a person."

"I'm not a person either," I replied, and walked forward into the mystery.

As I left, something small and bright blue caught my eye by the door; I bent to pick it up. It was a toy rabbit, a tiny figure from a block set. I turned to offer it to my hostess.

"You have a child?"

"I might," she replied, accepting it. "Another personal detail you don't want to think about, you see? Not sexy at all. Thank you for your patronage, sir. Good night and happy New Year!"

I walked back past the crowd of mortals on the Dam. There were more of them now, still whooping and celebrating. Vendors sold hot drinks, sausages, parade horns, gnome hats, dance-lights. Wire screens, vast as city blocks, were mounted on the sides of buildings and displayed New Year's jollity from other cities as though they were occurring simultaneously, creating a sense of worldwide party.

I found an all-night coffeehouse some blocks away and edged into a booth at the back. It was dark and quiet there. I ordered coffee and pastry, and watched from the darkness as the New Year came upon us, the bright child in his banner emblazoned HAPPY 2093!

Celebrate while you can.

Hendrick got his shots on January 2. On the fifth of January he started kindergarten.

I took him to school. Anna and Geert were dismayed by the crowd of kameramen in the street, didn't know what to do, what to say. But what were Doss and Waters paying me for, after all? I shrugged into my overcoat, took Hendrick by the hand, and escorted him down the steps.

He looked pale and frightened, but he went without question. Children endure so much, so steadfastly, once they learn to abandon hope. He stared unsmiling into the blank avid eyes of the kameramen and let them See him for a moment before following me as I pushed through the mortals.

And there the gunman was, as I'd known he'd be, the heavy-set young man in the green shirt, holding up the bag with the Amsterdam Wire logo, stepping suddenly too close. As I reached out to break his wrist, before the shouting started, I heard Hendrick saying quietly: "That one's not a kameraman. See his eyes? Here it comes. Good-bye—"

But the gun went off, in accordance with recorded history, pointed up and away from Hendrick. It broke a window in a villa across the street, and I knew without bothering to look up the unnerving pattern the shattered glass had formed, like a six-pointed star, for this too was in accordance with recorded history. I heard the scream, as much in frustration as pain, of the would-be assassin. I heard the whirring of the kameramen as they ran close to frame our struggle (no attempt to help me!) except for the one who turned his devouring face up to the broken window, catching that unforgettable image. And, at last, here were a few police.

And Labienus, to manage statements, so that I was permitted to walk on at last towing Hendrick after me, down the quiet street toward the waiting car. I bowed my head, striding along, feeling Hendrick's hand twist in mine as he looked back.

So I too entered recorded history, of course with my face well hidden: that dark overcoat flowing back from those striding legs, the stiff arm extended to the boy who turned to peer over his shoulder so somberly into the cameras. By that evening a billion mortals had seen the image.

They were waiting for us at the school with tremulous applause, for of course Labienus made certain that word of what had happened preceded our arrival. That was where the reaction set in. I was trembling, sweating, and really in no mood to shake all the tiny hands extended to me; but I had saved Hendrick's life, and the more enlightened citizens of Amsterdam wanted to thank me. I was given flowers. Toddlers were put into my arms and told to kiss me. The teachers kissed me. I disengaged as politely as I could and retreated to an empty office, to mop my perspiring face and endure, until it should be time to take Hendrick home, being the hero of the hour.

And what a brief hour it was.

Oh, we had waves of positive publicity from the murder attempt. The gunman had been acting alone, but was associated with the Church of God-A, a cult calling for more than zero population growth. They resolutely denied they had any intention of bringing this about by violence, though they admitted they were opposed to Hendrick's existence on principle.

There was a great deal of self-congratulation within Amsterdam. Once again its good citizens had shown themselves tolerant, humane, and enlightened! Hendrick got on well with his playmates. Anne Frank was invoked again, wan smiling ghost to give her blessing on another little outsider.

On his third day at school Hendrick developed a slight fever, a mild headache. I escorted him home. Anna was furious, positive his illness was a reaction to the unnecessary vaccinations. Geert wrung his hands. Before nightfall, however, the boy's splendid superior engineered antibodies had clearly done their trick. His fever fell, his headache went away, he was fine.

Not so his classmates.

Three children showed up at the school on the fourth day. The rest were at home, violently ill. By nightfall most of them had died.

Most of the teachers were dead by the following morning, and all the children had died. The illness spread through their families. Their families died. Drastically enforced quarantine measures seemed to contain the outbreak, though it was also possible that the plague killed its hosts so quickly that it was unable to spread effectively after a certain point.

The Wire coverage was heartbreaking: images, from happier days, of the smiling little faces. There were around-the-clock broadcasts as people cowered in their homes. Ratings soared. Rumors spread quickly as only the electronic media could spread them, especially with a captive audience.

Once it had started, it didn't take long.

The Amsterdam Center for Disease Control assaulted the question immediately. The obvious conclusion to be drawn was that the outbreak was somehow associated with Hendrick, since he had survived it and none of the other children had. From the moment that theory was widely known, the public had decided.

Useless for Anna and Geert to protest via voicelink that Hendrick had come into contact with plenty of people from the day of his birth, without harming anyone; we couldn't get any of the other doctors who'd worked with them to come forward and make a statement in their support. Useless to point out that Hendrick had been ill, too, and that undoubtedly only his unique antibody system had enabled him to recover. Anna and Geert were not professional entertainers, they spoke poorly, without stage presence or vocal training. Though Labienus repeated their statements an hour later, the first stammering denials were the ones that had the most impact.

Moreover a biologist, who spoke well and who *did* have stage presence, was interviewed immediately afterward. He put forward his opinion that Hendrick's much-touted immune system might be responsible. Perhaps, somehow, it had perceived his little classmates with their ordinary coughs and colds as dangers to his survival, and manufactured a toxin to eliminate them.

This was immediately accepted as a glaringly obvious fact.

The truth came far too late, as we were being evacuated; and no one listened, I think, but Hendrick and I.

Labienus was hurrying Anna and Geert through their packing. Hendrick was already packed. I was buttoning him into his coat in the flickering light of the Wire images, for it had been deemed unsafe to turn on any of the other household lights, and in truth we only dared keep the Wire on because we needed the constant flow of information.

Abruptly a grim-faced commentator broke in over the latest "news" (endless recapitulation of everything that had already been shown) to announce that investigators had uncovered a possibly significant fact that might prove Hendrick wasn't responsible for the plague after all. The first instance of illness had occurred at the school *before* he had ever arrived. He had got there late the first morning, due to the attempt on his life. During the time we were making statements to the police, as his future classmates waited for Hendrick's appearance, one of the children had been taken ill and sent home, escorted by a teacher because her mother was too ill to come for her. She had never returned. The teacher who had escorted her home was the first to die.

I had never heard this. These details had never become part of recorded history. I stared, astonished, at the images, forgetting to hand Hendrick his mittens. He took them from me, patiently, and pulled them on.

Then I was Seeing, through the eyes of a kameraman, the Disease Control investigators in their protective suits, emerging from the house where they'd just found the mother and child dead.

I knew that house. I'd been inside it. It was in the red light district. The kameraman was running close to get a shot through the window, before being pushed back by police. The only image he was able to frame that was clearly recognizable was a travel poster on one wall, its subject a city in North Africa.

The commentator was unable to interview any of the investigators, but the suited figures rushing to and fro in the background lent weight to his expressed opinion that this might explain at last the origin of the plague: for the child's mother was a licensed prostitute of African descent, and she may have contracted the disease from an African customer, likely enough in view of the plagues that had decimated so much of Africa's population in recent years . . .

I had kissed her. Children, teachers, had kissed me.

It really is remarkable how our immortal senses take control at such times. I rose like the perfect machine I should have been and shut off the Wire. I took Hendrick's hand and led him through the dark house to wait by the back door. We could hear Labienus helping Anna and Geert carry their bags downstairs. They were stumbling, dropping things. There were already barricades at the end of the street and crowds assembling there, shouting at the police.

How sad, how sad, the poor girl had been exposed to a virus and unwittingly passed it on to me, and I'd—

But I'd have known if there had been anything wrong with her.

We heard the first shots fired in the front street, not what you'd expect at all, an insignificant-sounding popping.

"There it goes," said Hendrick, almost calmly. He was in shock, his dark eyes enormous. "All locked up now. I told you so."

I had scanned the mortal woman before our encounter. She hadn't been carrying any virus.

"Here, here!" whispered Labienus, shepherding Anna and Geert before him. "Out to the car. Now! Nils will drive you to a safe location." He looked into my eyes and transmitted: *You've got the blood effects ready?*

The woman hadn't been carrying any virus. I, however, had.

It didn't feel like rage. It felt like a white flare, so intense it was, so unlike a human emotion. I stared back at him.

Was it in the Theobromos you gave me? I transmitted.

His face told the truth, though he hastily transmitted back: *What? Don't be ridiculous! Get them out of here, now, we can't waste time on this.*

How true. We couldn't waste time, not when history was dictating that Anna and Geert and the child escaped from their house at nineteen hundred hours precisely, exiting through the back and making their departure in a rented car driven by Hendrick's bodyguard.

The perfect automaton went briskly down the back steps, opened the doors of the waiting Volta, took bags and loaded them into the boot while the Karremans family scrambled into their seats. He shut them in, and climbed behind the wheel to take them to their appointment with history.

As we drove away, a faint transmission came from the dark house: *I'll explain when we rendezvous.*

How pleasant to have an explanation offered.

How heavily I'd been perspiring in the school. And with the woman.

The last act played out quickly.

I drove the mortals to their previous home in the country, the loft apartment above the laboratory where they'd done their work. The apartment was closed up now, though the laboratory was still in use; it was within commuting distance and the Karremans had planned to go back to work after Hendrick was in school full-time.

We let ourselves in and they took shelter upstairs, in the rooms where Hendrick had played as a baby. The place can't have afforded him any comfort of familiarity now, dark and empty as it was. I remained below in the laboratory, ostensibly to stand guard but in reality following through on what I had been told was the point of this entire operation: locating and securing all the files, all the project notes for the Karremans' work with recombinant DNA. History would record it as lost in the course of the evening's events.

The Company knew otherwise, naturally. The Company knew that a man placed in the event shadow—for history did not record what happened in the laboratory during the hour the Karremans family cowered upstairs—might remove the data on Hendrick's creation to a safe location for later retrieval. Anna's and Geert's work would be saved, would pass into the possession of Dr. Zeus Incorporated, presumably to be of some benefit to mortal humanity at some unspecified time in the twenty-fourth century.

Though I had no real idea of what would be done with the knowledge. We're told so little, we operatives struggling through the past. Our masters assure us it's better that way. Easier on our nerves.

I seemed to have no nerves left in the forty-five minutes I searched through the laboratory. Eventually I found the files, or at least their backups, neatly labeled in—what else?—a file box. I carried it out into the night, ran with it to the nearest drainage ditch, dug a hole in the snow and buried it. Then I returned to the laboratory to keep my own appointment with history.

Not long to wait. Glancing at my chronometer, I saw that the mobs would by now have stormed the house and found it deserted, but set it afire anyway and gone looking for the monster and his wicked creators, pausing only to raid the Civil Guard arsenal. Thanks to the splendid media coverage Labienus had masterminded, a good many people knew exactly where the Karremans' laboratory was. Yes: here came the line of headlights through the night.

Car doors slamming. Shouted consultation. Upstairs, inaudible to mortal ears, Hendrick's whimpering, Anna's stifled sobs. Heartbeats pounding, both within and without, for the attackers were frightened, too.

So it was a brave man who climbed back into his utility vehicle, after pounding had failed to force the door, and simply drove it through the wall.

He died almost at once. Pointless to shoot him, I suppose, but I had no choice: history stated that he was shot by Hendrick's bodyguard before he had time to jump from the cab of his vehicle. It stated further that other members of the mob, pouring in through the breach he'd made in the wall, promptly gunned down the bodyguard.

So I took my pose there in the dark, as their shots went wide, and I thumbed the electronic device that set off the little detonations in my heavily padded clothing. The blood bags exploded. I toppled forward, as dead as I would ever be.

The mob advanced cautiously, fearful. There came an echoing clatter of feet down the stairs. Who was running down the stairs? This hadn't been mentioned in any of the accounts, and of course I couldn't turn over to see.

"*Make it be over,*" I heard Hendrick crying in desperation. "Make it be over now!"

Geert and Anna were close behind him, frantic to pull him back out of danger.

Deafening barrage of shots. They died there, on the stairs.

I hope it was over quickly.

Certainly I could hear no failing heartbeats, no last gasps in the moment of profound silence that came when the shooting stopped. The mortals seemed stunned at what they'd done. At last somebody had presence of mind to say: "We'll have to burn this place. It's the only way to keep the plague from spreading!"

Yes! That was a plan all of them understood. It was done quickly, because some of them had thoughtfully brought along accelerant as well as guns. They dumped it around, ran back out through the breach, and somebody lit a firecracker—perhaps left over from New Year's Eve—and tossed it in. Very effective: a roar and a fireball at once.

I winked out to the lavatory at the back of the building. Forcing the window over the basin, I crawled out and dropped into the snow that had drifted behind the wall. No need to worry about the telltale print of my body in the drift. It would have melted away within the hour, as the laboratory became an inferno.

I fled, secure in the knowledge that my escape wouldn't be spotted. History recorded otherwise, after all. Pausing only long enough to retrieve the file box from the ditch where I'd hidden it, I ran away, back toward Amsterdam.

One oughtn't to think at such times. Undeniably a foolish thing to do.

I thought and thought as I ran, you see, with the result that by the time I reached the outskirts of the city all my questions had resolved into just two: Could I do it? How was I to do it?

Hard to find a fire hot enough, intense enough. Probably even the fire at the laboratory wouldn't have been of sufficient heat. No bonfires permitted nowadays, in safety-conscious 2093, and most homes were heated with electricity.

As I marched along, I came to a shop licensed to sell liquor. It was gated and locked against the night, but the lock could be forced; and the shop contained everything I'd need, which was to say rows of bottles of alcohol and little packets of hotpoints to start the fire. Yes. Would the fire cleanse away my filth?

Undoubtedly, if it burned away all but the indestructible skeleton within me and the augmented brain protected within my ferroceramic skull. I wouldn't die—I was immortal, after all—but I might be so badly damaged the Company would be unable to repair me. I might spend the rest of eternity in a bioregeneration vat, only marginally alive. Better than I deserved, to be sure, but I hadn't many alternatives. I wasn't even certain I could force myself to remain there in the fire. They made us such cowards, when they made us deathless.

I had set down the file box and was wrestling with the lock when Labienus stepped from the shadows behind me.

"Let it go, Victor. It was a wretched business, but it's over now."

I turned to stare at him. He scooped up the file box and tucked it securely under one arm. He met my stare.

"Why?" I demanded.

"Why were you used as the carrier or why weren't you told?" he inquired. No attempt to brazen out the lie. I hadn't expected that. He smiled slightly at my confusion.

"What's the first rule we learn, Victor? That *history cannot be changed.* History recorded that the Karremans plague would kill a certain number of people. History recorded that the Recombinant would be killed, along with his creators, and their research lost. How was the Company to alter any of those historical facts? We couldn't, of course.

"All we could do was work within the historical record, to place ourselves in the position of greatest advantage and thereby control the situation. You see? But it was decided to do more than simply take the research files. Wouldn't it be better to ensure that there was no Karremans plague after all? No unknown and uncontrollable virus evolving from a Recombinant's body? There'd be no way to change the historical facts as known, those little victims must die—but wouldn't it be much less dangerous for humanity if they actually died of something controllable? Something we could deactivate once the historical facts had been *apparently* matched? We were minimizing the potential for a greater disaster, Victor, you see?

"Terrible that the tragedy had to occur, certainly. Terrible that it will galvanize all the nations of the world to forbid any further research into work of this kind. Impossible to change these things. But at least this way we've been able to derive something positive from it! The research has been saved. And the 'plague' will never spread further, because we know it never existed in the first place."

So, once again, Dr. Zeus Incorporated had become the beneficiary of mortal suffering. I leaned on the grate, longing for those bottles of vodka and aquavit behind the glass. I wondered what Labienus would do if I grappled him close, if I forced his mouth open with my own and spat my misery down his throat.

He narrowed his eyes, perhaps picking up the image from my thoughts, and continued: "As to why you were chosen for the job—well, really, Victor, it must have occurred to you by now that you're unique among our operatives."

"I'm an ordinary Executive Facilitator," I stated.

"Oh, Victor, so much more than that! You have a talent none of the rest of them have. You were augmented to do in fact what that poor child was assumed to be doing: your body can produce customized toxins in response to specific stimulus. Surely that affair in San Francisco gave you a clue, beyond what we were permitted to tell you at the time? Budu attacked you, and you immediately manufactured a virus to disable him."

"And the woman, here?" I demanded. "The children? What threat did they present?"

He cleared his throat.

"Well—none, of course, but their deaths were a regrettable necessity. There was nothing in the Theobromos. You'd have detected any adulteration, you know that. Your ability is programmed to activate when certain signals are transmitted. Do you recall when I shook your hand, New Year's Eve? You felt, perhaps, a slight shock? No? But your body responded to the order I gave it by producing what history will call the Karremans Recombinant Defensive. As we had intended it to do, I might add. Nothing was ever out of our control."

"You're saying, then"—I fought to keep my voice steady—"that the Company is able to make my body generate poisons without my knowledge. At any time."

"Exactly so."

"Why was this thing done to me?" I asked.

"Now, now, you're taking entirely the wrong attitude! Though you can be excused, in view of what you've just been through." Labienus smiled indulgently. "The Company was considering a special-threat design, and Aegeus felt you were the nearest match to the desired psychological profile."

"Did he really?"

"Oh, yes. Of course, you still underwent years of tests to see if you'd be emotionally up to the work. Placed in certain situations to see how you responded. Why, when you were still at Eurobase One, hardly more than a neophyte, there was a drone named Lewis—"

"I remember." I closed my eyes. "Please. Enough."

Labienus seemed to feel it was safe to step close and place a comradely hand on my shoulder. He was correct; however extraordinary my revulsion might be, I hadn't the will, just now, to attack him. If only he'd go away, I could get on with my immolation. Myself I hated most of all.

"Now then," he continued, "you'll be relieved to know, I'm sure, that you're no longer manufacturing the virus. It's served its purpose. You can go on to your next assignment without endangering any other mortals." He drew a small case from an inner pocket and put it into my nerveless hand. "That contains your new credit ID. You're to report to the Herengracht HQ before daylight, for a change of clothes and a shave. The Section Head there will brief you on your next posting. I'd discard that coat before you go much farther, however. You're a little conspicuous."

I looked down at the bullet holes, the imitation blood.

When I looked up he was gone.

A little nonsensical voice sang in my ear: *Victor. Vector. Virus. Victor Veneficus . . .*

Like the good machine I was, I slogged away through the night and found my way at last, sick and chilled, to the Herengracht HQ. Van Drouten, red-eyed with weeping, let me in and was very kind to me. She stuffed me full of a hot breakfast, and I managed to keep it down until I was alone in the lavatory.

I showered. I shaved. I put on clean pajamas and slept, in a quaint little room at the top of the house where Van Drouten had once hidden Jewish children, and woke to find Facilitator General Aegeus sitting on a chair beside my bed, regarding me with cold eyes. I'd so admired him, once.

There were recorded voices speaking in the room. It was the conversation Labienus and I had had outside the liquor shop.

When the voices stopped at last, Aegeus spoke briefly and to the point. He informed me that Labienus was a liar, the leader of a genocidal cabal within the Company. *He* had augmented me to produce viruses, intending me as a weapon for his group. My own loyalty to our masters was now suspect, by association.

It was expected that Labienus would shortly offer me a chance to join his inner circle. I would accept his offer. I would monitor the cabal's activities. I would keep Aegeus informed on what they planned to do next . . .

And perhaps one day I might be trusted again.

———

How to trust either one of them? I suspect there is no solution to my particular dilemma. Not at the present time, at least.

I proceed with extreme care, as indeed one ought when one may become a source of disease at any moment, quite unawares. It has necessitated some changes in my personal habits. Obviously, I can never engage in intimacies of any kind again.

It is not a pleasant life. And it continues, for I am unable to die; and so the pain never goes away.

History took its course, and recorded that the plague had been generated by Hendrick's overpowerful immune system. Horrified by the tragedy, all the nations of the world signed the treaty that would outlaw forever any further experimentation with recombinant human DNA.

The Karremans became infamous, their story dramatized to its full potential to shock, horrify, and entertain. After the manner of storytellers, the filmmakers altered the facts for greater mythic appeal: in the American version of the story, Hendrick (or the Recombinant) was depicted as a perfect Aryan type, blond and blue-eyed, coldly adult in his manner. Anna was a lesbian, Geert an alcoholic. I was played by a hulking actor (bodyguards must be huge, mustn't they?) as a simple-minded muscleman, faithful to his doglike death.

But all that came later.

Amsterdam mourned, and it had so much to mourn. So much was buried with all those white coffins.

All the same, the city had justly earned its reputation for tolerance and common sense, and in time those virtues reasserted themselves. Anna and Geert were never to be vindicated, but Hendrick was recognized for the innocent victim he had been.

A statue was erected on the site of the house where they'd tried to live. The sculptor utilized the famous image taken that first day of school, after the murder attempt, and there it stands to this hour in black metal: Hendrick being pulled along by the hand, turning to look back, his little face sad and enigmatic. Dynamic, the grim striding figure that drags him relentlessly forward, the folds of its long black coat flowing out behind.

The sculptor has chosen not to give the figure a face.

EPILOGUE

Labienus opens another file case.

He regards a field photograph taken by an operative, of a street in what can only be San Francisco. Before a hotel, a young mortal woman is being helped down from a carriage. She is heavily pregnant. From her clothing and the rest of the setting, the photograph would appear to have been taken in the early 1860s. And here is a second picture, a portrait of a man, taken much later: perhaps the first quarter of the twentieth century?

Another face inhuman, but much more subtly so. Smiling, but the deep-set eyes are as cold as Budu's. There is something suggestive of a shark in the too-boyish grin. Labienus's frown deepens.

A loose cannon. A compromise. An unacceptable exception to the rules.

What had Aegeus been planning? Some kind of parity with the old project *Adonai*? Take an extraordinary child, gift him with extraordinary resources, and put him in a position to affect world events to the Company's advantage?

If so, Aegeus had been successful. The really awful part was that it had been a public success.

"Spoiled millionaire's brat," Labienus mutters. He looks down at the face of William Randolph Hearst. Crass, naïve, arrogant, *American*. Given unlimited attention from the moment of his birth, an only child who had but to point at something and, if money could buy it, it was his. Where was the shaping discipline? Where was the inner pain to spur him on to great deeds? He should have been profitless to the Company, a crashing failure for Aegeus. At the very least, he should have become an empty-souled Charles Foster Kane.

Instead he's been a rampant success, a monster with a heart solid as a diamond, voraciously alive, motivated, powerful, breaking even Company rules with comparative impunity because of his usefulness. Posing as his own descendant, he has rebuilt his empire. Hearst News Services is an invaluable tool for the Company, and the Hearst museums throughout Europe continue to accrue as much priceless art for Dr. Zeus as the most dedicated team of Preservers.

The idea that the child had been wanted and loved by his parents might figure in the equation, somehow, never even occurs to Labienus.

He flips on through the dossier. Here are the later pictures, with the big American in modern dress, still strangely old-fashioned looking. Smiling at museum openings, scholarship awards banquets, *orphanage dedications* for God's sake. Immortal, and immature enough to believe he could improve the world. Labienus shakes his head.

There's the fool smiling on the steps of the National Museum of Tunisia, on the occasion of its grand rededication. Here is an insert of the priceless Carthaginian artifacts he (or rather, his paid experts) had tracked down and restored to the museum. Did he imagine for a moment he would win their love? The American really has no grasp of history, has he?

Carthage hadn't changed much since the third Punic War. Labienus had gone there on a whim, celebrating the two-thousand-three-hundredth anniversary of its destruction, and even in 2154 there weren't many amenities for tourists. No trams at all to the infamous Tophet; he'd had to walk more than a mile through an ankle-turning wilderness of spiny weeds and broken stone before he'd come to the site.

Labienus stood surveying what had been Baal-Hammon's shrine. Vague rectangles in the pale rock, broken stele, long-eroded pits from bygone archaeological digs. And, underneath his feet to an unknown depth, the crumbled bones and ashes of thousands upon thousands of mortal children.

Closing his eyes, Labienus could still hear the voices:

"They're a morally inferior race as well," Cato had told him, glaring over his wine cup. In the villa's atrium, a fountain babbled quietly and slaves played soothing music.

"What, because Dido lay down for Aeneas?" Caecilianus shouted impatiently. He was a young member of the *populares*. "That's no reason to trounce somebody we've already defeated! The Carthaginians have changed. Hannibal's so much history. They're peaceful merchants now, and they'll stay that way—"

"If you please," Labienus had said. "Let the honorable Cato speak his mind." He said it in such a way as to imply a broad wink to the younger guests sprawled around his table, but the truth was that Labienus rather liked Cato. The old mortal might be a warmonger, but he was ruthlessly pragmatic. "Why would you say our ancient enemy is morally inferior, dear Cato?"

"Their religious practices are an offense to the holy gods," said Cato, staring down Caecilianus. "As is well known. They worship Cronus. The old baby-eater, you see? Over there he's got some damned Eastern name, Baal or Moloch if I remember rightly. Your 'peaceful merchants' have a huge bronze image made of him, a bull-headed figure with a gaping mouth and cleverly articulated arms, and do you know what they do?

"They build a pyre inside Moloch so intense he glows red-hot, and then they place their firstborns in the thing's hands and some priest pulls a lever. Up go the arms and the children fall screaming through Moloch's mouth, into the fire."

Caecilianus winced. Cato pressed his advantage: "And then, the Carthaginians clash cymbals and skirl pipes as loudly as they can, to drown out the cries of their little victims!" The other guests grimaced. They weren't soldiers; only politicians.

"Oh, that's too horrible," cried Caecilianus. "Nobody would do that."

Labienus looked at him and smiled, thinking of the infants his legions had put to the sword: little Gauls, little Nubians, little Greeks, all in the name of the Pax Romana.

"Believe it, young man," insisted Cato. "And that is only one of the reasons I say, as I have said and will say again—"

"*Carthago delenda est!*" they all shouted, including Labienus, who could remember a time when Cato's ancestors had not only sacrificed children but eaten them.

In the end, Cato had finally had his way.

It had been a long siege, and it had cost a lot of money. Caecilianus and his fellow *populares* had complained about that; they had complained, too, about the underhanded means and ridiculous pretext Rome had used to justify the war. Further justification was needed.

So Labienus strode through the ruin of Carthage, pausing now and again to cheer on the legions in their good work, sometimes even setting his own torch to purple hangings, or directing the crews that toppled walls. He was there to see that Dr. Zeus got its share of the loot, of course, but he was also there in his official capacity as the nearest thing Rome had to a journalist, gathering reports for the Senate.

This was why he made his way now to the temple of Baal-Hammon, stepping over the sprawled bodies, the pooled blood that reflected bright fire climbing, and smiled as he came.

Marcus Gracchus was waiting for him on the steps of the temple. Blood ran down the steps, a thick stream flowing. Two legionaries stood alongside, supporting between them a man in chains.

"Ave, Labienus." Gracchus saluted. He took his helmet off, wiped his face with a bit of torn curtain: fine stuff, sea-green and cloth of gold.

"Ave, Gracchus!" Labienus bounded up the steps and surveyed the prisoner. "So this is my interviewee? He doesn't look much like a high priest."

Gracchus squinted at his men. "He was a lot more impressive before the boys had a bit of fun with him. Well, where do you want the bastard?"

"Are all the temple buildings secured? Find us an administrative office," said Labienus, and five minutes later he was comfortably ensconced in the high priest's own chair, pouring himself a glass of the high priest's own wine. The high priest knelt before him, blinking through blood from a scalp wound. The legionaries stood just outside the door, sullen because they were missing out on the temple loot. Labienus tasted the wine.

"Mmm. Falernian, isn't it?" he asked the priest, in the priest's own language. The priest raised weary eyes. He was past shock.

"Yes," he replied. "Roman wine."

"You ought to have bought more of our wine. You ought to have bought our olive oil, too. It might have prevented all this," Labienus said, gesturing widely with the cup. "Trade imbalance is worse than a few elephants over the Alps, you see. Takes bread from the mouth of the Roman olive grower. We can't have that."

"What will you do with me?" the priest asked.

"Ultimately? Parade you in a triumph, I imagine. We'll want to clean you up, first; you're certainly not very imposing as you are." Labienus looked the priest over critically. "What you've got on, is that your ceremonial regalia?"

"Some of it," said the priest. "The legionaries took the rest."

"Tsk! Not splendid enough at all. We'll have to make you up something in cloth of gold for the triumph. Rome likes a good show. It wants its villains larger than life." Labienus set the wine aside and leaned back, surveying the priest. "Now, why don't you tell me all about the worship of Baal-Hammon?"

"He is our lord of the fertile fields," said the priest, his voice trembling. "He is the Good Father, the consort of Tanit. To him we offer our first fruits, and the young of the beasts."

"How many babies do you burn in a month?"

The priest blinked. "It depends," he said. "In the fever season, sometimes one every day. Other times, we can go a month without a child-offering, if it pleases the Lord."

"Do you kill them before they go into the fire, or drop them in alive?"

"What?" the priest cried. "What are you saying? They're dead! We offer them to the Lord because they're dead! Holy gods, is this why you hate us? You think we kill children?"

"No, no; we hate you because you sell olive oil at lower prices than we do," Labienus explained. "But if everyone believes you kill children, we can run you out of business and even the *populares* can't complain."

"You must understand, these are babies who have *already* died!" the priest insisted, horrified. "Miscarriages. Stillbirths. All who die of sickness or mischance. How could we let their little souls go into the darkness? We give them back to the Lord, he takes them through the fire, and they become his angels."

"He takes them through the fire. That would be in the great bronze idol, the one with the head of a bull?"

"A bull?" The priest frowned. "Baal-Hammon hasn't got the head of a bull. You're thinking of the Egyptians."

Labienus withdrew a pair of gauntlets from a pouch at his belt. He put them on and half rose in the chair, just far enough to reach out and slap the priest.

"Baal-Hammon has the head of a bull, and you feed him children," he said. "You place them in his hands, and they're dropped into a fire in his belly."

"No! Come into the temple and see for yourself!" said the priest. "He has a beard, and a high crown—eating children, what kind of minds do you Romans have? We put the babies in the Lord's hands. He lowers them into the holy fire and gives them life again! I have seen them smile, before they pass through to Paradise! This is all a misunderstanding—"

Labienus hit him this time, hard enough to break a tooth.

"Listen to me, very carefully," he said in a quiet voice. "You feed your firstborn children to Baal-Hammon. That's what you'll tell everyone in Rome. You deck the poor little things with flowers, and then you drop them screaming down his gullet, to be roasted alive in the bronze furnace. Your own people hate you for it. They were happy to be conquered by Rome."

"No," said the priest, clutching his jaw. There were tears in his eyes from the pain. "I think—long ago, people used to offer human sacrifices. I have heard of it being done. But we never did. And never children. Why do you—"

Labienus hit him again.

"You're not listening," he said patiently. "I want you to tell me the truth. The truth is that you burn your own children alive. You see? It's very simple. Tell me that truth."

"But I don't—"

Labienus raised his hand. "Tell me the truth," he repeated. "I can call the legionaries in here with a word, and you know what they'd do. If you tell me what I want to hear, things will be much more pleasant. Your tooth's giving you agony, isn't it? I can have a dentist see to it. Rome has excellent dentists, you know. We're a civilized nation."

"We have dentists, too, you son of an ape," wept the priest.

"Not any more," Labienus pointed out. "Now, tell me the truth. You offer up sacrifices of living children to your bestial god, don't you? Trust me, the hour will come when you'll say it, and you'll believe it, too. The only thing you can control, my friend, is how much pain you go through before that hour comes. Think carefully."

In despair, the priest shouted: "The Lord will punish Rome, Roman! He'll send plague, and brimstone, and armies for her destruction!"

Labienus grinned. "Yes. Rome will fall, in her turn. Does that make you feel better? Now . . . tell me the truth."

Who says history cannot be changed? thought Labienus smugly, opening his eyes to regard the bleached wasteland. There was no salt covering the ruin to the thickness of a common soldier's toe—that would have *really* cost money, beyond any spin doctor's ability to shut the complainers up. But the landscape was just as white, and Carthage had been poisoned just as effectively, as though it were true.

And Baal-Hammon, in his persona as bull-headed monster, had served Labienus's purposes wonderfully well. How far his horned shadow had been thrown! Out beyond the classical world, into the feverish minds of medieval scholars and princes of the church, yea, even unto the televangelists.

The Company had profited, too, of course; its coffers filled with plunder from the sack, and its investments in Roman olive oil futures yielded heavy dividends.

Labienus felt a mortal approaching him, now, and turned to see a shabby little man in modern Tunisian dress peering at him speculatively.

"Monsieur, may I offer the services of a tour guide?" he inquired, and without waiting for a reply scurried closer. "You know where you are? Famous sacrificial altar of Baal-Hammon! Look!"

He drew a holo device from his pocket and switched it on. Hazy and transparent in the midday glare, computer-generated figures knelt to offer a swaddled bundle to their awful horned god.

"Then, Romans invaded and began their genocidal persecution of my countrymen," said the man, changing the scene to a blurry diorama of Roman armies sacking a town.

"You consider yourself a Carthaginian?" Labienus regarded him scornfully, scanning the mortal's genetic makeup. Some Euro-mongrel, Almerian and Balearic; he hadn't a drop of the ancient blood in him. "Are you proud of being descended from people who sacrificed children?"

"Ancient times," the man explained, looking a little uncomfortable. "Carthaginians had not yet heard the word of God. But Romans were *much* worse, killed millions of children. Carthaginians at least believed they were giving them as servants to their gods. And all nations have given children to their gods, in all times everywhere!"

"That's certainly true," said Labienus, deciding he was amused by the mortal. "And sacrifice is relative, isn't it? What do mortals bear them for, anyway, but to be of use?"

"It is every son's duty to do his father's will," agreed the mortal solemnly.

Unseen all around them the little ghosts were standing, not merely the lost children of Carthage but of Rome and Britain, of every nation on earth, watching, an army of specters gray as ashes, silent. No need to play the cymbals or the pipes now to drown them out, no need to tell them *Hush, don't cry! Don't shame us!*

An image flashed into Labienus's mind, memory of an illustration by Edward Gorey: Death, in the formal costume of a governess, skull-faced, grinning pleasantly at the viewer as she holds her umbrella aloft. Gathered around her feet are her tiny listless charges, a flock of children in old-fashioned clothes. Their eyes are vacant. They stand together like so many stuffed penguins.

The mortal children had done the job their parents asked of them, gone wide-eyed into Hell in exchange for victory, good harvests, gold, status, love. *Pro patria mori.* And they were fortunate, after all, compared to the children taken by Zeus.

"What if one of those children stood before you now?" said Labienus. "What do you suppose he'd have to tell you, about eternal life in the service of the gods?"

The mortal blinked at him.

"Would you like to purchase a holocard, monsieur?" he asked.

Labienus laughed. He bought a holocard and the mortal went away.

Nothing matters but the work. Yet the work is meaningless.

History cannot be changed. Yet history is a tissue of lies.

And if one can't leave the world, and if there is no better place, then the world will have to do for Paradise. No reason, then, not to shape the world to one's own desires, is there? But it will take scouring fire to purify it, and seas of blood to wash out its imperfections . . .

So. What about this third boy, old *Adonai* revived at last?

Yet is there really a place for him now, at this end of the long corridor of time? It's hardly an age for heroes. No sweeping religious upheavals in which he might immolate himself, like Nicholas Harpole; no British Empire whose burden he might shoulder, as Edward Bell-Fairfax had done. Only a dwindling and pusillanimous global village, bickering feebly with its colonies on Luna and Mars . . .

Though there will be *real* nastiness erupting on Mars . . .

The rotten tree must fall; what wedge might be placed, to cause the profitable trunk to topple in just the right direction? What lord with a golden voice, and absolute confidence in his ideals?

What if the woman were brought in again, in her fatal role of catalyst? *The Botanist Mendoza* . . .

Labienus glances up at his wilderness, distracted by something at the edge of his field of vision. He frowns.

"Damn!" He goes to inspect the window where the frantic mortal had stood. Smudged on the outer surface of the glass are a pair of handprints and . . . yes . . . that blob can only be the print of the mortal's nose. Disgusting monkeys!

He puts his head on one side, considering. Which of his subordinates has displeased him lately?

Spoyka! he transmits.

Yes, sir! The reply comes hastily.

Report to room 218 with a rag, a bottle of Windex, eighty feet of rope, and a rappelling harness. Further orders to follow.

Immediately, sir!

Labienus folds his arms and gazes out at the view. His smile has returned. Room 218 is two floors above his office. To reach his window, the man will actually need ninety feet of rope. Can he be creative, or will he suffer a painful accident?

Either way, it ought to be fun to watch.

ABOUT THE AUTHOR

KAGE BAKER has been an artist, actor and director at the living History Centre and has taught Elizabethan English as a second language. Born in 1952 in Hollywood, she lives in Pismo Beach, California, the Clam Capital of the World.